Praise for Cindy Dees

"There's action and hot attraction galore. . . .
Dees does a terrific job of advancing the overall
series while lending her unique talent to her
vibrant individual contribution."

—*RT Book Reviews*
on *The 9-Month Bodyguard*

"A solid, suspenseful plot, tormented, vulnerable
characters, and beautiful, compelling writing
will keep you turning the pages."

—*RT Book Reviews*
on *Deadly Sight*

"Dees brings readers into an action-packed
world, with superhuman operatives . . . this is
a book you can't put down."

—*RT Book Reviews*
on *Flash of Death*

THE
DREAMING
HUNT

CINDY DEES
AND
BILL FLIPPIN

TOR®
fantasy

A TOM DOHERTY ASSOCIATES BOOK
NEW YORK

This is a work of fiction. All of the characters, organizations, and events portrayed in this novel are either products of the authors' imaginations or are used fictitiously.

THE DREAMING HUNT

Copyright © 2016 by Cindy Dees and Bill Flippin

All rights reserved.

A Tor Book
Published by Tom Doherty Associates
175 Fifth Avenue
New York, NY 10010

www.tor-forge.com

Tor® is a registered trademark of Macmillan Publishing Group, LLC.

ISBN 978-0-7653-7031-0

Our books may be purchased in bulk for promotional, educational, or business use. Please contact your local bookseller or the Macmillan Corporate and Premium Sales Department at 1-800-221-7945, extension 5442, or by e-mail at MacmillanSpecialMarkets@macmillan.com.

First Edition: September 2016
First Mass Market Edition: August 2017

Printed in the United States of America

0 9 8 7 6 5 4 3 2 1

THE
DREAMING
HUNT

CHAPTER

1

He was a fraud. Even his name, Will Cobb, was a lie. If any of the soldiers lounging around the common room knew who he really was, they'd arrest him in a heartbeat and put him to permanent death . . . or worse. Why hadn't his father or grandfather warned him that hiding in plain sight from the Empire would turn out to be such a nerve-racking business?

He might feel safer if his friends were aware of his deception. But for their protection he had to keep up the charade even for them. It was exhausting. It was also becoming increasingly dangerous. He'd caught other people's attention now. Powerful people. Some of whom would, without hesitation, destroy him and his companions to prevent them from succeeding in their quest.

Will glared around the common room of the Heart building out of general principles. He did not like tonight's business in the guild of healers, and he made no effort to hide his distaste for the proceedings. But desperate times called for desperate action.

Their nemesis, the deposed governor, Anton Constantine, was on the loose and would do everything in his power to take revenge against them. Not only had they been instrumental in ousting Anton but they'd stolen the treasure the greedy noble coveted above all else right out from under his nose. For that, he would pursue them to the ends of Urth and obliterate them.

Anton thought they'd found gold. But they'd found

something much more valuable—memory of a legendary king who could stand against the ex-governor's precious Kothite Empire. Of course, Will and his companions still had to find a way to wake the Sleeping King before Anton destroyed all memory of him. Or destroyed them.

It wasn't that he worried for himself, even though he was no doubt Anton's main target. But Rosana . . . he worried about her.

He was still furious with the gypsy healer for giving up a piece of her spirit to save his life in their desperate flight from the Sleeping King's lair. She knew to keep her spirit firmly where it belonged and not to tempt fate by ripping out part of hers and using it in a manner for which it was never intended.

Not that he was in any position to cast stones at her for doing the unnatural. He fingered the thumb-sized wooden disk grown firmly onto his chest. No sane person voluntarily carried around a tree spirit inside himself, either. Of course, he was grateful to Rosana for her sacrifice. She'd stabilized the unnatural union of his spirit with Lord Bloodroot's. Which was a boon. For weeks before her stunt, he had hovered on the ragged edge of death.

Now that he was not continuously nauseated and violently ill, High Matriarch Lenora wanted to attempt a ritual to transfer the shard of Rosana's spirit from him back into the gypsy girl where it belonged. He was all for the transfer. But he could not help being suspicious of the whole business of high magic. Forest bred and humbly raised, these fancy magics were foreign to him. They smacked of the Empire with all its wealth and power. Or mayhap that was Bloodroot speaking. It was becoming increasingly difficult to separate his thoughts and feelings from those of the irascible truant.

Torches guttered in their sconces every time the Heart building's door opened, casting hellish light into the corners of the wide, low-ceilinged common room. Two burly Royal Order of the Sun guardians—charged with defending the Heart, its healers, and most importantly, its resurrection

Heartstones—stood guard while High Matriarch Lenora painstakingly laid out five large, overlapping circles of colored silk rope upon the floor. The braided ropes were marked with intricate signs that helped shape and focus the powerful magical energies summoned in rituals. Each circle would call and contain a particular flavor of magic. As the high matriarch wasn't entirely certain what she was doing this night, she was calling upon many types of magic all at once.

Which was *not* reassuring. The whole notion of exploring a way to restore Rosana's spirit made him twitchy. A ritual like this had never been attempted, and no scroll of instruction existed for such a thing. Lenora was making it up as she went. Which likely passed beyond desperate into foolhardy.

At least Raina was going to be present in case things did not go well. Another member of their little party of adventurers, she'd sought the Sleeping King for reasons of her own. Her magical skills were considerable. She was an archmage in the making and could heal a small village singlehandedly. He had faith, given the sheer volume of spirit magic she could summon, that Raina would keep them all alive through this ritual.

Still, his gut rumbled that the whole thing was a load of glittering unicorn dung. He was half-tempted to storm out and leave them to their smoky mirrors and useless spells. It wasn't that he didn't believe in magic. By the Void, he was rapidly becoming a formidable caster himself.

It did not alleviate his doubts and concerns one bit that Guildmaster Aurelius himself had come out of his hallowed guildhall to consult with Lenora over the particulars of casting tonight's ritual.

Bloodroot had been able to take the piece of Rosana's spirit without any fancy rituals. Surely, the tree lord could give it back if he so chose. And the whoreson had *better* so choose if he and Will no longer had need of Rosana's spirit to stay alive. Gruff humor rumbled somewhere deep in his belly. Will cursed back at the truant silently.

He should take Bloodroot back to the Forest of Thorns from whence he came and get rid of him once and for all. Of course, there was the small problem of the enraged tribe of orcs who called the Forest of Thorns home. The Boki. Will-self's lip curled in hatred of the cursed orcs who'd murdered his parents. But the other self trapped within him, the Bloodroot-self, reacted fondly to thought of the Boki, who revered him. *Bah. Orc scum.*

Lord Bloodroot was one of the thirteen tree lords of the Great Circle. Or at least he had been until the other tree lords turned on him and hacked his tree to bits. Bloodroot's spirit, housed in one of those bits of the great bloodthorn tree's heartwood, had nearly killed Will before Rosana pulled her healing trick a few weeks back.

Will glanced over fondly at the gypsy, where she conversed in whispers with Raina. The two healers had grown close in their mutual efforts to keep him alive while they completed their quest. They'd found King Gawaine, or at least a dreaming echo of him, not surprisingly in the dream realm. Will was still not entirely clear on how extra-planar spaces existed, but he'd seen the evidence of one such place with his own eyes.

Apparently, he and his companions now needed to find the Sleeping King's regalia and his physical body on this plane if they were to actually wake him. But those problems could wait for another day. First, they had to get Rosana's spirit back where it belonged.

Raina's blond hair shone pale in contrast to the gleaming sable of Rosana's as they giggled at some joke. As if the gypsy felt his gaze upon her, Rosana looked up just then and smiled at him, her big, dark eyes worried. His irritation softened somewhat. If this cursed ritual would fix her, he would play nice and cooperate. And if it made her smile at him, all the better.

Rosana stepped wide around the ritual circles and rested her hand surreptitiously upon his forearm. Warmth and a feeling of rightness spread through him at her simple touch.

She murmured, "How do you feel today?"

"Fine. Whatever healing you did to me in that cave holds steady."

"You will tell me immediately if you begin to weaken or sicken again, yes?"

That must have been at least the hundredth time she'd said that exact same thing to him. "Of course. I'm an open book to you, sweet gypsy rose."

She gave his shoulder a playful swat. "On the verge of a deadly ritual and still you flirt with me? You're incorrigible, Will Cobb."

"Only with you, Rosie."

She smiled up at him, a warm sparkle in her gaze. "What am I to do with you?"

"Love me always and never leave me."

"Always and never," she whispered back.

Her characterization of the forthcoming magic belatedly struck him. "Exactly how deadly is yon ritual?" he demanded abruptly.

She shrugged, but a shadow passed through her eyes. "Well, of course, there's always a small risk of a flaw in the outcome. Or . . . ," she trailed off.

"Or what?" he demanded.

"Or a backlash," she mumbled.

"What *sort* of—"

He broke off as a commotion erupted at the door. The Royal Order of the Sun guards admitted the shining, golden-skinned solinari—sun elf—Aurelius. It was a wet, blustery night but the rain and wind did not seem to have touched his impeccable presence.

Rosana took advantage of the distraction to glide away from Will's side. Avoiding answering his question about backlashes, no doubt.

"Welcome, Guildmaster," the high matriarch greeted him formally.

Aurelius bowed back courteously in the elven fashion, remarking, "I see the circles are prepared. I brought you the magical components you requested." He held out a cloth bag, which Lenora passed to Raina. "And here is the other thing we spoke of." He pulled a leather tube from the folds of his cloak that Will recognized as a scroll holder. It looked old. Desiccated. Lenora took the case with a word of thanks, handling it with extreme care.

"A moment with you in private, High Matriarch?" Aurelius murmured.

Will frowned. He knew that tone of voice. The elf wanted to talk about secret things. And Will would bet all the gold he owned it had to do with tonight's ritual. What hadn't Aurelius told him about this casting? Will's gaze shot to Rosana smiling and chatting with Raina inside the ritual circle, and his gut clenched in sharp fear.

The high matriarch and Aurelius slipped out of the common room and into a small office. In quick decision, Will made his way unobtrusively to the kitchen and, when no one was looking, darted into the pantry beside the office. He climbed on a barrel and pressed his ear to a thin spot high on the wall.

Lenora was speaking. "Just how dangerous is it?"

Aurelius answered carefully in the tone he used when he was avoiding a subject, "—am worried that both of their spirits are unstable. You do not know much of Will—"

"I have a good idea exactly who he is, old man."

Will was shocked to hear her take that tone with his guildmaster.

"You cannot possibly—" Aurelius started.

"You forget that I am an Imperial genealogist. By his skills alone I could guess who Will Cobb really is, even if he were not the spitting image of his father at that age. For that matter, I know who his mother was, as well."

"You do?" Aurelius sounded shocked.

A pause. Then, her voice low enough that Will had to hold his breath to hear her, Lenora murmured, "The Heart has tracked the pastoral line of Serica's family for generations for the same reasons we have tracked the Delphi line."

Will all but fell off the barrel. Lenora knew who he was? And she had not turned him in to the Empire? Could she be trusted with this knowledge or not?

Aurelius hissed in a sharp breath. "We must have a long chat about this after tonight's ritual is concluded. I will be fascinated to hear what else you can tell me of young Will's parentage."

A lengthy silence stretched out. Will heard noise behind him as if someone might be headed for the pantry, and he scrambled down to look busy. The footsteps retreated across the kitchen, and he hastily resumed his listening post on the barrel.

"—about the piece of Rosana's spirit that is trapped within the boy?" Lenora was asking.

A heavy sigh. "He collects too much of others' spirits within him. I am concerned that Will is becoming a vessel. I have seen this before with Tarses, and it did not go well. Will is no more meant to carry around these energies within him than the general was meant to hold that ice elemental."

He'd heard of General Tarses, of course. Everyone had. The bards sang tales of his conquests all the time. Tarses conquered the elemental continent, Pan Orda, for Koth and was attacked in his moment of victory by the lord of ice, an elemental creature called the Hand of Winter. The general had survived the attack and returned home in triumph, only to die in battle soon after, if the songs were to be believed. A tragic end for a great man.

The high matriarch was speaking again. "—you have any idea the potential of the children you've thrown together?"

"That would be the point," Aurelius replied dryly. "Who else could possibly succeed at the task we have set for them?"

"Do they have any idea?"

"No. And it must stay that way. They must continue to believe they are just normal youths. They must not in any way call the wrong attention to themselves. Everything depends on it. *Everything.*"

"You have put a great load on young and untried shoulders, Guildmaster."

"Believe me, I wish it were not necessary. But there is no one else up to the task." A pause. "We need to get that shard of Rosana's spirit out of Will before we send them into the wilderness once more. Otherwise, he risks losing himself to the alien spirits within him. It is the only reason I am allowing this ritual to proceed."

Lenora sounded amused when she answered, "The last time I checked, this is my house."

Will heard footsteps retreating from the office, and he hurried out of the pantry, as well. He slipped back into the kitchen just as one of the Royal Order of the Sun guardians poked his head into the room. "There you are, boy. High matriarch's looking for you."

Will grabbed a sausage roll off the long table and followed the big man docilely back into the common room, but his thoughts whirled. What was a pastoral line? Who had his mother really been before she'd become the humble wife of a cobbler in a muddy little village on the edge of nowhere? He knew she was a talented scout and a skilled archer. And unfortunately, he'd seen firsthand that she knew how to use alchemical gas poisons. She'd used a fear gas to force him to flee his parents the night they'd died at the hands of the Boki. Of course, his father had been the greatest battle mage in Dupree and leader of the colony's Celestial Order of the Dragon before he'd fallen afoul of Anton Constantine and become a fugitive.

What of the coming ritual? Would the piece of Rosana's spirit inside him ultimately harm him? So far it had done nothing but improve his health radically. But would it stay that way if this ritual failed?

As he moved to stand beside her, Rosana shook her head at the bun in his fist. "You're hungry at a time like this? My stomach is doing flips and flops. I could not possibly eat."

Not far from the circles on the floor, Aurelius took a seat in a comfortable chair someone brought for him. Will had argued heatedly with the guildmaster—also his adopted grandfather—over this ritual, insisting instead on returning to the Forest of Thorns to seek a solution less dangerous to Rosana. But Aurelius had been adamant that he was not going to risk his only grandson's life, nor the gypsy girl's, on the questionable hospitality of the Boki. Aurelius believed the Boki would just as soon kill Will and cut Bloodroot's disk off his chest. Truth be told, he reluctantly agreed with his grandfather.

"How dangerous could a ritual backlash be?" he asked Rosana low as a waiting quiet settled over the room.

She winced. "If we were lucky, you and I would only die and have to resurrect. But with both of the casters' experience, I'm sure we will be fine."

"Both?" he asked, surprised.

"Well, yes. Raina will assist Lenora. She can perform high magic and summon more magic than everyone in this room combined. The high matriarch would be silly not to let her help with the casting, just in case . . . "

He finished the thought in his own mind. Just in case something went terribly wrong and they needed to power through the ritual by brute force—or in case Raina had to restore them all to life. A deep sense of foreboding washed over him as he stared at the overlapping circles on the floor. This wasn't even foolhardy. It was insane.

The high matriarch called from across the room, "We are ready, Will and Rosana. Let us begin."

Raina stepped reluctantly into the small area where all five circles overlapped. This moment represented everything she'd tried so hard to avoid in her life. Ever since she'd shown massive talent as a healer, other people had been trying to fashion her into a tool for their own uses. She'd run away from home, given up her noble rank, her family, even her identity, for a chance to forge her own path in the world.

Ending up in the Heart had not been ideal, but landing in the White Heart had been a stroke of luck. It was the pacifist, diplomatic order within the healer's guild and enjoyed close protection by the Royal Order of the Sun. Her White Heart colors allowed her to move freely and in relative safety wherever she chose to roam.

The White Heart was known for dabbling in politics, which suited her purposes, as well. And it had the added benefit of making her untouchable by those who would have co-opted her power for their own ends. The downside was that she nominally served the Kothite Empire, which she despised. It was an uncomfortable arrangement at best. But life was turning out to be fraught with arrangements that left her less than thrilled.

"Get comfortable," the high matriarch instructed her, Will, and Rosana. "This may take a while."

Will sat on a narrow stool a Royal Order of the Sun guardian brought forward. Rosana perched beside him on another. On a small table between her and the high matriarch, Raina carefully laid out the magical items whose energies would be drained to help fuel the ritual.

"What's all that?" Will demanded suspiciously.

Raina answered, "Distilled essencia. Etherium manacles. Spinneret of a veilweaver, threads of an aethercloak. And of course you know this one: sap of an ancient bloodthorn." She gestured at a small glass tube of liquid, so dark a red it looked nearly black.

The high matriarch pulled Aurelius's scroll tube out of her sleeve, carefully unrolled an age-stained parchment scroll upon the tiny table, and weighted down its corners with the small stones. Raina read the first few lines and was impressed. It described how to cast a nature circle from an extremely rare form of magic.

Lenora glanced at her. "Shall we begin?"

Raina was not clear on why the nature circle was necessary. She could see logic in using spirit and curse circles. Rosana could cast both types of magic, and as such, they would be intrinsic to her spirit. The time and glamour circles had more to do with powering the ritual than with specifically helping fix Rosana. But nature? Did it matter to the gypsy somehow? Or was that a nod to the Bloodroot spirit within Will?

One by one, Lenora activated the circles, blending their energies into a dome of magic encompassing all four of them. It would serve to contain the otherwise wild and uncontrollable high magics.

"Once I draw forth the magic from the items on the table, I will begin adding my own magical energies to it. That is when you will start adding your magic to the ritual, Raina."

"Yes, High Matriarch," Raina murmured dutifully, privately amused. As if she didn't know how this worked. She'd been casting high magic since she was a child. She might only be sixteen, but her home in Tyrel seemed a lifetime away. She missed them, her bossy older sister, her little brothers and father, even her domineering mother, who had ultimately driven her to run away from home.

A prickle of energy passed over her skin as the spirit circle activated, adding its energies to the shell around them. Will glanced over at her, and she smiled reassuringly at him. He returned the smile, but the expression did not reach his eyes. She saw his fingers squeeze Rosana's.

She secretly envied them their young love. It had always been her fondest wish to marry and have a family, but joining the White Heart had pretty much made that impossible. Her childhood sweetheart was still in Tyrel, but she was expected to go wherever the Heart sent her, healing whenever and wherever her skill was needed. It would be hard to settle and have a family while roaming the width and breadth of a continent the size of Haelos.

"Let the magic flow into you as it builds, Will," Lenora murmured.

He looked as if he sincerely tried to do so. But all of a sudden, the ritual magics were twisting and writhing wildly, whipping around all of them like the tails of angry cats. Not all the circles were activated yet! Would the existing circle magics be enough to contain whatever was going wrong inside them?

Will clawed at the disk upon his chest with his fingernails, even though he knew full well that he could not pry it off his skin. "Bloodroot," he gasped. "Stop this ritual."

"We risk a backlash if we stop it now," Rosana replied nervously.

"He doesn't want the spirit shard removed. He's fighting it," Will panted, obviously in searing pain. "This isn't right."

"Heal him," Lenora ordered Raina, her concentration fully upon the magics she was trying and failing to corral and calm.

It was too dangerous to use common magic inside a shell of ritual magic, so Raina made do with spreading a healing salve on Will's chest just where the disk attached, its red scars streaking outward from the disk more angrily than usual.

Understanding broke over her as rage flowed out of the disk and into her fingertips as bright and strong as the magics flailing around their heads. "Bloodroot does not wish for this ritual to continue. He wants the shard of Rosana's spirit to stay where it is."

"I would have my healer whole," Lenora snapped.

She didn't think Bloodroot gave a care for Rosana's wholeness or for the high matriarch's desires, which meant this ritual was doomed to failure before it barely got started. All that remained to be seen now was how bad the backlash would be.

CHAPTER
2

G regor Beltane, landsgrave of Lochnar, huddled on the hard bench in the prow of the rowboat as two of his most trusted men rowed him across the great lake to the island that marked the center of his land holdings. The oars dipped into the black water silently with only thin trickles of dripping water marking their rhythmic lifts from the water.

A muted rumble of thunder in the west announced that more rain would be forthcoming momentarily.

It had been a while since he'd made this secret journey. With Anton Constantine ousted and replaced by Lady Syreena Wingblade, he'd been forced to stay in Dupree for weeks to get a read on the new political environment of the colony.

This was a good night to check on the hidden tower. The miserable weather assured that no one would be abroad and spot him sneaking off to the island where the White Tower was hidden. It had been painstakingly smuggled here stone by surreptitious stone hidden in the ballast loads of Black Ships from the continent of Koth far across the Abyssmal Sea and reassembled here on the island with utmost care. The tower had been magically camouflaged behind trees and foliage with just as painstaking care.

He wondered sometimes who on Koth dared work against the Empire to send the tower here. Those nameless souls must have been very brave, indeed, to suborn the Emperor under his very nose.

Gregor had never been inside the tower, but that was not his purpose as Keeper of the Tower, a secret position that had passed down through his gypsy family for generations. His duty was to safeguard it until its ancient magics were finally released. Sometimes, he dared to wish he knew when that day would be and what the magics would actually do. On other days, he wished himself well clear of anything that might be perceived as a threat to His Resplendent Majesty, Emperor Maximillian the Third, the ageless and immortal ruler of the Eternal Empire of Koth.

The prow of the rowboat thudded against the dock jutting out into the lake. He stood, caught his balance, and jumped onto the dock. He snagged the rope one of his men tossed him and tied off the line efficiently as the first drops of rain began to splat against his face.

The soldiers secured the oars and prepared to disembark while he strode ashore, his boots breaking through the crust of wet sand and sinking heavily into the beach. Gads, it was dark tonight. No hint of moon or starlight alleviated the impenetrable blanket of black overhead. He turned around to tell his men to bring torches and was just in time to glimpse a pair of dark forms rising silently out of the lake on either side of the dinghy. They grabbed his men from behind—covering their mouths in the process—and dragged them over the side of the rowboat and into the water. So quickly and silently was the attack executed that he barely heard a splash as his men slipped below the surface of the lake.

Had he not been looking directly at the stealthy attack when it happened, he'd have had no idea where his men disappeared to. As it was, he lunged forward to the edge of the lake, drawing his sword as he went. A brief gout of bubbles was the only sign of his men's passage.

Frustrated, he pulled up at the edge of the lake. He was not skilled in underwater combat nor did he have a potion in his pouch for breathing underwater. Blind and unable to breathe, he would be less than useless at attempting a rescue of his men. Who had the ambushers been? And why had they taken his men?

"Show yourselves, cowards!" he bellowed in futile fury.

This time, four black shadows rose from the thigh-deep water. The texture of scaled skin caught his eye. Gills slanted on their necks. Burly bodies were silhouetted darkly. *Merr*. Gregor swore under his breath. What on Urth were the mostly water-dwelling humanoids doing attacking him and his men? There had never been any Merr in this lake. The local lizard-man clan claimed this water, and the two races were bitter rivals.

The first rule of combat against water dwellers was to force them onto dry land. He backed up the shore toward the thick wall of trees and shrubs that hid the tower. If the Merr planned to kill him, they would have to do it on his turf.

He spotted two warriors with distinctive coral blades gleaming pale in the darkness. A third had the glowing hands of a caster, and the fourth was just stripping off a thin pair of gloves. A poisoner, then. Certain Merr developed skills in delivering alchemical poisons by touch, and he'd heard an entire school of dueling existed among Merr poisoners.

The caster opened up with a curse spell intended to make him more vulnerable to weapons damage. These Merr must have mistaken him for human. Gypsies who served the Empire were rare but not entirely unheard of. He had no great love for Maximillian, but his position within the Empire allowed him to look out for his fellow gypsies.

As the curse magic struck him, he called upon his gypsy blood to resist it. The flash of magic fizzled around him without ever touching him.

"Gah," the caster growled. He called out something to his cronies in gurgling syllables.

Gregor turned and sprinted for the tower and its defenses. He leaped over a patch of warded ground and skidded to a halt on the far side facing his foes.

The two warriors charged after him, and the first one hit the glyph. An explosion of heat slammed into Gregor, but the Merr warrior fell to the ground, burned into a blackened husk. Nasty business, incineration glyphs.

The second Merr warrior roared a battle cry and charged past his fallen comrade, coral sword raised.

Ever an efficient man, Gregor wasted no time with fancy footwork. He merely dodged the first swing of the deadly blade by ducking low. As soon as the sword whooshed overhead, he lunged in low and fast with his off hand, burying his dagger in the creature's side. He'd expected the toughness of the scaled hide and put all his weight behind the blow. He threw up his sword and caught the coral blade on its downswing with his own steel, forcing both weapons high overhead as he twisted his dagger, gutting the Merr.

The coral blade fell away, and he slammed his sword down onto the back of the creature's neck. The scales there were as tough as armor, however, and his blade bounced ineffectually. He yanked his dagger free and jumped back. The Merr, staggering, brandished his sword chest high in an erratic weaving pattern.

Using an underhanded swing that bypassed the wavering coral blade, Gregor's sword gathered speed and force, culminating in a thrust to the throat with all his weight behind it. The tip of his sword sank through six inches of meat, stopping only when it fetched up hard against the creature's spine.

Magic crackled against Gregor's back, but he recognized the vibration of curse magic and resisted it yet again.

The impaled Merr went limp, abruptly reduced to dead meat upon his blade.

Another blast of magic slammed into Gregor's back, this time high-level curse magic designed to cause debilitating pain and render him unable to defend himself. He resisted the spell once more, but he could not resist the caster's magic indefinitely. He turned and called magic of his own to hand. In quick blasts, he threw three silencing spells at the caster in case the creature had active shields of his own against magic.

The caster appeared silenced for the moment, but Gregor suspected his foe would remedy that momentarily. The poisoner was moving off to one side, flanking Gregor. Perfect. Gregor slid left, forcing the poisoner even farther to the right. One more step. . . .

Poof.

A glyph exploded that would trap the poisoner's foot in place, preventing him from further movement, which would give Gregor the breathing space he needed to deal with the blasted caster. He started to turn toward the magic user when, out of the corner of his eye, he spied the poisoner pulling out a small wooden box and withdrawing a vial. Gregor hesitated. Mayhap he should jump the poisoner first while the caster was silenced.

The poisoner pulled some sort of spiny quill from his belt and dipped it in the vial. He took a step with his one free foot to throw the quill and sprang the second half of the trap. A wooden framework dropped down from its hiding place in the tree branches above, dozens of razor-sharp blades lashed to it. The weight of the frame and the razors would slice anyone beneath them into tiny strips, killing him or her instantly.

Gregor gaped as the poisoner, in his last, desperate instant of life, launched the quill at him. It was an innocuous little thing, barely longer than his hand and not even a finger's width in diameter. It grazed his neck, barely scratching it.

But then the poison coating it struck with the force of a great hammer. He gasped at the power of it, even as he recognized the curse-based flavor of it. He threw everything he had into resisting the poison as he staggered backward, his equilibrium wrecked. The trees spun around him and the island tilted beneath his feet. He stumbled and fetched up hard against something cold. Stone.

Dying. He was dying.

Fight the poison.

Slipping.

The door beneath his cheek felt cool. Soothing. As if the White Tower stroked his skin gently.

He exhaled with one last dying rattle of life expelled.

In that suspended instant between life and death, the tower door gave way, opening of its own volition, and he tumbled forward. Into blackness. Into nothing.

Rosana watched fearfully as Lenora doggedly erected the fifth and final ritual circle, this one created of nature magics. For an instant, a separate dome of green magic formed just over the green rope on the floor, and then its energy flowed into the larger shell, blending with the whole.

Rosana started to breathe a sigh of relief, but it turned into a gasp of pain as a spot over her left collarbone suddenly felt as if it had been stabbed. The ritual circle, now showing hints of green, stabilized overhead. But Lenora had no sooner mopped the sweat off her brow, and Raina had no sooner thrown a relieved glance in Will's direction than faint streaks of dark red began to run through the magic, almost like . . . veins.

She'd *known* this ritual was a bad idea, no matter how dangerous Anton might be and no matter how badly they needed Will and her at full strength before they headed out again on their quest.

"What is it?" Will asked urgently, staring fearfully at the encroaching streaks. Not what but who, and whoever they were, her blood sang darkly in recognition of them.

Lenora was staring at Rosana as if she had grown a second head.

And that was when she noticed that the streaks of red in the circle's magic were starting to align. And they formed a starburst pattern with every streak pointing directly at her gypsy heart.

"No, no, no," Lenora muttered. "More energy, Raina. Those . . . things . . . are eating the circle."

As Raina complied, the red streaks thickened and turned

a brighter shade of red. If anything, adding magic to the ritual seemed to empower the invading veins of old magic even more.

Aurelius jumped to his feet, his entire body glowing as if he prepared to perform some great magic.

"No, Aurelius," Lenora bit out. "Do not try to absorb it."

"What is it?" the solinari demanded.

Lenora responded slowly, her voice questioning, "Rosana? Do you know?"

She swore under her breath. Recognition vibrated deep in her bones, but she knew without a shadow of a doubt that she had never actually seen such a thing before. Why couldn't her life go back to boring and conventional like it had been before she was attacked by orcs and rescued by Will Cobb on a dark road last spring? She'd never wanted anything to do with strange magics and tree lords and sleeping kings in the first place. For all she knew, Will and Raina had hallucinated their whole encounter with the Sleeping King, anyway.

Waking the king was not her quest, and it should not be theirs, either. Let powerful people like Guildmaster Aurelius and High Matriarch Lenora chase after ancient hearth tales if they so choose. But she and Will had their entire lives in front of them. If he would but stop chasing the whole crazy idea of waking up some long-dead king, the two of them could settle down, handfast or even marry, and start a family.

One of the streaks separated itself from the dome of magic and slashed at her. She threw up her forearm and felt a searing cut across her arm. "Magic," she gasped. "That felt like magic."

"What kind of magic?" Lenora demanded urgently as more streaks began reaching down out of the arcing shell of the ritual circle toward her. *Only her.*

Will tried to jump in front of her as one of the tendrils whipped across her face, leaving a thin, burning line of pain behind. Reluctantly, she pushed him back and faced the waving ropes of magic herself. Like it or not, no one else in the circle had what it took to tame this attack.

She felt the power of the angry streaks pulsing through her veins like liquid fire. It was hot. Vibrant. Seductive. Without knowing why she did it, but unable to fight the compulsion, she fumbled at her belt for the small knife she used to trim herbs and cut lengths of bandage. Will lurched to stop her, but before he could grab her wrist, she slashed the inside of her forearm with the sharp little blade. She held her dripping arm over the red rope defining the curse circle on the floor and let her blood run onto the curse signs painted onto the circle. Her blood sizzled as it hit, evaporating instantly and unnaturally. If she was not mistaken, the streaks overhead retreated slightly.

"What are you doing?" Will demanded.

"I have to feed it; else it will grow until it consumes me," she ground out painfully.

"Should all of us feed it?" Raina asked, reaching for the sleeve of her shirt.

"No!" Lenora cried. "Just her."

The matriarch was right. Their blood was too tame. Too civilized. This blood magic needed primal energy. The dark energy of her people, amassed over generations of oppression and suffering.

"Old blood fuels old magic," she muttered, her focus entirely on sending her blood onto the rope at her feet.

"I won't allow you to kill yourself for me," Will declared forcefully.

She glanced up at him. "It's not really your choice, is it? If necessary, that is exactly what I will do."

CHAPTER

3

L andsgrave Leland Hyland prowled the halls of his
manor house restlessly as rain pounded outside. His
ancestral seat felt empty tonight. Hollow. It had been
thus ever since his only son, Kendrick, had been kidnapped
by Kerryl Moonrunner, a powerful nature guardian. What
was the world coming to?

Leland studied the map of Dupree, the Imperial Kothite
colony clinging to a tiny corner of the great, largely un-
explored continent, Haelos. He'd been carefully tracking his
search for Kendrick upon it. Scouts and runners had initially
been sent to the northeastern part of the colony in search of
a clue to Kendrick's whereabouts. His son had been taken
from a party of adventurers in the Forest of Thorns in search
of the Sleeping King. At least the quest had been partially
successful, but stars, the price of it. His son, gone. Taken . . .

He'd long searched in secret for the legendary king said to
be an ancient ruler of these lands. Prophecy foretold that
the king would wake one day to lead his people to freedom.
The people of Urth certainly needed freedom from the
shackles of the mighty Kothite Empire that ruled almost the
whole of Urth under its unyielding iron fist.

When Will Cobb, the son of his old friend Tiberius De'Vir,
and the young arch-mage Raina of Tyrel had shown up on
his doorstep, he hadn't hesitated to send his son to help them
finish the quest that he and Tiberius had failed to complete.
If only he had known how it would turn out. Would he still
have sent his only heir, his boy? It was one thing to sacrifice

his own life for the good of his people. But Kendrick, as well? It was more than his broken heart could bear.

Thank the stars his wife was not alive to see this day. Losing Kendrick would have killed her. By the Void, it was killing him.

He would send out a new batch of scouts on the morrow as soon as the rains abated. And he would bid them to search farther afield. Somebody, somewhere, must know something about the fate of his son.

His gut twisted with guilt at diverting resources that had been allocated for seeking the Sleeping King's regalia to the search for his son. Young Will and Raina had learned that the regalia was necessary to restore the king's spirit to his body. Aurelius could not openly divert Mage's Guild resources to the hunt for regalia any more than High Matriarch Lenora could. Thus, the task had fallen to him to quietly advance the quest. Until Kendrick had gone missing.

The three great Culkellen coursing hounds that were his constant companions and currently dozing in front of the fire lifted their heads in unison, announcing the arrival of someone. Leland looked up to see his seneschal standing in the doorway.

"M'lord, ye've a guest. Rather, a party of 'em. Shall I tell them to come back in the morn at a decent hour?"

"Who are they?" His stomach leaped. Scouts, mayhap? With news of Kendrick? Who else would show up at his door at this hour?

"I dunno. But they's rough-looking sorts. Roguish. Shifty."

Scouts, for sure. "Show them to the trophy room. I'll take their reports immediately."

Leaving the wolfhounds to their naps, he strode to his receiving hall eagerly. Its familiar, rustic comfort washed over him. Trophies from decades of hunting and gifts collected over a lifetime of public service adorned the wood-paneled walls: the head of the Boar of Hyland Heath, the Spirit Stag's antlers, a huge furred skin from the Bear of the Wylde Wood. The great hewn oak beams spanning the ceiling felt heavy overhead tonight. Or perhaps it was merely the weight of worry pressing down on him.

"Here they be, m'lord," the seneschal announced from behind him.

Leland whirled, expecting to see the familiar faces of his men. But instead, five rakasha—white tiger changelings if the fine striped fur on their faces was any indication—prowled silently into the hall.

Their wet clothing was, indeed, rough. Fraying at the edges. But their weapons—high quality at a glance—gleamed. Sheaths well oiled. Grips smooth from use. He scanned their faces, his gaze returning to the big, powerful-looking one with the matching pair of swords in his belt. He frowned. "Do I know you?"

"Name's Gorath. Don't think we've ever met." The big rakasha gestured at the female wearing a bulky pouch, but displaying no other weapons, to his right. "My sister, Mara. And those are my three brothers."

"What's your clan?" Leland queried. He'd definitely seen Gorath somewhere before. He just couldn't place the face.

"That's no matter to the likes of thee," the tiger changeling growled.

"Hey, now," the seneschal protested. "You cannot speak to the landsgrave thus—"

Gorath backhanded the aged seneschal viciously, dropping the fellow like a stone to the floor.

Leland might not have been a youngling himself, but his reflexes were still battle honed, and he had not been one of the greatest warriors in the land for nothing. He leaped for the nearest weapon, a Boki battle thorn—a heavy club covered thickly with razor-sharp thorns hanging beside the Boar of Hyland Heath. It wasn't a decent weapon against swords but better than his bare hands by far.

"This ain't gonna be much of a fight," one of the brothers complained as the four male rakasha took up battle stances. "He's an old man, and a weakling human at that."

Gorath muttered, "The Hart of Hyland is fierce. Do not underestimate him."

Smart fellow. Without sound or warning, Leland leaped toward the nearest rakasha, raising the great battle club as he jumped. He raked the weapon lightly across the fellow's face. For a heavy weapon, it actually called for a delicate touch in its delivery. The vicious thorns completely shredded the rakasha's face into a mass of blood and gore with that single blow. The cat changeling screamed as the poison intrinsic to the bloodthorn burned into his flesh, and he dropped to the floor, bleeding profusely.

The metallic swish of swords being drawn filled the air. The club was heavy and cumbersome—far too slow to defend against lighter, faster swords. He jumped back from the rakasha fighters, parrying the first flurry of blows clumsily. He was outnumbered, and as the cats fanned out to flank him, the tactic showed they were no amateurs at ambush.

He needed a wall at his back. Space in front to operate. A ranged weapon. To hold them off and stop them from rushing him all at once. Without looking over his shoulder, he reached for the silvani moonbow and quiver he knew to be hanging there. He yanked both off their pegs. Not his first choice in a weapon, but he was competent with a bow.

He nocked two arrows at once and shot them at the closest rakasha male, one of the remaining brothers. The fellow howled and went down as one arrow pierced his thigh and the other struck in the soft flesh of his groin.

"It burns! By the Void, it burns. Get it out of me!" the downed rakasha howled.

The female—a healer, apparently—ran over to him and yanked the arrows free as Leland loosed a third arrow at another one of the brothers. Although this rakasha flinched a little as the moonarrow struck his shoulder, he merely reached up and yanked the missile free himself and threw it to the floor.

The middle brother pounced, and Leland dodged to force the attacker through the pooled blood on the floor. The cat's boot skidded, throwing him off balance. Leland dodged the awkward upward swing, using the bow to block it. The slender wood shaft broke in his hand, and Leland threw himself backward, away from the next swing of lethal steel. He slammed into the long council table and landed on top of it. He spun his legs around and leaped off the far side of the table as he flung the broken bow aside.

Gorath raced around the end of the table to loom in front of him, and the remaining male stalked him from behind.

Leland grabbed a dragon's tongue spear favored by lizardmen. Its head forked into two points, hence the name. He lunged, jamming the double points into Gorath's chest. The blow should have dropped the cat changeling, but it did not. Odd.

Leland yanked at the weapon, but it would not come free. Forced to abandon it, he retreated, looking around frantically for another weapon. He became aware of barking, growling, and the scrabbling of great claws raking frantically at the door across the room. His hounds. If he could get over there, let them in, they'd even the odds. He backed away from Gorath toward the remaining brother who'd called him old and who was now regarding him rather more cautiously than before.

Across the table, the female had opened her pouch and fumbled within it. Given that her hands were not glowing with magic, he guessed she was an alchemist. Once she started lobbing gases at him, he was done for. He needed to do something to even the odds, and fast. He reached for the pendant hanging from a chain under his shirt. Where was the cursed thing? Gorath was almost upon him, and he had no shield or weapon to parry even the simplest blow. His fingers closed upon warm metal, and he blurted out the activation word just as both rakasha fighters leaped.

A darkness spell poured forth from the pendant, enveloping the room in a blackness so thick and impenetrable that no shape nor shadow could be seen within it.

Long trained in the art of blind fighting and a great deal

more familiar with the layout of this room than his attackers, he ducked Gorath's wild sword swing and slid to the side around the big rakasha. He groped the wall and found the sword mounted beside a ram whose life the blade had taken. The grip fit his hand to perfection. Ahh, he remembered this blade. Nice balance. Weighted close to the hilt, just the way he liked his swords. It made for a fast blade tip.

He turned to face his attackers. Rakasha had the extraordinarily keen scent of their kind and would locate him soon enough. He wasted no time sliding to his right, closer to the smaller brother. If he could eliminate the other brothers, isolate Gorath one-on-one, he would stand a better chance against the powerful warrior.

He flicked his blade wide around the rakasha, playing the child's game of tapping a person on the shoulder while standing by the other one. Predictably, the rakasha swung right, giving his entire left side undefended to him.

Leland swung for the body, but at the last second, the rakasha must have sensed the blow coming and threw out a gauntleted forearm to catch the blade. With shocking speed, the changeling parried, slicing across the meat of Leland's left arm. It burned but not with poison. That was a boon, at least. The wound felt deep but not mortal. And the arm still functioned. He set aside the pain and fought on.

The sword came at him again, and he parried and riposted blow after blow. The unnamed rakasha brother was fast even without benefit of seeing his foe. Leland made a short, chopping swing, channeling all his skill and intent into delivering a deadly blow to his foe. The blade bit through the rakasha's leather jerkin, tasting flesh. The power of the blow drove the blade deep into the creature's side, guiding the edge unerringly between ribs and into the vital tissues below. The attacker went down with a howl of agony.

Leland yanked at the blade, but it had sunk deep, and the rakasha's bones and gristle did not release it easily. Gorath charged, and Leland had no choice but to abandon the blade and flee.

He raced around the table, gauging its length in his mind. He charged across the open space of the room, hurdling the low table between the pair of big chairs by the fireplace. Something whizzed past his ear and smashed against the wall before him with a crash of breaking glass. He dived and rolled to the side lest the gas from the broken alchemy globe find him.

He jumped for the carved wooden chest in the corner and threw up the lid, picturing the contents in his mind. Thank the Lady he was a creature of habit, always packing his war chests in the same way. He grabbed a handful of alchemical potions in his left hand and had just reached for a spare sword when something slammed into his right leg, low. The power of the blow knocked his foot out from under him, and he went down hard on his right shoulder. His entire arm went numb, but by some miracle, he managed to retain a grip on the sword.

He rolled and barely avoided the pouncing weight of the big rakasha. His arm was partially trapped beneath his body, but he managed a truncated swing at his foe nonetheless. The tip of the sword nicked something, and the rakasha snarled in rage. It felt as if he'd cut the cat's face.

It wasn't much, but it bought him time to roll to his feet and smash the flat of his blade into the side of the cat's head with considerable force. He sensed the cat staggering and going down to one knee, shaking his head, dazed.

Another glass globe exploded on the wall above his head. Liquid ran down the paneling, the wood sizzling as a metallic odor of acid rose from it. That had been entirely too close for comfort. Worse, the alchemist had moved in front of the door and the hounds.

Leland ran toward the far corner of the room to draw her away from the door. But his right leg was not working properly, and his boot squished, full of blood, with each step.

As he half ran, limping, he tucked the sword under his arm and used his free hand to unstopper one of the potion vials. He tossed the contents down, shuddering at the awful taste of an alchemy shield.

Something light slammed into his back, and the tinkle of broken glass trailed behind him. A dim flash of light accompanied the magic of his alchemy shield being burned up. He swore as the flash gave away his position, and he dived to the side. His injured leg barely held his weight, and he staggered, stumbled, and righted himself awkwardly.

He unstoppered another vial and chugged the contents as he heard the female rakasha muttering the command to activate a gas poison behind him. Another globe struck him in the back. Gads, she was fast.

He turned to face her as he drank his third, and last, shield potion. He sensed Mara standing at nearly the far end of the room, lobbing her globes with considerable strength to be reaching him all the way down here.

He dodged an incoming globe and envisioned the walls on either side of him for likely weapons. All that hung on the wall nearby was the pelt of a great black cave bear. He snatched it down, and as yet another poison flew toward him, he lifted the pelt to catch the glass globe. The rare and terribly expensive fur disintegrated in his hands as acid ate through it.

He had to do something to stop her or at least slow down Gorath, who was rising to his feet even now. He was no expert at throwing daggers, but he remembered a brace of them down the wall. Better, he was able to reach the door and throw it open. His hounds charged into the room furiously, but stopped, confused by the total darkness.

Using his enhanced, blind-fighting senses, Leland both sensed and heard Gorath raising his nose and taking a long sniff. And then the big cat changeling turned toward him and advanced stealthily. He frowned. He sensed the cat holding his clawed hands in an unusual above-and-below defensive pose.

Anton. That was where he'd seen the big rakasha before. Memory burst over Leland of that odd defensive style. Gorath and several of his Clan Kithmar kin had been with the governor in the Forest of Thorns last spring at the clandestine meeting between Anton and the Boki thane, Ki'Raiden. The meeting whereat Anton made a deal with the Boki traitor to assassinate Landsgrave Talyn. *That* was what this attack was about. An assassination engineered by his longtime nemesis, Anton Constantine.

In his momentary distraction, Leland missed sensing an incoming globe and was not fast enough to dodge. It broke against his arm, and his magical shield lit up. Worse, the seneschal was beginning to rouse where he had fallen by the doors, groaning aloud. Gorath reacted sharply to the sound and charged toward it.

Leland swore and jumped to protect his man, snatching up a small, ceremonial shield no larger than a dinner platter as he passed by it. Diving forward, he was able to throw the shield in front of his man and deflect Gorath's first blow. But the second one caught Leland across the back. The worst of it was stopped by spine and ribs, but it was a large cut, and his body arched backward instinctively, contorted in fiery agony.

He had to move. Use the darkness to escape. But his right leg refused to jump when he commanded it to. He staggered, half fell toward the far wall, and banged loudly into the row of wooden chairs lined up there for petitioners.

Gorath corrected direction and ran for the noise. Dregs. Leland fell backward into a chair and rolled aside just as Gorath's sword skewered the chair back. In the second it took the changeling to yank the tip free of the wood, Leland reached desperately for a weapon, anything with which to defend himself. His hand brushed across a trophy upon the wall. Collected antlers shed each year by the Spirit Stag. He grasped one, and as he finished falling to the floor, it broke off in his hand. He took a desperate backhand swing with his left arm and slashed its pointed tip across the back of the rakasha's knee, partially hamstringing him.

Swearing viciously, Gorath swung his fist in Leland's

general direction. Dregs. The rakasha had extended his claws. Like all cat changelings, Gorath had four razor-sharp claws embedded in his fists that could be extended upon command. Leland threw up his improvised weapon, but the blow was too strong, delivered with too much force for him to block it. Gorath's claws slid up the short length of the antler and slammed into his right shoulder, burying themselves in the muscles that controlled his arm. The rakasha yanked viciously, raking the claws through muscle and sinew, shredding the joint completely.

The limb fell useless to Leland's side as a gush of hot blood poured over his chest and down his back, his fingers frozen around the antler. The room began to spin and he grew light-headed in the span of a few seconds as his life's blood poured from his wounds.

He. Must. Not. Die. Kendrick needed him. No one else had the resources to mount a full-scale search for his son nor to recover him from the powerful nature guardian who'd kidnapped him. Leland clung to consciousness by the thinnest thread, fighting with every ounce of his will to overcome his wounds. To stand. To fight. To win.

Something hit him lightly in the chest, no harder than a sparrow's wing brushing against him. He felt, rather than saw, the gas cloud envelop him. And then there was nothing.

G orath righted himself, swearing luridly. The landsgrave was supposed to be surprised by their ambush and not fight back, and certainly not with such ferocity. Leland Hyland was said to be an old man. Hells, he would hate to have faced the man in his prime.

"Are you alive, Gorath?" Mara called anxiously.

"Aye. The others?"

"I cannot see."

"Jack went down first. Find him."

As Leland's life expired, so did the darkness spell. Lamplight shone once more throughout the destroyed chamber.

The hounds charged Mara, who was closest to them, and she threw all the remaining gas globes in her hands at the beasts.

Gorath leaped forward to the whimpering, burned creatures, slashing their throats open viciously. *Cursed, foul beasts.* They could bleed out like their master. With their last heartbeats, the three hounds dragged themselves on their bellies toward Leland's body, trying and failing to reach his corpse before they died with howls gurgling uselessly in their slit throats.

Meanwhile, three crumpled heaps marked where his brothers had fallen in the fight. "Heal them!" he ordered Mara urgently.

She was already racing to Niall's side, closest to her. She poured a potion down his throat, but entirely too slowly.

"Faster!" he bit out.

"I can only do this so quickly without spilling the potion and wasting it," she snapped back. Niall groaned and rolled over at her feet. She moved to the next body and repeated the process with their brother Paco. But this time, nothing happened.

She swore and dug frantically in her pouch for another vial. Gorath swore, as well. Life potions were expensive and hard to come by. If Hyland weren't already dead, he would gut the man for killing his brother *and* for costing them a pretty pile of gold by having to burn a life potion.

Mara poured the potion down Paco's throat. Gorath held his breath until his brother lurched of a sudden, gasped violently, and commenced swearing.

"Hurry, Mar. He went down first," Gorath snarled, pointing at his closest brother in age, he of the mangled face. He must have bled out after Leland shredded him with that cursed thorned club.

She moved to their last brother's side and crouched beside the corpse, taking in the massive pool of blood that had spread a full body's length beyond their kin. "No use even bothering with healing potions here. I'm going straight for a life potion."

A *second* life potion? *Curses upon Hyland and all his kin.*

Mara poured the second expensive potion down Jack's throat, but nothing happened.

"What's wrong?" Gorath growled, prowling over to take a closer look.

"I got to him too late. He's dead."

"You mean he's going to have to resurrect?" Gorath demanded in fury.

"That's the way of it."

He was going to dismember the landsgrave's dead corpse and burn the pieces—

Curses. This was not how Hyland was supposed to die. He had to clean up this mess and do what he had been paid to do. He knew as well as anyone the danger of crossing Anton Constantine. Anton was vicious and merciless to any who dared stand against him. He might have been deposed as governor of Dupree and be a fugitive, but he still had power and resources. One would never know from whence came revenge once Anton was well and truly provoked.

He swore some more and satisfied himself in part by trashing the remaining furniture, smashing what was still intact into kindling.

"By the Great Beasts, what a fiasco," Mara muttered as she strode over to Hyland's corpse to examine it. "Did you have to kill him, Gor?" she complained. "I don't have any more life potions. The Slaver's Guild has an order in effect to capture him and bring him in to face charges of treason. Bringing him in would earn me great rewards and go a long way toward getting me a promotion in rank."

He needed to distract her. Draw her away from Hyland's body so he could do what had to be done. "Do you need to go be with Jack's spirit and offer it field resurrection? The sooner he's up and around, the sooner we can all be quit of this place."

"Good point." She hustled across the room and knelt at their brother's side, blessedly with her back to him.

Furtively, Gorath pulled two vials out of his pouch. He poured the first, a life potion, down Hyland's throat. As the man drew a gasping breath, he coughed to cover the sound and used the butt of his belt dagger to knock the landsgrave unconscious. Then, carefully, he unsealed the second vial and poured the viscous, red-black fluid inside it down Hyland's unresisting throat. With a single, long inhalation, the landsgrave died. For good this time, if Anton's description of the poison's effect was accurate.

He stuffed the empty vial back into his pouch just in the nick of time, for Mara came over to stand beside him. She stared down at the landsgrave's corpse. "Odd. He seemed so determined to live. But I do not sense his spirit hovering near his body. It is as if he has already moved beyond the Veil."

"Huh. Odd," he echoed. At long last. His family's debt to Constantine was paid in full. The Kithmar clan was finally free of Anton. Exultation roared through him.

"I'll feed the servant a forgetting potion and then slit his throat. You start hauling in the other bodies," she ordered irritably. She gave the landsgrave's corpse a kick with her booted toe on her way past him.

Gorath hoisted the first body from the wagon over his shoulder, a badger changeling corpse in a torn and bloody Dominion tabard, and carried it into the landsgrave's house. He dumped it next to the pool of blood where his deceased brother lay and headed back to the wagon.

Why Anton wanted to frame the fierce changeling horde that was the Dominion for this murder was a mystery to him. Gorath supposed that, if he'd had no clan of his own, mayhap he would've gone into the wilds in search of service within the Dominion. But as it was, he dumped another body—this one a wolverine changeling—on the floor with a shrug. The four parallel red slashes emanating from an animal paw that made up the Dominion's symbol gleamed up at him from the creature's black tabard.

Too bad they could not get Anton to compensate them for the expensive life potions they had been forced to use. Not to mention if Jack's spirit didn't have the sense to approach Mara for a field resurrection, they would have to pay the Heart richly for resurrecting their brother. Sure, the poor didn't have to pay, but the Kithmar were well known as successful—and rich—slavers. They would be expected to give lavishly to the Heart's coffers in return for their brother's life.

Irritated at the high cost Hyland had inflicted upon them, he picked up one of the side chairs and gave it a good heave. It smashed satisfyingly into a wall hanging, tangled with the tapestry tassels, and tore the entire hanging down from the wall. On the way down, the rod crashed into an oil lamp and knocked it out of its sconce. The lamp's glass reservoir broke, splashing hot oil over the crumpled tapestry cloth. The burning wick landed in the midst of the heap, and the whole flared up in flames.

"Gor. *Ath*," Mara complained through clenched jaws.

He went over to the tapestry and grabbed a corner of it with the intent to pull the thing outside. But as he yanked, a shower of sparks and burning embers flew up, some of them alighting in the curtains. The thin, expensive silk ignited, and within the space of a breath, a wall of flames climbed toward the dry, old wood of the rafters.

"You've set the place on fire," Mara snarled. "Put it out before the whole manor goes up in smoke and all our work is for naught. Hurry."

He searched for a bucket of water near the hearth, but none was at hand. "Sorry, sister," he mumbled, not feeling sorry at all.

"We have to get out of here before the village rouses and the locals come to put out the fire. The whole point of this was to make people think the Dominion did it."

Grumbling, he ducked out past the fire, which had spread to three windows and several chairs. He dumped the last body as flames climbed a second wall now and licked hungrily at the ceiling.

"You'd better hope your fire does not destroy the details Anton insisted on," she huffed as they gathered their surviving brothers and ran for the woods.

"To the Void with him," Gorath panted back. *To the Void with all those noble types.*

CHAPTER

4

Will sat warily, and Rosana did the same beside him. Nothing about this ritual had gone well so far, and a looming sense of foreboding clung to the circle and its occupants. Lenora looked vaguely gray about the edges, and Raina frankly looked exhausted. But as soon as the thought occurred to Will, she got up from her stool and moved around the little table, reaching into her belt pouch as she came.

"Let me bind your arm, Rosana," she murmured. "It's still bleeding."

Will watched anxiously as Raina swabbed away blood still trickling over Rosana's wrist and fingers. A long, narrow cut along Rosana's forearm became visible.

"There is nothing unusual about the wound?" he asked anxiously.

Raina glanced up at him. "Nay. It's just a cut. Her blood is the unusual bit."

"How so?" he started.

Without warning, Raina froze. Her knuckles went white, and Rosana made a tiny sound of protest. The blond human girl's gaze was distant, horrified, staring at something he could not see. Since when did she receive visions?

Rosana groaned, and he lunged forward to grab her as her legs began to collapse.

And then a vision flashed into his mind's eye. A glimpse of darkness so vast and black and empty as to suck the very soul from a man.

"What the—" he gasped.

Men's voices shouted nearby, but trapped in the vision Will only peripherally registered swords swinging clear of sheaths.

"No!" Lenora called out strongly. "Do not interrupt the circles! Stay where you are!"

Will blinked hard, forcibly jerking his mind back from the margin of the abyss. The Heart's common room came into focus once more. But it was as if two entirely separate places occupied the single space. A shadow of that other place, an endless black void, overlaid the Heart common room with its wooden floors, broad beamed ceilings, plaster walls, and anxious-faced healers.

Ephemeral creatures were taking form throughout the room, passing over from that other realm into this one, quickly gaining form and substance. He reached reflexively for his staff, but it was not slung in its usual place across his back. Will swore and snatched Rosana's dagger from its sheath as he leaped in front of her.

A transparent humanoid man dressed in white robes with a long white beard and carrying a lit lantern stood near the Heartstone. The Royal Order of the Sun guards dived to put themselves between him and the stone, but the apparition merely smiled gently as they passed through his ghostly image.

A commotion on the other side of the room caused Will to turn sharply. Rosana cringed against his side as a man dressed all in black, as grim and forbidding as the man in white had been welcoming, appeared momentarily. The apparition held a black scourge coiled in his right hand, the hungry, braided leather whip deadly looking. The man stood with his feet braced apart, his left foot a little forward, his weight back as if he prepared to flay someone.

Raina moaned and fell to her knees as a third and even more frightening image came into focus at the very edges of Will's ability to see it. The figure was large and also cloaked all in black. But this one carried a silver-bladed scythe mounted on a black pole nearly as tall as the being himself. He seemed to be part of the infinite darkness Will had glimpsed, a creature made of the very essence of that sucking void. Of death. *Reaper.*

Will had heard legends of such creatures but never dreamed they actually existed. He'd thought they were made up to scare children into staying abed at night. Surely he, of all people, ought to know by now that the old myths were based more in fact than most people knew. Nonetheless, he was shocked to his core by the reaper's appearance.

"Help me," Rosana muttered at him as she knelt beside Raina.

Will reached down and grasped both girls by a hand to haul them upright. But as he did, it was as if a magical circuit of some kind had been completed. Magic zinged between all three of them, greater than any of them individually. The disk affixed to his chest seared his skin as if it would burn a hole in him. Rosana and Raina reached for the wood piece simultaneously. How did they know it burned him?

Rosana's hand got there first, and Raina's landed on top of the gypsy's. A wave of healing poured into him, which was passing strange since normal healing had little effect on him these days.

Overhead, an ominous sound started, commencing as a low rending noise and crescendoing into a mighty crack of sound. Anyone forest-born knew it for the splitting of wood. Will looked up quickly, startled, in time to see the great, central oaken beam supporting the ceiling of the Heart common room open a great crack down its length to the accompaniment of that awful rending noise. It was as if the brief collision of worlds had proved too much for the mighty beam.

Will looked away, back in the direction of the reaper, but the great black being had vanished, along with all the otherworldly apparitions. The common room was just a room once again.

The Royal Order of the Sun knights alternated between looking around the room frantically for otherworldly attackers and casting doubtful stares upward at the now split beam.

"I thought you were not supposed to cast common magic inside a ritual circle," Will muttered low to the girls. *They* hadn't caused the beam to fail because of something they'd done, had they?

"We didn't cast any magic just now," Rosana replied, startled.

And yet, he felt invigorated. Healthy. Exactly as if he *had* been healed. "You did not heal me when you two laid your hands on me?"

"No," both healers replied simultaneously.

Frowning, he rose to his full height, and the girls' hands fell away from his chest. Something had definitely happened when they both touched Bloodroot's disk.

Someone brought a ladder, and one of the Royal Order knights climbed up to the cracked beam to take a closer look at it. Apparently, he was a trained combat engineer. The three knights put their heads together to confer about repairs to the building.

"Where did that creature go?" one of the Royal Order of the Sun guardians demanded. He and his companions brandished their swords in the general area of where the reaper had briefly appeared.

"He is still there," Raina answered tiredly. "You just cannot see nor touch him."

"Where?" the guard demanded.

"Beyond this plane. In the Void," she replied. "He is always there. This building is a nexus where souls frequently leave our plane to cross over into his."

"How come we could see him just now?" the guardian demanded.

Lenora was the one who answered thoughtfully. "Some great disruption in the fabric of life in Dupree has torn it a little. The tear allowed us a glimpse beyond the Veil, into the Void, before it was repaired. Raina, you and I have been pulling large amounts of spiritual magic from that web of life for over an hour. We may have been the catalyst for those . . . visions."

Will sincerely hoped that was all they had been. Just hallucinations. But he just as sincerely doubted that was the case.

"Did I tear the Veil somehow?" Raina asked in dismay.

"I think not," the high matriarch answered promptly. "Something else caused that." She took a deep breath and then announced, "This is becoming too dangerous. I am sorry, Rosana. I cannot in good conscience allow this ritual to continue. We will have to find another way to restore your spirit to you."

And high time it was, indeed, to end this madness. *Praise the Lady.* Will balled his fists tightly, frustrated with the outcome of this fiasco. Intellectually, he understood the high matriarch's decision. Both she and Raina looked about ready to collapse. But curses, he'd been counting on Rosana being whole once more. There *had* to be a way to fix her. He would find it, come hounds or high water. It was the least he could do for her. She was willing to sacrifice her life to save him. And he was willing to do no less for her.

Raina lay in the dark, frozen with terror in her narrow bunk. Something powerful enough to attack a ritual while not even in the same room had come for them tonight. Who or what had that kind of power? The actual fabric of magic, the veil between the planes themselves, had been torn. Anything that powerful could crush her and her friends like so many ants underfoot.

She'd known in a vague way that attempting to wake the Sleeping King would also wake powerful forces opposed to the idea. But now that the reality was upon her, she had to question the wisdom of carrying on in their quest. The Kothite Emperor himself would throw his full might at them when he got wind of what they were up to. And surely he would, at some point. The Empire had eyes and ears everywhere. No matter how careful and secretive they were, she and her companions were bound to catch someone's attention eventually. She just hadn't expected it to be this soon.

Breathing hard, she lay in the half-dark listening to the sounds of the Heart chapter beyond the curtain separating her little alcove from the common room. The building was never still. People came and went around the clock seeking healing or trading for healing scrolls and potions. A constant murmur of voices, bangs, shuffles, and other man-made sounds enveloped her. Usually, she liked how it reminded her of her family's crowded, noisy manor house far away in Tyrel.

But tonight, she just wished for a little silence in which to quiet her mind. As exhausting as the physical demands of summoning so much magic had been, her nerves still jangled too badly to let her sleep. How on Urth had anyone interrupted that ritual? It had actually been going very well until that first surge of . . . disturbance, for lack of any better way of thinking of it. She'd been calling and molding spirit magic for as long as she had memory, and she'd never encountered anything like the ripple that passed through all the spirit magic in the land. It was as if a piece of her own soul had torn loose and been destroyed.

And then the attacks on the curse circle that had panicked Rosana and whatever had happened to put Will on the floor in writhing agony . . . she'd have called them backlashes if the ritual hadn't continued on as it had.

She'd never heard of anyone or anything that could corrupt a ritual like that. But then, she'd never heard of any of the stuff six months ago that she and her friends were currently elbow deep in. Like it or not, they all had enemies now.

Should they consider stopping their search for the Sleeping King's regalia? Did they dare stop? They were already so deep into treason that none of them would survive capture by Imperial forces of any kind. They already had no homes, no families, no names left. At this point, they had little to lose by continuing on.

She pulled the thin blanket up around her ears. Not that it blocked out the low groans of whatever injury had just stumbled in. The flow of sick and hurt people through the building never stopped. She yanked the blanket all the way over her head.

Stars, she really hated the Heart sometimes. She'd just wanted to live a normal life. To grow up at home in her beloved Tyrel, marry her childhood sweetheart, Justin, and raise a family. She'd never dreamed of *this* for herself.

She glared up at the White Heart tabard hanging on its hook beside her, its pristine white bright in the light leaking past her curtain, the royal blue Heart symbol on it a dark shadow in the dim alcove. And she'd certainly never dreamed of joining *that* order.

Her thoughts circled back to the failed ritual. She had cast plenty of high magic rituals before, but none had ever made her feel so trapped or claustrophobic. The magics tonight had suffocated her, pushing in until she'd been hard-pressed not to bolt from the circle. That same restlessness overcame her now. With a resentful glare for it, she snatched her tabard off the hook and dragged the White Heart colors over her head. She jammed her feet into her boots and headed out into the common room.

A lizardman healer looked up in surprise from the wounded man he was healing. His green scales and broad, kind face were markedly different from Sha'Li's black scales and heart-shaped features. His eyes were dark with compassion and concern for his patient.

"Can I assist you, Brother Lizmorn?" she mumbled, checking her irritation. No sense taking out her foul mood on everyone around her.

"No, thank you. I've got this. And you tired yourself out with that ritual. Rest, Initiate Raina."

If only. On cue, the walls of the common room and the low, heavy-beamed ceiling with temporary braces propped all along its length started to close in on her. She had to get out of here. Grabbing her cloak from its hook by the door, she made for the exit. At this time of night, the wizard's lock was in place around the entire building, and a Royal Order of the Sun knight was pulling door duty, wizard's lock key in hand to let people in or out of the building.

"Going somewhere?" he asked her.

She recognized him, a red-haired barbarian warrior newly come from serving with Lord Justinius—commander of the entire Royal Order of the Sun. "I'm just stepping out, Sir Hrothgar. I need some air."

"It's too late for a young girl to be roaming the streets of Dupree alone."

"Nonetheless, that's exactly what I intend to do. The

wizard's lock, please." She didn't often resort to the polite but firm noble's tone of command her mother had perfected and which she imitated now.

Frowning, Hrothgar lowered the lock, and the faint glow around the doorway disappeared. But then he surprised her by tossing the key to Lizmorn. "You've got the door while I escort the White Heart."

"I've no need for an escort," she protested. She really just wanted to be by herself for a little while. Was that too much to ask?

The knight ignored her and threw a cloak over his armor. He took up an imposing white shield emblazoned with the Royal Order's symbol—a red field with the heart-and-sunray pattern upon it—and drew his sword.

Oh, for the love of the Lady. "I'm not going into battle," she grumbled.

He merely shrugged and opened the door for her. Stubborn barbarian.

With a huff of exasperation at the ruination of her plan to be alone, she stepped past him. The night was chilly and damp, and she breathed deeply of the cold, fresh air. Resolved to ignore the warrior pacing behind her, she hurried down the steps and across the broad square in front of the Heart building.

The city of Dupree was laid out like a wheel. The governor's palace and the huge square around it made up the hub. Broad avenues led outward like spokes to smaller squares, each one housing the headquarters of a different Imperial guild. The space between the spokes was a warren of twisting side streets, businesses, and dwellings crammed together willy-nilly to make a sprawling city.

It was into this morass of winding streets she plunged with Hrothgar in tow. Her White Heart colors virtually assured her that no one would harm or harass her here. Not only was the tabard known and respected by all, but she, herself, had gained acclaim as a prodigious healer in the great riots just prior to Anton Constantine's fall. It probably didn't hurt, either, that she resembled her mother, Charlotte, who had been a great beauty renowned throughout Dupree in her youth. And then, of course, there was the burly, menacing, and well-armed knight stalking her heels.

She wandered the deserted streets, enjoying the shine of wet cobblestones and the way tendrils of fog curled at her feet as she neared the shore of the great Bay of Dupree. She fancied that she could hear the voices of the sleeping people of Dupree whispering to her as she moved among them.

Her claustrophobia dissipated, leaving her so exhausted she could hardly stand. She paused on a street corner to orient herself and realized with a start that she was just around the corner from Leland Hyland's town house. The landsgrave had been like a father to her since she had come here, protecting her and advising her in her quest to find the Sleeping King. He'd been the one to convince her to join the White Heart, as well. It was mostly for him that she tolerated the confines of the colors.

Her entire being felt drained. Empty. The long walk back to the Heart loomed, and she was abruptly so fatigued she could not fathom making the long trek back to her own bed. It was not as if she could ask Hrothgar to carry her home on his shoulders. Although she had no doubt he would if she asked him to. The Royal Order of the Sun took its duty to the White Heart extremely seriously, which was ironic in its own way. Some of the most violent warriors in the Empire protected the exclusively pacifist arm of the Heart.

"Sir Hrothgar, would you mind if I spent the night at Hyland's house?"

"That would be acceptable. The landsgrave and his troops are capable and honorable men. They will keep you safe at the forfeit of their own lives."

She shuddered at the notion of anyone sacrificing his or her life for her. But then, that was exactly what Hrothgar was sworn to do. A frisson of guilt rippled through her for dragging him out here in the dead of night into a city that was far from safe. "I suppose you would be much relieved if I got behind high walls, would you not?"

"I would, Initiate."

She was disappointed when Hyland's night watch informed her that Leland was currently at his manor home in the country. They were quick to offer her usual chambers to her for the night, however.

The lure of sleeping in a soft bed all by herself in a quiet room was too much to resist. She bade good night to Hrothgar and murmured to the watch soldier that she would show herself to her room. She headed wearily up the stairs, kicked off her boots, and crawled into bed, asleep almost before her head hit the pillow.

Her dreams were strange and disjointed. They were punctuated by loss, grief, and violence she was helpless to prevent. Eventually, the nightmares exploded into a great conflagration that burned up everything she'd been dreaming of and then consumed her.

Frightened, her dreaming self fled the fire and burst into a white, featureless fog. It swirled around her, plucking at her clothing and nipping at her skin. It was insidious and malevolent, the fog, seeking to steal something from her. She moved forward cautiously. Fear drove her to walk faster and faster and then break into a jog and finally into a full-out sprint of terror. But always the fog was there, attempting to insert itself into her mind and steal her most precious memory. She mustn't let it! Panic clawed at her as she tried to outrun the encroaching thief—

She stumbled and nearly fell as green, springy grass sprouted abruptly beneath her feet. The fog rushed back from her violently, unveiling a forest glade of such beauty that she could hardly bear to look it at.

A tall, dark-haired elf as beautiful as the glade turned quickly to face her and took a concerned step forward as she slumped in abject relief. It was *him*. He still lived. Or existed as a memory, or whatever it was he did in this dreaming place.

"Raina, welcome. What is wrong?"

"Wrong?" she echoed. "Why do you ask? How did I get here?"

"You summoned me to your dream."

She stared at the Sleeping King. "I summoned *you*? But how?" she asked blankly.

A faint frown crossed his noble brow. "Apparently, you are deeply disturbed by something. Enough so that your distress reached out to me of its own volition."

"Oh, dear. I'm sorry I bothered you, Your Majesty. I didn't mean to."

"I am glad you did. And call me Gawaine. My kingdom has not existed for millennia." He gestured to a pair of bent willow chairs she had not noticed before. Or mayhap they had just appeared beside him under the spreading boughs of a magnificently flowering tree she did not recognize. "Come. Sit."

She moved forward, staring at him. She remembered him as handsome from the first time they'd met, but not like this. She sank into one of the chairs, and he did the same.

"What troubles your dreams, Raina?"

"I helped cast a ritual this evening. It went badly."

"Did it backlash? Were you hurt?"

"Not exactly. Bloodroot did not want us to perform the ritual and resisted it, causing Will a fair bit of discomfort. Then, when the nature circle went up, it attacked Rosana and wanted her blood. And later, there was a . . . rip."

"What sort of rip?"

"Is it possible that I could have seen into the Void?"

Gawaine looked startled. "The actual Void?"

"For a moment, it was as if the mortal plane tore away. In its place, I saw some sort of spirit guide. A man dressed in white and carrying a lantern. And I saw a scourge and a reaper. Beyond them yawned a blackness so dark and deep I could not draw breath while I gazed into it. And within it lay death." She shook her head. "It was probably just my imagination. I must have exhausted myself trying to keep the circle intact."

Gawaine frowned. "Death's creatures are around you all the time. They wait where the material plane meets the Void and collect spirits as they pass beyond the Veil from your world into theirs. I do not doubt that what you saw was real. The question is, why did you see it?"

She had no answer for that.

"Can you still see the Void and its keepers?"

She looked around the grove in alarm, and Gawaine chuckled. "You will not see them here. This is the land of Nod. The dream realm only indirectly touches the Void." Gawaine was silent for a time in the leisurely way of his race. Then he murmured, "How goes it in Dupree?"

"In a word, chaotic. The governor was deposed and fled from arrest. He hides, probably somewhere in the colony. And knowing Anton, he plots mischief. The new governess seems a lamb after Anton, but we have yet to see if a wolf hides beneath her fleece or not."

Gawaine smiled a little at that. "Will Cobb and your friends?"

"Will and Lord Bloodroot seem to have achieved a truce. Will's health is stable. Or at least it is as long as Rosana and I periodically join our healing and give it to him."

"She's the gypsy girl you told me about?"

Raina nodded.

Gawaine made no comment, but she got the feeling he knew more than he was saying about how her magic and Rosana's were working in unison to help Will.

She continued, "My kindari protector, Cicero, has gone back to Tyrel. Being so close to the Empire made him uneasy."

Gawaine's lips twitched. "Is he perchance an outlaw?"

Raina shrugged, her eyes twinkling. Far be it from her to give away her dear friend's secrets.

"I am glad his sword protected you. What of the lizard-man girl?"

"She's got her Tribe of the Moon mark and is very smug about it."

"Good for her. Lunimar's cause is worthy, and my uncle has great need of brave warriors to his service."

His *uncle*? A greater being said to harness the power of the moon itself? Gawaine hadn't made the reference in a way that invited questions, hence she did not pry. She was not deeply familiar with the Tribe of the Moon, other than having heard the secretive group served nature in some shadowy and not entirely legal way.

"Have you found your missing friend?"

"Kendrick? No. Eben—he's the jann I told you about—is frantic."

"And you?" Gawaine asked quietly. "How are you?"

She glanced up at him and was arrested by the intense way he was studying her. As if he could see right inside her soul. It was simply not possible to prevaricate in the face of that penetrating stare.

She answered with bald honesty, "I am frustrated. Worried. Unsettled. We spend too long in Dupree wasting time in training when we should be out searching for what we need to finish waking you." Realizing how whiny that sounded, she added, "But the rest of my friends are safe. I have a place to stay, and the men who were chasing me before cannot touch me now that I am White Heart." A fact she took great pleasure in.

Thwarting the Mages of Alchizzadon was no easy feat. But she would be twice cursed before she went along with their plans for her. For generations the women in her family had been selectively matched with powerful mages to produce ever more gifted daughters. The mages planned to use her to breed the next generation of magically enhanced women for her family and had gone so far as to pick out a mate for her—a bland, boring man half again her age whose name she didn't even know.

"Why are you unhappy?" Gawaine asked astutely, cutting to the core of the issue.

She was *not* going to complain about her fate to a king who had been killed and trapped in this prison for thousands of years, stripped of kingdom, title, and name, and long forgotten. "I will grow used to the White Heart and find happiness in my work."

"Ahh."

She winced as he gazed at her knowingly. He commented, "It is hard being a living symbol, is it not? People always tugging at your sleeve. Always draining you of magic. Always expecting you to heal them."

"I do not mind healing," she blurted. "It is just that sometimes I would like to be alone. I would like to be . . . me. It is as if I have become a walking White Heart tabard and am no longer a person."

He nodded gravely. "It is the same when you become a king."

She paused, arrested. She had never thought of it thus. But she could see his point. A king was a symbol. A protector, judge, and leader. People would always have expectations of him. Place demands upon his office. They would not see him as a man.

Even now, thousands of years after he had died, she and her friends were still coming after him, demanding that he wake and battle against the Kothite Empire on their behalf.

"Your Majesty, I am so sorry," she murmured formally. "Please allow me to offer my humble apologies—"

"For what?" he interrupted.

"Will and I barged in here to your resting place all set upon finding and waking you, and we never stopped to ask if you even want to be awoken."

Warmth lit his eyes. And understanding. "No apology is necessary. You are concerned about the welfare of your land and people. I cannot fault you for that."

Silence fell between them. Birds overhead sang songs so achingly sweet they made her want to weep, and the fresh scent of wild geraniums wafted to her. The peace of this place was profound. Perfect. She soaked it in through every pore of her skin.

Eventually, he spoke rather more seriously than she'd expected. "I believe the White Heart is the perfect place for you to fully develop your unique talents. Perhaps you can take comfort in knowing that you are exactly where you need to be."

Easy for him to say. He had all this peace and quiet to surround him. She asked carefully, "Should we stop looking for your regalia and your body?"

"I cannot make that decision for you. You must choose your own path and weave your own thread into the great tapestry of history as you see fit."

He was avoiding giving her an answer. Amused at such an intimidating being dodging a question from her, she persisted. "Would you refuse to return to Urth if we succeed in rejoining your regalia and body to revive you?"

His dark eyes glinted in answering humor at the shared joke of her making him squirm a little. "No," he answered eventually. "I would not refuse to walk the land once more. It is not for me to say how or when the fates will choose to use me."

"Stars willing, they will use you to destroy the Emperor."

He frowned for an instant before his brow smoothed once more. "Be careful what you wish for. There may be greater evils than the Emperor in the world."

"If the peoples of Urth are freed and can work together, I cannot imagine any threat we cannot face and defeat."

"Ahh, the idealism of youth. I have missed that."

"But you will come back and help us?"

He nodded once, slowly.

She sensed his reservations, though, and did not push the issue. She was not impertinent enough to ask if he would agree to be king once more, if he would lead a rebellion against the Kothites, if he would restore freedom and hope to the oppressed peoples of Urth. For now, it was enough that he'd agreed to be awakened.

"Is it possible for me to do this again?" she asked. "For me to dream of you and find myself here?"

"I see no reason why not. Or I may dream of you and find myself in your dreams from time to time."

Comforted that this would not be the last time she saw him, she drifted then, leaving his grove and losing herself in the fog, which was no longer malevolent, but merely misty and soft, cool upon her skin.

CHAPTER
6

N ice desk," Will commented as morning sun streamed in the window to illuminate the highly polished oak. "Is it new?" He'd accidentally blown up Aurelius's previous desk with magic the first time he'd visited the guild-master's study. That had been the day he'd found out who his father had really been and that Aurelius had legally adopted his father. Which made the guildmaster his grand-father.

Aurelius's mouth twitched humorously, but his words were dry. "Thank you. It was high time for me to redecorate." The solinari held out his hand. "Give me your staff."

Frowning, Will passed over the copper-tipped wooden pole to his teacher. He'd hoped Aurelius would speak of whatever had happened at last night's failed ritual. But apparently, they were going to talk about the weapon his father had made for him instead.

"Tell me about this," Aurelius ordered.

What was so interesting about an oversized stick to a mage of the solinari's prowess? Aloud, he answered, "My father constructed it a long time ago out of an old staff for a friend of the family, a forester named Adrick. He fashioned it to be a spear. When the Boki invaded Hickory Hollow, Adrick was killed and dropped it. I scooped up the spear to defend myself, and a Boki scout hacked the tip off with an axe. I defeated him with the broken spear, ran for the village to find my parents, and we fled to the woods."

"And you say Tiberius repaired the broken end and clad

it in this copper cap all with a single magic spell in the woods?" Aurelius asked skeptically, studying the metal sheath in question.

"Aye." Although not edged, a metal-clad staff made a formidable weapon in the hands of a decent staff wielder. And Ty had made sure by various sly training methods that his son was a great deal more than decent with a staff.

Will supposed it had been too risky for his father to teach him swordplay. After all, his family's lives had depended on doing absolutely nothing to draw the attention of the Empire. Had a boy from tiny Hickory Hollow, tucked on the edge of nowhere, suddenly exhibited superb mastery of swords, far too many questions would have been asked.

"Can you teach me the magic my father used to repair it and bond that metal to the shaft?" Will asked.

Aurelius frowned. "Your father was a fair pyromancer, I'll give him that. But even I do not have the skill to do what you say he did to this weapon. Unless . . . " He asked abruptly, startling Will, "Do you know this wood?"

Will stared at the blond shaft whose grain was shot through with reddish brown and faint hints of gray. "It's hickory."

Aurelius snorted. "If I'm right, that's not the half of it, boy."

"And the other half?" he asked when his teacher did not continue. Elves did have an annoying way of taking their time making a point. Mayhap it had to do with their exceedingly long life spans. They were in no rush to do much of anything.

"Oh, it is hickory, all right," Aurelius finally replied. "From Stormcaller himself, if I do not miss my guess. He is the grandfather of all hickories in Waelan."

At hearing the name "Stormcaller," something fierce stirred in recognition deep in Will's gut, even as he was certain in his mind that he'd never heard the name before.

Aurelius continued, "This wood is copper infused. See the glint of it in the sunlight if you turn it just so? Leave it to your father to give you a weapon perfectly suited to your talents."

Waelan? Where was that? And copper infused? What did that mean? And why did he know the name Stormcaller without ever having heard it?

Aurelius glanced up, one eyebrow cocked as if he expected a barrage of questions from his notoriously impatient apprentice. Stubbornly, Will held his tongue. As the silence stretched into a contest of wills between them, amusement glinted in the elf's golden gaze.

"So much like him," Aurelius finally muttered in disgust.

Will took the remark as a great compliment. At one time, his father, Sir Tiberius De'Vir, had been the premier battle caster in the entire colony of Dupree and a dragon of the Celestial Order of the Dragon in Dupree. At least he had been before Tiberius, Aurelius, the landsgrave of Hyland, and a nulvari assassin called Selea Rouge had infuriated Anton Constantine by trying to find the Sleeping King. Before Tiberius had taken the fall for them all, been sentenced to annihilation by Constantine, and been forced into hiding with his wife and infant son.

Aurelius continued, a note of resignation in his voice. "Tree Lord Stormcaller and his hickory grow in Shandril, which lies within the kingdom of Waelan. On Koth."

Another tree lord? Like Bloodroot? Will's gaze shot to his staff as the rest of Aurelius's words registered. His weapon hailed from Koth itself? The distant continent, home of the Kothite Empire, loomed mysterious and sinister in his mind. And he possessed a tiny sliver of it?

Aurelius took on a lecturing tone. "Stormcaller is said to have been infused with copper by giants. Infusion is a magical process whereby two unlike substances are bonded together at the most fundamental level. The resulting substance retains properties of both original elements. In this case, the copper within the wood conducts energy with great efficiency. Ty must have suspected that you inherited his talent for channeling magic."

"Channeling?" Will frowned.

"Casting magic through yon staff. Like a lightning rod in reverse."

Understanding burst through him. He had spontaneously sent blasts of magic through the staff toward foes when his life was in mortal danger, but without really knowing how he'd done it. "Can you teach me to do that on command?"

A sardonic smile curved one corner of the elf's mouth. "Now that you fall under the auspices of the Mage's Guild, I can teach you anything the guild has control over. Which encompasses the entirety of magic, excepting healing, Will Cobb."

Eagerness flashed through him, along with caution. The use of his assumed name was a sharp reminder from Aurelius that he could never claim to be his father's son, never use the name De'Vir within the Empire, no matter what talents he might have inherited from his father.

The guildmaster looked up at him gravely. "What is this weapon's name?"

Will frowned. "Why would a glorified stick have a name?"

"Because this *stick* is well on its way to becoming an artifact. Discover its name and you will command its special powers."

"What kind of special powers?"

Aurelius shrugged. "I have no idea. This weapon is not listed in any inventory of artifacts that I have ever seen. I could not begin to guess what abilities the staff's original maker imbued into it. It is possible, of course, to enchant items after the fact of their creation, but it is difficult, expensive, and usually temporary. This one appears to have been gifted at the time of its making. Given where that wood comes from, and who has handled it over the years, there is no telling what it will do when fully woken."

Woken? "Will it be . . . sentient?" Will asked in dismay. He already had one sentient being within him to deal with.

"Not in the way you mean." Aurelius surprised Will by

gathering a fair bit of magic between his golden fingertips and murmuring an incant Will had never heard before.

"What are you doing?" he asked.

"Hush. Watch and learn." Aurelius concentrated intently upon the weapon and began to feed the mass of magic he'd gathered carefully into the staff. The precision of the solinari's control of the twisting, writhing energy dancing on his fingertips was impressive. Will didn't have anywhere near that degree of surgical precision. At the moment, he could mostly gather up great gobs of energy and heave them at broad targets. He could generally hit something human-sized or larger. But Aurelius was wielding his magic as delicately as an artist painting a fine work of art.

Lines began to appear on the surface of the staff. They were dark brown as if they'd been burned into the wood. But whether Aurelius was creating the lines or merely revealing them, Will could not tell. Glowing, intricately woven lines began to appear on the copper cladding of the staff's tip.

At long last, Aurelius sat back. Will was shocked to see a droplet of sweat course down his grandfather's golden brow. His staff was now covered in beautiful, interweaving lines that reminded him of vines and stylized leaves. But the geometric forms were so intricate that his gaze could not follow a single line within the pattern for any length of time without losing its way.

"What did you do to it?" he asked.

"I revealed its true nature. Mind you, I have not fully woken it. You will need its name to do that."

"How do I find its name?"

"Were you the philosophical type, I would tell you that its name will reveal itself to you when the time is right—"

Will snorted.

Aurelius continued blandly, ignoring Will's interruption, "But you are too much like your father to accept such an answer. Hence, I shall tell you merely to search for its name until you find it."

"Where?"

"Your mother and Adrick hailed from Waelan as did the wood in the spear shaft. I might start by uttering Waelanian names to it. Mayhap it will respond."

"Whoa. Wait. My mother came from *Koth*?"

"She never told you?"

"No!"

"Ahh. Then you did not know Adrick introduced your mother and father to one another and was, perhaps, their oldest and dearest friend? He found Hickory Hollow for them to . . . retire to, I believe."

To hide in, more like. Will's shoulder blades slammed against the back of his chair. Well, *that* certainly explained a lot. No wonder his parents had always been so generous to the woodsman and had tacitly let Adrick teach Will forestry, tracking, and combat skills. It also explained how Adrick had always seemed to materialize when trouble came to call in Hickory Hollow. Like the night Adrick had been killed— the same night the Boki had come to kill their old enemy, Tiberius De'Vir.

"Magic can, in fact, spontaneously attach itself to an item," Aurelius said in a lecturing tone.

Will's attention snapped back to his teacher. "How?"

"Great deeds draw great power to them. Likewise, a magic item involved in great deeds draws magical energy to itself. Over time, the magic of a weapon or piece of armor or an enchanted item can gradually expand and multiply through use. Once changed enough, such items are classed as artifacts. They earn—or are given—a name, and often, their magics become permanent within them."

"So if I kill a dragon with it, my staff will gain power?" Will asked incredulously.

Aurelius laughed. "Most definitely."

"Has anyone ever killed a dragon?"

"Of course."

"Anyone living today?"

Aurelius abruptly waxed sober. Grim, even. "Yes. Our most resplendent Emperor has."

Will's jaw sagged. A *dragon*? The Emperor? How on Urth could any rebellion by normal mortals defeat a being powerful enough to kill a dragon? Was the dream of freedom from Koth utterly ridiculous, after all?

"Enough of this dangerous talk. I summoned you here for a lesson."

Will sighed. Back to memorization and endless, dull exercises summoning pea-sized balls of magic and doing nothing with them.

"Today we shall consider the source of magic," Aurelius intoned.

Will sat up a little straighter. He'd long wondered where it came from, even since before he knew he possessed a talent for it.

"The Decirum teaches us that magic is inherent to every living thing."

"Meaning what?" Will asked blankly.

"Meaning that magic exists naturally within in every living object. It is all around us. In us. Infusing the entire world we live in and everything in it."

"And this Decirum is . . . what?"

"It is ancient knowledge, passed down through the ages. Think of it as the fundamental theory of magic. All we know of magic and its use comes from this body of information."

"Is it written down? Can I read it?"

"It is written in our flesh and bones. In instinct. Our purpose in the Mage's Guild is to teach acolytes how to access this deep understanding."

It all sounded like smoke and mirrors to him. But if pretending to understand it meant that Aurelius would teach him how to channel magic through his staff, he would nod and smile like this Decirum thing made perfect sense.

Aurelius lectured, "Because magic is imbued with life energy, it does not act like, say, a rock. When you throw a rock, it travels straight, without thought or intent, in whatever direction you toss it. But when you cast magic, you must take into account that it moves with intent of its own."

Will had experienced this. Casting magic was like tossing water from a spinning bucket. The magic writhed and wobbled and refused to travel straight. Only the will and mental power of the caster marshaled its chaotic movement into orderly flight toward a target. Of course, shapes, colors, and signs helped pull in magic, and physical objects like wands, rods, and staffs helped channel the outward flow of it.

Aurelius continued, "Even the air that magic moves through influences it with its own innate magical energy—"

The office door opened without warning, and Will and Aurelius looked up together, startled. Drake Bruin, who had served under Will's father in the Celestial Order of the Sun, stood in the doorway. "My apology for the interruption, but Selea Rouge sends word that you are needed at Landsgrave Hyland's house."

"What is the reason?" Aurelius asked quickly.

"His message did not say."

"When do Leland and Selea need me?"

"Now."

Aurelius stood with an alacrity that conveyed the depth of his alarm at this summons from Selea personally. "Are you coming?" the solinari asked Will a shade sharply.

"Uhh, yes. Of course." Will leaped up from his chair as his grandfather swept from the room. Bruin followed them down the stairs and held out Aurelius's cloak in silence. Unspoken was the offer of the drake's sword, as well, should his guildmaster have need of it.

"You are a good man, Bruin," Aurelius murmured as he took the garment and swung it around his shoulders. "But you are needed here. Guard the guild in my absence."

Bruin executed a short bow of obedience.

Will grabbed his own cloak from a hook by the door. An unseasonably cold, wet spell had descended upon Dupree overnight. He hurried after Aurelius, who had not waited for him and now strode across the broad Mage's Guild Square. Luckily, he'd attained his father's height and more in the past few months, and his long stride carried him to his grandfather's heels quickly.

Something bad had happened. He could feel it in his bones. And obviously, Aurelius felt it, too.

CHAPTER
7

Anton batted away the hand creeping up his arm seductively. He'd been forced to use a precious love potion on his prisoner as the most expeditious means of transporting her in secrecy to their final destination. The jann girl, Marikeen, was far too powerful a magic caster to leave with her free will intact while he transported her. And the cost of the silence poisons it would take to keep her from casting magic at him for the several-day journey was prohibitive.

He was not likely to have access to either an alchemy lab or supplies to make more love potions for a long time to come, which made it doubly a shame to have to burn one on this recalcitrant young woman. Particularly since, as much as he would relish the sweet revenge of bedding a young, beautiful female attached to the household of his greatest enemy, she was more valuable untouched as currency in the purchase of favors and power.

Anton tripped and stumbled. He righted himself, cursing, and paid closer attention to his footing. He hated skulking around in the woods like a common criminal. Yet another grievance to lay at the feet of his enemies. They would all pay for this. Although, if all had gone according to plan last night, his greatest enemy was dead. His triumph at having finally destroyed Leland Hyland assuaged his irritation at least a little.

* * *

He looked around expectantly. The clearing, situated at the base of a small waterfall, was empty. Where was Tholin? How dare he keep his governor waiting! No matter what anyone else said, as long as he lived, *he* would be the true governor of Dupree. That avarian woman they'd put on his throne had better enjoy the title while she had it, for he *would* have both throne and title back.

"This place is very beautiful," Marikeen purred from behind him. "I have a special affinity for water. You remembered that, didn't you? Oh, my lord, you are so considerate. I do not deserve you. I would do anything for you." The blue striations in her skin swirled a little.

He raised a hand. "Enough. I am here to meet an important friend."

Marikeen's gaze glittered with intelligence for an instant before the effect of the potion took over and her gaze melted into adoration once more. He'd long wondered how much women under the effects of his love potions remembered when he let the potions wear off. His impression was that their memories fogged over. But Marikeen had been enslaved less than a single cycle of the moon and was no unschooled peasant girl.

No matter. She would either serve the man he planned to give her to this night or she would die. And from what he knew of the jann girl and her brother, they were both survivors. Odd ducks, those jann. Elementally aligned, their skin reflected their elemental affinities. Marikeen's caramel-colored skin displayed blue whorls indicative of a mainly water-aligned jann.

A rustling in the brush behind him made him pivot sharply, gas globes in hand. "Who goes there?" he demanded.

"Stow your poisons, Anton. It is only me."

"Tholin. I nearly killed you." He sagged in relief. It had been a very long time since he actually worried about being bodily attacked by anyone. The day would come again, though, when fear alone would make people steer well clear of him.

The mage's hand glowed brightly with magic, which faded slowly as he strode into the clearing, grinning. "You could have *tried* to kill me. Mayhap you would have succeeded, mayhap not."

Anton scowled, in no mood for Tholin's humor today. "What news?"

"A greenskin force was seen in Talyn last night, moving south. Also, I heard rumors of a Black Ship sailing for Haelos under orders to make haste."

Anton jolted. "A Black Ship?" He devolved into a spate of cursing. The regular tax collection ship wasn't due for months! It would ruin everything if one of the mighty warships got here too soon! He paced the clearing in high agitation while his lieutenant looked on warily.

He could not *believe* he was so close to his goal and might be foiled yet again. The governess was as weak as a kitten, and if all had gone well last night, she was stripped of all her landsgraves. One solid attack by the Boki would be the end of Dupree. Then he would swoop in and rescue the colony, restore order, and be redeemed in the eyes of the Emperor. But now some Black Ship captain might gain all the glory that was supposed to be his!

He would have to move up the timetable of the attack. Whatever greenskin force the Boki had already assembled would have to be enough for an invasion of Dupree.

Tholin interrupted his turbulent thoughts. "Who's the girl? She doesn't look like one of your usual playthings."

"She is no plaything. A love potion merely brought her amicably to this rendezvous."

"She is an enemy brought low, then?"

Anton ignored the question. From whence the girl came was none of Tholin's affair. The mage looked around the clearing nervously as if he expected Boki to jump out and attack them. Little did Tholin know that the coming marauders worked for him.

"What can I do for you this night, my lord?"

Anton fingered the tattoo in the middle of his forehead, silently invoking their connection as members of the secretive Coil crime syndicate. His tattoo depicted a green viper wrapped sinuously around a golden sword. Not only was it his family's crest but it was also a sign of leadership in the Coil. A golden rattlesnake tattoo wrapped around Tholin's arm, its fanged head resting on the back of his hand, marking him as a longtime Coil member.

Anton replied, "I have brought this girl for you. A gift." Marikeen wailed, and he snapped at her, "If you love me, you will do this for me. Tholin is a good friend of mine, and he can be a good friend to you."

Again, the moment of curiosity in her eyes, maybe even speculation. And then the puppy-like worship took over. "Of course, my lord. If that is what you wish."

Tholin burst out, "What use have I for a cast-off love slave of yours?"

"She is not my love slave," Anton snarled. "I need her to disappear for a while. Somewhere she will remain safe." Somewhere she would be difficult to find, but not so deeply buried that she could not act as bait. The girl would unquestionably draw her brother and his companions out into the open, but Anton hoped she would draw out a hidden fish lurking much deeper than those annoying children. A much bigger fish. *Much* bigger. After all, he knew who Marikeen's father was.

Tholin frowned and reached out to take the girl's hand in his. A momentary glow of magic indicated that he'd cast a spell upon her. A startled look crossed Tholin's features, and he cast considerably more magic into her unresisting hand this time, using his finger to draw a sign on the back of her wrist. The sigil glowed briefly and then blinked out of existence.

"What do you see?" Anton demanded. This man hadn't been his first choice for Mage's Guildmaster in Dupree for nothing. At least he had been until that buffoon Henrik

Volen had been appointed in Anton's place to be the first governor of the newly formed colony some twenty years ago.

By the time Anton had managed to murder Volen and replace him as governor, that cursed solinari, Aurelius, had been too deeply entrenched in the position of guildmaster to dislodge and give Tholin the job. Ultimately, Tholin had proven more useful to Anton in the Coil and in acting as liaison to an even more elusive bunch: the Cabal.

Truth be told, Anton knew little of the Cabal and their goals except that they collected the most powerful magics in the land to themselves and seemed bent on achieving something as yet unknown to him. Two things he did know, though. One, they were formidable, and two, he was in dire need of allies at the moment. Hence, his gift to Tholin of a young elemental magic user who he suspected was on her way to becoming a great mage in her own right.

"You did not lie, Anton. She is, indeed, a mage."

Tholin was holding out on him; he'd seen more than mere magic in the jann girl. And if Anton had doubted that for a second, all doubt was dispelled when Tholin said briskly, "What can I do for you in return for you bringing her to me?"

Tholin never volunteered favors or, heavens forbid, gold to anyone unless he was getting the better end of the bargain. The girl must be even more talented than he'd guessed.

Pursing his lips, Anton answered, "I am currently experiencing difficulty in procuring the ingredients I need to make alchemical potions." Given Tholin's sudden eagerness to get ahold of Marikeen, Anton went for broke and added, "In particular, I need sanguine fruit."

"Sanguine fruit?" Tholin echoed. "From bloodthorn trees? Whatever for?"

It was the key ingredient in creating spirit death poison that would permanently kill a victim. It was by far the most difficult recipe he had ever mastered, and by far the deadliest. He had used up all the sanguine fruit his Boki contact had given him to make four spirit death poisons, one for each of the landsgraves who held land in the Lochlands of Dupree. But Tholin did not need to know any of that.

Anton shrugged. "I just need some of the fruit. You asked what you could do for me; that is what you can do. Get me that fruit."

"I'll see what I can do. Bloodthorns only grow in the Forest of Thorns, though, and the Boki do not take kindly to intruders in their territory."

Anton nodded, not mollified but pretending to be. He did not like the sensation of having been bettered in a business deal. Not one bit.

Tholin's voice, pitched to kindness and directed at Marikeen, startled Anton out of his sulk. "The first thing we must do, child, is get that slave mark off your cheek."

The girl dipped her head in silent gratitude.

"Then we shall see to your training. You know the potential of the magic within you, do you not?"

"Yes, I do," she answered bluntly.

Anton looked back and forth between them suspiciously. What potential? He already knew she was on her way to real power someday. But what else had that whoreson, Tholin, seen in her? He should take her back. Keep her for himself. Greed to possess her magic gnawed at him.

Marikeen turned to him and asked calmly, "When exactly will the love potion wear off?"

He blinked at her, stunned. Had she somehow managed to defeat the enhanced version of the poison he'd personally invented and refined? Water mages did sometimes have the capacity to purify liquids, including human blood. Had she spontaneously cleansed her body of the poison? He should study her. Take her back to his lab . . . oh, wait. He did not have a lab anymore. He did not even have his stash of ingredients with which to brew the simplest of poisons.

"End of next week," he mumbled in belated response to Marikeen's startling question.

Distress blossomed in her dark gaze. "It is no matter. I

shall love you till the end of time, potion or no. I cannot leave you, my lord."

That was more like it. Blind devotion. If only he could feed the whole blasted colony his love poisons.

"Come, child," Tholin murmured, urging her gently away from him. "I'm going to introduce you to a few of my friends. They study magic, and I believe they will be eager to speak with you. Afterward, you may return to Anton if you wish."

"Do you promise?" she gasped hopefully.

"You have my solemn oath," Tholin replied earnestly.

Raina was perplexed at this summons by Selea Rouge—a master assassin, no less—of her and Rosana to Hyland's house. Even more perplexing, there was no sign of Leland Hyland, who was more father than mentor to her, when she and Rosana arrived at his home. Eben was already there, waiting for them in the formal sitting room.

"What's going on?" she asked him.

The jann looked as confused as she felt. "I have no idea. Selea kicked me out of Leland's study, emerged with a fistful of messages he told Hyland's men to deliver, gave orders that he was not to be disturbed, and retreated into the office. He's still in there."

Will and Aurelius arrived looking alarmed, and the solinari had the courage to ignore Selea's edict not to be disturbed and knocked on Hyland's study door. Selea emerged looking so grim that Raina's blood ran cold. The nulvari rarely showed any emotion at all, let alone this open distress.

Selea looked around. "We're all here, then. Hyland's man had trouble finding Sha'Li. She is submerged somewhere, and he was only able to ask a lizardman on shore that word be passed to her to join us here. My news is too urgent to wait for her, though."

Raina braced herself as he continued, "I have received reports within the hour that all four of the Lochland landsgraves were attacked last night by assassins."

She gasped in consternation.

Selea continued grimly, "Delphi was killed but lifed, and her killer was chased off. Beltane was attacked and is missing and presumed dead. Talyn has disappeared without a trace."

He paused for a moment, gathering himself to share the last news, the most important news, about the one they all knew and loved so well, Leland. The length of that painful pause told her enough. Horror flowed over her and through her, choking her until she could not draw breath.

The words fell out of Selea's mouth singly like pebbles falling into water. "Hyland is believed dead. His manor house was burned to the ground. His body was recovered, and his spirit has neither been sensed nearby nor attempted resurrection."

A silence so deep and profound that no breath was possible fell over them all. It lasted for one final, desperate moment of denial, and then the moment broke, and the grief crashed in on all of them.

Each breath felt like a hot knife stabbing Raina's side as a silent scream started in her skull and would not stop. Into that backdrop, a single thought formed. *He cannot be gone.*

But her heart told her without question that Leland had passed beyond the Veil, and this time he would not be coming back. The last time he had died, only the news that his son had been kidnapped had pulled him back from the Black Gates of the Void and the welcoming arms of his long-dead wife beyond.

But this time . . .

No. He was gone.

Selea moved out of the sitting room, leading the group to Leland's private study. The spacious workroom was as warm and welcoming as ever. How could its master be dead? Should not the very walls be weeping?

A commotion of sound and movement heralded the arrival of a visitor.

"Sha'Li!" Raina cried in surprised pleasure. She hadn't seen her lizardman friend in a long time. The black-scaled girl who'd accompanied them on their quest to find the Sleeping King wrapped Raina in a hug that nigh crushed her ribs. Stars, Sha'Li was strong. But then she'd been warrior trained from birth.

"A little air," Raina wheezed.

"Sorry," the lizardman girl muttered. Whether she referred to the over-strong embrace or the loss of their mentor, Raina could not tell. She nodded in return, her throat too tight for words.

Eben turned from beside the fireplace, his caramel-toned skin more mottled with elemental markings than usual, his face wet with tears. Raina moved silently to the big jann. They held on to each other in shared grief for a long time. They'd both lost a father this day.

But poor Eben had lost his sister to slavers barely two months ago, and then his best friend and surrogate brother, Kendrick Hyland, had been kidnapped soon after. Now this. Her heart broke for him. It was more than one person should have to bear.

Rosana and Will spent a long time hugging, as well.

"What? No one the lizard comforts?" Sha'Li demanded in disgust.

Laughter broke the spell of grief engulfing the room. Raina sighed. "Ahh, Sha'Li. I have missed you. Where have you been?"

"In nearest water soaking I have been. And eating my fill of nice raw fish, not that swill you humans call food."

Surely, she had not just been bathing. Raina would lay odds that her friend's new Tribe of the Moon symbol, recently appeared upon Sha'Li's cheek, had earned the lizardman girl a raft of new training. Although in what combat arts, she knew not.

"You've been in the Dupree harbor?" Will asked skeptically.

Sha'Li rolled her eyes. "No, stupid human. In Glass Lake I was. Fresh water my kind prefer. Only filthy Merr in salt water delight."

Selea and Aurelius had been murmuring quietly in a corner, but then Aurelius's voice rose, cutting across the other conversations. "Who did it?" Aurelius asked tersely.

"I am no seer. I do not know everything," Selea protested. "I am only certain it was not a guild-sanctioned hit."

"But you have a good idea of who did do it," Aurelius accused shrewdly.

The nulvari shrugged. "Anton is the obvious suspect. He would have hired killers from outside the Assassin's Guild, of course. I imagine he would attempt to cast blame for the attacks on others. It would not surprise me if his killers were specially chosen for their ability to sow discord and panic throughout the colony."

Raina piped up. "Will the new governess believe accusations against the former governor without solid proof, though?"

Selea sent her a penetrating look, and Aurelius murmured reluctantly, "Doubtful. She is a Kothite noble herself. She will be reluctant to think the worst of a fellow Kothite."

Reluctant herself, Raina asked the obvious next question. "What details have your sources passed to you of the other attacks, Master Selea?" She wasn't certain of the nulvari's title within the Assassin's Guild, but it was widely assumed that he was some sort of master assassin at a minimum.

"A house guard in Delphi field-resurrected successfully. He describes his attacker as a snake changeling wearing Dominion colors."

"Dominion!" the group exclaimed collectively.

"Aye," Selea answered. "Jethina Delphi confirms that a snake changeling and a male human whose face she never saw attacked her. The remains of several Dominion-marked changelings were found partially charred in the wreckage of Leland's manor, as well."

Will burst out, "What in stars' name does the Dominion want with Dupree?"

Even Raina knew the answer to that one. The faction of animal changelings, purportedly bent on defeating the

Kothite Empire and conquering all the colonies for itself, believed that might made right. Dupree was weak, its old leadership recently deposed, its new leadership not yet established. Now was the perfect time for a Dominion strike.

She spoke thoughtfully. "Is the timing of this Dominion attack too perfect, perchance?"

Will and Sha'Li both scowled at her, but Rosana, of all people, nodded in thoughtful agreement. "Suspiciously perfect timing, indeed, for the Dominion to rise up now. Anton used Boki before to give himself an excuse to make war. Why not use the Dominion to make war, now?"

Aurelius frowned. "Subtlety has never been Anton's strong point. He's a thug at heart and has always surrounded himself with equally direct thugs. He sees what he wants and takes it."

"What does he want, then?" Raina asked.

"That's easy," Eben answered grimly. "Revenge."

Sha'Li scowled, the fine scales on her face lifting to lend her a menacing aspect. "Revenge he has, methinks. Three of the four landsgraves missing or dead. A brand-new governess who of this place knows nothing. In his mind, cut off is the snake's head. What plans he next, then?"

"I have one more report of note," Selea announced quietly.

Something about his tone of voice made Raina's blood freeze once more.

He continued, "From Talyn Keep, I have received news of an incursion. A Boki attack. A large, bloody one. However, it is only a first report and badly garbled. It may be nothing."

Or it could be a full-scale war party. The Boki were livid at the recent invasion of their traditional home forest and Anton's slaughter of their kind. To their immense credit, the Boki had thrown their men, women, the old and infirm, even their children at defending the site of the portal to the Sleeping King's dream prison. It had been a bloodbath for the Boki to keep Anton out of the secret cave.

Talyn was the northernmost holding in Dupree and encompassed the Forest of Thorns that the Boki called home. If the orcs had left their forest and attacked Talyn Keep, there was no telling where they might head next.

Something bothered her about Talyn's disappearance. If the Boki had killed Landsgrave Talyn, they would have made a ritual of it, loudly and publicly feeding the nulvari landsgrave's spirit to one of their bloodthorn weapons. If the reports were true that Talyn had disappeared without a trace, then the Boki had not succeeded in killing him.

Will spoke heavily, voicing the thought they all were having. "If the Dominion and the Boki attack Dupree simultaneously, the colony will be crushed."

The mere thought of the death toll that would come from a double invasion made Raina physically ill.

Eventually, Aurelius broke the heavy silence. "What do we know of Gregor Beltane's disappearance?"

Selea answered, "Two of his men resurrected. They report being attacked by Merr in Loch Narr. Apparently, they were dragged off their boat, pulled underwater, and drowned. They saw nothing of what happened to Gregor."

Sha'Li hissed. Her scalp scales lifted into a crested ridge that ran from the top of her head down the back of her neck and disappeared into her jerkin, making her look even fiercer than usual.

"Gregor's not a fighter I would relish tangling with," Aurelius commented. "He cannot have been an easy takedown. Do we have any reports of Merr resurrecting recently?"

Rosana spoke up sheepishly. "I stole a peek at the death log. No Merr have resurrected in the past week anywhere in Dupree."

Eben added, "For that matter, Landsgrave Hyland is—was—a formidable warrior. How many Dominion bodies were found in his house?"

"Four," Selea answered.

Will smiled a little. "Not a bad showing for a man alone and ambushed."

Eben said heavily, "This will kill Kendrick. But he deserves to know. We *must* rescue him and let him know his father is gone."

Selea frowned. "The prudent thing would be to put the search for Kendrick and Marikeen on hold for a while. Now is no time to be gallivanting about the colony. Not with Dominion and Boki forces marauding and Anton out there somewhere."

Eben and Sha'Li exchanged a loaded look and moved to stand side by side in solidarity. Clearly, they hated the idea of stopping the search for their friend. Raina hated it, too, but none of them were skilled enough adventurers to continue the hunt without more training.

Aurelius added, "Not to mention you all have your educations to attend to. Later, when you're all ready, we can search for the regalia."

Eben spun to face the solinari, glaring. "To the Void with your regalia. We cannot stop searching for Kendrick and my sister! Kendrick would keep searching for any one of us. The hunt *must* go on."

"I understand your frustration, Eben," Aurelius replied. "But we have no leads. As soon as we have something solid to go on, I will not stop you from looking for Kendrick. But in the meantime, you all need more training. The stakes have gone up; the risks are greater than before. The five of you are known now, and you have enemies. Certain people will do everything in their power to stop you if they suspect you may be on the trail of the Sleeping King."

Namely, Anton Constantine, Raina thought.

While she found the elf's logic unassailable, loyalty to their friend Kendrick rebelled in her gut. He'd been a good-hearted youth, well on his way to becoming a man much like his father. Not to mention he'd been charming and personable. She did not know Marikeen and had only glimpsed her once in a slave market, but out of general principles, she worried about Eben's sister. The girl had no one else but her brother to save her from whatever fate had befallen her.

When she'd faced the prospect of running away from home, Raina had been a young girl, alone and afraid. She still thanked the stars daily that the kindari elf Cicero had come to her rescue and escorted her safely to Dupree. But Marikeen had no such rescuer. Raina fully understood Eben's urgency to go after his sister. However, she also understood Aurelius's reservations. The world was a dangerous place and becoming more so every day for their little group.

Eben was not so circumspect. "I will not sit here twiddling my thumbs while everyone else studies applied theory of underwater basket weaving until you deem us ready to go forth and save the world. Kendrick and Marikeen are kidnapped. Missing. Enduring who knows what hardships or worse. They cannot afford for us to wait a single day to find them!"

Sha'Li spoke up. "Truth speaks Eben. Go we must. Now."

Rosana cast a distressed look first in Will's direction and then in Raina's. For her part, Raina glanced over at Will. Of all of them, he and she best understood the perils ahead of them if they wished to find the Sleeping King's regalia and wake him. They'd survived their first attempt to wake the king by a hair's breadth. Next time, they could not expect to be so lucky.

Doubt glinted in Will's eyes. He knew he needed more training to unlock his talent for magic, which had gone largely untapped before now. She, too, was just learning the full scope of her powers, not to mention the full power—and responsibility—of her tabard.

A strange animal, the White Heart. Often called fanatics and peaceniks, her order's mission was to defend life. She was expected to heal a Boki as quickly as a human, a Dominion changeling as quickly as a citizen of Dupree. Had she been present at Hyland's ambush, she'd have been duty bound to heal both the landsgrave and his murderers. If Anton Constantine himself fell at her feet, she was obliged to heal him; hence, the White Heart was universally liked, trusted, and granted safe passage.

The intense neutrality of her position made her able to travel pretty much anywhere with impunity. But it also threw her order squarely into the middle of the stickiest political situations in the colony. White Heart members were frequently called upon to negotiate between disputing factions in last-ditch attempts to prevent violent conflict or even to step in front of swinging swords to stop it.

She was yet to fully understand the dynamic between her order and the knights of the Royal Order of the Sun. The order was charged with defending the Heart—particularly the chapter houses, Heartstones, and healers. Apparently, any time a White Heart member came to harm, the swift and sure retribution of the Royal Order of the Sun was a terrible thing to see. She gathered that the threat of angry knights coming to call was part of what kept members of her order safe from harm.

That, and her kind were walking healing batteries everywhere they went—she more than most. The women in her family had long been bred to be powerful mages and she was no exception. At full strength she could heal a small village by herself; moreover, her ability still seemed to be growing.

Raina said to Eben, "The Sleeping King can take on Koth and possibly win. Our goal of waking him reaches far beyond ourselves and our friends. We must think about the good of everyone—"

The jann cut her off. "Cut out that White Heart tripe. We're just a bunch of kids. How on Urth do you expect us to overthrow Koth? That is far, *far* beyond our abilities. But we *can* find our friend and my sister. Why do we sit here and argue when time is slipping away from us?"

Will, of all people, interceded to support her. "Have some faith in yourself, Eben. You have more potential than you know. We all do." He looked around the group, making eye contact with each of them. "We may be young, but we are talented. And we *are* young. We have speed and strength and stamina. Belief in ourselves. We can find the king's regalia and wake him. I know we can."

Sha'Li scowled more darkly than usual. "Die we can, as well, Will. Too dangerous is what you propose."

Raina frowned. Since when did Sha'Li doubt their quest? What had the Tribe of the Moon and her fellow lizardmen been preaching to her while she soaked in Glass Lake?

"And you think going after your friend Kerryl Moonrunner is any less dangerous?" Will exclaimed. "Lest you forget, he dropped *all of us* with hardly a fight and made off with Kendrick."

"*Nothing* do you know of Kerryl—" Sha'Li started hotly.

Raina interrupted the burgeoning shouting match, asking quietly, "What would Kendrick want us to do?"

Eben looked on the verge of exploding. If she was not mistaken, the colored striations across his flushed cheeks were actually swirling. "That is not fair," Eben ground out. "Kendrick was—is—a noble fool."

"Why is it unfair to take into account his desires, noble or otherwise?" she asked reasonably.

Warily, she eyed Eben's fist flexing and unflexing around the pommel of his long sword. She moved over to his side and placed a light hand on his sleeve. "Be calm, my friend. We shall rescue Kendrick and your sister. But we must live to reach them first. What if we take a short break here in Dupree to pursue more training for all of us, then we go forth in search of both the regalia and Kendrick when we have a lead on one or the other?"

The jann stared down at her, his dark eyes turbulent with rage and despair. "They are my only remaining family. I *must* go after them now."

She stared up at him for a long moment. If her childhood sweetheart, Justin, were kidnapped and missing, she would not wait patiently for her companions to complete a course of training, either. "Please, Eben. Tarry but an hour. Eat supper and think on your decision a bit. If you still wish to leave, I will do anything in my power to help you."

He scowled down at her, but a note of indecision had

entered his voice as he rasped, "For you, I will stay for supper. Then I go."

As reprieves went, it was not much to work with. But it would give the others a little time to talk sense into the jann. While they waited for the meal to be served, she noticed Aurelius had moved into the adjoining office and seated himself at Leland's desk. Through the open door, she spied him intently studying something spread across it.

She followed him into the room. "Why did you not intervene in our argument?"

"All of you must believe in what you do and be totally committed to it, or you will fail and Sha'Li will be correct. All of you *will* die. I can make persuasive arguments or even order you to stay or to go. But that would serve no good purpose. Not only do *I* need you to succeed, but you are correct—*everyone* needs you to succeed. You have to work this out for yourselves."

She supposed she could see his point, but that didn't mean she had to like it overmuch.

"I suppose someone ought to sort through Leland's papers," Aurelius said heavily. "And better I than someone who might take Leland's private opinions amiss."

Which was to say, someone who would expose Leland posthumously for working against the Empire. She joined Aurelius at Leland's desk and saw a map spread wide upon it. Dupree plus a bit beyond the borders of the Lochlands were depicted. Notes in Leland's hand were scattered across the map, mostly along roads and traders' routes. "What did Leland track so meticulously?"

"It appears he mapped the routes upon which he sent scouts in search of his son," Aurelius replied.

She exhaled a painful breath. Stars, to have lost both father and son one right after the other, it was hard to bear. How Eben stood the agony was beyond her. Aurelius opened desk drawers and rummaged in them until he came up with a big leather-bound journal. He opened it across the map and commenced reading Leland's entries. His expression grew steadily grimmer as he read. Finally, he cursed under his breath.

"What have you found?" Raina asked.

He turned the journal to face her. "Look at this."

She glanced down the page, and gasped. Report after report from Hyland's scouts spoke of unusual greenskin activity. Groups of goblins, hobgoblins, ogres, troglodytes, and a variety of other creatures were apparently leaving their traditional homelands and stealthily converging upon Dupree. More to the point, Leland's spies reported seeing Anton Constantine meeting up with several of the groups.

"He's really doing it, isn't he?" she breathed. "Anton Constantine is organizing a massive greenskin insurrection. There will be a second Night of Green Fires, won't there?"

Aurelius nodded tightly. "It looks that way."

Stars above. The first Night of Green Fires had nearly destroyed Dupree, and it had been battle ready with strong leadership. They were now led by a single, elderly landsgrave who was no warrior and a completely untested governess not to mention decimated ranks within the Haelan legion itself as Anton's loyalists had deserted to follow him into exile.

Raina asked, "Will the new governess believe us if we warn her?"

Aurelius exhaled heavily. "If only I knew her better, I might be able to answer that. As it is, she is an unknown. Stars know, the people of Dupree need her to believe us."

Although it was not as if the recently deposed governor, Anton Constantine, had left much behind by way of resources for the new governess to defend the colony with.

"Do not speak of this to the others. We cannot afford for any rumors to get started through a careless remark." He added soberly, "I will speak with the governess in the morning."

"Look here." Raina turned the book to face Aurelius. "This scout, the one Landsgrave Hyland sent northwest, has not reported back in a while."

The solinari referenced the map, drawing his finger north across the map, skirting the western edge of the Forest of Thorns and Boki territory. "She last reported from this outpost. The scout's name is Tarryn."

"Tarryn?" Eben exclaimed from the doorway. "She searches for Kendrick?"

"You know her?" Aurelius asked.

"Aye. She's kindari. Clan Lion. A scout for Hyland, and a good one, too. Old friend of Kendrick's. Had quite the crush on him."

"Leland's notes show her searching west of the Forest of Thorns for him."

"And you say she has missed reporting in?" Eben asked sharply. "Something is wrong, then, or else she has found a trail and follows it too quickly to send word back to her liege."

"You cannot know that—" Raina started.

Eben cut her off. "I know Tarryn. She would be tireless searching for Kendrick. She has found something."

She could just as easily be dead, but Raina was loath to point out that possibility. Eben needed some shred of hope, no matter how slim, to cling to.

A simple dinner was served, and Raina watched the jann furtively throughout the meal. As she'd feared, the tight set of his jaw did not ease one bit. The somber meal concluded, and Eben pushed back his chair impatiently.

Raina rose from her seat with him. "I understand. You do what you must. At least let me cast some protective spells on you before you go. They will last a few days and see you safely on your way."

"Thanks be," he muttered.

She really ought to warn him of the natives on the move toward Dupree. But Aurelius had ordered her to say nothing. Instead, she took both of Eben's hands in her own and stared intently into his eyes. "Listen to me, my friend. There are dangers abroad you do not know of and which I cannot

speak of. Promise me you will be more cautious than see[s]
necessary."

He stared back at her intently, obviously hearing a hid[-]
den message in her words but just as obviously missing its
exact meaning. "I will exercise utmost caution."

"As if we were still in the Forest of Thorns caught between
two armies," she murmured.

"Even so?" he asked in surprise.

Selea moved past, and Raina painted on a false smile as
she murmured, "Even so."

Aurelius approached, carrying a beautifully worked suit
of armor bearing the Hyland crest, and Eben groaned. The
elf spoke implacably. "He would want you to have it. And
where you are going, you will need it."

"No!" Eben burst out, his voice breaking. "I cannot wear
that. It is his."

Aurelius momentarily looked as shattered as Eben
sounded. None of them could quite believe Hyland was gone.

Tears clogging her throat, Raina hugged Eben and then
stepped back. "Safe travels to you. Don't make me have to
come after you, too."

He rolled his eyes at her.

Raina frowned. "Eben. Should ill befall you, you would be
sorely missed. We are your friends. We would come for you."

"Exactly. And that is why I must go after Kendrick."

"There is a wise way to go about these things." She made
no attempt to disguise the implication that there was also a
foolish way to go about it.

Eben didn't look swayed, and his expression remained
bleak. Raina knew what it was like to feel utterly alone in
the world, and her heart went out to him.

"If go you do, so go I," Sha'Li declared stoutly. "Leave
me behind to rot you will not."

Eben gave her a look of deep gratitude. They were an
unlikely pair but had become good friends over the past
months of shared danger.

...lea exclaimed from over by the fireplace.

...e?"

...stop me," Eben warned the nulvari. "I would

...o draw blood under Leland's roof." He flipped

...nain he always wore around his neck to fasten his

...op me not, either," Sha'Li warned, her claws slither-

...partway out of their sheaths.

"At least provision yourselves properly," Selea exhorted. "And send back reports as you—"

The nulvari broke off, stepping forward abruptly to lift the blazon on the chain Eben wore. "Where did you get this?" Selea demanded angrily, brandishing the medal.

Aurelius stared at the campaign medal, as well. "It could be a replica."

"Check it," Selea snapped at the solinari.

Aurelius cast a spell upon the enameled metal disk that Raina thought to be a Pan Ordan campaign insignia, although she was no expert on such things. A thunderstruck expression crossed the guildmaster's face. "Where did you get this?" It was his turn to demand.

Eben frowned. "It was said to belong to my father."

Aurelius's jaw actually fell open. He and Selea exchanged a long, wordless look fraught with dismay and disbelief. Raina wished she knew what silent conversation they were having with one another. The blazon would have been given to officers who led the military campaign by the Kothite Empire to conquer Pan Orda, or to regular soldiers who performed heroically in the attack upon the elemental continent. What was so significant about that?

"Where will you go first?" Aurelius asked as his hand fell away from the medal.

So. The elves were not going to stop Eben and Sha'Li, were they? Fond as she was of Kendrick, she could not understand why Aurelius and Selea would split the party being trained to seek the Sleeping King's all-important regalia. The pieces they knew of—his sword and shield, bow, signet ring, and crown—supposedly contained magics that would help rejoin Gawaine's spirit to his body. By sending Eben and Sha'Li away, were they abandoning the quest to wake the Sleeping King? Her gut clenched in panic.

"We go north," Eben declared, tucking the blazon into his shirt. "To the Forest of Thorns where Kendrick and the madman who kidnapped him were last seen. And then west to discover whatever trail Tarryn follows."

"Kerryl Moonrunner his name is," Sha'Li disagreed. "And mad he is not. His reasons I know not, but intelligent and cunning is he."

"Friend of yours or not," Eben warned her, "I will kill him if he has harmed Kendrick."

Sha'Li showed the whites of her eyes in what Raina surmised was distress, but the lizardman girl made no verbal reply. The pair swept out of the room, and silence fell over the remaining party.

And now they were three. Where they had once been seven strong and confident in their teamwork, now it was just Will, Rosana, and her, and the strange link between them that kept Will alive. How were they to finish their all-important quest to wake the Sleeping King with only the three of them to continue on?

Tarryn crouched behind a thick clump of sharp-leaved holly bushes, peering stealthily through the greenery at the fire in the distance through the trees. Four men sat around its meager light. But more to the point, one visage among them she knew as well as her own. It belonged to Kendrick Hyland. *Finally.* She'd found him. And no easy task it had been. Greenskins had been *everywhere*, and she had spent nearly as much time dodging them as she had tracking Kendrick.

She eased forward, her doeskin moccasins soundless upon the detritus of the forest floor. A long pause. Another step. Another pause brimming with the predatory patience of her kind.

According to the reports, Kendrick had been kidnapped by some sort of nature guardian. Was one of the men at the fire that man? Who were the other two? And who was the female? At a glance she did not seem human. Was Kendrick restrained in some way? Chained or shackled? Had he, stars forbid, been slave marked? The wild rage of her race that always simmered in her gut heated up considerably at the notion.

Her patience nearly failed her as she crept step by painfully slow step closer to the ring of light illuminating the dark shadows of the forest. She had moved well beyond the margins of the Forest of Thorns toward the west. These trees were nowhere near as ancient as the mighty bloodwoods of the Forest of Thorns. The thin branches overhead let in sufficient light for thick underbrush to thrive among the tree trunks, which worked to her benefit by providing her ample cover, but worked against her as brambles and vines caught at her clothing.

She got her first good look at the two slender men sitting side by side on a fallen log. They were exact mirrors of one another. Twins, then. Kendrick sat in profile to her. His cheeks were leaner than before, his features more mature. Gads, he was handsomer than ever.

Mentally shaking herself, she turned her attention to the last man. He appeared to be of middle age but looked as powerful as an ox. He had the thick chest and muscular forearms of a woodsman. Surely, that must have been Kerryl Moonrunner, the nature guardian. Beside him sat a woman with distinctly green-toned skin, scantily clad in clothing that appeared to be made of . . . leaves? Was that a *dryad*? Tarryn frowned. Where was this one's tree? No tree in this clearing had the size and perfection of form associated with dryad-inhabited trees.

Kendrick's familiar voice drifted to her sharp ears on the chilly night air. "Tell me more of this threat you sense coming toward us."

Tarryn's heart jolted. Was Kendrick trying to warn her that Kerryl Moonrunner would be able to detect her coming? She'd heard stories of nature guardians talking to animals and trees and drawing magic from the forests themselves, but she had always dismissed them as silly hearth tales.

Kerryl was speaking. "—as great a danger as you can imagine in your worst nightmares—the threat gathering to attack this land is worse. I do my best to prepare for it. That is why I took you and made you into who you are. Your talents are needed for the fight, boy."

Kendrick's brow furrowed slightly, like it did when he was thinking hard. The fire hissed quietly, and Kerryl jumped up to pace back and forth behind the log he'd been sitting on. Tarryn forced herself to remain utterly still and not to shrink back farther out of sight. Movement captured the eye long before the shape of an unmoving shadow did.

Kendrick asked, "Do you feel any remorse at all for forcing me to this path? Did you ever consider asking me if I would help you oppose this coming evil?"

Kerryl scowled. "I could not afford to have you say no."

"You insult my honor."

She'd never heard Kendrick so angry. Terrible outrage vibrated in his voice, along with a note of something she'd never heard from his before. Bitterness, mayhap? Or grief? She could not be sure. For the moment, she dared not take her unblinking gaze away from the nature guardian to study Kendrick's expression.

"Pierre. Phillipe. Go forth into the wood."

In unison, the twins stood. Each man was lean but looked wiry and strong. They would be lightning fast in a fight. Dangerous.

Kerryl's voice dropped into a deep timbre of command. "Bring my next soldier to me." He grasped his left arm with his right hand as he gave the order, and she spied a faint glow from between his fingers. He wore a bracer on his left forearm that appeared made of leather. Intricately carved into it were images of every animal she could think of. So detailed were the depictions that she fancied the beasts cavorted around the man's arm on the leather band.

The twins moved off to her left but not before she saw that each of their left eyes glowed an alarming shade of red. She had never seen the like. The pair disappeared quickly into the trees.

Now was her opportunity to make a move against Kendrick's captor and free her friend. She took a silent step forward, hunting in the way of her lion-aligned clan, her attention focused intently upon her target.

Another step.

The undergrowth on either side of her exploded inward, and the twin brothers came flying out of the darkness, tackling her to the ground before she knew what had hit her. So vicious was their attack that they actually bit at her face and neck. She struggled with all her might, but to no avail. They were much stronger even than she'd anticipated.

One of them tore her short sword off her belt, and the other ripped her bow from her hand. Then one of them stepped on the back of her neck while the other sat on her. No matter how violently she struggled, she could not seem to throw them off. Quickly, they threw loops of thin, strong rope around her, trapping her arms and yanking sharply. Her shoulders were all but torn from their sockets.

"Augh!" she cried. "Kendrick, help me! It's Tarryn!"

A shout of rage and dismay issued from Kendrick's throat, the beginning of her name. But it broke off and became an anguished groan. "Nooo. Not now." The groan shifted and became a hoarse, unintelligible growl hovering on the edge of speech, just beyond comprehension. The sound was more chilling than anything she'd yet heard this night.

The twins jumped up, and between them, they dragged her through the trees, uncaring that she was scratched by branches and thorns as they thrust her into the clearing. She fell to her knees painfully and looked up at Kendrick crouching beyond the fire, his hand held up in front of him as if to ward off some great evil.

"It's me," she spoke urgently at his unseeing stare. "It's Tarryn. I've come for you."

He moaned. "Ahh, no. Not her. Do not perpetrate your evil upon her, I beg of you. Curse you, Kerryl!"

"That's enough out of you, boy," Kerryl snapped, fingering his bracer again.

As if on command, Kendrick's left eye glowed brighter scarlet than spouting blood. The right eye was still Kendrick's, but not Kendrick's. The fun-loving, charming youth was gone. And in his place was an embittered man consumed by helpless rage.

She looked away, unable to bear the pain in Kendrick's

anguished stare. She glared at Kerryl, not bothering to disguise her hatred for the man who had done this to the happy-go-lucky youth she liked so much.

"Who have we here?" the nature guardian asked. "A spy, methinks."

The dryad trilled in a high, bell-toned voice, "Nay. A friend of Kendrick's. Sweet on him, she is."

Tarryn scowled at the dryad. Her feelings for Kendrick were a closely guarded secret and most certainly did not need revealing to him.

Kendrick made a growling sound, but no speech issued from his throat. He snapped his jaw shut in obvious frustration.

Kerryl smiled. "Excellent. Her feelings for you will hold the two of you with me to look out for one another. The she-elf was quite skilled in approaching us. Another talented warrior House Hyland has provided me. Well done, wherever you are this night, my old friend, Leland."

For the first time, real fear for her safety erupted in Tarryn's breast. "What are you planning to do to me?"

"You, too, shall have the honor of serving in my army. Something strong. Cunning. Able to move quickly in many terrains and with excellent camouflage." He tapped a tooth with a fingernail, considering. Then his face lit. "An alligator speaker lives not that far from here, guarding a scion of the Great Alligator. And he is close to a source of more magical waters of change, in fact. Yes. That will do nicely, I think."

CHAPTER
9

G unther Druumedar grunted in disgust as the rain intensified from drizzle into a cold, soaking rain. A
foul night for a dwarf to be caught out late. Stupid of
him to ignore the gray clouds rolling in from the west and
not stop prospecting earlier to head home.

He could duck off the exposed cliffside path and take
cover under the trees covering the broad plateau atop the
Hauksgrafir, but to do so he would have to wade through
waist-high grass that would soak him to the skin. Not to
mention the weeds would foul in the mechanism of his mechanical leg. The artificial limb was cranky at best and un-
reliable at worst. But it was better than letting cursed Heart
healers use their black arts to grow him a new leg, thank you
very much.

The rain became a pounding downpour that gave him no
choice but to retreat to the cover of the trees. The exposed
granite of the path was becoming too slippery for him to
risk. Not with a fall of a thousand feet or more barely an
arm's length away.

As if that were not bad enough, a flash of lightning struck
so nearby the hairs on his arms stood straight up and he
fancied that his beard even tingled. Trading one danger for
another, he was. The forest was not a place to be at night.
Predators and monsters roamed the woods, and a crippled
dwarf would make a tasty treat for one of them.

Gor, it was dark under the dripping trees. Give him a nice,
dry mine with narrow, stone walls and rough-hewn ceilings

anytime over all this green growing stuff. *Bah*. He trudged along, cursing at the rain and the dark and himself.

But then he heard a noise. A snapping of branches behind him. Had to be something big and heavy to be making that sharp cracking sound. The noises were rhythmic as if someone stomped along behind him without a care for stealth. He frowned. Something wrong with those noises. . . .

And then it hit him. Those sounds were spaced too far apart for any normal-sized dwarf, or even a human, to be making. Whoever was taking those steps was large. Very large.

Ahh, no. By the Void. Not a yeren.

He looked fearfully over his shoulder, peering into the darkness, but saw no sign of a great, hairy beast walking upright like a man. Nonetheless he picked up the pace of his own steps considerably. For a creature twice the height and more of a dwarf, yeren could blend into their surroundings with shocking effectiveness. In these mountains the beasts had long, reddish-brown hair that looked much like the dead pine needles carpeting the forest floor.

The cracking noises stopped. Had the thing taken to the trees? He'd heard tales of them swinging through the branches hand over hand with their long arms, strong enough to crush a man. Gunther broke into a shambling run.

Something massive thudded heavily to the ground in front of him. By the spirit of the mountain, it was a yeren as he'd feared. The creature was huge, with a big, hairy belly and disproportionately long arms. Its face was simian and covered in hair, its eyes more intelligent than Gunther expected. And it looked angry.

Gunther skidded to a stop and commenced backing away from the giant beast. He thought briefly about reaching for the pickaxe slung across his back, but the yeren would tear him limb from limb before he could do the slightest damage to it.

When the beast made no immediate move toward him, he turned and ran. He darted to his left toward the lowest-hanging branches and thickest scrub brush he could find. His only hope was to use his smaller stature to duck under obstacles that would slow the pursuing yeren down. Mayhap he could find a rock or burrow to hide in where the beast could not reach him. The tactic worked until Gunther burst into the open. Desperate, he took off running down the bare stone path, ignoring the needles of rain slicing hard against his skin.

The beast bellowed in rage behind him. Stars, the yeren was close. It would burst out of the woods any second and be upon him. He could not see where he was going but ran on blindly, anyway. Stopping or even slowing spelled sure death.

The beast burst out of the trees in front of him, and Gunther tried to stop, but his mechanical leg buckled under the strain, and he pitched over on his side, tumbling head over heels straight toward the cliff.

He grabbed for anything to stop his fall, his fingernails scrabbling uselessly at the wet stone. His legs flew into open air, and the edge of the path gave way beneath him with a sickening collapse of saturated ground.

He pitched over the edge of the cliff.

Thankfully, it was not quite a vertical drop at this spot. He gathered speed, bouncing from outcrop to outcrop, sliding down steep rock faces, fetching up against tiny ledges until they gave way beneath the force of his fall, and then continued crashing down the mountainside. Desperate, he grabbed at every rock and root he could in a blind effort to gain enough purchase to stop his descent.

At long last, he fetched up hard against a rock ledge broad enough to hold his entire body. He lay there, panting hard, waiting for it to collapse out from underneath him. But it held.

Gingerly, he reached for the rock wall beside him. Grabbing an outcropping and doing his best to take weight off the ledge, he cautiously pulled himself upright, plastering his torso to the cliff face.

How far down the mountain he'd scraped and skidded, he had no idea. Hundreds of feet, it felt like. He risked a peek over his shoulder and drew back sharply. He'd caught the very last bit of the mountain before the steep face turned into a truly vertical cliff plunging many hundreds of feet to the valley floor below. Had he missed this precarious ledge, he'd have been a goner. What a humiliating way for a dwarf to die—falling off a mountain he'd known his entire life.

He turned his attention to making his way back up the rock face to safety. Did he dare try it? Would that cursed yeren wait at the top for him or move on? Mayhap he should wait out the night here. Were yeren nocturnal or did they hunt in the daytime, as well? If only he'd listened to the hearth tales over the years.

Cursed rain was coming down harder than ever. And the temperature had dropped precipitously. In fact, if he was not mistaken, those were strings of sleet starting to pepper his back, making seeing up the cliff face impossible. Worse, this north-facing section of mountain was coated in moss that turned to green slime when a man grabbed at it. The stuff made climbing a nightmare even in the best of light and weather, especially for a one-legged dwarf.

He reached down to punch his mechanical knee into a straight and locked position. Cursed contraption and its needlessly intricate moving parts didn't much like the moisture: must remember to oil it when he got back home. *If* he got back home.

Still facing the rock wall, he felt his way along the ledge as it narrowed to mere inches in width. He reached to his right, seeking hand- and toe-holds stout enough to support the weight of his stocky body. Of a sudden, his right hand plunged forward into nothingness, and he all but fell off the blasted ledge before he caught his balance.

What was this? He edged a bit more to the right. Felt again. An opening of some kind in the cliff face. Huh. The stone face gave way to a crack. Crawled all over this cursed pile of rock his whole life, he had, and never had he spied a cave in this place. Of course, no sane dwarf would venture down the slope this far, so close to the edge of a fall into nothingness. Blasted yeren. Might its offspring all be runts who got hunted down and turned into rugs.

He waited out a particularly violent sheet of rain and then dashed the water away from his eyes. A crevasse of some kind opened into the mountain at an oblique angle. Had he not been standing exactly here, he would never have spotted it. That overlapping outcropping of granite would hide it from any soul standing in the valley and peering up at the mountain, too.

Experimentally, he wedged his body into the hidden crevasse. It was a close fit, but he was able to make his way a few feet into the mountain. He paused to shake the worst of the rain out of his bushy hair and red beard.

Gor, the darkness was thick. Not that his kind minded a little dark. Dwarves were no strangers to Under Urth. He pushed a little farther into the crevasse, stopping to untangle his clothing and pouches from sharp edges and to shake off the dripping rain again. If nothing else, mayhap he would find a dryish overhang under which to wait out the storm and then climb back up the mountain to safe ground.

He burst into open space without warning. He stumbled forward and fell a half dozen feet, face-first, down a steep slope into what felt and smelled like a cave. A dry one, praise the Olde Ones. He took a moment to catch his breath, the mountain's cold soaking through his thickest wool cloak and leather jerkin as he sprawled on the stone floor.

Laboriously, he pushed up to his hands and knees. The mechanical joint stuck but then gave way without warning. He caught himself clumsily, cursing himself for being foolish enough to use an ancient wonder without understanding its inner workings. He'd found the false leg tucked in a dusty corner of a sundry shop not long after he'd lost his own limb in a mining accident. Folks told him to let the Heart regrow him a new leg, but he didn't trust the Heart, not one bit. Lackeys of the cursed Empire, one and all, them healers.

He lit one of his small hand torches by feel, using the flint and striking stone from his pouch. Raising the guttering light high, he studied a ribbon of darkness winding away from him into the heart of the mountain. He'd been prospecting this pile of rock fifty years and more, and he'd never heard of a natural passage into the mountain. No map marked it nor dwarven lore spoke of it.

He pulled his cloak closer about him. By the blade of Battle Brand, the weather'd turned foul of a sudden. Caught him out on the mountain like some rank amateur, it had. No choice but to hunker down and wait it out. A cold and hungry night stretched before him. And not a single gem to show for his misery.

The wind shifted, driving sheets of rain into the angled opening as if to force him deeper into the crevasse. Might as well have a look farther in. He had nothing better to do until the storm passed. This called for a prospecting torch, which cast light bright enough to discern even the smallest vein of mineral within stone. No respectable miner was ever without one.

As soon as a spark caught greased cotton and the big torch flickered to life, he recognized worked stone around him. He lifted the light higher to inspect the walls. They were old, for sure. Errock work, if he had to guess. The deep dwarves were known for their use of broad-headed picks like the ones that had created this space. His kin, the kelnor, favored narrow-headed picks like the one slung over his shoulder. But errock were not known for working so high up inside a mountain. These realms were left by tradition and treaty to his kind—the hill dwarves.

The errock had a secret mine in kelnor territory, did they? It would not be secret for much longer if he had anything to say about it. Cautious now, he eased deeper into the passage. It opened out soon enough into what turned out to be quite a large space. A mine.

A thick layer of powdered grit covered every surface, and the air tasted stale. Hadn't been worked in a while, then. Was it played out? Had the errock taken all the treasure and gotten away without discovery? The kelnor council was going to have something to say about this, all right. Growling into his beard, he inspected the space more closely.

He spied tailings on the floor and picked up a few shards to take a closer look. Iron ore. Surely the errock didn't climb the treacherous cliff outside, hide the entrance to this place, and risk infuriating the kelnor who claimed this region of Waelan just to mine common iron.

Intrigued despite his ire, he continued exploring. *Ahh, Druumedar. It's greed twisting your gut, and there's the way of it.* Wary of letting it get the best of him, he moved on cautiously.

He came to an intersection of tunnels leading deeper into the mountain and stopped, shocked. What was this? A full mining complex? Soundings taken by striking the bedrock with singing hammers had never indicated any tunnels in Hauksgrafir. Only the most accomplished of master miners could create tunnels that soundings did not detect. Someone had gone to great lengths to disguise the presence of this place. But who? The errock made their homes deep underground. They would not have operated this far above the surface unless they had found something truly extraordinary.

The main tunnel branched, and he chose to follow the one with the most smoothly worn floor. Marking the wall of the tunnel that would lead him back to the cliffside cave with a piece of chalk, he lifted his torch and headed deeper into the mountain.

Before long, this tunnel widened into what looked for all the world like a miner's village. Small alcoves opened off the main chamber, and stone outcroppings carved into rough benches rose out of the floor in a circle around a shallow pit still blackened by ancient fires. His sharp prospector's eye spotted bits of pottery, a rusted nail here and there. Someone had definitely lived here or at least worked here.

Scowling, he stumped around the space looking for clues as to who'd carved out this mine and what they'd been doing here. The local elders were emphatically not going to be happy to hear about this place.

The good news was it appeared very old. Long deserted. He found a series of narrow post holes augured into the floor. Some sort of forge must have stood next to the blackened fire pit. A narrow, blackened shaft that looked suspiciously chimney-like disappeared up into the ceiling above it. Why on Urth would anyone build a forge inside a place like this? The effort required to haul in the forge itself, let alone bring in enough charred coal to properly fuel it, boggled the mind. Were the errock mad?

He moved farther into the big cavern, and his torchlight glinted off something shiny. A sluggish trickle of water seeped down a wall and into a knee-high basin. The water filling it was black and still. Curious, he plunged his pick-axe into the pool, and it was deep, sinking well below the level of the floor without touching the bottom. A quenching pool. This had definitely been a forge at one time. But for what? And why?

He moved back to where the forge must have stood and raised his torch high. That was when he spotted the circular array of blue glints overhead. Turquoise. And where there was turquoise, there was copper. A dozen veins of the stuff seemed to run together exactly over the spot where the ancient forge must have stood. Odd.

Copper was no rarer or more special than common iron. What, then, was the secret treasure of this mountain?

Frustrated, he moved away from the center of the cavern and commenced methodically searching the side alcoves. He found more evidence of dwarven occupation—a beard bead or two, a broken cup on a roughly hewn shelf over what must have once been a sleeping platform.

At the far end of the huge chamber, there had been a cave-in. As a prospector, cave-ins were particularly interesting to him because they quickly revealed large, previously unseen layers of rock and ore that would otherwise have remained buried.

He poked around the rockfall. The collapsed rubble pile was not tall—it had fallen outward more like a wall collapsing than rock sheering off in an avalanche pile. Still, he could not see the exposed face behind the rocks, curse it. Awkwardly, he picked his way around, over, and through the debris. A faint flash of green caught his eye. *'Ey? What's that?*

He clambered on top of a boulder and spied a smooth curve of stone that looked worked. In fact, it looked finely carved. He took a step toward it, and his artificial leg chose that moment to lock up. He pitched forward, falling clumsily and landing heavily on his side.

He shouted hoarsely as a green eye glinted back at him. He scrabbled backward, feeling about frantically for the torch, which had rolled away from him and was guttering badly, threatening to go out.

He righted the torch and got it burning properly again, and then he thrust it forward at the creature peering out at him from under the stone.

Nothing moved.

Cautiously, he leaned down to peer into the shadows. It was an eye, all right. But this time he saw it was carved of some precious stone. Now that he looked closely, all the stone fragments around him appeared to be carved and smoothed into a statue-like finish. That looked like a leg over there. And an arm . . .

Huh. With a bracer buckled to the stone forearm. Except the bracer was not part of the carving. It looked to be made of metal of some kind. He gave an experimental tug at the bracer, and it lifted away from the shockingly realistic arm beneath, complete with bulging muscles and corded tendons in the elbow and wrist.

At first glance, the bracer was little more than a bent piece of metal. Copper if the green patina covering it was any indication. A finger-long gash marred it right across the middle, though. He shoved it into his pouch and reached for a big, curved piece of rock to push it aside. A metallic ringing announced that another piece of metal lay under it. He rolled over what turned out to be the statue's incredibly realistic stone torso and spied a larger metal piece. This time a breastplate in the same copper as the bracer.

Now who would make a copper suit of armor? Any apprentice armorsmith knew that copper was far too soft a metal to stand up to the rigors of combat or even a good swing from a tempered steel blade.

He poked around a bit more, and some distance away, he spied a round stone. It turned out not to be stone at all, but a head still wearing a copper helm. And both were shockingly intact. The face was so lifelike down to the last little detail that he fancied he could feel stubble on the carving's cheek above where its beard began to grow. Each hair in the intricately woven and beaded beard had been meticulously carved. He'd never seen or heard of chisels that could texture stone so finely. The mouth had tiny flakes where the statue's lips had been chapped—whether by wind or lack of water, he could not tell. Even a few hairs inside the nostrils were faithfully rendered.

The model for this piece had definitely been a dwarf. But the features weren't errock nor kelnor. And although he'd met but a few of the reclusive terrakin dwarves in his day, the face staring up at him didn't look entirely terrakin, either. Bah. He was no art critic. It was a dwarf, and he'd leave it at that.

He had to say, the armor pieces felt pretty solid. He put his full strength into trying to warp the breastplate and didn't achieve the slightest flexion. And when he whacked the helm with the flat side of his pickaxe, he didn't leave a mark on it, let alone a dent.

Using the edge of his cloak, he rubbed away the worst of the dust and grit covering the pieces, but he still could make out no details. Harrumphing, he limped back to the quenching pool. His stump hurt where the false leg attached. The tumble down the cliff, and now this latest fall, had wrenched it violently.

He should toss out the mechanical leg and use a traditional wooden one. Except a gnome had offered this one to him. Not only had he been intrigued by the encounter with a member of the nearly extinct race, but he'd been intrigued by all the intricate moving parts that seemed to serve some secret purpose.

The gnome had stubbornly refused to tell him what any of the extra gears and levers and boxes did. And he never could turn his back on a good mystery. He'd been tinkering with the leg, trying to ascertain what the extra bits did, to little avail. He had learned how to throw a clever lever that engaged a gear in the knee joint, allowing him to lift a man's worth of extra weight beyond what his good leg would do.

And speaking of curiosity, he dipped the bracer into the water and scrubbed it vigorously to remove the worst of the grime. It had clearly been fashioned to protect the back of a warrior's hand and forearm. Slits on each edge of the piece would have been where leather buckles had attached it to a mailed glove most likely.

What he'd initially thought were bits of dirt clinging to the thing turned out to be incredibly intricate decorative details covered in dust. As he cleaned the green piece thin, twisted ropes of copper emerged, along with tiny beads of copper that formed a complex geometric pattern across its surface.

He gave the breastplate and helm the same scrubbing, and beautifully inlaid patterns began to appear. If he was not mistaken, the inlay was also copper, but of a distinctly different color and composition from the base piece. All three pieces were light and well shaped, and despite their damaged state, incredibly strong. The quality of the craftsmanship was extraordinary, even to his jaundiced eye.

Huh. No errock had made such a thing. They were stonemasons and gem cutters first and foremost, not metal artists, and definitely not armorsmiths of this caliber. Reluctantly, he admitted to himself that no kelnor smith he knew of could replicate a piece this magnificent, either.

Hmm. Mayhap this piece, this place, were better brought to the attention of the *other* dwarven council. Not the local miner's consortium that answered to the Imperial Miner's Guild but the immensely more secretive and cautious group the Empire knew nothing about. Now that he thought on it, this hidden and entirely unmapped place could prove highly useful to the resistance. And in the meantime, it was a fine place to wait out the storm on the mountain and that cursed yeren.

He eyed a small pile of ancient coal in its stone cradle by the fire pit. Mayhap it would still burn. He built a pyramid of the stuff near one of the sleeping platforms ringing the chamber, primed it with a smear of grease and a handful of crystalized pine resin, and thrust his torch into the whole. Good dwarven charcoal, that. It lit up as if it had been made yesterday and was not older than the hills.

As the fire cast light at the ceiling of the main cave, metallic flashes caught his eye. A circle of metallic posts was clearly visible in the gray rock of the ceiling among the strange veins of turquoise. Too regularly spaced to have been nature-made, the posts were sunk almost entirely into the granite with only a handspan length of each protruding. Now what purpose did those serve? For surely the makers of this cave would not have gone to such trouble to install them way up in that cavernous ceiling just for decoration.

He trimmed a timekeeper candle for eight hours and carefully extinguished his torch. Finding his way out of this warren of alcoves and tunnels would be nigh impossible if he lost all his light sources. He stretched out on the sleeping platform and watched his little fire's smoke curl upward toward the ceiling. Who put a forge deep underground, anyway? Never mind the difficulty of hauling fuel down here to feed its fires. Where did the smoke go once it entered that narrow chimney?

Irritated at the complete lack of answers, he rolled himself in his cloak. His final thought before he fell asleep was to wonder on the last dwarf who had slept in this exact spot and what had caused the fellow to depart, leaving no known trace of this place behind.

Will was tired and out of sorts today. He and the others had failed to talk Eben and Sha'Li out of haring off into the wilds in search of their friend Kendrick. He was secretly jealous of the pair. If only he could have found a way to accompany them. But Aurelius had kept a sharp eye upon him last night, as if sensing Will's yearning to sneak away.

The guildmaster had all but personally tucked him into bed on the upper floor of the Mage's Guild. Surely, it had been no accident that Aurelius gave the door guards orders in front of Will that no one should pass in or out of the guild without his express permission. Not that the order had prevented Aurelius from disappearing from the guild on some secret errand of his own bright and early this morning.

Will chafed at being stuck in a city, sitting through dull lessons on magical theory as if he were a stripling schoolboy. He would much rather be stomping through the woods in search of adventure.

"While we are examining gifts from my parents, Guildmaster," Will asked formally that afternoon, "perhaps you could tell me more about this hand shield?"

"Where did you get it?" Aurelius asked, examining the object Will had handed him, a gently concave disk slightly larger than his spread-fingered hand. It was made of clear, golden amber, and Will had always thought it resembled an optic lens, except for the wooden bead embedded exactly in the center of it. The bead was carved into the likeness of a hickory nut, portrayed accurately down to the last, minute detail. Thin metallic straps crossed the amber disk's surface, attaching the piece to the back of a fingerless leather glove.

Will had already figured out that the item had talismanic properties that helped him control and shape magic into spells. He'd never seen his mother cast magic, but the hand shield had been hers until she gave it to Will the night they fled their home and ran from the Boki. He fingered the braided leather bracelet that held the green stone bead he used as his regular talisman. The bead had been a gift from Adrick, his parents' best friend, the bracelet itself fashioned by his father.

He answered Aurelius's question with, "My mother gave it to me just before . . . well, before." He couldn't bring himself to say the words *before she died at the hands of the Boki*.

Aurelius smiled a little as he rubbed his thumb across the smooth amber surface, but Will sensed it was more in remembrance than pleasure. "As I recall, this was a gift to your mother from the Amber Mages, whom she served."

"The Amber who? She served them?" Will spluttered. Was there no end to the secrets his parents had kept from him?

"Aye," Aurelius answered casually. "Serica came from a long line of Amber Mages. Although she was not magically gifted herself, she used her considerable skills as a tracker and alchemist to serve them."

"Who or what is an Amber Mage?" Will demanded.

"An order specializing in an ancient . . . art, for lack of another word. They retain knowledge of how to encase a living target entirely in amber."

"Does that kill the target?" Will had seen bits of leaves and even insects trapped in orbs of ancient pine resin that had hardened and become amber over time.

"I have heard that their targets remain fully alive and conscious within their amber prisons."

That was terrible. He shuddered to contemplate being trapped forever, unable to move or speak. "Can a target safely be released once it has been encased in amber?"

"In my experience, most magics that can be done can also be undone."

In other words, Aurelius did not know.

Will watched the solinari turn the golden-hued hand shield this way and that in the morning sun streaming into his office. Hints of green flashed when the light hit it just so. Those had always fascinated Will, dancing within the liquid gold of the talisman.

"I do believe this amber is infused," Aurelius commented in mild surprise.

"With what?"

"Copper of Ymir, if I do not miss my guess. Powerful stuff. Aids greatly in the transmission of magic. It seems both of your parents were intent on outfitting you as a proper mage."

"Too bad they didn't see fit to train me as one." It still rankled with Will that lads half his age were apprenticed to the Mage's Guild to learn the art of casting magic. If only his own talent had been nurtured earlier. No telling how much more powerful a mage he would be by now.

"Do not be bitter, Will. Your father spent your entire life laying into you a magnificent foundation for the study of magic. It is why you progress so rapidly now."

If this was rapid, Will would hate to experience the study of magic learned slowly. He was going half-mad with impatience at the snail's pace Aurelius set with him. It was enough to make a forest-raised lad snort with disgust.

Raina watched in amusement as Rosana barely managed to hold back a snort of disgust. The high matriarch was delivering a long after-lunch dissertation to the gypsy about the dangers of dying from overcasting or from attempting to channel more magic through one's spirit than one was capable of managing. The lecture struck Raina as coming a wee bit late, given that Rosana had already torn out an entire chunk of her spirit and passed it to Will by way of Lord Bloodroot.

She did get the feeling from time to time that Lenora was holding out on them, not sharing sensitive information and analysis of local political matters. Whether the woman was merely guarding secrets or guarding political turf was anyone's guess.

Raina's early education with her older sister had done a remarkable job of preparing her to see and understand the complex goings on in a big city like Dupree. Still, she resented owing the Mages of Alchizzadon a debt of gratitude for that education. In return for the mages breeding the women of her family to be powerful magic users, her family had educated its women as if they would one day be queens.

Her desire to free herself and her sister from the breeding program had led her to seek a great mage of old, said to be locked in a sleeping stasis. Of course, the great mage Hadrian had not been the one she and Will had eventually found. Instead, they had found the echo of an ancient elven king. Funny how the fates worked. She started with one goal in mind—saving the women of her family—but now she worked for the good of all the people of Haelos. Of course, the risks were commensurately higher, as well.

No one could tell her what would happen to a White Heart member who opposed Koth. Traditionally, her order was immune to any and all interference from the Empire. But what if a White Heart member engaged in outright rebellion? Then what? Raina's guess was that even White Heart colors would not protect a healer from treason.

She spent the afternoon helping the Heart's potion makers mix curatives for headaches, hangovers, and minor injuries. Tonight was the anniversary of the Night of Green Fires, and there would be a run on healing potions before the night was out.

The Memorial Festival of Remembrance of the Boki Incursion of Dupree was the formal name of the annual celebration. The more common nickname referred to the fires the greenskin invaders had lit all across the colony, burning out homes, barns, and buildings in their orgy of destruction. Tonight, bonfires would be lit across the colony to commemorate the Boki invasion that had nearly wiped out the young colony almost two decades ago.

It had become the custom to throw specially formulated salts into the bonfires to turn the flames green. She supposed it symbolized the greenskin army of Boki, goblins, hob-goblins, and other nonhuman races going up in flames, as they'd ultimately been defeated. Or perhaps a more optimistic interpretation might be that the life force of Haelos itself had prevailed and the people and land had survived the assault upon it. Either way, the Heart common room would be full of drunks and brawlers looking for healing before the green fires burned down to ash.

Sure enough, it was an insanely busy evening, and she never got to sit down for more than a few seconds at a time. The deluge of the revelers finally began to diminish, and a special midnight supper was laid for the healers, who were all hungry after manipulating magics for hours.

Raina had just sat down at the long trestle table in the kitchen with the other healers when a great sound of horns blowing erupted outside the building. The older healers leaped up with cries of dismay while the younger ones looked around in confusion, asking what was going on. Sir Hrothgar burst into the kitchen breathing hard. His face was red as if he'd been running full out.

"What's amiss?" Lenora asked sharply. "Why are the Haelan legion's battle horns blowing?"

"All healers are called to the aid of the Imperial Army by order of Lord Justinius of the Royal Order of the Sun," he declared between pants. "The Boki are attacking Dupree."

10

If the Boki intended to cause chaos, attacking late at night at the end of a drunken festival just as Dupree settled down to sleep off the celebration was a brilliant choice. Will strode along beside Aurelius as the revelers still abroad ran every which way, heading for home to bar their doors while others streamed out of their dwellings to see what all the fuss was about. Great, magically amplified horns blared across the capital, signaling to the various military units that made up the Haelan legion to assemble.

And then the attack signals were blown.

Women screamed and children cried, men shouted, and rumors flew thick and fast around Will as he hurried after his teacher. Dismay coursed through him. On the one hand, he despised Boki. He would love to kill the ones specifically who murdered his parents. On the other hand, he did not wish death upon the entire race. Hundreds of their kind had sacrificed their lives defending him and his friends so they could complete the first step of their quest to wake the Sleeping King.

He also could not forget that the orcs had good reason to be furious with the Empire, and with Dupree in particular. How was he supposed to indiscriminately cut them down now?

The rage he had nurtured over his parents' murder bubbled up, coaxing him to embrace it. To loose it upon all Boki. But then something deep inside him reminded him that the Boki were not monsters. Nor were they ravening beasts with no souls, no feelings, no traditions, no pride. They were not animals. They were men. Warriors. Honorable foes.

"Curse it, Aurelius," he ground out as the solinari paused to let a squad of soldiers run past. "How are we supposed to kill them? The Boki helped us. They're not savages."

"And now they come to kill men, women, and children in retribution for Anton's attack. We must defend those who cannot defend themselves."

"But—"

The elf turned swiftly and grabbed Will by the shirtfront, right over where Bloodroot's wooden disk grew into his chest. With surprising strength, Aurelius hauled Will close and bit out low, "Draw no attention to yourself from the Empire, boy. Your quest must not be foiled because you choose to take some noble—and doomed—stand on behalf of the Boki. They, of all people, would understand that the quest is greater than you or your honor. Greater than them and their honor."

"So you want me to sally forth and slaughter them?" Will demanded.

"No one said you have to kill them. You merely have to defend the citizens of Dupree, like a loyal member of the Mage's Guild. Do not disgrace me or the guild. Do not disgrace your father nor the order he served. Do your duty. Act as the Empire expects you to. Understood? Do not be a hero."

Will could not bring himself to mutter something dutiful in response; therefore, he said nothing at all.

"You must fight as if you hate them. As if they are nothing more than filthy greenskins to you. Give the governess what she expects." As Will drew breath to protest one last time, Aurelius added, "Think about your parents. Remember Hickory Hollow. This night is when you even the scales for that night. Put the rest of it out of your head. You *must* do this."

But *how*? He felt as if he were being stretched between opposing teams of oxen and slowly torn in two. How was it possible to both despise and admire a foe? To hate and respect simultaneously? It was as if the two spirits within him warred for supremacy, neither yielding, each tearing at the other until nothing of him remained intact.

Aurelius didn't sound any happier about having to do combat against the Boki than he. Reluctantly, Will gripped his staff more tightly, his mother's amber hand shield secured over his left hand, which left his right hand free for casting magic. Into the breach, then. But he had a bad feeling about this night's work.

Raina had no desire to see combat ever again. It was a bloody, soul-sickening business, and she would not have enough skill to heal every wounded person in this night's battle.

"Stay back from the main melee, Raina," the high matriarch murmured. "I would not have your life put at risk."

Easy for Lenora to say, but in fact it was her duty to put her life at risk. White Heart Brother Balthazar had died multiple times to prove to the Boki that the White Heart would defend life to the death for all sentient beings of all races. Never mind that the Boki thought him as mad as a hatter. She could do no less. Her colors could do no less.

The chaos in the streets was unbelievable. If Leland were here, he would have found a way to muster order from this mess. He'd have ordered the locals who could not fight into their homes and those who could into the squares with whatever weapons they could find. He would have used experienced soldiers to lead small groups of volunteers.

But the militia was gutted by the recent desertions of those loyal to Anton, and no one knew the governess. She was unproven, and they would not listen to her once the battle spilled into the streets. Then it would be every man for himself.

Raina had no doubt this night would be a bloodbath. She'd seen Boki fight before. They were skilled, strong, and focused. Formidable foes to even the most seasoned soldiers.

Once the Boki got past the militia to engage the local popu-
lace, the people of Dupree would be slaughtered like lambs.

The tenor of the shouting changed pitch, and new urgency
entered the distant roars. Faint sounds of metal clanging
became audible, and Lenora ordered her healers to fan out.
They approached Slaver's Square on the northwestern edge
of the city, and the broad boulevard they jogged along opened
onto an impromptu battlefield.

It was fully as bad as Raina remembered. She winced as
Hrothgar ordered a contingent of healers to stay behind
while the rest continued on with him, and she glared at Lenora as the high matriarch directed her to retreat from the
square.

It felt strange to run away from wounded and dying men
like this. In fact, it felt *wrong*. She moved up beside Lenora.
"I think I should go back there and help those people."

"Other healers were left to help them. You are needed
elsewhere."

Raina frowned. "Why does it matter where I heal? I'm
White Heart. I'm supposed to heal them all."

"Even you have limits. You will be applied strategically
to the battle."

"By whom?"

"By Justinius, if I don't miss my guess. He and his men
came into the city earlier today. They spent the afternoon
discussing with the governess and Krugar how to best defend the city from just such an attack and redeploying the
Haelan legion along the city walls. The timing could not
have been better."

Had the governess listened to Aurelius, then? And just in
the nick of time? She fervently hoped so. Perhaps they had
a fighting chance of surviving this night, after all.

Will was surprised when Aurelius and the contingent of
Celestial Order of the Dragon guardians veered away
from the sounds of combat in Entertainer's Square ahead of

them. Was he to be spared the terrible dilemma of what to do, after all?

"Where do we go?" Will panted.

"Governor's palace, according to the new defense plan the governess, Krugar, and Lord Justinius drew up this afternoon," Bruin answered tersely.

This afternoon? That was convenient.

The Mage's Guild was to guard the governor's palace. He supposed that made sense. The orcs would look for the strongest, most capable warriors, with the most status, to slaughter. Those spirits would be fed to the shards of Lord Bloodroot shaped into weapons that the Boki carried. Where else to find the greatest warriors than at the home of the war leader of the entire colony?

Their party arrived at Anton's palace—Will wondered if it would always be known for the man who'd built it instead of the person who occupied it—and the great portcullis was lowered, the iron-clad wood gates behind it tightly sealed. Their party was let in through a one-man postern gate after a tense delay while the locks and bars on the other side were undone for them.

The Mage's Guild party stepped into a courtyard filled with mustering soldiers. It sounded like a giant hive of buzzing bees.

"Come," Aurelius ordered.

Will followed his grandfather across the bailey toward a tall tower. A soldier opened the door at its base for them, and Aurelius hurried up the stone spiral staircase inside. From here, the city looked peaceful. Quiet, even.

"Report," Aurelius snapped at the nearest man-at-arms.

"Three-pronged invasion from the north, northwest, and west. Columns are maybe three hundred strong each of Boki warriors, assorted goblins, hobgoblins, ogres, and other greenskins. Our advance scouts report maybe a hundred Boki overall in each column, and there are several Boki mages in each column."

"Thorns," Will muttered.

"What?" the guard asked, surprised.

"The Boki call their battle mages thorns. It's a title. Zars are their raiders. Thanes are their equivalent of knights. Kis are their leaders. Like landsgraves."

"Boki knights," the soldier snorted in humor. "That's a good one."

Will cast a grim glance at Aurelius, who shook his head fractionally in warning to hold his tongue. He obeyed but with a sardonic twist to his mouth. If that was all the better the fellow thought of the Boki, yon soldier was in for a rude surprise before the night was out.

Still. He was confused. Why had only a few hundred Boki come to wreak vengeance on Dupree? He knew as well as anybody just how many Boki there really were hidden away in the Forest of Thorns and just how formidable a fighting force they were.

The soldier listed off a half dozen units that had been sent to the Slaver's, Entertainer's, and Miner's Guild Squares to act as mustering points for any civilians who could come out to join them. Will wondered at how many able-bodied men and women would hide in their homes and refuse to fight for the Empire. There was no love lost for Anton Constantine in most quarters, and for sixteen years he had been the face and voice of the Empire in Dupree.

Aurelius sighed. "Syreena's too newly come to know who to call upon to rouse the locals to fight. If only Hyland—" He broke off the thought without finishing it.

Will agreed. Hyland would have been able to draw every able-bodied fighter in the city to defend Dupree. But as it was, the new governess would have to make do with Anton's ragtag legion, recently gutted from bottom to top by the defection of Anton's flunkies and followers.

Of course, a bevy of hotheaded lads who merely wished to crack a few green skulls for fun would turn out for tonight's battle. But they would be no match for battle-hardened Boki.

Will commented low to Aurelius, "Maybe there are

enough citizens who remember the last Boki insurrection
and will fight for their lives before it is too late."

"Maybe," the elf replied doubtfully. "Human memories
are notoriously short."

Will winced. Aurelius was right. Already, the Night of
Green Fires was mostly an excuse to feast and drink. He'd
been but an infant himself the last time the Boki had come
to call on Dupree.

Pain began to build in his head, becoming a white-hot ball
of agony in the center of his skull, radiating shards of tor-
ment outward to encompass his entire being. If it did not
abate soon, he would go mad. *Curses, Bloodroot. If this is
you, cease and desist. You're killing me.*

Raina nearly plowed into Hrothgar's back as he screeched
to a halt in Miner's Guild Square. The barbarian spoke
over his shoulder. "Our scouts believe the leaders of the
attack are here. If we can hold off this column of Boki, the
others may lose focus. Be diverted and ultimately defeated."

Boki diverted? Raina highly doubted that would happen,
but she kept the observation to herself. She followed the high
matriarch up the steps of the Miner's Guild to gain a better
vantage point on the battle before them.

The noise was unbelievable, the wails and screams of the
wounded unbearable to her. But something else came to
Raina's ears in the din that made her stop and look around
frantically. It was the whispers again. They were urgent, trying to communicate something just beyond her understanding. *But what?* She strained to hear them, to make out their
warning, but it eluded her.

"Fall back!" someone bellowed from the middle of the
square. The jumble of soldiers and townspeople fighting
desperately in front of her stumbled backward toward her
position.

"Retreat, Heart!" Hrothgar shouted as the combat threat-
ened to swallow them.

Wounded and dead bodies were strewn across the square.

Rather than retreat, Raina pushed forward, calling magic to her hands.

"Not yet!" Hrothgar yelled, grabbing her tabard and yanking her back. "Come with me!"

"But—"

"Go with him, child!" Lenora called. "In battle, the White Heart follows the Royal Order of the Sun's orders."

Raina scowled. Neither the Heart nor the Royal Order of the Sun commanded the White Heart to break its vow in any circumstances, according to Brother Balthazar and Leland. But new as she was to the colors, she hesitated to disobey.

Unhappy, she fell back with the other healers. She did manage to heal a few minor wounds here and there around her, and she was relieved to see that several healers had lagged behind enough for the Imperial lines to catch up with them and get healing. She watched in admiration as three combat healers threw magic rapidly at the worst of the injured, casting on the fly as they ran.

A high-pitched child's giggle trilled in her ears, and Raina looked around wildly. No child should be abroad in this chaos. He or she would be slaughtered! She strained to hear the child again, and the whispers surged forward, filling her ears. *Go away, curse you! I have to find that child!* But the harder she concentrated on hearing the child again, the more her ears filled with maddening, wordless cacophony.

Hrothgar grabbed her arm and bodily dragged her from the square, ignoring her frantic protests that a child was nearby and in danger. He snapped something about her being the child in danger and left her no choice but to stumble along beside him.

It dawned on her that he was manipulating whom she had physical access to. He was making sure that all her healing went to the colonial forces and none of it to the greenskin attackers. This must have been the strategic management of the White Heart Lenora had spoken of earlier. Outraged, she started to tell him she was wise to his tactic, but the entire

Heart contingent took off running full out just then, and she had no choice but to follow along.

They burst into governor's square, and Raina couldn't help but screech to a halt in dismay. On one side of the square, a crowd of soldiers and townspeople clustered. They looked jittery, yelling catcalls and insults across the square. On the other side of the open square, a restless mob of Boki and assorted nonhumans stomped and grunted, yelling back their own insults and invective.

The whispers were louder than ever here, and she actually clapped her hands over her ears to block them out. The noise grated like sandpaper against her eardrums, and no amount of ignoring it made the voices go away. She was losing her mind. They would drive her mad if they did not quiet. Desperate to distract herself, she stared at the battleground before her and focused intently on how the forces were laid out. If healing on battlefields was to be her future, it behooved her to understand how lines formed and moved and how commanders deployed their troops.

It looked as though the governess had elected to concentrate all her forces on a single, great confrontation with the Boki. One fight for all the gold. It was a dangerous strategy. Although she supposed the alternative, letting the Boki hack away at the remains of the Haelan legion bit by skirmishing bit, wasn't any better a choice.

"We must make our way around the square to the Imperial Army lines. Be quick now!" Hrothgar ordered.

Raina hesitated. From here, she would have a clear path straight to the front lines when the two forces closed on one another. That would be where the worst of the casualties would happen. Her healing would be of most use there.

Lenora spoke sternly to her. "Do not mistake the neutrality of the White Heart for aiding the enemy."

"Exactly who is the enemy here?" she retorted. "We invaded their lands and slaughtered their people. This is retribution. While I do not condone that, either, the Boki are the aggrieved party."

The high matriarch spoke low and urgent. "Now is not the time or place to debate politics. You are Heart. The Heart serves the Empire. To do otherwise would be disastrous, not only for every member of our order but for common people everywhere. They need us. And to serve them, we must stay clear of the Empire's wrath."

She might not like it, but she could not fault Lenora's logic. Exhaling hard, she followed the Heart party around the square. With a heavy heart, she allowed herself to be herded behind the lines and managed.

Hrothgar and the others would make sure to put so many of their own wounded in front of her that she would never reach the Boki wounded. Or she would be so depleted of mana—the magical energy to fuel her spells—that, by the time she got there, she would not be able to heal more than a handful of the enemy.

She only hoped the White Heart emissary to the Boki, Balthazar, was somewhere behind that seething mass of Boki warriors. He would even the scales at least a little.

We must go," Aurelius murmured to Will. "Syreena's troops will need every bit of help they can get."

That was no jest. To Will's eyes, watering from the pain in his skull, this battle looked to be a disaster in the making. The colonial forces didn't stand a chance against a Boki force of the size converging in the great square before them. Not to mention, the invaders looked and sounded *pissed*.

Flashes of memory of the night his parents were killed and his village torched intermingled with images of Boki dying in droves, their bodies lying in literal piles before the secret cave entrance that led to the Sleeping King. Rage and terror pounded through him, and he felt himself coming unhinged. He could not do this. He *must* do this. *Kill. Show mercy. Run. Fight.* His mind whirled crazily, the whole world atilt around him.

As if Aurelius read his mind, the elf muttered, "Do not overthink it, boy. Live or die. Kill or be killed. Once you enter combat, do not hesitate, do not question. Just fight to win."

Ty used to say the same thing in almost the exact same words. The advice resonated within him, settling the encroaching madness. He supposed, at the end of the day, it was not a bad thing to respect, or even like, a foe on the battlefield. It lent a certain honor to the exercise of beating each other's brains out.

He breathed deeply and attempted to empty his mind completely. If only he understood his symbiosis with Bloodroot more fully, mayhap he could exert more control over these increasingly frequent episodes of internal conflict—

Now was not the moment to think on that.

No thought. Just action. Fight. Win. Live.

Aurelius arrayed his mages in the second rank of troops where they would be close enough to the front to cast magic at their foes but not within weapon range of the Boki. Will also noted that the Celestial Order guardians and knights stayed close enough to collapse back around Aurelius and defend their guildmaster at a moment's notice.

Will was interested to see the great battle mage at work. From what he'd heard, Aurelius had epic skill in combat. As orders were shouted down the lines, Will reviewed the spells he'd learned recently—how to deliver metered amounts of magical damage, and the specialized spells of a battle mage, spells for weakening, slowing, and immobilizing targets.

The three main prongs of the invading force poured into the square, and heretofore unseen Boki, who must have been marauding in the side streets leading to the square, pushed into the space behind their brethren.

Oh, this was not good. Will tried to count greenskins and got lost somewhere in excess of two hundred Boki warriors. In his experience, the militia would need four or five skilled soldiers for every one Boki to have a fighting chance. Although there were upward of a thousand locals on this side of the lines, many of them were civilians or new conscripts to the Haelan legion. The Dupree forces had a decent number of battle mages and healers, but would that be enough to turn the tide in their favor?

He took a closer look at the horde and realized with a start that it was comprised of more goblins, ogres, and other races than actual Boki. That was strange.

He studied the Boki themselves. Curiouser and curiouser. He didn't spot many grizzled, heavily scarred orcs. Boki warriors wore their scars like trophies: the more experienced, the more scarred. Shamans also seemed to be in seriously short supply.

"Something's wrong!" he called to his grandfather. "These are only youngsters and inexperienced fighters. Where are the real Boki warriors?"

Aurelius took a hard look at the enemy columns and then nodded tersely at Will. "Maybe this is a splinter faction we didn't meet in the Forest of Thorns."

The Boki had factions within their ranks? That was news to him. At least someone in charge was alerted to the possibility that this was a trap. Of course, it was also possible that the Boki hadn't bothered to send their best fighters because they didn't think they would be necessary for the defeat of Dupree.

Aurelius yelled to his men, "Find their casters! Call out as you spot them!"

Will spied a line of white tabards spreading out behind the Imperial lines. The Heart. Rosana would be among them. Panic for her safety nearly overcame him. He resolved to fight his way across the lines until he spotted her and then to stick to her like glue.

He spotted Raina, parked behind a burly Royal Order of the Sun warrior, and she looked none too happy. She'd gone all save-the-bunnies since she'd put on those colors. Probably was having a heart attack over the loss of life to come. Her peaceful sentiments were noble, but affairs of state were inherently violent. Wishing for everyone to get along and love one another was pure fantasy. *This* was the way of the world.

Tonight, the city of Dupree would live or die, and possibly the entire young colony with it. The governess would prove her mettle in battle, or she would fail before she ever really established herself.

P rincess Endellian mentally winced when High Lord Inquisitor Laernan was announced into Emperor Maximillian's small throne room. Her half brother was never
the bearer of good tidings. Not to mention her father had
been volatile ever since word of Anton Constantine being deposed in Dupree had reached the Imperial Court. Bad news
was the last thing the Emperor's uncertain mood needed
right now.

She did not for a second think that Maximillian was actually worried about Haelos. If anything, she sensed a hint
of entertainment in his mental emanations when he was not
primarily irritated. One of the great risks of immortality was
boredom. And humans were terribly predictable most of the
time. Her father had so successfully cowed them that they
barely posed a challenge anymore.

Laernan glanced quickly around the golden throne
room—a miniature version of the Great Receiving Hall in
the center of the sprawling Imperial Seat—and seemed relieved that only she and her father were present. Along with
a line of deaf guards, of course.

"What have you for me today?" her father asked his chief
inquisitor pleasantly enough.

"A prophecy, Your Resplendent Majesty."

"From a Child of Fate?"

"Aye, Your Majesty."

"Let us have it, then." Her father sounded supremely dis-
interested. And for good reason. The Children of Fate had

been singing dire fates for Maximillian and the Eternal Empire of Koth for years now. The refrain was growing old.

Laernan bowed his head and then said, "It goes thus:

Unto an ancient kingdom shall a new Empire arise.
Borne on the wings of falcon great, the old is swept aside.
Great Totem, mighty Haelos born, warrior wings shall
fill the night.
The stars shall fall within his wake and all is set aright."

Her first inclination was to shrug off the latest prophecy of doom and destruction, hence she was surprised when Maximillian asked Laernan to repeat it and then proceeded to wax thoughtful.

A falcon? General Tarses, mayhap? Her father had been fond of calling his favorite general his falcon. Her heart leaped in hope that her lover of long ago might finally return, but she quashed the reaction before her father could sense it.

Or the new governess of Dupree, perhaps? She was some sort of avarian. A bird changeling. Was she the falcon who would bring a new Empire to an ancient kingdom? If so, her father would be well pleased. The governess had risen from squalor to become an Imperial noble. She owed all she was to the Empire.

But what if this falcon was someone else? What if this was yet another warning of impending doom to the Kothite Throne? Gah. She had no patience for prophecies and double-speak. How her father abided such tripe was beyond her.

She knew, of course, what his answer would be if she asked why he tolerated such things. He would shrug and remind her that his subjects paid attention to seers and prophets; therefore, he did the same. Frankly, as seers went, the Children of Fate were more prescient than most. And indeed, by the rules of the Accord, if enough mortals believed a thing, it could come to pass according to their beliefs. Still. She had trouble crediting her almighty father with believing any of it.

Although he had reacted forcefully to the Prophecy of the End, as it had come to be called. Given by a Child of Fate oracle under torture nearly twenty years ago, it had been the first prophecy to forecast the end of the Kothite Empire at the hands of a nameless one who would supposedly emerge from the wilds to break the shackles of Kothite rule. *Absurd.* Her father was stronger than ever.

She had to admit, though, that the Children of Fate were known to be uncannily accurate. Laernan readily admitted that his prisoners had some sort of special connection to forces beyond the Veil of Time. Even her half brother, son of the King of Kufu, ruler of the Sands of Time himself, could not generate the same connection across time.

Reluctantly, she turned her attention back to this latest mumbling. What of the totem reference in this falcon prophecy? Archduke Ammertus, leader of the invasion force that had been sent to take Haelos, had broken the Great Circle he'd found there. The surviving totems in Haelos were in disarray and no threat to the Empire. Was the Falcon Totem on the rise once more, perchance? A single totem could not possibly threaten the entire empire. Last she'd heard, a Falcon Totem had emerged in Pan Orda. Was that the falcon in the prophecy, perhaps?

Bah. She would discount the whole riddled mess were it not for her father's continued interest in the Children of Fate.

"How goes the hunt for new Children?" Maximillian asked abruptly.

Laernan frowned slightly, which spoke volumes. "They continue to be scarce."

She picked up on a faint nuance in his voice that spoke of Children hiding. Or perhaps fleeing Koth. Odd. Children of Fate would not have the resources to dodge the Emperor's hounds or to escape Koth on their own. Surely, they did not receive assistance. Who would dare? The notion of anyone resisting her father's will was laughable.

For his part, Maximillian did not seem perturbed. "Continue running the hounds."

"I shall inform the Master of Hounds, Your Resplendent Majesty," Laernan replied formally. He murmured something about retiring and returning to his work. She did not envy him spending all his time, day in and day out, tearing into the minds of unwilling victims. She got the impression he did not enjoy his work, but he was unparalleled at it.

No sooner had Laernan bowed his way out than the chamberlain announced another arrival. And this one made her father sit up straighter on his throne. Captain Kodo, captain of the Black Ship *Victorious,* fresh returned from Dupree.

The captain must have worked his mages mercilessly to spur on the wind elementals and water elementals who propelled Black Ships at greater than normal speed. Usually, it took nine months or more to cross the mighty Abyssmal Sea that separated Koth from Haelos and return again. But Kodo had completed this round trip in an unheard of six months. It was dangerous in the extreme to make the crossing so rapidly, even for a Black Ship.

"Report, Kodo," Max ordered.

"As already reported, based on information given to me by First Advisor Ceridwyn Nightshade and several Imperial guildmasters, I was forced to remove Governor Constantine from his position and place him under arrest."

"What is this information you speak of?"

Kodo handed over a black, leather-bound journal to her father. Maximillian perused it at length while all in the throne room waited in silence.

Maximillian looked up. "Where is Nightshade? Why is she not standing in front of me to present these accusations?"

"Shortly after First Advisor Nightshade handed over those

notes, a minor riot broke out, and I was diverted containing it. By the time calm was restored and I sent orders to the palace for Ceridwyn to present herself to me, she was gone. Nobody could give me any information regarding where she might be."

"And where is Anton?" Maximillian asked, looking over Kodo's shoulder expectantly.

The captain answered regretfully, "Anton fled the scene moments after I removed him from power. The riot I mentioned flared up at my proclamation, and he used the . . . confusion to make his escape."

Endellian got the distinct impression that the word Kodo had wanted to use was *celebration,* not *confusion.* So. The natives celebrated their governor's fall, did they? Her father did not seem surprised at that silent revelation.

Kodo was speaking again. "To date, Constantine remains at large."

"Find Constantine and Nightshade and bring them both to me. Commandeer as many troops as you need and offer whatever reward is necessary to apprehend them."

Kodo bowed in silent acquiescence to the order.

Max's fingers drummed the arm of his throne, a sure sign that his patience had worn thin. "So. The first advisor vanished, and Anton ran. Then what transpired?"

"For lack of any other suitable noble, I named the ranking Kothite noble present interim governess until you can select a permanent governor."

"Syreena Wingblade," Max murmured thoughtfully. "How do you judge her capabilities, Kodo?"

"She will rule with a lighter hand than her predecessor. Production in the colony will drop although income from that quarter may, in fact, rise."

Endellian's brows shot upward. Kodo dared to intimate that one of her father's governors had been dipping his fingers in the coffers? Graft and corruption must have been rampant in Dupree for Kodo to be so bold. Not that she was surprised. Anton had always seemed a slimy character in her estimation. Constantine was a known pet of Ammertus, who was not exactly renowned for his stability or law-abiding nature.

Kodo continued, "Given time, I believe she will calm the colony."

"Any other news of note?" Maximillian asked.

"I did hear a rumor that a certain escaped prisoner was seen beyond the Estarran Sea."

Endellian's heart leaped. *Tarses had been seen?*

She still thought of him fondly, even if she also understood the necessity for Maximillian to keep him under wraps and believed dead by all. A charismatic and likable leader, Tarses had been too successful for his own good. The entire Imperial Army adored him to the extent that he actually posed a potential threat to Maximillian's throne. And then there was the whole business of the ice elemental Tarses had tried to absorb. There was no telling how it had changed her father's old friend. But surely it had.

Although he'd considered Tarses his closest friend, Maximillian had been forced to banish him to a secret prison in Dupree and circulate a story that Tarses had been killed in battle. The Emperor simply could not allow such an unpredictable person to exist. Still, she missed him.

Ironic that her lover was now a nameless fugitive, disappeared into the wilds. Almost as if he were being shaped by the prophecy of the end itself. Not that any mumbled vision by some fortune-telling hack actually had the power to shape the future against the will of her father.

Maximillian spoke briskly to Kodo. "Have special hounds prepared. Send a contingent of your best troops with them to the Estarran Sea and beyond. Find him. Bring him back to me in utmost secrecy." Her father sounded as satisfied as a cat with a bowl of cream all to itself. The news about Tarses had pleased him greatly. She held no illusion that her sire's contentment derived from the anticipated return of his old friend. Rather, he enjoyed manipulating events to circumvent that old prophecy about a nameless one coming in from the wild.

"So shall it be, Your Resplendent Majesty," Kodo murmured obediently.

"One last task, Kodo. Find and destroy the Falcon Totem of Haelos and the Great Falcon of the Pan Ordan Circle of Beasts."

Kodo looked visibly startled. As well he should. Such acts would be open provocations to local nature-aligned forces on both continents and undoubtedly cause unrest in both places.

"Is this a problem?"

"No, Your Majesty. Uhh, so shall it be." The order obviously had taken Kodo by surprise. However, the captain's duty was not to ask but merely to obey.

So. Tarses had shown himself, had he? For surely, the only way any rumor of him had reached this room was because he willed it so. She sometimes wondered if Constantine hadn't engineered Tarses's escape. Apparently, there had been an uprising of monster races, and a group of orcs had overrun the prison and released all the prisoners.

Her father had long had the means to fix Tarses's problem and remove the elemental magics from within him, if someone could but catch up with the fugitive general and bring him in. On one hand, she greatly wished for him to be fixed. Her father's plan had long been to install her in Pan Orda as its queen with Tarses as her consort to help keep order on the sprawling and fractious continent. It was a plan she greatly favored. An itch to get out from under Maximillian's thumb tormented her. And personally, she was quite fond of Tarses.

But on the other hand, she feared for his safety if he emerged from hiding. He posed a real and dangerous threat to Maximillian's throne, and her father would never tolerate that, no matter how fond of his falcon he might be.

What were the odds that Laernan should retrieve a prophecy that spoke of a falcon and, moments later, word of General Tarses's whereabouts should surface? A chill whisked down her spine. This was *exactly* why she despised soothsayers and portents.

A chamberlain stepped forward, and Maximillian looked at him expectantly. "Commander Thanon has arrived and awaits your pleasure as ordered, Your Resplendent Majesty."

"Send him in."

Endellian observed the young officer, a paxan who'd distinguished himself by leading his own regiment of elite shock troops in battle. He did not look old enough to have amassed the chestful of blazons from military campaigns and medals for valor that left no doubt as to the nature of the man wearing them. Thanon made a crisp bow and rose with athletic fluidity when her father gestured him up. The mark around the closed third eye in the middle of Thanon's forehead was Grand Marshal Korovo's. He was commander in chief of all of Maximillian's military forces.

"I have a mission for you, Commander Thanon," her father announced. "I need you to lead your regiment to Haelos with all due haste. I shall arrange for a portal to drop you near Dupree. Captain Kodo, here, sails in the morning in the Black Ship *Victorious*. He will bring you the bulk of your equipment and supplies."

"It is my honor to serve Your Resplendent Majesty."

She was surprised at the officer's brevity. Most who came before her father felt obliged to bury her sire in great, horrible soliloquies of praise that were made all the more obsequious by being patently insincere.

Maximillian smiled a little. Perhaps he was reminded of another talented military officer from long ago. Had Tarses ever been this intense and focused? She thought back. Yes. Yes, he had.

"Your primary task shall be to help the Haelan legion restore order and bring quiet to the colony. Additionally, I need you to be my eyes and ears. Learn the new lay of the land."

"So shall it be, Your Majesty."

Interesting. Her father felt a need for more players on the game board in Haelos. Did he have reason to believe that events were accelerating on that problematic continent?

Her speculations were interrupted when Maximillian told her briskly, "Summon my councilors. We must discuss this business of who shall rule Haelos. It is imperative that the new governor get control of the situation quickly."

She rose to her feet. "Of course, Father. Right away."

Ready?" Aurelius murmured over his shoulder. "They'll come any minute now. Yon Boki battle leader has his forces nearly whipped into a killing frenzy. They'll go quiet just before they charge so they can hear the order and go together."

Will stepped up beside the guildmaster to have a look. He did not recognize any of the Boki warriors shouting and waving their clubs. He muttered to his grandfather, "Does it not strike you as odd that they are spending so much time posturing? That is entirely unlike the Boki tactics I saw in the Forest of Thorns."

"Mayhap they act differently when defending their home," Aurelius replied distractedly.

Will frowned. The Boki in the Forest of Thorns had been serious, focused, and organized. Yes, there'd been some shouting and club waving, but nothing remotely resembling this. Frankly, the display he witnessed now looked more like a grand show than actual combat. As if they intentionally tried to engage the attention of as many Haelan forces as they could . . .

The Boki were fully clever enough to pull off a distraction tactic.

"Are you sure this is their main battle force?" he asked his grandfather.

Aurelius's full attention swung to him. "Explain yourself."

"This is *nothing* like how they acted when led by their thanes and thorns. And where are the thanes and thorns? They should have a dozen of them at the front of their line, and I see *not one* experienced battle leader." He added forcefully, "This is a trick."

"We must follow our orders," Aurelius snapped.

"Let me challenge the leader to single combat and get this fight started," Will declared.

"Absolutely not. You are my only living heir. I will not allow you to risk your life like that."

"They killed my father. Your adopted *son*. And my mother."

Aurelius whipped around to face him, golden eyes blazing hotter than the sun. "I *know*," he growled. "You are fated to great deeds, but not this night. You must trust me. Let them stay over there out of reach."

A voice from Will's other side said cheerfully, "I can make them come over here."

Will turned sharply. A slender young man dressed in a random assortment of ragged clothing grinned at him mischievously. "Who are you?"

"Travesty, if you please. Wandrakin minstrel and master of the jest."

"How will you bring yon orcs to me?"

"Easy." The wandrakin cupped his hands around his mouth and shouted across the field, "Hey, you big, green lump of rat turd! Yeah, you! The one with the big red club and a face so ugly your mother wouldn't suckle you. No wonder you're so scrawny."

The orc standing at the head of force of greenskins roared, and his face twisted in rage.

"You're so stupid a sheep can outsmart you!" Travesty shouted. Hoots and catcalls up and down the Dupree line seemed to lend the wandrakin energy. Literally. It was just on the edge of his vision, but Will thought the wandrakin was actually channeling the words in an almost magical way. Twisting them into something weapon-like, imbuing them with intent. With emotional power.

The wandrakin shouted, "Stars, even a moss-covered rock can outsmart you, and it would be a less disgusting wad of green slime than you!"

The lead orc roared, and the rest of the horde picked up on the howl of fury. Will gripped his staff more tightly as the Boki yanked a short, curved dagger out of his crude belt. He thought to kill the Haelan legion with that little toothpick? Will swished his staff experimentally, testing its range. As long as he could keep his foes beyond the arc of his staff, Will would control any fight he engaged in.

The lead orc brandished his dagger in his fist, shoving it high in the air. And then the creature plunged the blade into his own ear with a scream of rage and agony.

Will lurched in shock. "Why did he do that?" he exclaimed.

"The wandrakin taunts him," Aurelius answered grimly. "The orc puts out his own eardrums rather than let young Travesty lure him into an unreasoning battle rage from which he cannot escape. Which," he added grimly under his breath, "lends credence to your assertion that this group is under orders to distract the legion and keep it here, not to engage the governess's troops in bloody battle."

Will swiveled to face his grandfather. "Taunts are real?"

"Observe and learn," Aurelius muttered, nodding at the young wandrakin, who was still shouting invective at the Boki battle leader in a steady stream. The words twisted and writhed through the air, growing in power as they traveled toward their target. It was akin to watching magic, but the source of the power was markedly different. Language itself seemed to be the point of origin.

"Your troops are without balls. Your wife is a wart-covered goblin. And your children are idiots!" On and on the insults went, growing ever more outrageous. Will had never seen nor heard the like. He would laugh his head off if that strange power didn't vibrate through every syllable.

The orc shifted the wicked dagger into his off hand.

"Quickly," Aurelius urged the wandrakin. "He's about to put out his other eardrum."

For a moment, desperation crossed young Travesty's face. "He's resisting powerfully. I need something personal to him. Something that causes him pain. A failure of some kind. That would push him over the edge."

Will knew just the thing. He leaned down and muttered quickly in the wandrakin's ear.

"Yup, that'll do it," Travesty responded, nodding.

"Hurry," Aurelius urged. "This day's victory or loss may come down to this moment. You must succeed, youngling."

Travesty grinned impudently at Will's mentor. "Watch this." He bellowed at the top of his lungs so every living being on the field could not fail to hear him. "The son of your greatest enemy stands here beside me, alive. You all *failed*. You could not erase the lineage of your foe. You and your entire tribe were not able to kill one lousy stripling lad."

The orc's dagger hesitated. Travesty cursed and sweat popped out on his brow.

Will leaned forward and muttered in the wandrakin's ear urgently, "Tell him the son of the yellow dragon lives."

Travesty screamed, pitching his voice in a timbre that even evoked soul-deep agitation in Will, "The son of the yellow dragon lives! Here he stands, you stupid lout!"

That was it.

The orc bellowed like a minotaur and charged, shocking his troops and leaving them behind for a stunned moment before they gathered themselves to follow their leader.

The result was an arrow-shaped charge by the Boki line with the enraged orc alone, well in front of the rest. Will gripped his staff tightly, took a deep breath, and charged.

But Aurelius also signaled to Syreena's battle commander just as Will leaped forward. Horns blew, sounding the charge, and a mass of Dupree regulars and militia charged in a coordinated mass toward the oncoming thane. Will was not able to break through and get to the front of the line to meet the Boki in honorable battle. Which was no doubt Aurelius's intent. Curse him.

The need to avenge his mother and father, the pent-up grief and loss, the pure, clean rage of hatred poured through Will. The wooden disk embedded over his heart burned like acid, feeding upon his fury, gorging upon it. And hate came back to Will from the disk, magnified a hundredfold. Bloodroot was the guardian of death and destruction. This battle, this moment, fed his soul like nothing else.

The tree lord's power surged through Will, almost too much for his mortal vessel to contain. His head felt as if it would split in twain. His entire body felt as if it might explode. He yelled at the top of his lungs, giving voice to it all.

The orc leader's speed and strength, along with his surprise head start, meant he crashed into the Dupree line a good dozen man-lengths in front of any of his troops. Colonial soldiers and militia swarmed the Boki, hacking ferociously at him from all directions. It was at least twenty on one.

Seconds later, the entire Boki and Dupree lines crashed into each other with a deafening explosion of sound and fury. Weapons clanged, men shouted and cried and screamed. Orders were bellowed, horns blown to direct troop movements, and the moans of the wounded and dying began to rise from the ground. Blood flew everywhere, and the smell of it filled the air. The paving stones beneath Will's feet grew slippery, running with blood in a river of death.

Where was the leader? What was the real plan out here? The orc was surrounded by a mass of soldiers hacking at him from all sides. Even the greatest Boki warrior could not withstand such a lopsided assault for long. Ty had always told Will that sufficient quantity would win out over quality every time in a fight. Now he knew what his father had meant. The orc's leather armor and then the natural armor of his own tough hide were sliced to ribbons by dozens of blades chopping into his body.

The Boki seemed oblivious to the wounds springing up all over him, caught as he was in the grip of the battle rage Travesty had provoked. Will had seen some tough Boki in his day, but never had he seen anything like this. The orc's left arm was all but severed above the elbow, his right thigh hacked in multiple places by massive gashes that would have felled a lesser creature. A dozen arrows stuck out of his hide, his nose and jaw were askew, and smaller wounds without count crisscrossed his green hide. The orc roared with every swing of his mighty axe, mowing down locals around him like stalks of wheat, ripe for the harvest. It was a terrible and beautiful sight to see.

Will's paltry staff was swept aside by the torrent of blades ebbing and flowing around the Boki. He was pushed back from the bristling mob as the orc went down under a pile of shouting attackers.

Blades continued to rise and fall madly. Great arcs of blood swung wide of the scrum as the Dupree defenders hacked their enemy to bits. The violence of the orc's end stunned Will. It even seemed to rock the Boki line itself. The green charge faltered. Broke.

Units of infuriated Dupree regulars and irregulars barreled into the abrupt chaos of the greenskin line as it fell apart. It devolved into a gigantic melee of dozens of smaller skirmishes. It was almost as if that taunt had affected everyone within earshot of it.

Mage's Guild and Heart members spread across the field of battle, flowing from one pocket of fighting to the next, lending assistance as needed but focusing most of their efforts on the most dangerous combat.

The volume of blood was incredible. The only battles Will had seen before had taken place in wild places where the earth soaked up the blood quickly. But here, in a city with paved streets, it ran in rivers along the curbs and winding across the squares. It smelled of iron death and made the streets slick and treacherous.

Aurelius's battle mages and the Royal Order of the Sun knights teamed up to move methodically across the square, eliminating each pocket of fighting as they came to it. Will had gotten separated from his grandfather during the fight, and somehow he didn't think that had been an accident. The worst of the fighting centered upon Aurelius and several Heart knights.

Momentarily at a loss for what to do or where to go, Will scanned across the field of battle. The greenskins were retreating before the onslaught, standing and fighting until hard-pressed and then dropping back to the north. He frowned. Since when did Boki ever retreat, and since when did greenskins in general retreat in such a disciplined fashion? He frowned. Were the Haelan troops being led northward on purpose?

Why?

What lay to the south of their current position? Certainty bubbled up in his gut that some ruse was afoot. The Boki would not randomly attack Dupree in a suicide mission like this. They had a purpose in mind. But what?

Aurelius's thoughts must have been running in the same vein, for he materialized beside Will. "We can spare you here. Why don't you go have a look on the south side of the city? If these Boki do, indeed, distract us here, that is where they wish to divert our attention away from."

"Yes, sir!"

"Be careful. I would take it much amiss if aught were to happen to you."

He grinned at his grandfather and took off running.

Following the instinctive certainty in his belly that the Boki were perpetrating a trick, he raced down a southbound avenue, unfamiliar with this part of the city. The sounds of fighting diminished behind him. Apparently, all the invaders were in the northern part of the city. A few civilians darted about, but for the most part, the streets and alleys in this section of Dupree were deserted.

He burst out into the great open practice field for the Haelan legion. It reached all the way down to the shore of the Bay of Dupree and was bounded on the other three sides by the legion's barracks and headquarters. Why on Urth would the Boki and their minions go to such trouble to draw the battle away from *this* place?

He slowed to a walk, catching his breath as he traversed the dirt field, pounded hard by countless boots marching and drilling over the years. Great hulking buildings ringed the field, silent now, emptied of soldiers who'd gone forth to defend the city.

A slight movement caught his attention ahead, down by the shore. He dropped to his belly, cursing the lack of cover out here. Cautiously, he lifted his head. Two long, low dugout canoes were pulling up to the banks of the field. Were those the vessels called ryslu? Two Boki jumped out of each of the long dugouts with their pointed prows, narrow bodies, and blunt sterns. No wonder colonists called them thornboats. They were shaped like great spiny thorns.

He prayed the slight undulations in the field would hide him from view of the four Boki now racing along the field's margin. The orcs disappeared around the end of a great stone building with iron bars across all its windows. The armory.

He jumped up and ran lightly to where he'd last seen the raiders, pausing at the corner to peer around it. The four orcs stood in front of a door of some kind. A magic user threw a spell at the faintly glowing portal, and the light of the wizard's lock extinguished. Another orc raised a massive axe and hacked at the door. Sparks flew. Must have been an iron-bound portal. They were breaking into the Haelan legion's armory? What on Urth?

The big orc and his axe smashed through the door, and the Boki disappeared inside. Will could go for help, but by the time he found any troops, convinced them to come back here, and returned, these orcs would be long gone.

His natural curiosity took over. He had to know what they were up to. He sprinted down the alley and slipped into the building.

Although the space felt large, it was so full of shelves and racks filled with anything an army might need to fight a war that he could only see a little way in any direction. Cautiously, he moved forward.

There. A faint noise ahead and to the left. His old woodsman's skills came in handy as he slid from shadow to shadow.

A circle of light shone ahead. He moved down a parallel row between shelves full of small barrels. He crouched down and peered between them.

He swore to himself. These orcs were big, brawny, and scarred enough to be experienced warriors. Worse, they all carried wooden weapons fashioned of the distinctively hued bloodthorn wood. Only the most accomplished Boki fighters carried pieces of Bloodroot's destroyed tree.

The Boki were sawing into the lid of a chest between the iron bands wrapping it. One of the Boki was just putting away a set of tools he recognized as trap picks. They were breaking into a trapped chest? What would the Haelan legion store inside such a thing? The chest in question was covered in dust. Whatever was inside was not something the legion used often.

As he looked on, the Boki broke through the lid. With a grunt of triumph, an orc reached inside and pulled out a fleece-wrapped object. It was about the length of Will's forearm and looked heavy. The orc reached inside again and fished around before announcing, "Jus' one. No mo'."

The magic user unwrapped the skin to reveal a pie-shaped wedge of carved stone. It was black and glossy with gold veins running through it. So much magic poured off the thing that, to Will's trained eyes, it lit the space brighter than the torch. He thought he felt air moving across his skin, and yet no hair on his head stirred. Perhaps that was the energy of the magic pouring forth. The mage grunted in satisfaction. Will had no idea what that stone was, but it could *not* be good that the Boki were stealing it. He must find a way to stop them!

The mage rewrapped the stone and tucked it into a crude pack, announcing, "We go, Zar'Mok."

The biggest orc nodded and gestured for the strike team to move out. Frantically, Will pointed his staff at Zar'Mok's ankles and fired a blast of magic. The Boki cried out and collapsed. Will stood upright and threw a bolt of force damage between the barrels at the nearest Boki. The orc howled.

He turned and took off running before the mage could get a bead on him. A bolt of magic sailed over his head, and he ducked around a corner. Heavy footsteps pounded behind him. Curse it, he'd forgotten how fast they were.

Something heavy—a club, maybe—slammed into his back. He staggered, righted himself, and kept running. But the footsteps were noticeably closer now. And then they split. *Dregs. Not good.*

A club swung around the corner of an intersection ahead, and he skidded to a halt, but not in time. It caught him a glancing blow on his shoulder, spinning him around. Like a trapped rat, he darted off in another random direction.

A Boki materialized in front of him. He swung his staff and caught the orc's club on its shaft, directing the blow up and away from his head. He'd never tried it before, but Will desperately channeled magic *down* the shaft of his staff toward its base, flinging it toward his attacker.

Thank the stars, it worked. The Boki stumbled back, snarling in rage and pain.

Will whirled, but three more Boki raced up behind him, and one got in a glancing blow with his club to the side of Will's head. He was dazed and trapped, frantically trying to regain his wits to defend himself at a minimum. One of them raised the torch high so the others could see to kill him.

Zar'Mok grunted in surprise and then poked at his own chest above his heart. "Sapling human. Vessel o' Bloodroot. No kill 'im. We go."

Dazed, Will stared in disbelief as the burly orcs moved away from him, jogging toward the exit. Whatever that wedge of stone was, it had been worth bringing a thousand greenskins to Dupree on a suicide mission. He had to get it back.

Stumbling drunkenly, he headed after the fleeing Boki. He stepped outside, and the fresh air and bright light helped clear his head. He took off running after his prey, his steps steadying and picking up speed. He rounded the corner into the big practice field and spied the Boki partway across the open space. They were getting away!

He sprinted at full speed. It was going to be a close thing to reach them before they gained the safety of their dugout ryslu canoes. He gathered magic as he ran. When he had enough, he slowed enough to cast a disarming spell at the caster carrying the skin-wrapped stone. The orc fumbled and dropped the piece, and the others screeched to a halt as the mage scrambled to retrieve it.

Will caught sight of a third small boat approaching the shore and cursed under his breath. The last thing he needed was for this bunch to get reinforcements. As it was, he couldn't take on four seasoned Boki alone and realistically hope to live. He kept on running, though. He had no choice. He had to get that stone back or die trying.

Wariness flowed through Thanon as he and his men stepped through the portal onto the main pier in Dupree. It was clear at a glance that all was not well in the city. For one thing, no one came to meet him and his men. As in *no one.* Not a harbormaster or even a dockworker to inquire as to who they were. For another, he thought he heard the sounds of fighting somewhere in the direction of Governor's Square, or maybe slightly north of there. And third, as he looked down at the ground, the runoff water from a recent rain was tinged red.

Thanon ordered his men into the city to check on the governor's safety. They jogged off in formation while he appropriated a dinghy and rowed for the headquarters of the Haelan legion just to the west of the docks. He'd been ordered to report to Captain Krugar immediately when he arrived in the colony, and so he would. It was also his best bet for receiving a military status report.

He rowed his boat toward the gravel strand edging an expansive practice field. As he approached, he spied four large, battle-scarred orcs running away from a human warrior. He drew closer and saw the telltale forehead scars of Boki. That legendary tribe's fame had spread even to the shores of Koth. The human with the staff must be a mighty fighter to terrify them so.

His landing craft scraped bottom just as the Boki turned to face their attacker. He leaped ashore, drawing his crystal long sword as he did. He raced up the strand as the human youth fired off a blindingly fast series of disarming spells at his Boki foes and then wasted no time diving in with a staff to pound on the momentarily weaponless orcs. Nice tactic.

Roaring with rage, the Boki scooped up their weapons and charged the human.

Time to even the odds. Thanon attacked the exposed backs of the Boki, laying into them pell-mell. One of them turned to face him, blocking his sword blow with some sort of small, heavy-looking object covered in skin. Thanon's sword reverberated off what felt like stone. Swearing, he made a hard turn to slash his blade into the thigh of another Boki.

The orcs jumped back, attempting to flank both him and the human. Sensing the tactic almost before they did it, Thanon jumped forward to place himself beside the human. Something fast moving and metallic swung for his head, and he barely managed to duck beneath its deadly arc before it would have smashed into his face.

What in the name of the cursed was *that*? The human had taken a swing at him, but he hadn't telepathically sensed it coming. He was never taken by surprise in battle. His entire life had been spent honing his paxan mental talents into an uncanny battle sense that both felt and perceived the moves his foes were going to make a split second before they actually made them. Compliments of his mental edge, he always flowed seamlessly into and through a battle, working in perfect concert with his own men, and he was always in the right place at the right time to do the most damage to his foes.

The metal-clad staff snapped back the other way and

clipped him painfully on the side of his knee. His leg collapsed, and only his superb fitness and reflexes kept him on his feet. Good grief, the kid was fast with a staff.

The biggest Boki closed on him with a howl of rage, a huge red-hued club raised high. The orc was going to feint a mighty downward swing with the club and use that dagger hidden in his off hand to gut him. That was more like it. His battle intuition was back in place where it belonged.

He sidestepped the club while blocking the wickedly fast dagger with his sword. All in one movement, he swung his shield off his back and into position on his left arm, backing away from a second Boki trying to flank him on the left. That cursed staff nearly nailed him again.

"I fight *with* you against the orcs," he snapped, irritated.

"Sorry," the young man grunted, grappling with a Boki warrior, holding off the orc's spear with the shaft of a nice-looking staff.

They had no more time for conversation as the four Boki took up positions on all sides of them, an attempt to confuse him and his impromptu battle brother-in-arms. The Boki magic user cast some sort of damaging spell at Thanon, but his armor held and absorbed the attack. He took a quick swipe at the mage with his sword, backing the fellow up enough that the orc mage would not be able to bring a weapon to bear against him, which left him one-on-one with the big Boki with the club and dagger for the moment.

Except the Boki put away the dagger and pulled a spiked mace off his back with his off hand. Thanon sensed that the orc was at ease with either weapon in either hand. Mustn't underestimate the danger of that mace, then. He settled lower in his fighting stance and again expanded his awareness to encompass the human now fighting at his back.

He sensed *nothing*.

The Boki charged, flailing both mace and club at him, and Thanon thrust his shield from side to side, catching the worst of the blows on its sturdy surface. The sheer weight of the Boki's attack drove him back, though, until his shoulder blades nearly touched the human's. The orc mage cast another blast of damage at him, and he felt his armor start to give way. Another bolt like that, and he would be in serious trouble. And he couldn't reach the Boki mage, as the fellow hovered out of sword range and gathered magic for another shot at him.

"Switch places," he told the human. "Get the mage." He desperately hoped the young battle mage at his back understood that it took a ranged attacker to beat another ranged attacker. There was no time to observe the niceties and ask, however.

He and the human spun in a half circle, the sudden maneuver catching the pair who'd been engaging the human by surprise. He got in a deep cut across one's side. His deadly sharp crystal blade dripped with blood.

He both heard and felt a massive crackle of magical energy discharge behind him. Out of the corner of his eye, he saw a bolt of magic slam into the Boki mage's chest. This kid could channel magic? His respect for his nameless battle brother increased sharply.

He sensed which of the two orcs facing him was least skilled and unleashed a flurry of sword blows at that Boki. The orc fell back under the onslaught as bloody gashes opened on his arms and shoulders.

But then both Boki facing him charged, bellowing, and he scrambled to hold them both off as they attacked all out. These Boki definitely lived up to their reputation as skilled fighters. He heard several fast magic spells from the Boki mage behind him and an answering barrage of magic from his companion. A smell of ozone began to stink around them, a result of the volume of magic being cast.

Thanon dodged the wounded Boki's charge easily enough, but the other one was fast and strong, overran his shield, and got right on top of him. Long swords were perhaps the deadliest of all weapons, but they had one great weakness. They were useless when an attacker got inside their swing radius.

Abandoning the weapon, Thanon grabbed the big Boki around the neck. The orc's naturally thick skin was bumpy and hard. He would not be able to choke the Boki, but then he did not need to. Using a skill learned from Grand Marshal Korovo himself and honed over years of practice, Thanon projected a command into the Boki's mind to die.

The orc's battle enraged stare met his, and then an instant of surprise registered as the orc's body followed the command. The creature's legs collapsed, and he crumpled to the ground.

The other Boki warriors cried out in rage and dismay. The biggest one yelled, "Run!"

All three of the remaining orcs took off for the shore as Thanon bent down to scoop up his sword. For bulky creatures, they moved shockingly fast.

"You all right?" he asked his human comrade-in-arms.

"Yes. You? Do we pursue?"

"Can we catch them?" Thanon asked. He glared at the sturdy battle canoe that all three orcs had leaped into and were now paddling strongly. A riptide caught the vessel and flung it away from the shore at a high rate of speed. The small landing craft he'd commandeered earlier wasn't strong enough to handle a current like that.

"We couldn't catch them in your rowboat," the human declared in disgust. "And we'd likely die trying. Or at least get dumped overboard. And I have no skill at underwater combat. I'd be useless."

"I doubt that," Thanon declared. They watched the Boki turn to parallel the shore at a distance that ensured no magic of the human's could reach them.

He turned to take his first good look at the human battle mage. Dregs. The kid couldn't be more than twenty summers old. He could handle a staff like that *and* channel magic? More to the point, how was it he'd been completely unable to sense the youth's intentions during the fight? He didn't know whether to be impressed or suspicious. Either way, he was intrigued.

"Name's Thanon." He held out a gauntleted hand to the youth.

"Will. Will Cobb," the human replied, mopping sweat off his forehead and flashing an amber hand shield the likes of which he'd rarely seen. The mystery deepened.

"Well met, Will Cobb. Are there more of these Boki in need of killing?"

"There was a large greenskin force up in Governor's Square a few minutes ago. Although I expect they've been driven out of there by now. But we can probably find ourselves a few more if you're in the mood to test your blade."

"Lead on."

They took off at a jog along what Thanon recognized from studying maps of Dupree as one of the main avenues toward the city center. His men should be up this way somewhere. Once the governess was safe, his unit would head for where the fighting was worst and charge to the front.

"This kind of thing happen often around here?" he asked as they ran.

"Last time we had a full-scale Boki invasion was almost twenty years ago. You just have excellent timing." Will Cobb grinned at him, and he grinned back.

They crossed Governor's Square, which was littered with the bodies of goblins, hobgoblins, and ogres. Only a few orc corpses were visible across the broad square.

The sound of skirmishing erupted down a side street as they left the north side of the square. As one, they veered toward it. He and Will smashed into the cluster of mixed-race greenskins harrying a party of townspeople and made short work of them, laying out nearly a dozen of the invaders. As the thanks of local citizens rang in their ears, they moved on.

It took close to an hour to work their way all the way to the North Gate of Dupree, mopping up clusters of fighting as they went. There, Thanon met his men, apparently assigned by Captain Krugar to guard the gate while the Haelan legion sallied forth into the countryside in pursuit of the fleeing invaders. Which was a smart call. His men were not familiar with the local area, hence were best used to defend the city against any attackers who thought to circle around Krugar and his men.

He had a word with his squad leaders to confirm that none of his men had been lost in combat. A few had wounds serious enough to send them to the Heart, but that was all.

"Can you point me at the Heart?" he asked Will. He had a general idea of how to get there, but he was not averse to a local guide. Memorizing a map could only get a person so far.

"I'll take you," Will answered. They took off walking back to the south and Will asked, "Who are those soldiers? I don't recognize the blazons."

"Talons of Koth. The elite shock regiment of the Imperial Legion of Koth."

"When did *they* get here?"

"Within the hour."

"Who commands of these Talons of Koth?"

"I do."

The human youth missed a step, recovered, and stared at him in obvious alarm. "Uhh, I'm sorry, your lordship. I didn't know—"

He laughed and slapped Will on the shoulder. "Call me Thanon. We met on the battlefield where skill determines equals and betters, not titles and ranks. And you are plenty skilled to have earned my respect."

They resumed walking toward the Heart. "You earned my respect, as well," Will said formally.

"Relax. I like you. And you acquitted yourself well against those Boki. Where did you learn to fight like that?"

"I'm an apprentice in the Mage's Guild."

"Gads. I'd hate to see their adepts in combat if you're only an apprentice." He grinned at Will, who grinned back.

"The guildmaster is a pure caster, and he's unbelievable on the battlefield." Obvious pride rang in Will's voice.

"That would be Aurelius Lightstar?"

"You've heard of him?"

"Indeed. I've come to see him."

"Why?" Will blurted.

"Imperial business." Lest the youth take offense at being brushed off, he added, "After I check on my men, what say you show me to the pub with the best ale in town and we trade a few war stories over a pint?"

"That'll be the Prancing Unicorn Tavern."

It turned out that both of his injured men were fully healed by the time Thanon reached the Heart House. He sent them to the North Gate with word to join him at the Prancing Unicorn when they could. He trusted his men completely to handle themselves in his absence, a fact his men took pride in, as well.

His military career had taken him to the ends of Urth, and he was no stranger to the rough conditions in these frontier towns. As they went, Dupree seemed reasonably civilized. But then, Anton Constantine was said to have carved out quite a corrupt little kingdom for himself in Haelos.

The Prancing Unicorn was empty after the night's violence. However, the tavern was spacious and the mugs clean. He and Will sat at the end of a long table by the fire and were served quickly and politely. Of course, his chestful of Imperial blazons might have had something to do with that.

Speaking of which, Will was studying the insignia intently. "I don't recognize that one."

Thanon looked down to where Will pointed. "Mindor campaign."

Will frowned. "You're paxan, though."

"Yes, and my kind in Koth are loyal to the Empire. It's the paxan of Mindor who resist Imperial rule."

Will tactfully changed subjects. "So. What's your best war story?"

"Well. That would undoubtedly involve a bold and buxom lass in the Imperial Seat who led me a merry chase a few years back."

"Did you love her?"

He raised his pint, grinning. "Not enough to turn down a posting to Pan Orda, for which she vowed never to forgive me." He took a pull of the frothy ale. Not bad for a local brew. But then he was a soldier. He wasn't picky.

A disturbance at the door turned out to be a dozen of his men piling into the tavern. They swarmed around him and Will, jovially ordering food and drink.

Will spent the next hour teasing stories out of him and his men on their various campaigns and exploits while Thanon observed the young battle mage closely. The youth was smart and focused and seemed to thirst for travel, adventure, and glory. His men took a liking to him, too, especially after Thanon recounted how the two of them had engaged in pitched battle against four Boki and Will had protected his back. Will fielded his men's questions about Boki combat tactics, and he was impressed with how well the kid knew Boki ways of thinking and fighting and correlated the two.

He turned over in his mind why he could not read Will's intentions in combat but came up with no explanation. The kid had a special mental defense of some kind, though. That was for sure.

The night aged into the wee hours, and it was time to get his men some rest. They would not leave until he did, though, concerned as they were for his well-being, and he for theirs.

"Will Cobb," he declared. "Would you consider joining my unit? I can offer you all the training you desire in magic or combat, along with seeing the wide world, honor and fame, and a decent living. What say you?"

His men raised their mugs to endorse the offer loudly.

Will's face lit with interest. But then his expression fell. "I'm afraid I'm promised to the Mage's Guild, else I would be sore tempted to accept your offer."

"Ahh, well. That's easy enough to remedy. The guild-master will not always control you, perhaps sooner rather than later. Come with us, Will Cobb. Earn the glory you were meant for."

12

R aina slept through much of the next day, waking only to eat and then go right back to sleep. Draining herself of her formidable well of magic was exhausting in the extreme. A frantic Rosana woke her for supper. Will was not at the Mage's Guild, and no one had seen him since last night.

"You've checked the death log?" Raina asked quickly.

"Aye. He hasn't resurrected." The gypsy continued in an aggrieved hush, "The high matriarch won't let me go look for him. She says if Will's hurt he'll come to us and that the Mage's Guild is busy with the cleanup and repairs."

"Are wounded still coming in?"

"Aye."

"Then she surely won't let me go look for Will," Raina replied.

"You need to eat," Rosana declared practically. "You know how much healing takes out of you."

In spite of her worry for Will and the voices lurking just beyond her fierce concentration on holding them back, she ate heartily and felt better. Raina was just finishing a second plate of fried fish and fresh greens when a messenger from the Mage's Guild arrived at the Heart House. And not just any messenger.

Drake Bruin, commander of the Celestial Order of the Dragon in the city of Dupree, brought the request from Guildmaster Aurelius for Raina and Rosana to join him at

Leland Hyland's house at their earliest convenience. Which was polite elf-speak for *now*.

Of course, the high matriarch gave them permission to answer the summons. Hah. So much for Lenora not letting them out of the Heart! Bruin hustled them across the city, Raina and Rosana like a pair of ducklings following their mother.

Rosana asked Raina under her breath, "Why do you suppose Aurelius summons us?"

"No idea," Raina replied low. "But it must be important for him to have sent a drake of the Celestial Order to fetch us."

"It's always an emergency with him," Rosana muttered. "I've had enough of running around in the woods for a lifetime."

She expected Rosana had not seen the last of running around in woods if the gypsy wished to be with Will. Although his reasons were different, he was as set on waking the Sleeping King as she was. Speaking of which, Raina really could use a dreaming conversation with Gawaine about what threats lurked near, ready to take advantage of the colony's weakness. But he remained stubbornly hidden from her, whether by his choice or not, she had no idea.

Aurelius had taken up residence at Hyland's town house while he worked at wrapping up Leland's business affairs and saw to the most urgent matters of running the Hyland landhold until the governess appointed a new landsgrave. It seemed fitting that Leland's friends and protégés still gathered at his home and continued the work dearest to him of rescuing his son and finding the Sleeping King.

Hyland's postern gate opened at Bruin's knock to admit them to a small courtyard. A tall figure emerged from the house to meet them, and Rosana all but knocked Raina off her feet as she bolted past, sprinted across the cobblestones, and threw herself at him.

Will. Thank the stars.

Bruin grunted in disapproval beside Raina as Rosana

threw her arms around Will's neck and the two kissed passionately. Raina murmured to the older knight, "They're happy. Where's the harm in that?"

"Personal entanglements cloud the mission. Make a warrior vulnerable," he retorted.

The words were a dagger to her heart. Her fondest wish was to have a family of her own someday. But not only did White Heart members travel too much and apparently not live long enough to have families, the nature of their work made families a risk to them, as well. In the same way a family would weaken Bruin or Will, a family would weaken her.

"Go inside, child," Bruin said kindly, as if he sensed the direction of her thoughts. "The guildmaster is waiting for you."

Reminders of Leland, her mentor and friend, were everywhere as she followed the old Hyland steward to Leland's study. A book carelessly left sitting upon a table where Leland had last laid it down. A cloak hanging in the hallway that still carried his scent. His study was almost more than she could bear. His maps and mechanical toys littered the big desk where he had left them.

Thankfully, before she could dissolve into the tears she was desperately fighting off, Aurelius came into the study accompanied by two men.

The first was so arrestingly attractive she could not help but gape. His hair was the color of antique gold and flowed around his face like a lion's mane. His eyes were piercingly blue, his features a vision of manly perfection. He was fully as tall as Will, but muscular with the maturity of full manhood. He moved with the grace of a dancer and the strength of a warrior.

But it was the third eye in the center of his forehead, announcing him to be of the paxan race, that stopped her cold. It was *open*. She'd heard rumors that it was not even possible for paxan's closed third eyes to do that. Obviously, those rumors had been completely wrong. Of course, she'd also heard that all open-eyed paxan were put to death by the Kothite Empire. What was he doing in Dupree, then, if that were even partially true?

His third eye looked just like his other eyes, a bright blue that shone intelligently as it swiveled in concert with the usual two, taking in the room alertly. Like a bodyguard might do. Her dear friend and sometimes bodyguard, Cicero, used to scan rooms like that. But he'd been forced to flee the heavy Imperial presence in Dupree and had returned to the wilds of Tyrel that were her home and his. She felt his absence keenly. Especially now, when they'd lost both Kendrick and Leland, and Eben and Sha'Li had left for parts unknown.

It was a struggle to rip her gaze away from the open-eyed paxan and take note of the second man partially hidden behind him. But as soon as her gaze lighted on the other, she found herself fully as fascinated.

He was also a paxan but with the traditionally closed eye. At first glance he seemed to be a relatively young man; but as she looked more closely, a miniscule web of fine wrinkles around his eyes announced him to be older than her first impression, perhaps closer to middle age. But then she met his gaze. His eyes were so lively—playful, even—that it was hard to reconcile any aging at all with the youthful vitality emanating from him.

"These are the children I was telling you about," Aurelius said. Respect vibrated in every syllable of his words. Enough so that she did not even take umbrage at being called a child.

The two-eyed paxan moved farther into the room. "Introduce us if you will, Aurelius."

On a first-name basis with the guildmaster? A man of status, then. Raina dipped into a short curtsy her mother had taught her to use with noble persons of uncertain rank. It elicited a chuckle and a nod of acknowledgment from the guildmaster's guest.

Rosana followed suit with a curtsy, and Will made an elven semi-formal bow, which he performed admirably smoothly. Now where did he learn to do a thing like that growing up on the edge of the wilderness as he had? Not to mention, where did he learn the nuance of choosing that particular bow for this particular situation?

Aurelius said with obvious pleasure, "This is my friend, Phinneas. He is a scholar of the Oneiri Order, which is a gathering of paxan scholars to study and share knowledge. Phinneas is perhaps the preeminent scholar in his field alive today."

"And what might that field be?" Raina asked courteously when Aurelius did not elaborate.

"Later," Aurelius murmured pleasantly with a glance for the steward.

Phinneas spoke smoothly over the awkward moment. "This is my companion, student, and bodyguard, Rynn." He gestured at the godlike specimen standing tall beside him.

The younger paxan nodded politely, and Rosana sighed slightly beside her. Raina reluctantly had to admit to feeling a similar reaction.

Aurelius gave the steward instructions for supper and ushered the servitor out, closing the study door behind him. Raina waited through the obligatory pleasantries Aurelius and Phinneas exchanged according to elven traditions of courtesy. Raina did not know much of paxan culture, but like the elves, the paxan were a long-lived race. It made sense that they, too, would take their time with social conventions.

Finally, the conversation wound its way around to Will, Rosana, and her. Aurelius startled her by saying, "These are several of the youths I wrote to you about."

"And the reason I came with all due haste to see you, my friend. Tell me more of their adventure."

Was that what it had been? An adventure? Several of their party had died, they'd all suffered terribly, and countless Boki had died to defend them. Her White Heart sensibility forced her to reluctantly acknowledge that many of Anton's hired mercenaries had died, as well.

Aurelius continued, "While young Rosana stayed behind to guard the gate they found, Will and Raina journeyed into the dream plane. With your indulgence, I would like them to tell you what they saw there in hopes of you identifying some or all of it."

Raina stared at Aurelius in horror. The secret of Gawaine's existence and particularly the secret of where they had found him must not be shared with anyone! Gawaine had been clear. They were to trust *no one* with news of his existence.

Aurelius sent her back a rather withering look of his own. He said mildly, "I asked Phinneas to make the rigorous journey to Dupree to speak with you of what you saw in hopes that he could shed more light on what you encountered."

"Thank you, Guildmaster," she replied with entirely false gratitude. "Unfortunately, I do not know either of these men, and I find myself reluctant to speak of our . . . *adventure* in their esteemed presence. No offense intended, gentlemen."

Phinneas nodded slightly, but a smile flickered at the corner of his companion's mouth.

Aurelius huffed in as close to exasperation as she'd ever seen him. "Phinneas, do you vouch for the trustworthiness of your man, Rynn?"

The paxan did not answer the question but rather spoke directly to her. "Are you aware that it is death for my kind to be born with an open eye? If Rynn should be seen by any Imperial official while we are here, he will be arrested, sent to Koth, and tortured. Then, the Empire will either forcibly close his eye, crippling him for life, or, if they are feeling merciful, he will be put to permanent death."

To the tall paxan, she said solemnly, "I am White Heart. I will do everything in my power to save you from such a fate. You have nothing to fear from me."

The smile broke loose this time, flashing at her with such

brilliance she momentarily lost her train of thought. Were it not for that open third eye, this man would have legions of women all over the Empire swooning at his feet.

Aurelius commented, "Phinneas has studied the dream plane for longer than I have been alive. If anyone can tell us what exactly you saw, he can. We need all the help we can get to understand what is happening both there and here."

"Indeed, my order is deeply concerned at recent developments in the dream realm. We've not seen the like before," Phinneas added.

If only she didn't agree so strongly with both men that events were in motion extending far beyond the visible, she would walk out of here right now and drag Will with her. But as it was, she sank unhappily into one of the armchairs before the fire. Three more had been pulled into the room for this meeting, and everyone but Rynn took a seat.

Rosana looked up at the beautiful paxan in distress. "You will not sit?"

"I am best prepared to defend my mentor on my feet. I am accustomed to standing for long periods of time. Do not worry about me."

Raina bloody well worried about him. Aurelius clearly did not know this Rynn fellow as well as he knew Phinneas. Even if the bodyguard did have a death sentence prominently in the middle of his forehead.

"If you could describe the dream plane from when you entered until you stopped being attacked," Aurelius prompted.

Ahh. Well, all right, then. Aurelius was not going to make them speak of Gawaine. She could live with that.

Will started by describing the door they had passed through with a spiderweb of dream catchers stretched across its surface.

Phinneas commented, "Old, native magic. Tribal."

Raina suspected Boki thorns had built the door, so that agreed with her conjecture. But she was not about to tell that to this paxan scholar. Will described the giant, four-armed troll that had attacked them just inside the door.

Rynn nodded as Will described cutting off the troll's possessions—a pouch, belt, and necklace—and the beast weakening with the loss of each. "Phantasm," the open-eyed paxan declared. "When one of them takes on the aspect of a creature who once lived, possessing physical objects that belonged to the creature makes the phantasm stronger. Exponentially so."

"Then you know what happened to the troll when we killed it?" Will challenged.

Raina's gaze snapped to Will's face. So. He did not entirely trust these paxan, either, and tested them subtly. Was Bloodroot giving warning to him, mayhap?

Rynn answered in a voice as mellifluous and gorgeous as the rest of him, "Your troll turned to mist and dissipated. It is what phantasms do when killed."

"Then a hydra attacked—" Will started.

She interrupted him. "Do not forget the wall. And the gem."

Phinneas turned his bird-bright gaze on her. "What wall, child?"

"It surrounded us in an arc that trapped us in front of the door. It looked made of . . . this will sound strange, but made of . . . " She searched for words to describe the strange substance. "Burning crystal."

Phinneas sucked in a sharp breath. "Crystals all the colors of fire as if flames were trapped in time and made solid? Caught between a crystalline form and a flame, midflicker?"

"Exactly!" Raina exclaimed.

"How did you pass this wall of fire crystal?" he pressed.

"We hit it," she answered. "Just once. It made this strange ringing sound that went on for far too long. As if it were summoning the hydra that eventually showed up." She recalled the way the tone had jangled every nerve in her body with a feeling of wrongness. And the gigantic, four-headed beast with its long, swinging necks had appeared, making the massive troll that had nearly killed them all look puny.

She fell silent, lost in memory of the horror that had coursed through her, the certainty that they were all going to die. Will took up the tale. "Sha'Li—she's our lizardman friend who was with us—recognized it. When one of the heads spouted a gout of fire, we knew it for a fire hydra."

"How many heads?" Rynn asked quickly.

"Four."

The paxan warrior sucked in a breath between his teeth. "That's rough. How did you defeat it?"

Will continued grimly. "Sha'Li charged it. And was promptly incinerated into a pile of ash without ever harming the beast. Thankfully, she resurrected with Rosana in the cave outside." It was his turn to fall silent in unpleasant recollection.

Raina took up the tale. "The hydra started to speak. Its heads repeated a rhyme over and over. Will's mother used to say it to him as a boy, and he recognized that it spoke of the lady's breath flower. He knew the look of the plant and found some growing behind us. He picked a bunch, burned it, and blew the ashes at the hydra."

"You defeated a fire hydra with *flowers*?" Rynn burst out.

Raina shrugged. "No weapon or skill we had was going to scratch that beast, let alone take it down."

Phinneas nodded, a certain respect entering his gaze. "Unconventional. Perhaps that is why you succeeded where others failed."

"Truth be told," she confessed, "we had barely any strength or skills left to call upon by the time we arrived on the dream plane. Anything else seemed worth a try."

Phinneas frowned thoughtfully, steepling his fingers before his mouth. He spoke slowly. "It is possible that your very lack of strength is what gained you entrance to a plane that only the strongest usually survive. Interesting." He shook himself and then murmured, "I digress. Go on."

Raina picked up the story. "The hydra dissipated as soon as the flower's ashes touched it. But it did not go up in a poof of mist like the troll. It went up in a great blast of fire, big enough to engulf a house."

"Except there was no heat from the fire," Will added. "And as soon as the hydra burned up, the crystal wall came crashing down."

Raina nodded. "And when the whole thing was done shattering and the hydra's fire went out, a gem was left behind, sitting on the ground."

Phinneas leaned forward in his chair staring intently at her. "Describe it," he said tersely.

"It was bigger than my fist. Egg shaped. The color of fire. All the hues of flames flickered through it. And it . . . pulsed. Like a heart."

"Do you have it?" Phinneas demanded.

"Umm, no. A creature came racing out of nowhere and grabbed it."

"What creature, child?" With each question he fired at her, Phinneas was growing more tense.

She thought back desperately. "The being looked almost like a piece of the fog. It was shaped like a large humanoid but made entirely of, well, air. It broke off from the rest of the mist and scooped up the fire gem."

Phinneas leaned back in what looked like dismay. He spoke heavily. "I know not what it was, but that was no simple fire gem, and that was no simple bit of mist. I expect it was a very clever phantasm, indeed, to have taken on the form of a large elemental."

Aurelius asked quietly, "What sort of elemental, and for what purpose?"

"I do not know. But it obviously gathers items imbued with elemental powers. Because fire magics would not help a wind elemental, one must surmise he scooped up the stone for his master."

"Who is his master?" Raina asked.

"That I do not know, either. But there have been reports that great elemental forces are at work on the dream plane."

Aurelius interjected, "Why do elementals cross over to the dream realm? It is not their place."

"That is an excellent and worthy question, my friend," Phinneas answered gravely. "The dream plane is the one most closely linked to the material plane and the easiest to cross into this world from."

"Are you suggesting that some sort of elemental invasion force is being assembled in the dream realm?" Aurelius asked, aghast.

"I'm sure it's not as dramatic as all that," Phinneas answered mildly.

Raina frowned. "What would happen if an elemental fire creature, possibly a phantasm, got ahold of that gem? What power would it gain?"

"I cannot say. But it could not be good."

Based on what she'd gleaned from Eben, she knew that elementals were eternally at odds with one another. One element gaining a significant advantage over its opposing elements—even on another plane—was a potential source of serious conflict or even violence.

Phinneas murmured, "What I do not understand is why the dream realm put creatures of such unusual power in your path."

Rynn added, "And immediately after you arrived. Before you showed your intentions to anyone there."

Raina traded glances with Will. They knew full well why the plane had tried so desperately to expel them. The creatures of the dream realm had been protecting the Sleeping King, perhaps one of the greatest treasures hidden in the realm. But since neither paxan had phrased their observations as a question, she refrained from offering any explanation.

"Continue," Aurelius prompted them.

Will took up the story. "We walked a little way through a

white fog and came into a forest. A man riding a great black lion came up to us."

Raina held back a snort. The man had charged them and all but run them down before they could identify themselves.

"Did he have a name?" Phinneas queried.

"Aye. He called himself the Laird of Dalmigen," Will answered.

Phinneas threw himself backward in his chair and stared back and forth between Will and her. "The laird himself?" the paxan finally gasped.

Will shrugged. "He had a black lion on his shield that was gold. And he called his lion Aegenis."

Phinneas sent Aurelius a look of incredulity. "I see why you sent for me." To Will, he said, "Tell me of him. What was he like? Was he stern? Fearsome? Noble in demeanor?"

Raina leaned forward and spoke before Will could. "What do *you* know of the Laird of Dalmigen?"

"He is one of the oldest and most powerful guardians of the dream realm. His purpose has been lost to history, and he does not make appearances oft in modern times. My colleagues and I have conjectured that whatever he guarded has also been lost to time, hence threats to it are few and far between. Beyond that, I know he is described in the annals as a just and fearsome knight, a flawless defender of his charge. Did he truly carry a spear longer than his beast?"

Will nodded. "He called it a lance, and it was at least twice the length of his lion. He carried it under his arm against his side with the tip well ahead of his beast's nose as it charged."

Rynn sucked in a breath and murmured, "The strength that must take."

Raina supplied, "He was built powerfully. Although he claimed to be failing with age, I saw no evidence of it. When the drakken came, our friend stayed behind to help him.

Cicero reported that the laird fought ferociously and with extraordinary skill."

"A drakken?" Phinneas exclaimed. "What color?"

"How big?" Rynn asked at the same time.

Will answered before Raina could intervene to stop him. "Green. The first one was huge—the size of a house—but the second one was even larger."

"Second one?" Phinneas sputtered.

"Is it possible that Hemlocke herself sent them?" Rynn breathed. "Has the Green awakened?"

A green *dragon*? For surely that was what Rynn referred to in those hushed tones of awe. Foreboding skittered down Raina's spine. Everyone knew dragons were purely the stuff of myth and legend. Although she had seen things in the past few months that challenged her notions of what did and did not exist, she simply couldn't credit the idea of dragons being real. Even the dragon-like creatures she and Will had seen on the dream plane were, at the end of the day, imaginary. For what were dreams but random hallucinations of sleeping minds? The drakken must have been manifestations of children's hearth tales, given form by the insubstantial nature of dreams and the dream realm.

"Who are you?" Phinneas asked into the deep silence that had fallen over the room.

Will looked alarmed and silently passed the question to her with a beseeching look. She'd known for some time that there was more to Will's ancestry than he spoke of, but she had never pressed him for details. For her part, now that she was protected from harm by her White Heart tabard, she could afford to speak of her true identity.

"I am the second daughter of a minor house far west of here at the edge of the civilized world. An insignificant holding called Tyrel." She added, choosing her words carefully, "Will comes from a village in the Wylde Wold. And Rosana has been in the Heart for most of her life."

The healer's guild was known to take in young children

who showed magical talent to raise and train. The Mage's Guild did it, as well. Raina had been lucky enough to be born into a family whose women were mages and could train her at home.

Phinneas assessed them for a long time. Neither she nor Will was inclined to volunteer more information about themselves for the man to mull over, and silence reigned once more.

At long last, Phinneas asked heavily, "Is there more?"

Raina answered quickly lest Will say too much. They had come to the part of the story in need of careful editing. "There was a cliff and some giant falcons. Eventually, we fell through the fog. When we emerged from it, we had landed back at the dream catcher door."

"Did you accomplish what you intended to on the plane?" Phinneas asked abruptly.

A leading question. Will looked at her in distress. He, too, saw the trap. She answered carefully, "The journey seemed to stabilize Will's health, which had been failing until then. So, in answer to your question, yes. We accomplished what we needed to."

"And your failing health, boy? What was the source of that? You look like a strapping lad in fine fettle."

Will glanced over at Aurelius. The solinari nodded, and Will pulled open the laces of his shirt to show the paxan the wooden disk affixed to his chest just over his heart. "It is a piece of heartwood from an ancient tree and contains a tree spirit. It grows into me and cannot be removed without killing me. However, the alien nature of a plant in my human body was poisoning me until our journey to the dream realm stabilized my . . . *symbiotic relationship* with the disk."

"Extraordinary."

Raina had to agree with Phinneas. The fact that the disk had not killed Will still amazed her. Two such different spirits should not be able to coexist in the same body. And yet, he and Bloodroot managed it. She could not imagine the mental and physical fortitude that took. He had confessed once that it was painful and he felt sick all the time. If Will was occasionally grumpy or even surly, she could forgive him for it. If she didn't miss her guess, Bloodroot's connection to rage and destruction tended to bleed over to Will, too. Rosana was good for him. She made him happy. Distracted him from his misery and anger.

Phinneas stared long and hard at Will's disk. "I can only guess at why the denizens of the dream realm took you so seriously. Perhaps because of the particular entrance you used. But it is clear that they did. Whatever you are about is clearly of extreme importance."

Alarm exploded in Raina's gut. He mustn't figure it out. A knock on the door announcing the arrival of dinner stopped the conversation abruptly, to Raina's vast relief. They'd been venturing onto treacherous ground.

Over supper, Aurelius and Phinneas chatted about trivial matters, mostly gossip and speculation about who the new landsgraves would be. Will and Rosana put their heads together during the meal, murmuring to each other, which left Raina to sit back and observe. If Aurelius and Phinneas spoke obliquely of anything important during the meal, it passed over her head. She did note that Rynn was every bit as keen an observer as she was. He also observed every nuance of the conversation. He would not be one to underestimate.

As the meal was winding down, Phinneas announced, "I would like to send my man, Rynn, with you to assist you with your future endeavors."

"What endeavors would those be?" Raina asked boldly. She did not want an outsider traveling with them and certainly not one who would attract as much attention as a gorgeous, open-eyed paxan.

"I am sure I do not know, child. But I do know Aurelius, and he obviously thinks your work to be of vital importance. Furthermore, something dangerous gathers power in the dream realm, toward what goal I know not. But I do know you children drew a great deal of attention when you visited the dream plane. I worry that whatever force grows in strength there may come for you. Rynn is gifted at and experienced in navigating and fighting there."

What was his angle? Did he send Rynn to spy on them, help them, or hinder them? Were they Imperial spies or not? She asked cautiously, "How would you describe your relationship with the Empire?"

Phinneas laughed heartily. "Well done, child. A feint within a feint." He, too, chose his next words carefully. "Within my race, there are many factions. Many paxan who are native to Koth support the Empire fully, while those native to Mindor . . . do not."

Mindor was the home continent of the paxan and wandrakin, and to her knowledge, it had not fallen to the Empire.

"As for Rynn and me—" A pause. "You will understand if I cannot be fond of policies that would put my favorite student to death for the mere fact of his existence."

She leaned back in her seat, intrigued at his choice of words. He had skirted as close to criticism—which was, of course, treason—as anyone would dare to speak aloud anywhere in the Kothite Empire. But he had stopped well short of saying he opposed Koth.

Aurelius spoke up. "Your colors notwithstanding, Raina, you and your companions will need protection going forward. Rynn is an accomplished warrior in addition to having extensive knowledge of the dream realm. I believe he can be of assistance to you."

She glanced over at Rynn, who seemed as shocked by this turn of events as she was. In fact, he leaned down to murmur to Phinneas, "But, my master, who will protect you if I leave your side?"

She approved. Loyalty was an important trait.

"I will be fine." Phinneas reached out and touched his student on the temple. Rynn's eyes closed as if he was watching some moving image that Phinneas inserted directly into his mind. She'd heard of the paxan having extraordinary mental powers. Something called a mind touch. Was that what the two paxan did now?

Rynn's eyes opened, and he looked troubled. "As you wish. I will go with these humans and guard them with my life."

Will spoke quickly. "Rosana will accompany us, and hopefully, our lizardman and jann friends will rejoin us. Will you guard them, as well, paxan?"

"Aye," Rynn answered solemnly. "You have my word of honor on it."

Gunther fidgeted nervously in the line of dwarves awaiting permission to pass the roadblock a squad of Imperial soldiers had erected on the Imperial highway. He would not have traveled this route if there were any other way through the great pass south toward Waelan. But he did not have weeks to scale the mighty peaks to either side of the valley, assuming he could even make the climb with his cantankerous mechanical limb.

His turn to pass the roadblock came. Schooling his voice in politer tones than he usually took with troops in the black and red of Koth, he said, "What can I do for you lads, to-day?"

"We're searching for contraband and banned weapons."

"Just got my prospecting pick for poking at rocks and a short dagger for cutting my meat."

"We'll be taking a look in yon pack ye're carrying, old man."

Call him old, would they? Scowling, he reluctantly handed over his pack. The copper helm was buried at the bottom of it. He wore the breastplate beneath his shirt and the broken bracer on his own arm beneath a leather bracer. But the helm had been too big for him, and without a full set of armor to attach it to, it tended to turn to one side and blind him.

"What's this?" the soldier exclaimed, pulling the helm from the pack.

"Just an old hat I found a while back. I'm taking it as a gift to the grandkids to play with."

The soldier turned it this way and that. *Curses*. Why had he cleaned the thing up, anyway? He should've left it filthy and unpolished so it would pass as junk. Sure enough, the strange veins in the copper caught a shaft of sunlight, and the intricate designs worked into the metal flashed into view. "Did you make this?"

"Gor, me? Naw. I'm just a poor prospector."

"Mighty fine piece of workmanship for a toy. I'm thinking this is the property of the Empire. All weaponsmiths are required to offer their output first to the Imperial Army. It was an oversight if this piece weren't appropriated."

Panic tore through him. "'Ey now. It's just a helmet. No armor to go with it or nothing. And who wants copper armor, anyway? It's too soft to be of any use," he added in desperation.

"Move along, old man." The soldier handed off the helm to another soldier sitting atop a wagon filled with confiscated loot. His helm was tossed into the back and disappeared from sight. Gunther contemplated making a grab for it, but there were five soldiers, and he couldn't outrun humans even if he'd had both legs and been decades younger.

"Go on. Get going," the confiscator ordered him. "You're holding up the line."

Furious, Gunther stumped away from the checkpoint. At least they hadn't gotten his breastplate and bracer. Heaping dire curses upon all their heads, he moved away from the soldiers. One day. One day his kind would rise up from the earth from whence they came and destroy the Empire of Koth and all who served it. By the mountain, he hoped he lived to see that day.

Fueled by rage, he made excellent time and reached Svedburg, a decent-sized town tucked into the lower slopes of the Groenn's Rest Range, just as the sun touched the peaks in the west. He stopped in a tavern for a bite of supper and a pint of ale before continuing on to his final destination. Once full dark had fallen, he headed for the Haltekrag, a pub where those he sought this night were known to congregate.

It turned out to be a smoky, dark tavern lit only by a roaring blaze on a hearth that stretched nearly to the low-beamed ceiling. The customers were as rough as the place, all dwarves, all eyeing him suspiciously. He scowled back and made his clumsy way to a table in the back.

It took nursing three pints of ale to finally spot what he sought. An inconspicuous door in the corner opened to let out a gray-bearded dwarf. From his vantage point, Gunther spotted a long table in the back room filled with more graybeards.

He tossed back the dregs of his ale and made his way to the door. He banged on it with his fist, and it cracked open to reveal a surly looking fellow completely blocking the narrow opening. "Who goes?"

"Name's Druumedar. Gunther Druumedar. Prospector up on the north face of the Hauksgrafir. I need to talk to the council."

"They meet in Waelan, first day of each month. Make your petition to them."

"Not the margrave's council, you fool," Gunther growled low. "I found something pertaining to *our* kind. Something *important.*"

"Wait there." The door closed, and he stood before it feeling like a fool. He'd come all this way, gotten robbed by the Empire, and now they weren't even going to listen to—

The door opened again. "Enter."

He stepped inside, and every eye in the room turned in his direction. Suspicious silence filled the space. The fire in here was considerably less smoky than the one without, and its flickering light danced across the ceiling as he stared back at them.

"State your business, Druumedar," one of the dwarves snapped.

"Mind if I sit? Been walking all day on my mechanical leg."

Harrumphing, the speaker gestured him to an empty seat at the base of the table. The assemblage stared at him skeptically. Didn't think a one-legged prospector had anything worthy to say to their snooty selves, eh? Hah! He'd found them, hadn't he? Not that he begrudged them their secrecy. For these were the local leaders of the dwarven resistance to the Empire. With the wind screaming down off Hauksgrafir tonight, the fire guttered and flared intermittently, increasing the clandestine mood in the room.

"So, Druumedar," one of the dwarves bellowed with false joviality. "What brings you to our table this blustery night? Shouldn't a fellow like you be at home and long abed?"

A fellow like him? A cripple? Half a man? Why, that bellowing windbag full of elf droppings . . .

Fury began a slow burn in his gut. Rather than open his mouth and give vent to his irritation, he unbuckled his leather bracer, unlaced his sleeve, and unstrapped the copper bracer he'd found inside the secret tunnels of Hauksgrafir. He tossed it onto the table. It hit with a musical clink of metal on wood. A sound that made every dwarf in the room look up with interest.

"What's this?" Bellowbreath asked.

"You tell me. Have any of you ever seen the like?" Gunther demanded truculently.

One of the other dwarves leaned forward. Picked it up. Turned it over carelessly. "It is a copper bracer. Not that copper would do a soul any good in a real fight."

As if he didn't already know that.

The other dwarf continued, "Too damaged to wear, what with that big gash in it. Nicely worked, I'll grant."

"Nicely worked?" Gunther growled, his voice rising. "Name me one smith alive today who could fashion such a piece!"

Another dwarf took the gauntlet and turned it over with the stained and callused hands of a craftsman. He held it up to the fire and shards of green fire flashed throughout the room like a crystal catching sunlight.

Many voices exclaimed at once, demanding to know what had just happened. The smith turned the bracer this way and that again in the light of the fire, but the green flash was not repeated. Finally, the fellow laid it down on the table once more, with marked reverence. Everyone stared at the piece as if it might jump up and bite them.

"That, gentlemen," the old smith declared ponderously, "is hardened copper. Ain't never seen it in the flesh before, but my great-grandpappy whispered of old knowledge lost of metals forged like that."

Gunther frowned and declined to mention the abandoned forge he'd found the piece in.

The old smith was speaking again. "Making of copper armor is an ancient dwarven secret. Kept its existence from them cursed Kothites, we did."

Gunther stood and unlaced his shirt. "That's not all. I found this breastplate and a helm that a bunch of twice-cursed soldiers confiscated from me."

"Where'd you get it?" the smith asked urgently.

"Like I said. I'm a prospector. Work the north face of the Hauk, mostly. I took a tumble down the mountain and found the entrance to an abandoned mine. Looked like errock might have worked it."

That got grunts of surprise and displeasure from the lot of them.

He continued, "Found a busted-up statue partly buried by a cave-in. The armor pieces were on it. The helm, breastplate, and bracer were the only pieces I found. Might be more of the suit under boulders I couldn't move, maybe the rest of the suit was destroyed."

"May I send this bracer to my cousin?" the smith asked. "He's a master smith and would be most interested in it."

"Our compatriots in Rignhall should see this," someone else objected.

"Send the bracer to one, the breastplate to the other," a white-bearded dwarf pronounced from the far end of the table.

Gunther harrumphed. If anyone was taking his armor pieces somewhere, *he* would be the one doing it. He'd found them. They belonged to him now. But he did not relish a long journey. Dangerous. Expensive. Cursed annoying on one leg and a stump.

He glared down the table at the old man but was startled out of his general irritation by the wisdom gleaming in the dwarf's return stare. "You came to us for help, did you not, Gunther Druumedar?" the man asked.

"Aye," he answered reluctantly.

"Then let us help you. Let us send the bracer to friends of our cause. You shall take the breastplate to Sven's cousin."

Their cause? Did the old one refer to the rebellion? Was he to be admitted to its incredibly secret ranks, then? Satisfaction coursed through him. He would be honored to take the Empire down a peg, he would. "Done," he declared.

"Wouldn't be flashing that breastplate about, if I were you," the smith who'd examined the bracer mumbled. "Draw the wrong kind of attention, you would."

"From whom?" Gunther demanded.

"Everyone," the geezer wheezed.

If the Empire coveted his strange copper armor pieces and would interfere with his learning about them, that alone was reason enough to take the armor—or at least a piece of it—to Rignhall and learn everything he could about it.

"Right, then," he announced, lacing his shirt over the beautifully inlaid breastplate. "Rignhall, you say? And where exactly will I find your compatriots?"

Will walked through the streets of Dupree the next day in awe. The amount of destruction the Boki had caused in their brief incursion was truly impressive. Although, as he glimpsed a few people scuttling furtively into alleys, their shirts stuffed full, mayhap the greenskins had gotten some help from the locals in their looting and pillaging.

He'd told Aurelius about the break-in at the Haelan armory, and his grandfather had sworn him to secrecy regarding the theft. Which was passing strange. What could a carved stone tucked away in an old chest in a dusty corner mean to anyone? No telling how it had gotten there or how long it had been there. What game was his grandfather playing at?

Will returned to the Mage's Guild, and the door guard announced, "The guildmaster is looking for you. Said to send you to his office straight away upon your return."

He jogged up the stairs to Aurelius's office and knocked on the glowing door. The magic winked out, and his grandfather called, "Enter."

Will stepped inside. As always, he took a moment to breathe in the magic permeating the space.

"There you are," Aurelius declared. "I wish to speak with you about your father's name."

Will winced. It was a sore subject with him that he'd been forced to give up calling himself by it. Dropping the name his father had given him seemed disrespectful of the dead. "What of it?"

"People have been talking about your resemblance to Tiberius. I've told them you look like a thousand other peasants in the colony and that your people must hail from the same region of Koth that De'Vir's did. I believe I have squelched the rumors for now."

"Thank you, Grandfather."

The solinari nodded solemnly. The moment of intimacy shimmered between them and then passed. Aurelius gave himself a little shake. "Nonetheless, you will have to lie low for a while. In the meantime, I am going to increase your weapon training."

Curse his father. Why couldn't Tiberius just have trained him through his youth? By now, he would have been one of the finest warriors in the colony had his illustrious sire shared but a portion of his knowledge and skill with his son. As it was, Will could hardly stand to think about how long it would take him to become a competent warrior. He was just now becoming a half-decent staff fighter, and his father had spent Will's entire youth teaching him that much. How long would it be until he mastered other weapons with more complicated fighting styles? Years? Decades? Ever? Would he even live that long?

Gah. More negative thinking. Did it come from Bloodroot or him? He could hardly tell the difference anymore. Rubbing at the wooden disk embedded in his chest, he halfheartedly cursed Gawaine for making him choose to either keep or lose the blasted thing. He would dearly love to blame someone else, or even unkind fate, for sticking him with the thing . . . but no. He'd chosen this path for himself.

Gawaine said the spirit within the disk could teach him skills he would never master on his own. Perhaps one of those skills would be armed combat. He waited hopefully for some sort of response from within his gut, but today he got nothing. Curse Bloodroot, anyway.

Aurelius announced without warning, "Enough of lectures and book learning. Now you must learn how to use what your father and I have taught you."

"My father taught me nothing."

Aurelius pursed his lips. "You do not give your father enough credit. Now and again I see flashes of something . . . " Infuriatingly, the elf did not continue. Will knew of what Aurelius spoke, though. Sometimes, he seemed just on the verge of remembering something buried deep within his mind, forgotten to conscious knowing.

His grandfather continued, "While I am a competent combat caster, I do not combine weapons and magic. Hence, I am not best suited to teach you how to fight. Also, I do not rely on stored magics. Scrolls, scroll books, potions, and decanters are outside my area of expertise."

Will had already been taught the rudiments of reading a printed magical scroll, absorbing its stored magic, and then casting it. He was still clumsy at it, but the basic idea was not difficult. As for magical potions, anyone could uncork a vial and drink. He supposed a decanter with many doses of a potion could be trickier. It probably wouldn't do to guzzle down the whole thing if only a sip was needed. He could picture how furious Rosana would be if he ever drank down a dozen doses of healing when he needed only one. He smiled until Aurelius spoke again, distracting him from pleasant thoughts of snapping gypsy eyes and rosy cheeks.

"In order to teach you the kind of combined weapon and battle magic mastery you will need to protect yourself and your companions, I have asked perhaps the finest warrior in Dupree besides your father to have a look at you. To ascertain if there's talent in you for advanced training. He is a wind magic caster. If you show some talent with combat magic, he may teach it to you."

"Who is it?"

"Captain Krugar."

"The captain in Anton's militia who caught us in the Forest of Thorns?" he demanded in dismay.

"The same."

"Are you mad? He will kill me on sight!"

"Krugar never actually discovered your true identity. He knows you only as a boy from the woods, my apprentice, and possessed of more talent than my men can train. And he is a first-class weapons master. He will be good for you."

Will seriously doubted that. And if Krugar should ever happen to figure out exactly who he was, the Imperial Army officer would lop Will's head off without a second thought. What on Urth was his grandfather *thinking*?

Gabrielle, Queen of Haraland, wanted nothing more than to explode up out of her seat and storm out of this sham session of the Council of Kings. It wasn't as if the council would ever dare gainsay Maximillian. Oh no. They made a fine science of sussing out exactly how he wished for them to vote, and did so with alacrity. Besides, the matters Maximillian deigned to pass to his Council of Kings were of little real import. Crumbs cast before pecking chickens.

She looked down from her perch in the gallery overlooking the council chamber at her husband, Regalo, King of Haraland and one of the most respected members of the council. His posture was tense. Tired. He was an accomplished peacemaker, but this year's session of the Council of Kings had been particularly fractious. He'd been run ragged trying to smooth ruffled feathers and make deals happen behind the scenes. Deals that were ultimately meaningless in the face of Maximillian's utter control of, well, everything.

Normally, she would have made her excuses and stayed home. But just before Regalo had been scheduled to leave for court, an unusual pack of Imperial hunting hounds had come to Haraland's ports bound for Haelos.

One of the handlers, with whom she'd flirted just enough to render the fellow talkative, had let slip that this batch of hounds had been specially trained to seek out elemental beings. He hinted that there was even more to their training than that, but no amount of flirting cajoled specifically what or who the beasts were bound for Haelos to hunt. Which was even more worrisome.

She had to find a way to get word to the Eight about this development and hope they could pass it to the northern colony in time for any elementals on the wrong side of Koth to hide or flee. If only she knew more of the Eight. She knew they had been at work for a long time to quietly undermine the Kothite Empire from within. Which hinted at members of the resistance at the Imperial Court itself. Because of the Emperor's sweeping mind powers and ever-present scrutiny of his subjects, the Eight moved with glacial slowness, affecting events in only the subtlest and most innocuous of ways.

But that extreme caution left her without any means of passing along her urgent news in a timely manner. It nigh killed her to wait through the weeks of preparation and travel from Haraland to the Imperial Seat. Worse, her only contact with the Eight was not even in the Imperial Seat when she and Regalo arrived. She could only hope that her unusual presence at court was enough to signal her handler that she had news for him.

Of course, part of the reason she stayed as far from court and the Emperor as she did was to protect her knowledge of the Eight, scanty as it was, from falling into Maximillian's hands. The last part of her reluctance to come here was hatred. Of the Empire's utter control over everyone and everything. Of the rampant depravity tolerated at court. Of privilege and excess, unfettered ambition and breathtaking greed. She hated all of it.

At home, when she was sure she was alone and no one could read her mind or her facial expression, she indulged in thinking lushly vile, deliciously awful thoughts about Maximillian. Which was perhaps why being back at court and having to completely suppress all those thoughts and feelings chafed her so sorely.

Thankfully, she fretted in the Imperial Seat for only a few days before she received word that Talissar, consort to the Queen of Quantaine, had been seen stepping off a ship. Immediately, she sent him an invitation to come for tea in the Haraland chambers.

Lest anyone mistake the invitation for an assignation, she'd come to the gallery of King's Council Chamber so any reply from Talissar would be appropriately public in its delivery. She fingered the heavy Octavium Pendant on its long chain around her neck. It had been a gift from the elven prince who was her recruiter and only direct contact with the Eight, even to this day.

Supposedly, the pendant protected the wearer from his or her mind being intruded upon and read. But she doubted any magical item could withstand the terrible mental power of Maximillian himself. She'd heard tales of him making entire armies drop dead in their tracks, simply by willing it so.

She started as a voice murmured, "Mine eyes rejoice to behold thy stellar beauty, Your Highness."

Startled, she looked up to see the spectacularly beautiful face of Talissar, as if her thoughts of him had willed him to her side. "Well met, my lord," she replied courteously. "Do you also grow bored with the proceedings below?"

"My queen and your husband seem to have the debate well in hand. The air waxes close and stuffy here in the gallery.

Might I importune thee to stroll with my humble self in the gardens?"

"That sounds lovely." She pitched her answer in a tone of relief for any eavesdroppers and fanned herself with her silk fan for emphasis. "You must tell me how Lyssandra fares."

"My queen is well, and thy graciousness in inquiring after her health will please her mightily."

"Do give her my warmest regards. She must come visit us again soon."

They wandered outside into the Imperial Gardens, which were as grandiose in scale and opulence as the rest of the Imperial Seat. The entire palace and grounds were built on a city-sized platform called the White Crown Plaza suspended between the eight mountains known as Thoris's Shield. The platform spanned the width of the mighty Crystal River. Giants were said to have grown the graceful and delicate fretwork of stone arches that supported the massive plaza.

They walked far enough into the Gardens of Nations to leave behind most casual visitors. Talissar spoke to her under his breath, his lips never moving. "Hast Haraland also received orders from Maximillian to double the usual ironwood harvest this year?"

"Yes," Gabrielle answered in a similar fashion. "The foresters are furious and say it will deplete the ironwood stands excessively. I gather Maximillian plans to begin construction of another Black Ship?" The only object whose construction required anywhere near the amount of ironwood being ordered was one of the mighty, seafaring ships. The oceans of Urth were storm-tossed, dangerous at best and impassable at worst. Only ships built of the nearly indestructible iron-infused wood stood any chance of surviving an ocean crossing.

Talissar smiled slightly. "Our resplendent Emperor doth not share his plans with this lowly elf. I would not presume to speculate on his purpose. I merely stand and serve."

And plot against Maximillian. She smiled back, amused. It was a rare treat to speak or even allow herself to think so irreverently of the Emperor with another person. "Shipping overall has increased greatly in Haraland this year."

"Indeed? What manner of cargo swells thy port?"

"Imperial hounds and their masters brought in from Pan Orda. A new lot. This pack excels in tracking the scent of elemental beings."

"Interesting. How many were there?"

"Eight beasts and two hunters."

Talissar drew in a sharp breath behind his pleasant expression. As well he might. "I shall most assuredly relay that information with alacrity."

"To whom?" she asked curiously.

He merely smiled gently, and frustration soared through her. She spoke bluntly. "I've been part of this organization for a very long time. I want to know more. Do more. Who are the Eight? I think I've earned the right to know."

"My dearest lady. Prithee, do not mistake my reticence as a lack of trust. It is, rather, my high esteem for thee which thusly stills my tongue. The less any one of our number knowest, the safer the greater organization and its goals remain. If an octopus should lose a limb, is he not still able to swim? But if a man should lose a leg, is he not crippled?"

She made a sound of impatience at his flowery analogy. He was trying to flatter and distract her. She was made of sterner stuff than that. "I would like to meet one of them."

"Thou hast met our leader. Many times."

"What? How is that possible?"

"He moves among us, of course."

"Right out in the open?"

"Where better to hide?" Talissar asked shrewdly.

Good point. So. The leader of the Eight was at court, was he? A noble, then. Or at least some kind of high functionary. No, he must be noble. Who else would have the hubris to believe he could oppose Maximillian? At least she knew the leader to be a man now. That eliminated half the possible candidates. He would have to be someone intelligent—although maybe not visibly so. Mayhap he played the dimwit to throw the Emperor off the trail.

Assuming Maximillian even searched for rebels and conspiracies in his own home. Surely, he did. The Emperor was nothing if not paranoid.

Talissar chuckled. "I vow I hear the cogs and wheels awhirl in that nimble mind of thine, my lady. I would remind thee to do nothing to call attention to our cause."

"I would never!" she exclaimed in quick horror.

"Perchance one day, our leader will choose to reveal himself to thee. But until that happy day, we two must remain, as ever, small islands stranded in a sea of ignorance."

She huffed, entirely dissatisfied with his brush-off. Mayhap it was time for her to take action to prove her usefulness to the Eight. She had thought upon how she might do that long and hard, and she had an idea. Taking a deep breath, she felt her ribs contract around her lungs, a sure sign of nervousness.

Steadying her voice, she murmured, "I have an acquaintance whom I wish to approach. I know her to be a like-minded soul to me in every way that matters, and she is my oldest and dearest friend. I trust her with my life and beyond."

Talissar's eyebrows first shot up and then lowered thunderously. He spoke urgently. "This is not how we work. Thou *knowest* this."

"Indeed I do know this, my lord. I also know that she could be of immense value as an ally."

He muttered in resignation, "Who is it?"

"Lady Sasha, wife of the ambassador from the Heartland to the Imperial Court."

Talissar gave away no reaction whatsoever. None. He was perfectly still. Perfectly unreadable. And yet, his utter lack of a reaction spoke more loudly than any expression of surprise could have. He resumed walking along the garden path. "Tell me of this friend of thine."

Yes. He was interested. He hadn't dismissed her suggestion out of hand. Which meant he also saw the value of bringing a high-ranking Heartland noble, who was influential in her own right, into their group. Sasha was privy to the innermost workings of the Heart's diplomacy by way of her husband, Rafal. And she genuinely did have a kind heart. Gabrielle knew firsthand that her friend had no love for the Empire and its casual atrocities against life.

In answer to Talissar's inquiry, she replied, "Sasha is a gypsy by birth. She was taken in by the Heart as a foundling and raised in the house. She showed an early talent for magic and was trained as a healer. As you no doubt are aware, she rose far and fast within the Heart and serves it loyally."

"Not an uncommon story," Talissar commented. "Pray, enlighten this humble elf if thou canst. From which gypsy tribe dost the ambassador's wife hail?"

Gabrielle mentally lurched. A man of Talissar's race and rank knew that there were, in fact, tribes within the gypsies? Most perceived gypsies as the lowest scum in the Empire—thieves and cutpurses, the villains of children's hearth tales. And yet, this prince knew that gypsy society was complex and ordered? The only reason she knew the same was because of her close friendship with Sasha.

"She hails from the Lom Clan, I believe."

"Indeed?" That news sent Talissar's eyebrows sallying forth toward his hairline. "The rarest of all gypsy clans, by far. Ancient practitioners of old magics, as I recall."

Old magics? Sasha had never spoken about any such thing with her. Truthfully, Gabrielle was only vaguely aware that such magics existed. They, too, were mostly the stuff of children's bedtime stories.

"Mayhap a careful conversation with thy friend would be in order," Talissar mused. "Employing the utmost in delicacy and discretion, of course."

"Of course."

"Utter privacy must be ensured."

They walked a little more while Gabrielle's mind turned to the problem of exactly how to approach Sasha. But Talissar interrupted her ruminations by murmuring, "Mine eyes rejoice to spy the pendant that was my honor to gift to thee. Prithee, continue to let that lucky strand clasp the tender column of thy neck, particularly in these climes where oblivi are plentiful."

"Oblivi?" she echoed. "What, pray tell, are those?"

"Creatures whose sole purpose is thus: deletion of memory. Were thou to discard yon bauble, an oblivi would come for thee. It would invade thy mind, and thou wouldst suffer instant loss of certain recollections most precious to thee. They would drift away with the languid certitude of dandelion fluff upon the wind."

Alarmed, she clutched the pendant on its long chain in her fist. He turned their steps back toward the palace complex, announcing an end to their secret conversation.

She was disappointed she had not extracted more information from Talissar but frankly was surprised at how much she had managed to get him to reveal. Perhaps his approval of her request to approach Sasha signaled that she was finally trusted enough to become more deeply involved in the plans of the Eight.

"Remember, Your Highness. Gently steps he who would leave no trail."

"I will not forget, Prince Talissar."

Raina woke late and felt as if she'd taken a drubbing from a brace of staff fighters when she finally hauled herself out of bed. The whispers had been so loud last night that she could not go to sleep and, once asleep, had woken over and over to their echoes in her skull. If only she knew their purpose, mayhap she could find a way to quiet them.

The number of wounded coming in after the Boki incursion had finally slowed to a trickle, and High Matriarch Lenora had declared a day of rest for everyone in the Heart. Which meant Raina had no training today.

Lenora had hinted last night that perhaps Raina should make an excursion into the countryside in her new role as a White Heart healer. But before she ventured beyond the walls of Dupree, she had one task to do. A task she had been avoiding for months.

In the name of procrastination, she ate a leisurely brunch and even took a walk through the medicinal herb garden. She wasn't particularly gifted with plant lore, but she was gradually memorizing the appearances and uses of various herbs.

Unable to delay any longer, she made her way upstairs to the scroll copying room and laid out parchment, ink, quills, trimming knife, and blotter on a big work table. In the bright light streaming through the glass-paned window, she sat down to write a letter to her mother. Cognizant that the mages who'd been in league with her mother and who'd forced her to leave home would likely read the letter, too, she struggled to organize her thoughts.

She had fled Tyrel rather than let the Mages of Alchizzadon force her to produce female children for their selective breeding program. They thought they were creating a queen for a great mage of old, Hadrian, an ancient human who had fallen into stasis eons ago and whose body the mages still guarded and hoped to rouse one day. She, however, had wanted no part of her family's long-standing tradition and had run away from home rather than allow herself to be used thus.

The mages, of course, had given chase. It was part of why she'd chosen the path of the White Heart. In these colors, the knights of the Royal Order of the Sun, and most people who knew of the White Heart, would protect her from being kidnapped and dragged back to Tyrel.

Thankfully, Gawaine had known and explained to her the actual purpose of the Mages of Alchizzadon's breeding program, a purpose which had been lost over time. Today, she must find a way to explain it to her mother, and indirectly to the mages themselves, in such a fashion that they believed her. Given her mother's stubborn devotion to the cause, she feared Charlotte would refuse to accept any part of her explanation. Her mother would likely accuse her of making up the entire tale to get herself and her sister out of doing the mages' bidding.

It wasn't that the mages were entirely wrong in their thinking. But, as Gawaine had pointed out, stories tended to distort with the passage of time. Details got lost or embellished until the original truth bore little resemblance to the later hearth tale. So it was with the original purpose of the Mages of Alchizzadon.

Nowadays, the mages believed their purpose to be primarily that of breeding a queen worthy of their long-lost king, Hadrian. They still remembered correctly that he had been a great mage possessed of extremely powerful magic. Dangerously so. The mages believed that only a woman possessed of exceptional magic herself could survive bearing Hadrian's children. Which might also, in point of fact, be true.

However, the important detail that had gotten lost over time—and which Gawaine remembered—was that the women of her family had been bonded to the people of Tyrel in a magical ritual by Hadrian.

Her life energy and that of all her female relatives was linked to the life energy of the people living in the lands that had once been Hadrian's. Gawaine believed it was this link that was the source of her extraordinary magical power. He also believed that it was not the women of the House of Tyrel who needed to be more magically powerful. It was the bond itself between Raina's female relatives and the land that Hadrian had wished for the mages to nurture and protect. Ironically, the mages' breeding program had actually strengthened the bond over time, even though that had not been their stated purpose.

If it would appease the Mages of Alchizzadon and stop them from pestering her or her sister, she was all in favor of accepting Gawaine's version of the ancient story. Now to convince her mother to do the same.

It took her most of the afternoon to craft the letter to her satisfaction. First, she apologized for any grief she'd caused her family by her abrupt departure. She assured Charlotte that she was safe and sound within the White Heart and enjoying her continued training. Then she did her best to explain how the mages had strayed from the truth in their recollection of ancient events. It did not help that she barely understood the concept of a bond between Hadrian's subjects and his lands herself. And she was still a bit fuzzy on how the women of her family figured into all of it. They were apparently the keepers of the bond itself.

She needed to reveal to Charlotte in general terms the credentials of whom she'd gotten the information from, but without revealing Gawaine's actual identity or where and how she'd met him. Ultimately, she settled on referring to him as a notable scholar with direct access to ancient knowledge. Hopefully, that would be enough to get her mother to listen.

She hinted in the final paragraph of her letter that she was working on getting what the Mages of Alchizzadon would need to rouse Hadrian from his ancient slumber. In return she asked for time and space, and for her family to be patient a little while longer. Which was to say, she was tacitly asking her mother and the mages to stop chasing after her.

She assumed it went without saying that she still would not participate in their breeding program to create ever more powerful female mages within family line. It was as close to an offer of truce as she could bring herself to offer her mother and her old enemy.

The coup de grâce, of course, was that she was going to ask the Royal Order of the Sun to deliver the letter. Lest her mother and the Mages of Alchizzadon fail to accept the terms of her offer, the Royal Order of the Sun colors would be a stark warning that she was untouchable now. Assuming that Charlotte or the mages didn't just ignore her colors and snatch her, come what consequences may.

It was a calculated risk letting her mother know where she was. But by the time this letter reached far-flung Tyrel, Raina and her friends should be well away from Dupree and safe from her mother or the mages' clutches. Not that she actually expected they would be satisfied by her explanation of Hadrian's true intent for them. But maybe they would consider employing subtler tactics henceforth other than kidnapping her and dragging her by the hair, kicking and screaming, back to Tyrel.

She blotted the letter, rolled it, and sealed it with blue wax and the White Heart seal. She was just sliding it into a leather scroll tube when Rosana burst into the workroom.

"Raina. News! Eben and Sha'Li have returned. They didn't find Kendrick, but they got a lead on where Tarryn went. And they ran into a whole lot of greenskins who were jumping any settler they came across. Apparently, Eben and Sha'Li had some close calls. They're back in town to resupply, but then they want to go back out. They've asked us to go with them to find Kendrick and Tarryn."

"Where are they now?"

"They've gone to the Mage's Guild to let the guildmaster and Will know what they found."

"And Rynn," Raina added with a grin.

Rosana grinned back. "Aye. And the pretty paxan. I'm almost looking forward to traveling unknown roads again. Gah, how I hate being trapped in this city."

Raina knew the claustrophobic feeling. Although she supposed it was even worse for the gypsy for whom wandering was in her blood. Raina's impatience to get on with finding Gawaine's regalia and waking him made pure torture of each day she was forced to sit in the Heart building enduring lectures on how to bind wounds and how to properly represent the White Heart's special status within the Empire.

The pressure to take action had built up to such a point within her that she felt nigh ready to explode from it. Maybe that was what those cursed voices inside her skull were telling her.

It was time to go.

CHAPTER

14

Will stared doubtfully at the powerful man doffing his cloak before him in the practice yard. Krugar was barrel-chested with arms wreathed in muscle. Not especially tall, he nonetheless looked like the kind of warrior no one possessing any sense tangled with.

Likewise, Krugar studied him intently, obviously sizing him up. "Aurelius tells me you've got talent, boy. Is that true?"

Will shrugged. "I would not know, sir. I just do my best."

"Staff and magic? What flavor?"

"Umm, force magic."

"Ever fought with a bladed weapon?"

"Not much, sir. There's not much use for wielding a sword where I come from." Deeply wary of this Imperial officer recognizing him, Will cloaked himself as thickly as he could in his homespun, peasant-from-the-woods upbringing.

Krugar moved over to the weapons stand at the side of the practice ground and picked up the longest and heaviest staff leaning there. He hefted it, finding its center of balance, and assumed a relaxed stance before Will. "Let's see what you've got, then."

Nervous, Will settled into a fighting stance of his own, his hickory-and-copper staff at the ready. Krugar moved forward casually, but his staff snapped forward so fast that Will barely had time to bring his own weapon up to catch the blow. Another snap, this time with the other end of Krugar's staff, and Will grunted as the wooden pole struck his thigh painfully.

"Faster hands, boy, else I'll mark you black and blue."

Will couldn't tell if Krugar meant that as a warning or a threat. Either way, he hadn't been this hard-pressed since the last time he'd sparred with his father. A pang of grief momentarily distracted him, and he barely leaped back out of the way of a flurry of blows.

"Don't waste my time, boy."

Ty's training took over. Will's mind cleared, and the entire world narrowed down to Krugar's staff. Peripherally, Will registered his foe's footwork, balance, and center of mass. The next time Krugar moved in on the attack, Will caught the tip of the soldier's staff with his weapon, guiding it down the length of his staff with a sweep and turn that brought Will into position to tap Krugar smartly on the ribs before the man spun away.

Krugar's bored expression gave way to a certain interest. The soldier came in again on the attack. Will recognized the feint and flowed into the correct countermove automatically. He could not count how many times he had practiced this exact sequence with his father.

Another attack. Another response from deep within Will's muscles and memory. And with it came recollection of long ago uttered instructions from his father. "Defense is fine for marking time in a fight. For fatiguing an enemy. But to win a fight, you must go on the offense."

Of its own volition, the tip of his staff danced in an intricate pattern, tracing a sign in the air that actually seemed to glow as he drew it. Somehow he knew that, were he to trace the sign again, it would grow in power. Spying a tiny opening in Krugar's offside defense, Will pounced, jabbing the magical sting into his opponent with the tip of the staff. Krugar was forced to leap back awkwardly to avoid the magical attack, and Will—anticipating the movement correctly—landed a quick blow to Krugar's calf. As the soldier lurched to protect his flank, Will rapped him smartly across the knuckles. Had this been real combat, he'd have hit the fist hard enough to numb the hand and force his foe to drop the staff.

As it was, Krugar swore and stepped back, pausing the sparring to shake out what Will knew from personal experience to be painful tingling in his fingers. He did his best not to grin at the soldier. No sense infuriating a man who could no doubt retaliate in such a way as to make his life miserable.

"Who are you?" Krugar asked while they waited for his hand to regain feeling.

"Apprentice to the Mage's Guild—"

Krugar cut off his stock answer. "Who trained you to fight?"

"Oh. That. Well, most of the boys in the hollow messed around with staffs. We sparred all the time. At least when we weren't cutting and hauling timber, and chopping wood, and planing lumber—"

"Are there more boys who can fight like you in this hollow of yours?"

He shrugged modestly. "None of them could best me."

"Let's go again. This time, full out. No pauses until one of us taps out." Krugar pulled a metal-backed gauntlet out of his belt and donned it over his off hand grimly.

Will knew the term "tapping out" from his father. It referred to declaring oneself defeated and surrendering. Not that Ty had taught him to believe in any surrender short of death in actual combat. In response to Krugar's gloves, Will fished his mother's amber hand shield out of his pouch and slipped it on. The soft, fingerless glove slipped over his left palm, fitting his palm perfectly but leaving his fingers entirely free to move. Odd. He remembered this glove fitting well when he was but a lad, as well. He used to play with it when his mother took it out to clean and oil it. The leather must have stretched to accommodate his larger hand.

Will left his casting hand bare as he would do in actual

combat conditions. He took up his staff once more and dropped into a defensive stance. Subtle heat pulsed through the hickory staff and into his hand shield. It was almost as if the two items were old friends sharing a warm greeting with one another. He did not often wear both items at once. He could not actually use the shield while wielding the staff, but he sensed he might need it before this sparring match ended. An enchanted gift from his mother and a magically enhanced gift from his father—of course the two items recognized one another.

An odd sense of comfort settled around him. They were still with him, his parents. If not in body, then in the skills and training they had passed on to him, and in the fighting spirit they had imbued in him.

If only they were still alive. What he wouldn't give to be trained by them, knowing what he did now about the world and about their hidden abilities. Anger rolled through Will at the Imperial Army colors standing before him. He hated everything that Krugar represented. The fellow wanted full-out combat? Then full-out he would have.

Will did not wait for the soldier to attack. He leaped forward, battering at his foe with a barrage of fast strikes. To his credit, Krugar met him blow for blow, blocking everything Will threw at him. It was as if their training and skills had been cut from the identical cloth. For every move Will knew, Krugar knew the countermeasure, and vice versa. The courtyard rang with the knocking of their weapons, and Will peripherally registered an audience gathering in doorways and windows to watch.

Neither he nor his foe yielded an inch as the battle aged. Sweat rolled down Will's face and his lungs and legs burned, but determination to take down this Imperial bastard fueled his body anew whenever it began to lag. Krugar's face settled into lines of determination every bit as grim. On and on they fought, raging back and forth across the yard, first one of them on the attack and then the other.

Eventually, Will began to despair of ever breaking through

Krugar's defenses. As fatigue began to override his mental discipline, he became aware of his staff growing first warm, then hot, in his grip. Magic crackled down its length, seeking escape from the veins of copper eagerly channeling the energy.

He . . . would . . . not . . . cast . . . magic.

This fight was about sinew and strength, speed and cunning. He would win this on his own merit, curse it.

So much magical energy built up in his staff that he could barely maintain his grip upon the wooden shaft. Finally, it was too much. He threw the tip of the weapon up toward the sky and let loose a mighty bolt of force magic into the heavens.

It took only an instant, but that instant was enough for Krugar. The soldier snapped his staff around, catching the shaft of Will's weapon and sweeping it aside. The other end of Krugar's staff swung lightning fast and struck Will so hard on the ear that he dropped to the ground, stunned.

His head rang and stars danced before his eyes.

"Do you yield?" Krugar demanded from above.

"Aye," Will replied sourly.

Immediately, Krugar's raised staff lowered. A hand appeared before Will's eyes. It would be poor sportsmanship not to take the offer of help. Grumpy, though, he took the officer's hand and let Krugar haul him upright.

"Not bad, boy. Not bad at all."

But he'd lost. In a real fight, he would be dead right now. Failure was unacceptable in actual combat. Of course, in a real fight he would have aimed that massive bolt of magical damage at his foe and not discharged it harmlessly into the sky. His bruised pride took some small comfort in that knowledge. But then he spied the fading glow of magic in Krugar's fist as well. Light blue.

Wind magic. "Could you teach your magic to me?"

"Kinetic magics like your force magic are entirely different animals than the elemental magics. It takes a certain knack for it to corral the elemental paths."

"I'd like to try," Will replied intently.

"Next time. I also want to try you at the sword. Your moves, your balance speak of a sword fighter's stance. You'd take to the blade well, I think."

It made sense. His father had been one of the preeminent swordsmen in the land by all accounts. It had just been too dangerous for Ty to teach bladed combat to Will. "I would like that, sir."

It galled Will to admit it, but he looked forward to learning swordplay from Krugar. The man obviously knew what he was about with fighting.

Aurelius stepped out of a shadowed doorway into the courtyard and immediately, the other mages hanging out of the windows and doors melted from sight. "What do you think, Krugar? Does he have something worth developing?"

Krugar assessed Will for a long moment. "Aye. He's too old to begin serious training as a weapons master, but he's too talented not to train up as far as he is able to progress."

The guildmaster nodded. "My men report that he does not know how to get started in a fight, but once he's in motion, he's a natural."

Will's gaze snapped to his grandfather. Was *that* what the Celestial knights thought of him?

"He reminds me of a Casted warrior I saw once," Krugar said ominously. "How did this boy come by his skill? You did not implant it in him magically, did you?"

Aurelius sucked in a sharp breath. In an offended voice, he declared, "The Casted do not actually learn their skills; rather their abilities are implanted magically. I promise you, Will comes by his naturally. Furthermore, the Casted burn out quickly, leaving little more than a hull behind. I ask, does yon lad fight like a Remnant?"

"Nay, Guildmaster. I meant no offense. But he has the same unconscious quality when he calls upon a complex skill. As if he learned it but then forgot it long ago and only just now is recalling it." He spoke the words as if still convinced that Will was some sort of unnaturally dangerous freak.

Will looked back and forth between the two men who were measuring one another skeptically as if they both thought the other one not being entirely honest. He spoke up cautiously, "I assure you. I have memory of the hundreds of bumps and bruises it took to become skilled with my staff. It was a long road spanning many years."

Eventually, Krugar looked away from Aurelius and smiled a little. "He reminds me a little of myself at his age. Overeager. Undisciplined. Unfocused. But there's a seed of talent within him. It remains to be seen if the seed will germinate and grow, however."

Will's teeth ground together at Krugar's assessment. He'd gone toe-to-toe with the best fighter in Dupree for better than a quarter of an hour, hadn't he? If he hadn't had to discharge that stupid magic build-up, they would still be fighting.

"—be back tomorrow to work with him. Same time acceptable to you?" Krugar was saying.

"He'll be here." Aurelius added dryly, "And he will have his magic under better control on the morrow, as well."

Will winced. His grandfather had seen that, huh?

"Come, Will. It is clear you need further training in how to suppress your magics in addition to summoning them."

Gunther scowled at a brace of children who whispered among themselves as they stared at his mechanical leg. He stumped past them, ignoring their pointing fingers. Someday they would appreciate the value of being alive in spite of one's scars and imperfections. But not yet. For now, they were merely impudent brats.

It looked and felt strange coming down out of the mountains into the lowlands of Kel south of the Groenn's Rest Range. Everything was so blasted green and moist. Even the stones were covered with bright moss. He missed the windswept peaks and barren granite cliffs of his home. Kel was soft and gentle with low rolling hills, misty mornings, and picturesque villages tucked into forest glades. Gah. His beard felt as if it were starting to mildew.

Humans were abundant, pale skinned and soft cheeked. They fit this place. He breathed a sigh of relief when he arrived at the village that was his destination and heard the familiar clang of a hammer on steel. Following the sound, he spied a good-sized smithy. The familiar sizzle of hot steel meeting cold water and the gasping of bellows announced that the smith was at his anvil.

He'd not wielded hammer and tongs since the accident. Weapon smithing had proven too strenuous for him on a single leg, and he'd had to give it up. Now and again, though, an itch to forge a good sword came over him, and this was one of those moments. As if in wry response, the stump of his leg ached where it had been severed. The rain that had been threatening all afternoon commenced as a drizzle, and Gunther ducked under the roof covering the forge.

A barrel-shaped dwarf, sleeves rolled up to reveal massively muscled forearms, glanced up between rhythmic blows on some metal piece. He grunted to acknowledge Gunther's presence but then went back to work.

Over the next few minutes, the rain intensified to a loud, steady drumming against what must be a metal roof. His stump continued aching, and he looked around for a spot to sit. He spied a short barrel with a lid on it and dropped onto it with a grunt.

The smith held up some sort of oversized buckle in his tongs, turning it this way and that. He plunged the piece into the trough of water beside his anvil and steam rose along with the sizzle of quenching metal.

"Can I 'elp thee?" the smith growled, wiping his hands on his jerkin.

"Are you Halvar Langskaag?" Gunther replied.

"Aye. An' 'oo's askin'?"

"Druumedar. Gunther Druumedar of the Hauksgraffen Druumedars."

"The Hauk? I got me a cousin over that way."

"Aye, he's the one who sent me here. To see thee."

The smith picked up a short-handled iron shovel and

pushed ashes over the glowing coals, stoking the forge against the cold and damp. "Let's go inside. Hoist an ale. Cursed rotten day to be outside."

Gunther followed the fellow into a sturdy stone cottage next to the forge. The thatched roof absorbed the rain sounds, and deep silence embraced the two men. The smith fetched a pair of mugs and filled them from a tap on the side of an ale barrel.

"Whot brings ye all the way to Kel on a foul day like this?"

"This." Gunther unlaced his shirt to reveal the breastplate beneath. He unbuckled it from the matching boiled leather backpiece he'd fashioned to pair with it. Carefully, he laid the copper piece on the rough plank table in front of the smith.

Halvar took one look at the breastplate and shoved his bench away from the table abruptly. He leaped to his feet and rushed to the windows, slammed the shutters closed, dropped the locking bar across the door, and checked inside the cupboard and under the cot in the corner before coming back to the table warily.

He leaned close to Gunther and whispered yeastily, "Where'd ye get that?"

"You know what it is, then?"

"Seen the like afore. Where'd ye get it?"

"Found it."

"*Where?*"

"In an abandoned mine."

" 'Tis death to possess that thing," Halvar muttered direly. "And there's plenty o' folk who'd kill thee to take it from thee."

"Why? Your cousin called it hardened copper. What's that?"

"Just what it sounds like."

Now he was only a miner these days and spent more time with rocks than people, but he knew an evasion when he heard one. This bloke, Halvar, wasn't being square with him.

"Your cousin sent a letter for you." Gunther fished the dirtied parchment roll out of his pouch and passed it across the table.

With a harrumph, Halvar took the letter and clumped over to the hearth with it. Holding the paper up to the firelight, he broke the wax seal and read the letter. "He says you're a trusty type. That I can speak freely wit' ye."

The smith threw several pieces of split oak on the fire and sat down once more, picking up the breastplate to turn it this way and that in the fledgling flames. The firelight picked up the intricate inlay of darker green copper stretching across the broad surface in winding knots that must have taken forever to painstakingly craft and pound into the plate.

"First, tell me exactly where ye found this piece."

"In an old mine, like I said." He was reluctant to tell anyone exactly where the mine was, however. No need to set off a flurry of prospectors looking for more of this rare copper until he knew if he'd stumbled upon a fortune for himself.

"Was there a forge in this mine? Or mayhap next to it? On a mountaintop?"

"Why a mountaintop?"

"The lightning, man, the lightning. How else would storm copper be forged?"

Storm copper? He frowned, not understanding. "There was a forge in the mine. Or there used to be. All that was left was a bunch of auger holes where the anvil must have been, a quenching pool, and a pile of charred coal."

"And a chimney? With copper rods all around it?"

"Short rods sticking out about a hand's span with turquoise deposits all around?"

Halvar nodded. "The turquoise is formed as the copper rods channel the lightning bolts."

All at once, the working of the ancient forge came clear in Gunther's head. He always had been mechanically inclined, and that one piece of information filled in the missing gap in his understanding. He asked eagerly, "Did lightning strike raw metal that the smiths worked later? Or did smiths work items first and then get them lightning struck?"

"My guess is that pieces were mostly forged first. They were finished after the metal was infused with lightning's power."

It made sense. "Cold quenching would seal the magic in the metal, methinks."

Halvar nodded. "When this cursed rain abates, I'll take ye into the mountains. Introduce ye to them who might know more."

Gunther lurched. It was a generous offer. Or mayhap Halvar was trying to horn in on his discovery. Learn more of where Gunther'd found the bracer so he could search for more pieces of the rare copper for himself.

"Are you saying you know who made yon bracer?"

Halvar's face went more tightly closed than a clam over a boiling pot. He knew something about the makers of storm copper. "Looks like rain the rest of the night. If'n it clears in the morn, we'll head out then. Ye can bunk down by the fire if ye want. I got no bed for ye, though."

"Floor's good enough for me, and grateful I am for a roof o'er me head and the warmth of a fire. But if ye'll just tell me where to go, I'll make the trek and find yer friend mesself, thanks."

"No one up that way'll talk to an outsider, even if he wears a beaded beard. Ye'll need the introduction." Halvar got up and moved over to the big kettle hanging over the fire. He gave its contents a stir with a big, wooden spoon. "You want a nip o' stew?"

Gunther never had been one to say no to a hot meal. He nodded his assent. But as soon as Halvar's back was turned and the fellow was occupied spooning stew into bowls, Gunther scooped up the breastplate and buckled it back about his person. He'd been sleeping in it ever since those cursed soldiers confiscated the helm, and he wasn't about to change that habit now.

So. The piece *was* old. As he'd suspected. But lightning-infused copper? Who'd have guessed such a thing existed? Maybe when he got up into the mountains, someone would tell him more about the creators of the ruined forge—and the storm copper.

Lenora looked up from the unrolled parchment weighted down upon her desk as Raina knocked upon her open office door.

"You summoned me, High Matriarch?"

"I've received a letter from Emissary Balthazar."

Raina nodded politely and sank onto the edge of the chair before her desk. Well-mannered girl. She could cast circles around all of them, and she knew it, yet she still demonstrated respect for her elders.

"This letter was penned at the demand of the Boki warlord. It is an edict to all outsiders to stay out of the Forest of Thorns or be put to immediate death, no warnings, no questions asked."

"Nice of him to let us know," Raina replied wryly.

"While he had access to paper, ink, and a messenger, Balthazar took the opportunity to report that there is friction within the Boki ranks. Apparently, Will Cobb's appearance among them with Lord Bloodroot's spirit in him has caused much discord."

"I can imagine. When we first arrived, there was a pitched argument with some wanting to kill him on the spot as an impostor, and others defending him as Bloodroot's chosen one. When he fought Ki'Raiden's son, Ki'Agar, to a draw, the disagreement only seemed to deepen."

"Balthazar says that some Boki think Will must have cheated to hold his own against Ki'Agar. Furthermore, as long as Bloodroot chooses to hide inside a puny, weak human, he is not worthy of their reverence."

Raina looked taken aback, as well she should. They had all assumed Will's link to Bloodroot would protect him from Boki recriminations for possessing a piece of their sacred tree lord. If their assumptions were wrong, though, it would mean Will Cobb was in mortal danger from Boki who would stop at nothing to rip the heart of Bloodroot off his chest.

As if that were not worrisome enough, Lenora took a deep breath and got to the meat of the report. "Balthazar also says there is a deeper split within the Boki leadership. Some support the youngsters who engineered the recent attacks, and others revile them."

Raina leaned forward. "So it *was* a splinter group! I could not believe the senior Boki leaders would support an invasion of Dupree. They know all too well the wrath of the Empire and have no wish to feel its bite."

"Balthazar agrees with you. He says the Warlord of the Boki does not wish to confront the Haelan legion and is livid that a faction has disobeyed him by raiding the settled lands. The warlord is sending thanes to neighboring areas, possibly to separate the hotheads from one another and possibly to form new Boki outposts."

Raina nodded. "They will consolidate their power beyond the reach of Koth and grow their armies in the safety of the wild forests."

"Balthazar also reports that the warlord's daughter Ka'Anka is now seventh thane. She and her sister Du'Ynda apparently are gone on some secret mission having to do with recovering the Great Boar that has gone missing from the Forest of Thorns." She looked up at Raina. "Remind me what those ranks are?"

"Ka's are sub-thanes, if you will. Du' indicates a scout."

Lenora shook her head. "I have trouble keeping all their ranks and titles straight."

"At least you do not underestimate the complexity and richness of their society because they are green skinned," Raina replied dryly.

Lenora smiled. "Spoken like a true White Heart member." A pause, then, "Tell me this. Do you believe these factional divisions within the Boki pose an ongoing threat to Dupree?"

Raina frowned. "The Boki were enraged when Anton invaded their lands. And many, many of them died to—" She broke off.

What had Raina been on the verge of saying? Died to do what?

"Died to defend their home and repel Anton," Raina finished lamely.

That was *not* what the girl had originally been thinking.

Raina continued, "In spite of their recent defeat at the hands of the new governess, or maybe because of it, I expect many of the younger Boki to be spoiling for blood revenge. I cannot guess how effective the elders will be at sitting on them. What does Balthazar say on the subject?"

"He predicts more trouble."

Raina looked worried, as well they all should. The Boki had nearly destroyed the colony on the first Night of Green Fires. Boki and other greenskins had swarmed the colony and burned everything in their path. The most recent attack, although much smaller and ill-coordinated, had still caused plenty of damage and loss of life.

"One last bit of information. The Boki warlord is aware that Anton contracted with Ki'Raiden secretly. The warlord does not trust the Viper and worries that Anton may attempt to use Ki'Raiden again."

"Has the warlord taken action against Ki'Raiden, then?" Raina asked.

"Apparently, he has been promoted to fifth thane but sent out of the Forest of Thorns to a remote location for now."

"So Ki'Raiden is still a threat," Raina murmured. "I must warn Will . . . and Bloodroot."

"I think that would be wise. As would staying safe within the walls of this city be until the Boki problem settles down." Not that she expected for a minute that Raina and her friends would do so. After all, they were young. Brash. Convinced they were immortal. That said it all.

What secret mission was Aurelius training them all for, anyway? Surely, it was not a simple jaunt through the countryside that the Mage's Guildmaster had in mind for his young protégés. Of all people in Dupree, she, as an Imperial genealogist, had perhaps the best idea of just how special a group it was. Every last one of the youths had an extraordinary lineage yet not one of them knew the full extent of their own identity.

But they would learn. The day was coming—sooner rather than later—when they would all have to find out exactly who they were and what they were born to do.

And then they would all see if the training she and Aurelius and Krugar were frantically cramming into the youths was enough or not.

Justin staggered a little as his feet touched solid ground once more. After several days aboard a rocking ship, the earth felt as if it rolled and heaved, while the great Estarran Sea behind him was the unmoving thing.

"Ready to go?"

He sighed. The Royal Order of the Sun knight, a barbarian named Hrothgar, never seemed to tire. Ever. Even confined to a small cargo ship, the fellow still managed to be exhausting company. They'd bumped into one another on the road at the southwestern margin of Dupree, and the gregarious barbarian had quickly figured out that Justin hailed from close to where Sir Hrothgar was headed.

It was lucky for the Heart man because Justin knew exactly where to find the recipient of the letter the Heart knight was charged with delivering. Not so lucky for him, though. Hrothgar had more or less ordered him to act as his guide and take him to Tyrel.

Justin had set out months ago from Tyrel to track down his childhood best friend, but he'd found no trace of Raina in any settlement west of the Estarran Sea. He'd crossed the body of water separating the mostly unsettled west from the more heavily populated lands of Dupree and had promptly heard stories of a young girl who was shocking everyone with her powers of healing. That sounded like Raina, all right. He'd been bound for Dupree to check out the rumors when Hrothgar derailed his plan.

"Come, Justin. The daylight grows short. We need to reach the Heart before dark," Hrothgar declared.

He rolled his eyes and hoisted his pack over a shoulder. "This way." He led the Heart knight westward through the rough waterside town of Bannockburn. There were a few more landing points farther south, closer to Tyrel, but this was the last even remotely safe one.

They came to a dilapidated, one-story building sided in rough wood. It was covered in a layer of dust like every other person and place in this forsaken slice of nowhere. The roof needed work and the front porch looked ready to collapse in the next strong breeze. Truthfully, it was no more run-down than any other structure in the town. But the Heart symbol was freshly painted upon the door, and the place had an air of energetic bustle about it.

The Royal Order of the Sun fellow at the door exclaimed in surprise when he spied Hrothgar approaching. For his part, Hrothgar bellowed back, "Luthien! As I live and breathe. Have they made a knight out of you yet?"

"Just barely. And I see they've knighted you. Were they so short on candidates for promotion, then?"

The men shook hands, slapped each other's shoulders, and were generally collegial with one another. Justin slipped inside mostly unnoticed and accepted a bracing bowl of rice, beans, and spicy sausage sauce from the healer on duty. Drained after the rough sea crossing—and he didn't care if the Merr sailing their boat had declared it jolly fine weather and a right smooth ride—Justin was happy to crawl into a bunk and pass out while the Royal Order of the Sun knights traded news.

Well before dawn the next morn, a jovial voice enjoined him to rise and shine as his blankets were summarily torn off his body. Justin groaned at Hrothgar and stumbled to his feet. The knight shoved a meat pastry into his hand and hustled him out of the Heart house before Justin even fully woke up.

They walked inland to Lake Stillwater, which took most

of the morning. There, Justin negotiated with the local Merr for a boat ride south along the Scholl River, past the Scholl Swamp, to the northern border of Tyrel. A bargain was struck, and Sir Hrothgar passed over the agreed-upon silver.

Once more, Justin forced his land-loving body onto a boat. This time, it was a sleek, oversized canoe. While one of the gilled fish men handled the tiller, at least two more Merr swam beneath the vessel, pushing against bars protruding underwater from the hull.

Justin was fascinated watching the Merr's lazy-looking kicks with their webbed feet. The canoe skimmed over the lake, seeming to barely touch the glassy surface of the water. He'd never seen anything move this fast, and the fine spray carried on the wind of their passage was exhilarating.

"Kind of discomfiting, isn't it, realizing how clumsy we humans are in water compared to them?" Hrothgar commented. "Never tangle with a Merr underwater. Of course, they're skilled fighters on land, too. But in water, they're murderous. Never seen the like."

To their west, the beginning of the Sorrow Wold towered over the riverbank, dark and forbidding. He'd grown up on stories of the strange and violent creatures who lived within its shadowed borders.

The day aged, and the river carried them beyond the forest and into a dank, smelly swamp. The channel of the river remained clear, but even their Merr guides looked around nervously. Apparently, this was lizardman territory, and only some sort of uneasy truce gave these Merr permission to carry their passengers through the area at all.

"We almost there, boy?" Sir Hrothgar asked as the sun began to dip in the west.

"We'll make Tyrel by nightfall. It's still a two-day walk to our destination after that," Justin answered.

"And you're certain Lady Charlotte will be there?"

"She rarely leaves home. Her estate may be small, but she manages it diligently."

"When you were last there, did Lady Charlotte perchance entertain any long-term guests?"

Justin snorted. "Aye, although they weren't so much guests as intruders."

"Tell me about them."

He frowned, unsure of how much about the men was secret. But then, those secrets were not his problem to keep, and furthermore, he hadn't liked the visitors. "There were two. Both mages. From a place called Alchizzadon. They seemed to think they had some claim upon one of Lady Charlotte's daughters."

"Raina," the squire stated with a confidence that startled him.

"Aye. Just so. She ran away from home rather than do what they wanted her to."

Hrothgar commented thoughtfully, "Now the letter in my pouch makes more sense."

"You know the contents of a letter?" Justin asked, startled.

"Aye. That way, if the actual parchment is lost, I may still deliver the message and discharge my duty."

These knights were all so tense about duty and honor. Not that he didn't admire the nobility of it all. But the necessities of life—shelter, food, scraping together enough gold to pay taxes and still have enough coin to buy an ale now and again—rated much higher in Justin's world. In most people's worlds, if he had to guess.

Once back on land, Hrothgar set a ridiculously fast pace that strained even Justin's youth and stamina. They marched deep into the night and were up and on the road once more well before dawn kissed the sunward horizon.

The familiar rise just north of Tyrel Keep came into sight near twilight. The night watch hailed Justin from the north tower of the keep, and the two of them were let in the postern gate. The guards knew him, and Hrothgar's Heart colors earned him speedy admittance.

"This way, Sir Hrothgar," Justin said formally. Lady Charlotte, Raina's mother and mistress of Tyrel, had scant patience for a lack of manners in her vassals.

Supper was just winding down and the hall mostly empty. The kitchen wenches moved among the tables, gathering armloads of wooden plates and trenchers, while the keep's dogs jumped about underfoot after scraps.

Sir Darren had already left the table, but Lady Charlotte was still there. And beside her, Justin glimpsed the familiar, gruff visage of Kadir, the Mage of Alchizzadon responsible for Raina running away from home last spring.

"Yonder is Lady Charlotte and one of the mages of whom we spoke." Justin pointed out Raina's mother and Kadir and then turned to head for the kitchens. He would have no trouble charming Cook out of a plate piled high with sandwiches, a brimming mug of hard cider, and whatever sweets might be lurking about the cupboards.

"Not so fast, Justin Morland," Charlotte called out.

He sighed. Turned to face his mistress. Bowed from the waist. "How may I serve you, my lady?"

"What news of my daughter?"

"None, I am sorry to say; however, I also found no evidence of any harm befalling her, either. I believe her journey has carried her far beyond these lands and out of reach"—he spared a sarcastic glance for Kadir and finished harmlessly enough—"of my paltry inquiries."

"Go eat. Then I would speak more with you in my office."

"Yes, my lady."

But the summons, when it came, was not from Charlotte. Rather it was from Kadir, the elder of the two Mages of Alchizzadon who had been in residence ever since Raina disappeared. A servant stated deadpan that Justin was cordially invited to join Kadir in the tower room he had apparently appropriated for his own use whilst he was installed in Tyrel Keep.

Justin choked down the rest of a slice of cake, licked the sweet, gooey icing off his fingers, and followed the fellow to Kadir's door. The servant melted away as Justin lifted his knuckles to the wooden panel. Not fond of the visiting mage, was the fellow? No surprise.

"Enter," a deep voice called in response to his knock.

Justin let himself into the round, high-ceilinged office. The stone walls gave off a chill tonight, and he pulled his cloak forward.

Kadir sat at the desk that dominated most of the space. He held a parchment flat with one hand while he rubbed his eyes with his other hand. The man looked aggravated, and mayhap tired, but not the least bit sinister. Justin was not fooled, however. This was a powerful magic user from a secretive and powerful order of mages.

Before she had run away from home, Raina muttered mad accusations about a secret program to selectively breed massively talented female mages for some unknown purpose—and of her refusal to be one of those girls. He still did not understand it. But if Raina had opposed it strongly enough to forsake everyone and everything she had ever known, he was deeply suspicious of the man seated at the desk now.

"Sit," Kadir ordered tiredly.

Justin scowled but obeyed.

Kadir held the letter flat, perusing it at length before finally looking up. He then said the last thing Justin would ever have guessed to hear from such a man. "I need your help."

"Whatever for?"

"What's your name?"

"Justin."

"Raina's beau. Yes?"

"We grew up together. Were always close. But I'm not sure I would go so far as to call myself that—"

"She's sweet on you. I saw it, and I don't have time to tiptoe around niceties."

He shrugged. "Then yes. She is." At least she had been before he'd turned down her plea for help and forced her to run away from home all by herself. An act he would bitterly regret until his dying day.

"Raina is in serious trouble."

Alarm quickened Justin's pulse. "How?"

"You may have noticed that she possesses certain magical gifts beyond the ordinary."

He snorted at the obviousness of that remark.

Kadir continued, "However, Raina does not yet have mastery over all the aspects of her gift. More accurately, if she does not receive further training in how to control her abilities, she will eventually be driven mad by them."

"How so?"

Kadir leaned forward, and his voice dropped as if he spoke of secrets now. "She has a certain link to the people around her. It allows her to see and hear more than a normal mortal such as you or me. She sees into the hearts of others. Or at least she will, once she knows how to shape and use her talents. And she will begin to hear the echoes of spirits. However, without certain vital training that my order can give her, she will gradually lose the ability to differentiate between that which is real and that which is merely a manifestation of spirits invisible and inaudible to the rest of us. She will go mad."

"What can I do to help her?"

"I need you to find her. Convince her that the Mages of Alchizzadon only wish to help her, to save her sanity. And then bring her home."

"How?"

Kadir shrugged. "She likes you. Wants to be with you. If you bring her back here, I'm sure I can convince Charlotte that you are the best man for her daughter. You may have Raina."

"Should not Raina have some say in this plan for her life?"

"You must convince her that this is the best and only course of action for her. Use your charm. Use her feelings for you. Do you not wish to be with her, as well?"

That was not the point. It was this whole business of planning her life for her that had sent Raina running for the hills the first time. Mayhap the girl herself should have a choice.

If only he knew where she was. He would go to her secretly. Tell her about this latest plan for her. Ask her if she wished to come home or not. Unlike the mage seated before him, Justin would let her choose whatever path she wished. And then, he would walk it beside her if she would have him.

"Is that letter about her?" His impression had been that the letter was Heart business—hence, a Royal Order of the Sun knight delivering it.

Kadir snorted. "The letter is *from* her."

"Where is she? Is she safe? What did she say?" he blurted.

Kadir gestured at the parchment, now rolled up again on his desk. "She wished to inform her mother that she has joined the White Heart and, as such, can no longer assist us with our primary goal."

"What primary goal would that be?" Justin asked cautiously.

Kadir sighed. Studied him at length. And then surprised Justin by actually answering. "My order studies the relationship between spirits and the links to their physical forms."

Ever one to speak his mind, Justin asked, "What on Urth does that mean?"

A reluctant smile tugged at Kadir's mouth. "For your purposes, it means that my order had been associated with the House of Tyrel since before time has memory. The women of this house are . . . very special. You may have noticed they have an extraordinary gift for magic."

He responded dryly, "It is hard to miss."

"Raina more than most. Members of my order wish to . . . *study* her. To learn the source of her magic. To . . . duplicate it. Help her learn to . . . manipulate it."

The man was lying to him. Justin felt it in the slight hesitations between words, the careful way certain words were chosen. "You wish to harness her magic for yourself and use it to your own ends," he retorted bluntly.

Kadir's eyes narrowed. "Yes. That is correct."

"So, the real danger to her is from your kind, then?" Justin pressed.

"It is more complicated than that."

"Explain." He probably ought to be treading far more gently around this powerful mage whose hands were starting to glow faintly along with the runic marks tattooed, or maybe ritually etched, upon his neck and face.

"My order suffers from a certain division in its ranks. I am considered to represent the more moderate faction of the two."

"Stars preserve us all if you're the moderate one!"

Kadir did smile at that. "Just so. The second faction holds beliefs heretical to the rest of my brethren. And they will react rather strongly to the news contained within this letter."

"How so?"

"They will not care that Raina now wears the symbol of a protected Heart order. She has revealed her location to us by the origin of this note, and the heretics will be all for sallying forth and kidnapping her, White Heart colors or no."

Justin frowned. "Doesn't the Royal Order of the Sun take a dim view of anyone messing with a White Heart member?"

"That is an understatement. However, my brethren will not be deterred."

"What will they do with her if they successfully kidnap her?"

Kadir leaned back in the big wingback chair and looked off into the sluggish fire for a long time before his dark, grim gaze turned back. "They will drain all the magics from her, and they will take her special gift that is the source of all her magics, killing her in the process. They will find a way to store her gift until a more cooperative vessel can be found to contain the power. And then they will transfer her magic into a more malleable person."

"Kill her?" Perhaps taking a death would be worth it if she gained her freedom from these monsters in the process. "She will resurrect, though. Yes?"

"No. Her gift is so intrinsic to her spirit that removing it would destroy her. She will die permanently."

Justin rose out of his seat. "Get rid of that letter now. Burn it. Do not let these heretics know where she is!"

Kadir stared at him. Slowly, he began to nod. He rose to stand beside Justin before the fire. The mage was a big man, but Justin had grown in the past few months while he'd been on the road searching for Raina. They stood eye to eye with one another.

"And if I burn the letter, you will help me?"

"Yes."

"I have your word?"

"My solemn word of honor. Just burn the cursed thing."

Never breaking the lock of their stares, Kadir tossed the parchment onto the flames with a flick of his wrist. Justin's gaze dropped to the letter to watch it burn. The paper caught and flared up, blackening and curling, consuming the words that would get her killed. He used the iron poker to stir the fire, breaking up the charred bits of parchment until not a single pen stroke would be legible later.

Kadir murmured, "That will only buy her a little time. A White Heart member of her ability is bound to draw a great deal of attention. She will become famous throughout the land. Eventually, even in their remote corner of the colony, the heretics of Alchizzadon will hear of her. And then they will come for her and destroy her."

"But for now, we have time on our side. Enough to warn the Royal Order of the Sun to guard her closely. Enough to warn her. Correct?" he asked urgently.

"Mere knights cannot stand before the ritual powers my brothers will summon."

Kadir spoke the words with such quiet certainty that Justin accepted the observation as truth without question. And it sent a chill through him that had nothing to do with the brisk evening. "How can I help her?" he asked grimly.

"Not only do I need you to get close to her, convince her to let me help her control her power, but I also need you to watch over her."

"This I will gladly do. But how can I protect her if knights of the Royal Order of the Sun cannot?"

A conspiratorial twinkle entered Kadir's eyes. "I will make you one of us."

"A Mage of Alchizzadon?" Justin squawked. "I cannot even cast magic!"

"I can fix that." Kadir tossed out the words dismissively, as if it would be child's play to teach him magic. Justin had secretly tried to learn it for most of his life. And he knew for certain that he had no talent for it. At all. Kadir continued, "I happen to know plenty of magic runs in your blood."

Justin stared, stunned. How did this stranger know the first thing about his blood?

The mage was nodding now, warming to his own plan. "I shall mark you with secret symbols of our order. When the heretics approach Raina and see your marks, they will know they are being watched. That they cannot just take her and make her disappear without their actions being seen, known, and reported."

"Will that be enough to stop them?"

"Stars, no!" Kadir exclaimed. "I shall also have to mark you with defensive runes that will slow them down significantly. Enough, perchance, that the Royal Order of the Sun might stand against the heretics with your help."

"How am I supposed to get close to Raina if the Royal Order is guarding her day and night?"

"Ahh. Well. Clearly you must join the Heart."

"Wait. What? First you wish to turn me into a mage, then turn me into one of you, and then you want to make me a Heart man?"

"That, or she will die."

White Heart, I need healing. White Heart, healing if you please. White Heart, my husband is hurt. My child is sick. Something's wrong with my wife . . ."

Raina was starting to cringe every time she heard the words "White Heart." She did not begrudge the people around her their healing. What good was having all this magic if she could not use it to help others? But the tugging on her tabard was ceaseless. Everywhere she went, be it a shopping trip or a formal function at the governess's palace, people saw her colors and lined up to receive healing. And the more magic she cast, the louder the voices in her head became.

Even today, on a simple errand to an apothecary shop, she'd already been stopped twice en route by locals begging for healing. Raina had volunteered to go out and buy herbs for a batch of healing potions in hopes of escaping a steady stream of sick citizens to the Heart for help with a nagging fever and cough that was going around. No such luck.

The apothecary shop reminded her of one like it back in Tyrel with its dusty sweet smell and rows of large jars filled with seeds, dried leaves, powdered roots, and the like. A girl maybe five summers younger than Raina in age stepped out from behind a leather curtain as an older woman, probably the grandmother, weighed the herbs Raina needed and recounted the silver coins she'd laid on the work table.

No sooner had the girl slipped into the front room than Raina noticed something odd about the child. A vague glow surrounded her entire body like a nimbus. It was not the glow of magic; Raina knew the look of that all too well. Rather, this light hovered right at the edge of her ability to perceive it, so faint and transparent that if Raina looked away and looked back, it took her eye several seconds to readapt and find the light again.

For her part, the girl stood stock-still, her gaze glazing over as she stared at nothing. Her face paled, and a sheen of perspiration abruptly made her skin glisten. Sir Christian, a big, bluff Royal Order of the Sun knight who was Lord Justinius's man but who had been drafted to act as her escort since Sir Hrothgar was out of town, jumped forward to assist the younger girl.

Raina's healing training quickly diagnosed some kind of seizure. But that odd glow strengthened until she became half-convinced the light was in some way confining the child. Which was crazy, of course. Confining magics were high level and readily visible to even the most untrained eye. They looked nothing like this.

The girl began to mumble. Except her lips did not move. And the whisper of sound was unlike any human voice Raina had ever heard. It tickled her brain without ever seeming to pass through her ears. How was that possible? Was this some sort of psionic communication directly from the child's mind into hers?

The sounds took shape, forming words. Although they were joined together in seeming haphazard fashion, Raina could not find any actual meaning in them. They were gibberish.

"What are you trying to tell me?" Raina asked urgently. Had the whispers finally found a human outlet for their insistent message?

"The child said nothing," Sir Christian declared, looking back and forth between Raina and the young girl.

"But—" Raina broke off. "Did she glow for a moment?"

"What nonsense is this?" Sir Christian growled. "Of course she did not glow. If she had, my sword would not be resting quiet in its scabbard. I would be standing between you and yon child." In fact, he took several quick steps forward to place himself between Raina and the girl. Although who was being protected from whom, Raina could not say.

She leaned to one side to peer around the big knight. "Are you all right?" she asked the girl. "Do you feel ill?"

The child shook her head, although she was starting to look frightened.

"Never mind me. I'm sure you're in perfect health." Perplexed, Raina took the folded paper cone of herbs from the grandmother and left the apothecary. She stopped at the Mage's Guild to recount the odd occurrence with Will, but he and Aurelius were busy in some sort of training session with Captain Krugar.

Raina satisfied herself with penning a short note to Will describing what she had seen and heard. Mayhap in his Mage's Guild training he had run across something similar to explain the odd incident. Disappointed, she left the guild and turned her steps toward the Heart building.

What was afoot with all the Imperial training Aurelius was cramming into Will? It was as if the solinari did his best to distract Will from his true purpose, to pull his attention off the quest to wake the Sleeping King. Mayhap Aurelius attempted to lead his adopted grandson away from the dangers of continuing with the search. No doubt an urge to be like his father must run strong in Will. And she supposed Bloodroot's bloodthirsty streak must be loving all the weapons practice.

But it felt as if their little party was being torn apart, as if their quest was slowly but surely being forgotten, subsumed in the day-to-day demands of their individual training.

Even Eben and Sha'Li had been convinced by Aurelius and Selea to suspend their search for a few weeks, to properly provision themselves, to train some more, and wait for a solid lead to come in. Aurelius was teaching more of elemental magic to Eben, and who knew what Selea was teaching the rogue lizardman girl.

Did some greater force, invisible to them but powerful nonetheless, drag at their feet, holding them back from completing their quest? Or mayhap some malevolent force worked more subtly, confounding their path and turning their footsteps aside.

Who wished for them to fail? It was not a question she had ever really considered. Obviously, the Emperor would not be thrilled at the appearance of a rival for his throne. The former governor, Anton Constantine, had been no fan of their quest, although she suspected his objections had more to do with his insatiable greed than any great care for protecting the Empire.

If only Hyland were still alive. What she would not give

for one more hour seated next to him in front of a roaring fire, sipping mead, talking out such matters with him. Feeling lonelier than she had in a long while, she trudged back to the Heart. An exhausting afternoon of stirring a steaming pot of brewing potions over a hot fire awaited her.

And so it went. She studied healing, ran errands, worked around the Heart, and healed a steady stream of people wherever she went. The constant drain upon her magic left her continually fatigued and ravenously hungry. The voices were always with her now, lurking in the background of her mind, waiting for an unguarded moment in which to surge forward and drive her mad with their incessant babble.

At least she had become highly proficient at diagnosing common illnesses and injuries over the past few months and at fixing them with a quick burst of magical energy. Her sleep deprivation gradually deepened into a state of complete exhaustion.

Stars knew, she had begun to imagine that her name had morphed into "White Heart." The symbol on her tabard was starting to feel permanently imprinted upon her flesh.

She missed her friends. They would have teased her about the odd experience with the girl until she laughed over it. She barely saw any of them anymore. Will was immersed in his daily lessons with Krugar; and when he wasn't jumping around trying to kill the soldier with some weapon or another, he was busy with magic casting lessons. As a result, Rosana was grumpy and out of sorts most of the time.

When he wasn't taking magic lessons of his own, Eben lurked around Hyland's old house, by turns tense and depressed, waiting for a scout or bounty hunter to send back word of a sighting of Kendrick or Marikeen. The muscular young elemental grew more morose and antisocial than ever as the days passed with no news of his friend or his sister. Even Sha'Li began to seem like a ray of sunshine by comparison.

If the gorgeous three-eyed paxan, Rynn, was still in Dupree, he was lying extremely low. Not only did Raina never glimpse him, but not even a breath of rumor about a handsome open-eyed paxan was to be heard.

She had to get out from under the heavy thumb of the Heart and continue the quest to wake the Sleeping King. But how? She dared not try it alone. Of course, it was not as if the Royal Order of the Sun ever left her unattended for more than a few seconds. As she searched for a way to escape her constant bodyguards, the days continued to slip away one by one as summer aged toward fall.

Anton scowled at the dripping black trees around him. He hated the great outdoors, and he hated being alone like this with no one to guard his back. He felt vulnerable and small. And he despised both of those sensations. He did not even have the benefit of a slave, loyalty ensured by one of his special enslavement potions. He was a Kothite noble, or at least he should be one, and here he was toting a pack containing all his worldly goods upon his own back and *walking* like a common peddler. It was a travesty.

Thankfully, the plentiful gangs of greenskin bandits he'd encountered out here had left him alone as soon as they realized his identity. As well they should. He was financing their marauding. He had to admit they were not doing a half-bad job of it. He'd run across multiple burned-out homesteads and ransacked villages in the past few weeks. It was gratifying to see the havoc he'd wreaked.

Too bad they hadn't managed to sack Dupree, though. Now *that* would have caused chaos the colony would never have recovered from. At least not until he took control again and brought back order. He did have the satisfaction of having eliminated three of his most annoying foes. And even if Jethina Delphi had survived, she was too weak without the support of the other three landsgraves to cause any trouble. She was an old woman. She would die soon enough of her own volition.

Frankly, he was disappointed that the guilds and minor

landholders under the dead landsgraves had not demanded his return to power already. It would have been a heady thing to ride a wave of popular support back to the governor's palace. *His* palace. Ungrateful louts, all of them. Before he was done, they would yearn for a return to the peaceful days when he'd been governor. They would *beg* him to come back and rule them all.

A few more minutes of hiking brought him to a beautiful waterfall in a lush forest glade. Had a bevy of slaves gone before him to lay a picnic feast, and a half dozen musicians provided entertainment while another half dozen dancing girls did their best to seduce him, he might have enjoyed this spot. But as it was, he curled his lip in distaste for the *greenness* of it all.

He suspected his associates were amusing themselves at his expense, choosing these out-of-the-way meeting places with nary a building nor human comfort in sight. He would take note of every veiled insult, every small jab they leveled at him. And he would have his revenge tenfold for every pin they stuck in him. Nay. A hundredfold. If not today, then someday. He could be patient. Particularly when sweet revenge lay in the balance.

The steady roar of water plunging over a precipice and crashing to the pool below gave him a minor headache and put him in an even surlier mood. By the time movement across the clearing announced the arrival of his associate to this unholy meeting, he had achieved a truly foul state of mind.

Anton moved over to the water's edge where the noise was loudest. "About time you got here. You're late," Anton declared irritably.

"I am so sorry to have inconvenienced you, Governor."

He could not tell if the man was being sarcastic or not. Either way, he was mollified by the title that was rightfully his. "I need you to place an agent with the Boki in the Forest of Thorns. If my contact there does not do as he is told, I'll have him killed."

The contact nodded. "We have traders who pass through that area regularly."

"No simple traders will have access to Ki'Raiden. I need a spy-assassin among them."

"Ki'Raiden? I thought we were done with him."

Anton snorted. "He gains influence among his kind. If I can bring him to the Empire as an ally, like I did with the Kithmar—who were royalty among the rakasha—Maximillian will have no choice but to reinstate me." He added avidly, "With full honors. And maybe even an apology. Or maybe he will declare Dupree a kingdom and crown me its first king—" He broke off. No need to reveal his long-term schemes to this peon.

The man frowned but bowed his head briefly. "I shall put an agent in place, m'lord." He asked unhappily, "And the other thing?"

"I need information."

The fellow visibly relaxed. "Ahh, well. That is easy enough. We have informants in every corner of the colony and beyond. What do you wish to know?"

"Not so fast with your smiles and promises of success, my friend," Anton retorted. "A group of young adventurers traveled into the Forest of Thorns several months ago. They found something that belongs to me. I want them captured. Questioned—no, tortured—until they sing like birds. I want to know everything they saw. Everything they heard. What they found. What they learned. And what they *took* from me. I want it back."

The black serpent tattooed on the Coil contact's forearm writhed and twisted as the fellow clenched and unclenched his fist. "What you ask is somewhat more difficult than I anticipated."

"I need it done quickly. Quietly."

The black snake wiggled uncomfortably. "Is there not something else we could do for you instead? Our expertise lies more in commerce. Intelligence gathering. Financial transactions."

Anton leaned in close, forcing the man to lean back from the waist. "I require *this* of you. And I require it *now*. I will do whatever it takes to rule this colony again."

The fellow stared, then shook himself, saying carefully, "Of course you will, my lord. And the Coil will do everything in its power to help you regain your position as governor."

Of course they would. The Coil profited immensely when its leader controlled the purse strings of the entire colony.

"How will we let you know what we have learned?"

Anton's reply was swift. "I'll be watching you. I will contact you."

16

Will could not remember what it was like to wake up in the morning and not be sore from head to foot. He ought to be grateful for the grueling training to which Captain Krugar was subjecting him. But the soldier kept talking in terms of years of this intense practice before he would master any one weapon, let alone a wide array of them.

At least Krugar had started teaching him how to cast wind magic. It was devilish hard to get the hang of calling power from the moving currents of air instead of from that easy, instinctive place within him from whence force magic came.

Today, he trudged along reluctantly behind Aurelius to the Heart to be introduced to the Heartstone. His grandfather had been appalled to discover by chance that Will had never undergone the Ceremony of Introduction. It was an ancient ritual that most people performed as children to become familiar with Heartstones and know what to do should they ever need to resurrect.

Will was always intrigued by people's reactions to his grandfather. They were fascinated by his glittering golden skin but wary of getting caught staring. Will gathered that the solinari race in general was strongly supportive of the Empire, considered to be loyal citizens. The Sunset Isles, native home to most solinari, was considered to be a rich enclave of kothite loyalist sentiment.

Not that any place under the rule of Koth admitted to anything else. At least not publicly. To even think treasonous thoughts was a crime punishable by death. Speaking them aloud meant death to the speaker's entire family, both close *and* extended, and likely death to friends, acquaintances, and possibly, the traitor's entire village.

The elemental continent, Pan Orda, and the changeling continent, Kentogen, were said to have mostly repelled Koth. Both had been invaded in the past few decades by Imperial legions and temporarily conquered. But the moment the bulk of the invading legion had withdrawn, both continents had risen up against the Imperial occupations attempting to gain permanent footholds. Rumors abounded that Koth was preparing to return to both continents and invade again. But then, rumors had been floating for as long as Will could remember that a full Imperial legion was bound for Haelos at any minute to conquer the rest of it, too.

They arrived at the Heart, and his grandfather led him to the ornate central dome built in the central courtyard of the Heart compound. The structure was several stories tall with an elaborately carved façade and a tall spire over the center.

They stepped inside, and he was galled to see the domed edifice filled with children ranging from perhaps ten to twelve summers and their beaming parents. He towered over the other initiates, which had the one benefit of allowing him to glower at his grandfather unimpeded.

Aurelius refused to acknowledge Will's silent disgust.

The high matriarch came into the room in full, formal Heart regalia, all white clothing with a beautifully embroidered Heart tabard edged in gold thread to indicate her rank. She stopped at a large stone altar draped in white cloth.

No fewer than eight Royal Order of the Sun knights stood around the altar, and Lord Justinius himself, commander of the Royal Order of the Sun in Haelos, moved up beside the high matriarch. Another half dozen Royal Order of the Sun squires ringed the room, and Will had noted at least that many more just outside the Heartstone cupola.

Lenora gave a short speech about the wondrous gift of Heartstones to the peoples of Urth and how grateful she was that all people could live full and complete lives, free from fear of premature death, thanks to the miracle of resurrection. He listened more closely as she launched into an explanation of how resurrection worked.

"If you die, your spirit separates from your body and spends some time wandering this plane before it finds its way beyond the Veil to the spirit realm. During that drifting time, you may see bright points of light and be attracted to them. Don't be afraid. Go to them. Small lights are healers trained in helping spirits return to their bodies. A big, bright light that shines across the land is known as a Glow. It comes from a Heartstone. The larger the stone, the farther its Glow is cast. All you have to do is step into the Glow, and the stone will do the rest. It will draw you back to this realm, reform your body, and send you back into it. You will wake up in a Heart chapter as if you've woken from a nap."

The children nodded in wonder, but Will frowned. He wanted to question her closely about how the stone magically re-created bodies, how spirits returned to bodies, and most importantly, where the stone drew its magic from. But Lenora did not solicit any questions from the children. Rather, she had them line up and one by one, stick their hand down into an opening in the top of the altar, and touch an actual Heartstone. So *that* was why all the Royal Order of the Sun knights were present.

He hung back until all the children had touched the stone and their attention turned to the tea and cookies laid out on tables across the room. Lenora smiled encouragingly at him as he pulled a face and stuck his hand into the box. The stone felt like any other stone at first, cold and hard, carved and polished into a smooth sphere. He splayed his palm across its surface, and that was when its magic jangled up his arm painfully.

He jerked his hand back.

"What is amiss?" Lenora asked.

"Is it always painful like that?"

"Painful?" she echoed.

Lord Justinius challenged, "Painful how?"

Aurelius materialized beside him, frowning. Will answered the knight slowly. "It felt like . . . saw teeth zinging up my arm. Not as if it wished to hurt me, but as if it did not like me touching it." He didn't add that the energy shooting up his arm had actually felt sentient. And that it had communicated dislike for him.

"Touch it again," Lenora ordered, placing her hand in the box before him.

Reluctantly, he reached inside the box. The stone felt warm this time, vibrating in . . . agitation, maybe? His discomfort at the contact was more pronounced, not just a physical pain but a soul. In spite of his resolve not to, he yanked his hand back again.

Lenora observed, "This is a Heartstone from Koth. But Bloodroot is native to Haelos."

"So did it not like me, or does Bloodroot not like it?" Will asked.

"More to the point," Aurelius interjected, "can Will resurrect through it or would it reject his spirit?"

He stared at his grandfather in horror.

Lenora spoke slowly. "I think it would resurrect him. The experience might be unpleasant or even painful, though, since Will's energies and the stone's are not synchronized with one another."

She *thought* he could resurrect? But she was not certain? Splendid. Just splendid. He'd always assumed that, should his adventures go terribly awry, he could at least resurrect somewhere and then disappear like his parents had and start a new life. But now he might not be able to come back from death *at all*?

Well, that certainly cast the whole quest to wake the Sleeping King in a new light.

Was starting a rebellion worth risking his permanent existence?

Or more accurately, how badly did he want to live in a place where the Empire held no sway? He honestly could not envision such a place. Through the summer's calm in Dupree, the idea of waking the Sleeping King and fomenting a rebellion to throw Koth out of Haelos had begun to seem completely absurd. Maybe they would all be better off just getting on with their lives and forgetting about childish quests. The new governess was proving to be a great deal more reasonable than her predecessor and had already reversed the worst of Anton's excesses.

Even his grandfather seemed in no rush to have him continue the quest. Aurelius kept arranging for more and yet more training sessions stretching out for months or possibly years to come.

Rosana and Raina were safe in the Heart. Eben had taken over many of Hyland's trade dealings, Raina's friend Cicero had returned to some remote forest in the west that he called home, and stars knew where Sha'Li was or what she did with her days. She'd earned the Tribe of the Moon mark on her cheek, though, and seemed content now that she had it. They were all in good places and their lives were stable. Perhaps abandoning their quest was for the best.

But no sooner had the thought crossed his mind than a dark and terrible sense of foreboding rose up, starting at the soles of his feet and climbing through his belly. Something bad approached. It was time to move on from this place if he did not wish to be crushed by it.

Whether or not the feeling was Bloodroot's doing, he could not tell. But the warning lay heavy on his heart and would not lift. Trouble was coming for him. And soon.

Endellian looked down at the list of summonses her father had issued for today. It was far below her station to act as his personal secretary; however, the position gave her priceless insights into the inner workings of the court. She was privy to every detail of how Maximillian ran his Empire, and she saw every thread he tugged in his never-ending game of manipulating his web of power.

High Hunter Lovak, Master of the Hounds, was due to

arrive in Maximillian's trophy room any moment. Nobody dared to be other than exactly punctual with her father, of course. The location of this meeting was somewhat unusual; Maximillian usually preferred to receive his subjects in one of his throne rooms. All of them were designed for maximum intimidation, built as impressive displays of the limitless wealth and reach of the Kothite Empire.

Not that her father's trophy room was any less overwhelming to the uninitiated. Every corner of the vast space was crammed with one priceless artifact after another. The entire history of Urth and its peoples could be told in that one room.

Lovak was the breeder and trainer of a line of magical hunting hounds who could track unusual trails. They had successfully been trained to hunt individuals with specific magical gifts, to hunt psionicists, even to hunt mystical creatures.

She wandered over to the dwarf encased in amber that stood just beside the adjoining door to her father's small golden throne room. She'd always found the awareness shining in the fellow's eyes fascinating. What must it be like to be eternally trapped like that? Never moving, never speaking, never dying? Truly, it must be a fate worse than death to be trapped inside one's own mind forever.

"Ahh, there you are, daughter. I require your grandson for this next audience."

Her grandson, Broccar Gyrkin, was the only son of her daughter by Tarses, Jaelanna Tarses. Both Jaelanna and Broccar had inherited the general's jann race. She bowed her head in acquiescence and spoke over her shoulder to her foster sister, 'Nandu. "Fetch Broccar to us immediately."

The blue dragon, trapped in human form, bowed low, managing as she always did to infuse the gesture with a certain irony. 'Nandu was a source of private irritation to her. She understood why her father had hatched a dragon and hand raised her at his court but that didn't mean she had to enjoy sharing his attention with a foster sibling. Particularly when

Maximillian had set 'Nandu to watch over her in case Endellian should ever contemplate seizing the Golden Throne for herself. The dragon was also a reminder—intentional or not, she could not tell—of her inability to master the awesome power her father had used to hatch and control such a being. Maximillian held the dragon's leash, and Maximillian only.

A door opened to admit High Hunter Lovak. The fellow had mostly finished his obeisances to the Emperor when Broccar joined them. Endellian watched her grandson fondly as he displayed a pleasingly muscular leg to Maximillian in a bow. Trained practically from birth by Ammertus in the arts of combat, Broccar was a magnificent gladiator of a young man, proud and strong and brave. He took after his grandsire Tarses.

Maximillian was speaking. "—would have you train four new braces of hounds, Lovak. One to hunt totems. Another to hunt Great Beasts. And the last two—I would have you send one to Pan Orda and the other to Haelos."

Lovak asked, "What will the last two be trained to hunt, Your Resplendent Majesty?"

"Jann."

Lovak frowned faintly at that. Hunting beings of a common race was well beneath the superior abilities of the magically enhanced canines descended directly from the Great Mastiff, a Great Beast of Koth. "We already have elemental hounds and hunters proficient at hunting similar beings."

Maximillian smiled slightly. "Ahh, but I seek one jann in particular."

Endellian's heart leaped in her chest. The only jann her father would take a personal interest in finding would be his favorite general, none other than Tarses. Was that why Broccar's presence was required? Could the hounds catch the scent of a bloodline, mayhap? She would not put it past Lovak's hounds to be capable of such a thing.

Maximillian touched the intricately carved helm mounted on a table beside him. The piece was the pale, translucent blue of glacial ice, cold and wet to the touch, but it never melted. Not a single drop of moisture ever fell to the table below. Moreover, a faint blue glow emanated from the helm as if light shone through it from behind. "This vessel contains the essence of the Hand of Winter. Or at least a portion of him. Unfortunately, it is too bulky for your purposes."

The story went that, after his conquest of the elemental continent of Pan Orda, General Tarses had attempted to absorb the power of the Hand of Winter, an ice elemental lord, into himself. Why he would try such a thing, she could not fathom. It was apparently some sort of jann ritual.

At any rate, the Hand's spirit had been too much for Tarses to handle, and he had begun to lose himself to the ice elemental who, instead, began to absorb Tarses into himself. A mage standing close to Tarses, a solinari . . . what was his name? She cast back in her memory . . . ahh, yes. Aurelius.

Aurelius, correctly realizing what was happening, had dived forward and absorbed some of the energy of the Hand of Winter into himself in a heroic act. He had used the solinari race's unique ability to absorb magic and hold it temporarily before recasting it to absorb the energy of the ice elemental, hold the elemental's power, and then cast it into this helm, which had been made specifically to contain the spirit fragment of the Hand of Winter.

Aurelius had siphoned off enough power that Tarses was able to regain the upper hand and absorb the remainder of the ice elemental's spirit without incident. Supposedly.

Endellian had to wonder what having the spirit of so great a being inside oneself had done to her lover. She was one of only a few people who knew that Maximillian had worried about how the ice elemental changed Tarses. It made the general unpredictable. And Maximillian could not tolerate such a trait in anyone. Not so close to the Golden Throne.

Maximillian broke her train of thought. "Broccar, can you absorb a portion of the essence contained within this piece and then pass it into another object? Say, this crystal bottle?"

Endellian froze, appalled. The creature whose essence

was stored in the carving had nearly destroyed Tarses. She would not lose her grandson to the Hand of Winter, also. Intellectually, she knew Broccar to be gifted with more than merely his jann race's talent for elemental energy. Like his grandsire, he was able to absorb echoes and shards of essences left by elemental beings long departed. However, she also knew that the greater powers of Kothites diluted from one generation to the next. Case in point: her own lesser powers compared to her sire's.

She knew the markings upon Broccar's skin to be unusual. He held elemental energy in his striations and discharged it at will, losing the markings in the process. It did not hurt that he also had a portion of her extraordinary will, inherited from Maximillian. Perhaps the combination of his powerful grandparents' traits would be enough to do what Maximillian asked of him.

Broccar intoned, "It would be my honor to transfer this energy."

Maximillian nodded. "Proceed."

Endellian could not help tensing as Broccar laid his hands upon the ice helm. The blue glow within the piece raced to where his hands touched the ice, drawn to his flesh like iron filings to lodestone.

Lovak gasped as pale blue markings, as iridescent as the helm itself, appeared on Broccar's hands and forearms, swirling across his skin in the way of jann elemental marks. The glow within the carving diminished as the markings grew.

Broccar lifted his hands away from the helm, giving them a little shake. But as she knew would be the case, no moisture flew from his fingers. He murmured, "Into that crystal bottle, you say?"

"Just so," Maximillian confirmed.

Broccar picked up the small, beautifully carved bottle. It cradled nicely in her grandson's big, callused palm. He unstoppered it, concentrating intently. The blue markings gradually disappeared from her grandson's flesh, and a faint blue glow filled the bottle. Broccar stoppered it and passed it to Lovak.

"Let your hounds get the scent of that," the Emperor ordered. "The jann I seek contains the rest of this spirit inside himself."

"And when the hounds find him?"

"Bring him to me."

Her heart leaped at the prospect of seeing Tarses. Never had she thought to do so again.

Lovak went through the usual bowing and scraping, murmuring about what an honor it was to serve and vowing to succeed or die. But Endellian ignored most of it. Rather, she gauged her father's mood as this audience concluded. He seemed well pleased with Lovak's assurances that his hounds would have no trouble tracking any of the prey Maximillian had set them upon.

When the door had closed behind Lovak, she asked her father a question that had been bothering her for some time. "A number of years ago, you created a magic item of great power—a staff topped with a green rose. I believe its purpose was to cleanse General Tarses of the ice elemental's spirit and restore him to his original self. Whatever happened to that?"

Maximillian's exquisitely embroidered robe billowed as he whirled to face her. He looked intensely irritated, and she recoiled, startled at the strong reaction her question elicited.

"The staff has been discharged recently. But not into my falcon, else the spirit shard in yon helm would have dissipated. Indeed, I dearly desire to know who was the recipient of its magic. Instruct Kodo to investigate the matter upon his return to Dupree and report back to me."

She nodded and turned to escort her grandson from the room.

But Maximillian surprised her by saying, "You did well today, Broccar. Stay. We have much to discuss. You may be just the man to complete your grandfather's work in Pan Orda."

Her father thought to send Broccar to reassert Imperial rule there? His original plan had been to install her as queen of Pan Orda with Tarses as her consort. But Tarses had put an end to all of that with his impulsive stunt.

Broccar in charge of Pan Orda? Well, well, well. That was quite a development. And not to her disliking in the least. She could count on Broccar's loyalty to her. With him in control of Pan Orda, that would put an entire continent effectively in her pocket. Maximillian's pocket, she corrected hastily. It was not as if anything would ever remove her father from the Golden Throne and place her upon it.

Still. Satisfaction coursed through her as she went in search of Kodo.

Eben chafed as he sat through a mind-numbing meeting of the Merchant's Guild. Today's thrilling topic was how to get outlying villages to pay for repairs on potholes in the major trade roads passing through their settlements. It was enough to make a fellow wish for an orc attack or a good chase through the woods fleeing Imperial soldiers.

As if that were not bad enough, a series of minor Merchant's Guild functionaries had come in from remote parts of the colony to report on trade opportunities in their various regions. He listlessly made note of which village was in short supply of ore for its smithy, which one had a surplus of grain to sell, and the like.

Yet another nervous, rotund merchant cleared his throat to speak. Eben was going to fall off his chair from the boredom before too much longer.

"—new trade opportunity this autumn and winter with groups sheltering in the forest nearby, which is itself a magnificent natural resource—"

The Merchant's Guildmaster must have been as bored as Eben, for he interrupted, droning, "What kind of groups? And what supplies will they need? Give us specific examples."

The fellow hemmed and hawed for a moment, and then

his face lit up. "On my way here, I ran into a curious crew led by a rather strange forester. I would say he spoke to the animals if'n my eyes did not deceive—"

Eben sat up sharply. "Where? Was there a young human fellow with him? Maybe twenty summers in age? Handsome? Strong?"

"Well, umm. Err, yes. As a matter of fact, there was a youth like that. And a weasely looking pair of twins. Longest, most pointed noses you ever saw on humans. And a girl. An elf of some kind with brown designs drawn on her face."

Eben was out of his chair like an arrow shot across the room and had the man by the shirtfront before he was aware himself of having moved. "Exactly where did you see this group? And when? What day was it?"

The man stammered, "Out p-past Southfield. W-west side of the Wylde Wold on the Unicorn's Run. Shepard's Rest it were."

"How long ago?" Eben demanded. Belatedly, he realized he was choking the fellow, and he turned the merchant's shirt loose.

The fellow tugged his shirt down and smoothed it back into place as he took a nervous step back from Eben. "Well, now, lemme think. Woulda been two days before I left to come here, which was Saturday last, so that would make it two Thursdays past . . . and today being Monday, that would make it ten, no eleven, days past," the merchant announced triumphantly.

Eben grimaced. A week and a half was a long time for a group on the move. They could be anywhere by now. He asked urgently, "You say they're planning to winter over in the Wylde Wold?"

"They was buying supplies like they's a-plannin' to. I don't see five people carrying all that gear and food very far on they's backs. I'd say as they has a camp close by and is squattin' there fer a spell."

Eben turned and raced out of the room, heedless of the

calls of consternation following him. *Finally*. A solid lead on Kendrick. And mayhap, even Tarryn.

He had to get out to Shepard's Rest before Kendrick and Tarryn disappeared yet again. Time was the enemy now.

Sha'Li was on Raina duty today. The Royal Order of the Sun had all its members running around the countryside chasing down greenskins and killing them. Which made the back of her neck crawl, truth be told. Although her coloration was black, her race skirted uncomfortably close to being lumped in with the goblins, ogres, orcs, and other nonhuman races the Royal Order of the Sun was currently slaughtering.

Lizardmen might think of themselves as an ancient and noble race with a rich culture and heritage, and their mythology might have them descending from dragons, but that did not mean the Empire or its lackeys saw them the same way.

The Tribe of the Moon did most of its work in the wild places, defending nature and the people who lived in harmony with it, so there was not much for her to do here in this city of stone that felt dead beneath her feet. To pass time, she'd been sparring with any lizardman in or around Glass Lake who would give her a fight, learning more about disarming traps, and honing her ability to move stealthily. And of course, Selea Rouge was teaching her the finer points of assassination. But she was so bored with training she was half-tempted to suggest to Raina that the two of them make a run for it and flee Dupree this very minute.

Today, Raina had been sent to the home of some important slave trader to heal the members of the house, several of whom had fallen ill. It had taken the human healer about ten minutes to cure everyone from the mistress of the manor to the lowest of the servants of some sort of fever and hacking cough that had put them all abed, looking even paler and more deathly than humans already did.

She snorted. The only reason it had taken Raina that long

to heal them all was because they were sissies about getting their healing slowly enough so it didn't hurt. She shook her head. How such soft, weak creatures dominated all others on Urth, she could not understand.

They'd barely left the slaver's house when Raina asked, "What's that place?"

Sha'Li looked in the direction her friend did and spied a broad, open-walled barn large enough to house the entire combat floor of a small Diamond. "Slave market," she spat in disgust.

"Do you mind if I stop in there? I'd lay odds the ailment I just healed in that house either comes from yon slave barn or has spread to it."

"Not a good place for you, it is." Sir Hrothgar would be deeply annoyed if he found out she'd let Raina venture into such a place. Which was almost reason enough to let her friend go there.

"I won't be long," Raina said over her shoulder, hurrying toward the big shed. Scowling, Sha'Li strode after her.

"In front let me go, at least," she demanded, tugging at Raina's elbow. Extending her claws, Sha'Li led the way into the shade of the slave market.

"I've been to one of these before, you know," Raina declared. "The day Kendrick bought Eben from the slavers who took him and Marikeen. Kendrick didn't have enough gold to buy Eben's sister, too but said the slavers would not hurt her because she was so valuable as a slave."

"To her what happened?" Sha'Li asked, curious.

"Rosana thought she escaped her slavers during the riots just before Anton was deposed. But Eben has had no word from her, and no one has seen her since."

"Alive I hope she is."

"Me, too." Then, Raina mumbled, "I'd forgotten how awful these places are."

Sha'Li looked around in deep distaste. No matter if most fell into slavery through actions of their own—crimes committed or taxes unpaid. The people chained like work animals to long hitching posts stretching the width of the building were a dispirited and bedraggled lot.

Supposedly this was a relatively clean, bright, and well-kept market where the slaves were fed, washed, and warm. *Still. Chains.* She commented tartly, "Heal them you should not. Only increase their value you do. More money into pockets of filthy slavers you put."

"You may be right." Raina sighed. "But I cannot bring myself to watch any human being suffer so and not take action to help them."

"Soft are you."

"Aye. Which is why I make a point of having a friend as strong in spirit as you."

Sha'Li scowled out of general principles but was secretly pleased.

"All right, Sha'Li. Let's do this. I promise I'll be quick about it."

Raina hurried down the rows as promised, spewing healing like a steam vent spitting mud in the swamps back home. But she stopped, and Sha'Li nearly plowed into her as they came upon a row of children. They were scared and dirty, and most of them had colds. Raina healed them gently, taking her time with casting healing into each one of them so it would not hurt. As they reached the end of the row, Raina lifted a written tag upon the ropes of the last child. She lifted it, frowning. "This says they're already sold. To whom?"

A slaver who happened to be walking past stopped. "They's likely Krugar's kids."

"Captain Krugar? Of the colonial militia?" Raina blurted in surprise that mirrored Sha'Li's.

"Aye."

"What use does he have for a bunch of children?"

"Oh, him. He buys all the kids he can lay hands on. Been doing it for fifteen years or more. Slavers know ta bring all the young'uns here. Pays top price fer 'em, Krugar do."

"With children what does he?" Sha'Li demanded suspiciously.

"Puts 'em in the legion, 'e does. Raises 'em and trains 'em up. Far sight better life than most slaves end up gettin'."

Sha'Li took a quick head count. There were eleven children in the row. If, say, ten children per week was about average, that meant he was putting on the order of five hundred youths into the militia annually. And he'd been doing so for *years*. A substantial percentage of the entire Haelan legion was likely to feel deep, personal gratitude to Krugar for saving them from a worse fate.

Raina looked thunderstruck.

"What think you to cause that expression?"

The slaver wandered off, and Raina muttered low, "Think about it. Krugar has turned the loyalty of a large chunk of the Haelan legion away from the Empire, away from the general in charge of the legion, and even away from the governor. It is loyal to *him*."

"A rebel is he, or merely angling to take over the legion one day?"

"That is an *excellent* question. Clearly, he is a man who bears watching."

Bah. She was no lover of intrigue and secrets. "Finish healing these wretched souls, shall we?" Sha'Li muttered in distaste.

The last row of slaves awaiting sale was mostly big, burly men, scarred and hard-looking. They lounged casually, seemingly unconcerned about their fates.

A half dozen well-dressed men turned down the row with a man dressed like a noble in the lead.

"Bogatyr," Raina muttered.

"Who?"

"Head of the Dupree Entertainer's Guild."

Sha'Li tensed as she realized the man and his entourage were headed straight for her and Raina. "Go now we must."

Behind them, Bogatyr boomed, "Fine lot of fighters this week. Good fodder for the Diamond. New season's starting up in just a few weeks. Could use a few more gladiators to round out the schedule. What do you say, boys? Any of you interested in testing yourselves against some filthy green-skins?"

A shout went up from the row of men they'd just left behind.

Raina rolled her eyes at Sha'Li, who rolled hers back, and they headed for the exit.

The slaver who'd spoken with them before sidled up to them. "Thanks be to ye fer the healin', White Heart. Just doubled me take, ye did. I owe ye."

"No thanks are necessary." Sha'Li heard the sarcasm in her friend's voice, but the slaver seemed to miss it.

"Still. I pays me debts. And I likes ye Heart types. You's good to us regular folk. Al'ays treated me and mine righ'. Gonna do ye a favor." His voice dropped to a low rasp, and he mumbled from behind unmoving lips, "I gots a tip fer ye. Them Kithmar—you know—them white tiger rakasha slavers wot shows up now and again?"

The same Kithmar clan who'd been in league with Anton during his invasion of the Forest of Thorns? Sha'Li's ears perked up.

"They takes side jobs from time ter time." The slaver drew a finger across his throat in a slitting motion and whispered, "Ye catch me drift?"

The Kithmar took contracts to kill people? To her knowledge, they were not sanctioned assassins. Next time she saw Selea, she would have to mention it. Mayhap he would take action to stop them if they were taking unsanctioned hits.

"Way I hears it, they's mighty miffed coz a certain personage they used ta do business with is cutting them out of his new action."

Anton was stirring up trouble again? Oh, joy.

"What's this personage up to now?" Raina asked.

"Dunno. I jus' know 'im and them Kithmar's on the outs."

Sha'Li was glad to leave the miserable place. But as they made their way across the expanse of Governor's Square, a man in rough woodsman's garb fell in beside her. Sha'Li was stunned to see a deep green Tribe of the Moon mark on the fellow's right cheek. Slowing her pace, she fell a little behind Raina, who was distracted watching a group of acrobats perform.

"Greetings, friend," he mumbled.

"To you the same," she muttered back, aware that he was staring at the moon and star mark on her own cheek. Its white coloration was unheard of among tribe members.

"I'm to deliver a message to the black lizardman girl: do not forget that our kind protects the protectors of nature."

She stared at the man. "What means this nonsense?"

"When the time comes, you must protect Kerryl Moonrunner. His work must continue."

Raina had continued to walk on, and Sha'Li stopped to stare at the man. "He kidnapped our friend. We want him back."

"You must choose between your friends and your tribe."

"Betray my friends you ask of me?"

"If you wish to retain that mark, you will be loyal to the Tribe of the Moon above all. Will you keep your vows or not?"

"Of course I will," she blurted. She was angrier and more scared than she dared let on. Obviously this was a warning shot across her bow that she'd been skirting dangerously close to putting her friends ahead of her family. But to betray her friends . . . that did not sit well with her.

Troubled, she looked up at the woodsman. "Who sends this message to me?"

A shrug. "I do not know. I am merely the messenger." A pause, then he blurted, "Is your mark really white, or is that just a trick of your coloring?"

She shrugged in return. As if she had any idea why Lunimar had chosen to turn her mark its unheard-of color. Tribe marks were known to appear in gray, red, green, silver, and gold, even in black, but never white.

The man spoke in a whispered rush. "I was also told to share a piece of information with you. The Coil is asking around about some kids who went up north a while back, a tribe-marked lizardman among them."

"Asking what?" she demanded.

"What they found. Where they are now."

She hissed in a sharp breath.

"I'd lie low for a while if I were you. Go for a nice, long swim somewhere else."

Outright alarm blossomed in Sha'Li's belly now. "For the message and warning, thanks be."

"We take care of our own." The man peeled away from her into the crowd crossing Heart Square and disappeared. Sha'Li hastened to rejoin her friend.

Raina asked, "Who was that?"

If only she could talk to the healer about the strange exchange. Raina was so much better than she at understanding hidden meanings and nuances of politics. She didn't like that her tribe brethren were keeping secrets from her. What exactly was Kerryl Moonrunner doing that was important enough to abandon Kendrick Hyland? Besides the fact that he was of noble blood, Kendrick was innocent of any wrongdoing. One of the Tribe of the Moon's main tenets was "Protect the Innocent."

She had a bad feeling about this. How was she supposed to help Kerryl Moonrunner without harming her friends?

And then there was the news about the former governor. Anton was hunting them, was he? That was an unpleasant wrinkle, indeed.

Rynn rarely moved about the streets of Dupree in the daytime on account of his open eye. It was not as if he could pull a hat down over his third eye. Its lid never closed, and anything that touched the eyeball directly caused him excruciating pain. Furthermore, covering his third eye with a patch caused him dizziness and disorientation. He was meant to function with all three of his eyes in the same way that humans were meant to function with both of theirs.

If forced to go out in public, he usually wore a circlet made of intricately twisted wire that formed a cage over and cleverly disguised his third eye as if it were part of the headpiece. Even with the circlet firmly in place, he still wore his hood pulled far forward to hide his face from passersby. His appearance usually drew so much reaction from females that it was impossible for him to move anywhere without drawing a great deal of attention.

He hurried to the tall gate in front of Hyland's house and knocked. One of Hyland's men let him in, and he left the street in deep relief. "Is Guildmaster Aurelius here by any chance?" he asked the guard.

"Nay, but everyone else in Dupree is. Come join the party."

Rynn halted sharply. "Who is here?"

"Young master Will, Initiate Raina, Sister Rosana. And Eben just barged in here with his hair on fire demanding to see the guildmaster. Guess you'll have to wait in line to see Aurelius, you will."

Rynn stepped into Hyland's study. Although Aurelius had been taking care of Hyland holding's most urgent affairs from the room for some time, it would always be Leland Hyland's office in his mind. The man's spirit was imprinted in every corner of the room.

"Rynn! What brings you here?" It was Rosana, the pretty gypsy girl who liked Will.

"I need to speak with the guildmaster and was hoping not to have to go to his guild to do so."

Raina, the other healer, piped up. "Will sent a note to him a quarter hour ago requesting his company here at his earliest convenience. He is a busy man, and we may have to wait a while, but I'm confident he'll come when he can. Can you tarry a bit?"

"I can."

Eben spoke from the far end of the room near the fireplace. "The only person missing now is Sha'Li. Mayhap we should send for her, as well."

Raina answered, "She has gone to her lodgings to fetch her belongings, and then she will be along."

Some emergency was clearly afoot, which was alarming, given the nature of the connection between these youths. The others clustered in two small knots, murmuring among themselves. He sighed, feeling very much the outsider. He had not yet earned his way into their confidence. Until then, he would have to be patient. Which was a challenge given the underlying panic vibrating throughout the room.

The door opened behind him to admit Guildmaster Aurelius. *Hmm. That was fast.*

He listened with interest as Raina told her news of Anton being up to some new mischief, Will warned of a terrible foreboding that had come over him, and Eben finished by sharing news of a promising sighting that sounded a great deal like Kerryl Moonrunner, Kendrick, and the missing scout, Tarryn.

Aurelius asked, "And what brings you here, Rynn?"

"I have word from a reliable source that a Black Ship is en route to Dupree bearing a pack of Imperial hounds."

Aurelius's eyes lit with comprehension, but Will asked, "What's special about Imperial hounds?"

Rynn looked over at the impossibly young, forest-bred human. "The Emperor's hounds can track anything and anyone. They are known, in particular, for tracking psionicists." He added lightly, gesturing at his third eye, "Like me."

Aurelius added, "No place in the colony will be safe for Rynn. They are relentless in pursuit of their quarry. Once they catch a scent, only death can stop them."

Eben spoke up. "I propose that we head west to Shepard's Rest. We can check out the lead on Kendrick and take Rynn away."

Aurelius nodded thoughtfully. "It does seem as if events are conspiring to push the lot of you into motion once more. I only hope the additional training you all have received will be adequate to keep you safe."

Will shrugged. "It will have to be enough."

The door opened, and everyone in the room turned, tensed, toward the intruder. The lizardman girl Sha'Li burst in. She ground to a halt, staring back at the party as everyone stared at her.

"What? Grown flesh my face has?" she demanded.

Ahh. Nicely done. Sha'Li's comment effectively broke the tension in the room.

"What news have I missed?"

Eben spoke eagerly. "We leave for the west. A merchant out by Shepard's Rest has seen Kendrick and Tarryn."

"Ready to go am I. Leave now, shall we?"

A plan was quickly formed for Rosana to accompany Aurelius to the Heart. While he had a private word with High Matriarch Lenora, she would pack her and Raina's belongings and bring them back to Hyland's house so Raina would not draw the attention of the Royal Order of the Sun. Will would go to the Mage's Guild to get his possessions, and Sha'Li and Rynn would raid Hyland's storeroom and pull additional provisions for the entire group.

It was hard to believe that so much rested upon the shoulders of a group so young and inexperienced. If he had not seen the evidence himself that these youths had already been touched by extraordinary forces, he would have questioned his marching orders from his secret superiors. Not the paxan Oneiri, who were secretive in their own right—his *other* superiors. The ones he never spoke of, not even to Phinneas, his mentor and closest friend.

But there was no denying this group's odd credentials— Will's strange connection to a tree spirit, Raina's impressive magics, Sha'Li's rare, white Tribe of the Moon mark, Rosana's strange rose markings that possibly marked her as the one he sought. He did not know yet if Eben was in some way special, but he made a mental note to observe the jann closely.

He noted when Raina subtly signaled Aurelius that she needed a word with him alone. The two stepped into the small solar attached to Hyland's study and closed the door. He shouldn't have eavesdropped, but this group had so many secrets, and it was his assignment to discover them. Using his mental powers at the full extent of their abilities, he probed the girl's mind as she spoke to the solinari.

"—something I must give to you for safekeeping." She was reluctant to hand it over, whatever it was.

A light inhalation of surprise from Aurelius when he saw the object.

"I can't think of anyone else whom I would trust its safety to."

"I'll put the Sleeping King's crown in the safest spot within the Mage's Guild treasury. After last spring's break-in, we've significantly increased its security measures. I'll make sure a Celestial Order man is on guard around the clock as long as this rests there."

"Can you disguise it in some way?" the girl asked. *Ahh. Clever idea.*

"Yes, if the crown itself will let me."

"Here. Let me commune with it." The girl could speak to an object? This crown was sentient, then? Whose was it? Surely not *the* Sleeping King's.

"I think it will tolerate being disguised in a deceptive fashion," she said.

"I'll see to it personally," Aurelius promised. Rynn heard them moving and raced to the desk, where he sat down and busied himself pretending to study a map.

"Dinner should be ready soon. Do you join us?" Aurelius asked him.

"With pleasure." They moved into the dining room, entering just as one of the house guards came in from the hallway.

"Excuse me, Guildmaster. You have a guest who says he's here on Imperial business."

Aurelius replied to the guard, "Give us a moment and then send him in." The solinari glanced warningly at Rynn, who nodded and moved quickly back into Leland's office, closing the door behind him.

He pressed his ear to the panel.

"Guildmaster Aurelius Lightstar?" a new voice asked briskly.

"Yes. I believe we have not met, Commander."

"I'm Thanon of the Imperial Legion of Koth, commander of the Talons of Koth. You are hereby summoned to present yourself to his Most Resplendent Majesty, Emperor Maximillian the Third, with all due haste. To that end, I have the ritual components necessary to transport you to the Isle of Nissa, from whence you shall travel by portal to the Imperial Seat."

Horror shuddered through Rynn. No one came back from an Imperial summons. It was tantamount to the most terrible kind of death sentence.

Aurelius spoke with admirable calm, though. "If I might have a short time to put my affairs in order here? After the untimely demise of the landsgrave of Hyland, I have been managing his estates for the governess. I will need to let her know I am leaving."

"Of course, Guildmaster. Say, first thing in the morning?"

"Very well. Thank you for your understanding, Commander Thanon."

The Imperial Army officer was shown out, but Rynn stayed hidden to be safe. Aurelius came in and said grimly, "I need to speak with Phinneas immediately. I will wait here."

When Rynn returned with his mentor, Raina was upstairs, the others had left, and Aurelius was alone in Leland's study. The solinari rose when they entered but did not sit back down. Rather, he began pacing nervously.

"As I'm sure Rynn told you, I am summoned to court to appear before Maximillian."

"My sympathies," Phinneas responded soberly.

"Let me be blunt. I need more than your sympathy. I know things that I would rather not have come under the Emperor's direct scrutiny. Can you remove them from my mind?"

Phinneas pulled a doubtful face. "I can conceal thoughts and erase memories from all but the most intense scrutiny. But should the Emperor himself tear into your mind, there is nothing anyone on Urth can do to conceal what rests there."

"I must ask you to try, if you are willing."

"If I put all my power into erasing a single memory, I might be more successful."

Rynn sympathized with Aurelius's dilemma. How did a man choose from a lifetime's worth of thoughts, memories, and learned bits of information to erase? With a nod of decision, Aurelius sat down at Leland's desk and pulled out a piece of parchment. He wrote quickly upon it a single paragraph. He folded it, sealed it with wax, and pressed his signet ring into it.

Then, to Rynn's surprise, Aurelius passed it not to Phinneas but to him. "Hide this in the safest place you know; and if I return, give it back to me."

He bowed his head in acknowledgment and took the folded note.

"Help me, Rynn," Phinneas said. He stepped forward and laid his hands on Aurelius's head alongside his master's as Phinneas intoned, "Show us what it is you wish to forget, my friend."

Rynn was stunned at the revelations as he probed the guildmaster's thoughts. Will Cobb was both his grandson and the son of an Imperial fugitive. But that wasn't the memory that terrified the solinari. The memory he'd chosen to lose was one of High Matriarch Lenora revealing to Aurelius that the youth's mother came from a long-lost line of pastors, whose purpose was to care for and speak for the Great Trees and their tree lords. If Maximillian learned that, Will Cobb was *dead*.

And then there were no more memories. Just waves of forgetting, one piling on top of the next. But no matter how many they sent into the solinari's mind, Rynn feared they would not be enough.

W ill inhaled deeply. He hadn't realized how much he missed the rich manure odor of fresh-plowed dirt. By the Lady, it was good to be out among the fields and crofts and forests once more, away from the crowded buildings, cobbled streets, and stench of humanity that was Dupree.

He was tired of waiting around. Tired of not taking action to find his friend. Tired of having the quest to wake the Sleeping King hanging unfinished over his head. Tired of endless lessons and lectures on the nature of magic and its sources. Of the exhausting, demoralizing practice sessions with Krugar.

More and more recently, though, his lessons with Krugar had been following the same pattern. Krugar would show him the first step or two of an attack or counterattack, and all of a sudden, Will would be executing the entire sequence, having had no idea at all that he'd ever learned it and locked it away in his muscles' memories. It was as if Tiberius had taught Will all the pieces of being an accomplished warrior but had failed to teach him *when* to use which piece. It was incredibly frustrating.

Every time he did it, Krugar went silent and grim, eyeing him as if he was some sort of dangerous creature. Krugar and Aurelius would exchange a loaded glance and sometimes a faint nod from one to the other. If nothing else, his training sessions had seemed to build a rapport between Krugar and Aurelius. They kept telling him to listen to his muscles and trust his instincts. But most of the time Will feared the only instinct speaking to him was an irascible truant with no care whatsoever for his host's weapon training.

Bah. He knew how to use magic, and that was what mattered in a fight. Granted, magical energy was finite whereas the number of swings in a sword was limited only by a warrior's stamina and strength. Still. Magic was a potent tide turner at the very least.

He and Rosana had slipped out of Dupree with the flow of homeward-bound farmers and laborers who lived in the villages nearby, and no one even gave them a second glance. He liked the idea that people saw them as a couple. He'd never expected to think of such things, but mayhap he should consider proposing to her. They could settle down someplace quiet—not in Dupree, where a death sentence lay upon his head—build a little house, start a family in a few years. It would be a good life.

Will was stunned by the amount of destruction outside the city walls. Practically every structure they passed was damaged—windows smashed in, roofs collapsed, fences destroyed, or the buildings burned down. The greenskins who'd invaded the capital of Dupree had not spared the surrounding area from their marauding. A smell of fire still hung in the air, and a general pall lay over the countryside. Bloated corpses of cows and sheep and goats still littered fields, and circling vultures wheeled in spirals overhead.

The memories conjured by all this death and destruction were almost more than Will could bear. The night his parents had been killed had looked much like this except lit by the ghoulish light of torched houses and tainted by the smell of blood and sound of screams.

He did not wish to appear weak to Rosana, so he set his jaw and strode onward, in a hurry to leave it behind. She seemed to understand his need and was uncharacteristically silent beside him as she hustled to keep up.

They rejoined the others at the rendezvous point they'd set. Everyone seemed disturbed by the sights they'd seen upon leaving the city. Subdued, they agreed to travel late into the evening to put more distance between themselves and anyone who might attempt to pursue them. In particular, the Royal Order of the Sun.

Raina was apparently not allowed to take off her colors. Doing so would indicate resignation from her order, or something like that. She had, however, covered the bright white of her surcoat with a dark cloak. She was growing into a beautiful young woman, though, and her striking golden hair was hard to miss. He doubted that she'd left the city unnoted. Word would get back to the Royal Order of the Sun that she had fled Dupree. Hopefully, the high matriarch would be able to convince the knights not to give chase.

It was like old times as twilight turned to dusk, and dusk turned to night. They fell into their usual marching order with Will and Eben up front, Rosana and Raina in the middle, Sha'Li and Rynn—the paxan in place of their absent friend Cicero—bringing up the rear. They walked a paved Imperial highway, rendering countertracking unnecessary.

The moon rose, lighting their steps along the West Road, which actually ran slightly northwest between the Lochlands and Delphi. Hyland's chef had hastily prepared them a marching supper for tonight, and they munched on the tasty picnic that could be consumed while walking. Night hid signs of the recent invasion, and everyone's mood improved considerably.

As for Will, every passing mile lightened the load upon his shoulders a bit more. Not that the journey before them was free of peril. For surely there would be danger. And of course, there was Lenora's concern that he might not be able to resurrect, should he die. But even with the grim specter of permanent death hanging over his head, it felt good to finally take action.

"What say we find a stopping place before long?" Rynn suggested. "The road before us is long, and we would do well to pace ourselves."

"Tired already, paxan?" Will challenged. "The road will be long, indeed, if you are."

Rynn answered so mildly as to make Will's comment sound a little foolish. "I but thought of the healers who are unaccustomed to heavy physical exertion."

He scowled into the darkness. The man tried to make him look bad in front of Rosana, did he? Will asked the healers solicitously, "Are you tired? Of course, we will stop if you are." There. Take that, Three Eyes.

Raina shrugged. "I've been stomping around Dupree for weeks in an effort to build my strength in case I got a chance to escape."

Escape? She felt trapped in Dupree, too, then? Or mayhap it was the White Heart that trapped her. He could never bear the constant babysitters the Heart forced upon her.

Rosana spoke up soothingly. "I, too, feel fine. Perhaps we should walk another hour or two. Then we can find a nice spot to stop, yes?"

Sha'Li added, "A good place I know a few miles on. To it I'll take us."

The lizardman girl's good place turned out to be a bramble-clogged, rocky, bug-infested clearing next to a deep, quiet stream. If a soul could rightly call this mess of brush and thorns a clearing.

Rynn pulled a gigantic machete out of his pack and chopped at the brambles with shocking efficiency. Will thought to get out his long sword and help, but by the time he fumbled at the ties holding it across his pack and unsheathed the blade, Rynn had a spacious area cut back. Plenty of room for all five of them to spread their bedrolls. Sha'Li was already heading eagerly for the stream to sleep underwater, shedding her outer clothing as she went.

Thankfully, the night was warm, and they had no need of a fire.

The paxan declared that he would take the first watch and sat down with his back against a tree, machete across his upraised knee. *Show-off.* Will noticed Rosana and Raina staring at the handsome paxan, and then their heads going together as they whispered and giggled. Surly, Will volunteered for the second watch—the least desirable of the night watches for it interrupted a person's sleep the most. So there, pretty boy.

By the Lady, it felt good to sleep upon the ground under the stars once more, with a night breeze rustling through the trees for a lullaby.

Raina woke abruptly, alarmed, as something blunt poked her in the side.

"Wake up," a voice whispered. *Rosana*.

"What is wrong?" she whispered back, reflexively gathering magical power to her hands.

"Nothing. Get up quietly and come with me. You won't regret it."

Frowning, Raina rolled out of her warm bedroll. Dawn was just lightening the forest, and the stream they'd bedded down beside burbled quietly as she followed Rosana across it, leaping from stepping-stone to stepping-stone.

On the other side of the stream lay a tiny clearing within a grove of white-barked birch trees. In the middle, Rynn stood in profile to them, shirtless. His fists and forearms were encased in gauntlets that had to have been custom-made to fit the contour of every powerful muscle beneath. They appeared to be made of some sort of crystalline material covered by a fine fretwork of swirling metallic strands. As his hands passed through the air in a fluid and beautiful dance, the crystal caught the first morning light and reflected shards of rainbow color.

Rynn's lean-waisted torso rose to a pair of broad shoulders wreathed in muscle. The whole was tanned and perfect, glistening with sweat. He held a lunging pose with his front knee deeply bent, his back leg stretched out behind him. He glided from one pose to another and all the while, his hands wove those intricate, beautiful patterns. Raina fancied that he wove magic in the air for it seemed to shimmer around his hands. Or maybe that was just his unusual gauntlets causing a trick of the light.

Rynn commenced what could only be described as a combat dance. He punched and kicked, jumped and blocked phantom attacks, but one movement flowed so seamlessly into the next that it reminded her of the ballet dancer she'd seen once as a child. She did not know much about unarmed combat, but she guessed she was looking upon a master of the art.

"Beautiful, yes?" Rosana breathed.

"Yes," Raina replied fervently. The way the man's muscles bunched and stretched, the way he exuded grace and power, was mesmerizing.

A hand landed on Raina's shoulder without warning, and she jumped about a foot straight up into the air. Rosana let out a squeak beside her, as well.

Sha'Li stood behind them, looking back and forth between the girls and Rynn. "Problem there is?" the lizardman girl asked low.

"Nay," Rosana whispered. "We're watching the paxan exercise."

Sha'Li stared at Rynn, the expression in her eyes perplexed. "Why?"

"Because he's beautiful to look at," Rosana answered impatiently.

Sha'Li turned her attention to the paxan who'd moved into a strenuous series of jumps, spins, and kicks almost too fast for the eye to follow. The sequence ended, and Rynn stopped, his chest rising and falling rapidly. Sweat dripped from his brow and ran down his torso in rivulets. Veins corded over his bulging muscles, and Raina had to admit he was one of the most attractive beings she had ever laid eyes upon.

Sha'Li tilted her head first to one side and then the other. Eventually, she announced, "Nope. See it I do not. Ugly as dirt are all flesh-covered land walkers."

"Are you *crazy*?" Rosana whispered. "He's magnificent."

A reptilian version of a snort. "Magnificently ugly. Interesting to spar with he might be, though. Fast hands. To watch out for the feet, must I remember. Fast are those, as well."

Rosana turned in indignation to Sha'Li, gesturing back toward Rynn. "Really? You can look upon that and all you think about is *fighting* him?"

The lizardman tilted her head quizzically once more. "What think you when you watch him?"

Rosana threw up her hands in disgust. "I will never understand your kind."

Raina grinned. Personally, she'd long ago stopped trying to understand Sha'Li. The lizardman girl had a deep sense of honor, was intensely loyal to her friends, and seemed willing to do whatever it took to wake the Sleeping King. That was enough for her.

"What practice performs he now?" Sha'Li whispered.

Raina turned to look at the handsome paxan again. He'd sat down cross-legged in the middle of the clearing, hands resting on his knees, staring at something across the clearing. Very slowly, cautious hop by cautious hop, a large hare emerged into the clearing. Eyes bright and nose twitching, it approached Rynn.

She held her breath. She'd never seen a wild animal approach a humanoid like that before. The animal stopped right in front of Rynn, stretched up on its hind legs, and very carefully touched Rynn's cheek with its whiskers.

Rynn smiled, and the spell was broken. The hare dashed away and disappeared in the brush. The paxan rose in a fluid motion to his feet and started across the clearing toward his shirt, which lay atop a bush.

Raina and Rosana scampered back to camp giggling while a grumpy Sha'Li headed back to the stream. Raina thought she spied Will glaring at Rosana from between slitted eyelids before rolling over and emitting a loud snore.

R ise and shine, Druumedar! The rain's lifted, and the day's a-wasting!"

He jolted awake. A rough cottage took shape around him.

Right. The breastplate. A journey to learn more about its maker. The two men ate and buttoned up the cottage in efficient silence and then headed out.

They trekked due north through the lilting beauty of Kel toward the front range of Groenn's Rest. The path grew steep and narrow as they climbed out of the misty forests and into the highlands above the tree line. Fog filled the valley behind them, making it resemble a witch's cauldron. So far, his leg hadn't pulled any tricks, which was fortunate. His left shoulder hugged a granite cliff face, and his right shoulder hung in midair above a sheer drop into that cloud-like soup. The trail made a sharp switchback, and now his right shoulder hugged the cliff.

"How much farther?" he grunted. The air was getting thin up here, and his breathing was starting to labor. He'd been down out of his mountains for too long. Going soft, he was.

"Not far," his guide puffed back. Nice to know Halvar was huffing, too. It was no good suffering alone.

Gunther came from western Waelan where the mountains formed the end of the Groenn's Rest Range. They were gentler affairs for the most part with broad valleys, long, narrow lakes, and easily hiked slopes. But these monsters in the heart of the Groenn's Rest were young and sharp, shoving aggressively toward the heavens. Like the jagged bones of a spine, they divided the southern forests of Waelan and Kel from the northern deserts of Scythia and Shakkar.

Maybe a half dozen switchbacks later—he'd lost count—a broad plateau opened up without warning. Finally. They'd topped the ridge. Triumph surged through him. Not bad for a one-legged old man.

He looked to the north. The distant line of soaring, snow-capped peaks was magnificent. His dwarven soul yearned to climb among them, to plumb their treasures and to feel their heartbeats in the soles of his feet.

At one end of this flat space, an upthrust of granite, maybe fifty feet tall, rose up out of the plateau like a huge, snaggled tooth. Colored veins streaked the rock, running down its steep sides like sparkling ropes of jewels, blue and green and brown. Copper that would be. He could smell it from here.

"The whole mountain wouldn't be that chock-full of copper, now would it?" he asked Halvar.

"What? Eh, no. They's veins of it throughout all the mountains in this region. Hard to mine, though. They run vertical and deep, right down into the heart o' the rock."

"Where's the smith I'm needing to speak with about my copper piece? Down there?" He eyed the path dipping away from them on the far side of the plateau, twin to the path they'd just climbed, snaking back and forth across the mountainside.

"Aye, in yon valley."

He eyed the switchback path warily. His mechanical leg liked going uphill a great deal more than going downhill. Gads. It was going to take a week to make the trek all the way down to the valley floor.

"Follow me," Halvar said, grinning all of a sudden. He strode over toward that upthrusting tooth of granite and disappeared around its side.

Gunther was not fond of surprises, thank you very much. He stepped around the corner and pulled up short as an opening in the stone face came into view.

A vague sense of déjà vu made him uneasy as he stepped into the cave beyond. His eyes adjusted to the dim light, and as they did, a dwarf-worked chamber came into view. Stone benches ringed the space, and decorative carvings climbed the walls and arched across the ceiling.

"Over here," Halvar said excitedly.

He sounded like a boy at a circus. Scowling, Gunther stumped toward the back of the space.

"Put your shoulder into this wit' me." Halvar leaned against a great stone slab.

As Gunther threw his weight against it, too, the slab began to move, slowly at first, and then more quickly as the roller it rested upon set into motion. Dim light fell into a second, smaller chamber, much more utilitarian than the first. It looked like a mine entrance. Several arched passageways opened off the chamber, the tunnels beyond plunging downward into the mountain. Halvar lit a small torch with flint and steel, and Gunther lit a torch of his own off Halvar's.

"This way." Halvar headed for the tunnel farthest to the right. They descended a set of carved steps for no more than two minutes before Halvar fetched up, announcing, "Here we are."

Gunther was getting downright grumpy over all this mystery. This had better be good. He stepped to Halvar's left and lifted his torch high, staring at the sight that greeted him. A gigantic pulley stood in the center of the cave, a twisted cable thicker than his arm wrapped around its ponderous circumference. Hanging from the cable was a bucket large enough to hold at least six men, if not more.

Halvar strode up to the bucket, which rested only a few inches above the level of the cave's floor. He reached inside the bucket, unlatched what turned out to be a panel in the side of the thing, and opened it inward. "Well, come on, then. Ye don' wanna *walk* down into the valley do ye?"

Grinning in wonder, Gunther stepped into the bucket. "How does it move?"

"Counterweights. I release this brake over here"—Halvar grabbed a long lever on the far side of the bucket hanging down from the cable overhead and threw it forward—"and off we go."

With a mighty squeak, the huge pulley behind them began to turn. They barely moved at first but picked up speed gradually until they were moving along faster than he could've run with both his legs intact. He was forced to hold his torch down into the bucket to keep the wind of their passage from blowing it out. The speed stabilized, and they rushed down the mountain in a ride that was nothing short of exhilarating.

Somewhere in the middle of the mountain, another bucket identical to the one they rode in whizzed past them, heading upward. Eventually, their bucket came to a surprisingly gentle stop in a chamber exactly like the one at the top of the mountain, giant pulley and all.

Except this one was filled with hostile-looking dwarves wielding wicked axes and spears. As pale skinned as humans, they had to be terrakin.

"Hands in the air. Come out real slow, or else we skewer ye," one of the dwarves announced.

"Halvar Langskaag of Kel," his companion declared, hands raised high over his head as if he believed the threat. Gunther followed suit with alacrity. "An' this 'ere be Gunther Druumedar of the Hauksgrafir. Brought 'im to ye, I did."

All eyes turned on him. "State yer business, Druumedar."

Not friendly sorts, these terrakin. Weren't even going to let him out of this cave without interrogating him, were they?

"I, uhh, come in search of information."

Harrumphs greeted that declaration. "What sort o' information?"

"About a piece of metalwork I found a while back. Folks in the know seem to think you be the ones to talk to about it. That your kind mighta made it."

"What piece?" the speaker demanded.

"It's a breastplate. I'm wearing it. Gonna put my hand down to unlace my shirt," he warned the armed crowd. Very slowly, he reached down with his right hand and loosened the laces on his shirt to reveal the top of the ornate breastplate.

"Yorick!" the leader of the bunch called.

A gray-bearded terrakin jostled through the press of his companions and moved over to Gunther. He bent down to stare at the triangle of exposed copper, tilting his head this way and that. Yorick growled, "Where'd ye get that, outlander?"

If the atmosphere in the room had been hostile before, it was downright murderous now. Swords slipped out of hidden sheaths sewn into coats and tabards, and the party behind Yorick took a collective step closer.

Gunther took an involuntary step back, his backside bumping into the bucket. "I found it in an abandoned mine in the Hauksgrafir. Asked the council about it; and they sent me here."

"Not the Miner's Guild Council?" Yorick asked quickly in alarm.

"Of course not. The *Kelnor* Council." Which was short-hand for the anti-Kothite forces who worked out of sight of the Imperial Miner's Guild.

"C'mon, then." Yorick turned and headed for the exit.

As quickly as the swords had come out, they disappeared. He and Halvar were herded forward through a cave and outside into an altogether unremarkable-looking village. The mountains loomed massive and close, like watchful sentinels.

Gunther fell in beside Yorick, and the rest of the crowd of terrakin drifted off, turning for side streets and doorways as they marched through the muddy village. A smithy came into sight, but Gunther was surprised as Yorick led him past it. "You're not a smith?"

"Aye, but no common smith am I."

The rest of the terrakin and Halvar peeled off toward the smithy, leaving him and Yorick to continue on alone. Behind him, Gunther heard bellows of greeting.

Beyond the edge of the village, a path turned off the road toward the mountain, ending at a rough wooden door in the base of the granite hillside itself. Yorick led him inside.

A forge stood inside the door, much like the one in Hauksgrafir would have been had it still been intact. But this one was fully equipped and brightly lit, a pile of hot coals glowing in front of a bellows. The smith gave the bellows an absent pull, and the coals flared, white hot.

"Lemme see your breastplate, then," Yorick said.

He removed his leather armor and outer shirt to reveal the entire bracer.

"Dwarven made, it be."

"And the makers? Who were they?" Gunther asked.

"Old ones."

"Did they work in other metals?" Gunther asked curiously.

"Nope. Jus' copper in these hills. Learned how to harden it up so as to make fer nigh-unbreachable armor. Mind if I clean that up a bit?"

"Not at all." He'd tried to buff the piece himself, but the pale green patina had stubbornly refused to yield to his efforts. With Yorick's help, he unbuckled the breastplate and removed it. While he stretched out the kinks in his shoulders, Yorick picked up the piece and started to hold it out toward the fire.

"Hey, now!" Gunther lurched forward.

Yorick grinned. "Not to worry. Takes a whole lot more than my fire to bother this old copper."

"So you've seen the like before."

"Aye. Time or two."

Gunther subsided, watching as the smith deftly turned the piece this way and that. After a few minutes, he whipped the breastplate out of the fire and dunked it in the quenching pool a few steps beyond the forge. A sizzle and a cloud of steam rose up. Working fast, Yorick clamped the breastplate to his anvil and scrubbed energetically at it with a buffing cloth. The patina gave way to rich, warm copper that turned out to be covered in an intricate pattern of tiny circles embedded in the copper itself.

"What are those?" Gunther asked.

"Pattern left by the hammer blows the smith made. Wildly difficult to master. No one I've ever seen has been able to duplicate the complication and precision of these old pieces. Course, no modern hammer makes a mark on this old copper, anyway."

"How'd this piece get made, then?" Gunther asked.

"Dunno. Had to be a whale of a strong smith to work it, though." He turned the breastplate and commenced rubbing it vigorously again. "Good-sized piece ye've got here. Only stuff like this I've ever seen was broken bits and pieces."

Gunther asked his host, "Have you ever heard of a whole statue clad in the stuff? Bearing an uncanny resemblance to a living dwarf?" He warmed to his topic. "Bigger than life size, but beyond that, perfect, so a fellow could see the whiskers growing in his ears and dirt under his fingernails. Like you'd expect the fellow to up and start talking any second."

The armorsmith jolted violently, staring. He looked around in alarm and crowded right up close to Gunther, whispering in his ear, "Say no more. Not another word. The Empire will already put ye to permanent death for having *seen* one o' them old statues, but to speak about it—they'll wipe out everyone ye've ever met. Unnerstan'?"

"What? Why? What did I say?"

"This old copper—Empire don't wan' nobody knowin' of it. That's why Halvar brought ye here to this hidden valley to live. So's them Imperials wouldna take ye, torture ye, and kill ye when they's done wit' ye."

"I have no wish to live here! My home is on the Hauk—"

"Not anymore. If'n ye wish to live, of course. Ye're in the soup if them Kothites ever find out about this piece."

Memory of the matching copper helm that Imperial soldiers had confiscated from him, not to mention the bracer the dwarven council had insisted on taking to pass up their chain of command, flashed through his head.

He was worse than in the soup. He *was* the soup.

Will's steps dragged as the West Watch Road became more and more familiar to him. There was the stream he'd stopped to drink at when he'd fled the village that terrible night when his parents were murdered. So terrified and alone he'd been. Bits and pieces of it flashed through his mind as individual trees and stones sparked memories.

Even out here, far from Dupree, signs of recent greenskin attacks were everywhere. Burned-out farms, a distinct lack of living farm animals, and far too many fresh graves in village burial yards signaled that the insurrection had been more widespread than just an attack on the city of Dupree. If this was Anton's doing, he was succeeding at making a mess of the colony.

The party moved quietly and camped in the most secluded and defendable spots it could find. On several occasions, they heard movement nearby and went to ground, hiding from the threat until silence reigned once more. Whether they'd heard simple goblins or trained Boki warriors, Will had no idea. Nor did he have any desire to find out.

Imperial patrols were nonexistent. The empire was plenty fast to collect taxes out here on the fringes of civilization, but stars forbid that it should provide adequate protection in return.

They reached the crossroads a mile east of Hickory Hollow, and Rosana looked around curiously. "I know this place.

That night Boki attacked our Heart caravan and you found me, Will. You and I passed through here, yes?"

"Yes," he answered shortly. He'd stood in this exact spot when he'd chosen to leave behind his old life and follow the quest his parents had laid for him instead of returning to Hickory Hollow.

"Your village lies in front of us, does it not?" Rosana persisted.

"Yes."

Raina piped up. "We should stop for a visit. Your friends and family will want to see you."

"A few friends. No family," he corrected tersely.

Eben frowned. "This is the place the Boki attacked, then?" He added quietly, "And where you lost your parents. If you do not wish to return there, we'll understand. We can take the Ring Road around it."

Rosana touched his arm sympathetically. "I'm so sorry."

It was not as if she'd actually opened any old wounds. They were already raw and bleeding. He shrugged. "The attack happened a long time ago."

"Not so long," Eben responded. "Less than a year."

Will really didn't need all of them poking at his painful past like this. "I'm fine," he insisted. "Can we just get moving?"

"In which direction?" Rynn asked soberly. "The fastest route to Shepard's Rest is straight ahead through Hickory Hollow. But if you would rather avoid it, this is the turnoff that will take us around the village."

"Oh, for stars' sake. All of you quit fussing over me, will you? We are bound for Shepard's Rest, and there we shall go. If our path happens to pass through a village I used to live in, so be it."

He took off marching toward the hollow, and after a moment's pause, he heard the others shuffle into motion. So what if the tragic events that had reshaped his life had happened in this place? So what if his parents had died in the woods just beyond the hollow? So what if he'd witnessed the murder of his family's closest friend and his own mentor atop that rise coming into sight ahead? It was just a place. A familiar place. *Home.* No. Just a place now.

The Knot rose before them. He looked up its rocky slopes expecting to see the great, spreading branches of the grandfather hickory that perched atop the promontory—

Where was it? Only dead gray limbs broke the silhouette of the ridge.

Oh no. No, no, no. Not the hickory tree his mother had loved so much. He took off running, clambering over the familiar boulders and scree as if the past year had not happened.

He topped the rise and stopped, appalled. Of all the losses he'd suffered, all the horrors he'd seen, all the blows he'd absorbed, this was one of the hardest. The grand, vibrant, massive tree that had been the namesake, symbol, and unofficial protector of his home was irrevocably dead. The trunk was split, the bark fallen away to reveal the bare, bleached skeleton of the tree. Not a single hint of green, growing vegetation clung to any part of it. A few of the largest lower limbs had crashed to the ground and lay askew around the naked trunk.

He turned away, sick to his stomach and sick at heart. The life force of this entire little plateau was gone. He felt it through his boots without Bloodroot's grief in his gut having to tell him it was so. This little grove had died.

Rynn frowned. "It looks like a dryad grove that has lost its dryad."

Too heartsick to care, he approached the far edge of the Knot. What of the town below? Would anyone still live there? Would all trace of his parents be erased? Was he the only remnant of their existence? Him and a half-mad quest to wake a long-departed king—a sad legacy, indeed.

Steeling himself to face utter devastation, he looked.

He stared down in shock. Not only had the village been rebuilt but it was at least twice the size of before. It was still muddy and squalid, but it bustled with energy. Men he did not recognize picked their way down the main street, and women he did not know leaned over new picket fences to talk with their neighbors. It was as if last year's fiery destruction of the Boki attack had never happened. *At all.*

Furthermore, the recent greenskin attacks had obviously not reached this place. A burgeoning sense of outrage started simmering in his gut. His parents had been *murdered* here. And there was no trace of it. How could all these people blindly move into the area, rebuild the village, and go on with their lives as if nothing at all had happened here? Peasants did not have the resources to—of course. The Empire had rebuilt this place. Forester's Guild, most likely. As if nothing had ever happened here.

His gaze slid reluctantly to the end of the row of cottages running south from the main intersection in the village. The last one on the end had not been rebuilt. Rain and wind and time had scrubbed the ashes away, leaving a patch of bare dirt where his parents' tidy little cottage had stood. A goat grazed unconcernedly in what had been his mother's kitchen garden, now a tangle of weeds.

All trace of the old Hickory Hollow had been . . . *erased.*

It was as if the Empire had just rolled over the tragedy, ignoring the loss of life, the ruined families, the individual stories that had been wiped out. They'd built new buildings and shipped in new peasants to work the lumber trade as if nothing had ever happened.

It was worse than if the village had been left a ruin. At least then some memorial to the fallen would remain, other than a dead hickory tree and its forgotten grove.

Hatred for the Empire and its callous disregard for human life drove like spikes into his skull. *This* was why he would finish the quest. *This* was why he would do everything in his power to help Gawaine overthrow Emperor Maximillian. *This* was why he would oppose the Empire with his dying breath.

Resolutely, he started down the hill toward the village that was no longer his home. He could not count how many times he'd walked this path. He remembered the lamp his mother used to burn in the window for him when he stayed out late roaming the woods around the village. It became visible just here in the curve of the path.

A new and heavy wave of grief filled his stomach, taking him by surprise. Had he actually been harboring a secret hope that his parents had resurrected and come back here to start their lives anew? Surely they would have sent word to him if they yet lived. After all, Will's father had known where he was headed after the attack. Ty had been the one to send him to Dupree to speak with Aurelius.

As unreasonable as it might be, his heart had apparently not accepted the evidence of his mind that all he had ever known was lost. Not until now. Not until he stared down on that barren little patch of dirt where his home had once stood.

His father would have rebuilt the cottage. And his mother would never, ever have allowed her garden to come to such ruin if she lived. No. His parents were well and truly dead and gone. The knowing sank into his bones, the weight of it driving him to his knees.

How long he knelt there, dry eyed in grief and loss too deep for tears, staring down upon his past and watching it drift away into the ashes of time, he did not know.

Eventually, he looked away and was surprised to see his friends standing silent vigil beside him. Even Rynn's head was bowed, his lips moving silently in what looked like some paxan ritual of remembrance.

Of a sudden, he felt old. A heavy sigh slipped out of his chest. "It is time to move on."

The others nodded and picked up their packs. He did the same, and they finished the long trudge down the slope into the hollow.

"Where did the Boki surprise you and your friend on the watch?" Rosana asked, sidling up beside him and slipping her hand into his.

"Back on that Knot where the hickory stood."

"It must have been a beautiful tree while it lived," Rosana said softly.

"It was." His mother always had loved that big, old tree. When there'd been talk of cutting it down during a particularly lean year to pay the village's Imperial taxes, his mother had argued stridently against it. His parents had anonymously donated much of their personal savings to cover the hollow's tax levies so that old tree would be spared.

"Can I 'elp thee find someone?" a male voice asked, startling him out of his reverie.

"We're just passing through," Will answered the watchman. Odd. Once, he'd known every single person in the hollow.

"If ye be needin' supplies, the general store be the building wit' the red sign ahead a piece. And if ye be needin' to wet your whistles, the inn be across the street from the store."

Rosana spoke up from at his elbow. "Thank you kindly, sir. I am a Heart healer. If any villagers have need of healing, let them come to me at the inn."

Will was startled that Raina had not been the one to make the offer, but a glance in her direction showed her clutching her cloak tightly over her colors. Wise. If they wished to pass unnoticed, they could not advertise her presence any more than they could advertise an open-eyed paxan among their number. A quick glance in Rynn's direction showed his hood pulled down low over his forehead.

The watchman moved away, and Will muttered to Rosana, "We have no time to tarry for you healers to put on a clinic."

"I wear Heart colors openly. Not stopping to offer a bit of healing to the locals would draw more attention than stopping. As long as Raina keeps her cloak on and does not do anything crazy, we will be done before you boys finish an ale."

As it turned out, Will downed two ales and a big bowl of stew before the girls finished healing a motley collection of sick and wounded souls. Rosana traded most of her healing potions in return for raw ingredients to make more. He grimaced at the prospect of enduring a smelly pot of brewing potions over the campfire tonight.

Raina murmured, "Are we ready to go, then?"

Will pushed to his feet. "I've got no more business in this place—"

And that was when his old friend Tam ducked in the front door. "Will? Is that you?"

An urge to laugh—and to flee—rolled over him. He endured a back-thumping welcome from the big youth and sank back down onto the bench. "An ale for my friend, here," Will told the innkeeper.

"Ye've got copper rattling around in thy pouch, 'ave thee?" Tam asked curiously. "Where'd ye go after the Boki attack?"

"My father sent me to West Watch Fort to report the attack. Then I got sent to Dupree with the news. One thing led to another, and here I am. What of the others from the hollow? How do you and the old locals fare?" He didn't know quite what to call the original dwellers of Hickory Hollow.

"Fine, mostly. Them Boki took some o' the men and sold 'em into slavery. But the Forester's Guild bought most of 'em out and brought 'em back 'ere. Guild built new cottages and brought in a bunch of new folk to harvest lumber. Times are good."

"And my parents—they did not return or pass through this way?"

"Naw, man. I'm sorry. A bunch o' them Boki scurried off into the woods yelling crazy things about some yellow dragon. We was able to slip most of the women and children into the woods while they ran around chasing yer mum and paw. Saved a lot of lives, that night, they did, leading the Boki a merry chase until . . . well, the Boki caught up wit' 'em."

"Were their bodies found? Buried? Can I pay my respects?" Will asked gruffly.

"Naw. Never found a hair of 'em. Just saw a bunch o'

flashes o' light in the trees and heard the sound o' swords clashing like mad. It went on fer a long time. An' then, it jes' stopped. Quick as they came, them Boki left. They took a half dozen o' the biggest, strongest men from the village an' melted away into the night. Craziest thing I ever saw."

"And Adrick? Was his body recovered?"

"Ole Adrick, the woodsman? He weren't 'ere that night."

Will frowned. So. The body of his parents' dear friend, who had died up on the Knot beside the great hickory, had also disappeared? Had the Boki taken the corpses as trophies, then? Mayhap, the orcs had fed all three of their spirits to their cursed bloodwood weapons. "And there's been no sign of my parents or Adrick since?"

"Naw, Will. It's sorry I am to say it, but they's dead."

He nodded grimly. "As I expected. I have not heard from them since. And you know my mother. She would move the sky and seas to find me and boss me around."

Tam laughed. "Aye, an' she would at that." The big youth clapped Will on the shoulder. "Whot've ye got yerself up to these days, then?"

"Not much. Getting by."

Will caught significant glances passing between Rynn, Raina, and Eben. The jann cleared his throat. "Excuse me, Will. It is time we get on the road if we would not get caught out after dark in the woods."

Startled by Eben's imperious tone, he caught Rynn's silent look, entreating him to catch on to the ruse. Ahh. Will leaned close to Tam as the rest of the party made its way to the door. "I'm guiding yon merchant and his party about the countryside, and they actually pay me for it. Can ye imagine that?"

"Sweet gig. Where can I sign up—"

He rose to his feet, cutting off any further observations from Tam. "Got to go. Be safe, old friend."

"Safe travels to ye, as well!" Tam called after him as Will ducked outside.

Rynn murmured, "I am sorry to pull you out of there like

that, but if you had stayed any longer, word would have spread that you were back, and the place would have filled with everyone who's ever known you."

Reluctantly, he conceded that the paxan was right. "I heard all I needed to, anyway. Let us be quit of this place, and the sooner, the better."

Gabrielle looked down in sympathy at her husband having to endure a session of the Council of Kings presided over by Princess Endellian. Regalo would have his hands full today keeping peace in the chamber with her running the proceedings. Each of the leading Kothites had a distinctive temperament of his or her own—Ammertus was full of rage and passion; Korovo was, by contrast, the soul of disciplined reason. While Iolanthe was the quiet observer who saw everything, Maximillian was all about force of will.

And Endellian—she was a pale version of her mighty father. She was gifted with at least a portion of her father's implacable will, but unlike him, she had no real outlet for enforcing it upon others. Eternally the heir-in-waiting, the princess was destined never to step out of her father's shadow—which Gabrielle guessed to be a cause of Endellian's underlying bitterness. Oh, Endellian was subtle about it, but her cynicism crept forth from time to time.

Like today. The council's discussion had turned to forthcoming conscriptions for the Imperial Army. Grand Marshal Korovo had just finished a deadly dull presentation on troop strengths and upcoming campaigns. He anticipated a return to Pan Orda to settle it down, and Mindor was restless and a potential threat. New trouble was apparently brewing in Kentogen, and then, of course, there was Haelos, in desperate need of a good quelling.

She would expect no less of Korovo. It was his job to see disaster at every turn and to prepare for the worst case. But she was alarmed at the numbers of conscripts he was discussing. It was nearly double what he'd asked for each of the past dozen years.

"Lastly," Korovo droned, "the Imperial Army is in need of horses and horsemen for future endeavors."

That made Gabrielle sit up straighter in her seat. Cavalry? The Imperial Army had not relied on horsemen for centuries. Maximillian was a believer in standing on the ground he conquered. That, and his marching armies of foot soldiers implacably rolled over everything in their path like advancing swarms of ants. They had no need of the tactical faststrike capabilities that cavalry provided.

Korovo was speaking again. "If we commandeer Antille's horse tribes, that should provide the initial numbers we need. Their expert horsemen can train future recruits as we commandeer more horses from other kingdoms."

Sasha leaned forward in the Heart ambassador's seat, which she occupied today in her husband's stead. Gabrielle noted the way her dear friend's fists clenched the carved armrests, and remembered abruptly that Sasha was a native of Antille's broad steppes.

Her friend asked tightly, "How many horses and horsemen will be left behind to hunt and work the fields and feed the people of Antille? Not to mention rebuilding the herds of horses? It takes nearly a year for a single foal to be born."

Endellian matched Sasha's forward lean. "It does not matter if the general takes every horse in the kingdom. He will get what he needs."

"And destroy Antille in the process?" Sasha ground out. "Is the trade worth it?"

"It is worth it if the Emperor's grand marshal says it is," Endellian snapped.

Sasha subsided, her knuckles still white on the chair arms.

Korovo picked up his presentation once more. "And on the subject of conscripts for the Imperial Army, as I have already outlined, significantly more soldiers will be required in coming years. The agreement of fifteen years ago between the Imperial Army and this governing body is no longer sufficient. That being so, my strategists have run the numbers, and here is a list of how many recruits we require from each kingdom annually. You will meet these quotas, starting immediately."

Clerks shuffled around the room, passing out pieces of parchment to each king or his representative to examine.

Gabrielle watched Sasha closely for her reaction. Not that she wished Sasha or the Heartland ill, but given the conversation she hoped to have with her friend soon, the angrier Sasha was at these new Imperial conscriptions, the better.

Oh, dear. Sasha actually paled as she scanned down the list. The numbers must be worse than anyone had anticipated. Gabrielle glanced at her husband. A brief look of relief passed across his face, followed by one of general disbelief as he scanned down the list. Haraland must not have been tasked too heavily, then. But the overall scale of the numbers apparently alarmed even him.

So. A great military expansion was in the works, was it? That did not bode well for the Eight or its hoped-for rebellion. Had Maximillian somehow gotten wind of it? Did she dare approach Sasha now, or should she pull her head into her shell like a turtle and hide for a while? Torn, Gabrielle glanced at Endellian and was surprised to see the princess studying Sasha intently.

Sasha looked up. The two women's stares clashed. *Gently, Sasha. Gently.* Endellian might look like a harmless young girl, but the princess was a viper, and her fangs were deadly.

"Your Highness, the Heart has a long tradition of accepting all who ask for shelter into its ranks. We cannot possibly provide this number of conscripts to the Empire."

"Well, then," Endellian answered in a barely concealed sneer laced with satisfaction, "the Heart shall have to go without initiates for a few years."

"Are you telling the Heart how to conduct its affairs, Princess?" Sasha's voice was abruptly silky and dangerously calm.

Alarm spiked through Gabrielle. No one confronted Endellian like this and lived. *Stop, Sasha!* she shouted silently at her old friend.

"Am I to gather, then," Sasha continued, "that the Eternal Throne is dissatisfied with how the Heart cares for the citizens of Koth?"

Iolanthe materialized beside Endellian. She must have been sitting off to one side out of Gabrielle's line of sight or mayhap behind the throne itself. The high preceptor leaned down to whisper in Endellian's ear for a moment. Seen side by side like that, their relationship to one another was impossible to miss. Endellian had her mother's dark hair, exotic features, and delicate bone structure.

The princess's features tightened for an almost imperceptible moment and then smoothed over as she listened to Iolanthe.

Endellian looked up. "I make no suggestion about my father's opinion of Heart performance or policy. I merely suggest that the quotas are the quotas. The Heartland may meet theirs any way it wishes, in the same way each kingdom will be expected to do so."

It was not exactly an apology, but Endellian had stepped back from the edge of the abyss. Had Iolanthe not been there to rein her in, though, Gabrielle wondered if Endellian would finally have gone too far this day. Maximillian's relationship with the Heart might be complex, but he steadfastly supported the organization. Would an Empire with Endellian at the helm have no such bond between throne and healers? If the Heart were to turn against the Empire—the implications were too staggering to consider.

And this was certainly not the place to entertain such thoughts. She fingered her Octavium Pendant, not wishing to test its power to conceal thoughts against the mental probing of Maximillian himself.

The council recessed after a round of ranting from various kings who felt they had been unfairly tasked with providing conscripts in comparison to other kingdoms. Gabrielle hurried from the gallery, eager to get Regalo's take on the morning's proceedings, and furthermore to look at just how many Haralanders would be required to sacrifice their lives to the Imperial Army.

Except when she got down to the antechamber, her husband was already mobbed by other kings wishing to speak off the record with her influential husband. There would be no private conversation for her and Regalo until tonight, at least. Assuming he managed to tear free of court politics before the wee hours of the morning, well after she'd collapsed of exhaustion.

A hand touched Gabrielle's elbow. Given that her guard did not leap forward to defend her, whoever wanted her attention was no threat. She turned to find a white-lipped Sasha standing there.

"Walk with me," her old friend ground out past clenched teeth.

She had never seen Sasha so angry. Gabrielle linked her arm through Sasha's, ignoring the political implications of such a move during such a charged session of the Council of Kings. To the Void with such things. Her friend was on the verge of losing control and needed her support.

Sasha dragged Gabrielle around the gardens at a gallop for some minutes before calming herself enough to slow her breakneck pace and speak. "Not only will all the orphans in the Heartland be forced into the army, but orphans all over the continent will be the first victims of this edict. No king will wish to strip his kingdom of men and women, full grown and trained in trades. The children will be thrown to the wolves first. Stars, Gabby. They're babes. And they will all be sent to war." Sasha's voice broke on what sounded suspiciously like a sob.

"How bad are the conscription numbers?" Gabrielle asked low.

"Bad. And the tax levies to feed and clothe an army of this size—do you have any idea how many peasants will starve?"

They traded grim looks. Both of them were old enough to remember famines in the past.

"And Endellian sits there all smug and unconcerned. As if she's enjoying squeezing the common people to within an inch of their lives," Sasha spat out under her breath. "How dare she tell the Heart how to care for the people—"

Gabrielle placed a gently restraining hand on Sasha's arm. "Not this way, my friend. Do not fling your rage uselessly to the winds."

"What would you have me do? Let them just take the children? An entire generation lost to these senseless wars?"

Gabrielle took a deep breath. This was the moment she'd been looking for. "Nay. There is another way. Fight back."

"Against Koth?" Sasha snorted.

For her part, Gabrielle merely stared levelly at her friend.

At length, Sasha's voice dropped, and in a tone of disbelief, she whispered, "Are you mad? You hint at treason."

Gabrielle's gaze never wavered.

"What? How? Tell me what I may do."

"I do not know much. Secrecy is vital. The entire organization must not fall if one person is discovered."

Sasha's eyes opened wide. "An *organization*?"

"As I said, I know little of it. The symbol by which I know it is always an eight-pointed star, a compass rose."

"Like your pendant!" Sasha exclaimed.

Gabrielle smiled and nodded. "From time to time, someone asks me to do something. Nothing to oppose the Empire outright. A tiny nudge of little consequence here or there. Pass on a bit of information. Suggest to my husband that a certain person is well suited for a posting to some position. I only hope that many, many people are all contributing tiny nudges that might one day topple the entire thing."

"I will help. You have but to ask, and I will do whatever I may, be it small or large. You know my heart better than anyone save Rafal, Gabby."

She looked deeply into Sasha's dark eyes. "Aye. And now you know mine. You must never speak of this to anyone, including your husband. You must not even think of it while you are at court."

"Think—" She broke off and then resumed in a heartbeat. "Ahh. Of course not." Sasha took Gabrielle's hand and squeezed it tightly. "Thank you for trusting me enough to include me in this. I will not fail you. I swear."

Gabrielle smiled as profound relief—and a sense of being in too deep to back out now—swept through her. "I never doubted you for a second, my sister." Though not related by birth, they were now tied together by bonds of treason that transcended blood.

"Is this why you steadfastly avoid coming to court?" Sasha asked conversationally.

Gabrielle turned to head back to the Hall of Kings in the distance. "Aye."

"Speaking of which, I'm feeling a sudden need to return home to the Heartland. I'm sure I have pressing business there awaiting my personal attention."

"Understood. I shall send correspondence to you there for the time being, then."

"By all means, dear Gabrielle. I shall look forward to your letters."

The cloaked figure crouched behind a refuse heap, nearly bowled over by the foul odor while the quarry slipped into the inn. It was no surprise that the target had chosen such a seedy establishment in the worst corner of Dupree to spend the night. Some of Anton's most disreputable associates seemed to favor this place. The cloaked watcher slipped farther into the bowels of the narrow alley, settling in for what would likely be a long night of fruitless surveillance while the quarry was peacefully abed, snoring. But such was the nature of the work.

A strong arm snaked out of nowhere, and a hand slapped sharply over the watcher's mouth. A sharp yank, and two cloaks tangled in dark folds of shadow on shadow.

"Very funny, One."

"Glad you're amused, Three."

"Your target's in the Boar's Tusk, too?"

"Aye. Yours?"

"Just slipped in."

"And he's Coil for sure?"

Three answered scornfully. "I walked right up to him in the market and saw the snake mark wrapping all around his forearm."

"Did you get close enough to see if it's a tattoo or a ritual mark?"

"Ritual. No tattoo artist could achieve such detail or richness of color—"

"I do not need a critical analysis of the thing's artistic value," One snapped.

"You asked."

They subsided side by side in silence and darkness for several minutes. Three ventured, "How long until Two shows up here, do you think?"

"I give it an hour. His target looked the type to enjoy the pleasures of a lady before retiring for the night."

"It does not seem fair that we have to sit out here in the cold and stench while the Coil's worst sleep like babes."

"You want their treasure? And to catch Anton's attention? Then we do the dirty work."

A sigh. "I know. It just gets old sometimes."

"Eyes on the prize."

A noise at the end of the alley made them both freeze abruptly. A swift shadow moved, and then Two stood before them, likewise cloaked in layers of dark, concealing wool.

Three commented dryly, "My eyes spy Number Two."

One chuckled.

"Did I miss something?" Two asked low.

"Nothing that bears repeating. Your Coil target also looks to be bedding down for the night at the Boar's Tusk, then?"

"Nay. He met another Coil type: a man slipping in through the city gates just as they were closed for the night."

One and Three stood up straight in interest. "Do tell," One commented mildly.

"A fourth Coil agent. I caught a glimpse of his wrist, and there's a snake head on the underside of it. He and my target were thick as thieves, if you'll pardon the expression. Whispered with their heads together all through supper and over more than a few pints of ale."

"Any hint as to what they hunt for Anton?"

"Nay, but Anton wants it bad. He's offering a king's ransom for it. The fourth fellow has apparently provisioned a wagon for the four of them to travel in secrecy into the west. They leave in the morn."

"Where to exactly?" Three bit out.

"No idea. But they plan to go disguised as gypsies."

"Disguise, is it? Subterfuge for the Coil? That is new behavior for them. Cursed inconvenient they must find it having to hide like the common criminals they are now that their leader has been deposed."

Three subsided, slouching against the dank stone wall. Anton's associates had spent the past two decades establishing a criminal network that stretched the width and breadth of Dupree. In some ways, Anton was more powerful now that he was no longer governor, for any pretense of acting lawfully was no longer necessary. He and the Coil could rage across the colony with no one to stop them. Why then would they bother with all this secrecy and skulking about having clandestine meetings? Clearly, Anton had some big new enterprise in mind. And if the three of them were clever and moved fast, they might place themselves squarely in the middle of it.

Stars knew, the new governess would not stop Anton. Poor woman had no idea the viper's nest she'd stepped into. A fitting analogy given that Coil members identified themselves by snake markings upon their hands or wrists. Excepting Anton, of course. His was clear as day in the middle of his forehead. A bold man, he was, to advertise his affiliation with the Coil so openly.

"We should go back to our room, then and ready for a journey," One was saying. "We have a date with four snake-bit gypsies."

Three snorted. It was not as if they had much packing to do. They all traveled light so they could move fast. They would figure out what this Coil team sought, and the three of them would beat the Coil to it. And then, when they had something Anton would pay dearly to have, they would have a conversation with the former governor and come to an agreement.

CHAPTER
19

R aina sighed in relief as Shepard's Rest came into view.
It had been a long and tiring afternoon traversing
the Unicorn Run, an ancient road that ran through the
heart of the Wylde Wold. Will had practically run from
Hickory Hollow, and his long-legged stride had been nigh
impossible to keep up with. It reminded her of traveling with
her kindari friend Cicero. His kind seemed to feel a deeply
annoying need to run nearly everywhere they went.

But nobody in the party was about to ask Will to slow
down. They all understood too well the demons digging their
spurs into his sides this day.

The party had agreed to splurge and stay at an inn tonight.
It would be their last chance for a hot meal and more importantly, a hot bath, from here on out. Shepard's Rest lay at
the western edge of the Wylde Wold, the far terminus of the
last Imperial trade route east of the Estarran Sea.

Oh, the Emperor claimed the whole continent of Haelos,
and quite loudly. But where the presence of soldiers ended,
so did the Empire's effective control. Tyrel, where she hailed
from, lay across the Estarran Sea in the west. The only time
her people ever saw the slightest evidence of the Empire was
when tax collectors came through every other year or so.

A few settlements, mostly of indigenous peoples, lay inland, farther south and west than Tyrel, but dangerous jour-
neys were necessary to reach them. Would Kerryl take his
captives beyond even the scattered settlements in the west?

The party discussed the question in detail as they drew close to Shepard's Rest. A few things they agreed upon: their prey would be on foot. Also, Kendrick's captor would likely stick to the forests in which he was most at home, which meant he might be more inclined to head north rather than west once he left Imperial-controlled territories.

Although Rynn carried considerable funds in his pouch, they had agreed as a group to draw as little attention as possible to themselves and to travel humbly as hired messengers delivering various letters and notices. To that end, Eben actually had letters for the local Merchant's Guild representative in Shepard's Rest. Aurelius had scared up some long-lost relative of the local innkeeper's and offered to write down a letter for him. That scroll rested in Will's pouch now.

Dusk was falling as they trooped up the wide steps of the inn from which the tiny village took its name. Raina noted the thickness of the stone walls and the stoutness of the iron hinges on the door. This was not an entirely safe place to live, apparently, last vestiges of the Haelan legion or no.

A dozen travelers ranged around the room in twos and threes, eating and drinking. Raina's stomach growled, announcing that the dinner hour had come and passed on the road.

A big, muscular man came out of the kitchen, wiping his hands on an apron and flashing the wicked dagger tucked in his belt as he did so. "Welcome to the Shepard's Rest. Whot'll ye be wantin' this eve?"

Eben answered for all of them. "Supper and a pint for me and my friends. And then a pair of rooms if you've got 'em."

"Female folk in one and menfolk in the other," the innkeeper warned. "I run a respectable place, I do. That'll be three silver, five copper for the lot."

"Perfect," Eben replied, counting out the coins carefully.

Raina noticed other heads in the room rising to listen to the chink emanating from Eben's pouch. Ahh. *That* was why Rynn had passed a handful of small coins to Eben before they'd entered the village. Had Rynn dug around in his much larger pouch filled with gold, they would have been at greater risk of being robbed. As it was, Eben's pouch made a pitifully small clink, and interest from the other patrons waned at the paltry sound.

They piled onto benches at a long table in the shadows by the stairs. This summer had been unseasonably cold and wet, and it felt more like a fall evening than a late summer night. The cheerful warmth of the fire was welcome.

Raina shed her cloak and was the immediate center of attention for every pair of eyes in the room. They'd talked about it before they reached Shepard's Rest. If she were seen here and then heard to mention heading in some direction other than the one they actually chose, they might be able to throw off any followers.

"Oy. Be ye White Heart in truth?" a man across the room asked.

"Aye, sir. Have you need of healing?" she asked patiently.

"Well, now that ye mention it . . . "

Behind her, she heard Will ask their host, "Have you seen a woodsman by the name of Adrick pass through lately?"

"Nay, lad. Not since the Boki attack last year. Word has it he was killed by that green scum."

"He dinna resurrect, then?"

She smiled to hear how quickly Will had fallen back into the local cadences of the region. She would likely do the same if she ever returned to Tyrel. Not that she ever planned for that to happen. Not until the Mages of Alchizzadon were long gone and had no more interest in her.

"Mayhap he moved along to greener forests." A pause, and then the innkeeper asked kindly, "Adrick a friend of thine?"

"Aye."

"Good man, Adrick. Any friend of his be a friend of mine."

Will fell silent, and Raina spied Rosana slipping her hand into Will's under the table. He hadn't spoken much of this Adrick fellow—a sure sign that his death had hurt Will more than he wanted to let on.

Raina made the rounds of the common room and was asked to go down the street to a hut where a woman was too ill to come for healing. Her male companions exchanged glances, and Rynn rose to his feet to follow.

The crofter's hut and its occupants were fully as miserable as she'd become accustomed to. The Kothites did not believe in sharing any of their prosperity with the peasants upon whose backs their mighty empire was built. She healed the middle-aged woman of a chronic case of fluid on the lungs.

As she straightened from the woman's sickbed, the woman's hand shot out to capture Raina's wrist. "Beware the wilds," the woman whispered. "Something's a-comin' from 'em. Gonna cause a powerful lot o' upheaval afore all's said an' done."

"Are you a seer, then?" Raina asked, startled.

"I catches a glimpse beyon' the Veil now and again. I see swords a-swipin' through chains. Blood. War." She shook her head as if to clear the image from her mind.

Raina nodded grimly. Whatever rose to oppose Koth was gathering momentum. The prophecies were coming fast and close now. Apparently, seers all across the land and of every skill level were catching bits and pieces of the coming rebellion. She and her friends had best hurry if they were to wake Gawaine in time for him to lead them to freedom.

"Thank you for the warning, madam. Take care of your family, and I will take care of mine."

Out of general principles, she asked the eldest son, a lad of maybe twelve summers, to show her to the low, thatched barn behind the cottage. "Do any of your animals ail?" she asked him.

"The milch goat ain't been doin' so great," he replied doubtfully.

Thank goodness. Goats she could do. Chickens and other domestic foul still mostly confounded her to heal. Something about their spirits was different enough from human that her magic did not seem to affect them in the same way.

"Let's surprise your mother and heal the goat, shall we?" she murmured to the youth.

"Really? They's been fretting about her."

The boy's goodwill secured, she laid her hands on the coarse-haired creature and commenced trickling healing slowly into the goat. While she did so, she asked conversationally, "I think a friend of mine might have passed through here a few weeks ago. Do you perchance see any of the travelers who come here?"

"I see 'em all. Remember 'em, too, I do. What does your friend look like?"

"He's about twenty summers in age. Tall, handsome youth. Travelling with a bearded man, and maybe a few others."

"I remember them. Two men who looked just alike, and an elf girl was with 'em. She were pretty. Snooty, though, like all elves."

Raina refrained from comment on that pithy observation and asked, "How long ago was it you saw this party?"

"They been through twice. First time were mebbe a moon cycle and a half moon ago. Second time were, lemme see . . ." He counted laboriously on his fingers. "Five days past. Movin' fast, they was. Bought a pile o' dry rations at the store and didn't stay but mebbe a quarter hour."

Less than a week's head start Kendrick and Kerryl Moonrunner had on them? That was good news, indeed. "Did you happen to see which direction they went?" she asked.

"West. Out into the wilds they said they was goin'. I mighta hid behind the hedge beside the inn and listened in on 'em a bit," the youth admitted shamefacedly.

Raina was tempted to throw her arms around the boy and give him a big hug. But she remembered Justin at that age, and he'd have hated being hugged by a girl. She settled for saying enthusiastically, "You did wonderfully. Thank you so much! I would love ever so much to see my friend. If he ever passes through here again, maybe you would give him a message for me?"

"I guess."

"Tell him the healer lady in white says to write her a letter care of the Heart. Can you remember that?"

"O' course," the boy replied scornfully.

"Your goat is all healed up and none the worse for wear," she announced. "And here. Take this loaf of bread and sneak it back into your mother's bread box for me, will you? It was supposed to be your breakfast in the morn, was it not?"

The boy looked at the loaf dubiously. "Aye. But she paid you wit' that."

"All the payment I need is the information you just gave me. It's worth all the gold in Dupree."

"I dunno. That be a lot of gold." He grinned, reminding her sharply of her childhood sweetheart, Justin, of a sudden.

She ruffled his hair and picked her way through the muck, grateful for the sturdy boots Hyland had given her shortly before his death. Bypassing the cottage, she made her way back to the road. Rynn waited for her in the shadow of a mulberry bush.

"I did not know you were an animal physician, as well," he said low.

She shrugged, able to look up at him comfortably because the shadows hid most of his shocking beauty. "Keeping the animals healthy means the children of the house eat. And if they eat, they do not sicken so easily."

"Practical as well as gifted, the lady is."

"I do what I must."

"I have met several of your kind in my day, but never have I seen one heal a goat."

"Really? Huh." They walked a little, and she added, "I'm not going to stop healing goats now that I've figured out how to do it. Where have you met other White Heart members? I've only ever met one, and he's a touch mad."

"Koth, mostly. More of your kind roam there than anywhere else."

"You've been to Koth?" she breathed. "What was it like?"

"Much like here, albeit more thickly settled and more . . . tamed."

"The Empire rules more heavily than this, then?"

"You misunderstand my meaning. The land itself is tamed. Wild forests are few, and only those creatures known and managed by the foresters are allowed to roam free. Farms and roads and villages occupy much more space than here."

She tried to imagine a world without wilderness and mostly failed.

"But in answer to your question, yes, the Empire rules more heavily there. Most people are blindly loyal to Koth and do not even think to question its rule. They have no memory of freedom and do not dream of anything . . . different."

She sucked in a sharp breath. His words were treasonous in the extreme.

"Do I shock you with my criticism of Koth?"

"How did you stay alive on Koth itself?"

She caught a flash of white teeth in the darkness. "By being exceedingly circumspect. And by not staying long."

"You were visiting, then? What could induce one such as you to beard the lion in its den like that?"

"Aurelius warned me that you are an inquisitive child. And I see now what he means when he says you do not ask a child's questions."

"I have had my seventeenth birthday," she retorted. "In my race, I am past the age when girls first marry and start raising families."

He shook his head. "You short-lived races. Always in such a hurry to do things."

"You would live fast too if you only had a single century to accomplish your life's work and make your mark."

"Is that what you aspire to do? Make a mark upon the world?"

Raina subsided, unwilling to admit to any secret ambition. Finally, she murmured, "My lot is cast. I am White Heart."

Rynn laughed under his breath. "You will never be merely

a healer, Raina of Tyrel. Your destiny is much grander than that, I do believe."

"Are you a seer, then? Tell me my future."

Rynn reached for the inn's door, pausing just long enough to grin down at her and murmur, "Saved by the door."

Endellian frowned at the storm copper helm the court messenger presented on one knee to her father. She'd thought Maximillian had successfully stamped out all knowledge of storm copper long ago. A piece of the rare metal hadn't surfaced in many years. Until now.

"I want the name of every single person who has seen that helm you hold," her father declared sternly. "From the moment it was uncovered until this very second. Its finder, every person its finder showed it to, the soldiers who took it for the Empire, anyone they passed it to, anyone who even looked at it. Understood?"

The messenger bowed deeply, albeit awkwardly with the bulky piece in his arms. "So shall it be, Your Most Resplendent and Magnificent Majesty."

"And leave that here." Maximillian gestured at the helm. "I shall add it to my private collection."

The fellow bowed his way out of the throne room and rushed away to do the Emperor's bidding. She wondered idly if the messenger knew that, as soon as the list was compiled, everyone on it, including the messenger himself, would be put to permanent death.

Raina scowled at Rynn's muscular back as they slipped inside the inn. Which was why she noticed the fractional tightening across his shoulders as he surveyed the common room. Peering around him, she noticed several new travelers had arrived in their absence. One, an avarian, sat on the near side of the hearth, and two humans dressed like warriors, or soldiers minus the insignia, sat on the far side, ensconced in a pair of deep armchairs in quiet conversation.

Rynn moved unobtrusively toward the stairs, pausing only

when he was mostly hidden from view and tucked deep into a shadow. Curious to see what had made Rynn so tense, she wandered over to the humans first, noting that Sha'Li and Eben appeared to have already retired for the night. Only Will and Rosana still sat at the table in the corner.

"Good evening, gentlemen," Raina murmured politely. "You were not here earlier when I arrived. May I offer either of you healing?"

"Thanks be, White Heart. I do have a wound partly healed upon my arm that could use a bit of work," one of the men declared. The accent was formal. Educated. Certainly not the rough cadence of traders from these uncivilized lands.

The fellow rolled back his sleeve to reveal three deep, side-by-side gashes.

"An animal attacked you?" she asked conversationally.

"Nay. Just a cursed magical hound. Nasty creature."

Alarm sluiced through her. No normal hound had made these marks. She'd seen wounds from bear claws, and they were not much more widely spaced nor much deeper than these. She detected a fair bit of ale flowing through this man's blood. Perhaps it had loosened his tongue and she could get him to tell her more. "Hereabouts? Should I be worried for my safety?"

"Nay. Beast got me on the ship on the way over here. Recently come from Koth, we are," the man bragged.

She made a sound that she hoped passed for being mightily impressed. "You've ridden on a Black Ship, then?"

"Yup, me and a whole company of handpicked men."

Company? This man was an Imperial soldier? Why the civilian clothes? A secret mission of some kind? Her alarm notched up even higher. "Well, I'm glad to know you're not going to be hunting the creature that gave you these," she murmured, trickling healing into the cuts as slowly as she could to draw out the conversation.

"Nay. 'Tis a man we hunt. A jann fugitive. And I don't care what Kodo says, we'll beat those hounds who are coming for him and find the bastard first."

"Silence," the man's companion hissed.

Raina smiled gently at him. "You've no need to be worried on my account. I'll carry no tales. After all, the Heart and the Empire enjoy a close relationship and always have."

The security-conscious soldier subsided and whether she wished it so or not, the other man's triple gashes were now merely a set of red marks upon his whole and healthy flesh.

"Nicely done, White Heart. I hardly felt that one bit."

And well he shouldn't have. She could not have healed a screaming baby any more slowly or gently. "Safe travels to you, gentlemen."

"And to you, White Heart."

She was vividly aware of Rynn waiting for her in the corner. He needed to get out of here before one of the Imperial soldiers spotted him and took notice of the eye obscured underneath his headband. But knowing him, he would stay to watch over her until she left. He seemed to take his bodyguard duties for their little party extremely seriously.

As she neared him, Rynn muttered, "Eat. They will notice if you do not."

"They" must be the disguised Imperial soldiers.

Will and Rosana were whispering and smiling together, and it did not take any great skill to guess at what they spoke of. Although now that she took a closer look, there was a certain brittle quality to their posture. As if they, too, had figured out the identity of the soldiers and now merely posed as lovers to keep an eye on the Imperial men.

She sat down beside them and reached for a meat pie off the platter on the table. The door opened just as she was finishing it, and a big man smelling of wet dog blustered into the room.

The Imperial soldiers groaned. "What are you doing here, Jameson?" one of them asked the newcomer in tones of round disgust.

"Same thing you are, I expect. Hunting."

"The hunter and his hounds with you?"

Raina gulped.

"Him and his beasties are running the Circle Road. They should be back in a day or two. But I caught myself a miserable ague and came in from the hunt to find a bed, hot food, and some rest." To punctuate his statement, he let out a juicy, painful-sounding cough from deep in his chest.

"You're in luck, man. Yon sits a right talented White Heart healer. She'll fix you up, won't you, White Heart?"

She choked on the remnant of crust suddenly stuck in her throat. "Umm, of course." Cursing mentally, she rose to her feet. The soldiers had called their jann quarry a fugitive, which ruled out Eben as their target—she hoped. Hyland *had* cleared up the confusion over Eben's short-lived enslavement from last spring, hadn't he?

If not, and she healed this bounty hunter to full strength, she might very well be sealing Eben's doom. Sacrifice Eben: sacrifice this man's health. How was she to choose within the confines of her White Heart oath?

Reluctantly, she pushed to her feet and moved toward the man who'd collapsed onto a bench after the coughing fit. She laid both her hands on his back, high, over his lungs, and began trickling healing into him.

Being careful to keep her tone light and conversational, she asked, "Are you the one racing your friends to catch a jann?"

"Those two hunt a jann fugitive," he declared scornfully. "My quarry, however, is not a jann, but rather a paxan."

Great. She stopped herself from glancing over at Rynn in the shadows.

"You White Heart types get around a lot. Ever meet or hear of a paxan named Olar? Open-eyed type. Middle-aged. Comes from Mindor. Might be talking about breeding psionic creatures."

"Wouldn't breeding psionic beasts be illegal?" she asked.

"Gor, yes. Breaks all kinds of Imperial laws. I hear it even breaks a bunch of paxan laws, too."

"What kind of Imperial laws does it break?"

"Only person allowed to breed psionic creatures is the

High Lord Hunter himself. Of course, he's pretty much the only person who can control the Great Mastiff of Canute."

"Great Mastiff?" she echoed, pitching her voice to sound impressed.

The soldier's rib cage swelled importantly under her hands. "Aye. One of the Great Beasts of Koth. Captured by the Empire and bred for our uses now. His pups are the very same Imperial hounds we're running here."

"Can I pet one?"

The fellow laughed until he dissolved into another coughing fit. When he finally regained his breath, he lifted his chin toward the Imperial soldiers. "Ask yon fool how well it goes to pet an Imperial hound."

Ahh. The great gouges on the soldier's arm that she had finished healing. Speaking of healing, she was quickly reaching a decision point where she could leave this fellow sick enough to be abed for a few days, or she could finish healing him. "Do you hunt only this Olar fellow, or any open-eyed paxan?"

"Why do you ask?"

She distracted the hunter by sending a surge of healing into him that should be painful enough to gain his full attention. The burst of magic also cleared out the last of his lung infection. "There. That should do it. Get yourself a hot meal, sleep in late tomorrow, and you should be fine when you arise."

The hunter drew an experimental breath. The sound of it was deep and full. "That's better! I am in your debt, White Heart."

"Promise me you will travel at a more temperate pace. Sleep more and eat better. You cannot keep up your strength if you are forever racing around the countryside."

He snorted. "Do not cluck and fuss over me, child. 'Tis the nature of the work. The hunter runs his hounds, and we follow."

She had a sinking feeling that she and her friends were

about to be the ones running. She glanced into the corner where Rynn had been. He was gone.

The First rubbed his thumb thoughtfully across the ancient patina of the copper bracer in his hand. He looked up at the gray-bearded dwarf shifting uncomfortably from one foot to the other before him as if his joints ached. "Sit, friend."

The dwarf dropped heavily into a chair, sighed with relief, and took a long pull from a horn of the same dwarven ale he'd just delivered to the First's chambers.

Only then did the First ask, "Do you know what this is?"

"Aye. A bent and broken old bracer. Copper."

He eyed the Octavium Pendant around the dwarf's throat with satisfaction. "It is much more than that. This is storm copper. It was made by an ancient race of dwarves called the rokken. They have been all but eradicated from Urth by the Kothite Empire. The metal is forged in rain and lightning and captures the awful power of nature's fury within it."

The dwarf's expression alternated between skepticism and interest.

"Where was it found, and by whom?" the First asked.

"In Groenn's Rest, on the Hauksgrafir. By a kelnor, Gunther Druumedar."

"And where is he now? Does he still live?"

"Aye. We sent him away as soon as we saw that old copper. Hid 'im with the terrakin resistance in the high mountains where he's out of reach of the Empire."

"And undoubtedly saved his life and that of his family and friends in the process."

"Aye. Just so."

"Not only is this storm copper," the First continued, "but the workings and symbols upon it identify it as belonging to the personal guard of an ancient dwarven king. A king whose resting place has been lost."

"Many resting places are lost with the passage of time."

"Ahh, but we need to find this one. I believe the king within it is not truly dead and gone, but merely sleeping. And I most deeply desire to wake him."

"A sleeping dwarven king? Never heard of such a thing."

"Exactly. Our beloved Emperor has carefully erased all memory of him. Which is precisely why I should like to wake him."

"Is he one of these rokken dwarves, too?"

"Yes, indeed. If this bracer belongs to one of his guards, perhaps more of his guards are near. Mayhap they can tell us more of where to find their king. If nothing else, they might be able to tell us where he fell and how."

"Wake the dog and he'll find his master, eh?"

"Just so, my friend. Just so."

"Gunther said he got that piece off a broken statue, though. Not a living guard."

The First nodded. "The same method that created storm copper also could be used on people. It turned them into storm copper statues, frozen within the metal, frozen in time. I believe it may be possible to reverse that process."

"That how the rokken king been sleepin' all this time without dyin'?"

The First smiled. Clever, dwarves were. Perhaps clever enough, even, to bring back the rokken king. Ahh, the problems that would cause for Maximillian. The existence of a rokken—and a king who predated Maximillian, no less—would sharply challenge the Great Forgetting and its planted idea that the Kothite Empire had existed forever and nothing had come before it.

Yes, indeed. If he could throw enough paradoxes at the minds of the people of Urth, no amount of oblivi would be able to counteract the breakdown of Maximillian's curse. First an awakened ethiri girl had come along. She was a boon he had not been counting on, but what were the odds a gypsy would encounter a magic item powerful enough to erase Maximillian's curse upon her? Beyond calculation, for sure. And now this bit of storm copper. The stars were smiling down upon him and his plan to end Koth.

The dwarf commented, "Gunther ran into a yeren not far from where he found yon bracer. If they's lurkin' in the area, we might have ourselves a hard time gettin' past them to find your rokken royal guard."

The First considered his resources briefly. "I can help with that. There's a White Heart member in the Heartlands who has good relations with the yeren. I have a contact who might be able to prevail upon him to help us."

"You talkin' about the Shaggy Father?"

The First nodded. "I am."

"Way I hear it, he's off-kilter. Thinks yeren be sentient and that the Empire should recognize them as people, not creatures."

The First took a pull on the perfectly aged ale, smacking his lips together in enjoyment. "You know how those White Heart types can be. Always trying to make friends with the unlikeliest sorts."

Sorts who would make excellent allies when it was time to move against Koth. Yeren were large, strong, and hunted by the Empire for their valuable hides. They would be all in favor of overthrowing the Kothites when the time came. Moreover, no one knew how many of them there really were. Because they were hunted so aggressively, they'd become deeply reclusive and secretive, staying to the most remote corners of Urth, hiding in caves, thick forests, and underground.

The First nodded in decision. "I'll send word to my contact to speak with the Shaggy Father. Convince him to help us. If he agrees, I'll send someone to collect Gunther Druumedar, who can then show the Shaggy Father where this bracer was found. They can search the area for more rokken of the old royal guard."

Yes, indeed. This could be the catalyst that brought down

the Great Forgetting and sparked open rebellion at long last.

R aina? Raina of Tyrel?"

She whirled, shocked to hear her name, let alone spoken by a stranger in a place such as Shepard's Rest. "Do I know you, sir?" She identified the avarian sitting by the fire as the source of her name. He was a hawk changeling by the look of his reddish hair feathers and prominent, hooked nose.

"Nay, but I know you. Or at least I know your mother. And you've got the look of her through and through."

"Are you Tyrelian, then?" she asked cautiously, searching his skin for the telltale runes of the Mages of Alchizzadon. Of course, this man could well be one of their agents and not bear the marks. For that matter, his runes might be on his back or some other part of him not visible to her now.

"I am not *from* Tyrel. I have merely been *to* Tyrel."

"You have me at a disadvantage. You know my name, but I do not know yours."

"I am Hawk."

"Well met, Hawk. How recently come are you from Tyrel?" Of a sudden, a burning thirst for some sort of connection to home coursed through her. "What news is there?"

"Nothing of note. Crops look good this year barring any late storms. Taxes are still too high, and more bandits than ever roam the Sorrow Wold."

"What of my family? My sister, Arianna? Is she still at home?" She could not come right out and ask if the mages had forced her sister to walk out into the wasteland as they had generations of her female ancestors.

"Aye. Arianna's as bossy as ever. Gonna give Lady Charlotte a run for her money in that department soon."

Given that Raina had run away rather than give birth to a new generation of Tyrelian women for the mages to manipulate to their own ends, she'd hoped desperately that the order would think better of discarding her older sister. Apparently, her plan had worked. That was a small victory, at least.

"No offense intended about your lady mother being bossy."

Raina grinned. "None taken. She is." Her mother's overbearing demeanor was legendary in Tyrel. "What news of Justin Morland? His mother works at the castle. He's of an age with me. Tall. Sandy-haired. Last I knew, he was training as a squire."

"I know the youth of whom you speak. Way I hear it, he left Tyrel."

"Where to?" she asked urgently.

"How would I know?"

She subsided, disappointed. She felt bereft, somehow, not knowing where Justin was. He had always been her anchor, but now he was gone. And he'd taken a piece of her heart with him.

"One of those mages, the ones in the blue cloaks, left about the same time as that young'un you asked about," Hawk supplied.

"Which mage?"

"The older one. The younger one, the one your eye slides off whenever you look at him—you know the one I speak of?"

Raina nodded grimly. He'd been hand selected to father her children. Which was *not* going to happen in this lifetime.

"He got left behind in Tyrel. He's teaching magic and whatnot to your little brothers, the way I hear it."

So. The mages had installed a permanent watch on Tyrel, had they? As if she would ever go back with them skulking around, lying in wait for her. Or, if she did return home, one day, it would be with a big contingent of Royal Order of the Sun knights around her. Defiance surged in her belly. She would never be anyone's pawn—

She checked the thought. In this tabard she was the pawn of plenty of people. But at least she'd gotten to pick who pulled her strings. It was better than nothing. New resolve to wake the Sleeping King coursed through her. Gawaine thought he might be able to help rouse the great human mage whose memory held her family in thrall, compliments of the Mages of Alchizzadon.

She could not fail. Her freedom from all of them depended upon it.

You are arrived just in time, sir. Proctor Elfonse has a visitor. All proctors are requested to attend a small reception for him."

"I'm sorry. Did you say a *visitor*?" Shock coursed through Kadir. Since when did the Mages of Alchizzadon receive visitors? In the hidden palace itself, no less!

"That is correct, sir."

"When is this reception?" he asked tightly.

"Now, sir. In the receiving hall."

Kadir groaned. He had been on the road for weeks. He was filthy and hungry and exhausted, and he wanted a bath, hot food, and his own bed, in that order. Of course, Elfonse would take great pleasure in catching him at a disadvantage like this. *Scheming sewer rat.*

The very last thing he wished to do at the moment was play politics with the more extreme elements within his order. Elfonse and the Collectors—the faction over which Elfonse was proctor—were going to get them all killed one day with their complete disregard for the laws of the land. The only thing that mattered to them was collecting enough magic to rouse the Great Mage. By any means and at all costs. Lunatics.

Personally, he was a Preservator. He was concerned mainly with safeguarding the lineage of the Great Mage, Hadrian. His kind felt the problem of rousing him was best solved organically, over time, by creating a line of mages powerful enough to wake him. It was to that end the women of the House of Tyrel and their exceptional magic had been carefully managed and maintained since before there was record of time.

As for the other line they bred—male seers—they drew from whatever talent they found throughout Haelos. Like the youth he brought into the fold this day with promises of being with the girl he loved. *Anything to bring them in,* Kadir thought sourly. But once the lad saw the extent of what he could learn here, the magic would seduce him away from thoughts of true love.

Of course, the flip side of that coin was that Kadir fully intended to dangle young Justin as bait to draw out Raina from whatever rock she thought to hide under, be it painted in Heart colors or otherwise.

Following the initiate sent to fetch him, Kadir reached the rarely used receiving hall. He grimly straightened his shoulders under the road-stained blue of his robes and nodded at a pair of acolytes to open the tall, double doors for him.

Dregs. It was not just Elfonse and a few of his cronies. The entire faction of Collectors looked to be present. A sea of navy robes crowded the spacious hall, and avid curiosity crackled in the air. Hidden and shielded as their enclave was, no daylight penetrated the palace's protections, and perpetual night cloaked every room. But today, the chandeliers overhead were crammed with hundreds of burning candles that cast a warm glow over the assemblage.

In spite of the crowd, Kadir spotted the guest immediately. How could he not? The man was taller than almost everyone in the room and strikingly handsome. Of course, what really captured his gaze was the visitor's unusual coloring. His skin was snowy white, as pale as newly fallen snow. But as the guest bent his head to listen to someone speak beside him, the candles cast shadows in every shade of blue across his iridescent skin.

He would have taken the visitor for an ikonesti were his features not so unmistakably human in shape and his ears as round as non-elven ears could care to be. Kadir passed through the crowd, using his height and bulk to plow his way politely toward the stranger. As he did so, he caught the faintest glimpses of other colorations in the man's skin, glints of silver and gold, red and brown, as if a diamond winked at him in rainbow flashes of color.

A jann, mayhap?

What extraordinary circumstance could have convinced the high proctor to let any outsider into the inner sanctum of the mages of Alchizzadon like this? In his entire lifetime, Kadir had never heard of an outsider being granted access to this secret place. Elfonse was as adamant as the next man about maintaining the secrecy of the Mages of Alchizzadon in spite of his single-minded focus on his work.

Kadir could not imagine what had changed so radically in his absence, then, that Elfonse had been able to convince High Proctor Albinus to allow this travesty.

"Ahh, Proctor Kadir. You are returned to us, and just in time for glad tidings," Elfonse intoned.

"I cannot wait to hear what these tidings might be," he replied dryly.

"Prithee, allow me to introduce you to our guest. He is a man who claims to have no name but whose interests run parallel to ours."

A man with no name? The mystery deepened. The order's seers had been mumbling about nameless ones coming in from the wilds for years now. Had this fellow caught wind of the prophecies and claimed nameless status as a ruse to gain entrance to these hallowed halls?

Kadir looked the stranger in the eye directly. The confidence and power he saw there shocked him. And truth be told, it daunted him a bit. "In what way do we share interests, sir?"

The jann glanced over at Elfonse, who nodded slightly, and then turned back to Kadir. He intoned in a rich, deep voice, "I have an interest in exploring the magics of this continent."

Hmm. The Gatekeepers of Alchizzadon would have something to say about that if they were here to defend their interests. But alas, that secretive portion of his order served elsewhere, standing guard over the Gates of the Realms scattered across the continent. Aloud, he asked, "What sorts of magics do you explore, exactly?"

The jann shrugged. "Whatever magics Haelos has to offer up."

Kadir studied him intently. That face . . . memory of it hovered just beyond the edge of recall.

"Ahh, Kadir. You are returned to us at long last."

At the thin rasp, he turned to face the elderly leader of his order, a small man shrunken with age, like a raisin, but with bright, black eyes still. "High Proctor Albinus, I am overjoyed to find you in good health upon my return. How do you fare?"

"I am well, considering the indignities old age heaps upon a soul. Have you any news to report?"

"I have word that our missing charge has landed in the Heart. The White Heart, to be exact."

Albinus absorbed that news for a moment and then began to chuckle. "Ahh, spirited this one is. Like her mother. One cannot help but like her."

"Like her?" Elfonse squawked. "She's completely out of control. The child must be brought to heel immediately. If Kadir cannot do it, I and mine certainly will."

Kadir retorted, "The Royal Order of the Sun will likely have something to say about that. Draw their wrath and that will be the end of us all."

Elfonse shrugged. "We'll take the girl without them finding out who did it, then. Once we have her here under lock and key, they cannot touch us."

Kadir scowled. He had an inkling the form Elfonse's bringing to heel would take. The man would drain Raina's magic from her until he killed her permanently and callously stored her magic for the day of great awakening. He started hotly, "You and yours shall not lay hands on her while I yet breathe—"

"Let us discuss this later," Albinus intervened mildly. "We ignore our guest."

Kadir was in no mood to make nice, and he glared at

Elfonse. At length, he calmed himself enough to ask his mentor somewhat more temperately, "High Proctor, I do not understand our visitor's reason for being here."

"His spirit is . . . interesting. And furthermore, he seeks advice from us based on our special expertise regarding the bonds between spirits and physical form."

"In return for what?" Kadir demanded bluntly.

Albinus pursed his lips, whether in disapproval or amusement, Kadir could neither tell nor give a care. "It is our purpose to learn all we can so we may share our knowledge with those in need."

No, it wasn't. They had never shared anything they'd learned with outsiders, not in the entirety of their existence. Why, then, did Albinus break the ancient tradition for this jann?

Creating a debt of gratitude, mayhap. Who was this jann that a favor owed by him was worth risking exposure of the entire order? Kadir studied the man's inscrutable features closely. To his credit, the jann remained unruffled under Kadir's open scrutiny. A man of substance. Education. Self-possessed and clearly accustomed to being in charge. A leader of some kind. Was he an undercover Imperial agent?

"Where do you come from, sir?" Kadir asked the jann.

"I have no home. I have, however, spent the last few years wandering about observing and learning the lay of the land. Which is how I chanced upon the name of this order and searched it out. I have come to believe that we could be of mutual benefit to each other."

Kadir harrumphed into his robe's collar. He'd long suspected that the high proctor kept secrets from the rest of them, but this went too far. Albinus had finally fallen off his rocking chair. The question now was, would he let Elfonse take the entire order down to ruin?

Will lurched fully awake, whipping his dagger out from under his pillow as a hand closed over his mouth.

"Gently," a female voice whispered. "Wake your friends. You must go, and now."

He blinked up at a beautiful young woman he'd definitely never met before. He would not have forgotten that face.

"Who are you?"

"A friend. And you and your companions need to leave now. Wake up that one"—she nodded in the direction of Rynn—"and I'll go wake your female friends."

Will noticed that Eben was already awake and getting dressed grimly. He apparently believed the girl's warning. "Wait. What's going on?"

"Prepare to leave in silence and haste," she hissed. "And hurry." The girl slipped out the hallway door before he could question her any further.

Will swung his feet to the cold floor and jammed his feet into his boots as quietly as he could. He crept over to Rynn, who roused at a touch, took one look at him, and commenced dressing. They moved about in the deep shadows cast by the sluggish embers of the fire, dressing and arming themselves as quietly as they could.

He cracked open the hallway door and peeked out. Empty. He slipped across the hall to the girls' room and eased the door open. A sharp claw hooked under his chin before his nose even cleared the doorframe.

"You're awake, then," he breathed at Sha'Li, not daring to move with that razor-sharp claw at his throat.

"Aye. Shortly we'll be down," the lizardman girl whispered.

The party congregated in the common room no more than three minutes after the girl first woke Will. The girl came out of the kitchen, and Eben whispered, "What brings you here, Richelle?"

Will looked back and forth between the two. Eben knew this beauty?

"The same thing that brings you here, I imagine. Looking for Kendrick."

"Any luck?" Eben asked eagerly.

"Keep your voice down," Rynn warned.

Richelle nodded. "The paxan is wise. I heard the Imperial

soldiers talking about all of you after you went to bed. They're planning to detain the lot of you—except for you, White Heart—and interrogate you as to what you're up to and where you're headed." She pressed a fat cloth bundle into Eben's hands that looked like food.

She continued, "I have a lead on Kendrick and the one who controls him. They are headed north and fast. They've left Imperial held lands and head into the wilderness."

"Why?"

"Who knows? To escape the long arm of the Empire, mayhap." She hesitated and then added in a rush, "Find him, Eb. Bring him home to us. My family owes a debt to the Hyland name; the Lady of Hyland saved my life. For the sake of our old friendships, find him for me. Will you do that?"

"I will do my best."

"There is one with them who intentionally leaves tracks. They are subtle, but if you hire a decent tracker, you ought to be able to follow the trail fairly easily."

Eben grinned. "Tarryn. She's an expert tracker and counter-tracker. I'll bet she's the one laying a trail for us."

"I'll tell the soldiers you're headed south. Go north with all due haste." She glanced over at Will. "I heard you mention Adrick earlier. You'll find plenty of help in the north-lands if you use his name. Adrick was well liked in those parts."

It occurred to Will to ask her how she'd heard him speaking earlier, but the urgency of the moment stilled his tongue. Eben seemed to be taking her warning seriously and was already moving toward the door. Rynn lifted the heavy lock bar and took a hard look outside before gesturing the others to follow.

"I'll latch the door behind you," Richelle whispered. "Travel swiftly and find that which you seek."

Will murmured a quiet thanks to the girl and followed the others out into the chilly night. He glanced up at the position of the stars. It would be hours yet until dawn. As the initial alarm of the unexpected wake-up wore off, fatigue settled in its place.

Eben led the party past the last few crofters' huts in Shepard's Rest while Sha'Li countertracked for the group. Who'd ever heard of erasing tracks in a village, for stars' sake? The Imperial scouts would undoubtedly be master trackers, though.

The road quickly turned into little more than a one-person-wide cow path. Before long, trees crowded in close upon them, and leaves overhead blocked out the sky.

The party paused to take a short rest while Sha'Li caught up with them.

Will turned to Eben immediately. "Who was that girl?"

"That's Richelle, daughter of the Dupree Slaver's Guildmaster, Kenzarr."

"The Slaver's Guild?" Rosana exclaimed. "She's Imperial?"

"Kenzarr and Leland Hyland were great friends. Used to go hunting together all the time. They had a falling out some years ago over something that happened to Kendrick and Richelle. Hyland's wife fixed it, but the distance between Hyland and Kenzarr remained. I got the impression that Kenzarr regretted it and wished to repair the chasm between him and Leland. But Richelle was always hanging around the house. She was like a sister to us."

"So you trust her information?" Will asked. "She won't turn us in to the hunters back there?"

"Why would she? She has nothing against us."

Rosana snorted. "Nothing except being the daughter of Anton Constantine's closest friend and ally. She's Imperial. And worse, she's Anton's creature. For all we know, he put her up to sending us into a trap. We should do the exact opposite of what she told us to do and with all possible speed."

Eben frowned. "I've known her most of my life. She's a decent sort. She and her father may be slavers, but they've got honor."

Sha'Li spoke up. "Honor enough to hang all our lives upon?"

"C'mon," Eben coaxed. "She owes the House of Hyland. And she gave us a direction to go. It's more than we had before. What can it hurt to see if she's right and we pick up Tarryn's trail?"

Will was annoyed when Rynn interjected, "I sensed urgency and genuine desire to help her." It occurred suddenly to Will to wonder what else Rynn could sense in all of them that he was not telling them. Could he see their secrets? Did he know about the Sleeping King? The identity of his father? The fact that an Imperial death sentence lay upon the head of every member of the house of De'Vir?

Eben nodded firmly at Rynn. "Exactly. I trust her. She and Kendrick and I were very close. She would not betray so many years of friendship."

Before daylight, any hint of a path had disappeared. Only Will's exceptional woodcraft allowed them to make their way forward through the increasingly dense forest thickets on nearly invisible deer trails. But, as Richelle had forecast, Sha'Li started picking up signs of a subtly marked trail. She estimated that it was several days old, but it represented hope, especially to Eben, whose spirits picked up markedly.

Will had grown up in this part of Dupree, and even he was shocked at how quickly all signs of civilization stopped as they headed north first, and then the trail they followed veered west. When they had set out from Shepard's Rest just a few hours ago, they were firmly in an Imperial colony. And suddenly, they were . . . not. Even the Forest of Thorns had not felt this completely uninhabited.

Some things stayed the same, though. An unknown enemy loomed in front of them, and they were on the run, being chased by Imperial forces. Again. The more things changed, the more they stayed the same.

20

Marikeen rubbed her cheek absently. Sometimes it still stung where the slave mark had been before. It was long gone, but the burn of humiliation lingered.

Speaking of lingering, her nose twitched at the odor of decay permeating the oddly shaped room around her. The walls were all curves and flowing lines with no square corners anywhere. The claustrophobically low ceiling looked like a stone clamshell that pressed down on her uncomfortably as if she were trapped deep underwater and being crushed by the weight of it. The carvings around the oval windows were of fish, eels, urchins, and other more fanciful underwater creatures that she did not recognize. She'd heard someone mention that this place was once a lizardman holding. Given that the structure squatted like a toadstool in the middle of a putrid swamp, she had no trouble believing it.

She looked around at the assembled mages who called themselves the Cabal. As best she could tell, this deeply secretive group was devoted to the idea of learning all it could about magic. An innocent enough mission on the surface of the thing. But she'd sensed from the moment she'd arrived at this magically disguised sanctum that their motives were nowhere near as pure as that. Many forms of magic were forbidden, either by law or taboo, and she suspected this bunch was interested in those magics most of all.

The man who had brought her into this group, Tholin, was not here at today's gathering. But as soon as the human calling himself Richard Layheart spoke to her, the reason for Tholin's absence became clear.

"What can you tell us of Anton's activities, Marikeen?"

Ahh. Tholin was also a Coil member and Anton's creature. She leaned back, considering Layheart's question. Were these people interested more in how much she'd registered while under the influence of one of Anton's infamous love potions, or were they more interested in spying on the former governor? Given Tholin's absence for this conversation, she gathered it was the latter.

"Anton spent much of the time that I was with him in search of rare components for making various alchemical poisons. And, of course, he spoke a fair bit about taking revenge for the slights perpetrated against him by various people he perceives as enemies."

"What orders did he give to his snake-tattooed associates?" A gypsy man with the brightly glowing hands of a mage asked that one. He'd been introduced to her as Victor Jedrin.

She turned to face him. And here it was. The choice she had thus far avoided. Did she cast her fate in with these powerful mages who had freed her from slavery and could teach her much, or did she hold out hope that her inept brother and his pathetic little band of friends would one day manage to find her and rescue her from whatever miserable path her life took her down?

Given that she'd been missing for months and had not heard a word from Eben or Kendrick, she had to assume they had given up searching for her. And now that Hyland was dead, if she went back to Dupree, she would have no benefactor to shield her from the consequences of her unknown parentage.

She took a long, slow breath. Held it a moment. Then answered, "Anton's last order to his Coil subordinates was to hunt down and bring to him a small party of young adventurers. Anton seems to think this group has stolen something from him. He wants it back before he kills them all."

"What do you know of these adventurers?" the tall paxan woman, Jewelin Palos, asked.

Marikeen shrugged. "I met two of them in the slave market. One, a human girl, called herself Raina. She fairly crackled with magic. If she's not an arch-mage, then I'm a goblin. She had with her a kindari bodyguard. Anton ranted about another, a human calling himself Will Cobb. Apparently, he is notable only for a strange piece of wood grown into his chest. A Tribe of the Moon–marked lizardman girl and a gypsy Heart member rounded out the party. And, of course, my brother, Eben, ran with them."

"You've a brother?" That was Keegan Stonefist. He was a dwarf, and as his name indicated, in place of one of his hands he had a carved stone piece in the shape of a fist. "Is he a mage also?"

"Not Eben," she answered with a touch of big-sister scorn.

"Has he got any special talents, then?" Stonefist pressed.

"Hard to tell. His stoneskin glitters a bit, which is unusual, and he can hold it for longer than most jann." She'd long suspected there was more to her brother than met the eye, but she did not yet know this group well enough to share that with them. Perhaps if they proved trustworthy, she would find a way to draw Eben into this organization with her.

"Humph," the dwarf grumbled in disappointment.

Richard Layheart spoke from over by the window. "An arch-mage could be interesting. I haven't seen one of those in a long while. What kinds of magic does she cast?"

"Anton was livid that she healed half of Dupree during the riots right before he was ousted. She's a spirit caster."

There was a collective nose wrinkling throughout the chamber. Healing magic wasn't anywhere near as interesting as the more dangerous magics.

"Thank you for sharing with us, Marikeen. Welcome to our group, and I shall look forward to seeing where your talents develop in the coming years."

Years? She had no interest in waiting *years* to develop her elemental magics further. She pasted on a smile nonetheless and nodded politely at the human. At least they'd taken that cursed slave mark off her face. She would find a way to convince them to teach her the rare and forbidden spells she craved knowing, and sooner rather than later.

The chamber's door opened with a crash, and a flamboyantly dressed human burst in carrying something large in his arms. The object was heavy based on how the man staggered a little under its weight.

"Look what we have found!" the man announced. "I told you taking over this place and searching it would yield treasure."

"What have you got there, Bogatyr?" Layheart asked with interest.

"Carved nullstone. And there's magic upon it." With a crash and a great puff of dust, the brightly dressed man dropped his load on the table.

Wedge shaped, it was made of some shiny black stone shot through with streaks of gold. Its face was dominated by a large runic symbol. Three arcs of odd, writing-like scribbles passed across its face, as well. Based on how the arcs went right to the edge of the piece and seemed to stop mid-etching, Marikeen surmised this was but part of a larger carving.

Based on the size and shape of this piece, and guessing the whole carving to be some kind of circle, the original piece would have been several feet across.

"Detect the magics upon it," Bogatyr demanded. "I can practically taste the power of it."

Layheart placed his hand over the rune-like shape on the stone, and magic leaped from his fingers. "Ritual magic," he announced eagerly. "Ancient. Powerful." The others crowded forward hungrily.

"What kind of magic?" Jewelin asked impatiently. She looked near ready to slap away her superior's hand and detect the magics for herself.

Layheart answered, "Too old to differentiate a specific

path. The magic is fractured, like this stone. The original spell upon the original stone must have been a thing to behold."

Stonefist piped up. "Since when do lizardmen cast the kind of magic you describe? They can barely read." The dwarf stroked the stone lightly, and a look of ecstasy entered his eyes.

"Unless that is an ancient form of their writings upon the stone," Jewelin commented. She ran a fingertip lightly over the carvings, and a shudder passed through her. Marikeen did not know whether to stare at the alien shapes on the rock or to be utterly fascinated by the greed with which these mages regarded the magics upon it. They seemed almost addicted to the magic.

Layheart declared, "Let us continue to excavate the tunnels under this place and see what else we may find. Mayhap more of those wedges are to be found." An anticipatory sigh of pleasure passed through the assemblage.

Bogatyr nodded briskly. "I will put my men to work on it right away."

Marikeen stared down at the stone, intrigued herself by the magic resonating from it. Stone magic was not her specialty, but even she could tell the magics before her did not originate within the stone itself. Some other being had imbued the stone with power so strong and deep that it had lasted far beyond the usual life span of such energy. It resonated deeply, drawing her to it.

Yes, she had made the right decision to cast her lot in with this group. Lust for more knowledge of magic like this pulsed through her. She was sick and tired of playing the dutiful good girl. It was high time and more that she finally stretched her wings and tested the limits of her talent for magic.

Rynn had informally been elected to take point as the party traveled into the wilds, which was fine with him. He was skilled enough at tracking to follow the trail that had been laid for them. Sha'Li was the best countertracker by far in the party, and she needed to bring up the rear, checking to make sure that they left no obvious trail for anyone else to follow.

Not that he expected to be followed out here. They had truly walked into the wilderness. Once the Circle Road and Shepard's Rest had disappeared behind them, so did all vestiges of the Kothite Empire. He hadn't felt this free, this safe, in a very long time. In celebration, he removed his headband with relish and stuffed it in his belt pouch.

As his sight normalized, the colors and energies that lay outside the range of his two-eyed vision leaped into view, and the world came alive around him in vivid clarity, tone, and depth. His stride lengthened and he breathed more deeply, finally able to be fully himself once more.

He topped a rise in the terrain just as a copse of trees thinned and opened up before him without warning. He stopped to take in the vast panorama at his feet. Undulating, golden grassland led into a broad swath of dark green velvet in the distance as forest resumed across the wide valley.

"Stars, that's pretty," Raina commented from beside him.

He smiled down at her, and she blinked back owlishly as if something had temporarily blinded her.

Will halted on his other side. "Sun will be going down soon. It's going to be right in our eyes if we try to cross that valley now. Not to mention, that's a pretty steep drop in front of us, and the stone looks loose. We'll need to find an easier way down. Maybe we should call it a day and make camp here for the night. We did trek a good portion of last night, after all. And Rosana looks like she's wilting."

Interesting pair, Will Cobb and the gypsy girl. Sometimes, when they were together and he wasn't quite looking straight at them, Rynn fancied that he saw a faint glow between them. It was tinged with a hint of green, and he attributed it to that strange disk affixed to Will's chest.

The young man was clearly smitten with Rosana, and she

was just as besotted with Will. He wished them luck finding happiness, although he expected fireworks aplenty awaited the pair before they found any measure of peace. Both of them were passionate souls, and he sensed that Will was prone to darker fits of temper than he let on. Maybe one day he could convince Will to try meditating with him. It would benefit the hotheaded youth.

Rynn had long counted himself lucky that his studies took so much of his time and energy, leaving him none free to pursue personal, intimate love in all its messy forms and complications. He chose, rather, to observe and appreciate everyone and everything, to seek and find beauty wherever he found it. To be in the world, but not of it.

"I think we should keep moving," Eben declared. "Kendrick is close by and waiting for us to find him."

"Certain of this we are not," Sha'Li replied. "Far away he may lie this night. Only hope we can that in the right direction we travel." Her tone was surprisingly gentle.

The lizardman girl was an interesting soul, although she'd seemed troubled of late. More withdrawn than usual if that was possible. Unfortunately, he didn't know her well enough to ask her about what was bothering her. Still, she was a good sort. Far kinder and more generous than most humans believed her kind capable of.

That white Tribe of the Moon mark was a dead giveaway to her true nature. He would lay odds it had to do with healing or spiritual connection—maybe something to do with repairing the Urth and restoring balance to living things.

Mayhap sometime he could ask Sha'Li for more information about the Tribe. What little he knew of its patron and founder, Lunimar, was that he was a greater being associated with the Moon's energies. Said to be the brother of the Green Lady, he was described as an avid protector of nature and creator of were-creatures.

Eben made a low sound of protest as the others chimed in with votes to stop for the night. The pain in the jann youth's voice struck Rynn sharply. Such agony was hard for anyone to bear without breaking. Perhaps Eben would benefit from a dream walk. If he were to lay down a few of his cares in the dream realm and leave them behind for a space of time, the young man might regain enough strength to bear the burden of his losses with more equanimity.

And then there was Raina, who'd confessed to him a few days ago that she was hearing voices inside her head and that they were starting to bother her. He'd promised to take a look with his special mental powers, but they hadn't had a calm enough moment since then for him to do so. He wondered if the murmurs in her mind were some sort of side effect of the massive amounts of magic she was capable of drawing to herself.

There was so much more he could do for all of them if they would only trust him. But he understood that things such as trust and friendship could not be forged instantly. He had to let them unfold naturally. Tomorrow morning, he would meditate on patience as he performed his martial exercises.

Eben's objections overruled, the party set about preparing camp with impressive efficiency. They had obviously done this many times together. He was relegated to hunting for small game to add a bit of meat to their evening meal. Sunset became twilight, and twilight became the gloaming before he returned to camp with two fat rabbits, skinned and dressed out, ready for roasting.

"There you are, Rynn," Raina commented. "I was getting ready to send the Imperial Army out after you."

It was nice to know they missed him when he was gone overlong. He handed over the rabbits and helped Eben rig a pair of forked sticks on each side of the fire. They placed his rabbits, threaded onto stout, green sticks, across the hot coals. The evening grew cool, stars began to twinkle in the gaps in the leaves overhead, and the savory scent of roasting hare filled the air. The moment was just about perfect.

With only a single crash of breaking branches as a warning, a great beast burst out of the trees and was practically

on top of the fire before Rynn could gain his feet. The others
fell backward off their logs and scrambled to draw weapons
as the giant hound set up an earsplitting howl of rage. Another bound and the beast was crouching, preparing to leap
over the fire directly at him.

It was a dog, but unlike any Rynn had ever seen. It was
huge, and massive jaws displayed great rows of teeth. The
beast had to weigh at least three times what a grown man
would and stood chest high to Rynn, who was not a small
man himself. The beast's coat was light brown, short, and
coarse, his hide flecked with foam from his huge jowls.

The beast's face was black, but it was the creature's eyes
that Rynn could not tear his gaze away from. They glowed
from within with preternatural intelligence. And the beast's
stare was locked directly on his third eye, never wavering for
an instant as the giant dog eyed him ferociously.

"That's an Imperial hound!" Raina cried.

Frantically, Raina cast a spell at Rynn that slammed into
his skin, burning as it raced across his body. He flinched as
the beast sprang into arcing flight and *passed right through
him*. What on Urth? Rynn looked down in shock only to see
that his body had lost its solid, corporeal form. Ahh. Quick
thinking, that. She'd cast a spirit form spell on him.

More crashing erupted around them, and three more
similar beasts burst into the clearing. As one, they leaped
for Eben, backing the jann against a tree, surrounding him
in a mass of snarling, snapping jaws.

Frowning, Raina cast a spirit form over the waist-high
backs of the beasts at the jann. His change from corporeal
to non-corporeal had no effect on the vicious creatures, however. The beasts seemed completely uninterested in the rest
of the humanoids in the clearing, all their ferocity directed
at Eben.

"If psionic hounds those be, why do they go not after
Rynn?" Sha'Li called out.

"Those are not psionic hounds," Rynn replied. "Trust me.
I have good reason to know what those beasts act like. Were

they psi-hounds, they would already be tearing me limb from limb and consuming my flesh for their supper."

"What are they, then?" Will demanded.

"Elemental hounds," Raina answered abruptly. "One of the soldiers back at the inn mentioned them. Where is their hunter?"

As if on cue, a man emerged from the trees. Rynn and the others whirled to face him. He wore a black tabard with a red torch insignia embroidered in fancy threads over his heart. The man's eyeballs were covered in a milky film where irises and pupils should be.

"He's *blind*," Will blurted.

Rynn was aware of Sha'Li slipping away and easing silently through the trees to position herself behind the blind hunter while Will, Rosana, and Raina moved between the hounds and Eben, effectively cornering all of them. It was courageous of them to put themselves in the way of the hounds, but they had no idea what those beasts were capable of. They were all going to die horribly. Even one of those beasts would give them all the fight they could handle.

Every cell in his body screamed for him to run for his life, but he stood his ground, out of sight and out of the hunter's mind, hopefully. It was what he got for letting down his guard and daring to enjoy the evening in the mistaken belief that they were safe. Safety for him while the Kothite Empire yet existed was an illusion.

"Not entirely blind, boy," the hunter replied to Will. "I perceive what my hounds do. And I can see well enough that they've found their quarr—" The man stopped, his blind eye sockets pointed unerringly at Eben and the four mighty beasts. "Who are *you*?" the hunter demanded in Eben's direction.

Raina stepped forward. "Why do you ask, hunter? Are not those your hounds? Do you not know who they track?"

"This is not the one they seek. And yet, my hounds never err. You will have to come with me, young man, while we sort out why they hunted you—"

Sha'Li struck so fast Rynn barely saw her move. One second the hunter was speaking about taking in Eben for questioning, and the next, he was crumpling to the ground, unconscious. Sha'Li stood there with the butt of a dagger raised shoulder high.

In the instant before all hell broke loose, Rynn cried out not to kill the hunter. Doing so would unleash the hounds from whatever mental restraints he exercised upon them. But he had barely gotten the words out when all four hounds leaped forward, intent upon devouring Eben.

He jumped forward, shouting, "Drop my spirit form, Raina!"

She did so just as he reached the beasts, who were giving Will and Eben more than they could handle even backed up against a tree that forced the hounds to stay in front of them.

Rynn leaped upon the back of the nearest hound, straddling it like a horse. He raised both fists, clasped them together, and slammed them down into the base of the hound's skull. The beast staggered and then whipped its head around, its enormous jaws clamping down on his lower leg. He felt the armor plate there start to crack. He smashed his fists into the beast's skull again, and this time the hound dropped.

But even taking the battle down to three hounds wasn't enough. The hounds forced the others to fall back, abandoning the protection of the tree. He leaped clear of the hound he'd been riding as it fell and all in one move smashed his right fist into the ear of the closest hound just as it lunged for Rosana.

His blow diverted its attention, and the open-mawed attack came at him instead. He ducked and avoided the teeth but not the heavy jaw, slamming into his face and throwing him backward off his feet.

A black, fast-moving shape flew past him, launching into another one of the beasts, both claws plunging directly into its throat. The hound yelped in pain and leaped off Raina, whom it had pinned to the ground, turning to attack Sha'Li.

The lizardman spit into the beast's face, and this hound

joined the first in squealing in pain. But neither beast stopped snapping and lunging, one pouring blood, the other slobbering in huge, sticky gobs. Rynn took advantage of the instant's respite to haul Raina to her feet.

"Don't go down again or you're done," he bit out to her as he turned to place himself in front of the healers.

The first hound he'd knocked out was already back on its feet, groggy, shaking its huge head, but regaining its senses far too quickly. All four hounds advanced upon them now, less frenzied than before but every bit as determined to tear Eben limb from limb.

Rynn and the others gave way before the snaps and snarls, swords and staff swinging frantically to hold off the beasts. He feared for his crystal gauntlets, but miraculously, they held under the force of the bites and blows the beasts peppered him with.

"The cliff!" Rosana cried.

"Idea I have!" Sha'Li called out in response. "Tease them into charging, and all of us when they come shall duck. Over the cliff we may send them."

"Let's do it," he grunted, kicking and punching and blocking for all he was worth.

There was no time for discussion or a vote. He could only hope the others grasped what Sha'Li had proposed and went along with it. If he was the only one who dropped his guard, he would die horribly right here on the edge of this cliff.

He stood upright and dropped both fists to his sides. The move startled the hounds, who paused momentarily as if to consult with one another. Rynn dared not take his stare off the beasts to see what his companions were doing. The success of this thing would depend upon split-second timing.

The hounds charged. They were only a single full stride away from the party, so it was more of a massive pounce than an actual charge. The hound in front of him flew up overhead and came crashing down toward him, fangs first, jaws wide open and claws outstretched.

"Now!" Rynn shouted, dropping flat upon the ground even

as the beast arced down toward him. He rolled frantically away from the cliff, which he felt crumbling beneath his shoulder. The beast caught him a glancing blow, and Rynn grunted in pain as claws raked across his back.

But then he heard and felt a sudden scrambling of claws on rolling rock. The ground trembled, and the sound of boulders tumbling joined the yelps and clawing below him.

"Back up!" Will yelled.

Still on his belly, Rynn raced on all fours like an alligator away from the cliff just as a chunk of it maybe twenty feet long and half that wide calved off and plunged down in a great crash of breaking stones, rolling dirt, and tumbling boulders.

The avalanche went on for long seconds and then settled. All went still and silent around them. He lay there panting, taking stock of his wounds. Nothing mortal, but he would need some of Raina's store of healing if he were to stand and walk anytime soon, let alone fight.

"Everyone all right?" Raina asked into the quiet.

Rynn lifted his head. A cloud of dust rose from the valley below and was drifting through the clearing. Sha'Li. Eben. Will and Rosana. Raina. They were all here. Praise the stars above and the sun below.

"We need to secure the hunter," he said. Excruciating pain shot through his jaw. Cursed hound must have cracked it when he whipped his head around and hit his face.

Eben grunted, "I'm going to need some healing before I can stand."

Raina pushed to her feet and stumbled over to Eben, healing herself as she went. She reached the jann and gathered a great ball of healing energy that she threw into him. Eben grunted again as Raina turned to Will and did the same. Rosana was already healing herself. Raina healed Sha'Li, who moved off fast toward the hunter, pulling the rope off her belt.

Raina came over and crouched beside Rynn. "You look the worse for wear, my friend. Fast or slow?"

"Fast," he mumbled. His jaw was already becoming immobile and waves of pain radiated from his leg where it had been bitten. Fiery agony across his back suggested that the claw marks there were rather deeper than he'd thought at first, and none of his limbs seemed inclined to obey his orders.

Raina slammed a crackling ball of magic into his chest, and it raced across his body, ripping at his flesh and knitting it back into place all in one agonizing instant. He sucked in a sharp breath in spite of his best effort not to react to the pain. Without the adrenaline of battle to numb the sensation, combat healing hurt almost worse than the injury.

"That should do it," Raina announced cheerfully, holding a hand down to him. She weighed half what he did and stood a full head shorter than he, but he appreciated the gesture enough to take her hand and let her give a mighty heave. He came to his feet easily, his body responding correctly to his commands once more.

He bowed over her hand, which he still held. "My thanks to thee, lady healer."

"It is I who owe you thanks. You distracted that hound when it would have killed me."

"All in a day's combat. We look out for our comrades and fight as a unit."

Eben called out from precariously close to the new cliff edge, "It looks as if the avalanche caught all the hounds, but we should go down there and make sure they're dead."

Raina made a small sound of distress in front of him. He sensed the conflict within her. As a White Heart member, she was responsible for the lives of the hounds. But loyalty to her friends and residual terror from being attacked urged her to let Eben slit the beasts' throats.

"I will see to it that Eben incapacitates them without killing them outright," he promised quietly.

She gazed up at him with big, dark eyes brimming with tears. "Thank you," she whispered.

He turned her hand loose and moved confidently to the

edge of the cliff. Rock climbing was a longtime hobby of his, and he eyed the scree and boulders littering the steep slope with a practiced eye.

He glanced over his shoulder. "Keep that hunter unconscious until we return, Sha'Li."

"Mine is the pleasure," she replied, grinning. In her reptilian face, the expression was macabre. A ferocious fighter, that girl was.

He half ran, half slid down the slope in a heart-stopping rush that put him at Eben's side in a matter of seconds. Just in time, in fact, to place a restraining hand on the youth's wrist as he raised his sword to hack off one of the hounds' heads.

"Raina," Rynn murmured.

"She's not here, and that thing tried to eat me."

"Raina saved your life and healed us all. In return, we owe it to her to respect her colors and her duty."

Eben glared at him furiously.

"I understand, friend," Rynn said sincerely. "I've been hunted by beasts like these before, and it is my fondest wish to slice them into a thousand tiny pieces. But if you kill these, the Empire will only replace them with ten more packs just like them. And," he added gently, "you will destroy Raina."

Eben's rage wavered.

"She loves you like a brother. Do not let her down."

"Gah." Eben spun and stomped away cursing fit to rouse the dead.

Rynn let him get the frustration out of his system and then suggested low, "We could, however, shift that outcropping of rock just up there and maybe bring down another chunk of the hillside on these mangy, flea-infested curs and bury them deep enough that it will take days to dig them out and heal their injuries."

A broad grin split Eben's face. "I'm liking you a bit more, paxan."

"Look, just there. See that boulder at the base of the outcropping? If we move it—"

"We'll need a lever," Eben interrupted excitedly. "Pull out that stone and the rest will tumble down."

They searched about and found a stout tree branch that had come down with the original avalanche. They placed its tip under the key boulder and in front of a knee-high rock they muscled into place. Then, together, they put their combined weight into pressing down upon the other end of the log. It took a couple of minutes of sweating and cursing and groaning, but at length, Rynn felt the boulder begin to shift.

"A bit more," he grunted.

Bracing his feet on the rock wall behind him, he pushed down with all his strength. The boulder gave way all at once, and a strong hand grabbed the back of his collar and yanked him out of the way as a larger piece of the rock wall than he'd anticipated came crashing down.

He threw his sleeve over his mouth and coughed violently along with Eben as a thick cloud of dirt and dust rose from the vicinity of where the hounds had fallen. In a few seconds, the dust cleared, and they were able to see their handiwork.

"Better," Eben announced in satisfaction. "That should hold those cursed mongrels down for a few days."

A huge pile of rocks and dirt completely covered all signs of the elemental hounds. It would take a team of men days to dig them out fully. Grinning, he banged his knuckles against Eben's as the jann held a congratulatory fist out to him.

"A job well done," Rynn declared.

"Are you two all right?" a female voice called down to them.

Rynn looked up to see Rosana lying down, peering over the edge of the cliff. "Just buying us a little breathing space."

"And getting a little vigilante justice," Eben muttered under his breath.

"Sha'Li says it'll be days before the hunter gets his knots undone up here. She conked him over the head again and says he'll be napping for a while. Raina and Will are just finishing packing up everybody's stuff. How long will it take you two to get back up here?"

"You four need to join us down here. The soldiers who travel with the hunters and their hounds will search the forest up there and find any tracks we leave."

"I'm not coming down that cliff!" Rosana squawked. Raina's face joined Rosana's in peering over the edge, and both girls pulled horrified faces.

"It's not that hard," Rynn coaxed. "You just start sliding and then run enough to keep your feet from getting buried as the dirt slides."

"No, thank you," Raina declared.

Will's head appeared. "It's not that bad. You two can do it. Unless of course, you're too afraid to give it a go."

"Hah." Sha'Li's dark visage appeared beside Will's. "Easy will it be. Raina will I help while Rosana you bring down."

Rynn ducked as the party's packs came sailing over the edge and tumbled down the slope, narrowly missing his head. Boots appeared overhead, then the hems of the split skirts the healers wore for traveling. Then all four of their companions lurched over the edge of the cliff.

As advertised, they slid the first part of the slope, picking up speed as they went. Rosana screamed as Will bodily dragged her forward, forcing her to run beside him as they kept pace with the sliding scree.

All four of their friends fetched up on the valley floor beside the mound burying the hounds. Raina looked frazzled, but Rosana looked up at Will, her eyes sparkling. "That was fun!" the gypsy declared.

Sha'Li, however, was more circumspect. "Down we are. Now. How to cross all that grass and no tracks leave?"

Rynn spoke reluctantly. "I do not believe that tracks will be the worst of our problems. In spite of slowing the hunter down by some days, he will free his hounds eventually and heal them. And then they will come after us with double the intensity of before. Next time, we may not be lucky enough to have a cliff at our backs that the hounds do not know of."

"Water," Will declared abruptly.

The others looked at him.

"Water throws regular hunting dogs off the scent of their prey. Why not elemental hounds? If we head for a body of water and cross it, that may confuse them. Or at least slow them down long enough to let us get away."

Rynn did not explain that there was no getting away from Imperial hounds. They would run themselves to death before they gave up the chase. Better to let the party have hope and do their best to elude the beasts instead of simply giving up and surrendering Eben to the hunter.

"It's worth a try," Eben said hopefully. "So where's the nearest big body of water?"

"The Estarran Sea," Raina said immediately. "But instead of going north, we will have to turn west."

"It takes us off Tarryn's trail," Eben objected.

"The necessity now is to elude the hounds, not find your friend," Rynn responded. "If we do not throw yon beasts off your scent, we will not live long enough to find Kendrick and Tarryn, anyway."

"No time have we for debate," Sha'Li declared. "Those mangy beasts and their master will not sleep forever."

"What if they perish of their wounds or starve before anyone finds them?" Raina asked, eying the stone mound doubtfully. "I cannot leave them here to die."

"Never fear," Rynn replied grimly. "The soldiers will find the hunter, and he will see to his hounds, even if he has to hire every person for miles around to dig. If we are lucky, this will buy us maybe half a week at best."

Rynn did not voice his fear that this hunter might have some sort of mental link to the second hunter they knew to be in the area. With a White Heart member in their midst, though, they could not kill the hunter on the ridge above nor the hounds below as his instinct told him to do. They must take their chances and hope the hunters were not connected.

The party turned its attention to the grassy valley stretching away from them. In the moonlight, it looked like a silver lake, its surface rippling gently in the night breezes. Far in the distance, rocky cliffs rose in a long line marking the other side of the valley.

Sha'Li shook her head. "Never will we without a trail cross all that fragile grass. Follow us without hounds a blind man could."

Rynn swore under his breath. She would know. She was as fine a countertracker as he'd ever seen.

"All night it will take to go around it, but tracks aplenty we will leave if through the valley we pass. Hours will we lose."

"Hours we cannot afford to lose," Eben added grimly.

"How long would it take us to walk across the valley if we had no care for leaving tracks?" Raina asked no one in particular.

Rynn gauged the distance quickly, using his third eye to triangulate the distance to within a few body lengths. "It is half a league plus or minus a few strides. A person could walk it in, say, thirty minutes were the land flat. But given the terrain, I would estimate the walking time to be an hour or more—"

"The terrain is not an issue," Raina interrupted. "Everybody line up, and I will cast spirit forms upon all of you. I will have to renew the spells several times as we cross the valley. But if I can find a rock to stand upon where I will not leave tracks, I will drop my form, cast new spells upon you, and then recast one upon myself. Once you are in spirit form, you will drift over the ground, neither rising nor falling. Think of moving forward and you will glide forward almost as if you are walking. Pretend you are a ghost. It helps. You will get the hang of it soon enough."

"Magic I like not!" Sha'Li declared.

"Tolerate it you will," Raina retorted. "Unless you have a better plan for crossing that valley quickly without leaving an easy trail for our friends, the Imperial hounds, to follow."

Sha'Li commented direly, "Track spirit forms they probably can."

Will added, "Yes, but following a non-corporeal trail should be slower than if we leave physical tracks."

Rynn did the math and was shocked by the amount of magic Raina was proposing to cast in this endeavor. Apparently, she had done the calculations, too, and felt it was within her ability. Aurelius had said she was an arch-mage, but it was hard to credit just how much magic she could summon until she casually proposed to keep six people in spirit forms for upward of a half-hour.

In short order, she cast spirit forms upon them. They were still vaguely visible, but their bodies took on a disconcerting transparency. They did, indeed, look like a pack of ghosts.

Will spoke first. "Let us not waste the magic. Follow me."

Traveling in this manner was actually quite easy once Rynn accustomed himself to it. Sha'Li asked, "If into one of you I bump, what happens? Pass through you do I, or something else?"

"I actually do not know," Raina answered. "Will, do you have any knowledge of how this magic works?"

"No, and I do not care to find out," he declared stoutly. Rynn shared the sentiment.

Not quite five minutes had passed when Raina called out low, "I found a good rock. I'm going to drop my form, and then as I call out your name, come to me and I will renew your spell."

The operation went smoothly, and they glided forward again. Four more times they had to stop for her to recast the spirit forms upon them. Gads, approaching three hundred simple healing spells she had just cast, and she didn't seem even the slightest bit fatigued or drained.

Somewhere in the middle of the valley, they crossed a river that looked swift and deep enough to cause them difficulty in crossing it. At best, it would have been a cold, drenching swim. At worst, it could have been a dangerous maneuver. As it was, we drifted over the black, roiling surface like wisps of fog, never slowing, never stopping.

They reached the first trees on the far side of the open valley and stopped, staring up at an imposing wall of boulders and broken stone. "Now what?" Rynn asked.

Raina answered, "Spirit forms will not float. We'll have to come out of our forms and climb the cliff, or preferably, move along its base and find an easier spot to ascend."

Rynn much enjoyed rock climbing, and he was a bit disappointed at not getting to try the cliff face. But he did not relish the idea of trying to get five amateur climbers with no climbing ropes or harnesses safely up the steep valley wall.

"Oh, dear," Rosana groaned as her legs collapsed and she fell in a heap on the ground.

The others staggered and stumbled around Rynn. Raina was the last to reform, but she was already sitting down on the ground when she did so. As Will helped her to her feet, she explained, "It's not usually that bad to come back into your body. It's just that we stayed in forms for so long that the transition back to normal hit us harder."

Eben replied, "It is the opposite coming out of my stone-skin form. I feel so light when it ends, it's as if I could fly."

"Like not these strange forms do I," Sha'Li grumbled.

Rynn grinned over at her. "Admit it. You're glad to be across that valley and not to have had to countertrack all of us through that dead grass."

Sha'Li shot him a credible scowl through her scaled features. "Fine. Admit it I do, ugly pinkskin."

His grin widened. He'd been called a lot of names in his life, but ugly had never been one of them. He rather enjoyed the sensation of being repulsive to someone.

"Well, that was fun," Will commented. "I'll keep that technique in mind the next time we encounter nasty terrain I'd rather not walk across."

Rosana glared at him. "Magic is no excuse for laziness."

Will grinned at her and tucked her under his arm, pulling her close to his side. Sha'Li rolled her eyes at the pair, and Eben wrinkled his nose at their obvious affection for one another.

As for him, Rynn didn't begrudge them their young love.

It was pure and innocent, and stars knew, few enough things in this world were either. Besides, his mentor, Phinneas, had foreseen troubles aplenty for both Will and Rosana before their quest was complete.

For that matter, Phinneas had foreseen trouble for them all. This group had attracted all kinds of attention on the dream plane already, and various factions were lining up, some to hinder them and some to help them. The fact that they'd drawn the notice of the Oneiri, who had sent their greatest warrior to protect these children, spoke volumes of the struggles that lay ahead of them.

So young they were for the heavy responsibilities upon their shoulders. So cursed naïve. He was precious little bulwark to protect them from the coming storm, and he had only his mind and his fists to save them from disaster. Which was not reassuring in the least.

The next two days were a nightmare race for their lives. Will stumbled along as quickly as his feet would go, so exhausted he could hardly see to place one foot in front of another. They barely stopped to eat, let alone to rest, and they snatched sleep in short naps that only seemed to make them all more tired. He was worried about Rosana and, from time to time, snuck equipment out of her pack and into his to lighten her load. But truth be told, she kept up as well as everyone else.

The terrain was rough, the forest thick with brambles, brush, and downed trees. But ever-present fear of Imperial hounds closing in on them spurred them to press on relentlessly. They all scratched their skin and tore their clothing, twisted ankles, and were bitten to pieces by swarms of gnats. Every noise in the forest made them jump and reach for weapons in fear that one of those massive hounds was about to leap out of hiding and tear their throats out. All in all, everyone was roundly miserable.

If only they knew how close the hounds were behind them. But there was no way to find out, so they could only assume the worst and flee as if the hounds were nipping at their heels.

On the morning of the third day, they woke up to rain. It made for cold and soggy going, but Sha'Li thought the rain would help mask their scent.

They had been walking for mayhap two hours when suddenly, the forest abruptly gave way to leaden gray sky. Rynn, who was leading the way, came to an abrupt halt at the edge of what turned out to be a breathtakingly enormous cliff.

Far below, a huge black body of water stretched away from them. No shore was visible in the distance. Just water and more water, draped in silver curtains of rain. They had reached the Estarran Sea. Now to find a way down the gigantic cliff and thence across the sprawling gulf that slashed inland into Haelos for a thousand miles or more.

Arcing gently out into the water to both their left and right, great stone cliffs towered in the misty rain, slate gray rock interspersed with veins of opalescent color. On the tip of the headland far to their left, a cottage sat like a tiny toy, dwarfed by the enormity of the cliff upon which it perched. Will estimated that the water lay at least a thousand feet below them.

To the right was some sort of massive timber structure jutting out over the cliff with pulleys and heavy chains dangling.

"That looks like a dock at the bottom of yon lift system," Rynn commented.

Will took a cautious step forward toward the edge and stared down in the direction Rynn was looking. There was no shoreline where water met stone, just a narrow strip of boulders and scree shed from the cliff face upon which great waves crashed angrily. But a broad, low wooden jetty poked out of some sort of dark opening in the cliff face between a particularly large pair of boulders.

He started walking to the right, paralleling the cliff in search of a way down. "There has to be a path for people to get down there."

"Steps I see," Sha'Li called.

Through the rain, Will made out a faint line of stripes descending diagonally down the cliff.

"What worries me," Rynn said, "is why there are these signs of civilization but no signs of people. Where are they?"

"Foul day it is. Inside soft humans stay, by fires huddled," Sha'Li answered scornfully.

The stairs turned out to be carved directly into the cliff face. They were broad and even, worn into smooth, shallow arcs by the passage of many feet and rendered treacherous by the rain. Each tread was wide enough for perhaps four men to walk abreast. However, there was no hand railing guarding the edge, and Will noticed he was not the only one hugging the cliff wall as they started down. Gusts of wind buffeted them as the rain pelted at their exposed skin, and it felt as if nature itself was trying to tear them off the cliff and throw them to their deaths.

Rosana, who was walking behind Will, mumbled fearfully, "I do not like heights."

Normally, they did not bother him, but today his stomach twisted and turned nervously like the wind swirling around them. "Do not look down. Concentrate on my back and watch the steps."

Perhaps it was fear firing his imagination, but the storm seemed to be getting worse. Rumbles of distant thunder rolled along the cliffs above, and the crashing waves roared below in a deafening cacophony of nature's fury.

Without warning, Rynn pulled up sharply in front of him. Will had to grab for an outcropping of rock beside himself to keep from running into the paxan's back. "What the—"

"Heads up," Rynn interrupted. "We have company." The paxan settled into a fighting stance in front of Will, his crystal-encased hands and forearms relaxed in front of his body.

There was precious little room to fight on these narrow stairs. If they were not extremely careful, someone was going to be pitched off the cliff to his or her death.

"What in the name of the Guardian of the Cliff are you people doing out here on the Steps on a terrible day like this?" a male voice demanded indignantly from beyond Rynn.

A short, stout human stood before them, squinting up the stairs at them through the rain.

"You'll fall to your deaths, for sure. Come in from the rain already and take the inside passage. Bunch of cursed fools."

Rynn glanced questioningly over his shoulder at Will, who shrugged in return. An inside passage sounded promising. Anything was better than continuing down these wet, slippery steps as the storm worsened around them.

About a dozen steps farther down the cliff, an opening loomed, leading into the cliff face. Rynn ducked through the low opening first, and Will followed suit. The party crowded into a relatively dry cave and shook the rain off like a bunch of dogs. The man who had led them in squawked as water flew in all directions and removed his cloak, revealing a purple-and-black tabard bearing the double mountain insignia of the Imperial Miner's Guild.

Rynn unobtrusively slipped his concealing circlet over his third eye, then gestured at Raina. "This is Initiate Raina of the White Heart, and we are her escort."

"And where might you be bound, White Heart? There are precious few people in these parts in need of your particular services. These here are the wilds, in case you hadn't noticed."

"That fact had not escaped my attention," Raina replied courteously, smiling. "I am on a journey of exploration. To that end, I am desirous of obtaining passage across the Estarran Sea to find out what lies beyond."

"Bah. Nothing worth your time lies over there. Just the odd settlement and a few bands of wild greenskins."

"As a White Heart member, greenskins fall within my area of duty," she replied gently.

Another grunt. "Waste of good healing, if you ask me."

Will was faintly surprised that Raina refrained from pointing out tartly that, in fact, she had not asked for the man's opinion.

He looked around the cave curiously. A half dozen passageways delved deeper into the cliff, and their guide led them toward the leftmost one. They paused to light torches they took from a basket sitting by the entrance to the tunnel and then proceeded downward on another set of steps much like those outside. Except of course, these steps were dry and did not offer the thrill of potentially falling to one's grisly death with a single misstep.

From time to time, a vein of pearlescent white shot through the dark gray of the walls, and as torchlight caught its surface a rainbow of colors shimmered in the translucent substance. Will restrained an urge to reach out and caress the beautiful stone.

After they'd been descending for perhaps five minutes, Raina stopped abruptly, frowning, and reached for yet another vein of that beautiful opalescent stone, laying her palm flat upon the rock wall and tilting her head to listen.

Rynn asked her, "What do you hear? Is it the voices again?"

Hear? Stone did not speak. Will frowned back and forth between the pair.

"Whispers," she answered. "Voices whose words I cannot quite make out. They . . . reverberate. Like echoes."

Rynn stepped near her and reached out with both hands to place them on either side of her head. His fingertips rested on her temples. "Do not try to understand the individual words. Let the greater meaning unfold as it wills, and do not fight it. Just let whatever comes, come."

She nodded between his hands, her frown easing slowly. What was that all about? She was hearing voices now? That could not be good. The last thing they needed was for her to go mad on them. He should know.

The party continued on.

The tunnel eventually opened into a huge chamber. A half dozen cottages would have easily fit within the confines of this soaring space. A collection of tables and benches tucked into one corner held a cluster of men who appeared to be chatting and drinking ales. A tavern, mayhap?

A line of men covered in stone dust, bearing axes and picks over their shoulders, clumped across the chamber and headed down one of many side passageways. Several of them wore Miner's Guild colors or insignia. The group was mainly different kinds of dwarves and humans.

"Where are you folks headed?" their guide asked.

Will and the others traded flummoxed looks among themselves, and Raina dived in to answer, "We'd like to go to the dock. I really do want to obtain passage across the sea."

"Well, then, you'll need to head down thataway." He pointed at a passage across the space. "But I would not go down there if I were you. Past these upper levels, lizardmen have been attacking the miners ever since we opened up an area of old caves. Them bug eaters seem to think they have some sacred right to them. They're demanding that we vacate all the caves they say is their ancestral places. Which is poppycock. They just want the rich veins of ore we struck. This whole cliff belongs to the Empire, it do." He spat scornfully.

Sha'Li had gone very, very still. Both Eben and Rynn moved closer to her, presumably to hold her back if she should attack.

The man continued heedlessly, "Making the Merr plenty mad, too, those lizardmen are. Had a few skirmishes between 'em, but for the most part, they's just spittin' and steerin' clear of one another. It ain't no fit place for a buncha kids to venture, White Heart colors or no. Best you stay out of the rest o' the mine altogether," he warned.

"But we need to cross the sea as soon as possible," Raina explained.

The miner shrugged. "If you get ambushed by lizardmen, no miners nor Merr will come to save you from those filthy greenskins."

Will heard the hiss from Sha'Li and the telltale slither of her claws starting to slip out of her fists. "Easy," he breathed at her.

The guide turned his back and stomped away to join the other miners in the makeshift tavern.

Rynn's eyesight was the best, so he went first into the darkness. Sha'Li went second. Forewarned of possible trouble, they moved slowly, easing downward into the bowels of the cliff. The passageway narrowed, and the stone changed down here. The walls were rougher, as if this was an active mine that had not finished being worked. They had just reached one of the wide landings marking a switchback in the tunnel when, without warning, a half dozen green lizardmen burst around the corner brandishing weapons. Rosana screamed a little, and even Will jolted at the creatures' sudden appearance.

"Our mines these be. Intruders you are. Leave at once or die."

Sha'Li pushed forward, elbowing Rynn aside. "Name thy clutch," she demanded truculently.

Hisses issued from the lizardmen's throats, and their spears lifted menacingly. But then one of them raised his torch high, and Sha'Li's black scales glistened like polished obsidian in the firelight. "Black Clan. White Tribe," he breathed.

All the lizardmen's torches lifted up high. They stared as if they had seen a ghost.

"Vouch for these others, do you, tribe warrior?"

"Aye. Vouch for them I do," Sha'Li replied.

And just like that, the lizardmen lowered both their torches and their weapons as meek as lambs. "The Elder will want to speak with you. Come with us."

They turned off the main tunnel and plunged deeper into the mountain. The passageway became rough, narrow, and dank. No way could Will work in these conditions every day. As it was, the weight of the mountain pressing in on him was making him intensely uncomfortable.

The lizardmen led them to a domed chamber cut out of the rock. He would have called it low and wide were the scale of the place not so large. The floor and walls were black stone and carved with long rows of intricate scribbles that looked like no writing he'd ever seen before. One of these leaped out at him, though. He saw it every day on Sha'Li's face. The Tribe of the Moon symbol.

Interspersed among the scribbles were pictorial panels carved with incredible detail. Most of the panels seemed to deal with a war between Merr and lizardmen followed by a reconciliation and peace between the two races. But among those, he spied a panel depicting what looked like a human woman before and after transforming into a werewolf.

Raina stopped in front of a panel showing an elf wielding a great longbow. "Who is this?" she asked their escorts.

One of the lizardmen glanced over his shoulder at the bas-relief. "The wielding of the Eliassan Strongbow that shows. The bow of an ancient warrior it was. Brought out in times of war by elves, for fires true it always does."

Will took a hard look at the bow. Stout and nearly as tall as the elf wielding it, that strong bow would take a strong man, indeed, to pull it, let alone fire it with any accuracy. Raina was concentrating fiercely on the carving as if memorizing every detail of the weapon and the elven warrior firing it. Did she think that might be Gawaine's missing bow?

Black stone benches rose from the floor of the cave in a huge circle, carved as part of its creation, apparently, and a fire burned sluggishly in the shallow depression inside the circle. They were waved over to the benches, and room was made for them to sit. As he took his place on a bench, Will noted fine golden veins running through the stone. It looked like the same stone the wedge in the Haelan legion armory had been carved from.

"What stone is this?" he murmured to Sha'Li.

"Nullstone."

He'd heard of it before. It had the power to absorb magic and was impervious to the effects of magic. It was said to be so hard as to be nearly unworkable, though. Legend had it that the rokken dwarves had been masters at mining and carving it. The modern Miner's Guild tightly controlled every sliver of the stuff these days. Gads. And these lizardmen sat in an entire cave made of it.

The lizardmen around them were several different colors,

which surprised Will. He'd thought they were all green. He asked low, "Eben, are the different colors in their skin similar to the differences in yours?"

The jann shrugged.

Rynn piped up with, "Different clans have different colorations. Whether that indicates some sort of elemental alignment, I could not say. However, red lizardmen come from the hot, dry places, and blue lizardmen came from deep, open water. They've been mostly eradicated by the Merr."

At the name of their enemy, hisses rose from the numerous lizardmen loitering in the chamber. They all looked as if they were waiting for something. And, indeed, a moment later, a new lizardman entered the space from another tunnel and made his way to the circle of stone benches.

As he approached the fire, Will saw that this one was actually brown in color, although as the flames caught his scales, a metallic glow closer to tarnished brass glinted. He looked old, although how he got that impression, Will couldn't exactly say—maybe the slow, stiff way he moved or the discoloration around his mouth and eyes.

The newcomer zeroed in on Sha'Li and sank to the bench beside her. "Welcome are you among us, sister."

"What place is this?" she asked the old one.

"Clutching ground of our ancient ancestors this is."

"Honored are we to be invited in," Sha'Li said formally.

Will looked around with fresh interest. How ancient were these ancestors of which the bronze lizardman spoke? Rumor had it that lizardmen were descended from dragons, but rumor also had it that dragon ancestry was a lie to try to gain social standing. Would that this actually was a dragon clutching ground. How many humans could claim to have seen one of those?

"What, tell me can you, of yon tribe symbol on the wall?" Sha'Li asked.

Going straight to the point, was she? Raised around his elven mother, Will was used to a fair bit of small talk before the real subject of any conversation came up. Not much for social niceties, these lizardmen.

"Ancient is that symbol. Carved by early members of the tribe chosen by Lunimar himself. With magic it is imbued. Yon panel shows Lyssa Wolfsong in her transformation to Lunimar's Gifted."

"Never have I seen so much nullstone in one place," Sha'Li said in wonder that mirrored Will's.

"Touched by a dragon's breath were these walls and hence formed the stone. Great and magical is the breath of our ancestors."

"Still active is the magic in the stones, then?" Sha'Li responded eagerly.

"Aye."

If Will was not mistaken, that was a warning tone the old bronze one had used, as if steering Sha'Li away from asking any more questions about the chamber and its symbols' magic.

"Of Tribe of the Moon and our kind, what can you tell me?"

"Many are we within tribe. Ancient is our kinship, one to another. Rare, however, is your white mark. Hatched have many clutches since seen has been that color. A sign it may be, that back is the white magic of your kind."

"What does it do?" Sha'Li asked eagerly.

"For healing does white magic stand. Purification and renewal its gifts are said to be."

"Bah," Sha'Li burst out, the ridge of scales along the back of her neck and over her head rising. "For combat raised and trained was I."

The old one shrugged. "And yet, white marked you be. With healers and warriors surround yourself you do. Like wolves and lambs, sharks and seals, always has it been. Giving of life and taking of life, together exist side by side. Both healer and warrior you may be."

Sha'Li subsided. After a pause, she asked, "How for this white mark was I chosen?"

"By your actions are you known."

Something in Will prompted him to speak up. "Actually, it's by her heart that she is known to us as our friend. And she is a credit to your race."

That brought all sound in the room to a screeching standstill. He felt the weight of dozens of stares upon him. The lizardmen were not used to compliments from humans, apparently. The rustlings and murmurs resumed, and Raina breathed to him, "Nicely done."

The lizardmen insisted on feeding them before they continued on their way, and a meal consisting of tasty fish and genuinely disgusting stewed seaweed was served to them. He noticed that Sha'Li moved off at one point to speak quietly with the old bronze lizardman. When she came back, she was carefully tucking what looked like a thin bronze plate into her pouch, although it was more oval in shape than round.

At length, the feast concluded, farewells were exchanged, and the lizardmen led them back to the wide tunnel they'd been traversing before. Rynn gestured for the party to reverse its marching order, leaving Will and Sha'Li to go last, which made sense if they were headed into the Merr-controlled portion of the cliff.

Before too much longer, the stairs ended in another vaulted chamber. But this one was more conventional in shape with large pillars to support the ceiling. The space was partially filled with huge, wheeled carts of ore, apparently waiting for transport. Trash littered the floor—bits of armor and broken arrows as if this had been the site of recent battle. It was lit from a large opening to the outside. The roar of angry surf and the smell of the sea were very close.

"Where are the merchants and shippers?" Eben muttered as they trod across the space. "Who looks after this storehouse?"

"Know that one, do I," Sha'Li replied eagerly from the back of the pack.

The others turned to stare at her. "Do tell," Raina declared.

"A Merr tribe the bay controls. Tiburon Merr," she added in disgust. The name meant nothing to Will, but given the way Sha'Li said it, he gathered they were a particularly distasteful flavor of the water-dwelling species, at least in the mind of a lizardman. The two races were forever at each other's throats, squabbling over water territories and generally snarling at one another. Will supposed that, at the end of the day, they were no more combative than humans were over control of land territories.

Raina piped up. "Why did those lizardmen react so strongly to seeing you, Sha'Li? Are you some sort of nobility within your kind?"

Will stared at the human girl and then at the lizardman girl. Now that she mentioned it, those lizardmen had reacted with something akin to awe when they'd spied her. And to be invited into the very space the lizardmen had kicked the miners out of?

Sha'Li snorted. "Elder or chieftain I am not."

They headed over toward the seaside exit to the warehouse. A stone ledge, perhaps ten feet above the waterline, ended in stone steps that led down to a huge, floating wooden pier that bobbed alarmingly on the surface of the water. Will mentally cringed at the idea of stepping out onto that heaving wooden structure.

Raina spoke up. "If Merr control the bay, then it will be from them we must hire a boat. Perhaps you should hang back a bit, Sha'Li, until we have secured passage."

"But information have I that helpful may be."

Everyone turned to look at her.

"The entire bay by Occyron the Six-Gilled is ruled. Clan chief of Tiburon Merr is he. Control most of the coastlines of Dupree do the Tiburon. Purchase passage from them you must. Lovers of the Kothite Empire they are not."

Raina nodded. "That is, indeed, helpful. Since Rosana and I prominently display our affiliation with the Heart, which is both Imperial and has no presence among the Merr, we are probably not the best choice to speak to these Merr. What little I know of the Merr is that they are generally a warlike people who revere strength and combat prowess. I worry that they will perceive Will and Eben as too young to be worthy of respect. Rynn, it looks like you get to negotiate on behalf of the group. And act fierce."

He replied dryly, "What makes you think I am not fierce in truth?"

Good point. From what little Will had seen from his beleaguered position in the fight, Rynn had fought well against the elemental hounds, particularly given that he'd fought with just his fists and feet.

The paxan removed his filigree circlet, exposing his third eye. Will repressed a shudder at the sight of that perceptive, observant eye so wildly out of place on Rynn's forehead. It did add to his overall menace, though.

Seasick already, Will watched Rynn pick his way down the wet stone steps to a large bell covered with a bright green patina. The paxan lifted a hammer hanging on a chain beside the bell and gave it a hefty whack. A loud gong rang out across the water. Will suspected, though, that the main sound was carried away underwater by the metal pole the bell was mounted upon.

"Now what?" Raina asked.

Rynn, who had bounded back up the steps and retreated with the rest of them to the relative cover from the rain inside the cave warehouse, shrugged. "Now we wait."

CHAPTER

22

Gabrielle watched Regalo pace the confines of the sitting room in their chambers at court. He looked as restless as a caged dire lion and as cranky as one. Not that she blamed him. It was not every day that the Emperor approached her husband to suggest that he might be torn out of his family's ancestral home in Haraland and sent to a violent, dangerous outpost in the hinterlands to serve as the first king of Dupree. Apparently, Maximillian was toying with the idea of turning the colony into a full-blown kingdom.

She had no idea whether the Emperor was serious or not. One could never tell with him. She did know he made a common practice of stirring up trouble by pitting his kings against one another in petty political struggles as a means of keeping them bickering among themselves. She supposed that, in Maximillian's mind, it was better to have his kings divided and at one another's throats rather than unified and at *his* throat.

It was a chaos the Eight were happy to help perpetuate. She'd already received a few rumors in scrawled notes signed only with the number eight suggesting that she share the contents with whoever she thought might be most interested. Which was a euphemism for her spreading the rumor to whoever would react most strongly and create the most strife among the peers of the realm.

"What did you say to Maximillian?" she asked.

for the hunter. But instead of a blind man, a half dozen Imperial soldiers burst out of the tunnel the hounds had come from. And they looked angry.

"Will! Watch your back!" he shouted, surging forward to meet this new threat.

Hound number one had other ideas, however, and a massively powerful vise clamped around Eben's left boot. He actually felt teeth through the thick leather as if a bear trap had just closed upon his foot.

A fist flashed past his face and slammed into the hound's nose. The speed of the blow stunned Eben almost as badly as the blow itself stunned the hound. The beast's jaws fell away from his foot. Two more quick fists from Rynn and the mighty beast actually stepped back to shake its head.

"You mustn't kill it!" Raina cried out from behind Eben.

"You can heal it later," Rynn called back.

And then the soldiers were on him and Rynn. The good news was that they got in the way of the hound who snapped and snarled behind them, trying to find a way through the dense line of soldiers.

It wasn't pretty. Even though Rynn was shockingly fast with his hands, and he wasn't half-bad with a sword himself, six on two just wasn't a winnable fight, particularly when it turned out these were no regular foot troops but highly trained fighters. The soldiers inexorably pushed them back toward a wall, encircling them with a bristling barrage of swords, spears, daggers, and axes.

The party might have stood a chance against the soldiers had not the hunter arrived, feeling his way through the tunnel opening. As soon as he appeared, the hounds went into a frenzy, shoving forward and shouldering aside the soldiers. In a matter of seconds, Eben and his friends had fallen back into a tight little knot, surrounded by a phalanx of soldiers and snapping hounds.

The hounds advanced upon him, snarling ferociously. As much as he wished to stand his ground, his mind cringed before their aggressive recognition of him as their quarry.

What was it about *him* that made the beasts so crazed? Raina leaped between him and the alpha beast, and shame coursed through him.

He had not been able to save Marikeen; had not been strong enough to protect Kendrick. Even his foster father, Leland Hyland, had died without any member of his family present to defend him or at least ease his passing. And now his friends were going to perish because he wasn't skilled enough to save them from this disaster he had brought down upon them.

"Step aside, Raina. They came for me," he declared. He raised his voice, calling to the hunter, who stood well back across the now quiet chamber, "I will surrender and go without a fight if you let my friends go free!"

"Why should I negotiate with you when you have lost, jann?" the hunter replied scornfully.

Eben opened his mouth to answer, but before he could form words, an explosion of magic erupted from one of the side tunnels, slamming into the backs of the soldiers and dropping four of them on the spot. One of the hounds went down, and a second one yelped and went down whimpering and wailing. Across the room, the hunter groaned and grabbed his midsection. Whether he'd been hit by the magic attack or merely felt sympathetic pain with his dog, Eben could not tell.

"Attack!" Rynn growled from beside him.

Eben brought his sword up and joined the fracas, which was much more evenly matched now. Will had gotten really fast with that staff of his, and for his part, Rynn was a blur as he spun and kicked and punched at close range.

The mages—three of them—who'd staged the surprise attack advanced into the room, hands glowing, as he and the others drove the remaining soldiers back and, one by one, dropped them.

"Who are you?" Eben demanded of the nearest mage.

"No time to talk. Come with—"

A flare of magic struck the mage in the back, dropping

him in his tracks. Rynn bent down quickly, laying his palm on the man's temple. Eben turned to follow the rescuing mages, but Rynn reached out with his free hand to halt him.

He looked questioningly at the paxan, who was frowning. Rynn muttered low, "They have malicious intent."

"Well, I should hope so. They're engaged in combat against Imperial soldiers."

"No. Malice toward us," Rynn bit out.

Eben's sword started to come back up, but abruptly, the two conscious mages' hands glowed brightly. Magic had the advantage of being deliverable from a distance. By the time he jumped forward and closed to sword-fighting range, or Rynn made it all the way forward to hand-to-hand range, they would be dropped in their tracks by that magic.

Now that he looked for it, definite violence gleamed in the duo's stares.

"Well, now," Raina drawled, "if it's magic we're going to be using today, let's use some real magic."

She held her hands up before her, and in an instant a bright blue ball of magical energy crackled and popped between her fingers, rapidly growing in diameter and intensity. What was she doing? She was White Heart. It was not like she was going to blast anyone with that impressive ball of power.

She took a quick step forward, and the mages fell back before her. The gathering of magic in her hands was now nearly shoulder wide and so bright Eben could barely look at it. Stars, he could actually feel heat rolling off it. The hairs on his arms were standing straight up. Gads, that was a lot of magic. More than he'd ever seen in one place.

From behind the mages, shouts became audible. Someone was charging down yet another tunnel, coming fast, and sounding intent on joining the battle.

The casters never took their stares off that ball of magic now spreading Raina's arms wide and still growing. Which turned out to be a mistake. A squad of lizardmen, perhaps the same ones from before, plowed into the backs of the casters, knocking them down.

The soldiers were just starting to revive, and the lizard-men jumped on the uniformed troopers, wielding claws and spears.

"Go!" one of them shouted. Apparently, the lizardmen were prepared to hold off hounds and hunter, soldiers and mages, all, so he and his friends could make their escape.

Rosana spun and ran for the cave entrance, the one leading down to the water. "This way!" she cried.

Raina flung the ball of magic down just in front of the hounds, and it exploded with a mighty crash like a bolt of lightning striking earth. The hounds yelped, noses undoubtedly singed, and jumped back momentarily. Will shoved Raina after the gypsy and followed behind her, disappearing from sight.

Rynn shouted at him, "Go, Eben! Sha'Li and I will bring up the rear!"

He nodded and sprinted for the stairs down to the dock. The bell started ringing frantically as he careened outside into the storm, which had worsened of a sudden as if even nature joined the attack against them.

Eben ran recklessly down the wet, slippery steps and onto the storm-tossed dock. Staying upright on this thing was almost worse than riding in a boat on rough water.

The sound of metal on metal made him spin, sword raised. Rynn and Sha'Li were retreating slowly, their flanks protected by a phalanx of hissing lizardmen, who appeared to be spitting some sort of black substance at their foes. Three of the soldiers were attacking Rynn, Sha'Li, and their escort, while the other three soldiers defended against the mages, who were casting spells as fast as the soldiers were able to activate their defenses. A hound snarled from somewhere inside the cave and then bounded into the doorway, filling the large opening with his stocky body.

Rynn and Sha'Li reached the steps. At a grunted command from the lizardmen, the pair turned and ran for the dock while the lizardmen closed ranks to hold the staircase. The soldiers had the high ground and pummeled the heads and shoulders of the lizardmen viciously. Only the attack of the mages from behind kept the soldiers from overwhelming their impromptu protectors.

"Eh? What's this?" a new voice shouted from behind him.

Eben spun to face this new threat. Through the slashing rain, he spied a silvery-blue-scaled humanoid standing on the end of the dock next to the bell, which had abruptly fallen silent. A Merr.

Will spoke urgently to the Merr, although Eben could not hear the conversation over the howling wind and crashing waves.

Thankfully, a boat rose out of the water just then, water streaming off it and out of it. The hull was long and pointed, albeit low to the water. The vessel looked fast but not stout enough to withstand the storm raging around it.

A dozen Merr materialized out of the water and climbed into the boat without any visible effort to heave themselves up and over the side of the vessel. How did they do that?

"To me!" Will shouted. "Hurry!"

Eben backed down the dock slowly in case Rynn and Sha'Li should be attacked again. A hand grabbed his arm urgently from behind. "Into the boat. Now," a sibilant voice ordered.

More hands guided him backward and down as he refused to take his gaze off his friends.

"What's this?" the Merr on the dock demanded as Sha'Li reached the boat. "You bring a filthy lizardman with you?"

"We agreed upon a price, and she is a member of our party," Will replied sharply. "Does the promise of a Merr mean nothing, then?"

The Merr hissed and jerked his head at Sha'Li to get in.

Rynn leaped into the vessel last, his balance so light and sure that the vessel barely rocked as he jumped aboard. The lizardmen defending their escape had stopped at the edge of the dock, unwilling apparently to set foot upon the heaving wooden platform. Or perhaps the dock was Merr territory. Either way, as the Merr shoved away from shore, the lizardmen grimly held their ground. When the vessel was perhaps thirty feet away from the dock, the lizardmen charged forward, shouting. Eben's last sight of them in the rain was a jumbled melee of Imperial Army tabards and green-scaled bodies rolling about in complete chaos.

Oddly, the hounds bunched in the door of the cave were looking off to the left in rapt attention. Their noses lifted to the storm, they seemed to be catching the scent of something. With a great baying of sound, they bounded down a narrow strip of rocky shoreline toward the south.

"What on Urth was that with the hounds?" Will demanded. "It's as if they caught another scent and took off after it."

"Let us sincerely hope so," Eben declared. He slumped in relief upon a bench seat stretching all the way across the narrow vessel. On each side of the boat, Merr manned oars, pulling strongly against the waves. How all six pairs of oarsmen were maintaining their unison, he had no idea. But with each powerful stroke, the boat leaped forward.

"Who were those mages?" Will demanded.

Rynn answered, "I probed the unconscious one's mind. Does the word 'coil' mean anything to any of you? It was strong in his mind. Along with intent to capture us."

"Capture us?" Rosana exclaimed. "Why?"

Rynn frowned. "I caught glimpses of a serpent. And a sword."

"Anton Constantine?" Will asked in worry. "His mark is a serpent wrapped around a sword."

Eben answered heavily. "I know of this Coil. It is the name of a criminal group that was headed up by our illustrious governor, Anton Constantine."

Everyone groaned.

Raina commented, "What makes you think he relinquished control of this group just because he was ousted as governor?"

"Good point," Eben responded. "Perhaps I should say he *is* in charge of this criminal group."

Rynn spoke up. "So an Imperial hunter and his hounds, the Imperial Army, this Coil group, and Anton Constantine appear to want to capture or kill us. Is there anyone else I should know about?"

Raina answered reluctantly, "Well, there is a group of mages from my home chasing me with the intent to kidnap me."

"Do not forget the Boki," Rosana added.

Unexpectedly, their Merr captain spoke up. "Those cliffs back there mark the western border of effective Imperial control. They do not control this sea nor do they occupy the lands on the far side in any meaningful way. I do not know much of this Coil group nor of the Boki, but the Empire will not chase you across this sea without permission from Baron Occyron."

Eben swiveled to stare at the Merr. "Even Imperial hounds will not go beyond the boundary of Dupree?"

"Well, now, I imagine dogs have no delicate sensibilities when it comes to political borders, but their handler will not venture into the west if he knows what is good for him."

"Why not?" Raina asked curiously.

"In the first place, he would have to negotiate with my kind to cross this body of water, which might or might not happen. And then he'd have to deal with hostile elements on the western shore that are more numerous and dangerous than he and his pups can handle."

"What kinds of hostiles?" Will asked.

The Merr shrugged. "All kinds. Some nastier than others." The vagueness and reluctance of the captain's answer made it clear he didn't want to elaborate on the threats they might face beyond the sea.

The Merr continued, "Now. If it's Imperial hounds you're looking to lose, we might be able to help somewhat with that."

"How?" Eben asked eagerly.

"A beastie who air scents is going to be able to track you across water. There's no telling how powerful these hounds' sniffers are, and it's possible they might even smell you all the way across the Estarran Sea. But there's no way they can sniff you under it."

Eben stared. "Under it?"

The Merr grinned. It was every bit as disturbing an expression on his scaled features as it was on Sha'Li's. He called out jovially, "Prepare to submerge, boys. We've got air breathers aboard."

All of the crewmen abandoned their oars except for one on each side of the vessel to steady the boat in the tossing waves. The remaining Merr unrolled some sort of clear, oiled tarp down the center of the craft and then, as one, hoisted the membrane overhead. It unrolled, revealing a row of narrow ribs sewn onto it. The sailors quickly bent the ribs and installed the ends in sockets along the sides of the boat. Most of the sailors startled him by diving overboard while one of the remaining Merr laid down a line of resin along the seam of wood and membrane, smearing it to form a seal. In short order, the boat had been turned into a watertight, airtight pod.

And then, by no means Eben could fathom, the vessel's tall, pointed prow dipped into the swells and caught. A great wave of water passed over the craft, and he ducked frantically along with his friends. But the membrane held in spite of its fragile appearance. They were completely under the surface now, and the light above was fading fast as they descended.

"Welcome to Estarris," the Merr captain intoned.

Eben looked around in awe. The water was mostly black with streaks of bubbles racing past now and then. The Merr crew held on to poles extending out from the sides of the vessel, propelling the boat with easy kicks of their webbed feet.

Rynn spoke up thoughtfully. "While we are in the business of throwing off the scent of the Imperial hounds, perhaps we should also engage in a misdirection exercise to further confound both hunter and hounds."

Everyone looked at him questioningly.

He continued, "Normally, one would board a Merr vessel with the intent of crossing the Estarran Sea, yes?"

The Merr captain nodded.

Rynn asked, "What if, instead, we make for Marhul? From there, we might hire passage on another vessel and sail north along the eastern shore. If we disembark north of where we were, perhaps we can pick up the trail of our quarry."

Eben had never been to the floating island of Marhul. Legend had it the city, a meeting point for Imperial merchants, Merr traders, and exotic merchants from far-flung lands, was built upon the hull of a leviathan.

Going there was not a half-bad idea. It was neutral territory, and the hunter and his hounds would not be able to attack Eben lest they violate treaties the Empire might have with the Merr.

Let the hunter fruitlessly spend his energy and time trying to figure out how to track him and his scent across the Gulf of Estarra when, in fact, neither he nor his scent would have crossed the sea at all. It was rather diabolical. The harder the hunter tried to reacquire his quarry's scent, the more he would fail. Eben suspected that failure was not an option for the hunter, ergo, the man would fling his hounds over and over at a trail that did not exist.

He nodded at Rynn. "I like it. A lot."

Grins spread among Merr and humans alike at the idea of outfoxing a brace of Imperial hounds.

The Merr captain gave brisk orders for the crew to come about and proceed north underwater. How they had any idea what north was down here in this featureless abyss, he couldn't imagine.

"You're sure the Imperial hunter won't follow us?" Eben asked the captain.

The Merr bared his teeth in what might be a smile or a threat display. "The only way to travel anywhere in or on this body of water is aboard our vessels or those we grant access.

All others we sink. I will put out word that passage might need to be . . . *scarce* for Imperial hunters and soldiers for a few days. I cannot hold them off forever, but I can give you a lead in your race against the Empire."

Rynn threw back his head and laughed. Sha'Li joined him first, and one by one the other members of the party joined in. Eben was last to start chuckling, and soon his belly shook with great gusts of humor. They'd done it. They had escaped what looked like certain capture by the hounds and, furthermore, had left the Empire behind. They still had enemies who might pursue them and unknown dangers ahead, but succeed or fail in their other quests, this had turned out to be a good day.

The silence down here was as deep and dark as the sea enveloping them. The pervasive water all around Eben overwhelmed his senses. He smelled it and tasted it, he felt it on his skin and in his gut. It was everywhere, pressing in on him, drowning him. Too much. The earthen part of him only faintly registered the seabed far below, obscured by the one element to which he'd always shown no affinity. Gads, he hated water.

As his stress grew, it twisted around him like living ropes, binding him more and more tightly. He was going to choke on it soon. If he did not find escape from all this wetness, he would lose his mind.

Mayhap he exhausted himself with fighting off the panic, or mayhap he was just tired from the fight. But either way, he slid off the bench, curled into an awkward ball in the bottom of the boat, and closed his eyes.

*A rise now, children of the elements," called a thunder-ous voice that resonated deep within Eben's spirit.
He looked around at the white mist obscuring everything beyond a small, verdant clearing. His friends slept around a campfire as they usually did, but he did not recall how they'd come to be in this place.*

Rising from his bed of earth, the air heavy with fog beneath the pines, he reached out to wake Sha'Li. She got up and squatted on her heels, holding her hands out to the fire. The strength of Urth flowed into his bare feet, and he drew a long, cool breath as Sha'Li poked at the fire with a stick, stirring glowing embers.

"Heed the call of Llyrando, the Crushing Wave. Come and be recognized," roared a voice in the distance. It pulled Eben forward like the rush of a mountain stream.

"Sha'Li, did you hear that?" he whispered. "Did you feel it?"

"Heed the call of Imogen, the Mother of Crystal. Come and be recognized," called another voice, clear and true.

"Wood this fire needs," Sha'Li remarked. "Alone is the cold heart that does not hear."

"What are you talking about?" he asked, confused. "Did you hear those voices or not?"

"Heed the call of Cyndra, the Crowning Flame. Come and be recognized," proclaimed yet another voice like a light in the darkness, showing him the way.

"Always told were we, listen not to voices in our heads,"

Sha'Li replied. He stared at her, completely flummoxed, as she tossed more wood on the fire. "Sleep again, Eben. Light comes early."

The breeze picked up strength, conveying warmth through his body while Sha'Li shivered by the fire.

"Heed the call of Arcus, the Coming Storm. Come and be recognized," sounded another voice. The call brought with it the feeling of a warm summer breeze, drawing him forward.

Frustrated, he muttered, "I know I heard that."

A tendril of fog rolled forward, nudging Eben to go. As he reached down to jostle Will, the first voice echoed in the mist, "Let those who would be free gather here. Do not fear your brothers and sisters."

As the mist around him cleared, Eben began to make out shapes. He saw buttes beneath rolling clouds, unmistakably the blunt crags of the mountain range known as the Wings of Haelos. Upon a platform-shaped butte that jutted out from the others stood a creature of cloud. Lightning flashed in his form while his edges flowed in the wind. To his left shimmered a woman in golden fire, to his right stood a man with arms like waves, and behind stood a female figure cut of crystal. Even at this distance, Eben could taste their elemental power, hear their substance, and feel their call.

He continued onward in the embrace of the breeze.

As the rest of the fog faded, he made out a vast army before him. Eben had never seen so many jann in one place. Looking west, he made out the silver sands of the Thirst, the great desert sprawling west of the Estarran Sea. Red-crested lizardmen stood among the jann there, and pyresti gathered on its shimmering earth. North, beyond the butte, Eben heard the sharp cut of crystalline facets in the breeze. He saw urthen dwarves bound to the power of stone, assembled with more jann and others hidden in the ktholes—the ancient underground rivers—of the crags.

"Welcome all, storm fellows, fire forged, stone born, and sea spawned!"

The thundering voice reverberated through Eben's heart. He continued drifting forward, noting people of many elementally aligned races in the masses before him.

A man in strange gray robes covered in runes appeared beside the elementals on the butte. On his right hand he wore a gauntlet of ancient design with four glowing blazons above the knuckles. Next to him, a shadowy form stood tall over a small child in rags.

The robed man shouted, "No longer shall we be divided! The boons granted to ye mark ye as offspring of powers more ancient than the interlopers who seek to divide us. Join us in taking back the powers of your birth. Join us in the freedom to be whatever you choose. Ye are the heirs to greatness!"

The assembly roared its approval.

It was then that Eben tasted snow. He looked back to the east and spied the white peaks of the Heaves, far away in Dupree. Upon the closest peak stood a man in strange armor with the look of a glacier, cold light escaping its plates. Whoever he might be, this man was more powerful than all the jann, ikonesti, and snowscales standing before him. The warrior spoke words Eben could not hear to those assembled at his feet and then strode back into the Heaves.

Eben started at the familiar touch of his sister's water energy upon his spirit. She was somewhere near. He looked around frantically.

Beyond the horde, a young woman pulled back the hood of a black mantle wreathed in bronze flames. Marikeen stepped clear of the crowd to stand before the assembled elementals and humans on the butte. Why could he not sense her before? Did that strange robe mask her?

"My great lords and ladies, I am called Marikeen. I stand before you a child of the elements, ready to do your will that I may claim my birthright."

He had found her at last! Eben cried out with all his breath, "Marikeen! Your brother is here!" He charged forward, pushing through the crowd as fast as he could. As he drew closer to the butte, it shrank until it was but a few heads above the horde. The Heaves and Thirst fell away, but the crowd remained.

The gauntleted man approached the platform's edge. "I see in ye great power, young Marikeen. Your offer doth please us. Upon ye we bestow the knowledge of summoning. From this night forth, ye may call upon the infinite forces of the pure ones to enact our will."

With that, the child in rags held out a strange book, glowing with symbols of power. The gauntleted man bowed his head in respect, took the book from the child, and handed it to Marikeen.

Eben still fought through the press of bodies as Marikeen opened the tome. Light poured from the pages, illuminating her face. Her elemental markings reflected the power emanating from the book, and as quickly as it began, the spectacle was over.

"Use thy new spell, young one. Show those assembled here your power," demanded the gauntleted man.

Marikeen called magic to her hands, the left one iridescent blue like the water mark upon her face, the right one arboreal brown. "Harken Guuri, Harken Wiisen!" Marikeen called.

Eben broke free of the crowd and ran toward his sister. Abruptly, he was picked up and thrown backward above the horde with the force of a hundred gales. For a moment, he spied the shadow that had been standing beside the child on the butte accepting a battle thorn from an orc bearing the markings of a thane, a horrible vertical scar across his left eye. Ki'Raiden? What was he doing here?

Even as Eben flew through the air, the shadow changed and formed into another Boki thane, older but with the look of Ki'Raiden about him.

Beside Marikeen, there appeared two creatures, a stone humanoid twice as tall as she and a writhing watery form. Elementals. A prideful grin wreathed her features.

In the suspended moment of his flight, Eben saw Ki'Raiden

hand a wedge of shiny black stone with golden writing on it to the child. Lastly, Eben caught a brief glimpse of Ki'Raiden holding out something blade shaped and bone white.

Eben's world turned black.

Into the darkness, the child spoke. "Such a fine prize, this Dragonfang. You shall have my support, Raiden, son of Daro, Ki of the Thornwold."

A sinister, childish giggle echoed through his mind.

Eben woke with a start. His companions all dozed around him. Sweat drenched his clothing. What in the name of the four elements had *that* dream been all about?

Will peered through the transparent shell and realized they were skimming along the tops of trees. Trees? Underwater? "What is that?" he asked in surprise.

"A forest," the Merr captain answered wryly. "What do you call a large cluster of trees where you come from?"

Will scowled. "We call it a forest, too." He paused, then added, "But it's underwater."

The Merr frowned. "That's Morvadul, the Forest Under the Waves. And aye, we have cities and farms and roads down here, as well. We are not savages, you know."

Apparently, he did not know. He'd never given much thought to how Merr might live underwater. He'd had some vague notion of them swimming about in packs like schools of fish, he supposed, hunting for whatever it was they ate. He turned to Sha'Li and muttered, "Do your kind have underwater cities, too?"

She threw him a look that could only be unadulterated scorn. "Of course, ignorant land walker." She added under her breath, "Nothing so grand as the Merr citadels, but plenty nice."

Huh. Who knew?

"Is that actual light I see overhead?" he asked in surprise.

Sha'Li glanced up. "Ascending we are. Feel it in your ears do you not?"

Now that she mentioned it, his ears did register a strange

sucking sensation. "Are we finally going to get out of this miserable prison?" he asked.

The Merr captain responded, "Do not impugn this vessel, boy. It's saving your ugly pink hide and those of your friends."

"You are correct, sir. My apology for insulting your fast, sturdy ship."

"This is no ship, lad. Merely a light cutter. Lucky for you we answered your call and not one of our surface cargo barges. They can't go undersea like this little lady."

In a few more minutes, they popped up to the surface of the water like a cork. The vessel dipped and bucked for several heart-stopping seconds before settling sedately on the surface. The Merr crew peeled back the membrane that had been their protection from the deep, and Will gratefully breathed in the fresh air.

The sun was setting in a grand display of molten fire across the now docile Estarran Sea. A light breeze ruffled his hair. Ahead of their vessel, a prickly black hump rose out of the water. As they sailed closer, Will made out what appeared to be an island covered in buildings. *Marhul.*

They drew near it and he spied docks radiating outward in every direction. Seagoing vessels of many shapes and sizes were moored there. Cumbersome, broad-beamed rafts huddled next to tall, sleek sailing ships. Narrow cutters like theirs were plentiful, as were husky vessels bristling with catapults and armaments. Obviously military ships of some kind. Except the markings were none he'd ever seen before. Did the Merr actually dare to float their own navy?

He asked in wonder, "How is it you have attack ships that are not part of the Imperial Navy?"

"We do not bow to Koth. The seas of Urth are *our* empire."

"What of the Black Ships?"

"They pay us tribute for the privilege of sailing our seas. In return, we allow them passage upon the surface."

He blinked. The Merr said that as if taking down a Black Ship would not pose any problem to his kind. Will said carefully, "I hear they are very sturdy vessels."

"I suppose."

Again, completely casual disdain for Koth's mightiest warships was evident. The captain turned his attention to docking his cutter then and spoke no more to him. Which was just as well. Will was speechless.

Marhul was crowded, the buildings jostling one another for space. It was bigger than he'd anticipated. A ring of storehouses lined the shore, testament to the shipping business that was the lifeblood of this place. As for the city rising beyond the docks, he estimated that it would hold several thousand people.

Will peered into the water in hope of catching a glimpse of the leviathan shell that the island supposedly rested upon. He did see something black and shiny, partly covered in swaying strands of algae, that could be the smooth surface of a shell. Or, it could just be part of the dock.

He jumped to the pier and staggered a little, as it seemed to heave beneath his feet. A natural sailor he was not. Eben led the way ashore wearing a grin that stretched to both his ears. It was good to see him smile again. Not that he begrudged Eben his stress and grief over the past weeks. Stars knew, Will was all too familiar with what it felt like to lose everyone a person loved in the world and suddenly be cast adrift.

By mutual, unspoken agreement, the party formed a tight phalanx with Sha'Li safely tucked in the middle. They did not need any trouble on this tiny island with nowhere to run or hide.

"What is that?" Rosana breathed.

Will followed the direction of her stare to see an elf unlike any he'd ever seen before. The pointed ears and refined features were definitely elven, but the rest? The woman's skin was the brilliant color of shallow seas upon a white sand beach. And were those gills beneath her chin? She reached up to adjust a pearl and carved shell necklace, and Will could swear he saw webbing between her long, slender fingers.

"That's an aquanesti," Rynn murmured. "If I am not mistaken, she is Shalri La'Quay, a representative of Islan."

"What is Islan?" Will demanded.

"An underwater aquanesti city." Rynn added under his breath, "And it's not polite to stare."

Will looked away hastily from the aquanesti woman. He'd never *heard* of such a race of elves. Merr were plentiful, carrying spears and nets slung over their free arms like he might carry a shield. His father had talked once about nets as weapons. A trio of Merr came at them carrying tridents taller than a man. They wore matching tabards, black with long turquoise triangles down the fronts, with a symbol of a black wave breaking onto a white beach over the breast.

"Black Tide," Rynn muttered. "Get out of their way and show respect."

Indeed, everyone scuttled out of the Merr warriors' paths like they were some kind of royalty. Will jumped aside with his friends, gaze cast downward just to be safe.

The crowd moved back together where it had parted for the Black Tide and continued on its way. "Who are they?" he asked Rynn.

"Elite troopers of the Merr Empire. You do *not* want to tangle with one of them in combat. Ever."

"Are there a lot of them?"

Rynn shrugged. "I would not know. But the seas are very big places. Every city-state of the Merr would have a contingent of them at a minimum, I should think."

Will glanced back over his shoulder speculatively. "And you say all Merr do not like Koth?"

Rynn grinned at Will. "The enemy of my enemy, huh? They'd make a formidable ally if they would ever agree to an alliance with anyone else. But they have never done so that I am aware of. They prefer to sit in the bottom of their oceans and let the surface dwellers squabble among themselves."

"Is that what we do? Squabble?" Will asked a touch bitterly. "It seems to me like we prepare for an all-out fight against an Empire that is determined to rule the entirety of Urth. Once they control all the continents, Koth will turn its attention to the seas. And then the Merr will be alone against an even more massive and powerful Empire."

"Since when does Koth limit its ambitions to Urth?" Rynn asked in a rhetorical tone.

Will stopped, stunned by the implications of that remark. He turned slowly to face the paxan. "What do you mean?"

"It is the belief of many among my kind that the Kothite Empire aims to control the other realms, as well." Rynn resumed walking, and Will was forced to follow along if he wished to continue the conversation and stay with the tightly bunched group.

"They wish to conquer multiple planes of existence?" Will demanded.

Rynn nodded. "Just so. If the Empire can conquer one, they will have a foothold to jump to all the others. Even now, the dream plane is in chaos. Factions are forming there to mirror those here on the prime plane almost faster than I can keep track of them all."

"What triggered the turmoil?" Will asked.

Rynn shrugged. "Your visit might have set a chain of events in motion. Of a sudden, players are moving upon the game board, both there and here. People are watching you. Some attempt to push you about as their pawns. Others wish to hinder you, others to help you."

"Which are you?" Will challenged baldly.

"Do you have to ask?" Rynn replied gently. "I have already put my life on the line for you, and I expect I will do so again before this journey's end."

Will sighed. It was petty of him to question Rynn's motives. Sometimes, though, it was frustrating comparing himself to the paxan's general perfection.

"Who's that?" Sha'Li asked sharply.

Will looked up and spied a two-toned Merr, white scaled on his face but black scaled on his arms and back.

"That's a Ballena Merr," Rynn supplied. "Orcan in nature. The blue Tiburon Merr are said to descend from sharks."

Sha'Li subsided, apparently disappointed with Rynn's answer. What did she hope the black coloration had indicated?

They wandered the streets, gawking at the array of exotic wares, from foreign garb and weapons to spices, rugs, jewelry, carvings, furniture, tapestries, and a hundred other items he did not recognize. Sweet perfumes and the pungent stink of fish wafted around them. If he'd thought Dupree was a city of many races, this place beggared the Imperial capital in that regard. He spied every imaginable humanoid race and a few more he'd never seen before.

"There's the Imperial Merchant's Guild," Eben pointed out. Will shuddered a little to see the familiar insignia on an imposing building. The last thing they needed was for some Kothite loyalist to spot them here and report their presence back in Dupree. The group veered down a side street rather than stroll past the guild house.

Gradually, twilight thickened around them, and the streets started to empty as people headed for home. Their exploration took them to the highest point of the floating city, and they spied a tall, white, gated house with elaborately carved spires jutting up into the sky.

"The residence of Nalor Eeth," Rynn told them. "He's the Merr in charge of the floating bazaar of Marhul."

"I'm hungry," Raina announced.

Ugh. Will's stomach was still far too unsettled for food.

Eben started back down the hill toward a tavern, but Sha'Li stopped the jann. "Not there. Instead, that one." She pointed at another tavern well down the steep street that led straight down to the shore.

"Why not the one I chose?" Eben asked Sha'Li.

"Rotten is the fish smell from the first. Fresh is the smell of the second."

By common consensus, the party headed for the inn the lizardman girl had pointed out. Its exterior was worn, the paint peeling and the wood timbers weather-bleached dull gray.

But a cheerful fire burned inside, the mixed company seated at the long trestle tables was merry, and the food—a rich, creamy seafood dish of some kind and crusty loaves of bread—was first rate. So much so, that Will's squeamish stomach was coaxed into trying a few bites and then diving into a plate of food with gusto.

A few Merr threw Sha'Li dirty looks, but she seemed to understand that she was on enemy turf and greatly outnumbered in this place. For once, she dialed back her truculence and ate quietly—if her enthusiastic slurping of the sauce off her plate could be called quiet.

"What's next for us?" Raina asked, leaning back in satisfaction after the meal.

Will's resentment flared when Rynn was the one to answer, "We can stay here a few days to rest and reprovision ourselves, or we can move on immediately."

Eben pounced on the comment. "I say we go on right away. As it is, we're going to have a hard time regaining the trail."

Will shrugged. "They were moving arrow straight to the north last time we had their trail. If we land and go due east, we ought to cross their path at some point."

Sha'Li frowned. "Very large are the wild lands. Very small are the chances of finding their trail."

"Then we'll have to do it the old-fashioned way," Eben declared. "Ask at farms and villages until we find someone who's seen them, then search for Tarryn's trail sign."

Sha'Li continued to look doubtful, and Will shared her skepticism.

Raina said speculatively, "Answer me this. Why, if Tarryn is Kerryl Moonrunner's prisoner, does he allow her to leave a trail at all? Correct me if I'm wrong, but he's some sort of greater nature guardian being. Surely he can see any track she lays down for us, no matter how sneaky she is about it."

Will stared at her. Sometimes, she thought of the most sideways things.

Sha'Li tilted her head thoughtfully, as did Rynn.

"What are you saying?" Rosana asked. "That Moonrunner is letting her lay a trail for us? Why would he do that?"

"Is it a trap?" Will asked. "Does he want to kidnap more of us?"

"For what purpose?" Rynn replied.

Will scowled at the paxan. He had no answer to his own question, else he would not have asked it. "How should I know? He's cra—"

"Not crazy is he," Sha'Li cut him off forcefully. "Following his own agenda is Moonrunner, but cunning and highly intelligent is he. Never forget this when dealing with him."

"I have no intention of ever dealing with him," he retorted.

"Deal with him we must if Kendrick we wish returned," Sha'Li said soberly.

"What's Moonrunner's angle?" Raina asked Sha'Li. "Why is he doing the things he is?"

"Nature he protects. This land he defends. Threats he sees and hears that others do not. Correct he usually is about such things." She paused, then added heavily, "Worried he is about something or someone who draws near to Haelos. Prepare he does for the coming storm."

Eben spoke slowly, in a troubled voice. "I dreamed of an army last night. Made up of elemental creatures. It was huge. And angry." He shook his head and then muttered, "But it was just a dream."

Rynn studied the jann thoughtfully while Will felt a shiver of foreboding up and down his spine.

Will drew his cloak close against the chill breeze racing across the open water. Ahead, the gray cliffs of the Estarran Sea's eastern shore rose out of the open water.

After an excellent night's sleep in rooms above the tavern they'd eaten in, the party had bought passage on a Merr cargo vessel about to leave for Medea, the paxan colony at

the north end of the Estarran Sea. But when Rynn had doubled the number of coins in his palm, the captain had agreed
to put them ashore somewhere along the northeastern coast
of the great body of water and to be quiet about it.

As the Merr cargo raft angled close to the wild northeastern shore of the sea, the cliffs grew and grew in scale. Will
asked no one in particular, "Is the entire Estarran Sea bordered by these massive walls of stone?"

The Merr captain answered him. "Only the eastern
shore is cliff-bound, lad. Even then, beaches and inlets interrupt the cliffs here and there. It is toward one of those
we sail."

As promised, the blunt nose of the wide, flat-bottomed
boat scraped lightly on what felt and sounded like sand a few
dozen yards from a narrow strip of beach. Although the rise
beyond it was steep and tall, it was weed-covered dune and
not sheer granite cliff.

Will and his friends removed their boots and socks. Clothing would dry quickly enough, but leather boots could stay
wet and miserable for days after a good soaking. He slid into
the thigh-deep water, gasping at the cold of it. Wading ashore
while holding his pack, boots, and staff overhead was awkward to say the least, what with the waves buffeting him
about and the sand shifting beneath his bare feet. But eventually, he stumbled ashore.

He turned to wave a farewell to the Merr crew, but the vessel was already a speck on the horizon, skimming across
the waves like a low-flying bird.

He turned back to study the lay of the land. Raina and
Rosana had already started up the dune, slogging through
the loose sand and laughing while Rynn hurried to catch up
and get in front of the two healers. Will scowled at the display of chivalry—or security consciousness. Either way, it
irritated him.

Taking advantage of his long legs, he chased after the
girls. He reached the top of the sandy ridge a few steps behind Rosana. From here they had a magnificent view of the

sea and of long, unbroken lines of cliffs stretching away in both directions.

"Isn't it beautiful?" Rosana breathed.

"Not half as beautiful as you," he declared gallantly, sweeping her up into his arms. They'd done it. They'd escaped the jaws of the Empire's hounds and could finally resume their quest. He felt light. Free. He drew Rosana close to kiss the laughter from her lips.

Sha'Li muttered sourly from somewhere nearby, "When finished swapping spit you are, proceed we shall."

Will set Rosana away from him regretfully but grinning unrepentantly. "You're just jealous that no one swaps spit with you."

"Kill you my spit would, human," Sha'Li retorted.

Raina, who'd come up behind him with Rynn, asked curiously, "Does that mean lizardmen don't kiss?"

Sha'Li scowled in as close to embarrassment as Will had ever seen from her. "Kill us our own poisons do not."

Of course, they all had to tease her mercilessly after that. The party set out to the east, away from the shore at their backs. Picking up the trail of Kerryl, Kendrick, and Tarryn was a long shot, but it was all they had. Stars willing, they had left all their pursuers far behind and headed in the entirely wrong direction.

The terrain undulated gently, blanketed in knee-high grasses. The winds coming off the great sea at their backs scoured the coast bare in spots, exposing rocky outcroppings that were their only real impediment to travel. A hardy tree here and there dared to stand against the elements, but those were twisted, stunted things that hardly resembled proper trees. Will thought that perhaps his disdain for the overgrown bushes that passed for trees in this place might come from Bloodroot. Or mayhap it came from his own upbringing in the great hickory stands of the Wylde Wold.

Their clothes dried quickly in the brisk breeze for which he was grateful. Even on a pleasant late summer day, damp clothing made for an unpleasant chill.

It was perhaps midafternoon when Rynn announced, "Storm's blowing in."

A storm? On this fine day? Will looked to the west, and sure enough, great, gray thunderclouds were rolling across the sea toward them. They needed shelter. But where?

Eben, who was on point ahead of them at the moment, called out, "I see a decent-sized outcropping ahead. If nothing else, we can shelter in its lee."

The upthrust of granite turned out to be the size of a cottage, and when Will and Eben rigged their tarp as half roof, half wall with the stone at their backs, it made for a passable shelter. The girls gathered what matted moss and dried animal dung they could find for a fire.

Rynn disappeared while the others hastily made camp, and fat drops of rain were starting to splat against the tarp before he finally came running back over a rise a few hundred feet east of them.

A lumpy sack bounced around on his back, and he grinned triumphantly as he ducked under the tarp. Will, who was sitting next to Rosana, felt her body melt a little as the handsome paxan's smile lit his face. Good thing Rosana had laid that big kiss on him earlier or he might have had to kill Rynn today.

"What've you got there?" Eben asked the paxan.

"I found a peat bog. Dug up as much as I could carry."

Will wrinkled his nose as Rynn reached into his bag and pulled out a brick-sized block of the stuff. It stunk to high heaven, like concentrated pig dung.

Sha'Li exclaimed, "Sick I may be if we have to burn that foul mess!"

Rynn grinned at her. "But warm you shall be while you puke, my friend."

Sha'Li froze, staring at the paxan. Will mentally shook his head. The lizardman girl would catch on eventually. They all considered her family.

The peat block Rynn added to the tiny fire the girls already had going did, indeed, give off a horrible stench. But it also gave off a decent measure of heat as the rain began to fall harder and the wind howled around them. Both boulder and tarp did their jobs, though, and protected them from the worst of the storm. They huddled shoulder to shoulder around the fire, holding their hands to the warmth and passing the time by speaking idly of their homes.

Will was surprised to realize that all of them had lost their families or left them behind in some irrevocable way. They were each alone in the world. It dawned on Will that this was his chosen family. They might be very different, but they were united in a shared cause, shared experiences, and a shared set of beliefs.

Rosana passed out strips of dried fish they'd bought in Marhul, and Will gnawed on the salty stuff thoughtfully. "What happens after we wake the—"

Raina cut him off sharply. "Will!"

He glanced up, startled, and then looked guiltily in Rynn's direction. "Oh. Sorry."

The paxan took a deep breath and exhaled it slowly. "I know you all are reluctant to trust me. But if Imperials catch me, they will rip my third eye out and torture me until I go mad as an example to all other paxan not to let my kind live. I have no love for Koth. And I have sworn to defend and protect all of you with my life."

Will muttered, "What harm would it do to tell him? If he stays with us, he'll find out, anyway."

Raina's gaze shifted to him. An entire unspoken conversation took place in her worried eyes. Gawaine had told the two of them to trust no one. To tell no one. Did they dare take this quiet paxan into their confidence? Aurelius had trusted Rynn enough to send the paxan along as their bodyguard.

Will felt the same indecision he saw in Raina's eyes. "It's up to you," he told her aloud. "If he's going to die to protect us, he has a right to know why."

She stared at him for a moment more and then nodded in decision. She said, "Rynn, have you ever heard a legend of the Sleeping King who will wake one day?"

"The one where he comes back in his people's moment of greatest need to save them from the terrible evil threatening to destroy them all?" he answered.

"That's the one." She took a deep breath. "It turns out the legend is true."

Rynn leaned back against the rock wall at his back. "Indeed?" he replied mildly enough.

Raina described to Rynn how the party had gone searching for the Sleeping King and ultimately found his resting place. As she retold the tale of their tribulations and deaths before they'd reached their goal, all the misery and fear and debilitating sickness that had finally overwhelmed Will came rushing back. And to think that the worst of their quest might still lie before them.

No. It did not bear thinking about. He was reasonably warm and dry, he did not feel sick, Bloodroot was quiet within him today, and Rosana was cuddled up against his side, her head resting on his shoulder. This moment was enough for now. Tomorrow would bring whatever challenges it willed, and he had no control over what came.

Rynn was even quieter than usual after the telling of the tale, commenting only, "You all have been busy, haven't you? No wonder the dream plane is in an uproar." At least the paxan didn't declare them all mad or delusional and leave them then and there.

Will took the first watch as the others settled down to get what sleep they could, huddled as close to the fire as they could get without being singed. The rain pattered quietly against the tarp now, and the darkness was heavy with no moon or stars to light the night. He put another block of peat on the fire to combat the sharp chill that followed the rain, reluctantly grateful Rynn knew how to find it.

He pondered the question Raina had stopped him from asking earlier. What would happen if they managed to wake the Sleeping King? Would there be a war? Ragtag armies of rebels clashing against the great Imperial legions? He'd seen the common folk of Hickory Hollow fight, and they could not even fend off a single orc raid. Granted, the Boki were formidable warriors. But so were the Emperor's soldiers.

If only the Boki would turn on the Empire. They'd be a powerful ally.

Allies. That would be the key. The Sleeping King would need allies aplenty. After all, his own army had been dust for centuries. But who would stand with a forgotten king against the might of Koth—

He spotted movement in the darkness. What predator would be out hunting in this terrible weather? The prey animals would all be hunkered down in their burrows, safe and dry tonight. There it was again. A tiny pop of movement as if some creature peeked over the crown of the rise some fifty feet ahead of him.

Normally, he would ignore such a thing. It could be just a fox out looking for mice and cautious of the human intruders into his domain. But tonight, Will's senses sharpened exponentially more than they should have at the sight of a fox.

He surreptitiously reached for his staff and loosened the ties on his cloak. If he leaped to his feet, he would leave its encumbering folds behind. There it was again, some forty feet to the right of his last sighting. That was quick for such a large movement. Unless there was more than one creature out there.

He reached out ostensibly to stir the fire with a long stick, but instead poked Eben across the fire. With his left foot, he nudged Rynn, as well. Both men's eyes popped open alertly and they stared at him questioningly.

He muttered from behind unmoving lips, "Something's just beyond the ridge. Several somethings. And they're being stealthy. Could be a pack of wolves, or could be something else."

Rynn nodded infinitesimally and rolled over, pretending to still be asleep. After about a minute, Will spotted another tiny shadow shifting where it should not be along the ridge.

"Wake the girls," Rynn breathed. "Ready yourselves for a fight, but don't be obvious about it."

Gabrielle pulled a gray, woolen cloak closer around her. The fabric was rough and plain, but it warmed her against the chill of the night and the fog lying thick over the lake. The bottom of the narrow kayak in which she sat was thin and chilled from the water cupping it close.

A lantern cast light mayhap a dozen yards ahead of the fragile vessel. Just enough to see the swirling tendrils of mist clutching at them. How the boatman knew his way, she could not fathom. Somewhere in the middle of this hidden lake lay a hidden island, and on it lived a hidden child. And it was her purpose this night to keep that child hidden. But to do so, he must leave this place and go where the Empire could not find him. An Imperial hunter and his hounds, trained to seek out Children of Fate, tracked the boy's scent only a few days behind her.

A sense of traveling into some nether region, neither life nor death, clutched at her. This place was ancient, infused with magics older than time. The mist itself felt magical caressing her cheeks, vaguely malevolent. An urge to order the oarsman to row faster nearly overcame her. But fear of what lay beyond the fog stilled her tongue. An ill night, this.

"We's almost there, m'lady."

"Please. No titles for me. I'm just Mistress Gabby." It was terrifying and exhilarating to leave behind her rank and the protections it offered. She gloried in being free, if only for a few hours, to act and think as she willed without fear that the Emperor would, at any moment, peer into her mind and pluck out her secrets.

The prow of the flimsy vessel scraped gravel, and her guide leaped ashore, taking his lantern with him. Darkness closed in around her, choking her.

"Take my hand now, mistress. Wouldn't want ye goin' fer a swim in that 'eavy cloak. Down ye'd go, ye would. Straight to the bottom o' the Hidden Lake."

She shuddered at the thought of death by drowning. "You'll wait here while I fetch what I came for?" she asked anxiously.

"Aye. Me and my boat'll be right 'ere. Be quick about it, though. We must be back afore dawn if'n ye wish to keep your errand secret."

She jumped for the edge of the lake but missed, and her foot splashed into icy, ankle-deep water. She stumbled, but the sturdy dwarf holding her hand righted her before she could fall and test his prediction of death by cloak.

She turned to face the island but could make out no details in the pall of mist hanging over the place. Cautiously, she moved farther ashore alone. A tingle of magic passed across her right palm, and she rehearsed battle magic incants that she hadn't used since she'd learned them decades ago. But she was careful to keep her hand tucked inside her cloak and out of sight as she proceeded up the gravel strand.

"Who goes there?" a voice called out of the darkness ahead.

"A friend. I was delayed by the storm earlier and am arriving late. I am expected."

"Who ye be visitin', then?" The voice was slurred as if its owner had been swilling ale for hours.

She bristled for an instant at being questioned so closely but then recalled that she was Mistress Gabby tonight, and the watchman but did his duty, even if he was too drunk to be of any use in an actual attack. "I've come to see a boy. He bears an hourglass mark upon his forehead. Do you know where I might find him?"

"Dafydd's but a lad. He'll be long abed." A long belch, and then the voice added in surly tones, "Come back on the morrow if'n ye be wantin' a reading from the boy."

"It is not a reading I want. I have urgent news for him and his family that cannot wait."

"Ahh. News is it, then? From whence and wherefore?"

"Please, sir. My errand is urgent. If you could just point me to where the boy and his kin live, I would be most grateful."

A heavily armored dwarf whose helm barely reached her shoulder emerged from the indistinct night in front of her, scowling. He bore a gigantic battle-axe in both hands and peered over it blearily at her, looking her up and down. "Ye look harmless enough. C'mon, then. Owain's house be on the far side o' the village."

The dwarf turned, stumbled, righted himself, and moved away from her. She hurried after him lest she lose sight of him in the featureless gray night. A hulking form came into view off to her left, and she started. It resolved into a rude hut. But her guide passed it by without a glance.

Several more huts materialized and faded away before the dwarf veered right and stopped before a round, stone-walled cottage with a high-peaked thatched roof. "'Ere we be," he announced.

He raised his fist to pound on the door, but she said quickly, "Let me. I'm a far sight less frightening than you showing up at their door in the middle of the night."

Scowling, the dwarf stepped back. "'Ave it yer way."

Using her left hand that was not glowing with magic, she lifted the hood off her head and knocked upon the sturdy oaken door. She called out softly, "Master Owain? Mistress? I'm a friend. I come bearing urgent news about your son."

In a few seconds, she heard movement inside. Water dripped off the thatch onto her head and neck like icy needles piercing her skin. She shivered but did not raise her hood.

A male voice spoke from the other side of the panel, low and threatening. "Get thee gone. It is late."

"I have news, sir. Of grave import to Dafydd."

"What news?"

The door did not open nor did the latch lift. She sighed, wishing she did not have to shout her tidings nor do so in front of the nosy dwarf behind her. No help for it, though. "An Imperial hunter and hounds approach."

She heard a feminine wail inside as the latch rattled and the door was thrown open. A disheveled, pale-haired man in breeches and a nightshirt stood there, wielding a wicked-looking scythe. He asked urgently, "How much time do we have?"

"It is not quite so dire as that. We have perhaps two days until they track your son here."

"Huh. You've not seen those beasts once they've acquired a trail. They move twice as fast as normal creatures and go twice as long. They'll be here on the morrow at best. We must go now."

The man moved away from the door, and she stepped inside cautiously. A thin, dark-skinned woman with a thick, black braid that hung nearly to her knees already moved around the tiny space, hastily throwing supplies into a leather bag. The man followed suit, stripping his nightclothes to don a shirt, sweater, and leather jerkin.

"Where did ye see the hounds, then?" he asked grimly as he awkwardly buckled his armor.

She moved over to his side, familiar with armor from having helped Regalo don ceremonial suits of it over the years. "Let me do that." He lifted his arm, and she buckled the row of straps attaching chest piece and back piece to one another. "Turn," she ordered, starting work on his other side.

The man shook his head. "There's no time to travel over-land. We'll have to ask the terrakin for help."

The woman stopped packing and stared at him. "We're not dwarves. They will not take us down the Shadow Kthole."

He shrugged. "Mayhap they will if we ask properly."

Gabrielle did not know this Shadow Kthole, although she recognized the old word for an underground river. Regardless, she did not think terrakin helped any but themselves. "I can take Dafydd far away from here where he will be safe."

"Where?" the woman asked sharply.

"The Heartland. The Heart will protect your son from the hounds and keep him out of the Emperor's clutches."

The man snorted. "No one can save the boy from the Empire."

"If that should not prove a safe destination, I have a friend who can send us across the Abyssmal Sea."

The man threw her a look both hopeful and skeptical. "Wake the boy, Ellyn," he said over his shoulder to the woman.

The woman climbed a ladder and disappeared into the loft overhead. She emerged in a moment, followed by a dark-haired, dark-skinned boy of perhaps twelve summers.

This boy, the last known Child of Fate in Koth, had been taught to prophesy by his father, also a Child of Fate, from the Kingdom of Kufu, home of the Sands of Time. Dafydd's natural father had apparently died saving his son from the blast of the child's first vision. But the raw power of prophecy had filled Dafydd, who was said to be the greatest seer in generations as a result.

The boy was all messy clothes and awkward limbs, not yet coming into manhood, as he climbed down the ladder. But then he looked at her, and Gabrielle's breath caught. Those eyes. So wise, they stripped away all her layers of deception and laid her spirit bare.

"You've come to save me from the Emperor," Dafydd announced.

"Aye. Just so," she replied.

He stared at her quizzically for a moment. "Where is your crown?"

"I have no crown," she blurted, taken aback.

He smiled slyly. "Not here, you don't."

She smiled back at him ruefully. "Clever boy."

"Your pendant. May I see it?"

She reached into the collar of her rough dress and pulled out the Octavium Pendant on its long chain. Its green gem caught the light of the single candle and flashed as if lit from within. The boy stepped close and reached out with a single finger to touch the glowing gem.

His voice took on a disturbing timbre, too deep and resonant for his age. "Never let this leave your person, lady in a crown, lest your castle tumble down around you, all revealed, all lost." He shook his head a little and grinned up at her, a twelve-year-old urchin once more.

A tug upon her heart of missing her own two children made her breath catch. But she asked the boy jauntily enough, "Are you ready to have an adventure, Dafydd?"

"Aye." He glanced over at the man. "Do we really get to ride the shadow river, Owain?"

"Dunno. You tell me. Will the terrakin say yes?"

The boy didn't hesitate. "Aye."

Owain grunted. "Let's go, then."

Gabrielle interjected, "I have a boat. Across the lake is a coach I have hired—"

Owain snorted. "Think ye we 'ave a seer in our home and don't have an escape of our own in place? Thanks be for the warning, but we'll be on our own way now."

She frowned, unaccustomed to being openly gainsayed. "It is vital that Dafydd make his way with all due haste to the Heartland. I can guarantee his safety there. We *must* keep him out of the clutches of the Empire."

Owain frowned back at her. "Look. If ye want to tag along wit' us, I suppose ye've earned the right by bringin' us word of the hounds."

She followed the family outside, prepared to argue further. She fetched up short, though, surprised to see the drunken town guard still outside. Except now he was standing strong and straight, his stare as sharp as a sword.

"Mistress Gabby, I've sent your man and his boat back to the mainland with instructions for your coach to be on its way. We'll use it as a decoy, should the hunter be tracking you to get to the boy."

Not a single syllable of the dwarf's words was slurred with drink. His eyes were clear and alert. "Who are you, sir?" she challenged.

"I, too, am a friend of the boy's. We have kept watch upon him ever since he came to this place." She opened her mouth to ask for the dwarf's name, but he forestalled her, saying, "The sooner we get Dafydd out of here, the less his scent will linger. Let us go and quickly."

Owain and Ellyn fell in behind the dwarf, whom they clearly knew and trusted. If she was to stay with the boy and personally protect him as she'd been ordered by the Eight to do, she had no choice but to follow along.

Their guide moved confidently toward what she judged to be the center of the island. He stepped up to a massive outcropping of black, wet rock the size of a house. He passed his hand over the stone, incanting something under his breath, and a crack appeared in the face of the rock.

The boy, Dafydd, ran his fingertips over the surface of the secret door and laughed in delight. "Oh, the hounds will be so frustrated. They will be maddened by my scent but will not be able to follow it into solid rock. Blood will flow as they dash themselves against this boulder."

Shuddering at the image conjured by the boy's words, Gabrielle hurried into the tunnel beyond the secret door. They lit torches while their guide sealed the entrance and said something magical to hide it once more. A passageway descended sharply before them, presumably under the lake. They walked for what seemed like hours, but in the darkness, lit only by the flickering torches, she had no sense of time passing.

At length, the tunnel widened into a chamber, and the chamber widened into a great, hollow space that hardly felt underground. A faint glow filled the gigantic space, seeming to emanate from the distant ceiling and unseen walls. Some sort of mossy plant grew beneath their feet, and a smooth road wound away from them. A stone cottage was visible a little way ahead, complete with a fenced yard and a small garden of gently glowing plants. It was a weird copy of the surface village they'd left behind.

"What is this place?" she asked in wonder.

"Welcome to Under Urth, Mistress," the dwarf commented ironically. "You will understand if I must swear you to silence on the location of yon entrance upon pain of death."

"Of course," she murmured, stunned at what appeared to be an actual village stretching away from them, at least as large as the one above.

They passed through the settlement and pulled up short at the bank of a fast-flowing stream, perhaps thirty feet across. They trod along its mossy shore until they came upon a widening in the river and a wooden dock protruding into the swift current. A dwarf dozed in a high-prow, sturdy-looking boat that could hold a dozen people.

Their little party, including the not-drunk guard, piled into the vessel as the helmsman cast off the lines and took his place at the tiller aft. No sooner had they taken seats upon low wooden benches affixed to the bottom of the craft than the boat shot forward, propelled at an alarming speed. Ellyn looked no more thrilled than Gabrielle to be flying along an underground river, but Owain and Dafydd whooped with joy and thoroughly enjoyed the ride.

They shot into a black tunnel so low that Gabrielle actually ducked as it closed in around them. The boat dipped precipitously and picked up even more speed. The torches were all but blown out and gave off only enough light to show seething rapids around them. They were going to die, dashed to pieces against the rocks bulging just below the fast-flowing water.

The boat dipped and bobbed like a cork, gathering even more speed. The dwarves seemed completely unconcerned, which was the only reason she did not panic entirely.

They burst out of the dark tunnel into a massive space that made the first chamber look like a mousehole by comparison. She could not even see a ceiling in the dim glow surrounding them. Their little tributary had joined a massive river running even faster than the first. She made out what looked like trees on the far bank of the black waters.

"Now's a good time for a nap," the night watchman announced. "Once we put ashore, we'll have a long, hard journey before us."

She stretched out on the hard planks of the vessel and pulled her cloak close around her. *What on Urth had she gotten herself into?*

Will nudged Raina and Rosana, who were asleep on either side of him while Eben woke Sha'Li. Without moving from prone positions, everyone readied weapons, and Will detected a faint glow from beneath the healers' cloaks as they gathered magic.

"Here they come," Will breathed. "Five of them." The attackers must have concluded that having several females in their party and only three men made this a winnable fight. Of course, it was a dreadful mistake to underestimate any of the women in their party.

"We should talk to them," Raina whispered.

"They're attacking us," Will snapped. "We fight back."

"Agreed," Eben murmured.

"We fight," Sha'Li chimed in.

"Raina's right," Rynn disagreed.

"You're outvoted, Three Eyes," Will ground out. "You said you would defend us with your life. So do it."

Rynn sighed. "So be it."

The creatures stalking them drew nearer, and Will focused all his attention on them, clearing his mind for the fight to come.

"I'll call our attack," Rynn murmured. "Patience, everyone."

The attackers moved slowly at first, approaching about

halfway between the ridge and their little camp before charging. Will tensed, sure that Rynn would call the countercharge immediately. But the paxan did not. The attackers were spread about ten feet apart, coming in at slight angles. Not that flanking this party would help the assailants. Will and his friends had been through enough melees to know how to keep their backs to one another and their flanks covered.

An eternity passed as the five dark figures grew larger. Claws gleamed in all their fists. Some sort of animal changeling types, then.

Finally, Rynn shouted as he jumped to his feet all in a single explosive lunge, "Now!"

All six of them leaped up and ran forward as one in a defensive arc with Will and Eben in the center. Sha'Li had one end and Rynn the other, with the two mages hanging back slightly but within an arm's length of the others.

Will focused mainly on the two attackers directly in front of him. He raised his staff high over his head as if to take a great, cumbersome downward swing. But as he ducked under the first swing of vicious claws, he snapped the bottom tip of his staff forward lightning fast into the jaw of his attacker. The fellow howled. His hood fell back to reveal a furred face bearing a resemblance to some sort of badgerlike creature.

Will had no more time to notice details for sharp claws raked across his thigh. The cuts were not deep but were intensely painful as he stumbled back. He reversed his hold on his staff and snapped the tip forward once more, this time in a neck-high blow that connected solidly with the one who'd sliced him. He didn't waste time swinging at the badger but just jabbed hard with his right-hand staff tip directly into the beast's face.

A crunch of bone told him he'd scored a serious hit. A painful shot of magic slammed into his back, and he hissed as Raina's combat healing found his leg wounds and cauterized them with searing, magical energy.

He jabbed back left with his staff, this time sending a blast of force magic down the copper veins of his weapon. His opponent staggered. From the left, Eben hamstringed the attacker's far leg, and the man went down, making horrible gasping noises.

Will half turned to finish off the badger, but Rynn had apparently already taken his opponent and was sweeping the badger's legs out from under him with a foot and then smashing a powerful fist into the side of the changeling's skull. The creature dropped like a rock.

Will was arrested by the look of complete serenity on Rynn's face as the paxan spun, fists held in front of him, seeking more opponents to crush with those fists of his. It was as if the paxan fought in some sort of trance. He had to give it to Rynn, though. The man was shockingly fast. And strong.

Will, too, spun, in search of more threats. But five shapes lay on the ground, two moaning, and three utterly still. "Let us tie them up before you start healing them, Raina," he ordered.

Sha'Li, who knelt over the last body on the end, pulled back the creature's cloak. "Bah! Dominion scum," she announced.

Dominion? Will stared down at the black tabard on the changeling's chest. A clawed, white paw shone in the upper-right quadrant of the beast's chest, and four jagged red lines trailed down the tabard as if the claws had slashed their way up the fabric.

Will's jaw dropped. "What is *the Dominion* doing here?" The group held its own nation-state on the continent of Kentogen formed entirely of animal changelings bent on world domination. And they'd come to Haelos? Why? Surely with the intent to conquer and subjugate. Great. The Empire and the Dominion were going to end up fighting over his home like dogs over a bone.

"The Dominion landed one of their floating islands somewhere in the north of Haelos a while back. They brought over an expeditionary force to join the already-existing colony," Rynn commented as calmly as if they discussed the weather.

What already-existing Dominion colony? Why didn't all the colonists know about this supposed Dominion foothold on Haelos?

Quickly, they worked together to truss up their attackers tightly enough to immobilize them. Interestingly, Rynn tore off strips of the attackers' cloaks to blindfold and gag them, as well. Come to think of it, that was a good idea. It would limit the amount of information these Dominion creatures could tell their superiors about their little party of humanoids, and it would hamper their efforts to yell for help, assuming anyone was close enough to hear their cries.

Raina healed each of their attackers just enough to make sure none of them would die. After all, her mission was to defend life, not blooming health. Her tabard required her to keep any and all living beings alive, but no more. Sha'Li efficiently knocked each changeling unconscious as soon as Raina stabilized his or her health. They appeared to be two badger changelings, a wolf changeling, a bear changeling, and maybe a wolverine changeling. Will wasn't sure about that last one, but the fellow had two broad stripes of lighter-colored hair running from his temples to the back of his head that reminded Will of one of the secretive and aggressive creatures.

He and the others packed up their camp as the rain intensified, and they set out cautiously over the ridge. They found the Dominion party's camp perhaps a half mile beyond the ridge in a small depression that protected the spot from the wind, but it had also collected a fair bit of water. Slogging through the mud, they retrieved the changelings' packs and searched them, taking all the food they found, along with rope, another tarp, and a stash of healing potions.

They were all too keyed up to go back to sleep after the fight, and besides, it was probably for the best that they got well away from the changelings before those claws of theirs sliced their bindings. Rynn and Raina had done their best to angle the creatures' fists so their claws would not reach their own bindings. But eventually, the five would rejoin one another from where the party had dragged each of them, and then the ropes would be dispensed with in a few quick slashes.

Perhaps the tactic of tying up the Dominion changelings would buy them a few hours to lose the patrol. Sha'Li conferred briefly with Rynn, and the two agreed that the intermittently heavy rain would make tracking them nearly impossible. Instead of moving slowly enough for the lizardman girl to countertrack, the party opted to maximize their speed.

They'd learned long ago not to let Will set the pace. His long legs and tendency to forget that the others did not have his stride made him run away from the party too often. That and the Bloodroot part of him reveled in moving fast. It was probably a novel experience for a tree accustomed to spending its entire life rooted in one spot.

Rynn set off at an entirely sensible jog, while Will chafed behind him. The logic of Rynn's pace became apparent as the others maintained the steady pace for the next two hours with only short rest breaks every quarter hour or so.

They stopped when a leaden dawn began to lighten the east. The rain gave way to drizzle and finally to just a damp chill. They stopped to eat, and Rosana broke out the rations from the Dominion packs—surprisingly tasty hardtack bread and strips of peppery jerky.

Reflecting back upon the night's attack, Will had to say that the party had performed admirably well. He hadn't seen how everyone else dropped their attacker, but it had been efficient and fast, well within their capabilities. His own reflexes had been faster than ever, no doubt thanks to Krugar's tutelage.

He commented to the party at large, "I guess all that training we had to endure the past few months paid off."

Eben offered him a palm, and Will smacked it with his

own. The jann grinned. "Those Dominion fur balls won't be messing with us again."

Rynn burst out angrily, "You have no idea what we've just done. The Dominion will come back with more warriors and crush us!"

"C'mon, Rynn. Don't be such a killjoy," Will cajoled. "We won. Be happy."

"We won nothing this day. We just made an enemy we cannot possibly hope to defeat. You are thoughtless *children*." He spat the word out like it was a curse. "You have no concept of the forces you're up against. The risks you face. You have *no idea* how much rides on you succeeding out here, and yet you're crashing around picking fights you cannot win and crowing about how great you did."

"Sheesh. Who tied your breeches in a bunch?" Will complained while the others stared at Rynn in stunned silence.

The paxan stared down each of them in turn. "Don't you understand? *Everything* depends on you. Centuries' worth of work is at stake here. People have died across multiple continents for generations to make what you're attempting possible. If you six complete your quest, maybe—just maybe—a rebellion has a chance of succeeding. But if you fail, all is lost. Everything will have been for naught. You hold the fate of us all in your inexperienced, naïve hands."

Will stared as Rynn paced in his agitation, continuing to lecture, "So forgive me if I cannot share your enthusiasm over having kicked one of the most dangerous hornets' nests in existence. The Dominion is huge, powerful, and aggressive. They also happen to be one of the few armies on Urth who hate Maximillian as much as any of you." He spun to glare at them all. "And you just made an *enemy* of them. How in the name of all that is blessed am I supposed to fix that?"

The party was silent in the face of his outburst. Will didn't know what to say. He'd had no idea that so much depended on them.

Eben frowned. "I thought we were just supposed to find some old elf and wake him up. And then our part will be done and this Gawaine guy will be in charge of organizing the whole rebellion thing."

Rynn said in a terrible, low voice, "Don't you understand? *You are the rebellion.* The six of you. Everyone is pinning all their hopes on you. Just you."

Will's jaw actually fell open a little. He glanced around at the others, and they all looked similarly shocked. He'd taken this quest seriously from the beginning—after all, his parents had died to set him upon it—but the whole rebellion was counting on them? They were the linchpin to it all? He caught himself gulping along with the others.

They were silent as they finished eating their cold breakfast and huddled together behind a quick, makeshift windbreak. The weather had turned cold overnight and felt as if it was going to get colder rather than warmer as the sun came up.

They took turns napping, and then they broke their minicamp.

Sha'Li ribbed Rosana quietly about getting lucky and hitting one of the Dominion changelings with a curse spell, and a subdued chuckle passed among them. Will was abjectly relieved that the lizardman girl had broken the thick tension that had hung between them after Rynn's outburst.

In addition to the much-needed comic relief, Will was glad to hear that Rosana had actually hit a target in the stress of combat. When he'd first met her she'd panicked easily and tended to cast her magic wildly. Frankly, she'd been a menace to her friends in a fight.

Despite his lack of weapons, Rynn had been blindingly fast with his feet and hands. The paxan also had nerves of steel and demonstrated an ability to think on his feet. And despite the paxan's forecast of gloom and doom, the group had fought extremely efficiently. Everyone had gained more skill. All in all, it boded well for their safety and success going forward.

He should be pleased, right? Then why, as he lay down for a short nap, did a deep-seated sense of disquiet vibrate through him? As if the hornets' nest they'd just kicked was about to become very, very angry.

Raina was sad when the open meadowlands gave way to light forest and more hills as they trekked east. Mostly they came across small farms scratched from the land by dint of grueling labor and sheer determination. The people were generally poor, dirty, and defiant. They would rather die out here of injury, disease, or simply working themselves to death than live under the fist of the Kothite Empire.

Her healing was a source of jubilation for most of the settlers they came across. A few expressed suspicion over her Heart affiliation, but nobody turned down her magic in the end. Health was too precious a commodity out here on the thinnest fringe of civilization.

When Sha'Li came running back to them from where she'd been scouting in advance of the party on a gray, drizzly afternoon with news that a village lay ahead, Raina was as stunned as any of the others. The forest around them was nothing like the mighty Forest of Thorns or even the dense tree stands of the Wylde Wold. This light forest was interspersed with clearings and small meadows. Sunlight and blue sky were visible, although today the view was silver strings of rain and clouds in varying shades of gray.

Weapons drawn and magic powered up, they rounded a bend in the rough path they'd been following. Indeed, an actual village sprawled in front of them. A lone man wearing a broad-rimmed straw hat trudged away from them pushing a handcart. Perhaps twenty structures huddled together along the muddy widening in the path.

"Is that a pub I see?" Eben murmured in glee.

Raina made out a wooden panel swinging from a post that might be in the shape of an ale barrel with a rough spigot. Smoke threaded lazily into the air above the shingled roof.

"We're being watched," Rynn muttered.

Eben crowded Raina a little closer to Rosana, and they passed the first cottages in a tight, defensive cluster. These were lawless lands, and their safety rested upon their own alertness and skill.

They ducked into the building, named simply Pub. It was low ceilinged and dark, with a sluggish fire losing its battle to hold off the damp chill. Two long, narrow tables with bundles of straw for seats filled the space. Half the bales, the ones closest to the fire, were occupied. A human woman of improbably large height and girth came out of the back room with six brimming mugs clenched in her fists. She plunked them down in front of a cluster of patrons, splashing foam and ale on the table. If any humans were descended from giants, surely this woman was one of them.

She looked up, and surprise came across her features. Her stare locked on Rynn, and she smiled, revealing a nearly toothless grin. What teeth still clung to her gums were blackened and rotted. "'Ey now, pretty boy. Come close. Let Mama Flora look at ye."

Raina smirked as Rynn winced faintly before pasting on his most dazzling smile. He said something inane about the barkeep being the most beautiful flower he'd ever beheld, and the woman simpered like a lass before laying a rib-cracking hug on the paxan. Raina faked a cough and threw a hand over her mouth to disguise the grin that broke across her face at seeing Rynn manhandled by their formidable hostess.

"Well met . . . madam . . . and might we . . . have some of . . . your fine ale?" Rynn managed to wheeze from the confines of Mama Flora's powerful arms.

"By all means. Park by the fire, my pretty boy. You scurvy dogs, scoot over," she ordered the patrons nearest the fire.

"That will not be necessary, my lady," Rynn interrupted. "Our vestments are warm, and we will be more comfortable over here, well away from the heat." He moved to the back corner of the room hastily. Probably avoiding another bone-crushing embrace from the proprietress.

The other members of their little party seemed to be having as much trouble keeping straight faces as she was. As Flora disappeared into the kitchen, they piled onto the bales of straw and managed to get seated before they all burst into gales of laughter. Rynn blushed beet red, which only made them all laugh the harder.

"Behave," Rynn finally muttered. "She returns."

Raina was impressed by the paxan's concern for the feelings of their hostess. At his core, he was a kind man, and she admired that. Flora set mugs of what turned out to be sour, well-watered ale in front of them, and she departed for the kitchen at Rynn's polite request for whatever food the house might have to offer.

In a few minutes, wooden boards loaded with a hard orange cheese, dry sausage, and hot, crusty bread were put before them. Raina dug in eagerly. The food was shockingly tasty. Or mayhap she'd been eating stringy game and dry traveling rations for so long that any real food tasted like manna from heaven. They'd nearly finished their meal, and she'd nearly remembered what it felt like to have a full belly when the front door opened and a cloaked and hooded figure blew in on a gust of rain.

Her own right hand started to tingle as magic danced across it, and she noted that Will's hand moved casually to his staff, which was leaning against the wall beside him. The others shifted slightly in their seats, as well.

The newcomer paused to gaze around the pub, and then he headed straight for the back corner of the room where she and her companions were seated. Rynn rose from his seat, and Eben followed suit. The two of them together formed a wall of muscle and sinew, and she had to lean sideways to see around them.

The man pushed his hood back, and she was startled to see a third eye—closed—in the middle of his forehead. Another paxan. She knew Rynn well enough to see his shoulders go rigid. Odd. Why would he be tense about meeting another of his own kind?

"Greetings, sir," Rynn said cautiously.

"And to you, traveler. Name's Olar. What brings thee and thine to these uncivilized lands?"

Rynn glanced around the room. "This seems quite civilized to me, good sir."

Raina noticed Flora puffing with pride in the kitchen door as she looked on with interest to the conversation. Now that Raina took notice, everyone in the room seemed to be taking deep interest in how Rynn would answer the newcomer's question.

"We're just passing through," Rynn said easily.

"Not many travelers pass through this way," Olar replied.

Rynn asked with just the right amount of casual disinterest, "How long has it been since *any* other travelers came through here?"

"Couple weeks," Flora answered helpfully from across the pub. "Two men. Skinny, weaselly sorts, they was. Not brawny nor bonny like you."

Raina was disappointed. That did not sound like Kerryl Moonrunner and Kendrick.

"Would you like to sit with us?" Rynn invited Olar.

Now why would Rynn do that? Intrigued, she watched the paxan pull up a bundle of straw and join them. Silently, Sha'Li pushed one of the wooden boards of cheese, sausage, and bread toward their guest. He nodded his thanks and nibbled at a hunk of the bread.

He turned to Rynn. "Do I recognize you? You have the look of—"

Rynn cut him off. "I would recall you if we had met, and

I do not believe we have. Let me formally introduce myself."
He held his hand out to the other paxan.

Olar took his hand, and Raina could swear the two men
shared some sort of silent communication. What did they
have to share in private? They released hands, and Olar's
tone of voice was noticeably more respectful when he asked,
"Where do you go, and how may I help you, young travelers?"

"Why would you help us?" Will asked suspiciously.

"Why not?" Olar shrugged. "One of my kind travels with
you as a friend. That is enough for me."

Rynn spoke low enough that his voice would not carry beyond their corner. "We track a friend whom we hope to
catch up with. He has been heading steadily north."

"That'll take you into Dominion lands. As soon as you
reach the Quills, you enter their territory. They claim the
Quills and everything north of it."

Raina jolted. She'd never heard of any permanent Dominion settlement anywhere on Haelos. "How long have they
been there?" she blurted.

Olar shrugged. "Long enough to build cities and estab-
lish roads and government and to breed native changelings.
Several generations at a minimum."

"Breed native changelings?" Sha'Li asked.

Olar took a long pull at his mug of ale. "Indeed. They
bring magical waters with them from their home on Kentogen. These waters transform a humanoid of any race into a
changeling of whatever animal is used in the ritual. The
Dominion has long practiced making changelings of the local, native species of creatures when they invade a place. It
ensures that their troops are suited to the climate, environment, and terrain. Brilliant strategy, if you think about it."

"How did they get over here?" Will asked. "Kentogen is
across a great ocean from Haelos."

"Don't know much about Dominion, do you, children?"
Olar commented.

Will scowled, and Raina caught herself bristling before she recalled that paxan could live many hundreds of years. Any human must seem like a child by comparison.

Their paxan guest continued, "The Dominion creates floating islands by carving off a chunk of land from Kentogen. They live on the island's resources while they float to their destination. It's slow, but they can move thousands of troops and colonists all at once. Makes for one whale of an invasion force."

"So there's an entire Dominion island sitting off the coast of Haelos?" she asked. She'd seen the best maps of Haelos that her father could lay hands on, and she'd never seen any island next to the northeast coast of the continent.

"No, young healer. It was destroyed some time ago."

"How?"

The paxan frowned. "I always assumed the Empire blasted it, but I don't actually know for certain. That's a good question. If you meet Goldeneye, you should ask him."

"Goldeneye?" she echoed questioningly.

"Leader of the Dominion in Haelos. Golden cobra changeling. *Not* a man to tangle with. He's related to one of the Great Beasts of Kentogen and has powers beyond those of any normal changeling I have ever seen."

"What sort of powers?" Will asked.

"For one thing, he can attack people by merely looking at them. Beware of making eye contact with him. And of course, he is the strongest fighter in all of Rahael. He will rule until someone else can defeat him and take his place."

Sha'Li sat up a little straighter. She must like the idea of a scaled reptile changeling being in charge of all the furry warm-blood changelings.

"What is Rahael?" Rosana asked.

"It is the Dominion colony you will enter if you continue northward. It lies on the Barbed Coast and is a great, sprawling place."

"Do only changelings live there?" Sha'Li asked eagerly.

"Stars, no. They have slaves of all races, and they do allow a few outsiders to live and trade among them. But it is a hard life for any who make a home there. They trust no one and live by rule of the strongest. Show the slightest weakness and they will crush you."

Raina shuddered. It sounded horrible.

Olar shrugged. "But you know what they say. He who hates my enemy is my ally. They hate the Empire as much as or more than our kind." He lifted his chin in Rynn's direction.

Rynn replied grimly, "Not all of our kind oppose Koth."

"Ahh, but your kind do, now don't they, enlightened one?"

Enlightened one. Was that some sort of paxan title for the open-eyed of their kind? Whatever it was, its use sent Rynn to his mug of ale for a long drink. There was no way he was drinking that swill for enjoyment. He was rattled by Olar's use of the title. Or mayhap it was Olar's bluntness that discomfited Rynn. Either way, she was amused.

When Rynn finally emerged from the mug, he asked, "And what brings *you* to these remote lands, friend?"

"I seek ways to raise all of our race to your far-seeing state." Olar gestured toward his own closed eye. "If you have time to tarry, I would relish speaking with you at length. Your kind are passing rare, and I have not had much opportunity over the years to ascertain the full extent of your kind's capabilities."

Rynn's expression and body language closed up tight, announcing clearly that the man presumed too much. Raina watched him closely as Rynn toyed with a piece of bread, tearing it into crumbs. Didn't like being a specimen, did he? She couldn't blame him. People sometimes treated her the same because of her gift for magic. Was that why he'd left Mindor and come to Haelos with Phinneas, his Oneiri mentor?

Eben surprised her by answering for Rynn. "Sadly, sir, we do not have time to tarry. Another time, mayhap."

Raina studied her jann friend with interest. His caramel-colored skin bore a flush that had little to do with his elemental striations. Eben, too, must know the burn of being an outsider and a freak. His compassion was admirable. So much of her life, she had been petted and protected, surrounded by family and friends. She was still coming to know the full pain and loneliness of having no home. Although Eben had been given safe shelter by Leland Hyland, she could imagine that it hadn't really felt like his own family or his own home. Eben and his sister had grown up among humans who had no idea what it meant to be jann.

Her gaze swiveled to Sha'Li. The lizardman girl was similarly a stranger among humans. Maybe that explained why Sha'Li and Eben had become good friends and seemed more at ease with each other than with the rest of the party.

The pub's door burst open on a blast of howling wind and swirling rain. The weather had gone from miserable to horrible outside. A young man dressed as a forester stepped in and shook himself off. Droplets of water flew in all directions, causing an outcry from those near him.

He caught his breath enough to pant, "I have a . . . report from south of here . . . sent by carrier pigeon. Strangers come this way. Two parties. Soldiers. A brace of giant dogs."

"What kind and how many?" Olar bit out.

"No room on a tiny slip of parchment for more details than that," the fellow replied.

Eben lurched to his feet first, but Raina and nearly everyone else in the pub were not far behind. Bales of straw got knocked over, and cloaks swirled every which way.

"How close?" Rynn asked tersely.

"Bird flew for under an hour, so less than fifty miles. The way I hears it, them Imperials move fast and don't stop much to rest. Maybe they took shelter from the storm, but my bird came on, anyway."

Olar grasped the man's forearm and murmured in gratitude that mirrored what Raina was feeling. She helped Rosana wrap the remaining food quickly in a cloth, and they stuffed it in their pouches as Will and Eben buckled on their weapons and Rynn tossed coins on the table.

They stepped outside into sheets of blowing rain. The customers of the pub were dispersing fast in every direction, which worked to their advantage. Their tracks would be difficult to distinguish from everyone else's. Unless, of course, those elemental hounds were on Eben's trail again.

"Come with us?" Rynn offered Olar.

"Nay. I've my own path to follow. Safe travels to you, young friends. Look out for Rynn and keep him safe, will you?"

Raina replied, "I think it is he who will keep us safe, but we all look out for one another, sir."

Olar gave her a short half bow and then whirled and took off running between the pub and the hut beside it.

"We must go," Eben said urgently. "Those cursed hounds will be upon us in no time."

The challenge now would be to stay ahead of the Imperial hounds and the soldiers accompanying them, and maybe even find Kendrick before they went too deep into Dominion lands and had to tangle with that dangerous bunch. Once more, she felt as if they'd jumped out of the stew pot and into the fire.

Over the next few days, the terrain grew rockier and the hills steeper and more continuous. When no elemental hounds leaped out of the wood to attack them, Eben gradually began to sleep easier. They circled well clear of a few isolated settlements, mostly squalid clusters of holdings scratched out of the dirt. From afar, the settlers looked like hard people with suspicious countenances. Not that he blamed them.

One night, the party jerked awake to the sound of wolves howling. Rynn, whose turn it was on watch, murmured that the beasts were not close and that all was well. Except when Eben fell asleep, he dreamed of a pack of Imperial hounds tearing him limb from limb while he screamed. He woke to Sha'Li's hand clamped over his mouth and Will shaking him.

The nightmare brought back full force his sense that those cursed hounds were stalking him with the intent to do in fact exactly what he'd dreamed of. He could feel their hot breath on his neck every minute of the day. He was unaccustomed to fear, despised it, but could do nothing to rid himself of it.

Matters had not been helped when Rynn casually mentioned that psionic hounds actually consumed their victims, absorbing their victims' psionic powers into themselves in the process. Surely, elemental hounds did something similar.

"We're out of water," Rosana announced one morning. "We must find more and soon."

Will answered practically, "We can always veer back to the last village and fetch water from their well."

Not a prospect Eben relished. The fewer people knew they were out here, the better.

"Unhealthy was that place. Thirsty I would go before drink their water I would. Bathe in it I would not," Sha'Li announced. She'd spent a fair bit of the morning complaining under her breath about how itchy and dry her skin was with no water available to soak in. She seemed capable of going for some time without a bath, but the lizardman girl most assuredly did not like doing so.

"What do you mean, unhealthy?" Raina queried.

"A taint I sense in that place. Like on my tongue a bad taste."

Rynn asked Sha'Li with interest, "So you have the skill of your kind to sense the unnatural?"

"No such skill have lizardmen," she answered.

"Not your race. Your tribe. Certain Tribe of the Moon members can sense things that go against the laws of nature."

"Really?" Sha'Li asked. Chagrin passed through her eyes. Didn't like showing ignorance of her own faction, did she? He could imagine how awkward it would be not knowing one's own abilities.

They resumed their trek with Will taking a turn in the lead, which Eben privately enjoyed. Will tended to set a hard pace that made the girls complain but which made his own limbs feel energized. The afternoon aged, and still no sign of water appeared. Just more towering pines whose roots reached deep enough not to need streams to feed them.

By noon the next day, the situation was becoming dire. His throat was parched, and his tongue stuck to the roof of his mouth. Everyone's lips cracked, and their voices roughened from lack of water. They stopped for a rest, and Eben flopped down on the ground, relieved to be in contact with the earth. It did not soothe his fluid-starved body, but it did soothe his spirit. There had to be water around somewhere. After all, they saw abundant wildlife as they hiked, and the land was covered with plant life.

His awareness flowed into the earth cradling his back and down into the ground. He felt layers of sand, clay, and gravel, and far beneath him, bedrock. He felt growing roots pushing into the soil and worms chewing their way slowly through it.

And moisture. He noticed dampness first. Eagerly, he followed the sensation deeper and off to his right. It became a seep and then a tiny rivulet of underground water. Where did it rise to the surface? He traced the tiny trickle intently . . .

There. Off to the east. "I know where to find water!" He jumped up and moved in the right direction, following the feeling. Or maybe it was the smell of water he followed. Or maybe it was merely insanity brought on by acute dehydration.

Drat. He'd lost the trail. He stopped, dropped to his hands and knees, and dug his fingers into the ground. He closed his eyes and concentrated. *There.* He found the trickle more easily this time and jumped back to his feet. It took him maybe ten minutes of alternately moving and stopping to check his direction before he came upon a tiny seep in the ground. It was no more than a puddle nestled in a stand of knee-high grass, really. But it was wet.

He dropped to his knees beside it in relief and was joined by the other members of the party in doing the same.

"Is it drinkable?" Rynn asked, directing the question at Sha'Li.

"Aye," she announced in relief.

"Fill the waterskins first and drink from those," Rynn directed. "Less waste that way." The advice was reasonable, but it did not prevent Eben from wanting to stick his face directly into the puddle and suck it dry.

Filling all six of their bone-dry waterskins emptied the seep of nearly half its water. But as they guzzled thirstily, it refilled. An underground spring must feed it, then.

Again and again they filled their waterskins and drank them empty until finally, they all had gorged themselves on the cold, sweet springwater. They filled every waterskin they had to capacity, and then Sha'Li cleared her throat.

"Possible is it that move away you all might? To wash, I desire, to end to this maddening itching."

After a short discussion, they agreed to pitch camp near the seep for the night and let everyone take a turn bathing, even if only to sponge off the sweat and grime of the past few days.

When Eben's turn came, he stripped down under the sweet-smelling pine boughs and distant stars and used a cloth to wash and rinse. He soaped his hair and then poured a skin of water over it. The rinse was icy cold and stole his breath away, but he felt like a new man.

The others in the party seemed equally refreshed. Finally, when they all settled down to sleep around a merrily crackling pine fire, Sha'Li excused herself and slipped away in the dark. She would no doubt spend the night soaking as much of herself as she could fit into that puddle. She would give the local wildlife quite a scare when they came for a nocturnal drink.

Silence fell over their little camp, the fire glowing silently. From across the fire, Raina asked, "How did you know where to find that water, Eben?"

He frowned. "I suppose I sensed it. I was lying on the ground wishing to find water, and awareness of an underground stream was just there. I followed it until it rose to the surface."

"Are you a dowser?" Rynn asked from his bedroll.

"Not that I know of."

"The only people I know who can sense water from as far away as you did are dowsers. And good ones at that," Rynn replied.

Him a dowser? He didn't even like water. It was high time and more that he went on a jann quest to find a source of elemental water energy and absorb it into his being, but he'd been putting it off for a while now. He'd mastered the other three elements but considered himself primarily connected to earth and stone energies. Shards of water energy felt strange to him. Foreign.

Rynn, who was bedded down next to him, rolled over to face him. The paxan spoke quietly. "When we were in the Merr cutter, you mentioned that you'd had a strange dream and wanted to talk to me about it when our situation calmed down. I haven't forgotten about it. Are you too tired to speak of it now?"

"No. I feel good. You?"

"I can go a number of days without sleep if need be," Rynn replied.

Hmm. Paxan thing, perchance?

"Your dream?" Rynn prompted.

Right. His dream. Eben recalled the odd dreaming experience once more, surprised to realize it was as vivid in his mind's eye now as it had been the night he'd had it. "It started with a white fog. And voices. And then a tremendous horde of elementally aligned people being mustered into some sort of army—"

Eben realized he was describing his dream in excruciating detail and broke off his story. "Is this too much information?"

"Not at all," Rynn replied smoothly. "Tell me everything you remember."

Eben resumed his narrative, doing as the paxan asked. He concluded with, "It felt as if I was really there with my sister. Like she's still alive and trying to communicate with me from wherever she is." He paused and then blurted, "Is that crazy?"

"Not at all. It sounds to me like you encountered a dreamer and not a phantasm of your sister."

"What's the difference?"

"A dreamer is a real person, like you, experiencing a dream that has taken their spirit to the dream plane. You were a dreamer in your visit to the dream plane, for example. A phantasm is a creature of the dream plane who has taken on an aspect similar to a person from our mortal plane. They may take that shape for only a few minutes or hold the shape permanently."

"Like a ghost?" Eben asked.

"Much more substantial than a ghost in the long-term cases. A phantasm who has held a form for a long time and taken on many aspects of the one they imitate can be indistinguishable from the real thing. They can also have most of the same skills and abilities."

Will piped up from across the fire. "Which is to say a phantasm can kill you as quickly as their real version can."

"Just so," Rynn replied.

Eben frowned. "But you think I saw the real Marikeen—well, the dreaming version of her?"

"Sounds like it. The next time you wish to visit the dream plane, may I suggest you let me take you there? I can distinguish a dreamer from a phantasm easily."

"Don't we go to the dream plane every time we dream?"

Rynn tilted his head to one side. "Technically, yes. But there are varying degrees of interaction with the dream plane. For example, Will and Raina physically walked onto the realm. They found a gate between planes and traveled from one to another. They were no longer on the mortal plane once they passed through the gate. Most people dream casually, and phantasms take fleeting forms shaped by those. The forms last only as long as the dream and then evaporate back into mist. Those are the dreams you may remember for a few seconds or minutes after you regain consciousness but forget when you fully wake."

Eben nodded, familiar with the phenomenon.

"Then there are deeper dreams. The ones with significance. Perhaps you desperately wish to get a message to someone, or mayhap someone has an important message for you. I believe this may be what happened in your dream under the sea, Eben. It might have been Marikeen reaching out to you or you reaching out to her."

"So how would you go with me into a dream?"

"You'll merely go to sleep, and I'll make the mental journey with you. Our bodies will stay here, asleep as usual."

"And we can do this anytime?"

"Yes. Assuming I am not too exhausted to concentrate sufficiently."

"Are you too exhausted now?"

"No."

"Can we do this journey thing tonight? I'm very worried about my sister."

"Done." And with that, the paxan lay down and pulled his cloak over his shoulders.

"What are you doing?" Eben blurted.

"Waiting for you to go to sleep. Ignore me. Just go to sleep like you always do."

Hah. Like that was going to happen now. Nonetheless, Eben closed his eyes and concentrated on falling asleep and finding Marikeen beyond the backs of his eyelids.

Nothing he did worked. He tossed and turned and fretted for what felt like hours. And all the while, Rynn lay beside him as still as death. The man might as well have been completely unconscious. It was maddening.

Surely, Rynn had given up on waiting for him hours ago. The paxan was probably lost in some dream of his own by now. Frustrated, Eben gave up trying to go to sleep and dream of his sister.

And, of course, that was when he drifted off. At first, Eben was aware of nothing. But then, the voices called to him again, beckoning him from his slumbers, Llyrando, Cyndra, Imogen, and Arcus.

The veil of the world gave way to the dreaming as the mists urged Eben forward. The same group of elementals stood upon a mound in a murky, black swamp that could only be Angor. And once again, a huge horde of elementally aligned mortals milled around them. If anything, the army had grown larger since last time he'd seen it. Upon the dark mound, the child was flanked by the Boki thane and the robed man with the elemental gauntlet.

From the west came the fire-touched, bringing offerings for the favor of the elemental lords and ladies. From the north came the stone-born, seeking to impress with their gifts of earth. From the south came the people of the winds, presenting trophies of the sky. All elemental nobles took their tribute from the treasures laid at their feet, all but Llyrando, for the east was silent.

"Bring forth your tribute that I may bestow my favor upon you," called Llyrando, his words washing over the spirit of those before him. Yet none came forth. "Come now, do you not see the power we offer? Did you not hear the words we taught to Marikeen, the words of summoning? Did you not—"

The Crushing Wave did not finish before another shouted from a ledge far away, upon the Heaves. It was an ikonesti warrior wearing ice armor, yet it did not have the same iridescent hue as that of his lord whom Eben had seen the last time. In this warrior's hand was a spear of glowing ice.

"We do not take a knee in the Heaves, pretender. Llylandril is the Mother of the Bay, and you are but an echo, a dream of what once was. Your time is long past. Go and leave this place while you still have form."

"What is this? You seek a duel with me? I, who ruled the raging rapids long before elves first touched Urth? I take no pleasure in laying you low, white one, but you shall feel my power."

The ikonesti launched himself, sliding across the snow

until he came to rest before the massive Llyrando. He declared loudly, "I am Kryth, Son of Winter, first Rime, born of the Long Snows. My people will know you for a false ancient when I take the heart of the wave."

Llyrando looked upon the other elementals, and the gauntleted one nodded. "Your people will only know the folly of their first Rime."

Battle was joined, Llyrando lashing out with his great arms while Kryth skated across the snow, striking the Crushing Wave with a strange ice deeply familiar to Eben. Since she was a little girl, Marikeen's first mark had begotten an inner light, identical to that present in the ice magic of this ikonesti.

The ice magic, which should have no effect upon the massive water elemental, was indeed freezing Llyrando. His arms grew ever more inflexible as Kryth assailed them with his ice bolts. The ikonesti closed the distance and launched his spear attacks. They, too, pierced the body of Llyrando, wounding the wave.

The elemental's cries seemed desperate, but Eben saw that while the attacks did harm Llyrando, he was baiting the ikonesti warrior. Llyrando pushed the waters of the swamp around, maneuvering Kryth to the perfect spot. What Kryth missed was that, as an elemental, Llyrando could channel power through any part of his body, including his legs.

Llyrando struck out with his foot, sweeping the young Rime from his feet and then pulling him in like a riptide. In a single moment, Llyrando's victory was assured as Kryth's spear flew away and the dark waters of the swamp bound him fast, preventing his baleful ice bolts.

"I shall make a brew with your blood, boy, to serve those who thought you my better," Llyrando bellowed.

Eben summoned the power of wind to mind, making the sign with his hands, but before he could transform and dash to Kryth's side, a familiar hand touched his sign, stopping him. A massive spear with the glow of the ice warrior's armor pierced the bosom of Llyrando, holding him fast.

In a single leap, the ice-armored warrior from Eben's first dream cleared the impossible distance between them, landing in front of the young ikonesti. Without even looking upon the massive elemental before him, the warrior addressed the elementals and humans upon the mound.

Marikeen whispered into Eben's ear, "Wait, Pebble. You will want to see this."

"Know this: I am the Lord of Winter, and the Heaves are mine. Should I ever hear your calls within their slopes, I will return and destroy all of you." With that, he plunged his hand into the chest of Llyrando.

In anger, the gauntleted man raised his hand, glowing with the colors of all the elements, to strike at the Lord of Winter, but the child laid hands upon the gauntleted man first.

She spoke, and his hand lowered, the power released. The gauntleted man threw back his hood, revealing a jann face of striking markings, bold and grand, unlike most of those in the horde below. In a respectful and sincere tone, he spoke. "The First Rime is yours, Great General of the Heaves. Take your champion. We seek no quarrel with you. You shall not hear our call again unless we be invited first to your land."

The Lord of Winter pulled his fist from the body of Llyrando, who in turn released Kryth. Both ice warriors turned their backs upon the shamed Llyrando. Kryth retrieved the ice spear, and cheers rose from the assembled warriors of the Heaves.

As the two ice warriors walked away, memory struck Eben like a lightning bolt, rolling forth from the deepest recesses of his memory. That voice, that glow. He had met that man before. The Lord of Winter was the one who'd saved Marikeen on the Night of Green Fire! There could be no doubt. Eben moved forward to follow the ice lord, but a hand on his shoulder held him back.

"Come, Pebble. There is someone I want you to meet," Marikeen murmured as she guided Eben toward the mound.

The horde parted for them, making way not for him but for Marikeen.

"Sister, wait. Are you well? Where have you been? What is that cloak you wear that I cannot sense you when its hood is raised? Who are these people? Come back with me, or tell me where I can find you," *Eben demanded urgently, reaching out to take hold of her.*

Marikeen slapped his hand away fiercely. "Don't touch me, Eben. You're not in charge of me. There is much happening here. You need to trust me, Pebble."

Pebble was what his mother had called him when he was little. Marikeen knew how much it meant to him and how it would irritate him if she used it. He loved his sister dearly, but sometimes she really got on his nerves.

This was her to be sure. No pretender would be able to get under his skin so quickly. But something was different about her now. She'd lost her girlish innocence and replaced it with something powerful in her demeanor. Eben wasn't entirely sure it was for the better.

They reached the mound and walked to the center, approaching the gauntleted man. Marikeen reached into her satchel, made in the image of her mantle, black fabric with bronze flames, and took out a large natural crystal that exuded a glow of old magic. "An offering for the ancients, mighty hand. We continue our search for the items you requested, and we have a promising lead on one of the pieces of the Grand Tympan."

The man smiled and motioned to the woman of crystal, Imogen, who approached.

"Well done, Marikeen," *the gauntleted man intoned.* "You and your compatriots in the Cabal have been most effective," *he stated as the Mother of Crystal took the stone.*

Eben fancied he heard new crystal growing in her as she held the glowing stone. It was as if Imogen was somehow becoming more . . . real.

The gauntleted man held out his right hand. "I know how to reward your efforts, young Marikeen. Come and receive *the gift of the ancient magics of blending, that you may entwine elemental energies in our service."*

Marikeen knelt before him. "I am ready to receive the gift of blending, great hand."

Eben moved to stop whatever was going on when the delicate but sharp hand of Imogen abruptly held him fast.

The man's gauntlet glowed, and he began to chant. Frustrated, Eben looked for another way to stop what was happening but instead noticed that the child seemed to be concentrating, as well.

The man laid his gauntlet upon Marikeen's head, and she screamed as power flowed into her. Eben lurched, and razor-sharp shards sliced into his skin, but he was unable to break free.

His sister's elemental marks, all four, burst with light through her robes.

"No, Marikeen! What have you people done to her?" Eben shouted.

Eben managed to tear his hands free, and he frantically made the sign of wind to escape the crystal vise. He flew to his sister's side. She crumpled as Eben embraced her.

"We have given her power, purpose, and position. The same we would do for ye, should ye choose to join us, Eben," the gauntleted man declared.

Marikeen pushed her brother away and straightened, gathering her strength. "I don't need your strength, Eben. I have strength of my own. Harken Guuri! Harken Wiisen!" Then she clapped her two hands together, one glowing brown and gray with the colors of earth, the other hand swirling in shades of blue and aqua.

This time, the two figures before her were made of mud, not earth or water as before, but a blend of the two. Eben stared in awe. To mix elements—the power that took was staggering. The pride on his sister's face was enormous, but he spied something else, as well, a combination of desire and vengeance.

"Take heed, Marikeen," the gauntleted man said sol-

emnly. "If you would blend opposing elements together, powerful forces will array against the unnatural taint of your creations. Take care as well not to blend more than two forces together lest they become unstable."

"Great hand, ancient ones, this is my brother Eben. He is . . . " Marikeen paused, searching for words.

"Everything you said he would be," Cyndra finished for her, a shower of sparks accompanying her words.

"He is one who bears a grand mantle," Imogen contradicted. "Your sister spoke highly of you, but even her words did not do you justice. I would have you carry my blazon, Eben. If you choose, wear this." Imogen held out a small faceted crystal cut like a three-pointed star. "It represents my favor. Join us and be rewarded beyond measure."

"Take it, Eben," Marikeen urged. "I want you with us. With me."

He had no choice, even if every part of his spirit told him this was wrong. He couldn't abandon his sister. He had searched too long and too hard. He could not lose her again. Eben nodded, taking the crystal from Imogen and placing it upon his cloak.

"So it begins . . . ," said the gauntleted man.

"What now?" Eben asked of his new acquaintances.

"Now," Marikeen said grimly, "we make them pay."

"Make who—" Eben started.

The gauntleted man cut him off. "Gather the items of power and purpose that we seek and you shall be rewarded a hundredfold, Eben. A great change is coming, and you shall be an important part of it, like your sister."

Eben jolted awake sharply, rudely torn from the dream.

"Sorry," Rynn muttered. "It was time to get you out of there. Before you gave an answer you would regret."

"Why?" Eben demanded. "She was going to tell me where to find her—"

"No. She wasn't. Your sister is in league with some powerful forces, and none of them bear anything but ill intent."

"But they're just dreams," he protested.

"Make no mistake. Beings from the dream plane are fully as powerful as any on the mortal plane. Particularly on their home realm."

Eben frowned. "As powerful as, say, dragons? Or elemental lords?"

"Absolutely."

Eben stared into the paxan's mesmerizingly turquoise eyes. He believed Rynn. And was afraid. Just how powerful were the elemental dream creatures his sister was involved with? And what did they have in mind to do with the enormous army they were assembling?

J ustin started as the door to his tiny room—more like a prison cell, really—burst open without warning. Hadn't these people heard of knocking first?

He'd been having serious misgivings about this whole project ever since arriving at Alchizzadon. The mages were so secretive that it made him suspicious. They were up to something they weren't telling him about. He could feel it. But what? And how did Raina fit in to their schemes? Surely there was more to it than needing her to have a couple of children for them. Any woman could do that. Why her, specifically?

Kadir stood in the doorway, as big and forbidding as always. "It is time. Come with me."

"Time for what?"

"We are going to wake your magic. And while I have the ritual casters gathered and the circles in place, we're going to mark you."

Justin gulped and followed Kadir out of the cell. It all sounded horribly painful. But he'd be twice cursed before he showed weakness to these mages. He got the impression this secret enclave was very large, but it was hard to tell with everything always shrouded in darkness and all the windows covered or obscured. "And you're sure this is going to work?"

"Your lineage is rich with powerful magic users. Frankly, I'm shocked your magic did not manifest naturally. Perhaps proximity to the women of the House of Tyrel had some effect on it. Hmm. I should look into that."

He followed Kadir, still mumbling to himself, down a trio of staircases into what had to be the bowels of the building. The entire place was appointed as richly as a castle, but everything—even the furniture and tapestries—had a look of extreme age.

"In here." Kadir gestured at a pair of tall wooden doors with iron-banded hinges. Dim light spilled out into the corridor.

Justin stepped inside and stopped in surprise. At least a dozen mages, dressed in the same dark blue robes as Kadir, their faces covered with runic markings, turned to stare at him.

"Is this the candidate, then?" one of them asked.

"Aye," Kadir answered.

An elderly man stepped forward. "And he understands that this will either work or he will die permanently?"

Justin's gaze snapped to Kadir. *Die? Permanently?*

Never breaking Justin's stare, Kadir answered the other man. "Yes. He understands."

He understood *now*. How kind of Kadir to get around to sharing that little detail moments before the cursed ritual. Death, huh? Was he willing to risk that to save Raina?

There was no question how he would answer that one.

He took another step into the room. "What are we waiting for?"

M y lord, we have a problem."

The First turned away from the window and its stunning view beyond the great plaza that held the Imperial Seat. "And what might that be, Talissar?"

"The Emperor has summoned the Master of the Dupree Mage's Guild to appear before him. Aurelius Lightstar portaled into the city a few minutes ago."

Lightstar. There was a name he had not heard in a while. After a brief moment of fame as the quick-thinking mage who saved General Tarses from his own folly, Aurelius had been posted to Haelos and faded into obscurity. Which was startling for a solinari. They craved glory like cats craved naps in sunbeams.

"Why was he summoned?" the First asked.

"I do not know. I have a source working on finding out, and I will let you know as soon as I get an answer."

The First responded gently, "Quickly, my friend. If Maximillian was in enough of a hurry to portal a minor functionary from a far colony directly to the seat, he will not wait long to speak to Aurelius."

"How much does the elf know?" Talissar asked.

It went without saying that he referred to the Eight's plans. Although Aurelius was not a member of their web of operatives, he was known to work toward the same ends, which made it the Eight's business to protect the solinari. Eventually, he answered Talissar gravely, "He knows enough."

"Can we cut ourselves off from him and those he knows?"

He frowned. "Rynn tells me that the party Aurelius has put together is the one to watch."

"Meaning what?"

"He believes they have found one of the sleeping kings. And furthermore, Rynn has found a person I specifically sent him in search of. As luck would have it, she is one of Aurelius's protégés."

"If I may ask, whom exactly did you send him in search of?"

"An awakened ethiri."

Talissar's sharply sucked-in breath was indicator enough that the elf understood the significance of *that* find. "Is one enough? Will she be sufficient to break the Great Forgetting?"

"I do not know. Therefore, I shall not pin all my hopes upon one young girl. We proceed as planned."

"Assuming we can protect Aurelius and all he knows from the Emperor," Talissar reminded him, bringing them back to the crisis at hand.

A rare feeling came over him. Dread. It was not often that he feared anything. But the idea of Maximillian uncovering even a piece of what they had spent so many years working on was worth fearing. The Emperor would not stop at permanently ending the lives of everyone Aurelius had ever known. He would relentlessly dig deeper, seeking out and destroying every last thread of resistance to Koth.

The Emperor had been increasingly tense over the past few years. His efforts to suppress the prophecies of his own demise had failed, and whispers were flying of a storm on the Imperial horizon. All Maximillian needed was one excuse to launch a purge of epic proportions.

He paced across the chamber and back in agitation. Everything they'd worked for so long and so carefully would be ruined. The entire house of cards would come tumbling down around his ears, and he would have to start all over again. Stars, the centuries of waiting. The excruciatingly cautious planning. The glacier-slow movement that was only just now beginning to add up to anything significant.

They were so close to having so many disparate forces aligned to move as one against Koth. If Maximillian uncovered their network now, they might never recover from it. Everyone was linked in, and everyone would be exposed. The Emperor's chokehold on Urth was such that he would eventually crush every source of potential resistance until none was left. This might be the last chance they would get at taking down the mighty, immortal ruler.

Aurelius must not go before the Emperor alone. And at all costs, Maximillian must not get inside his head.

"Word must be sent to Aurelius immediately to present himself to the Emperor in open court. Tonight, lest his Resplendent Majesty summon our friend to a private audience where I cannot protect him."

A state dinner was planned for that evening. Petitions would be accepted by the Emperor for a short while before the feast. It was a formality, and no actual business would be conducted during the session, of course. Usually it was a time for various official decrees and proclamations to be read in open court as a matter of law.

Talissar murmured, "We will be lucky to block a summons until tonight. Should we create some kerfuffle to distract the Emperor this afternoon, mayhap?"

"Yes, that would be wise. How easy would it be to stir up an argument between several kings over who will be the first king of Dupree?"

Talissar smiled a little. "Very easy, my lord. The kings squabble over it already. A few well-placed rumors and they will be at one another's throats."

"Excellent. And can you see to it that Aurelius's petition is heard tonight?"

"I think so," Talissar replied, frowning.

"Make it so," the First declared. "Everything depends upon it. *Everything*."

He watched Talissar leave the chamber, relieved to have

such a competent lieutenant in his secret army. He dared not move personally against the Emperor lest he draw undue attention to himself by the handful of people at court who might actually take note of him. He was just a messenger, after all. A servant. Not worthy of notice as a human being.

An hour or so later, another messenger in the messenger corps delivered a message to him without comment and left. The First tore into it nervously and hastily scanned the scrawled words. The reason Aurelius had been recalled to court was because a magical weapon of some kind—a staff, charged with some sort of ritual effect—had been discharged without Maximillian's permission. Apparently, the Emperor wanted to know why.

All right, then. Maximillian would be after a specific memory from Aurelius's mind. The First had to gain access to the solinari's mind and ascertain quickly whether or not the memory was worth shielding from Maximillian and what other knowledge might be tied to said memory that the Emperor needed *not* to see.

The problem with protecting Aurelius's mind from Maximillian's probing was to do it in such a way that the Emperor did not realize information was being shielded from him.

The First did not hit upon the solution until he was almost finished dressing for court. At formal events, messengers roamed the assemblage, secretly passing notes among the courtiers. However, for the sake of subtlety, messengers dressed so as to be indistinguishable from the courtiers themselves.

The trick was not to shield the information from Maximillian at all. Rather, he should use the Emperor's own blind spot against him.

It was a gamble. But if it worked, well worth it.

Quickly, he finished the tedious process of dressing for court. The primping, powdering, and perfuming were almost too much for him today. It was all so useless and ridiculous.

Of course, the pomp and ceremony were not useless from

Maximillian's point of view. The rigid rituals and rules of etiquette occupied most of his nobles' time and kept them from thinking too much about the actual state of the Empire. Which suited Maximillian's purposes entirely.

The First arrived at the Great Receiving Hall earlier than necessary, but he had to be in place before Aurelius arrived. Furthermore, he had to intercept the solinari before the Emperor noticed the mage and tore into his mind.

Not surprisingly, Aurelius waited to make his appearance until the massive hall was well crowded with nobles and functionaries. The solinari slipped in quietly, no doubt attempting to blend in with the crowd. Not that his glittering, golden skin was possible to miss in the sea of dull human flesh.

The First made his way over to Aurelius quickly—quickly enough that he actually had to touch the minds of those around him to make them forget his rapid passage. "Guildmaster Aurelius, isn't it? Welcome to court."

Aurelius turned to face him, a carefully polite expression on his face. "Have we met, sir?"

The First reached out and took Aurelius's hand. It was too familiar a greeting for men who had never met, but in the crush of people and the voluminous folds of their court robes, the gesture would go unnoticed.

Their palms touched, and the solinari frowned, perhaps sensing his urgent scanning of Aurelius's mind.

Great stars in the heavens. This man was up to his neck in rebellion. And it all centered around a group of youths— extraordinary youths—each with their own special gifts, individually enough to cause Maximillian enough alarm to take action. But together, the group would have to be crushed. No wonder a patina of panic overlaid all the solinari's thoughts.

It was an easy matter to find the memory of an ornate staff topped by a spectacularly carved green rose exploding in the hands of . . . ahh. The ethiri girl. Rosana. So *that* was how she'd been awakened. Maximillian's magic had removed his own curse from her. How ironic. Amusement flowed through him at the discovery. If only Maximillian could be allowed to see that he might very well be the cause of his own undoing.

But no. This was the memory that needed to be erased. Quickly, the First inserted a memory of himself standing in the corner of the Heart common room into Aurelius's mind as the solinari witnessed the staff's activation. When Maximillian saw the memory and him in it, the presence of the First would instantly and irrevocably erase the entire memory from the Emperor's mind.

His hand fell away from Aurelius's. His work done, he faded back into the crowd to observe the outcome of Aurelius's audience with the Emperor from a safe distance.

He'd barely moved away from the solinari when a soldier in Imperial livery approached Aurelius. At least the guard did not raise his voice and make a fuss over ordering the elf to present himself. But the guard did make it clear that his presence before the Emperor was required immediately.

Stars. He'd barely gotten to Aurelius in time. The First glided through the crowd, paralleling Aurelius and the guard as they approached the huge obsidian throne carved into the shape of a great, black flame rising toward the soaring ceiling. Maximillian sat in the chair carved into its base, the symbolism heavy-handed. The source of the Eternal Flame of Koth was the Emperor himself. Of course, the First knew differently. But he was in no position to say anything about Maximillian's real source of power.

Aurelius ascended the golden steps with barely perceptible reluctance. Which wasn't a bad thing. The Emperor would be suspicious of anyone who did not approach him with a certain reticence. The First shifted position slightly. He had studied the acoustics of this hall in enough detail to know exactly where to stand if he were to see and hear all the forthcoming exchange.

Aurelius bowed deeply. "Your Most Resplendent Majesty, it is an honor above all other honors to come before you thus."

"Rise, Aurelius Lightstar, and let me look at you."

Hah. Maximillian looked *into* his courtier, not at him. The First risked a cautious probe of his own to watch where Maximillian searched in Aurelius's mind. To make sure the Emperor did not find something that he had missed.

There. Max found the memory of the staff immediately. In an instant of rage and horror, Maximillian saw the girl's gypsy curse torn away and the ethiri beneath exploding forth. Maximillian looked around within the memory to see all who were present . . . the blank spot where the First stood . . . and then the entire memory evaporated. Gone. Every bit of it. The girl, the staff, the rose, the curse undone . . .

"So, Aurelius. I have seen into your mind. Now tell me what I have seen."

Aurelius's eyebrows twitched, indication of just how hard the solinari was thinking. The First dared not touch the elf's mind to give him a hint how to proceed. Not with the Emperor concentrating so intensely upon Aurelius's mind.

C'mon, Aurelius. Figure it out. If Maximillian could see the memory, you would already be on your way to Laernan's chamber of horrors.

"Where did it go, Aurelius? Where is my staff?"

Dawning understanding broke across the solinari's mind. An image of the staff leaning in the corner of some sort of locked treasure room blossomed in the guildmaster's mind.

If he could have cheered aloud without giving it all away, the First would have done so in that moment. Aurelius had summoned the *perfect* memory to mislead Maximillian. Images of fleeing looters, rioting in the streets of Dupree, and soldiers brawling with the locals filled in the rest of the gap in Aurelius's mind, unquestionably real and just as unquestioningly misleading.

Aloud, the guildmaster said regretfully, "Your Resplendent Majesty, there was a break-in to the Mage's Guild storehouse. I regret to inform you that the item in question disappeared. I take full responsibility for the theft—"

Maximillian raised a hand to stop the obligatory scraping and mea culpas, and Aurelius fell silent immediately. The man was no dummy and read the Emperor as well and quickly as any experienced courtier. There might just be a chance that the rebellion would escape this night intact, after all.

The Emperor leaned forward in his seat and lowered his voice so that none but those closest to him could hear—or anyone standing in the exact spot the First stood. "So you have no idea upon whom the staff was discharged?"

The moment of truth. Urgently, the First projected a single word into Aurelius's mind, doing everything in his power to wrap the word in his own essence, thereby shielding it from Maximillian's detection. *Lie.*

Both Aurelius and Maximillian frowned faintly. One because he heard the word, and one because he did not—or rather he heard it and instantly forgot it.

The First held his breath as Aurelius took a deep breath and spoke. "I do not know who received the ritual held within the staff."

Maximillian probed Aurelius's mind deeply, seeking truth. He must sense a lie. But without any other truth to replace it and the First's camouflage wrapped firmly around the lie, he could only accept the solinari's words at face value. The Emperor murmured, "Let us be frank with one another, Guildmaster. That staff was meant for one whom most think to be dead. An old friend of both of ours."

Aurelius gasped lightly. The Emperor must have projected an image of General Tarses directly into the elf's mind.

"I miss my old friend. I need you to find him. And when he is found, he needs to be . . . restored. You helped him once before. Can you do it again?"

The First shifted his stare to Aurelius. Could the powerful mage clear the taint of the Hand of Winter from Tarses? It would be an impressive feat. Perhaps the unique ability of solinari to absorb magic made such a thing possible.

"I will do my utmost," Aurelius responded soberly to the Emperor.

"Find him. Fix him."

Aurelius bowed deeply. "So shall it be, Your Resplendent Majesty."

The First exhaled the breath he had not realized he was holding. He had bought the rebellion a little time. But would it be enough? Maximillian's patience would not hold forever. And when he took action, blood would flow in the streets.

27

Raina was relieved to be lost in the wilderness with just the trees and her friends for company. Even if they did set a grueling pace in a futile effort to stay ahead of those cursed hounds. Except for the occasional bump or bruise, none of them required much in the way of healing, particularly now that she and Rosana weren't having to pour constant healing into Will and Bloodroot to keep the tree lord from killing Will.

Which was just as well. The voices in her head were with her constantly now and growing louder by the day. She began to wonder if she would be able to hear herself to cast magic around the din in her skull. Ever since they'd left Dupree, the mutterings had been getting steadily noisier and more insistent.

Any trail left for them by Tarryn had disappeared. They had taken the decision to go ahead and turn toward the north lest they overshoot Kerryl's path entirely. They could only assume that his destination with his hostages was in this general direction.

Summer was turning to fall around them, and the forests of paper birch, ash, and silver maple gave way entirely to the massive pines of the Quills. But before they disappeared altogether, the tree leaves turned from green to every conceivable shade of red, orange, and gold, shivering in anticipation of the winter to come. It was breathtakingly beautiful and the most peaceful place she had ever been. She might even go so far as to call herself happy out here were it not for the threat of hounds, or of meeting a Dominion patrol, or Kerryl Moonrunner himself.

She began to understand why the people in this region chose to live in tiny, squalid settlements. As dangerous as life might be out here, they were free of the Empire. Free of taxes and slavers and being under constant surveillance. If Justin were with her, she would find some remote village outside the Dominion lands to settle in and never go back to civilization. But he was not here, and she had a quest to complete. A responsibility to her family and the people of Haelos to see through.

The silence around them was expansive, interrupted only by the wind in the trees. Which was maybe why the voices were worse than ever tonight, whispering to her on the chilly winds of coming winter. As they walked through the day, she heard only snippets of voices in her head, but when they made camp, the whispers became deafening roars inside her head.

She sat by the fire one evening, frowning in concentration as she tried to make out words and meaning within the shouted syllables.

Rynn sat down next to her, bowl in hand, to eat. He asked around a mouthful of rabbit stew, compliments of Sha'Li's hunting skill, "Are you all right?"

"Why do you ask?"

"I sense your disquiet. And you've been distracted all day."

She glanced sidelong at the paxan. "How much can you sense?"

He shrugged. "Waking minds are guarded against my talents much more than sleeping ones."

"Does that mean you can poke around in our minds at will while we sleep?"

"It is not that simple. Nor is such practice ethical."

"Ethics matter to you, then?"

He turned his head to stare coolly at her. "You need to ask?" He sounded almost offended.

"No. I do not. I'm sorry. I'm just on edge tonight."

"I noticed," he commented dryly. "Why?"

She remembered his calming influence the day she'd heard the stones talking to her inside that cliff. In for a copper, in for a gold. She murmured, "The voices are starting to get the best of me."

"Tell me about them. What are they saying?"

"I cannot make out words. It's as if a great crowd of people is shouting all at once, making me unable to hear any of them."

"Echoes," he stated confidently.

Now that he mentioned it, that was a good description of the sound. "Yes. Exactly."

He nodded soberly. "For some reason, you have the ability to hear spirits that once were. Scholars among my kind argue over whether echoes linger from the past as disembodied things or whether they emanate from living beings as echoes of those people's pasts."

"I'm not sure I care which it is, if I can just find a way to make them be quiet."

"Do you mind if I take a look inside your mind? I might be able to do something to quiet them, if only temporarily."

"By all means."

He set his bowl down and placed his big, warm hands on either side of her head, his fingers threading through her hair to rest directly against her scalp. His touch was soothing, and her eyelids drifted closed.

Rynn's presence inside her mind was confident. Comfortable. She was in good hands. *Let's have a look at these echoes, shall we?* he projected into her consciousness.

Experimentally, she thought back to him, *"Yes. Let's."*

"Show them to me."

She stilled her thoughts and opened her awareness to the night around her, the same way she would if she were about to summon a large quantity of magic. The stars were cold pinpricks of light, the dew gathering on the grass chilly. There. The whispers were coming close again. She tensed.

"*Don't fight them,*" Rynn directed. "*Let them pass through you.*"

"*Easy for you to say. They make me crazy after a while.*"

"*Just for a minute or two while I take a look at them and trace their source.*"

The voices retreated sharply from her mind at the suggestion that he was going to find where they came from. But gradually, she relaxed and the voices came back. It wasn't so bad with Rynn's warm, calming presence inside her mind to act as a buffer against the battering noise.

After a minute or so, his hands slipped away, and she opened her eyes. He was staring down at her thoughtfully. "Where does your magic come from?"

"I beg your pardon?"

"When you summon magic, where does it come from?"

"I don't know. It just comes."

"Would you mind summoning some while I watch?"

"You mean to watch from inside my mind?"

"Correct."

"If it will help with the voices," she replied.

His hands came up to encompass her head once more.

It felt incredibly intimate calling magic to herself while someone else watched like this, from inside her mind. She summoned magic to each of her hands individually, holding them out to her sides so she wouldn't harm him where he sat directly in front of her, his muscular arms encircling her.

"Ahh," he sighed inside her mind. His satisfaction was palpable, flowing through her like a soothing bath.

His hands lifted away from her head. She looked up at him, abruptly aware of him as a person and not just a big, forbidding bodyguard.

"So here's the thing, Raina. Your magical energy comes from the same place as those echoes. I do not know if the echoes come attached to the energy or if, by summoning magic, you open a doorway that lets the voices through. But either way, the voices and your magic are linked."

"Why do other spirit magic casters not hear these voices,

then?" She raised her voice and called across the clearing to where Rosana sat with Will, hands linked and foreheads touching. "Rosie, do you ever hear whispers of people speaking inside your head, particularly when you're casting spirit magic?"

The gypsy looked away from Will and frowned. "No. Why do you ask?"

"See?" Raina turned back to Rynn. "It's just me."

"Yes, but you summon extraordinary amounts of magic. It may be that the echoes do not become audible until you pull forth a great deal of magic from whence it derives."

"I haven't been casting much magic for a while, though. There's been no need for it out here with just the six of us."

"I doubt that the correlation between use and volume of the voices is direct. You have opened a gate wide within yourself. It remains open at all times, the magic accessible whenever you have need of it. The more magic you know how to draw to yourself, the louder the voices in your head become."

"I don't know if I can stand hearing them all the time. What if they truly make me insane?"

"You can do exercises to calm your mind. I could teach you how to meditate. If we cannot silence the voices, mayhap you can make peace with them."

She nodded doubtfully.

He glanced over at Rosana. "It might behoove you to meditate with Raina and me, also, in case this phenomenon of spirit echoes begins to affect you, as well."

Will asked jokingly, "Would meditation shut up Bloodroot inside my noggin?"

"Perhaps," Rynn answered seriously. The paxan turned his gaze on Eben next. "And a bit of meditation would not hurt you, either, my tense friend."

Sha'Li announced forcefully, "Meditation I need not. Stand guard I shall while songs you sing and happy thoughts think."

Rynn grinned broadly at her. "You, my dear girl, do not

need my services. Your mind is pure in thought and clear in purpose."

"Really?" Sha'Li asked, sounding as startled as she ever did. The lizardman girl puffed up her chest a little and squared her shoulders as she strode off through the grass toward the latest seep Eben had found for them.

Rynn announced, "It is not too late for a lesson now in the basics of meditation. Close your eyes and do as I say."

Raina was so relaxed she was on the edge of going to sleep when Sha'Li's urgent whisper interrupted her meditation. "Something moves in the dark—"

It was all that Sha'Li got out before an arrow tip protruded through her throat and she pitched forward into the dirt at Raina's feet. Stunned, Raina dropped to her friend's side. Working frantically, she broke the fletching off the arrow, rolled the lizardman girl onto her side, and wrenched the arrow the rest of the way through her throat. A gush of hot blood went all over Raina's hands, and she steeled herself against panic at the sight of her friend bleeding out.

Shouts erupted all around her, and the party sprang into action as one.

She called life-renewing magic and slammed it into Sha'Li all in one movement. The telltale gasp of returning life came, and Raina hit her friend with another blast of healing. Leaping to her feet, the lizardman girl dived back into the fray, while Raina whirled to face desperate combat all around her.

Her impulse was to save her friends first. It wasn't noble, and it wasn't in the spirit of her colors. Except she knew and loved them. And besides, they were closest to her. It was not her sworn purpose to prevent her friends from defending themselves, merely to keep their foes from dying once the fight was concluded.

Her friends were directly in front of her for the most part. She would have to force her way past them to even be able to reach the assailants. She did halfheartedly lob a healing spell at one of the Dominion attackers lying on the ground. It hit the fellow but did not appear to have any effect. He must have been dead or dying. She made a mental note to check on him in a few minutes if the fight was not concluded by then.

Black-and-red Dominion tabards announced who their attackers were. But this time it was not a scouting party of five overconfident warriors. This time it was a squad of at least twenty, with a magic caster and an alchemist to boot. Her friends were quickly being backed into the fire, and she kicked dirt over it frantically lest they end up roasted as well as dead.

She hated feeling this helpless. Back in Dupree, Lenora had cast the rituals to remove all of Raina's damaging spells from her memory at Raina's request. It was not required of White Heart members to do that, but given the amount of mana she possessed, she'd felt it prudent to take the precaution. She felt a momentary stab of regret now that she could not blast everyone in the clearing.

The party was hard-pressed by multiple attackers. Gashes and blood sprang up on Will's and Eben's tabards, and even Rynn had three horizontal gashes across one of his shoulders from the swipe of a clawed paw. She cast healing at each one of them.

The party healed for the moment, she cast sleep spells at the nearest Dominion fighters, who dropped to the ground. Unfortunately, new Dominion attackers stepped over the prone forms and took up the attack where their companions had left off.

Without warning, a burst of magic rippled across her skin. Thankfully, she had up a magical shield of her own to absorb what felt like a silence spell. Without being able to incant aloud, she would not be able to shape magical energy into specific spells.

Quickly, she cast another magic shield upon herself, but in the meantime, Eben staggered and went down under a barrage of blows from at least four attackers. She threw a ball of magic at him and managed to hit his leg. He lurched back to consciousness, his health restored.

But her healing only prolonged the inevitable. No sooner had he regained consciousness than the changelings around him hacked into him viciously. Lying on the ground as he was, he had no means of protecting himself.

"Stop!" she screamed at his attackers. But they ignored her. She frantically cast healing at all her friends, flinging magic as fast as she could. But to no avail. No matter how fast she healed her friends, the attackers were able to slice them to bits again faster. There were just too many Dominion fighters. Too many weapons. No matter how well her companions fought, they were going to lose.

Three blasts of magic flew at her in quick succession. The first two she was able to protect herself against, but the third one froze her entire body in place, arm raised to cast magic at Rynn, whose bloody form had just been buried in a pile of Dominion tabards, his fists and feet still flailing grimly.

At least half their attackers were down on the ground, and several more were upright but badly wounded. She tried to talk, but her jaw was as immobile as the rest of her. She'd been paralyzed somehow. As she watched on in helpless horror, her remaining friends fell one by one, hacked and gutted into barely recognizable human forms.

Last to go down, Will cut loose with an impressive blast of magic that took out all four of the attackers on top of him, flinging them back, blackened and dead. But he did not get up from where he fell. A pack of Dominion beasts leaped upon his prostrate form and tore at it like hyenas feeding. She would have turned her head away from the gory sight, but she could not even close her eyes to stop herself from witnessing the terrible deaths of her friends.

Her terror was such that she had trouble forming thoughts. What would the Dominion do to her when this magical paralysis wore off? Would it be worse than the nightmare she'd already witnessed? If only she had a means of killing herself. A dagger lay on the ground a dozen feet away from her. Mayhap she could dive on it and stab her heart with it before the attackers did their worst to her. But the blade was probably too far away to reach before the creatures fell upon her. She gazed around frantically for some other weapon to kill herself with.

The thought vaguely passed through her mind that defending all life included her own life. Except she was already dead. Her attackers just hadn't gotten around to finishing her off yet. She was merely choosing a less violent and terrible means of accomplishing her demise.

Rosana was on the ground, but Raina could see her breathing deeply and evenly. Had she been magically slept, maybe? Was it possible that the gypsy would rouse and save their friends in a few minutes? Not that Raina would be alive to see it. Given the rabid way the beasts were starting to eye her, she would not live one more minute.

If only her captors would turn her loose, she would happily heal everyone. Surely, they knew that it was her duty as a White Heart member to do so. She watched in dismay as her friends' corpses were methodically searched and disarmed of all their weapons. No healing was given to them. The internal clock in her head that counted out how long everyone had been dead was ticking along at light speed. If they did not let her out of this paralysis soon, her friends and a good number of the Dominion would die.

She watched frantically as the remaining soldiers tied up her friends with glacial slowness. Were they going to life her friends or not? The Dominion magic caster waved his hand at her. "Tie her up. Kill her if she resists."

"Why should we save her? She's useless."

"Less than useless," someone else scoffed.

"The Heart pays to get its people back. They pay especially for the ones in white and blue."

A dozen inhuman stares turned her way. "But why?" one of them asked in blank disbelief. "She's as weak as a newborn babe—could not defend herself from even the simplest spells . . . has no weapon!" The last was spewed in tones of deepest disdain.

Her jaw sagged. They did not recognize the neutrality of

the White Heart? Soul-deep terror roared through her. She was completely vulnerable to these barbarous changelings. For the first time in her life, genuine fear that she was going to die permanently coursed through her. She had *no means whatsoever* of defending herself.

The reality of what it meant to venture into the wilds thus unprotected finally registered upon her in all its awful risk. This had been insane. White Heart members in their right minds should never venture into these places. Not unless they had a wish to die often and early. No wonder people commented that White Heart members never lived to see old age.

She was a lamb for the slaughter to these people. Sharp longing for Hrothgar or any of the other Royal Order of the Sun guardians in Dupree roared through her. And to think she'd spent all those weeks desperately wishing to get rid of them.

Rough hands grabbed her, and a rag was stuffed into her mouth. No! Now she could not heal her friends even if her captors did unparalyze her! Without words to help her shape the magic, she couldn't form spells that would do any good. Her hands were yanked behind her back, and she was bound, hand and foot. She shook like a leaf.

One of her captors shoved his snout close to her nose. "You and your fancy symbol mean *nothing* to us."

If she'd been afraid before, she was petrified now. She was well and truly on her own. If even the Heart itself did not reach out here, she had nothing to protect her except an oath meaningless to and scorned by these creatures.

The magic caster bent down to Eben and cast a tiny bit of healing into the big jann. Eben jolted to life and then sucked in a breath of agonized pain. His right shoulder looked terribly dislocated, and his entire body was covered with deep gashes and stab wounds. He might still be mortally wounded but be internally bleeding out slowly. He needed a lot more healing than that paltry dribble if he was to survive.

She could only watch on helplessly as, one by one, her

companions were lifed or healed barely enough to regain consciousness. Except for Rynn. When the Dominion got to his body, they blindfolded all his eyes, gagged him, and bound his hands and feet so he hung from a long pole. Then they lifed him and immediately hit him on the back of the head so he would not regain consciousness. All the while, the Dominion gave Rynn's limp form suspicious looks and his limbs wide berth. He must have put up quite a fight before he'd gone down for the Dominion to fear him even now.

The man who seemed to be in charge was strange looking. A porcupine changeling if she had to guess. In place of hair he had long quills that lay back flat against his skull at the moment. In battle, however, they'd stood up from his head in a deadly helmet of sharp points.

The porcupine changeling gave brisk orders to his men to get all the prisoners up and on their feet and to prepare to move out. Someone grabbed her arm roughly and shoved her forward. She turned to glare at the fellow and was backhanded for her troubles. She staggered and righted herself, the entire left side of her face on fire.

Angry, Raina glared at the changeling who'd hit her and then shifted her glare to the porcupine changeling in silent demand for permission to finish her work. It was all she could do not to summon magic to her bound hands, but she dared not act in a threatening way among these violent creatures.

His stare narrowed menacingly at her. "Cause me trouble, any trouble at all, and I will kill you and your friends. I will leave you for last to watch the others suffer as I torture them to death."

And she believed him.

Ceridwyn Nightshade moved quietly through the shadowed blackness of the trees. The stealth was necessary, for she had no doubt the Empire would dearly love to question her at length about the contents of the journal she'd turned over to Kodo a few months back. In it, she'd documented every single instance of corruption, embezzlement, graft, and outright theft she'd ever seen Anton Constantine commit. The governor had wrongly assumed that, by her silence, she tacitly approved of his behavior and that she must have been engaging in the same sorts of behaviors herself.

He would be wrong on both counts. Honor was not a code among her kind. It was tantamount to a religion among the nulvari people. Their first rule, memorized by every nulvari child as soon as they could speak, said it all:

> *Honor is spirit, together as one.*
> *Honor is fabric, invisibly spun.*
> *Honor is victory, silently won.*
> *Honor is all, the rest forever shun.*

Which was the reason she was out here tonight in Lochnar, skulking around like a common criminal. She was quietly investigating the assassination of Gregor Beltane. Her recently concluded investigation of Leland Hyland's death revealed that Dominion agents had almost certainly not been responsible for his death. Someone else had killed Hyland and tried to frame the Dominion for it. Not that she had any great love for those fur-covered felons. But she wanted the truth and sought proof of who everyone suspected had engineered Hyland's murder. Likewise, she was convinced that the assassination attempt upon Jethina Delphi also had not been a Dominion attack.

Which called into question who'd attacked Gregor Beltane. Her sources in Estarris were adamant that Occyron the Six-Gilled had not ordered a Merr hit upon Lochnar's landsgrave. Furthermore, they were adamant that if Occyron had sent his best warriors to do the job, they bloody well would not have been seen.

And then, of course, there'd been the Boki incursion that she'd narrowly pulled Landsgrave Talyn clear of. Those had not been top-drawer Boki warriors. She'd seen the thanes fight before, and they would not have stormed through the woods in a battle rage, heedlessly announcing their presence and giving warning to their target.

The way she heard it, the Boki invasion of Dupree itself had been pretty much the same. Although the orcs seemed to have stirred up the native greenskin population into a fine froth, that had not been the main Boki force that attacked Dupree. If it had been, the outcome of that fight likely would have been much different and certainly would have been much bloodier.

So. Someone was trying to increase tensions in the region. To convince the leadership of Dupree, and perhaps even the Empire in Koth, that the colony was under attack literally on all sides. The Dominion controlled the region north of Dupree. The Merr controlled the Estarran Sea that formed the long western boundary of Dupree proper. The Boki, while they made their home in the northern portions of Dupree, operated freely among all the greenskin tribes of the region surrounding the colony.

She smelled the lake before she saw it in the trees ahead, a faint glitter of water under moonlight. Loch Narr. Which was the old lizardman name for the lake, of course. But it had stuck with the coming of the Empire.

Beltane's murder had been the most perplexing of the four attacks on Anton's landsgraves. Beltane's body had never been recovered. For days afterward, Gregor's people had held out hope that they might receive a ransom demand from kidnappers or that he might resurrect somewhere nearby. But neither had ever happened. He'd just disappeared.

She crouched in the lee of a tall river birch to study where he'd been attacked. It was a good-sized lake. She could barely make out a structure on the far shore. Only a light shining through a window gave away its presence at all.

Loch Narr's surface was glassy smooth tonight. A small dock lay not far away to her right, several rowboats tied up at it, and a matching dock was visible on the heavily treed island in the middle of the lake.

Before she'd fed him a forgetting potion and erased all memory of the interview, Beltane's soldier had described rowing out to that island and being attacked as they disembarked there.

She hated the idea of being so exposed out on the surface of a lake in bright moonlight, but she had no choice. She'd come all this way to find out what had really happened.

Ceridwyn crept along the dock and picked the smallest rowboat to untie and step into. Settling the oars into the oarlocks, she eased away from shore. It did not take long to get the knack of rowing relatively evenly across the surface of the water. The quiet splash and drip of the oars, the smooth oak turning in her palm, the silence and the isolation were soothing.

The prow of her vessel thudded into the island's tiny dock clumsily, and it took her a few minutes to maneuver alongside it, steady the boat, stow the oars, manage to climb ashore, and secure the boat. She did not relish swimming all the way back to shore.

Right here was where the soldier said the Merr assassins had emerged from the water and taken down him and a second oarsman. The Merr had timed it well. The soldiers would have been distracted handling the boat and not on guard against an attack. The man said Beltane had already disembarked and been walking down the short dock when the Merr attacked.

Which meant Beltane had probably made it fully ashore. She traced his steps thoughtfully. He would have turned here. Maybe seen his men fighting.

Did he run back out on the pier to engage the Merr? It would have been the man's style to defend his troops. Except the soldier described being pulled under the water. To her knowledge Beltane was no expert at fighting underwater in spite of being a formidable warrior. Lizardmen had searched every square inch of the lake and never found Beltane's body or any evidence that he'd gone underwater to fight and die with his men.

If the soldiers had been going down or already disappeared by the time Beltane realized what was going on, that would have put him on shore and aware he was under attack. She glanced over her shoulder at the heavy growth just beyond the narrow strip of sand.

He would have retreated for the trees. He knew this island. Was a brilliant tactician. He'd have wanted to even the odds. Get the Merr on his turf. She trudged through the soft sand up the beach. There was no apparent passage through the brush to the interior of the island. She ended up crawling on her knees to get through the worst of it. Beyond the first barrier of thick bushes, the forest thinned out to something more reasonable, and a sandy path became visible.

Following the path, she expected to come out on the far side of the island but instead was shocked to emerge into a clearing in front of a tall, stone tower. The structure was white in the moonlight. Round. Very old-fashioned, with crenellations for archers around the top of it. Narrow windows spiraled up its side, suggesting rooms on perhaps three or four levels.

She'd never heard of Beltane having anything like this secret retreat in his holding. The front door looked like wood, but blackened with age, or maybe painted with some sort of tar. Hard to tell in the scant moonlight. She took a step toward the structure and all of a sudden, internal warnings sounded in her head. *Trap.*

Using her excellent low-light vision, she searched the ground and spied the faintest outline of what might be a pit trap just in front of her. Or it could be a pressure sensor stretching across the entire path. Either way, the white tower was not without defenses. Carefully, she circled wide of the traps, stepped over trip wires, and finally made her way to the front door.

It had no latch. No handle. No visible means of opening it. Frowning, she ran her hands around the margins of the wood panel. Nothing. Well, not nothing. A faint tingling passed through her palms to indicate that some sort of magic spell was attached to the door.

No sooner had she detected the magic and stepped back, frowning, than the door opened silently, swinging inward to reveal inky darkness.

"Who goes there?" a rough male voice asked from within.

"A friend. I mean no harm."

"That's what everyone who means harm says."

One corner of her mouth turned up wryly. "True. I come seeking understanding."

"Of what?"

"Who am I speaking to?"

"No one," the voice replied harshly.

She frowned. "Do you live here?"

"I am not sure I would describe myself as alive, but this is my home."

Was he a ghost? "Can you show yourself to me?"

Silence.

"I do not mean to intrude. I have come in search of answers regarding a friend of mine. He is said to have died here a few months ago."

More silence. Then, "What sort of answers?"

"Well, his body was never found. I'm worried that he might have been kidnapped and even now be languishing somewhere, waiting for a rescue that will never come."

"Ceridwyn?" the voice said hesitantly.

Shock coursed through her. She was disguised, wearing a deeply hooded cloak. Nobody could see her face. How did this disembodied voice recognize her? "Who are you?" she demanded, taking a step back and to one side, out of the direct line of fire from inside.

"Careful. One more step back and you will find yourself the victim of a most unpleasant pit trap."

"Did you see anything the night Gregor Beltane was attacked on this island?"

"Yes. I saw quite a bit."

"Tell me. What happened? Did he die? Did he get dragged under the water like his men?"

"What of his men?" the voice asked sharply. "Did they survive?"

"Both soldiers resurrected, telling wild tales of Merr rising up out of the water in silence to drag them under and kill them."

"Thank the Lady," the voice said in unquestionable relief.

She frowned. Looked up at the tower looming over her. It was old, the stones worn at the edges with weather and time. Symbols, so faint she could barely see them, covered the entire surface of the tower. She did not recognize any of the symbology, and as quickly as she looked at what seemed to be letters and words that might make sense, understanding slipped away from her. She felt the beginnings of a headache as she squinted at the markings.

Was the tower native to this place? It clearly predated the coming of Joubert Dupree to this land to claim it for Koth. Who had built it, then? It did not look lizardman in construction—their structures tended to be low, domed, and plain. Besides, why would they build anything on land?

"Who built this place?"

"I did. Or rather I rebuilt it here after it was dismantled and smuggled here stone by stone."

"I ask again. Who are you?"

"Apparently, I am the ghost in the tower."

"Do you—did you—have a name?"

The voice answered scornfully, "Of course."

"May I come in?"

"I don't know. You can try, I suppose. But be careful. The tower can be touchy."

The tower was in some way sentient? Eyebrows raised, she moved forward cautiously. Very slowly, as nonthreateningly as she could, she stepped across the threshold into a small, round room, ringed by a stone staircase following the curve of the wall. A man sat in a carved, upholstered chair with a high back and padded arms beside a barren, dark hearth.

She moved cautiously toward the matching chair and

caught her first full-on look at the man. And gasped. "Gregor? Is that you?"

"I cannot really say. Sit. I'm sorry I have no food or drink to offer you. Apparently, I have no need of either in my current state."

"What state is that?"

"I do not actually know. I was hoping you could tell me."

"Are you dead?"

"Don't know." He held out a hand. "Can you touch my flesh?"

She reached out and grasped his hand. It was warm and strong and vital. She slid her fingertips up his wrist. "A pulse beats in your veins, and your flesh has mortal substance."

"Hmm. I guess I'm not a ghost, then. That was my best guess."

"Why have you not gone back to your home?" she demanded. "Or to Dupree to let the governess know you live?"

He made a sound akin to a laugh, but a thousand times more bitter. "There's a small problem with that. You see, every time I attempt to leave this tower, I die."

"I beg your pardon?"

"It would be easier just to show you." Beltane rose from his chair and headed toward the open doorway she'd just entered. He spoke over his shoulder. "For what it's worth, I have tried every means I can think of to kill myself inside this tower, and nothing works. *Nothing.*"

He staggered as he got close to the door. Another step had him groaning in agony, gripping his belly. From between gritted teeth, he said, "I have not dared to actually cross the threshold as long as there was no one here to help me experiment. But if you would indulge me . . ."

"Anything. What do you need from me?" She rose in concern and moved over to support his elbow.

"Pull me back inside if this does not go well."

She frowned. "If *what* does not—"

He took one more step, his foot landing outside the doorway on the soft sand.

Without warning, Gregor collapsed. His face went slack, his breathing stopped, and the color drained from his face instantly. Shocked, she grabbed at his shoulders and rolled him onto his back to administer healing to him. She fumbled frantically in her pouch for a life potion, but as she did so, he blinked awake and stared up at her.

"Am I fully within the tower once more?" he rasped.

She glanced at the threshold. His feet lay just inside the doorframe. "Yes."

"And I live once more. Somehow, my spirit is tied to this cursed tower. As long as I remain within it, I live. But the moment I set foot outside, I die."

"I will bring healers to this place. We will figure it out. A ritual to separate your spirit from the tower's." It sounded strange even to her ears. But stranger things had happened before. Magic followed rules known only unto it. Particularly very old magics, which seemed to be what powered this strange edifice.

"No. No healers. Not yet."

"Mages, then. To study the magic and how you are bound to it."

"No. Nobody."

"Why not?"

"Assassins were sent to murder me. I can only assume that as soon as their failure is known, they will return to finish me off. Before I let anyone know I live, I would know who sent the killers to my doorstep."

"I believe I know who it was. All four of the sitting Dupree landsgraves were victims of assassination attempts on the same night."

Beltane lurched. "What happened? Did they all survive?"

"Delphi survived the attack with the aid of a spirit warrior tied to her family. Talyn escaped, but does not return to Dupree. Leland . . . " She trailed off. Gregor and Leland had been close friends over the years, bound by the shared loss of their wives and by similar codes of honor and care for their subjects.

She continued grimly, "Leland did not survive. Nor did he resurrect. He has passed beyond the Veil."

"Ahh, stars. Not Leland," Gregor moaned. "He was the best of us all."

She helped the grieving man to his feet and led him over to his chair. They sat for some time, Gregor's quiet grief the only sound intruding upon the deep silence of the tower.

Eventually, he said heavily, "And whoever ordered my assassination thinks he succeeded in permanently removing me, as well."

"Correct."

"We all know it was Anton who ordered these assassinations," Gregor declared.

"That would be my assumption, as well," she replied.

"I gather Anton has not been captured?"

"Correct. The Coil is powerful enough to protect him for as long as he cares to remain in hiding."

"Not to mention, many nefarious souls owe him favors above and beyond the reach of the Coil," he added bitterly.

"The spoils of a long and profitable career as a corrupt governor," she agreed.

"Tell me something, Ceridwyn. Why did you turn over your journals to Kodo? Why not keep them to yourself and blackmail Anton? You could have squeezed him for every copper he was worth. You could have had all the wealth, all the power—stars, you could have been governess if you played your cards right."

Her spine stiffened. "You do not know me very well if you think those things matter to me more than honor." She didn't bother to tell him she'd actually turned down the position of governess.

He waved off her indignation. "I mean no insult to your honor. You have always been the power behind the throne. You were the voice of reason whispering in Anton's ear when he would listen to no one else. The colony owes you a tremendous debt of service. What I am asking is whether you turned over those journals because you are a great friend of the Empire or because you have no great love for it."

She sat back hard in her chair, her shoulder blades slamming into the cushion at her back. That was blunt of him to come right out and ask where her loyalties lay. It was unlike Gregor, who was usually the soul of subtlety and discretion. But then, this man was trapped in a magical tower and thought to be dead by all. He had very little to lose at this point. And it was not as if he could leave this place, go to the authorities, and accuse her of treason.

She shrugged. "Anton has no honor." It was not a direct answer to his question, but it was as much as she could afford to give him.

"I gather, then, that you serve honor over the Empire. By which I assume you also mean you serve your people before you serve Koth."

He was not wrong, but she was shocked to hear him state it aloud.

"The thing about being locked up in a tower alone for several months is that it gives a man plenty of time to think. Too much time."

When he did not continue, she asked, "And what have you been thinking about, Gregor?"

"The past. The future of Dupree and Haelos."

"Have you reached any conclusions?"

"I have. If the people of this land are to live and prosper, they must throw off the yoke of Koth, and soon."

She stared at him, stunned. Never in her life had she heard anyone voice open treason.

He grinned lopsidedly at her. "What does it matter if I speak treason? I'm already dead."

True. But still.

"Will you tell the authorities where I am now? Have me dragged from this tower to my death?"

She answered slowly, "No, my old friend. I will not. Your secrets are safe with me." In a badly needed change of subject, she asked, "What is this place?"

"Just some old tower."

"It's obviously deeply magical. Its healing properties could be of huge value to the Heart—"

"I need you to do me a favor, Ceridwyn. In honor of our many years of friendship."

He was invoking their entire past, was he? "What favor might that be?"

"Tell no one about me. Nor about this place. Let us first find out what kind of poison killed me. I can tell you it was no ordinary poison. I've never felt the like. It was as if my entire spirit were ripped right out of me. Apparently, only remaining inside this tower keeps my spirit intact. Whatever that poison was, it *killed* me. As in permanent death. What kind of poison can do such a thing?"

She stared at him doubtfully. "I will ask my contacts within the Merr poisoner community if they know of a poison which does that."

"And find out if there is a cure, mayhap? Help me, Ceridwyn."

She nodded. "We will find a way to get you out of this place. In the meantime, do you need supplies? Food? Wine?"

"Those would be spectacular. I have not eaten since I fell into this place."

"That was months ago! How did you not die of thirst or starve?"

"Like I said. The tower sustains me. It does not keep my stomach from feeling as though it gnaws through my spine, however."

She stared at him in disbelief. What *was* this place? "I worry for your sanity, my friend."

He smiled a secret smile. "I am far from alone in this place. Many spirits have apparently suffered my fate over the eons and are trapped here." He hesitated and then confessed in a rush, "The spirit of my wife is somehow tied to this place. She is here. We have been catching up after our long years apart."

Ahh. No wonder he was in no big hurry to leave this place.

Their romance had been epic, almost to the point of being annoying at times, as she recalled. Absently, she agreed to his request to say nothing of his existence or of the existence of the tower. Until the mystery was solved, this tower of immortality was best kept secret from others who might find a way to use its power to their own ends—namely, Anton Constantine.

Will had endured a lot of pain and misery in his un-natural union with Bloodroot, but nothing had pre-pared him for the agony he suffered now. His left forearm was broken where he'd caught a mace on it, his nose was smashed, and something was wrong with his left hip. He had to lean to the right and drag his left leg forward every time he took a step. And if he fell behind his friends, who were similarly bruised and battered, one of his Dominion captors whacked him across the back or shoulders with a heavy cane of some kind. Only his thick, boiled leather jacket kept his back from being a bloodied mess. He cradled his arm protectively against his belly and stumbled along in a red haze of pain as best he could. He thought he fainted a few times, for he'd woken up staring at Dominion jackboots twice as rough hands dragged him to his feet.

Blessedly, as dark fell, they'd stopped to make camp. But of course, his captors pointed at a fire pit other slaves were build-ing and grunted that he must help build the fire and fetch wood from a stack on one side of the clearing. At least he wasn't being ordered to split logs with his arm the way it was.

He watched in dismay as more changelings in Dominion tabards poured into their camp over the next hour. Along with the onset of darkness came a sharp fall in temperature. Stars knew where his gear had gone, along with his blanket and bedroll, and he missed them as he shivered. A huge ket-tle of stew smelled heavenly, and his stomach ached with deprivation. He'd been allowed to stick his face in a creek earlier and drink his fill, but that did little to assuage his hunger. Easily two dozen new fur balls crowded around, talking and laughing with the crew who'd captured them. At least the mongrels thought they were dangerous enough and valuable enough to merit a substantial escort to wherever they were going. He took small satisfaction in that.

A young male, perhaps some sort of equine changeling, untied Rosana's gag and hands before passing her a bowl of something hot and liquid. Wow. How generous of their captors. They'd had nothing but quick stops to stick their faces in streams for the past two days.

Will rubbed his face as the gag was removed from his mouth and spat out the foul, greasy taste of the rag into the pine needles beside his boots.

"Eat," the young changeling ordered.

Will had learned early on not to resist their captors. The porcupine changeling in charge backhanded any resistance into submission, be it from one of his own men or from one of the prisoners. Will sipped at the hot liquid that tasted vaguely like boiled boots. Why the Dominion hadn't killed them outright that first night, Will hadn't a clue. Why bother kidnapping them like this?

He noted that most of the changelings who'd joined them were mammal and reptile types. He had yet to spot any insect changelings among the Dominion, and there were only a few avarians and rakasha. Discipline seemed reasonably good. Their camps the past two nights had been as clean as could be expected for a fast-moving patrol with prisoners. Even tonight, he spied very little loitering or lounging going on.

As he sipped at his broth, he noticed Rosana surreptitiously summoning magic beneath a fold of her skirt while keeping an eye on their guards. She reached toward him.

"You first," he hissed.

She glared at him but thankfully did not argue. She muttered under her breath, and the bruise around her right eye began to fade, and the swelling in her jaw went down. Then she reached out for him and commenced trickling healing magic into him surreptitiously.

The ache in his arm and his face subsided somewhat, and sitting cross-legged on the ground did not bother his hip so much anymore.

"Not all the way," he breathed. "Leave me bruised." The curs would no doubt kill Raina and Rosana if they thought the girls were healing their friends.

Rosana reached to her left and commenced healing Sha'Li. Luckily for the lizardman girl, her scaled skin did not show much by way of injury, and he expected Rosana would heal her completely.

He noticed that Raina had managed to get herself pushed to the ground very close to where Rynn lay, still trussed to the carrying pole and still unconscious. The paxan's badly dislocated shoulder joint suddenly looked like a proper shoulder again. As Will looked on, Rynn's bruises began to fade, too.

Like Rosana, Raina stopped short of healing the paxan fully. She shifted slightly, waited out a guard glancing her way, and then reached for Eben. Will would never again make fun of healers for being useless in a fight. They were worth their weight in platinum after one.

He breathed a sigh of relief at finally feeling semi-human once more. Not that it helped their predicament any. They were vastly outnumbered by Dominion changelings, who were skilled fighters one and all.

He was surprised when one of the newcomers, a badger changeling who strutted around and gave orders as if he were in charge of everyone, moved to stand over Rynn's prostrate form. The badger leaned down to tear off the blindfolds and remove the gag. "Put a sword to that one's throat"—he pointed at Raina, who was looking as disheveled as the rest of them—"and then wake up the three eyes."

Rynn lurched awake, fighting against his bonds. He subsided quickly as he took in where they were and that Raina was being held directly in front of him with a wicked dagger to her throat.

"I will not use my powers on you if you spare the White Heart's life," Rynn declared to the badger. "You have my word of honor." How did Rynn know that guy was the one in command? He'd been conscious for two seconds.

The badger changeling nodded tersely and then moved away. Rynn was untied from his pole and passed a bowl of boiled boot soup, which he guzzled down. The guy must have been parched as well as famished. Raina passed Rynn her bowl of soup, and Eben passed the remains of his to Rynn, as well. Will would have shared, but he'd already finished his foul supper.

They were allowed to relieve themselves in the bushes, and the six of them huddled close to the dying cook fire they'd been deposited in front of. Frost was in the air tonight if Will wasn't mistaken. He asked Rynn low, "The Dominion fears you. Why?"

"They respect natural adaptations like mine that make warriors stronger. And they fear my ability to get inside their minds."

Raina interjected, "You've been here before, haven't you?"

Rynn shrugged in a way that Will took to mean he had. Will leaned forward. "Where are we, then?"

"How long was I out?"

"Two days."

The paxan glanced at the tall, narrow pine trees rising around them. "We're deep in the Quills by now. Well into Dominion territory. What direction have we traveled?"

Sha'Li murmured, "North. Always north."

"Are they following Kerryl, or is he following them, mayhap?" Will asked.

Rynn shrugged. "Could be either. Although why he'd risk capture by the Dominion, I cannot fathom. He'll get no rescue from the Forester's Guild. The presence of a Dominion colony in Haelos is not something the Empire likes to advertise. It makes Koth look weak."

Will sat back on his heels, frowning. "Does he recruit, or mayhap kidnap changelings for his cause?"

"Perhaps," Rynn replied.

Eben muttered, "Will the Dominion give asylum to Kerryl and his prisoners?"

Rynn frowned. "If so, we will struggle to find them. This colony is home to thousands of people. It's the size of a margrave holding at least. There are villages, farms, encampments, roads, a port—everything a great army needs to sustain itself."

"Thousands of Dominion?" Sha'Li echoed. "Why have they not taken over Dupree?"

One corner of Rynn's mouth turned up sardonically. "And risk drawing the full attention of Koth and its legions? That would be suicide. They grow in strength for now."

"Where will they take us?" Raina asked low.

"I would think they will not take us to the capital. They are deeply suspicious of outsiders and will not wish for us to see anything in Rahael that we can tell about back in Dupree."

"As if we'll ever see that place again," Will commented bitterly.

"Oh, they'll let us go," Rynn replied. "For a price. The Heart will ransom back the girls, and they will likely try to ransom me back to my kind. I should think they will recruit Sha'Li—and perhaps Eben, for he is young and strong."

Will scowled. What? Did he have no value? If Aurelius were in Dupree, he would pay to get his grandson back. But he was in Koth, summoned by the Emperor, possibly never to return to Dupree. Will was completely without family, friends, or allies beyond those sitting with him right now.

Rynn leaned toward him urgently. "Listen, Will. The Dominion values strength and battle prowess above all else. If you have a chance to demonstrate your combat training, use every skill you've got. Lay waste to everyone around you with your magic and that staff of yours. Maybe, just maybe, they will let you live."

The equine changeling came over just then and cuffed Rynn sharply in the back of the head. "You do not speak in the presence of the leader," the changeling declared.

Will looked around in interest. What leader? On cue, a dozen changelings who all looked to be badgers—or wolverines, maybe?—came over and hoisted them to their feet. He and his friends were dragged across the clearing to another fire, this one blazing up into the night sky, obviously fed by resin-rich pine logs.

A changeling stepped forward, but unlike any other he'd seen so far. This one was taller than the others for one thing. And his skin was golden. Not like Aurelius's, but more like Sha'Li's. He was covered in tiny scales that glittered as he moved. And something was wrong with his neck, which was unnaturally long and wide. It was as if longitudinal folds of skin were collapsed along each side of his head, all the way down to his shoulders.

And his eyes . . . gads. They were large and gold in color with disturbing vertical black slits for pupils. He was a *snake* changeling. Surely, this could be none other than Goldeneye himself. Repulsed, Will stared, fascinated. A cobra changeling did not make for an attractive humanoid. If those folds of skin lifted and filled, they would look a lot like a cobra's hood. He did not think he wanted to see this man become agitated enough to display a hood, thank you very much.

"Kneel before the leader," someone growled from behind Will. Heavy hands on his shoulders forced him and the rest of the party down, and Will's knees banged painfully on the ground.

"Who have we here?" the cobra changeling asked.

The porcupine changeling who'd captured them stepped forward. "My lord Goldeneye, I tracked these humanoids and brought them to you, as ordered."

"You're telling me this sad bunch of misfits took out one of my patrols?"

The porcupine flinched. "They could not put up much resistance to me and my men."

Will snorted mentally. He and his misfit friends had dropped over half the Dominion squad, and they'd been outnumbered by changelings better than three to one. Four to one if Raina was not counted as a combatant.

"I know the red-and-yellow symbol on the gypsy." Goldeneye strolled over to stare down at Raina, who prudently was looking down at the ground. "But this blue and white. Are they the useless ones who do nothing in battle?"

The porcupine answered again. "Aye, m'lord. The yellow-haired human was worse than useless. Not worth the food to keep her alive. Shall I kill her?"

Will stared. Didn't they know what she was capable of? But then, if Raina's skills were measured purely for their fighting and killing potential, he supposed he could see the porcupine's point of view.

Goldeneye's almost nonexistent lips pulled back to reveal sharp teeth and a pair of long, needle-like fangs where his second incisors would normally be. Stars, was that supposed to be a smile? It was chilling to see. "Idiot humans pay best of all for the weak ones. Keep feeding her until word is sent to Briza. Find a Heart trader at the port and ask what he will pay for one in white and blue. Then make him pay double what he offers."

One of the wolverine types bowed and murmured in acknowledgment. He must be in charge of ransoming Heart members back to the Heart. The same wolverine murmured respectfully, "And the other girl? The red-and-yellow one?"

Goldeneye shrugged. "If they pay the usual price, they may have her. These healer types are too dimwitted to be of any use to us."

"I am not dimwitted, sir!" Rosana exclaimed.

Goldeneye's face swiveled to look at her, but the rest of his body did not move. It was eerie. "I did not give you permission to speak, gypsy." He glared coldly at her—and stars above, she stared back! *Look away, Rosie. Look away!*

"Why did you invade our lands, dimwitted child?"

She opened her mouth to answer, but no words came out. A mental groan rose up from deep inside him. Goldeneye had enslaved her.

"You may speak," Goldeneye told Rosana.

Abruptly, words spilled out of her mouth. "We did not invade. A friend of ours was kidnapped by a nature guardian, and we but followed his tracks to rescue him. We have no business with you. Release us immediately!"

Easy, Rosana, he cautioned her mentally. Rynn might have told them never to show weakness in front of the Dominion, but belligerence would not serve them well, either.

Goldeneye moved to stand before her, and Will realized again just how large a creature the Dominion leader was. "Do not take that tone with me, dimwitted pinkskin. I will not warn you again."

A chill chattered down Will's spine at the menace in those softly uttered words.

"Shall I kill her, my lord?" the porcupine asked eagerly.

Goldeneye's right hand whipped out so fast that Will barely saw it move. One second the porcupine stood beside his leader, and the next he writhed on the ground, his jaw broken and one side of his face smashed in. Goldeneye's hood flared, and abruptly he was all cobra and barely a man. It was possibly the most frightening sight Will had ever seen.

Will recoiled involuntarily from the violence and speed of the blow. They could never take this creature down. But then, that was the point, he supposed. The strong ruled by might and fear in these lands. And this one was the strongest of the strong.

Goldeneye's attention swiveled back to Rosana, who was staring at the ground now, horror written on her expressive features. "Heal him, pinkskin."

Rosana's feet stayed stubbornly in place for an instant, but then the enslavement visibly kicked in, forcing her over to the writhing porcupine's side. She knelt beside him and passed healing into his broken face until it began to resemble its previous ugly self.

Goldeneye said briskly, "Take them to the slave pens."

Terror shuddered through Will. In the Empire, slavery was everybody's worst nightmare.

A brace of changelings stepped forward aggressively to hustle them away when a new changeling burst into the circle of firelight. Something soft-furred, twitchy, and quick. "Bad tidings, my lord!" he cried.

Everyone stopped in their tracks, prisoner and captor alike, to stare at the youth.

"Speak," Goldeneye hissed.

"Someone has broken into your treasure trove and stolen—" The youth's voice faltered of a sudden as if it was just occurring to him that his news might enrage its intended recipient. He took a step back. "—something of great value to you."

"Tell me," Goldeneye ordered.

"The ampoules of untouched water from the homeland," the youth stammered.

Will cringed along with everyone else as Goldeneye's massive gold-scaled hood flared to its full breadth, a dark circle in the center of each flare on either side of his neck. His flat nostrils distended, his fangs bared, and a horrible hissing sound emanated from the back of his throat. *Great Green Lady, preserve them all from this beast.*

"Kerryl Moonrunner," the Dominion leader ground out in tones of rising fury. "This was his doing!" He pointed at Will and his friends and roared in a terrible voice, "Bring those captives back to me."

Rosana actually whimpered aloud, and Will barely refrained from doing the same.

"Do you work with him? With Moonrunner. Were you a diversion while he robbed me?"

"No, Lord Goldeneye!" Rosana all but sobbed. "I spoke true. We track him for he stole our friend from us."

Will held his breath so hard he started to become lightheaded. The snake changeling stared at Rosana as if he would strike at her any second, destroying her utterly. Without ever taking his mesmerizing, vertical-slitted glare off her, his right hand shot out. Caught the messenger by the throat. And squeezed until the changeling was a writhing, gurgling morsel of dying prey in his grasp.

"Please, my lord. Let the boy go," Raina gasped. "Kill me instead."

Rynn tried to throw himself in front of her, but two big, burly Dominion guards held him back by his arms.

Goldeneye's fist opened. The messenger boy dropped to the ground, gasping, and maybe dying, anyway. It sounded as if his throat might be crushed.

"If I let you go and send you to track down Moonrunner, you will recover my change water and bring it back to me." A long pause from Goldeneye. "If you do this, I will remove your enslavement from you, gypsy."

"Done!" Will declared from behind her. Anything to free her from the clutches of this creature.

Rosana half turned to throw him a quelling look. He supposed she was right. The last thing they needed was for two of them to get themselves enslaved to the Dominion leader. She turned back to Goldeneye. "Done. We will do this thing for you. You have our word of honor upon it."

"All of your words of honor?" the cobra changeling demanded.

Rynn placed a fist over his heart and bowed his head. Will followed suit, thinking better of speaking aloud again, given what doing so had earned Rosana. All the others followed suit.

"Done. Turn them loose. Take them to the last trail of Moonrunner, and release them."

"Our gear!" Will whispered to Rosana.

"My lord!" Rosana said to Goldeneye's back. "We'll need our gear and weapons to find Moonrunner and take your water back."

Goldeneye's stride paused mid-step. He ordered to no one in particular, "Give them their equipment." He strode away without looking back.

CHAPTER

29

Gabrielle expected that they would take the river until they were safely away from the island and then go back to the surface and proceed overland. But their dwarven guide had other ideas. It was impossible to tell exactly how much time passed, underground as they were, but she estimated that they sailed down the river for most of the night and a day.

She saw villages and forests float by, fields with some small breed of cow, and goats and chickens, farms and homesteads. It was an entire world down here. Some places were as dimly lit as a forest populated only by lightning bugs. Other places were filled with a dim blue glow from phosphorescent fungi lining the cave ceiling far overhead. And yet other areas were nearly as bright as a sunlit day.

Upon query, their guide explained that they used solar tubes, long shafts carved all the way to the surface and lined with highly reflective materials to convey sunshine downward. In these areas, crops were planted and villages clustered.

They docked in one such village as the sunlight failed and was replaced by a pale green glow rising from moss growing on the ground. Gabrielle, Dafydd, and his parents ate in a cramped tavern, served by a silent dwarven woman with a long, intricately braided beard, while their guide disappeared. By the time they'd finished eating, he had returned. Their hostess wrapped food in a napkin, and the guide grunted for them to go.

The thrill of the journey had worn thin for the boy seer,

and he drooped as they returned to the dock. This time they climbed aboard a wide, square vessel that floated more ponderously down the river.

"Make thyselves comfortable," their guide told them. "We'll be a while on the water."

A while turned out to be days. Gabrielle was stunned at the extent of this underwater network. Did the Eight know about this other world under the earth?

She lost track of day and night as they floated ever onward, a sluggish current carrying them inexorably away from the Imperial hounds hunting Dafydd. At least she hoped they were getting away. Although the boat did not move quickly, it did move continuously with only brief stops to drop off barrels, pick up new ones, and grab a bite of hot food.

After what she'd estimated to be five days, they finally docked in yet another nondescript village huddled next to the shore. "This be our stop," their guide announced to Gabrielle's vast relief.

If she did not see a boat again for a good long while, that would be fine with her. They followed a path through the village and into a forest of trees covered in narrow, silvery leaves. It dawned on her that the leaves were utterly still, with no breeze to ruffle them.

At length, they came to a stone stairway, broad and shallow, that turned out to be deceptive for the steps went on seemingly forever. Her legs burned with effort, and each step was agony before she finally spied a door in front of them. They stepped through it and into blindingly bright sunlight. Her body felt abrupt disorientation, accustomed as it was to the eternal twilight of Under Urth.

"Where is this?" she asked their guide.

"Heartland. That's where you wanted to go, right?"

Her jaw dropped. They'd just made a journey of *weeks* in a matter of days. The terrain was radically different, dry and rocky. The forests of Kel had been replaced by layered red stone worn into fantastic shapes by wind and time.

"Which way to the Citadel of the Heart?" she asked.

"It's the citadel you be wantin'? Well, now. She be that-away." He took off walking to what she guessed to be the south. He seemed prepared to take them to their final destination, for which she was grateful.

They hiked for several hours, and the day heated up with each passing mile. When she thought she was on the verge of melting outright, they came to a building by itself in the strange landscape and ducked inside its thick, stone walls. She should not have been surprised to discover that it was a Heart chapter house, she supposed.

In the common room, which looked like so many others she'd seen before, they sat at benches and were served a simple, bracing meal. They napped in bunks for several hours while the heat of the afternoon passed. Then, as the sun set, they resumed their journey.

The next few days passed the same way. They walked through the night and until it became too hot to continue, then retreated indoors to wait out the blistering afternoons. On the morning of the third day, they came upon a broad expanse of table-flat land, and in the distance a wondrous structure came into view. It looked tiny at first, but the longer they walked, the larger it grew.

It looked like a regular mountain from a distance. But as they drew nearer to it, Gabrielle made out façades and windows, great doorways and decorations all carved from red-and-gold-streaked stone. A gigantic palace had been carved out of the mountain itself. The *entire* mountain. The scale of the citadel was unbelievable.

At length, they finally reached the enormous structure rising out of the surrounding plain. A huge open portcullis beckoned, and they passed underneath it into a grand passageway leading into the mountain. A guard, wearing the white, red, and yellow of the Heart, greeted them politely.

"I am Gabrielle of Haraland," she announced. "Please tell Lady Sasha that I have arrived."

While Dafydd's parents stared in dismay at her, the man bowed deeply. "Welcome, Your Majesty. She's been expecting you." A flurry of activity accompanied the formal greeting, and a bevy of people, all wearing Heart colors, bustled around showing them into an elaborately carved antechamber. In just a few minutes, a familiar voice cried out her name.

"Sasha!" she replied joyfully. "I have brought you a talented young man and his family for safekeeping. Dafydd, this is my friend Lady Sasha. She will look out for you and keep you safe."

"Indeed we will," Sasha said kindly to both boy and parents. The next hour was spent in introductions to various Heart functionaries and settling Dafydd and his parents in quarters. But eventually, Sasha murmured, "A moment, Gabby, for a private word?"

"Of course."

They strolled down a long corridor lined with portraits of various high Heart officials based on the garb they wore in the paintings.

"I have received word from a mutual friend." Sasha fingered her own Octavium Pendant, and Gabrielle nodded in understanding. "There is a White Heart member, a man, who needs to be escorted into Groenn's Rest. The guide he will need is in Kel. I have sent for that guide to join us here."

"To what end?" Gabrielle asked low after checking that no one was within earshot.

"We search for a statue."

"A statue?"

"Of an ancient dwarf. Thought to be the personal guard of a dwarven king of old."

"To what end?"

"You and I are to find a means of releasing the guard from the stone prison he has been encased in."

Gabrielle frowned. "Do you know how to do such a thing?"

"A few trusted Heart historians research it for me as we speak."

"Am I to gather, then, that you go with us?" she asked hopefully.

"Indeed I shall."

Gabrielle smiled joyfully. "That will make the time pass much more pleasantly."

Sasha laughed. "You do not know the half of it. The White Heart initiate we will be traveling with is called the Shaggy Father. He is thought to be mad."

"Thought to be?"

Sasha shrugged. "He believes that yeren are not mindless monsters but rather are intelligent beings deserving of recognition as a sentient race."

"Yeren? The snow monsters who eat little children?"

"The Shaggy Father swears that the hearth tales of them as fearsome beasts are wrong. Apparently, we will get to find out one way or the other. We will have to pass through yeren territory to find the statue we have been told to seek out."

And she'd thought fleeing Imperial hounds had been scary.

Rosana followed their Dominion guide warily, half-afraid that somehow her enslavement to the snake changeling had been transferred to this fellow. He was joined by a pair of Dominion trackers who were shockingly efficient at following Kerryl Moonrunner's trail. Sha'Li spent most of the time with them, watching and learning.

For her part, Rosana spent most of the time trying to ascertain how Goldeneye's enslavement had affected her. They couldn't try to remove the curse as long as the Dominion scouts were with them, but Rynn promised under his breath to give it a try as soon as the scouts left.

The trail took them south and east to roughly follow the coast. Then it plunged south once more through the Quills. They moved at breakneck speed, rising before dawn each morning and hiking until long after dark each night. The changelings set a grueling pace that left Rosana exhausted every time they stopped to rest. It took them less than a week to pass through the towering stands of pine forest that formed the Quills and to emerge into lower hills that gave way to flatter and wetter terrain.

They reached the edge of a great expanse of forest growing out of shallow, standing water. It was there that the Dominion scouts abruptly lost the trail. They nodded their farewells and without ceremony turned away and headed back to the north. Rosana was immensely relieved to be quit of the black-and-red tabards.

"Learned much from them I did," Sha'Li declared. "But on my turf are we now." She turned back eagerly to face the swamp. "Track in this terrain can I, as easily as breathing."

"Umm, Sha'Li," Rosana said hesitantly, "I'm not exactly proficient at traversing swamps. Is it possible you could find us a dry path through this?"

The lizardman girl rolled her eyes.

"Your kind call us land walkers for a reason," Raina added wryly.

"Fine. Solid ways shall I follow."

It might be solid, but the path they trod was far from dry. The stagnant pools all around them were black and menacing, and Rosana shuddered to imagine what creatures might be lurking below the surfaces. The good news was their pace slowed as they headed deeper into the swamp.

"What is this place?" Rosana asked Sha'Li on one of the occasions when the lizardman girl circled back from having scouted ahead to join them.

"The edge of Angor's Swamp this is. A dark and dangerous place, not unlike my home."

No wonder Sha'Li seemed to be in such a jovial mood.

"A clear trail Tarryn leaves for us. Follow it any child could."

Rosana highly doubted she would have been able to see the trail sign on her own. Now and then she spotted a broken reed or foot-sized puddle that Sha'Li declared to be tracks, but for the most part, she managed only to watch her footing and not stray off the narrow trails Kerryl seemed to be following.

They made an uncomfortable camp at night by climbing into trees and tying themselves against the trunks to sleep. Not only was it the sole way to remain dry while sleeping, but Sha'Li declared it wise for safety reasons based on the creatures who roamed this place. The night sounds consisted of growls and screeches, clicks, chirps, and the occasional scream that was entirely unnerving. Rosana climbed down in the mornings stiff and sore, sure that she had not slept a wink all night.

Several days' walk led them deeper into the swamp. Long stretches of murky water covered by a film of lime green slime lurked beneath black-spined trees hung with vines and moss. It was as if death and decay lay over all of this blighted land. The paths they followed became narrow trails atop thin humps that the black water lapped at hungrily. The entire place gave her the creeps.

As the sun shone anemically overhead through a scudding layer of clouds, Sha'Li paused at an intersection between two crossing humps of raised ground. "A problem have we. Split has Kerryl's party."

"Can you tell which way Kendrick and Tarryn went?" Eben asked.

"Actual footprints do I see showing the humans going that way." She pointed off to her right. "But Tarryn's trail sign that way points." She pointed straight ahead.

"You're sure you're not mistaken?" Will asked.

Sha'Li threw him a withering look. "For yourself read the trail."

Even Rosana could see the trampled grass and broken reeds pointing down the left-hand path. There was even a clear boot print.

"That direction Tarryn *really* wishes us to go."

Reluctantly, everyone in the party was forced to admit that Sha'Li was correct.

"Perhaps she attempts to throw us off their trail because she fears for our safety if we take on Kerryl," Will suggested.

Rosana frowned. He had a point.

They paused in indecision for a minute more, and finally Eben said reluctantly, "We should trust Tarryn and Kendrick. If they wanted us to go that way, it was for some important reason."

Rynn added, "We can always come back to this spot and pick up their physical trail. Now that we're in these wetlands with a lizardman tracker, I'm confident we can track them without Tarryn's trail sign."

Sha'Li smiled a little at that. "Decided are we, then?"

Everyone murmured an affirmative, and they headed off to the left.

Before long, Sha'Li announced from the front of the party. "Two men we track. Narrow of foot, small in stature."

"The twins with the long noses the innkeeper in Shepard's Rest spoke of," Will declared.

Everyone relaxed a little. Two men would not pose much of a threat to their party, now that they were all fully restored to health and armed to the teeth.

A bleary sunset tinged a rapidly forming and putrid-smelling fog orange. Not long thereafter, Rynn made a sound of surprise in front of her. Rosana peered around his broad shoulders and spied the silhouettes of man-made structures in front of them. It looked like a homestead of some kind, a long, low cottage, a pair of barns, and several outbuildings. What manner of people chose to live in a place like this swamp? Apprehension skittered across her skin.

"Smoke I smell," Sha'Li announced low.

Rosana looked more closely and spied thin spirals rising from a half dozen sources ahead of them. Something was wrong. The narrow, raised path led to a rough-shored island of sorts, a low rise that sloped shallowly to the water on all sides.

Something long and flat slithered off the bank into the water with a tiny splash. They all froze, staring. Something else flashed, a white underjaw the size of her torso. Another jaw flashed in response as two enormous creatures bickered momentarily.

"Alligators," Sha'Li breathed.

A *lot* of alligators. Side by side, crowding the banks until there was hardly any space between them. Rosana had never seen one before, and now she was looking at a massive collection of the reptilian monsters. The shore was not rough in terrain at all. She was merely looking at the ridged and scaled backs of dozens of green-gray alligators. They moved restlessly, a seething mass of sinew and hide, as if agitated.

All at once, half a dozen of the creatures scuttled into the water, gave a single swish of their mighty tails, and disappeared from sight. Several more alligators crawled ashore to fill the gap. Oh, gads. How many more of the reptiles were lurking in that black water, just out of sight? Her skin crawled to think of it.

Sha'Li led them closer to the farm, and Rosana began to make out details. A huge alligator skull was mounted over the doorway of the house. A strand of individual claws was draped over the window beside the door, which hung askew, one hinge torn off.

The smoke came from the roof itself.

Sha'Li's claws were fully extended, Eben's sword came out of its sheath, and Will's staff came up in front of him. Rynn was walking more silently than usual, one foot placed carefully in front of the other on high alert. Even Raina's hands glowed as she dropped in close behind the fighters to heal them as need be.

Rosana called her own magic, summoning curse energies from her gypsy blood and rehearsing incants in her head as they moved forward cautiously toward the silent steading. The place looked lived in with benches, buckets, tools, stacks of firewood, and other plentiful signs of habitation about. But the farm itself was completely still with not a single creature moving except those agitated alligators down by the shore.

As they approached the buildings in the rapidly failing light, Rosana gasped. The home and barns were nothing more than blackened hulls, still smoking and even burning sluggishly in places. What had happened here? As they neared the cottage, a new smell intruded upon the sharp tang of smoke. She knew that stench. It was blood.

Everyone tensed. Eben and Sha'Li went left with Raina at their backs, and Will and Rynn moved right with Rosana on their heels. They approached the house from each side, peering through the ruined walls at utter chaos. What hadn't been charred and burned to ash was tossed around and broken as if this had been the scene of some horrific fight.

Rynn entered through a gaping hole in the far wall and picked his way through the ruins, lifting a plank here and there to peer underneath. The space was not large, and in a minute or two, he shook his head in the negative. Sha'Li and Eben backed away from the collapsed wall across the cottage and moved toward one of the barns. As soon as Rynn had rejoined them, Rosana and Will did the same, heading for what looked like a smokehouse.

Built of sturdy wood, this structure had survived the fire, albeit more blackened than it should be. Eben waved at them and indicated that the second house was empty, as well. All of them headed for the big barn.

In the deathly silence, Rosana heard Raina gasp. The White Heart healer dashed forward and knelt beside something on the ground that looked like a pile of rags.

They converged on the spot, and it turned out to be a woman of middling years. Dead. Very dead. Rosana watched the faint glow of a life spell fade off the body's waxen, pale skin. It was nice of Raina to try to renew the woman, but Rosana estimated that she'd been dead several hours or more.

They moved into the smaller of the two barns. The damage and chaos here matched that in the house. The place was wrecked. A goat pen beside the barn was bloody but empty, and the inside of the barn was liberally sprayed with blood. There'd been a whale of a fight in here. Somebody had bled a lot. But the barn yielded no more bodies.

They moved to the second, larger barn, and even Sha'Li groaned at the sight that greeted them as they rounded the doorframe. This must have been where the last stand had happened. Four humans lay dead in the middle of the space, two men, two women, all young, and one a boy barely sprouting his first mustache. They were hacked to bits.

While Raina checked the bodies for any indication that they might not be past the reach of a life spell, Rosana cast her awareness wide around her for any spirits that might be lurking nearby in search of a source of resurrection.

So far away from civilization, there would be no Heartstone Glow to draw spirits to it. However, a healer like she, who knew how to perform resurrections, could project a dim Glow of her own, which would attract any nearby spirits. They could linger near their bodies for up to several days before finally dissipating completely, unable to resurrect. The Heart tried desperately to spread enough healers out across the land so all people had access to resurrection. Only in the most remote corners of Urth—like this place—was access to resurrection a problem. No spirits came to her light, however.

They moved deeper into the barn, and Rynn made a makeshift torch of a length of wood and a rag he found on the barn floor. He held it out to Rosana, and she sent a spark of magic into it, lighting the greasy rag. It cast a heathen, guttering light on the scene of the massacre.

Without warning, Rynn fell to his knees, groaning. Rosana rushed over to him in concern, and as she drew near, she saw beyond him to the source of his agony.

"Ahh, no!" she cried. "Not the children!"

Five of them were huddled in the corner behind a big stack of hay, dead in one another's arms. Their little bodies had been brutally hacked apart, which was a cold mercy. These children had not suffered long. But their mouths still screamed in silent terror.

It looked as if something heavy had fallen beside them, knocking down part of the haystack, and then had been dragged away. A trail of bloody hay led all the way to what had once been a rear exit from the barn.

Sha'Li knelt beside the trail of hay and squinted down at it. But after a moment, the lizardman girl dashed angrily at her eyes before trying again. Was she *crying*? It was hard for Rosana to tell through her own tears.

"Stay back, Raina," Rynn said sharply. "There is nothing you can do for them." It was kind of him to try to spare her. But he did not know the Heart very well if he thought she and Raina would shy away from suffering. It was what the Heart did best. They bore the burdens and shared the pains of commoners' lives within the Kothite Empire. They stood beside simple people like this family had been, tried to alleviate as much misery as they could, and hoped to resurrect the rest.

But the Heart had failed these five children. They would be lost somewhere between this life and the Void, too young to pass through the spirit realm and find their way back.

Raina fell to her knees by the nearest child, a towheaded boy of perhaps six summers. "If these were my children, I would want someone to wash them and brush their hair, to lay them out tenderly and find a favorite toy to bury them with." Her voice broke on a sob.

They all helped with the heartbreaking task. The children ranged in age from perhaps four to ten summers. The adults had fought fiercely to defend them but in the end had failed. And they all had paid the ultimate price.

As they neared the end of their grisly task, Rynn said low and furious to Sha'Li, "Have a look around. Find out what or who did this."

"Those are edged cuts," Will declared confidently, looking down at the remains of one of the women. "Not a well-made steel blade, but something sharp."

Will, Rynn, and Eben busied themselves digging graves, and Sha'Li studied tracks, while she and Raina went in search of some small token to bury with each child. The pickings were slim and ended up being scraps of cloth from the mother's apron that had somehow escaped the fire. But it was better than nothing. They pressed a square of the fabric into each small fist and folded the cold little fingers around it.

They laid the entire family in a single grave, together in death as they had been in life. Rynn said something compassionate and moving over the bodies, but Rosana was too torn up to listen to much of it. Then Eben and Will set about the task of covering the bodies. They buried them deep at Sha'Li's instruction. Apparently, alligators were carrion eaters. Sha'Li told them grimly that only the fires had likely stopped the alligators from coming ashore and erasing all evidence of the attack before the six of them had arrived.

They were all exhausted and soot covered by the time they finished their sad task. Will built a fire in the open space between the buildings, and they sat on logs Eben and Rynn had rolled over beside the blaze. Rosana was glad for the big fire tonight. It held the dark at bay—and hopefully the alligators that were now roaring and rumbling ominously all around them.

Sha'Li joined them in a little while. Rosana did not know until that moment just how angry a scale-skinned humanoid could look. But Sha'Li looked ready to kill.

"What did you find?" Rynn asked in soothing tones.

"Goblin tracks and man-sized rodent tracks. A dozen. Maybe a few more. Unlike changeling tracks are these. On some of the tracks alligators lay, so a better look at the tracks I cannot get. Predators of alligators my kind be, but move away from the shore they will not, even for me. Extremely strange the creatures act. Refusing to leave the island they are."

"Do they guard clutches of eggs, perhaps?" Rynn asked.

"Wrong season," Sha'Li replied. "More there is. Two sets of narrow human tracks I saw, as well. With the goblin-rat beings they left this place, dragging a third person."

"You have a live trail for them?" Rynn asked sharply.

Will and Eben snatched up their weapons in unison. "What are we waiting for?" Will demanded. "I'm in the mood to kill a whole crowd of rats, and a few humans to boot."

Raina stared down at the fire miserably, and Rosana sympathized. This was one of those times when being White Heart tested the resolve of the strongest soul. Even after the massacring of children, Raina was still bound to defend the lives of the evil beings who'd done it.

Rosana said to her wryly, "Maybe you just don't have to defend their lives very hard this time."

Raina looked up and smiled briefly, but the expression did not reach her eyes.

"Sit down," Rynn commanded Will and Eben quietly. But there was steel in his voice. "We've had a long, upsetting day, and no one got any rest last night. We are emotional and would not focus in battle as we should. As angry as we all are at them, the murderers of this family will still be out there tomorrow. But tonight, let us look to our own spirits that are in need of solace."

Thankfully, Will and Eben subsided. Rosana shared their need for vengeance. It sang in her veins and burned in her heart. But she also agreed with Rynn. On the morrow would be soon enough to go forth and seek blood revenge for those innocent babes.

They each made peace with what they'd seen in their own way. Rynn moved off by himself to go through those martial dances of his and meditate. Eben and Raina went to sleep early after agreeing to take the middle watch, and Sha'Li slipped away into the darkness again. Whether she merely slid into the water to sleep for the night or performed some private Tribe of the Moon ritual, Rosana did not know and did not ask.

As for her, she stayed close to the fire, keeping it well fed and blazing up high into the night sky as the cold and damp closed in around them. Will sat silent beside her for the most part, clasping her hand sometimes loosely and sometimes squeezing it painfully tight. The fog cleared off somewhat, and she was able to look up at the stars and wonder what lay beyond them.

It was a long night, but Rosana eventually slept, and heavily. Some of the preserved food stores in the homes had not been destroyed, and they picked through the pantries to find dried meat, fruit, and nuts to break their fast. They met back at the fire and huddled around it eating; no one seeming inclined to move on with their trek yet.

"In first light, more I scouted," Sha'Li announced. "Here lived some sort of shaman, whose totem was alligator. Upon it he called for power."

That might explain the creatures' strange behavior in ringing the island and refusing to budge.

The lizardman girl continued, "Dragged from the barn and taken was he, I believe. Strange will it sound, but methinks the alligators came ashore and ate the corpses of the dead goblin-rats."

"Anything else?" Rynn asked.

"Not normal rodents were these. Giant for their species, abnormally long claws had they and dangerous bites. Mayhap poisonous, but certainly diseased."

"Are they some sort of swamp variant of rat?" Will asked.

"Nay. Creatures of this area I know well. Close to my home are we."

Indeed? What a miserable place to have grown up. No wonder Sha'Li was generally grim and surly in temperament.

Eben spoke grimly. "In what direction does the trail of these filthy killers lead?"

"Interesting is that. In the same direction as Kendrick and Tarryn travel, it leads."

That brought everyone to their feet in alarm. Rosana cried out, "The creatures who slaughtered this family are after Kendrick and Tarryn?"

Sha'Li frowned. "For once, glad let us be of Kerryl Moonrunner's combat prowess. Him, no rats will take."

"Let us be on our way and with all due haste," Eben declared. "Our friends are in need of rescue more than ever."

Tarryn slumped, dejected, by the fire. The cave in which they stayed did not draft well, and smoke was gathering by the ceiling, making the space feel even closer and stuffier. She was running out of time for a rescue. The twins, Pierre and Phillipe, should return anytime now. They'd been dispatched by Kerryl to fetch some local expert on alligators and bring him here. Kerryl wanted him to summon a great alligator whose spirit was going to be forced into her body. Or something like that.

Kendrick said a great boar had been bonded to him, magical in nature. Kerryl could actually force him to take on physical attributes and abilities of that boar. She'd seen the change overtake Kendrick several times now. He had only the tiniest sliver of control of himself in that state and was more beast than man. It was terrifying to think of becoming the same herself. A shallow bowl of beans and rice appeared under her nose, and she looked up.

"You have to eat, Tarryn."

"What if I refuse?" she snapped at Kendrick. "What if I starve myself and make myself too weak to survive his stupid ritual?" It was not his fault she was in this predicament, and he did not deserve her anger, but she could not help herself. She was tired and scared and did not want to become an alligator.

Kendrick sat down beside her, his shoulder rubbing hers. "You know Kerryl will find a way to make you eat, right? He'd torture me in front of you if he had to. He needs you."

"But why me?"

"You're a skilled scout. A brave fighter. Smart. And you're my friend. He may not say it aloud, but he respects you."

She snorted.

"Look. He made a mistake with Pierre and Phillipe, and he knows it. They were not men of sufficient honor to have been granted the powers he gave them."

"That's no lie." She despised the twins. They were devious, sneaky, and petty. She burst out, not for the first time since she'd been captured, "Why is Kerryl doing this to us?"

Kendrick shrugged and handed her the bowl. While she reluctantly began to eat, he said low, "I do know he's scared stiff of something. He won't speak of it, but he sees some threat lurking just beyond the horizon. He's convinced that the people of Haelos will not be able to defeat it and that he must start creating an army of enhanced beings to fight it."

"And that's enough for you?" she demanded. "You're just going to take the man who kidnapped us at his word and let him turn you into a monster?"

Kendrick sighed. "I've been with him longer than you, and this I know: he is not mad. I've seen the haunted look in his eyes when he speaks of this threat, speaks of what it will do to the people of Haelos. You have not."

She shook her head in denial.

"He told me once that when he saw me and my friends heading up into the Forest of Thorns, he knew events had been set in motion that would bring the threat he sees. Whatever threat he's preparing for, we somehow triggered it."

"Is that why you're letting him do this to you?" she asked, surprised. "You feel responsible for this unnamed threat and are sacrificing yourself to correct having triggered its arrival?"

Kendrick shrugged.

Hah. She was right. She argued, "He's trying to make you feel guilty for something you did not do so you'll stay with him and do his bidding."

Kendrick laughed without humor. "I do his bidding whether I wish it or no. His Band of Beasts gives him control of me and will give him control of you. Fight it all you wish, Tarryn, but you will do exactly what he says, as well."

"I do not wish!"

Kerryl looked up at her outburst from across the cave where he murmured with the dryad who came and went as she pleased, contrary to what Tarryn had been taught about the fae female's kind being tied to a single tree and unable to leave its immediate vicinity.

Tarryn lowered her voice. "I do not wish *ever* to do his bidding. And I cannot understand why you tolerate being his slave."

A commotion outside the cave announced the return of the twins. She rose to her feet along with Kendrick and Kerryl as Pierre and Phillipe, looking smug, staggered into the cave dragging an unconscious man between them. They dropped the human, a man of middle age wearing a bloody and gashed suit of alligator hide armor, to the floor.

"What have you done?" Kerryl exclaimed.

Phillipe, the one who usually spoke for the pair, replied proudly, "There he is. The alligator speaker you told us to bring you."

Tarryn winced. She'd hoped Kendrick's friends were close enough behind them to have seen her trail sign and gotten to the speaker before the twins did whatever they had planned for him. Apparently not.

"Why is he unconscious?" Kerryl demanded, moving to the man's side and checking his wounds. "And why is he all cut up?"

"Put up a fight, he did. Turned out he wasn't fond of the idea of coming with us."

"Tell me what happened. Everything." Kerryl did not have to touch the Band of Beasts buckled to his arm to make it clear that he'd given an order and it had better be obeyed.

Squirming a little, Phillipe answered, "We went out and hired those gobrats like you said to. Told them we only needed a half dozen or so, but they wouldn't let any go unless we took them all."

"How many went with you?" Kerryl ground out.

"About twenty," Pierre supplied helpfully. "And some goblins tagged along, too."

Phillipe scowled at his twin as Kerryl made a sound of irritation in his throat and growled, "Go on."

"So we took them with us to the farm. It was right where you said it was."

When Phillipe stopped speaking, Kerryl prompted, "And you told the speaker I needed his help and that you would lead him to me."

Pierre piped up again, "Naw. The gobrats saw the farm and ran ahead of us. Attacked before we caught up with them."

"Shut up," Phillipe muttered at his brother.

Kerryl, looking too furious for speech, glared expectantly at Phillipe, who whined, "I *told* them to hang back and let me do the talking. But they didn't listen."

"And?" Kerryl ground out.

"And they sort of overran the island. Chased the humans out of the cottage and ransacked it. A woman got dropped in the barnyard by the gobrats, and the rest of the humans retreated to one of the barns."

"Please tell me you bargained with the speaker to come out in exchange for his wife's body so he could restore her life."

Phillipe shifted his weight from foot to foot, and his gaze darted to the cave entrance. "Umm, not exactly. The gobrats, you see. Got carried away, they did. I guess the smell of blood excited them. They rushed the barn."

Kerryl spoke slowly, enunciating each syllable distinctly. "The speaker has a large family, as I recall. A brace of children ranging from grown ones to younglings. What happened to them?"

"They took cover in the barn. The eldest ones fought with their father. The young ones hid. But by the time we finally reached the island and caught up to the gobrats, the damage was done."

"*What happened?*" Kerryl's teeth clenched as he ground out the words.

"Like I said, the gobrats overran the oldest children. Found the hiding place of the youngsters. The speaker's a ferocious fighter, by the way. Mowed down a whole bunch of the gobrats—"

Kerryl cut him off. "The children are safe, though."

"Oh no," Pierre piped up. "They're all dead."

Tarryn gasped. Kendrick's left eye started to glow an alarming red, and Kerryl hadn't even commanded him to transform. A growl of rage rumbled in Kendrick's chest.

"Dead?" Kerryl bellowed.

The twins cringed, cowering against one another.

"We couldn't stop them," Phillipe whined. "The gobrats did it. Not us."

Kerryl paced angrily, spitting out a sentence with each trip across the cave. "*You* lost control of them. It's your fault those children died. I put you in charge. It was an easy task. Find the speaker. Ask for his assistance." He stopped pacing and whirled to face the twins. "And instead, you killed his entire family? This is a disaster!"

"But we brought you the speaker like you wanted."

"Now I will have to force him to summon a scion of the Great Alligator to me. And afterward, he will be my sworn enemy. Worse, if the other speakers get word of this, they will not help me. You have cost me some of my greatest allies!"

Tarryn had never heard Kerryl so angry. And for good reason. He resumed pacing, stalking around and around the cave like a caged beast.

Eventually, he stopped in front of Phillipe, looming over the smaller man. "Since you have ruined my plans for them, take these ampoules of change water with you and protect them at all costs, as well. But first . . ."

Kerryl rummaged in the pouch he'd been wearing ever since they'd robbed the Dominion encampment, pulling out a narrow tube made of glass and filled with clear liquid, which he tucked into his own pouch. "I'll need this one for Tarryn. The rest, however . . ." He devolved into mumbling under his breath as he pulled out the remaining tubes and commenced casting some sort of magic into them.

As Tarryn looked on, the liquid in the tubes turned a sickly shade of gray green and clouded over. Kerryl swirled them around, and after a minute or so, the murkiness dissipated, leaving the fluid in the ampoules clear once more. The nature guardian smiled briefly without humor. "There. That should give Goldeneye pause if he recovers these."

He tucked the ampoules back in the pouch and shoved the whole at Phillipe, who whined, "If Kendrick's friends find me wearing that, they will attack me for it."

"Then mayhap you should think on how to talk your way out of dying at their hands before they shed your blood," Kerryl snapped. "Go. Now. Before I change my mind and kill you where you stand."

Phillipe darted out of the cave and disappeared into the night, leaving his brother standing alone and looking lost.

Kerryl distracted her from studying Pierre, whose left eye was flickering faintly red, by asking, "Tarryn, did you do as I ordered and lay a trail to the cache? They will be able to follow it?"

Kendrick said his friends included an excellent lizardman tracker named Sha'Li. She had easily been able to follow the trail signs thus far. And now the lizardman girl was in her native, swampy terrain. "Absolutely," Tarryn answered.

"Then it is time. I shall revive yon speaker, have him summon a scion of the Great Alligator, and join your spirit with it."

Horror rushed through her. She was out of time. She looked to Kendrick for escape, or at least help, but his expression was implacable. He was not going to help her evade the fate Kerryl Moonrunner had planned for her? Then she was well and truly doomed. Despair coursed through her, overwhelming her last vestiges of hope.

Kerryl shook his head as he stared down at the unconscious prisoner. "This was supposed to be the start of creating a great army for the coming battle."

Pierre responded helpfully, "Do you mean an invasion of

Haelos by Koth? Even if they're angry at you, the speakers of the Great Beasts will still fight against the Empire."

Kerryl whirled, bellowing, "You fool! There are greater evils in this world than mere Kothites."

30

Justin looked around apprehensively at the spacious chamber Kadir had brought him to. It was circular with no windows and high ceilings. A round channel that encompassed most of the space was carved several inches into the floor. "What's that?" he asked, pointing down at it.

Kadir glanced up at him from the basket he'd set in the middle of the circle. "Holder for whatever material is laid out to confine the ritual magics."

"Oh." Kadir set out some sort of dried fruit-like object, and Justin asked, "What's that?"

"Ritual component."

"Oh." A carved stick of some kind and an amulet of some kind joined the fruit. They must be ritual components, as well. The same acolyte who'd brought in the basket carried in a large piece of art depicting a gentle landscape and hung it on a hook across the room. "What's that?" Justin demanded.

Irritation was evident in Kadir's voice as he answered, "A painting. It soothes me to look at it during rituals. Now be quiet and let me get this set up. I mustn't forget anything."

Justin waited impatiently while Kadir meticulously laid out the items he would need on a table inside the circle. The acolyte wheeled in a tall cot and placed it in the middle of the circle, as well.

To him, Justin muttered, "Why does that bed have wheels?"

"Easier to carry out the leftover parts if this ritual fails."

Justin's jaw dropped. He whirled to demand of Kadir, "Exactly how dangerous is this?"

Kadir stopped fussing over the components to glare at him. "I know ten times as much about ritual magics as those moron Collectors, who style themselves such great scientists and students of magic."

"Who are the Collectors?"

Kadir didn't deign to answer him, but the acolyte did. "Within the Mages of Alchizzadon, they are primarily focused on the collecting and understanding of magic. Particularly spirit magic."

Huh. They would've had a field day studying Raina had she let herself be taken by these people. No wonder she'd run away from home.

"Up on the table," Kadir ordered him.

"What will happen to me if this fails or backlashes?" Justin asked as he stretched out on the tall canvas cot.

"Not to worry," Kadir replied unconcernedly. "This will either work or you will no longer exist. No middle ground. There are more variables to this ritual than even I can count. I have accounted for all the ones I think might kill you. But I may have to adapt on the fly as this unfolds."

He stared up at the mage, who was starting to gather magic and forming a ritual circle around them. Justin had seen women do the same dozens of times back in Tyrel. But never had he been the target of a ritual. "How many times have you done this ritual?"

"Personally? Never. But I'm a genius at this stuff. I've thought of every contingency. Relax. This is going to hurt a little."

Justin sat bolt upright. "Hold on now. Never?"

Kadir pulled out one last item from the basket. He did so with great care, placing a tall cut-crystal bottle on the table with the other components. Lavender, vaguely glowing . . . something . . . swirled as gently as smoke inside the clear container. The mage explained, "This is a votive. And before you ask what that is, a votive is a magical vessel for storing a spirit."

Justin stared doubtfully at the bottle. "You're not going to put me in that thing, are you?"

"Exactly the opposite, my boy. I'm going to put the spirit in yon votive into you. The magical portion of quite an accomplished mage's spirit is trapped within the bottle."

The acolyte made a sound of eager anticipation, and Justin looked askance between Kadir and the assistant. "You didn't answer my question. What do you mean by never? You've never done this ritual, or are you saying it's never been tried before?"

"Oh, it's been tried before," the acolyte replied helpfully. "We're very good at putting spirits into bottles, but nobody's ever quite mastered getting them back out."

"Lie down, Justin, and be quiet. Don't distract me," Kadir ordered as he gathered a great, glowing ball of magic in his hands, adding to it from each of the components on the table. Justin was alarmed to see that there was no scroll of instruction for this ritual, apparently. But then this whole procedure was cursed alarming.

Kadir picked up the votive, and the gathered magic transferred to the surface of the bottle, making the entire thing glow brightly. He reached for the stopper. "Don't move, boy."

Justin gripped the edge of the cot with both hands and held his entire body rigidly still. He fixed a picture of Raina firmly in his mind's eye. This was for her. He thought of her that last day they'd spent together, laughing and her tickling him into telling her what her birthday present was going to be. He'd failed her once. He would not do so again.

Kadir poured the essence in the bottle onto Justin's chest. The lavender-gray stuff settled gently, spreading out across his skin, faintly warm. It felt not quite liquid, not quite gaseous. It sank into his pores lightly, like sunshine warming him.

And then it reached his blood. Without warning, liquid fire ripped through his belly, incinerating him with fiery agony from the inside out. An instant later, a great gout of the stuff reached his heart, and in a single convulsive heartbeat, the searing agony had been pumped to every corner of his body. It was unbelievable. He was being torn apart, individual cells burned alive.

He wanted to scream, but his throat was paralyzed from utter horror at what was happening to him. He wanted to leap up off the cot and run for his life, but his muscles were eviscerated into useless shreds of inoperative tissue. He could only lie there in sheer terror and endure while he died a death worse than anything he could ever have imagined.

Into the morass of agony, an image filled his mind. Of smiling green eyes. Blond hair lifting in a breeze. A generous smile and feisty spirit. The sound of laughter. The comfort of lifelong friendship. The knowing of a long future together to come. He clung to the image desperately, his only fragile lifeline to sanity.

The fire receded, leaving behind a sensation of every bone in his body being slowly pulverized. He panted under the weight of this new pain, unable to breathe as his chest was inexorably crushed.

Time lost all meaning as the agony stretched on and on. He might have lost consciousness at some point. But his entire existence fell away, reduced only to a state of pain, upon pain, upon pain.

And then it stopped.

Where he had once been, now there was only a vast, empty place. Darkness.

Had he died? Was this the spirit realm, then?

Raina had to work hard not to fall behind Sha'Li, who was tracking faster than she would have believed possible. At times the lizardman girl actually broke into a jog as she stared down at the boggy ground. But then, they were all determined to catch the vile beings who'd slaughtered those children. Apparently, the physical trail of the gobrats now ran practically on top of the signs Tarryn had left for them heading south and east, deeper into the swamp, which made it all that much easier to follow.

The going was terrible, at times they slogged thigh deep through black water and at others through knee-deep mud. But they pressed on grimly. Near midday, they stopped briefly at an upwelling of fresh springwater within the brackish swamp to drink and refill their waterskins.

"Into the heart of Angor the trail leads us," Sha'Li commented in a worried tone.

"Why's that a problem?" Will asked.

"Dark and dangerous is that place. Away from it all living creatures should stay."

That didn't sound good. And yet, the trail led arrow straight into the Swamp of Angor. And it wasn't like any of them were about to give up on catching the goblin-rats, particularly if Kendrick and Tarryn were in danger from them.

Raina was deeply unhappy over the whole business of tracking down the goblin-rats because she knew the others were set on executing vigilante justice upon the creatures. She had no idea how to talk them out of it. She fully understood their anger. Stars, she *shared* their anger; however, one murder did not justify another.

Perhaps she could talk the others into merely injuring the gobrats. Her oath was to defend life. As long as her friends didn't cross the line and actually take any lives, would she remain within the strictures of her oath? Perhaps technically, yes. But it would not be in the spirit of the oath. How was she going to stop them? Would she have to sacrifice her own life to protect the gobrats? Would it stop any of them? Stars knew, she was haunted by the sight of those tiny, lifeless bodies back on the island. If she were bent on vengeance, some White Heart member stepping in front of her would not slow her down.

Perhaps an hour after the water break, Sha'Li stopped abruptly, and Will nearly plowed into her. Eben did bump into Will and mumbled an apology. Raina just managed to stop herself before she knocked over Eben.

"What is it, Sha'Li?" Rynn asked quietly.

"High ground ahead."

Thank the Lady. Raina was more than ready for a break from wading through this interminable sludge. It was exhausting and, frankly, disgusting.

"Over there, look." Sha'Li pointed slightly to her right.

Raina peered in the direction indicated at a gap between a pair of black, moss-laden trees, whose spreading limbs hung low over the higher ground.

Rynn moved forward to stare where the lizardman girl pointed. "That looks like a cave entrance."

Now that he mentioned it, Raina did spy a dark maw beyond the trees.

"Does anyone live around here?" Will asked Sha'Li.

"No one. Of this, I am certain."

Rosana asked, "But that's where the trail leads?"

"Definitely."

"Fighters up front," Will murmured. He slipped his left hand into his amber hand shield and gripped his staff in the middle. Eben slid up on his left, lifting his sword. Sha'Li went first, not to follow the trail this time but to search for traps or trip wires.

They eased ashore, and Raina's legs felt almost weak, so much easier was the going on solid ground.

Sha'Li paused, crouching, to examine a singed spot in front of them. "Here a trap exploded, not long ago. A few days, mayhap."

"Has it been reset?" Rynn asked.

"Nay." Sha'Li rose to her feet and pressed on cautiously.

They passed under the two massive trees, and Sha'Li lifted a limp length of wire off the ground. "Disarmed trap," she breathed.

Twice more, they came across traps that had recently been tripped. Someone had clearly been here and had either removed what was inside the cave that had merited such protection or had no interest in protecting it anymore.

Just as they reached the cave entrance, a huge glob of mud in the vague shape of a man detached itself from the earthen outcropping that housed the cave. It swung a fist at Sha'Li, who ducked under it and came up jabbing at the thing's gut with her claws.

"No!" Rynn cried, but too late.

Sha'Li's claws sank into the belly of the mud beast, but as she tried to pull them out, they stuck fast.

Will started to swing his staff at the creature, but Rynn threw his crystal-gauntleted forearm in front of the weapon and caught the blow. "Your weapon will be trapped," the paxan bit out. "Use magic."

As if the creature had also heard him speak, its other fist glowed briefly, and some sort of magic bolt hit Eben. It flashed around the jann and broke into a thousand tiny sparks that dissipated harmlessly.

A mud fist slammed into Sha'Li hard, and she grunted in pain. With her claws trapped as they were, she could not use her quickness and agility to avoid the blows. Both mud fists drew back, preparing to strike again. Raina flipped a quick burst of healing energy at her friend.

"It's throwing stone magic," Eben bit out. "Meant to root the target to the ground."

Will gathered a ball of force energy. "Duck, Sha'Li!" he called as he threw damaging magic at the creature. The fists stopped mid-swing and instead swung at this new threat. Will danced back out of reach and sent another bolt of damage into the creature. The being's left side began to melt. One of Sha'Li's claws slipped free. The fists swung down at Sha'Li again, but this time she was able to dodge enough to catch only glancing blows from them.

Still, Raina sent another bolt of healing energy into the lizardman girl. Better safe than sorry. She'd discovered that it was better to overheal her friends and waste some of her plentiful mana than it was to let one of them go down and be lost to a fight, even for a few seconds.

Will gathered a larger bolt of magic this time and fired it into the creature. Most of the mud construct's right side collapsed, melting into a formless glob.

"Again!" Rosana cried.

One more blast from Will did the trick. The entire creature fell apart, losing all form and collapsing into a pile of mud that slowly oozed into a spreading puddle. Sha'Li jumped back, her second claw freed, wiping it clean on a patch of moss. For once, Raina did not have to worry about the ethics of healing or not healing a kill. This was not a living being but rather a magically animated pile of dirt.

"Shall we continue?" Rynn asked as they gathered themselves and adjusted their armor.

They stepped just inside the cave and paused long enough to make sure no more mud creatures waited within to ambush them. Although Will had handled the creature outside with relative ease, he could summon only a finite amount of magical energy, and the creature had taken a fair chunk of it if Raina had to guess. If only there were a way for her to share some of her seemingly endless well of energy with other mages.

The floor of the cave sloped sharply downward. Oh, goodie. They got to go underneath the swamp, apparently. The cave turned into a tunnel of sorts. It had brick walls arching into a low ceiling that leaked, dripping in numerous places. Several inches of water stood on the floor as the tunnel leveled out. They paused to light torches and then continued.

Will murmured, "Is it just me, or do those niches in the walls look like something or someone ought to be standing in them?" At least a dozen of the odd indentations lined the tunnel. She looked where he pointed. Oh, dear. He was entirely correct.

Eben commented, "They look like guard posts."

"Well, the last two ahead are not empty," Sha'Li said.

Rynn stopped to peer into the darkness in front of them. "The creatures in them look like some sort of man-sized fungus constructs."

Sha'Li groaned under her breath. "Mushroom men. Gases and dusts they expel with all sorts of nasty effects. Even love poisons have I seen from them."

Raina remarked dryly, "If these throw love poisons, we'll let Will and Rosana take the lead."

Will rolled his eyes at her. "Just be ready to heal whatever these things expel."

Raina's hands were already glowing brightly, and she nodded back to indicate she was ready. They moved toward the pair of mushroom men, standing motionless in their niches on each side of the passageway. As soon as Rynn and Sha'Li crossed the plane between the two niches, the creatures lurched an awkward step forward, sending a pair of gases outward.

Sha'Li and Rynn both gasped and staggered, and Raina threw two fast healing spells at them, followed by spells to purify blood of poisons. That did the trick. Sha'Li took a swipe at her mushroom man and sliced off a big, spongy chunk of it. Rynn threw a vicious kick into his, knocking an arm-like appendage off the creature.

The creatures spewed several poisons in fast succession. Will ducked and held a defensive position in front of Raina. Knowing him, he was prepared to leap in front of any gases that came her way. As long as she could throw purification magics as fast as the two mushroom men were throwing poisons, the group would be all right. Eben moved up beside Rynn and commenced slicing and dicing the creature that Rynn was pummeling.

Sha'Li dropped to the ground once before Raina could get cleansing and healing into her, but the lizardman popped right back to her feet as soon as Rosana peppered her with healing magic. Raina followed up with a blood purification spell and then spun to throw more of the same into Rynn and Eben.

It was fast and furious, with poisons and magic flying and weapons swinging fast and hard, gradually whittling the creatures down.

"Burn them!" Sha'Li called out as she took yet another poison burst in the face.

While Raina healed her, Rosana darted forward to plunge

her torch into the right-hand pile of mushroom pieces, and Will did the same to the left-hand creature's remains. An acrid stench rose as the fungus flared up, burning down in a matter of seconds into almost nothing. Just a pale dusting of ash was left behind.

"Well, that was fun," Raina said a little breathlessly. "Everyone healed up, or did I miss someone?"

No one spoke up.

"Can anyone tell me if those were living creatures or constructs like the mud creature outside?" she asked.

Rynn answered, "Once destroyed, they reverted to their natural state of being shapeless, insensate, unthinking fungus. I'm going to go with calling those constructs."

Sha'Li added, "No children have they. Nor villages, nor speech, nor organized behavior. I say they live not."

"That's good enough for me," Raina declared. If only it was going to be so easy when they got to the gobrats.

The party moved on. The tunnel turned a corner just ahead, and Rynn approached it first. She watched with interest as the paxan eased a small mirror on an extendable handle around the corner. Clever. If they ever got back to civilization, she would have to look into getting one of those for herself.

"Clear," Rynn announced.

They moved around the corner cautiously. Nothing exploded or jumped out at them or threw anything at them.

"It's a dead end," Sha'Li said in disappointment.

"What's that?" Eben raised his torch high to illuminate a spot on the wall where the tunnel ended. "It's made of stone."

He should know.

It looked like someone had scraped away a thick layer of dirt and debris to reveal an arched doorway. It was blocked by a stone carved to fit the opening. On the floor, an arcing line was freshly scraped to indicate that the door had opened very recently.

"A handle I do not see," Sha'Li announced.

Rynn stepped forward to trace the intricate carvings covering the stone lightly with his fingers. "Runes."

"Which are what?" Rosana asked.

"Drawings or carvings made to store magic and release it when properly activated. Everyone bring your torches in close so I can see these better." The group did so, and he continued, "My guess is we have to touch a few of these runes in the right order to unlock the door. Touch the wrong runes and something bad might happen."

"Maybe we should have the girls back up just in case," Will commented.

"Just because I'm a girl doesn't mean I can't take the same risks as you, Will Cobb," Rosana retorted heatedly.

"I meant no insult—"

Raina interrupted the budding spat, saying, "I will back up in case I'm needed to heal the rest of you."

Rynn said, "A few of these have been scratched recently, almost as if they've been marked. My guess is we should activate those runes in particular."

"Be my guest," Will replied.

Raina did indeed back up to the bend in the tunnel. The paxan tried the combination of five runes a dozen times, and eventually a distinctive click was audible. The entire stone door popped a few inches out of the frame, enough for Sha'Li to wedge her claws into the gap and tug the heavy stone door open. Raina held her breath, waiting for some threat to attack them. But nothing happened.

Holding a torch high, Sha'Li slipped into whatever lay beyond. "Clear it is," she called.

One by one, they slipped through the narrow opening into a small, stuffy chamber that looked carved out of a single, great boulder. No moisture seeped into this place. Will rolled a small boulder sitting just inside the door into the entrance to block the passage open, for which she was grateful. She did not relish the idea of being trapped in a tiny, dark cave underground to die of suffocation.

"A chest I have found," Sha'Li announced.

They gathered around a nearly waist-high chest carved right into the wall of the chamber, covered with a metal-banded wooden lid. Metal and wood alike were blackened with age.

"Have a care for traps," Rynn warned as the lizardman reached for the lip of the lid.

"Heal me Raina will," Sha'Li retorted, rolling her eyes. Which was, of course, true.

The lizardman lifted the lid a fraction of an inch and then peered long and hard into the gap. "Trapped this was. But no more." And with that announcement, she threw the lid fully open.

Raina braced for disaster, but none was forthcoming. "Is there anything inside?"

"Aye."

Sha'Li bent over the edge, her entire upper body disappearing into the chest. She stood upright, and in her arms was something long, wrapped in crumbling leather. Eben took it, laying it on the ground. Carefully, he pulled away the rotted skins to reveal a mace. It had nine intricately carved flanges made of some metal that all the colors of the rainbow swirled across as the torchlight danced on it. What looked like some sort of strange, unintelligible writing spiraled around the wooden shaft of the weapon, all the way down to the handgrip.

"Can anybody read that?" Eben asked.

Raina and Rynn both bent down close to study it, and both stood back up shaking their heads. Eben picked it up and turned it over in his hands. "Huh. Leather on the handgrip is in perfect condition."

Which was a surprise given that the wrapping was completely rotted.

Eben hefted the weapon experimentally. "Lighter than it looks. Nice balance. You want to give it a try, Will?"

"I've got no training with maces. Rynn, do you want to have a go with it?"

"Thank you, but I prefer to fight without weapons altogether and rely only upon my andreline crystal gauntlets and greaves."

"Looks like it's yours, Eben," Will declared.

Sha'Li had bent back down into the chest and this time emerged with a box holding a supply of potions. They were duly passed to Rosana to identify. She declared them healing potions and curse-based potions. They divvied out the healing potions among the non-spirit casters, and Rosana kept the rest.

A scroll book came out and was duly passed to Will, who said he would study the scrolls later where the light was better.

Another trip into the chest revealed an epistle of some kind with a Tribe of the Moon marking etched upon it. There was no question but that Sha'Li would keep the small book.

Sha'Li stuck her torch into the chest again, running it around the edges of the large space. "Almost missed that, I did," she muttered as she leaned down into the chest one last time. This time, she nearly fell into the thing as she reached far into a back corner. She emerged with a tiny wooden box that fit easily in the palm of her hand. It looked old, and the lid was cracked.

Sha'Li opened it and tilted her head to look down at the contents. "A ring of some kind, it is." The lizardman pried at it with her fingernail, but whatever was inside would not come out. The box was passed to Rosana, who also could not get the ring inside loose. The boys all had a go at it, and finally, the box was passed to Raina.

Raina examined the object inside closely. It did, indeed, look like a ring nestled in some sort of dark-colored fabric. The band was made of a milky white substance intricately carved all over its surface. The carvings reminded her of . . .

"No. It cannot be," she breathed.

"What?" Rosana asked. "Do you recognize it?"

"The carvings look a lot like the designs on the Sleeping King's crown."

Sha'Li leaned in close to stare at the band. "Right you are. Seen those shapes before, have I."

She recalled that Sha'Li had been the one to fetch the

crown from its hiding place. Curious, Raina ran her fingertip across the ring. It was warm to the touch. Vibrant. Enthralled, she lifted it, and it came out of the box as if it had been waiting for her. Without stopping to think about what she was doing, she slipped it onto the middle finger of her right hand. It was large, even on that finger, but then, all of a sudden, it shrank until it clasped her finger perfectly. *A magic ring.*

Something electric and familiar zinged through her, and her eyes widened in shock. "Gawaine," she whispered.

"What of him?" Will asked quickly.

"This was his."

They all stared at the ring that seemed to glow in the dim torchlight. So beautiful were the carvings upon it that they seemed to flow around the band. She tugged at it to put it back in the box, but the ring was having no part of coming off her finger.

"Leave it," Will said. "It's safer there than in some box."

"Particularly if it does not wish to come off," Rynn added wryly.

"Is there anything else in the chest?" Will asked.

Sha'Li shook her head. "Sorry I am, Rynn; no treasure is there for you."

The paxan smiled. "Trust me. I have everything I need or want already."

Raina frowned. It was odd, indeed, that there had been something in this chest for every single member of their party except the newcomer. Coincidence? Or not?

"We have tarried long enough here," Rynn said. "With each passing minute, our quarry draws farther away from us."

Raina winced. The moment of truth was coming soon when she would have to intervene to stop her friends from fulfilling their fondest wish to slaughter a band of murderous gobrats.

E ben hefted the mace yet again, still accustoming himself to the strangeness of it. Exquisitely balanced, it looked like metal but was far too light to be made of such a substance. He experimented, striking at a downed log harder and harder, and the delicate-looking flanges didn't bend or nick in the least.

As they moved away from the cache, Raina and Rynn discussed in low tones who might have opened up that cave for them, removed most of the protections upon it, and then left items for each of them like that. Always a conspiracy theorist Raina was, seeing intrigues within intrigues. He took the world at face value. Much simpler that way. He'd found a good mace, and he was pleased. It would come in handy when they caught up with those murdering rodents.

And they were getting close now. Sha'Li estimated that the tracks they followed were no more than an hour old. Given that it was drizzling and the tracks would be erased quickly by the rain, he trusted her estimate.

The terrain changed with less open water and more islets of dry ground separated by rivulets and muddy puddles. They found another cave, recently stayed in based on the warm fire ashes and bones from a recent meal thrown in a corner. Sha'Li was agitated by the tracks she found there.

"Kendrick and Tarryn here were. And Kerryl. The twins, as well. And a sixth set," she announced, following whatever she saw in the wet ground a little way from the cave. "A human. Moccasins he wears instead of boots. Lightly he treads, rolling from outside to inside of foot."

"A scout, then," Rynn commented.

Sha'Li shrugged. "Leading the way, he is." The party trailed along behind her as she led the way deeper into the darkest portion of the swamp lying south and east of them. "Odd," she eventually muttered.

"What?" Eben asked.

"Tarryn no longer the trail marks. Someone else the trail marks. Trained is this tracker, but not her. And—"

"And what?" he prompted when she stopped.

She pitched her voice low. "Animal tracks I see. Alligator sign. And our gobrats also follow Kerryl and company."

"Do they stalk Kerryl, or is this all some sort of elaborate trap to draw us in?" Eben asked.

She shrugged, but the whites of her eyes showed, and that was never a good sign.

A few minutes later, she murmured over her shoulder to him, "Close we draw. Prepare for battle we should."

Eben passed the word back to Will, who was behind him at that moment, while he grasped the marvelous mace more securely. Fixing an image of those murdered children firmly in his mind, he eased forward, staying close to Sha'Li, who moved stealthily now, claws extended. She paused, crouching a little. Eben followed suit, staring over her shoulder at what lay ahead.

A small fire burned, barely visible through the trees and brush. Four grayish creatures with only vaguely humanoid features sat around the fire, laughing and talking. Gobrats.

Dead. They were all dead.

Sha'Li slid right, and he slid left. Rynn moved off to the right, and Will came left with him, along with Rosana. Raina stood stock-still without choosing a direction, horror written on her face. This night, she would not get her save-the-bunnies way. These murderers would pay for what they had done. Justice would be served.

Eben crept within a dozen steps of the fire, pausing only

to spot Sha'Li and Rynn in position across from him. A nod from Rynn, and he charged. As inclined as he was to scream in rage and vengeance, these beasts did not deserve the courtesy of a warning. He and the others charged fast and silent, plowing into the party of gobrats with deadly results.

He decapitated the first one he reached. Hot blood spewed everywhere, and he was glad. They should all bleed like that family had bled. He took a mighty swing at the gobrat just rising from his seat on the right.

"Look out!" Raina shouted just as something heavy slammed into him, staggering him. He turned to face a much larger gobrat who had come out of nowhere.

Ambush.

The bastards had set up a few of their number as bait at that fire while the rest hid in the woods. All of a sudden, it was he and his friends with their backs to the fire fighting the furious attackers raging out of the woods.

"I'm hit!" Rynn called out behind him. No time to turn and check on him because three gobrats were attacking him viciously, swinging claws and biting at him with long, yellow teeth. Nearly as big as humans, they were strong and fast. They tag teamed well, also. One would go low for his ankles while the other two swung at his head. Were it not for the light, quick mace, which he could whip from side to side much faster than a regular iron-headed one, he'd have been in serious trouble.

As it was, one of the creatures got in a good swipe at his arm that severed the major muscles from his shoulder down to his elbow. The pain was incredible, and blood spouted everywhere. He fell back, shouting, "Healing!"

A hot blast of magic slammed into his back. There was a moment of even more searing pain as his wounded arm knit itself back together, and then he was able to lift and swing his mace once more.

Will swung his staff like a scythe, mowing down gobrats as they came at him. The weapon did not kill, however, and Eben jumped to the side again and again, using his sword in his off hand to finish off the creatures that Will dropped, temporarily stunned. The combination of sword and staff was actually quite effective.

But then something hit him lightly in the chest, and he heard the sound of breaking glass. "Alchem—" It was all he got out before he pitched forward and saw the ground coming up to meet him fast.

More heat. More pain. He blinked awake. No idea what had hit him before. No time to care. A gobrat was on top of him, long front teeth reaching for his face. Eben gave a mighty shove, and as he knocked the gobrat off him, he rolled to his hands and knees. Something heavy jumped on his back, but there was a shout from Will, and the weight disappeared. Eben scrambled to his feet fast, closing in on Will's right side.

"Alchemist in the woods!" he shouted. And the attacker would be cursed dangerous if he was allowed to lurk out there unseen and unchallenged, moving around the fight, lobbing deadly gases at him and his friends.

"Follow me, Raina!" Rynn cried from the other side of the fire. The pair worked its way left to close in on Will's other flank. Where was Sha'Li? Please let her be going after that cursed alchemist.

Another wave of gobrats came screaming out of the woods, claws high, and Eben, Will, and Rynn, standing tightly bunched, absorbed the brunt of the onslaught grimly. They protected one another's flanks with brutal efficiency. The gobrat attack broke, and the dozen or so standing creatures turned and ran for the woods.

"For the children!" Eben shouted, giving chase. Will picked up the cry and charged, as well. Rynn was quieter but also rushed forward. There was no time to check on the healers. He had to assume that they would come along, covering their backs. Indeed, he heard Rosana incant something behind him, and Raina called out some sort of congratulations to the gypsy.

The gobrats darted through the trees, and it was a mad

dash to catch them, hacking them in the back one at a time as they scattered.

Will grunted somewhere off to his right and went down. Eben would have circled back to him, but a big gobrat was right in front of him. Eben took a swing with his mace, reaching as far forward as he could while he ran. Something sharp came down across his arm, all but severing it in two. *Not again.* The big gobrat turned, snarling, as blood poured out of Eben's arm in a hot gush down his side and right leg.

He stumbled. Took a few steps backward. "Healing," he tried to shout. It came out a whisper.

Smiling viciously, the gobrat raised abnormally long claws and took a swipe at his face. Eben grabbed the mace out of his numb right hand with his left and threw it up desperately. The fine weapon deflected the blow, directing it harmlessly at a sapling to his right.

He began to feel light-headed, and the forest spun around him, tilting crazily. Something big and shiny crashed past him and slammed into the big gobrat. Rynn. Fists flying almost too fast to see, the paxan pounded the gobrat's face into ground meat and yelled something.

Eben fell. The wet ground felt cool against his cheek. Darkness raced forward, and he embraced it . . .

"Oww!" he complained. Gads, that healing had hurt. His whole right side felt on fire. He could barely feel his right hand.

"Get up," a male voice bit out. "I could use a little help."

Right. Battle. Rynn stood over him, frantically blocking the attacks of three gobrats who were almost on top of both of them. Eben scrambled to his feet, and fighting side by side he and Rynn were eventually able to dispatch the gobrats. Man, that paxan was deadly with his feet. Those crystal greaves of his made short work of everyone Rynn kicked with them.

"Alligators!" Will shouted from somewhere behind them.

Great. He and Rynn moved toward Will's voice, back-to-back and moving sideways. They crashed through the underbrush and stumbled into a knee-deep mudflat. They slogged through it before spying Will and Rosana, trapped against a tree and under attack from a pair of the reptiles.

Eben and Rynn charged forward. Rynn shocked Eben by actually landing on the back of the nearest alligator and grabbing its massive jaws in his hands. The creature twisted and rolled violently, but Rynn wrapped his legs around the beast and clung tenaciously to it as it thrashed.

Eben took a downward swing at the second alligator. His mace hit the tough hide and bit in; however, the flanges stuck in the base of the beast's spine. The alligator gave a violent swing of his tail, and Eben all but lost his grip on his mace before the weapon finally came free. Will whacked the alligator's jaw with his staff as Eben swung again. This time the mace caught the softer flesh of the alligator's belly, and the beast roared in rage. Will jumped forward, and using his belt dagger, he thrust it down with both hands into a spot just behind the big reptile's skull.

The alligator went still. Eben spun to help Rynn, but the paxan lay prone on the ground, bleeding out from a terrible gash in his side. His intestines were visible, and he was clearly mortally wounded.

"Raina!" Eben shouted at the top of his lungs.

She came running through the trees, her hands lit up like torches, her white tabard glowing in the night. She fell to her knees beside Rynn and laid her hands directly on the terrible wound. Huge amounts of magical energy flowed outward from her hands into the paxan, and Eben looked away in distaste as the flesh knitted before his eyes.

Sha'Li materialized out of the dark, breathing hard. "That way they've fled, and the alchemist with them. Wounded him I did, but killed him I did not."

"C'mon," Eben called to the others. Will took off after him, but Rynn was a little slower to rise. Raina was still healing him as the paxan climbed to his feet and regained his bearings. Eben saw no more of the paxan then, for he was off and running through the trees again, following Sha'Li as she flew through the undergrowth, leaped over rivulets, and circled wide around mudflats, clearly at home in this terrain.

Without her, they'd never have moved fast enough to catch up to the fleeing gobrats. But all of a sudden, they emerged into an open area under the canopy of trees. On the far side of the clearing, a thicket of vines and brambles formed a wall. Against it, six gobrats huddled in a tight phalanx, snapping and snarling. Behind them stood a human with an oddly glowing left eye.

As Eben looked on, the man's features shifted and transformed, his nose lengthening to a sharp point and long, yellow teeth emerging from his lips. His body deformed and hunched over, and long claws emerged from his fists. Humans did *not* have claws like that.

"Were-rat," Rynn called from behind them. "Beware of poison in his bite!"

Hopefully, Raina had come with them and was not still back at the fire, singing camp songs and healing all the gobrats they'd just dropped. No time to think on that now. The last of the vile creatures who'd murdered that family stood just across the clearing.

"For the children," Will snarled their rallying cry, advancing at a determined walk toward the clustered rats.

For the children, indeed. Eben gripped his mace firmly and moved forward, coldly gauging which gobrat he would gut first on his way to killing that were-rat. These gobrats were eminently more disciplined than the previous ones they'd fought. Or maybe it was something about being cornered that made them fight with such ferocity and focus.

Eben figured that he, Will, Rynn, and Sha'Li were about evenly matched with the six gobrats before them. Thankfully, Raina moved in behind them just as the alchemist began throwing gas globes at them. As quickly as he could injure them, she was able to heal them. It was not a comfortable fight, being struck by damage from the front and painfully sharp healing from behind, but it worked.

One gobrat fell, and then another. A third fell, and Eben and his companions abruptly had the upper hand in the fight as they gained a numerical advantage. They pressed forward, starting to swing for the alchemist. Eben nicked the fellow's cheek with the tip of his sword, and Will got in a good blow on the were-rat's casting shoulder. But then a strange thing happened. The were-rat stepped back against the wall of vines, brambles, and brush . . . and disappeared.

Confused, Eben had to yank his mace up to block a vicious swing he'd nearly missed seeing in his distraction wondering where the were-rat had gone. Focusing again on the foe at hand, he made short work of the wounded gobrat, using both sword and mace to crowd the creature against the wall of thorns while thrusting and chopping with both weapons.

"Where'd he go?" Will demanded.

Eben glanced around, and all the gobrats lay dead at their feet. Rynn was examining the barrier before them, and Eben followed suit, poking it experimentally with his sword. Thicker than the length of his mace, the wall was at least ten feet high and looked woven of living materials.

Will closed his eyes, concentrating on who knew what. Communing with that tree lord in his head, most likely. Mayhap Bloodroot would know how to pass through the barrier. Raina reached down toward one of the gobrats, hand glowing, and Rynn put a restraining hand on her arm.

"Justice has been served, White Heart. Do not undo it," the paxan said formally.

"You don't have the right to make that call," Raina snapped at Rynn.

"Actually, I do."

Eben frowned. What did that mean? Raina looked equally startled. By what right did the paxan administer high justice? Such a thing was reserved for high-ranking nobles.

Rynn turned away from Raina as if he did not wish to discuss it anymore and instead moved over beside Eben to ask, "Is your sword silvered?"

"Yes. It is." At Aurelius's urging, Eben had had his weapon coated in the expensive metal the last time he'd returned to Dupree. The solinari had been good enough to pay for it, too.

"Good. It typically takes silver to hurt were-creatures."

Eben shifted the mace to his off hand and gripped his long sword, with its shining silvered blade, tightly in his right hand.

"Tracks leading away from yon thorn wall," Sha'Li murmured, squatting on her haunches to examine the ground. She must have picked up the were-rat's footprints.

"Where did he go?" Eben asked.

"They," the lizardman girl corrected. "Three humans and an animal. Clawed feet it has."

"The were-rat?" Eben asked, surprised. How could the creature have slipped past them without them seeing it?

"Nay. Not the were-rat. A reptile," she corrected.

Frowning, Eben stared around the large clearing under the trees. Here and there, he spied small flashes of light. "What are those?"

Rynn looked up sharply. "What are what?"

"Those bits of light. There. And there." He pointed at them.

"I see nothing," Rynn replied.

Eben strode toward one of the lights. It was glowing a faint reddish color, and he leaned down to pick up its source, a narrow shard of stone lying on the ground. As his fist closed around it, shock rolled through him. He knew what this was. What on Urth was it doing here? He moved toward another light, this time picking up a silvery gray crystal.

"What are you doing?" Rynn asked.

Eben held out his open palm. "Do these appear to glow to you?"

"No, Eben. They are just bits of rock. Are you feeling all right?"

"They're elemental shards. They're scattered all over this area."

"What would something like that be doing here?"

"No idea. But I know what I see and feel."

"Let's go back to the others and show them." On their way back to the others, Rynn fished two potions out of his pouch and passed one to him. "Drink this. It will protect you against an alchemical attack."

Eben downed the potion as he followed the paxan back to where the others were gathered before the impenetrable wall. He held out the stones to Raina. "Do you see magic on these stones?" he demanded.

She stared at the rocks and then at him. "I see nothing."

"They're elemental shards," he insisted. "They glow. I can *see* it."

"Ahh. That explains it," Raina replied. "I know nothing of elemental magic. What are elementally charged bits of stone doing in a place like this?"

He frowned. "They can mean only one thing. Elementals have been active in this area. They've either been in combat here and lost bits of their energy, or they've performed some sort of elemental magic in this place and these are the scattered remnants of it."

Everyone looked around cautiously.

"I see an opening in the underbrush over that way," Rynn supplied.

"In that direction the tracks proceed, as well," Sha'Li offered.

By consensus, they moved off toward the open spot. But they hadn't gone more than a dozen yards when something fast moving flashed through the trees to their left. A twisting bolt of magic flew toward Eben, and the energy jangled through him painfully. But before it had reached his fingertips, healing magic hit him from behind.

Will took off running after the figure, and then suddenly, gobrats were darting at them from all directions. Excellent. The more that attacked them, the more that would die. Sha'Li took off after one, and Rynn took off after another. Raina raced after the paxan, and Rosana seemed bent on following Will.

Eben spied the were-rat and charged toward him. But where it he had been aggressive and vicious before, this time he seemed less interested in making a violent stand. Eben had no such qualms, however, and attacked him aggressively. But then an exact replica of the beast he fought jumped out of the darkness.

Two of them? Of course. The twins. He fell back as they swung their claws and snapped at him with those inhuman teeth. He concentrated his attacks on the less aggressive one while defending furiously against the better fighter of the two. Spotting the opening he'd been waiting for, Eben jumped forward as the first were-rat dropped his guard and plunged his silvered sword into the creature's belly. Eben put upward torque on the blade as he yanked it clear, broadening the stab wound into a gaping gash.

However, the move had opened up his right side to attack, and the second were-rat was on top of him so fast he barely had time to register piercing pain as those cursed teeth sank into the meat of his shoulder.

The bite wasn't particularly deep or painful. But in a few seconds, Eben began to feel somewhat nauseated. Well, hells. That was not good. He staggered back, bashing at the second were-rat with his mace. A downward chop of his sword at the rat's leg, and he forced the creature to stagger back himself, badly wounded.

The creature fumbled at a pouch and clumsily threw a gas globe at him, hissing in fury. The throw wasn't pretty, but at a range of only a few feet, the globe hit Eben's groin and broke, releasing a foul-smelling gas at him.

Something shimmered across his skin, and the gas dissipated harmlessly. Bless Rynn and his alchemical shield. A gobrat rushed toward him, squealing, and Eben was forced to back up. The were-rat paused to smear some sort of salve on his badly bleeding thigh wound, and Eben took the opportunity to turn and run.

Although it wasn't much of a run; it was more of a shambling jog. He really was starting to feel terrible. "Raina!" he called out weakly.

"Over here," her voice came from off to his left. He veered in that direction and saw Sha'Li engaged in a spitting contest with a gobrat. As he approached, she scored a direct hit in the creature's face, and it went down, screaming. She leaped on top of it just as something low and dark and fast moving rushed her at unbelievable speed.

"Look out, Sha'Li!" he yelled.

She rolled off her kill just in time to avoid being shredded by dozens of massive teeth as an alligator rushed her, jaws wide open. Instead, the creature plowed into the corpse of the gobrat. The jaws snapped shut with such power that the bite severed the gobrat in twain. Sha'Li scrambled backward, and Eben reached down to pull her to her feet.

"Terrible you look," she declared.

"Poisoned," he grunted.

"Incoming," she replied, spinning around him to place her back against his. Metal schwinged off her claws as he stabbed down at the alligator, death-rolling with half the dead gobrat in its jaws.

He caught a lucky break, and his blade jabbed the alligator in the pale underskin of its throat, sliding straight through into its brain cavity. The beast died on the end of his sword. Eben yanked the blade free but was shocked at how weak he already had become.

Sha'Li swore behind him. "Were-rat inbound. Move."

He took off running as best he could. Sha'Li, to her credit, stuck to his back despite his painfully slow pace. The were-rat closed with her, and she swore again. "My claws hurt it not," she ground out.

"Take my sword. It's silvered."

Sha'Li reached over her shoulder with an open fist, and he slapped the hilt of his weapon in it. Now without a blade to protect himself, he relied on his mace and dodging any blows that passed wide of the lizardman girl.

Will came into sight, hard-pressed by a huge alligator with a glowing red eye. A were-alligator? How were they to defeat that?

Raina was jumping around behind Will, blood running freely down her face from some sort of head wound, but she was pouring healing magic into Will practically continuously as he fought. Rosana was down, leaning crookedly against a tree, her right arm bending at a place it definitely should not. Broken. She vomited as he spotted her. Was she poisoned, as well?

Will's staff began to crackle with magic dancing down its length, and he jabbed it at the were-alligator desperately. A bolt of magic smashed into the creature, and it staggered back. In that momentary reprieve, Raina threw a bolt of magic at Will, a bolt of magic at Rosana, and a bolt of magic at Eben.

Eben was intensely grateful for the pain of her healing surging through him. But it wasn't enough. "I'm poisoned!" he called to her.

She responded by sending another blast of magic his way. This time, he felt immensely better as her magic purified his blood and cleared it of the poison flowing through it.

"Hit Rosana with one of those!" he called out.

Rynn came tearing into the clearing just then with a huge, four-legged beast on his heels. Gleaming tusks rose from the underjaw of a great, hairy snout. A muscular, bristled body on four short, sturdy legs announced the creature to be a boar. As it tossed its head and squealed in rage, Eben saw the red glint of its left eye.

"Switch," Sha'Li bit out, still at his back. "And take the sword."

He rotated left while she did the same, holding his right hand up over his right shoulder. His sword hilt smacked down into his palm. The turn brought him face-to-face with the were-rat once more. "You killed those children, and now I'll kill you," he snarled at his foe.

Apparently, Rynn's charge had carried him across the

clearing for he flashed into sight at the same instant Eben leaped forward on the attack. The two of them barreled into the were-rat from each side, sandwiching the beast in a punishing blow that caused bones to audibly crunch as they broke.

Wasting no time on niceties, Eben slashed the base of his blade across the creature's neck, slicing through tendon, muscle, and arteries in a killing blow.

Rynn spun away as Eben plunged his sword into the were-rat's heart for good measure. He looked up from the killing blow. Sha'Li and Rynn faced off against the were-boar while Raina tended to Rosana. Will sent bolt after bolt of magic down his staff into the were-alligator. It was clearly hurt by Will's magic, but it attacked, anyway, ignoring whatever wounds he gave it.

The reptile was easily twenty feet long, with longer-than-normal legs that moved almost like a human's. Its coloring was strange. Instead of the usual grayish green, this alligator's hide was pale green with almost golden undertones in the moonlight. Will swung his staff hard, catching the creature under the jaw hard enough to fling its entire head up and to the right toward Eben.

And that was when Eben saw the fine fretwork of russet brown markings covering its face. *Markings whose shape he recognized.*

Will used the alligator's momentary daze to gather a massive bolt of energy on his staff. The entire weapon glowed almost too brightly to look at.

"Will! No!" Eben shouted frantically. "That's Tarryn!"

Will glanced up at him, unholy fury glazing over his eyes, lost in the battle rage of the moment. He drew back his staff, preparatory to stabbing it into the were-gator in what would clearly be a deadly blow.

Eben lurched forward, shouting wordlessly in frustration and agony. Will was so lost in Bloodroot's rage that he was going to kill Tarryn. His friend. His childhood companion. His only link to the family he'd lost. Eben watched in horror as the staff started forward, deadly lightning flashing down its length.

And then, out of nowhere, a dark claw flashed across Will's throat. The staff dropped from his hands, and blood spouted from Will's severed jugular. Eben staggered to a halt as Will fell to his knees, a look of infinite surprise writ on his face. "Sha'Li?" he croaked. And then he pitched forward onto his face, dying.

"No!" Rosana screamed.

Rynn landed a spinning, crunching kick to the side of the were-boar's head, and its legs collapsed out from under it. "Confine it," the paxan ordered Raina tersely.

Raina jumped forward, throwing a tiny bit of healing at Will as she went, just enough to staunch the flow of blood from the gushing wound, but not enough to rouse him to consciousness. She threw the confining magic, which encased the creature from the neck down in a shell of magic. She moved to stand protectively over the were-boar. "I may have incapacitated this beast, but I will not let you kill it."

Abrupt, total silence fell around them.

"Look down at the were-boar at your feet," Rynn told Raina.

She did so and gasped. "Eben. Come here," she said urgently.

He moved across the clearing, looked down at where the beast had fallen, and could not believe his eyes. Where the boar had lain just moments ago, a human now lay in its place confined inside a shell of magic. Raina quickly released the young man from the spell.

"Kendrick!" he cried.

His best friend and brother blinked up at him, looking disoriented. Eben knelt beside Kendrick to embrace him, but the young man pulled back sharply.

Ahh, no. Stars, no. His left eye was beginning to glow a brilliant red.

Kendrick rasped, "Go. Now. Quickly, before I kill you all."

Gabrielle smiled as her dwarven traveling companion grumbled yet again, this time about the lousy footing of the path they trod. He was a stout, one-legged miner of the kelnor variety, with a salty mouth and a saltier temperament. She had grown surprisingly fond of him in the short time they'd been on the road.

They'd had to wait for several weeks while the messenger Sasha had dispatched to Kel found and brought back to the citadel a dwarf who had apparently passed on a rather notable bit of ancient armor to their anonymous colleagues.

The dwarf, named Gunther Druumedar, had eventually been found in the company of other sympathizers with their cause and been brought with all due haste to the Heartland—a fact about which he still complained often. Although she was not quite sure if it was the journey itself or the haste with which he'd been forced to make it that irked him so.

Sasha had come along on their trip south and east out of the Heartland to Vierre. The expedition had been made with all the pomp and fuss that could be expected of a queen and an ambassador's wife traveling in state. There had been house servants, cooks, porters, and guards enough to make them look like an Imperial legion on the march. Gabrielle's exit from the Heartland had been quite a change after her incognito arrival with the Child of Fate, Dafydd, and his parents.

Once in Vierre, Gabrielle and Sasha went to meet a man

by the name of Aran Rahor. At one time a Heart high patriarch, he'd given up that rank and accepted the lower White Heart rank of Serene to pursue his work with a species of creature called yeren. He was convinced the beasts were of significant enough intelligence to merit recognition as a sentient race by the Empire. The Forester's Guild, long a trader in valuable yeren hides, had opposed him every step of the way, and the matter was still unresolved.

Behind his back, most people called Rahor the Shaggy Father. Among some, it was a pejorative term referring to his unnatural closeness to the yeren. Among others, it was an homage to his unflagging work to get yeren recognized as a sentient race and protected from hunting.

An aging man himself, he'd proposed that his daughter, Mina, go with Gabrielle on her trek through yeren lands to ensure her safe passage. The daughter, also a White Heart member, apparently knew how to communicate with the yeren and also worked toward recognition of the creatures by the Empire.

Gabrielle said her farewells to Sasha on a sunny morning and set out from Vierre on the next leg of her journey. While Sasha returned to the Heartland with her entourage, Gabrielle, Gunther, a few porters and guards, and the White Heart initiate departed for the northeast and the high reaches of Groenn's Rest. Mina normally would have had a Royal Order of the Sun protector of some kind for such a journey. But instead, the young woman was accompanied by a gigantic, hairy beast who never left her side. Mina said his name was Kuango.

The red-brown yeren easily stood seven feet tall, with a big belly, long arms and a kind-looking, softly furred face. He made no sounds but used rudimentary sign language to communicate with Mina. The initiate said his throat had been injured when he was young, but did that mean most yeren *could* actually speak? At first, the creature had alarmed Gabrielle, but she'd already grown rather accustomed to his silent, hulking presence.

Sasha had also sent along with them an ogre-kin who'd

said gruffly to call him Olivar. Gabrielle had never been around anyone of his race before and learned in a matter of minutes that his burly appearance was deceiving. Behind the thick jaw, heavy brow, and yellow-hued, leathery skin lay a quick mind and dry wit. An avarian traveled with Olivar, who referred to the bird changeling as his apprentice. At what craft, Gabrielle had no idea.

The last member of their party was a taciturn lizardman. As the journey was long and the need to find that which they sought urgent, Sasha had arranged for the lizardman guide to speed their journey along.

To that end, they boarded a long, low barge poled along a sluggish river by a pair of lizardmen who worked for their guide. At first, the river was wide, bordered by marshes and reeds. But as they progressed, its banks narrowed and grew tall and rocky until the barge flew along in a deep canyon the sun barely penetrated. And then the banks closed in overhead, and they were completely underground.

"What is this?" Gabrielle asked the lizardman.

"An underwae we sail. Faster by far it is than walking, and less conspicuous."

That it was. She could not tell how long they let the fast-moving river carry them along, but it was at least a full day and a night if the number of meals they ate and the number of times the lizardmen at the tiller took turns steering the vessel were any indication.

When the river finally emerged above ground once more, it was night out, chilly and damp. Late night, then. They traversed another deep canyon, and nothing but shadowed rock walls were visible on either side of them. She huddled deeper in her cloak on her makeshift sleeping pallet and went back to sleep.

When she woke again, it was to bright sunlight. They were just emerging from the canyon into a green valley nestled between surprisingly tall mountains. They must have reached the beginning of Groenn's Rest, the tallest, youngest, steepest mountain range in all of Koth.

They sailed perhaps another half hour to the end of the valley, and then the river ended at a crystalline lake filled with shockingly cold water. They clambered ashore onto a beach made entirely of rounded slate stones no larger than her fist. It made for difficult walking, and she stumbled up the shore to grassier ground.

For the first time since she'd met him, Gunther smiled. "Ahh, it is good to be home. I've missed proper dwarven ale," he declared, patting his belly and grinning.

"Is it wise for us to be seen in villages and pubs given the nature of what we seek?" Gabrielle asked in concern.

He laughed. "Every dwarven steading in Groenn's Rest will have a few barrels of ale in the cellar. We drink it like humans drink water. It is the elixir of life to us."

My. He was in an expansively grand mood. She replied, "If that is the case, perhaps we should make a start on our journey toward where you found that bracer. We can stop for ale later after we've walked awhile."

She thanked the lizardman boatman and his crew and pressed a few extra coins into their hands by way of thanks. And then she turned to face the mountains. "The peaks are certainly high. Is there a way between them?" she asked Gunther.

He chuckled. "These here be baby hills. You've yet to see the real mountains. Once we top that pass ahead, then you'll see the heart of Groenn's Rest."

He turned out to be exactly correct. Later that afternoon when, huffing and puffing, she stepped over the summit of the pass he'd led the party through, she paused to gasp at the wonder of the massive, snowcapped peaks towering before them, nature's sentinels in all their wild glory.

"Please tell me I don't have to climb one of those," she panted.

Gunther grinned. "Not all the way to the top of one, at any rate. Just to where the tree line meets the snow line. That's where I was attacked by that filth—" He broke off. "Where that yeren jumped me."

Mina opened her mouth as if to speak but then thought better of it. Gunther had been throwing sidelong glares at Kuango all week, and Gabrielle suspected he was a lost cause when it came to learning to love yeren as friends and not food.

They stopped for the night at a prosperous-looking farm run by a human family. It turned out their eldest daughter had married recently and moved away, so they had a spare room they were willing to rent out for the night. Gunther and the others bedded down in the barn while she and Mina took the tiny room under the eaves of the rambling home.

If only their hosts knew the Queen of Haraland slept in their house, the ruckus it would cause. As it was, she enjoyed traveling incognito like this. Regalo would have heart failure if he knew she traveled abroad with so little protection and in such primitive conditions. But it was an adventure and a blessed relief from the strictures of royal life, particularly at court.

The next morning, they headed out and began the long climb up a mountain Gunther called the Hauksgrafir. A narrow forester's path crisscrossed back and forth across the face of the ever-steeper slope. Her thighs burned, and her lungs felt near exploding. But if a one-legged dwarf past his prime could make the climb, by the stars, so could she.

In midafternoon, Gunther stopped to survey their position. "I found the bracer in a cave well down that cliff over yonder. But I'd not like to make the climb down to it again. Nearly died, the first time I did. Sheer dumb luck that I fetched up on the last ledge before I would have plunged to my death. A woman like you, a city dweller, could never make the climb and live."

As much as she would like to disagree with him, she couldn't.

"Way I figure it, there must've been another entrance to the mine I found. Place that big couldn't have carried out all its production through the tiny tunnel and hidden entrance I used."

He stared at the mountain, thinking hard, and she did not interrupt him.

"I'm guessing the main entrance is nearly straight above us, maybe another three, four hundred feet up the mountain. In yon yeren-infested forest."

She gazed up. That would put them just shy of the snow line. Which was a blessing. She had not packed boots for tromping around in the cold and wet of a snowpack.

Gunther moved out, stumping to the front of the party on his odd mechanical leg. He led the way up a narrow forester's path. "Keep a sharp eye peeled, lads and ladies, for any cave entrances. Holler if you spot one."

It took them the better part of an hour to climb the three hundred feet higher. Not only did the path twist and turn, but the air was thin, and at times, the underbrush was almost too thick to pass through. No forester had been this way in a while, that was certain.

Gunther stopped. "Way I figure it, right around here somewhere; there must be a cave or a tunnel into the mountain."

They fanned out and found it in a little while. As it was getting late, though, they decided to camp in the large cave Gunther had found, its opening cleverly masked by overlapping stones that still left an opening a team of oxen could drive through.

Through the night, Mina and Kuango sat in the cave entrance. Three times, Gabrielle wakened to rumbling sounds outside that just tickled the edge of human speech. Were those yeren? She was too afraid to get up and find out.

First thing the next morning, they dressed warmly and prepared a brace of torches before heading deeper into the cave. Gabrielle was impressed by how Gunther never seemed to get disoriented or turned around while navigating his way forward.

For a while, they traversed a natural cave complex. But then the walls changed and became worked stone. They passed through large chambers that Gunther said were played-out mines. And then he stopped abruptly at an intersection of two crossing tunnels in the thick darkness.

"My sign!" he exclaimed, pointing at some chalk markings on a wall. Now that he mentioned it, the signs did look recent. He studied the markings for a moment, nodded to himself, and moved off down one of the side tunnels.

Before long, they emerged into another chamber, but this one held benches and sleeping coves and what looked like the remains of a forge of some kind. Olivar and his apprentice rushed forward to the forge and began muttering excitedly to each other.

"What is it?" Gunther demanded of the ogre-kin.

"Storm forge."

"You know how it works?" the dwarf asked eagerly.

"I may be a stormcaller, but that does not mean I know all there is to know about storm forges. What I do know is they're made to channel lightning through those copper conduits coming out of the ceiling right there."

Gabrielle and Mina waited patiently while the men oohed and aahed over the likely engineering of the full forge that had once stood here. But eventually, Gunther got around to commenting, "Over there, under that pile of rock fall is where I found my armor."

The party moved over to the small mountain of fallen stone and lifted their torches high. Kuango gestured urgently at Mina, who translated. "He says there's a big place behind it that smells different from the other places down here."

Gunther eyed the pile doubtfully. "It would take a mining crew a week to move that pile."

"Ahh, but we've got a yeren," Mina replied confidently. "If you will show me what stones to have Kuango move without causing the entire pile to come down on us, we'll be past that pile in no time."

It actually took what Gabrielle estimated to be an hour before a dark opening beckoned at the top of the rock pile. One by one they squeezed through it. She was amazed that

Kuango passed through an opening that was barely large enough for her.

They slid down the far side of the rock fall and lifted their torches high.

And gasped.

A room as large and ornate as any receiving chamber at the Imperial Court yawned in the darkness. Benches and decorative pillars, frescoes, and bas-relief hunting scenes were all exquisitely carved from the mountain's granite core. As they strode the length of the vast hall, their torches only lit a portion of the cavernous space at one time.

Which was why they'd nearly reached the far end before Gabrielle spied something that made her stop and gasp again. A statue stood on a raised dais beside a throne-like chair of massive proportions. But unlike everything else in the room, the statue did not look carved of granite. Rather it was fashioned from something darker, and gleaming dully. Metal, perhaps.

They reached the statue and examined it closely. The detail and perfection of the carving were hard to fathom. Each whisker, each pore, each individual eyelash managed to be portrayed with stunning accuracy.

Olivar reached out reverently to touch the suit of armor the statue had been carved wearing. "Storm copper," he murmured in awe.

"The suit of armor is made of this storm copper, or the whole statue is?" she asked, confused.

The ogre-kin tilted his head quizzically, staring at the face of the carved dwarven warrior. "I wonder . . ."

"Wonder what?" she prompted when he did not continue. She had a feeling she already knew what he would say, but the message from the Eight sending her and Sasha on this quest had made it clear that the true nature of the statue they sought must not be revealed to any outsiders.

"If the stories could be true, after all—"

"What stories?" she prodded him.

"Of living creatures being turned into storm copper statues, eternally frozen in metal until the day when they should be released again into the world by reversal of the—"

The room around them erupted into movement and filled with horrible screeching so piercingly loud she could hardly stop herself from clapping her hands over her ears and collapsing to the floor. From tunnels and other openings unseen to her, creatures poured into the hall around them.

Some were small and winged, no larger than dragonflies. Others bounded forward on four legs, dog-sized. But the largest ones made her cringe back toward the statue in horror. They were snakelike in shape and movement, with no legs, upright like humans but undulating forward like a sidewinder might proceed across sand. A haunting pink glow, visible just at the edge of her vision, came from them all.

The piercing noise they made was nigh unbearable. Olivar shouted something, but she could not hear it. The little flying ones were easy enough to bat away, and the medium ones, although annoying, were easily dispatched by Gunther's axe or Olivar and his apprentice's swords.

But the big ones were more problematic. It turned out they could move with blinding speed and dodge when edged weapons were swung at them. More frightening, though, was the way one latched onto the back of Olivar's head with its mouth in some sort of twisted parody of a kiss. His eyes went blank, and his sword tip wavered and dropped.

Gabrielle did not have cause to use magic often—there were servants aplenty who could cast whatever spells she required—but summoning the energy to her hand came back easily to her. She flung a ball of force magic at the creature attached to the back of Olivar's head, and it screamed, breaking away from him.

A swarm of the insectoid bugs was bedeviling Gunther, and at least eight of them had attached themselves to his head, as well. She threw a magical shield at the dwarf, and as the magic raced across his skin, the little creatures detached themselves from him. Once they were airborne, she chucked fire magic into the mass of creatures, singeing them and sending a shower of the creatures to the floor.

"Step on them!" she yelled at Gunther. He shook himself from whatever trance the creatures had lured him into and began dancing around awkwardly, stomping on the bugs with his mechanical leg.

She whirled as she felt something latch onto her leg. One of the middling-sized creatures was sucking on the back of her leg. Irritated, she shook it off and cast a ball of force damage down at it from a range of about one foot.

But then something large wrapped around her like a constrictor on its prey, and she felt something moist and cold on the back of her neck. She slapped her hand directly onto the creature's torso wrapped around her waist and cast a bolt of damaging magic into it. With a painfully loud squeal, the creature let her go.

The avarian apprentice to Olivar had out a pair of daggers and was whipping them around his head with admirable speed, taking out one of the insectoid creatures with every blow. As she glanced his way, however, one of the big ones wrapped itself around him and latched onto his head. The odd bit was that the avarian just stopped fighting, as if he'd forgotten what he was doing and where he was. Gabrielle took aim and fired a bolt of magic at the snakelike creature. It released the avarian, who just stood there once freed.

"Hit it!" she cried. "Stab it with your daggers!"

The avarian shook himself and then turned and stabbed at the creature.

Where was Mina? Gabrielle whirled and saw the White Heart member sitting on the ground, a blank look on her face, while Kuango picked up creature after creature and threw it violently against the wall beside him. The creatures were not going down, though. They bounced and came right back at the huge yeren, who was fighting maniacally to protect his mistress.

She ran over to the yeren's side and tossed magical

damage into each creature he momentarily incapacitated. Between the two of them, they made short work of the remaining creatures.

The entire attack lasted no longer than three minutes, but Gabrielle was completely drained of magical energy, exhausted, and ravenously hungry at the end of it. The party gathered together, taking stock of injuries. Mina, still acting dazed, managed to heal the various injuries that had been sustained in the battle.

Gabrielle turned to Olivar. "You were about to tell me about the storm copper that statue is made of."

"What statue?"

She frowned. "That one, right over there."

Everyone turned to look where she had pointed, blank looks on their faces. What in the world? How could they have forgotten finding it just a few minutes ago? Unless . . .

She turned to stare at the corpses littering the floor of the hall. Those must have been censors, and they'd been sucking the memories out of her companions. The one that had attacked her must have been prevented from removing her memory by Talissar's Octavium Pendant.

"The dwarven statue," she told Olivar. "You were telling us about old legends of living creatures being turned to storm copper and eternally frozen, alive, inside metal."

"I was?" A frown. "Oh. Now that you mention it, I do recall hearing such a story."

One by one, with her prompting them, the members of the party gradually remembered what had been going on directly before they'd been attacked.

"Can we take the statue out of here?" she asked no one in particular.

Gunther frowned. "If I brought in a miner's cart, we could wheel him out."

"Don't bother," Mina replied. "Kuango can carry the statue back to our camp."

Gabrielle was shocked that the yeren was indeed able to lift the large metal statue and hoist it over his shoulder with apparent ease. They had to push aside a little more debris and roll away a few stones to enlarge the opening back into the chamber with the forge, but then Kuango pushed the statue through and followed behind it.

"How come those creatures didn't suck out your memory?" Mina asked her as they hiked the dark tunnels back to the cave where they'd camped before.

Gabrielle shrugged. "I suppose it was the magic I summoned and cast."

"I summoned magic, too," the White Heart member replied, frowning.

"Maybe spirit magics didn't chase them away, but my damaging magic did."

"I guess so," Mina responded doubtfully.

Gabrielle silently thanked Talissar for gifting her with the protective amulet.

"What are we going to do with that copper fellow once we get him to the surface?" Gunther asked.

She glanced over at Olivar. "Is there somebody who might be able to reverse the process that turned this gentleman to metal?"

"If anyone knows how, it would be the dwarven smiths at the Great Storm Forge."

"And where might that be?" she asked, praying that the oblivi had not erased the memory from the ogre-kin's mind.

"Rignhall," Olivar answered firmly.

Justin opened his eyes. The ritual-casting chamber took shape around him. Kadir looked smug, his assistant looked shocked, and the painting that Kadir liked was still ugly.

"Welcome back," Kadir said. "Both of you."

He frowned. His forehead felt strange as he wrinkled it, and he reached up to touch it. *That was not his face!* He lurched upright, shocked.

"The melding of your spirit with the oginn's has caused certain changes to your physical appearance."

"An oginn?"

"An ogre mage. The name of the particular one you now carry within you was Damoc. I cannot tell you what his work entailed. It is a great secret of our order."

Our? Oh. Right. He was one of them now.

"You will still need lessons in how to use your magic, to shape it, cast, and manage it, before I send you out."

"Out where?"

"I have a job for you. A recent visitor to Alchizzadon helped himself to a collection of votives. We need you to track him down and let us know when you find him. A team of our mages will join you to get them back."

"Why would a person put a piece of his spirit in a jar?" he asked.

"We have several reasons for doing such a thing, and they are beyond your need to know until you have more experience within the order."

"I want to see what I look like."

Kadir nodded and sent the acolyte out to fetch a hand mirror. The youth passed the polished silver object to Justin, who held it up hesitantly.

His skin had taken on a sallow tone, and his jaw was heavier, squarer than before. His hair was unruly, probably from him thrashing around in the throes of the transformation, but it stuck up in a way it never had before. His eyes were still light blue, and he saw himself in them.

He turned his head side to side, and that was when he spotted the rune on his neck. It was a spiderweb of fine black lines on his vaguely golden skin.

"What in the name of all that is cursed is that?" he demanded. Now that he knew it was there, he became aware of a burning sensation on his skin.

"A rune. I took the opportunity to cast the ritual upon you since we were already doing rituals. I shall also have to teach you how to use its power. Come, Justin. I am hungry. And you have much to learn."

Sha'Li's cheek burned fiercely, and she slapped her hand over it, biting back a groan. Is this what it felt like to lose her tribe mark? She'd had to make a terrible choice. Her friend or the were-beast who had no control over his actions. Will or Kendrick.

It had been a split-second call. It was not that Will had less status in her mind because he was a human. But he'd been lost in his rage, not thinking clearly. He'd been on the verge of killing Kendrick, and she'd had no other way to stop him. And Raina was here. She would not let Will die. Handy to have around, that White Heart girl was sometimes.

The pain on her face diminished, and she removed her hand reluctantly. There would be no hiding the loss of her tribe mark from her friends. She might as well get the humiliation over with right away.

"Sha'Li!" Rosana cried.

"Gone is my mark, I know."

"Gone? It's glowing so bright white I can see it from over here," the gypsy contradicted her.

"What? Have it still I do?"

Kendrick snarled, a deep, rough growl that sounded entirely inhuman. Rynn knelt in front of the young man. "Fight the transformation, Kendrick. Focus on that calm place in your core. Your friends are here. They've searched high and wide for you, and they've rescued you."

"Don't. Understand," he panted. "Don't. Want. Rescue."

Eben stepped forward. "That cursed madman kidnapped you!"

"Not. Mad."

Something deep inside Sha'Li responded to Kendrick's struggle as he fought against the transformation trying to claim him. She moved to his side. Placed a hand on his shoulder. The turbulence roaring through him slammed into her, shocking her with the intensity of its violence.

"Not you, this is," she murmured. "Strong are you. Brave and kind."

He looked over at her, making eye contact with that disturbing red eye of his. "You're tribe, now?"

"So it seems."

"Can you fix lycanthropy, then?"

She blinked, startled. Lycanthropy? She'd heard stories as a child of tribe warriors who were gifted lycanthropes and could shift from human form to were-creature form and back. Some did it at will; some did it with the cycles of the moon to which they were tied.

"Know not how, do I. But elders of tribe I can ask."

"You've got the healing mark," Kendrick persisted. "Kerryl has spoken of it. He said that the reappearance of the white tribe mark after all this time is a harbinger of the coming storm. Your mark is prophetic."

Her? A prophecy? Not bloody likely. "What storm comes?" she asked curiously.

"Kerryl will not speak of it. He says it is a greater evil than

Koth, a greater threat to all life than the Empire, though. And you have been marked to fight it."

Sha'Li was staggered. She'd never been special, just a middling child of an average clutch, and a girl to boot. Her only oddity had been her determination to travel, to see more of the world than a dank little corner of a swamp in the middle of nowhere. Although if she were to be honest with herself, she'd always wanted to be . . . more.

"You've got the mark of the healer, Sha'Li. If anyone can remove this curse from Tarryn and me, it is you. I believe in you. If a way can be found, you will do it."

He felt and sounded as if he was slipping. The beast was slowly, inexorably, taking over his mind and soon would overtake his body.

"My thanks . . . for finding me . . . but I am at peace . . . with my fate. For now, I will stay with Kerryl . . . and learn more of this evil that comes." His words were interrupted by bestial pants as the change crept over him.

He gathered himself and said all in a rush, "Take Tarryn with you. She did not want this. Fix her, Sha'Li. She has just been changed; the curse should not have taken root as deeply in her as it has in me."

Eben knelt before Kendrick and took him by both shoulders. "My brother, you have a right to know. Your father was assassinated by Dominion marauders, likely hired by Anton Constantine. He did not resurrect. He is gone."

Kendrick stared at Eben for a second and then threw his head back and let out a roar of grief and rage so wrenching that Sha'Li's heart could hardly beat in her chest under the weight of his agony. She jerked her hand away from his shoulder, unable to bear the intensity of his pain any longer.

"Get." A snapping grunt. "Back."

And then the transformation was upon him. In a blink of an eye, Kendrick the human was no more, and in his place stood a massive, snarling were-boar bigger than any mundane boar she'd ever seen before and eminently more dangerous, for Kendrick's intelligence worked in the creature's mind.

They all took a stumbling step back.

The beast swung its huge, gleaming tusks aggressively at them once and then turned and plunged into the underbrush. Rynn tensed to give chase, but Eben spoke heavily from the ground where he knelt. "Let him go."

The night fell deeply silent around them as they mourned the loss of their friend. He had passed beyond them now, become someone and something they could not follow. They'd well and truly lost him.

So. Her white mark meant she was a healer, did it? She felt in her bones that Kendrick did not mean the kind of healing Raina and Rosana did. Her healing was something else altogether. She glanced over at Tarryn, lying on the ground. In her unconsciousness, she'd transformed back to human, as well.

"Restrain the kindari girl we must before wakes she does and kills us all."

Rynn threw her a grateful look. "You are the most practical one of us all, Sha'Li."

She pulled a length of stout rope from her belt and held it out to the paxan. That third eye of his made her skin crawl to look at, but he had an exceedingly kind heart. She liked him greatly in spite of his monstrous appearance.

In her experience staying busy was the best way to deal with grief. It gave a person less time to dwell on the pain while the heart accustomed itself to the loss.

"Healing we all need, White Heart," she said briskly to Raina. "And food you casters need," she said to Rosana. "A weapons count we need to make sure no swords or staffs we have lost," she told Eben. "And tell *not* the alligator of Hyland's death when she awakes. Another enraged werecreature we need not. As for you"—she looked down at Will where he was rubbing his newly healed throat—"a talk we must have."

Everyone seemed a little startled at her taking charge like this, but none of the others seemed up to the task at the moment, devastated as they all were by the loss of Kendrick.

She would grieve him in her own way, but later. Alone, in the privacy of nature and in the way of her people.

Will rose to his feet, and she made eye contact with him. He nodded and followed her a little way away from the clearing where Rosana was building a fire and Rynn and Eben were discussing how best to restrain Tarryn.

"What do you wish to talk about?" Will asked without preamble.

"Apologize first, I must. For attacking thee."

"I'd have killed Kendrick if you hadn't dropped me. It is I who owe you the apology, I think."

"Accept, I do."

"And I."

"Good we are, then?"

"We're good," Will said firmly.

"About my tribe marking wish I to speak. The other spirit within you, knows he aught of this white mark?"

Will frowned. "He does not speak to me as if he is a second voice inside my head. I only get impressions and feelings from him. I cannot ask questions and get direct answers, I'm afraid."

"Familiar with this color of mark is he, then?"

"Definitely."

"Knows he of what Kendrick spoke when he called me 'healer'?"

"Again, yes."

"Correct am I that my healing is not like Raina's?"

Will frowned for a moment. "Correct."

"Knows he exactly what my healing is?"

Will closed his eyes. If the expressions crossing his face were any indication, he was having some sort of argument with himself, maybe cajoling the Bloodroot part of himself to cough up the requested information.

Finally, he opened his eyes. "As part of your Tribe of the Moon training, has anyone ever taught you about taints?"

It was her turn to frown. It was a term she'd heard before. "Like bad water, I smelled?"

"That. And more." He said hesitantly, "Mayhap taints upon spirits? I am sorry I cannot be more specific, but Bloodroot can only send me images and feelings at best."

She shook her head regretfully. "Training in this I have none."

"Perhaps we should get you this training. Kendrick seems to think that you will be able to reverse Tarryn's taint, if that is what her condition is. And I'm inclined to believe him. Like he says, Kerryl Moonrunner is not mad. And Bloodroot within me agrees that Kerryl is anything but mad. Even if we do not like his methods, the man is cunning and intelligent, and we would be wise to listen to him."

Profound relief swept through her at those words. Finally. They'd seen the powerful, competent nature guardian she'd known and admired. If Kerryl Moonrunner said some great evil was coming, then she did not doubt it was. It was as if the last barrier between her and her friends had fallen. No more secrets did she have to keep from them, no more opinions keep to herself. They were all finally in agreement with one another.

On impulse, she stepped forward and gave Will a long hug. He looked staggered when she moved back. "No one tell I hugged you, or kill you I must," she grumbled.

Will laughed. "There's no shame in caring for your family, Sha'Li."

Family. The word sank into her pores like fresh springwater, clean and pure. And the mark upon her cheek felt a little warmer of a sudden.

"Of something else wish I to speak, but with everyone," she said gruffly.

Will clapped her in the middle of the back, and she hissed at him out of general principles. Laughing again, he led the way back to the clearing and the others.

Rosana had a fire going and was heating water. Sha'Li gathered a big pile of firewood while the gypsy made tea for all of them. They soaked the hardtack bread she passed out in the hot drink to soften it enough to make it chewable. It tasted like sawdust to Sha'Li, but it was sustenance. And she didn't feel like going fishing right now.

"What was it you wished to speak to all of us about?" Will asked her from across the fire.

"The cache that earlier we found."

"What of it?" Raina asked, turning the white ring upon her finger.

"Meant to find it, I believe we were." She hesitated and then plunged ahead. "Worked with Kerryl Moonrunner I have before. His signs, I know. In that place he was before us, and the way he cleared for us."

Raina nodded. "I was wondering why there was something of great value to each one of us in that trunk. Only Rynn, who Kerryl would not have known was with us, did not have a treat waiting for him in the chest."

Rosana spoke up. "Are you saying that Kerryl Moonrunner is *helping* us?"

Sha'Li shrugged. "In his own way, yes. His motives we know not, but failure he does not wish for us. At *something* wishes he for us to succeed. Very much."

A new voice spoke up from the shadows, startling them all. "She's right."

"Tarryn?" Eben exclaimed. "How are you feeling?"

"Worse than death," the kindari replied wryly.

Raina asked the elf cautiously, "Do you feel like you might transform again soon?"

Tarryn flexed her hands within the ropes binding them to her sides. "I feel fine for the moment. You will know if the change is coming because my eye will glow red."

Eben nodded. "We saw it in Kendrick."

"Is he safe? Where is he?" the kindari demanded.

"We talked with him," Eben explained. "He didn't want us to rescue him. He said he wishes to stay with Kerryl to learn more of what threat he sees coming. Kendrick told us to fix you, and then he left."

"Fool," Tarryn spit out. Her left eye began to glow faintly, a maroon tint in her otherwise light brown eyes.

Rynn said soothingly, "Focus on your breathing, Tarryn. Inhale. Hold the air in your lungs. Breathe out."

"My, you're pretty," Tarryn said to the paxan. "And who might you be?"

"I am Rynn. Sworn to protect and defend your friends and assist them in their quest."

The kindari smiled warmly. "Well met, Rynn. I am Tarryn." She added a little bitterly, "At least for now."

Sha'Li leaned forward. "What tell us can you of how Kerryl turned you thus?"

"It was a ritual of sorts. He had the twins, Pierre and Phillipe—they're were-rats and roundly horrible people—kidnap a speaker of alligators."

"We cleaned up the aftermath of that kidnapping," Will interjected. "Horrible's not the word for those two."

"I killed one of them," Eben volunteered.

Raina lurched. "Where? When?"

Rosana said unapologetically, "He's long past the reach of a life spell. And if we're lucky, the wretched creature will not find a place to resurrect."

"Has a spirit approached you?" Raina demanded.

The gypsy scowled. "Nay, and he'd better not. I would kill him again the instant his spirit entered his body. I do not believe his spirit would come to me; it would sense my hostility."

Sha'Li turned the conversation back to Tarryn's transformation. "Why did Kerryl the speaker need?"

Tarryn continued, "The speaker summoned a great alligator. Not a regular one, but some sort of scion of the Great Alligator. It was this body and spirit that Kerryl joined with mine. It looked mostly like a regular high magic ritual, except the magic was not the same. It was . . . green. And it worked somewhat differently."

"Nature magic," Raina commented. "Not much is known of it. Nature magic is shamanic and not hermetic like traditional magics."

Sha'Li had never heard the words before, but something

inside her confirmed that nature magics and the kind that Raina used were fundamentally different.

"It will likely take some kind of nature magic or shamanic effect to reverse whatever was done to Tarryn," Raina replied.

Will glanced over at Sha'Li and said, "We may have a lead on that. Kendrick asked Sha'Li if she could remove taints, and we think this may be a skill that tribe members can learn. If we can find a tribe elder, he or she might be able to teach Sha'Li how to do it—or at least tell her how to try."

Tarryn looked over at her hopefully. "You could fix me?"

Sha'Li shrugged. "Mayhap. Try I will, when knowing of its doing I have."

They bedded down for the remainder of the night, half the party keeping watch while the other half slept.

Over breakfast the next morning, Will asked the party, "Do we continue tracking Kerryl? We still must recover the change water from him to take back to Goldeneye so he'll fix Rosana."

Tarryn spoke up. "If it's the change water you want, Phillipe is carrying it in a pouch."

That caused a flurry of activity while the dead were-rat's body was located in the woods and searched. No pouch was in evidence, and Tarryn identified the dead rat as Pierre.

Rosana announced in satisfaction, "He has not yet resurrected. The Green Lady willing, he will not at all."

Sha'Li frowned. "How know you that?"

"His body is still here. If he had successfully resurrected, this body would have dissipated as his new body formed during the resurrection process."

She shuddered. Bodies forming and fading. Spirits floating around and then entering bodies. She had no wish to undergo resurrection, ever. Oh, she'd been introduced to a Heartstone along with all the other youths in her clutch in a city that had a Heart house with a stone. The one time she had died, she'd been too far from a Heartstone to sense its glow, and had field resurrected with Rosana instead. By the moon, she hoped never to have to use a Heartstone.

Raina asked practically, "How are we going to track Kerryl and Phillipe now that Tarryn is with us? It's her trail we've been following all this time."

Sha'Li answered scornfully, "A master tracker am I. Please."

Tarryn piped up. "I also am a tracker. And I've been traveling with the man for weeks. I know his signs like the back of my hand. I can track him, but if we get close to him, you should probably tie me up and knock me out so he can't command me to change with that magical bracer of his."

Eben nodded. "We will not let you hurt us or hurt yourself. You have my word on it."

Sha'Li thought that was a rather optimistic promise for the jann to be making. But Tarryn was effectively the only family he had until such time as he found his sister. She supposed it made sense that he would lay down his life for the kindari. It was Eben's way. Loyal, he was.

Will said stoutly, "Have at it, madam trackers. The day's a-wasting."

Raina was exhausted by the time they stopped for the night to make camp. The previous night's casting had taken a lot out of her, and she needed more food and sleep if she was going to recover fully.

Thankfully, Kerryl and his companions were sticking to solid ground as they moved deeper into the Swamp of Angor, which made following them slightly less miserable than before. The nature guardian was moving steadily southeast, which led Sha'Li and Tarryn to believe that he had some destination in mind. Tarryn also reported that Kerryl had mentioned searching for something important out here. He hadn't known where it was, though, and had needed the alligator speaker to take him to it.

There had been an alarming development when the trackers spied what they thought might be tracks of a pack of enormous wolves—or Imperial hounds. The last thing they needed was to be attacked by a hunter and his hounds out here. There would be nowhere to run or hide this time, hampered as they were by the swampy terrain.

But the tracks had crossed theirs at right angles, and Sha'Li and Tarryn agreed that the beasts had been moving away from them. Stars willing, the creatures were following the scent of some other quarry and not Eben's.

Raina stood first watch with Rynn and Sha'Li and was ready to drop by the time she finally lay down in her bedroll. Still, worry over Kerryl's plans and of being attacked by him and his beasts made settling down to sleep difficult. Not to mention those cursed hounds. And who knew what other creatures were out there, waiting to attack them?

She drifted off to sleep and was shocked to find herself walking through a familiar white mist. If phantasms and other dream creatures hid in the fog swirling around her this night, they did not reveal themselves to her. She walked for only a few minutes before familiar green grass appeared below her feet. Gawaine's grove took shape around her, as verdant and perfect as ever.

Tonight, he seemed to be waiting for her. He took a quick step forward when she appeared, saying, "There you are. Thank you for coming."

"You summoned me?" she asked, confused.

He smiled a little. "I did my best to call you."

"What can I do for you?" she asked politely.

He looked down pointedly at her right hand, and his face lit up. "So. You did find my signet ring!"

She looked down at the white ring clasping her middle finger. "I thought it was yours. It felt like you."

"Indeed. It is carved from the horn of Cerebus. My steed and friend. He was . . . is . . . the king of the unicorns. A magnificent creature. I should like to see him again one day."

"How did you know I found your ring?"

"Mine began to glow. And then it began to feel like you." He held his hand out, and on the middle finger of his right hand, an identical copy of her ring clasped his finger. His ring was giving off a faint glow that grew brighter as his ring approached her version of it.

"Where is my crown?" Gawaine asked. "It's not with you."

"I left it with Aurelius Lightstar for safekeeping. He's the Mage's Guildmaster of Dupree and a friend. I was worried that I might lose it if our travels did not go well."

"Have they gone well?"

"I would call it a mixed experience. We have attracted attention we could do without in the form of Imperial hounds. And we had an unfortunate encounter with the Dominion leader, a cobra changeling calling himself Goldeneye. Rosana is enslaved by him, and Kendrick does not wish to be rescued. But we draw close to Kerryl Moonrunner. He seems to be leading us to something."

Gawaine's face lit with comprehension. "Indeed, he does."

"Can you tell me what it is?"

"You will find it soon enough. And it will be self-explanatory."

Her stomach growled, and she frowned, embarrassed. "How can it be that I'm hungry in a dream?"

"You must have gone to sleep hungry. I can feed you here, at least. But you will still need sustenance when you wake. Come." He waved his hand, and a table appeared, laid out with all manner of food and delicacies.

"Ooh, raspberries! My favorite!" she cried. A great pile of the delicate, succulent berries sat before her.

"How have you been?" Gawaine asked after she'd eaten a bit. "I've been worried about you. When you gave away my crown, I lost my connection to you and could not find you."

He could track her through his crown? "Were you watching me?"

"Not exactly. I was able to check in on your dreams from time to time before."

"And now?"

"Now you wear my ring, and the connection is made once

more. In fact, because I wear a duplicate of that ring, the connection may be stronger than before."

"How is it you have a copy of this?" She turned the ring on her finger.

He shrugged. "The being who created this dreaming echo of me thought to create an echo of the ring, as well."

"Who created you?" she asked curiously.

"I cannot speak of it. I am sorry."

Fair enough. It probably had to do with great mystical powers and mythical beings far beyond her knowing, anyway.

He took off strolling around the margins of the grove, and she joined him, enjoying the serenity of the place. "You still have not told me how you've been," he said.

"Honestly, I've been better." She hesitated to tell him the full truth, but there was no one else who would understand. Rynn had been sweet about the voices and taught her how to empty her mind and focus on her breath, but even that was only a temporary fix at best. She blurted, "I think I may be losing my mind."

Gawaine stopped in quick concern and turned to face her.

"I've been hearing voices in my head. Although not voices exactly. Rynn thinks they're tied to the source of my magic. He showed me how to meditate, and it helps a little. But they are becoming too loud for me to hold back anymore."

"How long have you been hearing these voices?"

"For months."

"And they're getting worse over time?"

She nodded and looked up at him candidly, whispering, "I am afraid."

Gawaine took her hands in his. "Do you trust me?"

"Of course."

"Then believe me. You are not going to lose your mind. I have experience with hearing echoes. And you can learn to live with them. Not hear them unless you want to."

"How?"

"Let us listen to your voices together, and I will show you."

He laid his fingertips on her left temple. And of a sudden, he was there. *Inside* her head. It was different from Rynn's mind touch. This was much more personal, a much deeper connection, for she was suddenly aware of being inside his head, as well.

"Touch my temple," he murmured. Fascinated, she did as he instructed. His skin was smooth, his hair silky, the blood coursing through his veins vibrant. It was like touching . . . life.

"Let's hear these echoes of yours."

The tide of muttering voices surged forward, released at his command. Except it was ten times worse than it had ever been before. Stars! If this was how bad it was going to get, she was surely going to lose her mind. Fear surged through her.

But then Gawaine was there. "Watch me."

He opened his mind fully to the voices and then slowly but surely contained and suppressed them until they were barely audible. She couldn't say exactly how he did it, but she understood. He'd willed them into silence, and they'd obeyed him.

"You try it, Raina."

Of a sudden the voices were back, and she cringed away from them. Hesitantly, she opened her mind, and a deafening cacophony of sound pounded against her skull. She imitated what Gawaine had done, less quickly and less completely, but the voices receded. They *did* recede.

"Again," he said.

This time, she had more success and sooner.

"Now, without me."

Panic shot through her as he took a step back from her and the physical and mental contact between them was broken. She felt bereft. Did he feel the same way? She looked up with intent to ask. His dark gaze was intense. She would have been rocked by the unspoken message in it, but then the voices were back, screaming at her unbearably.

Closing her eyes, she opened the floodgates and then

determinedly closed them, exhaling in relief as the noise diminished to a manageable volume.

"You will need to practice. But in time, you can gain complete mastery over the echoes."

"Thank you."

He resumed walking. "My pleasure." The words were simple, but he packed them with meaning beyond the obvious. She barely kept her jaw from dropping open. So. He had felt the loss when they'd broken their mental connection.

"Events are accelerating," Gawaine commented mildly enough.

Thank the Lady. Safe conversational ground. "How so?" she responded.

"Major actors are stepping onto the stage. The Emperor himself mobilizes his forces. Although I do not believe he yet sees the exact threat. Nonetheless, he listens to the soothsayers and prepares." Gawaine bent to pick a flower, a sweet-smelling hedge rose, and handed it to her. "Here in the dream realm, powerful phantasms gather armies of followers. Elemental forces use their devotees to bring them items of power. The Dreamer himself is on the move."

"How does an army on this plane represent a threat to mine?"

"There are gates and portals between the two realms that an army could pass through easily enough."

She gulped. As if it wasn't bad enough to fear invasion by Maximillian's legions, now they had to fear an army from this plane? In a small voice, she said, "Rynn thinks it was our visit to the dream plane that caused the chaos here."

Gawaine shrugged. "These events have been building for a long time. Threatening to wake me has merely brought many of them to a head. Any number of beings believe your finding me is a sign that the time is coming to act."

"Why is that?"

"My waking would represent change. Under Kothite rule, the Urth has been, and will remain, static. It is how Maximillian maintains his grip on power."

"Change is a good thing, is it not?"

"It depends on your perspective, I suppose. Creative destruction may benefit the many, but not so to the few destroyed by it."

"Kerryl Moonrunner speaks of an evil greater than Koth coming if the Empire falls. That is not you, is it?"

"I should hope not. I have always done my best to work for the good of the land and its people."

Relieved, she asked, "What evil does he speak of, then?"

"That is not for me to tell. Just as it is not for me to decide if waking me is for the best. That is up to you and your companions."

"How can it not be for the best?" she exclaimed. "We have a chance to replace an evil, repressive Emperor with a noble and decent king."

"You are biased. You want me to wake because you have a connection to me, and I to you."

"Your Majesty, you cannot possibly be as bad a ruler as Maximillian."

"Call me Gawaine. You're inside my head and heart, for stars' sake. Of all people, you should use my name."

"Gawaine." The word felt awkward on her tongue. But mayhap she would grow used to it with time. "My statement stands. You cannot help but be an improvement over Maximillian."

He smiled a little. "If you promise only to use my name henceforth and never to use a title with me, I will concede the point."

She huffed. "Fine. I promise."

"Then I concede."

"Has anyone ever told you that you can be stubborn and exasperating?"

He chuckled. "My mother said so all the time."

They fell silent while she absorbed this new level of intimacy between them.

"A warning to you and your friends, Raina. The truly deadly players have yet to enter the game. Your journey will become much more dangerous and the fight much worse before it gets better. Prepare yourselves, and be careful." He sounded genuinely worried.

"I will pass your warning along to the others."

"The time is coming for me to awaken. But it is not yet. You have a little time still to find the rest of my regalia and find my body."

"I do not know how to proceed with that," she confessed. "We have no idea where to look for your gear."

He gestured at her ring. "Let that guide you."

She frowned down at it. "How?"

"Through it, you are connected to me. In the same way that you recognized it as mine, you will recognize where you must go to find the other items connected to my spirit."

As answers went, it wasn't much of one. She supposed she would have to take his words on faith and trust that when the time came, she would know where she had to go.

"You will wake soon from this dream," he said. Was that regret she heard in his voice? Or was it merely her own regret at leaving this peaceful glade and his fascinating presence that she sensed?

"Before I go, mayhap you have knowledge of something that would help us," she said hastily. "We have recovered a friend of Eben's whom Kerryl Moonrunner recently made into a were-alligator. Kendrick said that Sha'Li could fix her because of her white tribe mark, but Sha'Li doesn't know how to do it. Do you know how?"

"If I were there, I could do it myself. It is related to nature." He frowned. "If you find what Kerryl is leading you toward, Sha'Li will find the help she needs there to purge your friend's lycanthropy. It is, indeed, a skill certain Tribe of the Moon members can master."

"Why won't you tell me outright what lies before us?"

His frown deepened. "There are things that I cannot speak about even if I desperately wish to. Certain forces constrain me from saying the words aloud. The next time you visit me, perhaps we can speak more of the Accord."

The moment the last word came out of his mouth, the grove evaporated. The mist rushed in, and seconds later, she blinked awake. Whoa. That had been one forceful ejection from the dream. She sat up and looked around, disoriented.

"You all right?" Rosana asked.

The others were all awake, getting dressed and moving around the clearing and packing up camp.

"I told the others you needed extra sleep," the gypsy explained. "They agreed that you're useful to have around in a fight. Even if you won't let them kill stuff."

"Gee. Thanks." She looked down at the ring on her finger and for a moment thought it glowed a little. Sudden certainty washed over her, and she announced, "I know where we must go."

Will stood at the edge of an expanse of bog and wrinkled his nose. For the past two days, Kerryl's trail had stayed exclusively upon solid ground as they wound deep into the dark bowels of the swamp. But all of a sudden, he'd plunged into this great lake of muck before them. Even now, his trail was visible where he'd broken the film of scum covering the murky water.

"Do we really have to go that way?" he complained.

Tarryn sighed. "If only I could control my rage when I'm in alligator form, I'd be able to give you rides across it on my back."

"Thank you, no," he replied.

Sha'Li said cheerfully, "Walk it we must. In you go, land walkers." She'd been exceedingly chipper ever since her conversation with him a few nights back. "Splash not, or dwellers of the bog will you draw to us."

He did not relish the idea of fighting while mired to his thighs in mud. He didn't *relish* any of this. But Raina had been adamant that something of Gawaine's lay in this direction. And given that Kerryl's trail was leading right to it, he had to credit her assertion.

No help for it. They had to walk the bog. He hefted his

pack higher on his back and stepped in. Water filled his boots, cold and wet. It was just water. Except as he began wading through it, the consistency was more akin to syrup than water. Surprisingly, it never went deeper than about mid-thigh on him. The girls were in it nearly to the hips, but at least none of them had to swim weighed down by their wet clothing and gear.

The bog went on and on. At times the footing was firm, and at others, it felt like pudding. But always the water swirled around them, foul and filled with decay. After a time, his nose became immune to the rotting stench, which was a blessing.

"What is that?" Tarryn asked from ahead of him.

He looked past her and frowned. It looked like a wall of some kind, green and growing, stretching to the left and right in a curving arc with no end in sight. Not like a hedge, but more like a tremendous tangle of vines, brambles, tree branches, and other thorny vegetation.

Rosana made a pained sound from just behind him, and with a splash of water, he whirled to check on her. The gypsy pulled back the collar of her shirt frantically, thrashing around in the water. "It burns!"

Will's eyes snapped wide open, and he slogged over to her and stared at her collarbone. "Your green rose mark. It's glowing."

"There's magic in that wall of plants," Raina suggested. "Perhaps it's affecting your mark."

They approached the wall, and indeed, Rosana's mark glowed more and more brightly as they got close. Will didn't sense any magic in the wall, but he did sense the growing, living pulse of life running through it.

"Can you do your moving-the-vines thing on it?" Eben asked him.

Will stared at the knotted vegetation doubtfully. "I don't know. But I'll try." He reached out with his Bloodroot enhanced awareness and—

"Ouch!" Raina cried. "Something just bit me!"

The water around them erupted with movement as many small somethings attacked them.

"Told you not to splash, I did," Sha'Li said grimly. "Flesh-eater fish. Out of water we must climb and quickly, else eat us they will."

They ran for the wall as much as they could in the water, and Will frantically ordered it to make way for him. Rynn was kicking and stomping at the water, and the others followed suit. Something needle sharp stabbed Will's thigh, and he flailed, as well, all the while trying to concentrate on forming a passageway. It took a few moments and several more painful bites, but the plant life began to shift and untangle.

Tarryn grunted between kicks, "That looks like Kerryl's work. Now the question is whether he planned to let us all through or just Will."

"Mayhap if Will takes each of us through, we can all pass," Raina suggested breathlessly as she kicked and splashed.

It was worth a try. "Take my hand, Rosie." He had to turn sideways to pass through the opening without getting scratched to ribbons, but it obediently stayed open for the two of them to pass. Thankfully, no school of man-eating fish awaited them on the far side.

One by one, he walked all the members of the party through the wall. When he and Rynn passed through last, he told the wall to close, and it did so with alacrity. Raina had found a bit of solid ground and was healing the others already. He and Rynn took turns letting her trickle healing into their badly chewed calves.

Apprehensive, he looked around at more trees and more bog on this side of the wall. Enormous cypresses spread their branches wide, creating a dim and mysterious twilight world.

Inside the barrier, the standing water appeared to have given way mostly to mud. Thick and sticky, it looked like paste.

Sha'Li said low, "Movement I spy."

Will peered ahead and caught a flash of something. A pause. There it was again. Something moving up and down. They crept forward slowly, trying to minimize the sucking sound of their boots pulling free of the muck.

Without warning, Sha'Li grunted in what sounded like pain. She took a step back. Tarryn reached a hand past her and yanked it back as if she'd touched a hot kettle, as well.

"Look at that," Eben breathed.

Will looked where the jann was pointing off to the right of the two scouts and frowned. "It's a rock. Yes, that's weird in the middle of a swamp."

"It's *glowing*," Eben muttered.

Will stared at the upthrusting chunk of some light-colored stone carefully. "No, it isn't. It's just a rock."

"And there's another one." Eben pointed off to his left. "And another. They seem to be part of a large circle."

"Like a ritual circle?" Raina asked. "I do not see one."

"No," Rynn replied. "It would be an elemental circle, wouldn't it, Eben?"

"Yes. Exactly," the jann replied. "This one forms an energy barrier."

Will asked, "Any idea how we're supposed to cross it?"

Frowning, the jann slogged over to the nearest stone. He touched it and yanked back his hand, as well, grimacing. "Cursed water magic," Eben mumbled.

Will watched as his friend slogged to the next stone and touched it cautiously. "Ahh. Better. Earth energy imbues this stone."

"That's great," Will replied. "But can you get us past it?"

Eben closed his eyes. The jann's caramel-colored skin began to swirl with varying shades of earth tones. It took a while, but Eben eventually lifted his hands away from the stone, his face gray. Literally.

"Try now," he told Sha'Li.

"Willing to kill me are you, and not the others to risk?" this lizardman girl groused. "See I do, how this goes."

Harrumphing, she took a step forward and encountered no magical resistance.

The party continued onward. Without warning, a dozen figures raced out of the trees toward them as if unimpeded by the thick mud all but gluing him and his friends in place.

"Boglins," Sha'Li announced in disgust. "Mud-dwelling cousins of goblins." Her claws slid out to full extension, however, so Will gathered these bog creatures could still be dangerous.

The boglins used crude weapons ranging from rusty short swords to what looked like leg bones of some large animal to attack. They screamed and howled and were incredibly annoying as they darted in and out among the party, seemingly able to run along the surface of the mud without sinking down into it. They didn't pose any great threat as long as the group was vigilant and nobody took a surprise blow from one of them. Will easily caught all the weapon swings of his attackers with his staff, deflecting them effortlessly.

He took the offensive and swung at a few of the creatures with his staff, sending them flying. They were lighter than they looked. Most of the creatures stayed between the party and that up-and-down movement he'd seen earlier. It was almost as if they defended whatever he'd glimpsed.

Rynn said, "Let us discover what they guard. Perhaps it is what Kerryl wished for us to find."

It was awkward wading forward as a tight little group, all the while fighting off the rather maddening boglins. But step by step, they moved deeper into the mudflat. The cypresses overhead grew so thick that barely any light got through, which might have explained the boglins' large, protruding eyes.

"What on Urth?" Raina exclaimed.

Will looked up from the boglin he'd just sent sailing a dozen feet away to land with a plop in the mud. "Is that a horse?" He'd seen a few of the rare creatures in his life, but not many.

"No," Rynn breathed in what sounded like amazement. "It is a unicorn."

"His steed!" Raina exclaimed. "Cerebus!"

He had no idea what she was talking about and no time to ask, for three of the pesky boglins rushed him just then, screeching. He had to move smartly with his staff to block all of them as they swung their motley weapons at him.

Tarryn grunted in between dodging wild blows, "I thought unicorns were white. That one looks made of mud."

Will finally got another break in the sporadic fighting to glance over at the creature. Its head hung low, and it was mired past its belly in the mud. Now that Rynn mentioned it, a long, spiraling horn grew from the middle of its forehead. Its tip rested in the mud.

They moved a little closer, swatting away boglins, and Will made out a pair of great heavy ropes around the creature's neck and stretching to nearby trees. A pair of trees on either side of the beast behind it bore ropes that disappeared down into the mud. The unicorn's hind legs must have been bound, as well.

As they neared the small area where the creature was captive, it jerked its head up and snorted fiercely, nostrils flaring and eyes wild. It was hard to tell how tall it would stand on dry land, but it looked large and powerful.

"Anyone have experience with crazed unicorns?" Rynn asked dryly.

"I may have something that will calm it," Raina said. She started to move forward, but another wave of boglins came screaming out of the shadows just then, perhaps as many as two dozen.

One thing Will's father said to him over and over as a lad: quantity would beat quality every time on the field of battle if the numbers were skewed enough. He began to see what Ty had meant. He was hard-pressed to keep the creatures off him and even took a few nicks and bruises in the wave of attacks.

And then, out of nowhere, a blast of magic sent a half dozen of the creatures flying. What the—

"Behind us!" Rosana cried.

Three hooded beings in long cloaks glided *over* the mud toward them, coming fast. All that was visible of the people within were glowing hands. Will recognized the mages from the cave by the Estarran Sea. *Not* good.

"Oh no," Raina groaned. She began casting magic shields and got one up on Eben, Rynn, and Will before magic spells started flying in toward them. As if fighting boglins hadn't been hard enough in the mud, now they had to dodge magic spells with their feet all but stuck in place. It was a nightmare. Will fired a damaging spell back at the nearest hooded figure, which gave the nearest mage momentary pause. And then all three mages unleashed a barrage of magic at him.

Between his own protection spells and Raina casting frantic shielding spells on him, Will managed to stay alive for the first barrage. But then a second barrage of incoming bolts of magical energy smashed into his crumbling defenses.

The unicorn screamed behind him, and he gathered that a misfired bolt had caught the beast by accident.

"Don't let it die!" Rynn shouted at Raina as he dived in front of Will to take a particularly bright bolt of magic in the chest. The paxan fell to the ground, facedown in the mud, and started to sink into it.

"Raina!" Will shouted over the din. "Life Rynn!"

Eben was swinging his sword furiously at a new wave of boglins, and Sha'Li had worked her way around behind one of the mages and waylaid him or her as he looked on. But then the other mages spotted her and turned to spell her down viciously.

This fight had gone from annoying to deadly in the blink of an eye.

A bestial roar erupted, but Will could not tell from which direction because of the echoes under the trees and the overall din of combat. But then a huge, hairy form bounded through the mud, plowing through it toward the mages. Its shoulder caught Will a glancing blow as it charged past, knocking him down. He scrambled frantically to regain his footing and swore as he realized he'd lost his staff. He plunged his arm down into the mud, searching for it.

A boglin leaped at him, and left-handed, Will leaned over to one side, buried to the shoulder in the cursed mud, and cast a bolt of force damage, miraculously managing to hit the boglin. It sizzled as it fell over, dead.

"Will!" Raina cried in outrage.

Oh, she could get over it. The creature would have beheaded him before he found his cursed staff. He swore as another boglin appeared to take the place of the fallen one. Still no sign of his staff. *Quantity over quality.* He was going to *die* for lack of a stick to block the attacks of these monsters. And who knew if he'd be able to resurrect or not?

But then a bolt of curse magic flew past him, knocking over the boglin who was almost upon him. "Relax, Raina," Rosana said behind him. "It was a sleep spell."

He fished around frantically, and his foot hit something hard. He reached down.

There it was. His hand felt hard wood, pole shaped. He grasped the staff firmly and pulled it free of the mud. He wiped it quickly, but it did little good. The weapon was slippery and hard to hang on to, covered in mud.

That had been Kendrick in boar form who knocked him down. Where had *he* come from? Was Kerryl Moonrunner nearby, then? The hooded mages turned as one as Kendrick roared and charged them. Will took the opportunity to throw a substantial bolt of force damage at the back of the one he'd hit before. The mage staggered, went down. And the hood of the dark cloak fell to one side. Long, dark hair spilled out. A woman, then.

"Marikeen!" Eben shouted, lunging forward toward her with a mighty, slapping splash of mud. A brace of boglins jumped on her prone body as Will looked on in horror. He hadn't known it was Eben's sister!

And then another sound came from the trees. Growling. Snapping jaws. Snarling. That sounded like . . .

Oh, demons below, the Imperial hounds. They'd found Eben.

"Cut me loose!" Tarryn demanded. "I can help you. I can fight!"

"You'll turn," Rosana argued behind Will while he pummeled yet more boglins. Would these creatures never quit coming?

"Do we have a choice?" Tarryn asked in a terrible voice. "We'll all die if the odds are not evened and soon. Those hounds will kill us all if yon mages do not do the job first."

She had a point.

And then the kindari spoke again, her voice taking on a harsh quality. "I'm going to turn, anyway. You might as well let me help you. Point me at the hounds, and stay behind me. Away from my mou—"

Those were the last words she uttered.

Will looked around in alarm and leaped out of the way as a gigantic alligator, easily twenty feet long, surged toward him. He lost his balance, but Eben caught him under the armpits and hauled him upright, barely out of the charging were-alligator's path. The beast half ran, half swam through the mire, racing at unbelievable speed toward the Imperial hounds.

One of the hounds went down, yelping and flailing. It disappeared under the mud as Tarryn took it down in a death roll. There were a few flashes of muddy fur and flailing limbs twisted up with dark, leathery scales, and then the hound was no more.

Something rushed out of the trees at Will, and he was horrified to spot a glowing red eye. The other were-rat, Phillipe. Holder of the change water they needed to trade to Goldeneye for Rosana's cure. Grimly, Will turned to face him. The creature was unbelievably fast, leaping in on the attack and retreating before Will could strike him with his staff. Over and over, the rat darted in and out. But Krugar had taught him patience and a few tricks about learning an opponent's patterns and using them against him.

Out of the corner of his eye, Will saw the rest of the hounds dance away from the spot where Tarryn had attacked, sensing the threat. But they, too, stood to their bellies in the muck and were hampered in their movements.

Phillipe darted in again, feinting right and spinning away to the left. Behind him, Will glimpsed Marikeen and her friends facing off against the Imperial hounds. With the mages above the surface chucking magic at the Imperial hounds and Tarryn snapping at them from below, it was a fairly even fight. Mud flew everywhere as Will caught glimpses of a great reptilian tail sweeping the hounds' legs out from under them and the huge, flat head swinging from side to side, flashing long rows of enormous teeth. He could hear the snap of her mighty jaws from where he stood.

Phillipe came at him again, feinting to the right and spinning left again. Will made a point of delaying his response a shade, of making it look as if he'd barely managed to fend off the attack. *Do that one more time, you long-toothed rodent.*

One of the hounds broke off from the others, lifted its head, and seemed to catch Eben's scent, for his enraged stare zeroed in on the jann, and the beast charged. Rynn braced himself, his stance making it clear the hound would have to go through him to get to Eben.

The great beast bowled right through Rynn, lifting the muscular paxan into the air and tossing him aside like Will had been tossing aside boglins. The beast's great jaws swung toward Eben. And then it stopped. Turned.

Will glanced in the direction the beast stared. One of the mages had lowered her hood. Marikeen. The hound in front of Eben charged her while the other hounds went into a frenzy.

He nearly did miss catching Phillipe's feint and spin this time. *Focus, Will.*

The hounds seemed to have gone into some sort of a blood fury where they were impervious or possibly even immune to most of the magics the three mages threw at them. The barrage of magic was amazing, and in moments the air took on an odor of sizzled fur and singed wool.

Phillipe lunged at him one more time. Will dodged the initial attack and stepped left with blinding speed to catch Phillipe in the spin, striking a vicious blow across his foe's midsection with the tip of his staff. The rat doubled over, the wind knocked out of him. Will jammed the tip with all his strength into the base of the rat's skull. Whether the blow itself or the magic with it killed the were-rat, Will didn't much care. He scooped the pouch off the rat's corpse and threw the shoulder strap over his head.

He straightened just in time to see Kendrick, in boar form, leap at the mages and hounds. "No!" Will yelled at him. "They'll kill you—" It was too late; the great bristled sides and tusked snout of the were-boar joined the tumbling, snapping tangle of hounds and mages.

"Where's their hunter?" Raina called.

Will looked around frantically, swatting away a pair of boglins, as well. The blind man had to be nearby. The hounds would never leave him, and he would never leave them.

A tall figure slipped through the trees to their right, and Tarryn cried out, "That's Kerryl!"

Cripes. How many more of their enemies were going to take the field against them? A series of magic flashes through the trees suggested that Kerryl had engaged the hunter. Will had no idea who would come out the winner in such a contest.

The mages disengaged momentarily from the attacking hounds and, as one, winked out of visible existence. Whether they'd gone into spirit forms or cast invisibility spells upon themselves, he could not tell.

But the Imperial hounds went mad. They rushed off through the trees, no doubt chasing their quarry by smell. Kendrick charged after them, disappearing from sight. Relative quiet fell around them. A few boglins yipped in the trees.

E ben searched frantically for any sign of his sister, but she and her companions were *gone.* Marikeen had saved his life by taking off her magical hood and letting the hounds catch her scent. *Why* had she done that? He would much rather have the hounds after him than her!

Where was Kerryl? He wouldn't leave all of his were-creatures behind and flee like a coward, would he?

Eben took off toward where Tarryn had spotted Kerryl chasing after the Imperial hunter. If he could take them both down, two of his three most pressing problems would be solved. The hounds would leave off tracking him and his friends, and Kerryl's hold over Kendrick would be broken. Then all he had to do was find Marikeen and talk some sense into her.

He spied a pair of humanoid figures grappling ahead of him, and he slowed. But then a black shape suddenly loomed beside him, startling him badly. He recognized Sha'Li.

"Come away," Sha'Li breathed. "Back to the others we must go."

"Not yet. I have business with both of those men."

"Kill Kerryl you must not," she whispered urgently.

"Kill that bastard I will," he bit out.

She opened her mouth to argue further, but he was having none of it. He moved forward toward the fighting men, his sword in one hand, battle mace in the other. Both men looked the worse for wear and fought hand to hand, covered in blood and mud.

As he drew near, Kerryl got in a vicious punch to the blind hunter's jaw, spinning the fellow around and toppling him like a falling tree. Kerryl staggered back, a dagger sticking out of his side. The weapon looked small, and its angle did not point its blade at any vital organs. Nonetheless, Kerryl clasped the blade in pain. Perfect. One foe down and the other badly injured and distracted. He charged forward, coming in from behind Kerryl to take the nature guardian by surprise.

He raised his sword and was a bare instant from being in range when a voice rang out from the darkness, "Kerryl! Behind you!"

The nature guardian spun, throwing up his arm, and took

the edge of Eben's blade on the Band of Beasts. Except his blade did no damage to the leather gauntlet. Kerryl pulled the dagger out of his own side and swung it with his off hand, nearly gutting Eben.

But Eben managed to halt his forward momentum just in time to avoid running himself onto the dagger. Kerryl leaped forward, grabbing Eben's wrists and wrestling the weapons away from them both. Given that the nature guardian used no magic, Eben could only assume that Kerryl had depleted all his magic against the hunter. Thank the stars.

Although Kerryl was strong, Eben was a tiny bit stronger. Slowly but surely, he pulled his arms back in to his sides and began twisting his wrists free by slow degrees. He felt Kerryl's grip begin to weaken.

"Cease chasing me, boy," Kerryl grunted.

"Never. You took Kendrick and changed him. I'll kill you for that." Buoyed by his anger, he gave a mighty wrench, and his sword arm broke free of Kerryl's grasp. He lifted the weapon and took a mighty downward blow, chopping down toward the nature guardian's exposed neck with all the force he could muster.

His blade impacted something hard and sharp, sliding along its length and passing harmlessly by Kerryl's neck to catch at the base of the blade. He followed the short blade with his shocked stare, finding a fist, and beyond, a black-scaled face and anguished eyes.

Furious, he tore the mace out of Kerryl's failing grasp and swung it, a truncated blow given the proximity of Kerryl's body, but again, Sha'Li's other claw flashed out to deflect the blow.

Kerryl fell to his knees between them, breathing heavily, like a beast of burden that had been run to exhaustion and beyond.

Eben stared, stunned, at the lizardman girl. What was she *doing*?

Kerryl rocked back onto his heels, away from the weapons and claws locked over his head. He staggered to his feet while Eben and Sha'Li's weapons strained against one another. Without breaking his horrified stare at Sha'Li, Eben sensed Kerryl taking a step backward. Another step.

The nature guardian turned and fled into the night.

Sha'Li's claws retracted with a metallic slither into her fists, and Eben's weapons fell to his sides. He watched in numb disbelief as she turned without a word and disappeared into the trees.

They'd followed Kerryl and Kendrick for *weeks*. Kendrick himself had told them he was enslaved to Kerryl. Sha'Li knew Eben's fondest wish in life was to free his friend and brother, Kendrick, and she'd foiled him. She'd chosen that filthy, mad nature guardian over him. Over their friendship. Over her admiration for Kendrick, an innocent in all of this.

Eben could only draw one conclusion. She'd betrayed him. She'd betrayed them all.

W ill scowled as Rynn announced grimly, "Have a care. Tarryn is still out here somewhere in her bestial form. She will kill us as readily as she took down that hound."

"Where is it?" Raina asked. "The hound she killed. I must try to save it."

Will answered, "You will never find it. Tarryn could have dragged it hundreds of feet from here by now. Let the beast resurrect if it can." And good riddance it was.

Raina opened her mouth to protest, but the unicorn whinnied in alarm just then. "Help me cut the unicorn loose," she cried, wading urgently toward the beast.

It yanked violently against the ropes, snorting and shaking its head, in what looked like fury and panic. The creature was huge, its muscular back level with Will's nose. And it looked violent.

Raina held up her right hand, presumably showing the beast the ring upon her finger. Although if the ring was there, it was as covered in mud as the rest of her. But the unicorn stilled, breathing hard. Its great, brown eyes rolled, showing the whites, and its nostrils flared, red inside. But the trembling creature let Raina approach. Cautiously, she stroked its shoulder. It snorted under her touch, but it let her slide her hand to one of the thick ropes around its neck. Using the herb dagger from her belt, she commenced sawing at the heavy hemp.

"Let me do that," Rynn said. "It'll take you a week using that tiny thing." He scooped up one of the discarded short swords from the downed boglins and used its toothed edge to saw through the rope.

In the middle of the laborious sawing process, Eben returned to the clearing. He looked as if he'd seen a ghost. "You okay?" Will asked as he cautiously sawed at a rope around one of the unicorn's front legs.

Eben made a noncommittal sound.

"What of Kerryl and the hunter?"

"Kerryl dropped the hunter—" Raina lurched, and he added hastily, "But he did not kill the guy. As for Kerryl . . ." Eben paused, and then added shortly, "He got away."

"Where's Sha'Li?" Raina asked the jann.

"No idea."

"Should we go look for her?" Rosana chimed in.

"No!"

Will looked up, surprised at the sharpness of Eben's reply.

His jaw clenched, Eben went to work with his sword on the second rope on the other side of the unicorn's neck. The creature seemed to understand that they helped it and stayed still. Which was a boon. Will had never imagined that horses were this big or this intimidating.

"Can you talk to it?" Rosana asked him.

Will looked at her, surprised. "Me?"

"You have a connection to nature."

He tried to cast his mind outward, to touch the thoughts of the beast in front of him. Nothing. His talent lay in plant-based life, not animals.

Raina laid her hand on the unicorn's side and spoke

soothingly to it. "I'm going to find the rope around your hind leg now. Easy, Cerebus."

The unicorn's ears flicked back toward her as if he recognized his name.

"Pass me a sword, Rynn." Raina stuck her free hand out.

The paxan handed her the weapon, and she guided the blade below the muck to saw at unseen rope. Cerebus tossed his head from time to time, but he stood still while she went around to his far haunch and repeated the procedure on his other leg.

Will had been certain the beast would bolt the minute the last rope was freed, but strangely, it did not. Instead, it reached around and nudged Raina hard in the shoulder with its nose, nearly knocking her over.

"Why doesn't it teleport away from here to safety?" Rynn asked no one in particular.

Raina laid her hand on the beast's great, muscular neck. "Oh. Oh! I can hear him. The mud. It's magical. Keeps him from leaving. We must get it off of him."

"Where?" Will demanded. They were all covered in the sticky, light brown stuff from head to foot.

"There was clear water outside the thorn wall," Rosana offered.

"Can you lead it there?" he asked Raina.

She stared at nothing for a moment and then said, "He will come with us."

They slogged back to the tangled wall without incident. For the moment, the boglins were hanging back and merely shouting invective from the trees in high-pitched voices. The unicorn was much larger than Will, so when he asked the vines to move aside for them, Will specifically asked for a very large opening.

They stepped through the thorn barrier. He'd never thought to be so glad to see plain, old swamp. Will closed the gap in the wall and joined the others in scooping up handfuls of water and rinsing themselves off. Hopefully, the boglins would remain trapped on the other side.

They headed for a patch of high ground. The unicorn stood fully a tall as Will, its shoulders and hindquarters broad and wrapped in muscle. The creature's neck arched proudly, but this was no dainty creature of hearth tales. This steed looked like it could defend itself violently or attack as necessary.

Raina poured her waterskin over the unicorn's back. He shivered and stamped his hooves in response. A patch of white horsehair plastered to dark skin became visible. The unicorn threw his head, sending mud from his mane flying everywhere.

There was no way to avoid the sheets of flying mud. Filthy, Will and the others refilled their waterskins and poured them over the unicorn again and again. It was a laborious process, for the mud was stubborn, and the surface area in need of cleaning large.

They had most of the unicorn's left side cleaned off and had moved around to work on the creature's right side when, without warning, a boglin ran up out of the darkness and flung a bucketful of mud at the unicorn's clean side, splashing it all over the gleaming white hide, and then darted away into the shadows.

"Are you kidding me?" Will groused.

Rynn actually laughed. Will might have found it funny were he not more than a little intimidated by the stomping hooves and tossing head of the skittish equine.

"All right," Rynn said in amusement. "Everyone but the healers take up defensive positions around the horse while Raina and Rosana keep giving Cerebus his bath."

It was infuriating how the boglins timed their attacks to throw buckets of mud at both unicorn and defenders just when one or the other managed to get mostly clean. They came in waves that made keeping them back from the partially washed unicorn nigh impossible.

Somewhere in the seemingly fruitless process, Tarryn waded—on two legs—out of the shadows toward them.

"Good to see you," Eben said sincerely. "We were worried about you."

548 • CINDY DEES AND BILL FLIPPIN

Tarryn nodded but said nothing. Will wasn't sure what he would say if he'd recently been a gigantic alligator who attacked and ate everything in sight.

The next wave of boglins approached, buckets in hand. The first one tossed an arc of mud at Tarryn, catching her full in the chest.

"What the—" the kindari yelled. She growled, and Will was alarmed to see her left eye glowing scarlet as she looked around angrily. The boglins, en masse, dropped their buckets, squeaked in terror, and fled for their lives.

"Grab their buckets," Rosana suggested.

After Tarryn's return, the bathing of the unicorn went quickly. They rinsed out a half dozen of the boglins' buckets, and with Tarryn glaring watchfully into the swamp, the others finished cleaning the great creature.

Will stood back with the others to admire their work. "So. That's what a unicorn looks like, does it?"

The creature bobbed its head, but in rather more friendly a fashion, he thought, than before. Then it surprised him by stepping up to Raina and laying its nose on her shoulder as if using her for a headrest.

She tilted her head, listening. "He's grateful for his release and wishes to thank us. Is there anything he can do for us?"

Rosana spoke wistfully. "If only the legends were true that unicorns can fly people to the spirit realm. I would go there and bring back the spirits of the alligator speaker's children."

Raina frowned. "He says he can do that. Is that what you wish?"

Rosana's jaw fell open. "Will you come with me, Raina?"

The White Heart healer listened again. "He said it is not my destiny. But it is yours."

"How do I do this?" Rosana asked eagerly.

"Hold on just a minute," Will interrupted. "You're not going anywhere. Not without me. And going to the spirit realm is far too dangerous for any of us to attempt."

"How come?" the gypsy retorted. "You and Raina walked into the dream realm."

"As did Cicero and Sha'Li, and they both died," Will declared. "Sha'Li and Cicero are both accomplished warriors." He left it unsaid that she was anything but.

Rosana looked deflated. Thank the heavens he'd talked her out of her suicidal idea.

"I don't know about the rest of you," Raina declared, "but I'm hungry."

Will was famished. He hadn't thrown that much magic in a long time. Raina held a short consultation with the unicorn, who declared it safe for them to eat and rest. Apparently, now that he was free of the magical mud, his full powers were restored. He assured them that no boglin could throw mud on him again, nor that any threat would bother them this night.

Raina looked around at the trees and shadows looming menacingly around them. "Shouldn't Sha'Li have joined us by now?"

"She's fine," Eben snapped.

Will frowned. Usually those two were the best of chums. What was up with Eben's shortness? "Everything okay, Eben?"

The jann scowled. "Leave it alone. I don't want to talk about it."

They pitched camp right there in the middle of the swamp, crowded onto the only semidry piece of land in sight. Maybe it was pure exhaustion, or maybe it was the gleaming white stallion standing protectively nearby, but Will fell quickly into a deep and restful slumber.

Rosana pretended to sleep along with the others until she was sure she was the only one left awake. As quietly as she could, she crept around the sluggish embers of the fire and approached the unicorn. Stars, he was beautiful.

She whispered to him, "I hope you can understand me and know what I want. If there is a way, any way, to rescue those children, I must try. Can you help me?"

She could swear the unicorn nodded. "What do I do?" she asked.

The creature stepped lightly around the clearing to where Will and Raina slumbered. It reached down with its nose and touched the ground between the two.

"You want me to sit there?" she whispered, confused.

The unicorn put its nose on her shoulder and pushed down on it. Hard. All right, then. She sank down to the ground. Cerebus put his great face down close to hers and very deliberately closed his eyes. In a moment he opened them again expectantly. Did he want her merely to close her eyes or actually go to sleep? She would start with the first and see what happened.

She closed her eyes and immediately felt an odd sensation of falling. Screwing her eyes tightly shut, she put her hands on the ground to catch herself, except there was no ground. She looked around, and the swamp was gone. Everyone and everything was gone. She was . . . nowhere.

A voice entered her mind, startling her. "Do you hear me?" It did not sound human, that voice, and yet it was comfortable to her ears. Or maybe it bypassed her ears entirely. She could not tell.

"Cerebus?" she asked.

"Aye. Find the boy with the tree spirit and hang on to him tightly. He is your anchor to the mortal plane. His roots grow deep into the earth, and he will not tear free if you pull at him, even very hard. Find the white healer, as well. Her spirit magics are great, and you will have need of them where you go."

She reached out with her mind and took hold of Will's and Raina's hands. Whether she did it in physical fact or merely as a spiritual representation of the connection, she could not tell.

Without warning, another place took shape around her. It was not so different from the swamp in that it was dark and shadowed, with a feeling of eyes watching her. What was this place?

"You wished to go to the spirit realm to find lost children, did you not?" Cerebus said.

"Where is this?"

"Where lost souls go."

"Is it the Void?" She vividly recalled the brief glimpse she'd had of it when last spring's ritual to repair her spirit had gone awry in the Heart. It had been darker and bleaker even than this place.

"Nay. This is . . . in between. The spirit guide will be along soon to collect them and take them into the Void."

She looked around and realized with a start that five children of varying ages were huddled together not far from her. Even as she looked on, a man dressed all in white and carrying a lantern came into sight over a gentle rise ahead of her.

The high matriarch said in each Heartstone initiation ceremony that a spirit guide appeared as a man with a lantern and led away spirits that had passed on permanently. "No!" she shouted, rushing forward to join the children and stand between them and the guide.

"You have no business here," the guide said gently. "Move aside that I may take them to their rest."

"No!" Rosana declared stoutly. She was, without question, the least skilled combatant in their adventuring party, save Raina. But she would die fighting before she let this man take away children who'd barely had a chance to live and died through no fault of their own.

"If you try to stop me, I will have to call spirit warriors."

Oh, dear. She glanced around and spied a reasonably large boulder not far away in this strange landscape. She spoke to the eldest child, a girl of maybe ten summers. "Take your brothers and sisters and hide over there. And be prepared to run if I tell you to."

"That's what Papa said," the little girl replied.

"I'm here to take you back to your papa. He's alive and misses you very much."

"And Mama?" the girl asked eagerly.

"I do not know. Go. Hurry."

Rosana turned and was dismayed to see that the guide had

been joined by two large men dressed all in white, but wielding long swords in each hand. She probably ought to be scared out of her mind, but she had no time for it. Those children were depending on her. Quickly she reviewed the lessons Will had given her over the months about using her magic to fight. Wait until her foes were close enough to hit with reasonable certainty. Throw one low- to medium-level spell to test whether her foe had up some sort of magical shield. Throw subsequent spells in pairs in quick succession.

She did not know if her magics would even affect these spirit warriors. Either way, she had to try. The pair approached, not even bothering to split wide and flank her. They must have realized that she stood no chance against them.

The spirit guide and his warriors drew near enough for her to hit. She led with a sleep spell, which hit the right-hand swordsman. *Nothing.* Not even a flash to indicate that he'd had a shield up. She tried another curse spell, this time bigger. *Still nothing.* They were completely immune to her curse magic, which was her only effective combat magic. What help had it been to reach for Raina's spirit, then, if this flavor of magic had no effect at all in this place?

Her desperation grew into panic. She *had* to focus. *Had* to find a way to save the children cowering behind her. Every cell in her body screamed at her to stop these beings advancing upon her.

Onward they came, inexorably walking closer, swords at the ready. Frantically, she tried spirit magic on them. But if it did anything at all, it strengthened the warriors. They were almost on her now.

Panic made her wild, and she fired several spells in quick succession at the trio until she had to pause and catch her breath. They reached her. She braced for one of those gleaming swords to cut her in half, but instead, the warrior before her merely took her by the shoulders and set her aside. They continued walking calmly toward the children.

"No!" she screamed. "You shall not have them!" Too furious and panicked to think, she reached deep within her spirit, gathered magic, and threw it at the spirit warriors' backs without even incanting a spell.

A great, black gout of smoke went up, and the warrior pitched forward, falling onto his face. Rosana stared, stunned. What had she just done? And how? She tried again, throwing more of the black, writhing magic at the guide this time. Down he went.

The third warrior rushed her, sword raised. He took a running swing that she barely managed to duck in time to avoid being decapitated. She whirled around, dismayed to see that he was already almost upon her again. He reached out to gather her against his armored chest, to pin her arms and prevent her from casting. And then to crush the life out of her . . .

His plan was all there in his eyes for her to read, blank and staring as they were.

Desperate, she cast yet another blast of the strange magic that had come to her, and the warrior staggered. Fell a step back. She cast again. And again. Her spirit felt empty, drained, and that was when she called upon the link to Raina. It hadn't been to fuel her magic that the unicorn had intended. The link was meant to heal her.

The warrior staggered, and she threw one last blast of magic at him. He toppled over, sprawled on his back.

Frowning, she looked at her hand. What manner of magic was this? She'd never seen or felt the like. Its vibrations were unlike any magic she'd experienced before. And as part of her Heart testing to determine her talents, she'd been exposed to just about every flavor of magic known.

She released the energy without casting it, and it drifted away from her fingertips harmlessly. She rushed over to the children, cowering behind the rock. "Are you all right?" she asked.

They stared up at her with big, wide eyes, frightened. *Of her?* "I won't hurt you. I promise. I'm here to take you home—" she started.

"Impressive," a voice intoned behind her. She whirled

around, and this time the dark magic came to her hand instantly. Yet another being stood a little way away, staring down at the smoking bodies of the warriors and the guide.

Rosana could not tell if this person was male or female, humanoid or entirely alien. His/her features shifted and changed continuously. This person's garments were also immaculately white, but he/she wore in addition a long cloak lined in silver so shining bright it was hard to look at. "Who are you?" she demanded. "What are you?"

"I am an exemplar. These spirits work for me. At least they did until you destroyed them with your death magics."

"My . . . what?"

"Death magic."

"That does not exist. It is a myth told of times long ago when strange magics existed."

"And yet, you summoned it to your hand, and it came."

Rosana stared at her glowing fist. There was no denying that this was unlike any magic she'd ever felt.

"I have heard of you, healer. That you exist once more. You are . . . unique." A thoughtful pause. "I shall let you live."

"I don't care about my life. But I want these children sent back to the material plane," Rosana demanded. "They deserve a chance at a full and long life." She raised her hand menacingly. "Or mayhap we should find out what these strange magics of mine do to one such as you."

"Do not threaten me, child," the exemplar said mildly. Mildly enough that she was inclined to believe that he/she did not bluff. Rosana could not hurt this creature. But then the being intoned in a long-suffering voice, "Very well."

"Very well what?" she challenged.

"You may take them back if you will leave this place and stop attacking us. Find a light and lead them to it. But do not try to pass through it yourself, caster of death."

And with that, the exemplar vanished.

What did he mean by that? Do not try to pass through it herself? *Why not?* She collected the children and set out walking. Just over the next rise, she spotted a bright light shining in the valley below. She led the children to it and, starting with the youngest, showed them how to touch the light and let it take them back home to new bodies.

The eldest daughter went last. She paused before touching the light to mouth the words, "Thank you," before she was swept into the light and disappeared into a new life.

The wave of aggressive, motherly protectiveness passed, and suddenly Rosana felt utterly drained. Alone. Exhausted. And with no idea how to get back home. *Now what? Was she stuck here forever? Had she traded her eternal life for those of the children? While she would have loved to have a future with Will, she was all right with having sacrificed herself to save five young souls.*

As peace descended over her, Cerebus's voice asked inside her head, "Are you finished here?"

"Thank the Lady, you came for me!" she cried.

"Rather, thank the Lady's son," the unicorn replied.

Now what did that mean? "How do I get home?"

"Find the one you love. He is your anchor to that other reality. Follow the link."

She wasn't sure she knew how to do that, but she closed her eyes and focused on her feelings for Will. She opened her eyes. *And was still in the Shadowed Land.* "It didn't work!" she cried out to Cerebus. Except he didn't answer her this time.

Terrified, she tried again. *Her link to Will.* She concentrated on the empty space within her where she'd given a piece of her spirit to Will. She filled it with her feelings for him. Her . . . *love.* Huh. She'd fallen in love with the big, stubborn, awkward young man. With all his big ambitions and grand ideas, and suspicion and irascibility . . . and tenderness and compassion that he did not like to admit to.

The more she thought about how she felt about him and all the reasons why she loved him, the closer she felt to him. Of course he was her anchor. He would always look out for her, always be there for her, always bring her home. And with that thought, she blinked open her eyes.

Will was standing over her, looking as furious as she'd ever seen him. "Am I here? Am I really back?" she asked him.

"What did you do?" he asked in a flat tone that was either him so scared he could hardly speak or so angry he was restraining himself from doing violence.

"I, uhh, rescued the spirits of the alligator speaker's children. Cerebus helped me do it."

That caused Will to look over at the unicorn, who did in fact look exhausted, head low and hide slightly gray in cast.

Frowning, he held a hand down to her and lifted her into his arms. "Don't *ever* pull a stunt like that again without telling me first," he said in a ravaged voice.

"I did not mean to frighten you."

"What would I do if I lost you?" he ground out.

She mumbled against his chest, "I love you, too." She half hoped he didn't hear her. But his arms tightened in a crushing grip until she could barely breathe. He'd heard her.

Eventually, he asked, "Did you save them?"

"I did."

"What was the spirit realm like? Was it all shiny and peaceful like they say?"

"On the contrary. It was dark and menacing and very frightening. But I think Cerebus took me to the in-between place where spirits pass through to the Void."

"The Shadowed Land?"

She nodded.

"It is said that once the shadows touch you, you're never the same. Aurelius told me he thought that might be why Leland didn't resurrect this last time. The time before that he died, Raina talked his spirit into coming back from the Shadowed Land. But Leland never shook free of its hold." His arms tightened around her in concern.

"I am free of it." *She hoped.*

She waited until Will had stacked more wood upon the fire, crawled into his own bedroll, and was snoring lightly to pull her hand out from under her blanket. She concentrated on remembering the feel of that twisting, powerful magic and summoned it.

In the golden glow of the firelight she looked down at her fingers. And the magic writhing restlessly upon them was black.

CHAPTER
34

Gunther had well and truly had it with being dragged hither and yon, up and down mountainsides. He was sorry he ever found that stupid armor. Should've left it inside that mine. Now he was haring off even deeper into the mountains with a bunch of strangers and that statue.

The notion of being alive, but trapped forever, inside a hunk of metal was by far the most horrible fate he could ever imagine. Nope, when he died, he wanted to do it in his own bed with his back teeth awash in the best ale money could buy.

They topped the pass into the Rignhall Valley according to Olivar, their ogre-kin guide. Not a bad sort, Olivar, if a person could look past his vaguely monstrous appearance.

Gunther's irritation faded into wonder at the city suddenly sprawling at his feet. *Rignhall*. The City of Giants. Where canals were as plentiful as streets, and broad, flat-bottomed boats were used as often as one's feet for transportation.

They started into the city. All the roads were paved, and not just in crude cobbles. Nay, these paving stones were smooth and flat, their seams so expertly joined as to be nearly invisible. Grand stone buildings of ancient design towered above the broad canals, their workmanship every bit as fine as the road's. The structures had a shockingly delicate and airy feel to them. He allowed reluctantly that even the greatest dwarven carvers had never achieved such exquisite artistry in stone.

In between the great stone edifices, common structures

huddled, squat and ugly by comparison. The city sprawled in every direction, filling the entire valley. A distant roar of great waterfalls rumbled below the workaday din of the city, and a hint of mist in the air kissed his skin. They'd passed a great, rushing fall of water on their way through the pass, its top obscured in a rainbow cloud of the mist.

They walked until he judged they'd reached the center of the city. There, he stopped in amazement as he emerged into a square many times larger than any he'd ever seen before. The center of the open space was filled by a gigantic, symmetrical bowl, dipping below the level of the pavement. It was lined by some sort of metal cladding, and was perhaps three-quarters full of clear water. Smelled like rain, it did. The others in his party seemed similarly awestruck.

A local dwarf they'd passed on the road into Rignhall had said to follow the main road straight as an arrow through the city until it crossed the Rigngata. And there they would find the way to the Great Storm Forge.

Standing in the square now, he could imagine giants fashioning this great copper bowl. He asked a kelnor passing by if this huge basin was the Rigngata and got a hearty laugh from the fellow in response. "Gor, nay! This be a mere rain basin. The Rigngata be that way."

Frowning, Gunther stumped across the square with the others and continued onward. The place was farking huge. Fitting for giants.

They walked past several more canals and great stone halls, and abruptly, the city stopped at the banks of a massive lake. The only reason he could see across it was because of the height of the majestic mountains on the far shore. A narrow ribbon of stone extended right out across the lake, no more than a foot's height above the water. It appeared to float there, suspended delicately upon the surface. Whoever heard of stone floating on water?

Olivar started out confidently across the bridge with the others in single file behind him. Cautiously, Gunther set foot to the road. He fancied that he felt it give way slightly beneath his boot as if it were, indeed, floating. Bah. Silly fancy. Naught more. He trod ahead firmly, his attention fixed upon the far shore.

It took them nearly two hours to walk the Rigngata Road. But at long last, their feet touched solid ground once more. Great, ancient pines rose around them, interspersed with white-barked aspens, their leaves trembling in the slightest breeze. The air was pure and cold in his lungs, the sky so blue it almost hurt to look at. And the mountains—ahh, the mountains felt alive, standing as eternal sentinels to the grandeur of this place. Something deep in his soul sang the song of this land.

Olivar gestured at the narrow road leading up into the high pass between the mountains. "There lies our way."

Gunther was glad to climb into the heart of these mountains. Even if the stump of his missing leg ached, and even if he grew tired and sore from the trek. They climbed all afternoon and made camp on the side of the narrow path the road had devolved into. He grudgingly had to give the yeren Kuango credit. They'd fashioned a cart for the beast to pull the heavy copper statue in, but it still had to be hard work pulling the cart over the uneven and rocky path. The creature never expressed fatigue or displeasure at the task, but sturdily and steadfastly stayed right behind his mistress. Loyal pet, he was. And stronger than an ox.

The next day saw them to the top of the pass. Olivar stopped when they reached an open plateau just large enough to hold them all. They looked out in silence at the ring of great mountains surrounding the Valley of Storms. Each snowcapped peak towered impossibly high, scratching the belly of the heavens. Steep and forbidding, these were surely the grandfathers of Groenn's Rest.

Mist formed a blanket covering the floor of the valley below. They began the descent, and it was hardly less arduous than the climb had been. The path was steep and narrow, beset by stones that rolled underfoot and gravel that slipped beneath the unwary boot.

Late in the afternoon, a faint roaring sound became audible. They decided to make camp a little way beyond the fall where the sound diminished enough for them to speak and think. But he slept that night to the roar of crashing water.

The next morning brought them down into the mist. An enchanted land lay inside it, green upon green upon green. Lush forest, abundant wildflowers, and earth carpeted in a bright green velvet of moss. A fae place it seemed, too beautiful and perfect for the mortal realm.

Farther down the mountain, they emerged from the mist into a gently clouded valley of trees dripping with moisture and moss-covered marker stones beside the path, which had widened into a road once more. And people.

A dwarf came out of a moss-covered stone hut beside the road to study them suspiciously. He growled the meagerest of greetings and then retreated to his abode once more. Several more times along the way, they ran into locals, dwarves mostly of the terrakin variety. Plenty of reason they had to be unfriendly to outsiders. Of all races within the Empire, they had been most persecuted. The most unanimous they were as a race in their hatred of Koth, as well. It was rumored that some terrakin even refused to acknowledge the Empire and considered themselves in rebellion against it.

At length they came to a pretty little village with neat cottages surrounded by verdant gardens of vegetables, flowers, and fruit trees. Fat goats and fluffy sheep looked up at them from their grazing as they passed by.

"Where to, Gunther?" Gabrielle asked him.

"Given as this is a dwarven village, and seeing as how we wish to speak to the elders, the pub's the place to go." He led the way to an establishment announcing itself to be the Rokken Anvil.

Rocking it was, too. When they ducked inside, a drinking song was being bellowed by a crowd of dwarves. Miners by the looks of them. Grit was permanently ground into their skin, and their corded forearms and broad shoulders announced them to be strong and fit.

Mina chose to stay outside with Kuango and mumbled something about finding the stable. Gunther, Gabrielle, Olivar and his avarian apprentice crowded into a tight space the locals slid over to make for them on the benches. A comely barmaid brought out ales, and Gunther drained his with gusto. He joined in the next drinking song, delighted to be among his own kind once more.

The locals to his right asked him whereabouts he called home, and before long, they were engaging in animated conversation about the mineral composition of the Hauksgrafir versus the mountains hereabouts. When the question arose as to why he traveled with an ogre-kin, it was an easy enough matter to mention that Olivar was a stormcaller.

That caused a shout of welcome to go up to the ogre-kin and toasting to a stormcaller in their midst. From there, it was only a few more rounds of ale before Gunther was able to bring up the topic of storm forges and whether there might be a smith in the area with knowledge of the workings of one.

The dwarf beside Gunther was abruptly quite a bit less drunk and cast his voice low below the general din. "How'd ye know 'bout those?"

"We have need of one. Found a bit of storm copper in need of repair."

The fellow stared hard at Gunther, then at each of Gunther's companions in turn. He nodded slowly. "Come wit' me." The fellow threw a few coppers on the table, and Gunther jerked his head at his companions to come along.

The fellow led them outside into the evening chill and down the street to a private home. They were let into another gathering of dwarves, this one much more restrained than the previous crowd.

"Who've ye got there wit' ye?" one of the gathered terrakin asked their guide.

"Summat travelers. Come lookin' fer a storm smith. Got a bit o' storm copper in need o' repair." The announcement fell like a block of lead into sand, with a silent thud that was felt more than heard.

"Indeed?" the first speaker said mildly. "And how are you folks in the knowin' of this storm copper?"

Olivar spoke up. "I'm Olivar Worbal, Stormcaller of the Achensberg. The legends of storm copper are taught to all my kind. Along with legends of the Great Storm Forge and the master smiths who once used it. I am hopeful that at least some of that knowledge still exists, here in the Valley of Storms, said to be home of the Great Forge itself."

"Show us your storm copper," the speaker demanded.

"Show us a smith who can work it," Gunther challenged. Best to get these fellows to show their hands first before he and his companions revealed the existence of the statue.

Grim amusement flashed across the faces of the group seated around the fire. "Spoken like a kelnor," one of them commented.

"If that means I be cautious, or even a bit suspicious, I'll be taking that as a compliment," he retorted. "Our business requires it."

"Indeed?" the speaker replied. More interest sparked in this gathering's faces now.

To his surprise, Gabrielle stepped forward, fishing in her collar. She pulled out a chain, and on it hung a heavy, eight-pointed pendant with a large green gem in its center. "Do any of you gentlemen happen to recognize this? Or mayhap a figure eight turned on its side?"

As one, the front legs of every chair in the room thumped to the floor.

"Well, now. That changes things," someone said.

Gunther didn't know what that pendant signified, but those in the room surely did. They were whisked down the road to the inn and the barn out back. Kuango sat inside next to the wagon, eating. Mina sat beside him, apparently keeping him company.

Gunther threw back the tarp covering the dwarven statue. "Here's our storm copper."

An audible gasp went up.

Gabrielle spoke into the charged silence. "We were hoping

you might know how to unmake this fellow and return him to life."

The dwarves looked back and forth among themselves, and then as one said, "Magnus."

They covered the statue, and the dwarves peered warily outside before hustling them out of the barn. They moved down the street quickly and in silence, heading beyond the village into the cloud forest.

A low, thatched-roof cottage took form in the mist, and their guides knocked furtively upon the door, nervous even out here. Gunther was alarmed when the majority of the group took up defensive positions around the cart and the house, axes and maces in hand. Did some threat lurk in the woods, or were they just that intent on the safety of the statue?

A gray-haired dwarf opened the door, hair mussed and shirt untucked. Presumably, this was Magnus. They'd obviously gotten him out of bed. He took one look at the grim faces outside his door and stepped outside as one of the dwarves gestured for the oldster to come with him.

Gunther lifted the edge of the tarp, and the dwarf sucked in a sharp breath.

Magnus muttered, "I'll get dressed and be out in a flash. Gather every able-bodied person who can be trusted. This is the greatest treasure in the realm. No harm must come to it while we take it to the forge."

And so it was that a guard of nigh on a hundred dwarves escorted them deep into the valley. It was eerie, so many moving through the night fog with only the sound of jingling armor and the occasional scuffing of boots to announce their passing.

They walked for several hours, always gently downhill. And then, without warning, the column stopped.

"Send runners to the others," Magnus ordered.

A half dozen young dwarves nodded and took off running into the darkness. Before long, more gray-haired dwarves rubbing sleep from their eyes joined the gathering. Magnus climbed up on a tall rock with the help of some youngsters and spoke loudly enough to be heard across the clearing.

"We've work to do, lads. Some of ye need to stand guard, and others need to gather great, galloping loads of firewood—resin-rich pine and seasoned oak. The river gates must be closed to divert the river and the great rods brought out and put in place. And fetch the hammers. It's time at long last to fire up the forge!"

A great cheer went up among the assembled dwarves.

"Master Stormcaller, when all is in readiness, if you would do us the honors and call in the biggest storm ye've ever called, we'd be in your debt."

The dwarves scattered to their various tasks, and Mina hand-talked to Kuango, who gently lifted the statue out of the cart and carried it to a huge forge, built in the bottom of a bowl-shaped structure.

It took the rest of the night and all the next morning to gather supplies and light the forge. But at length, a great fire roared and steam hissed as water was let into a huge stone basin above the forge. Copper tubes the size of Gunther's arm were fit into openings in the roof of the forge, joining them to the long, copper pipes extending from the forge into each of the twelve mountains that formed this steep valley. A cart bearing eight smiths' hammers came into sight. Magnus and his fellow smiths reverently lifted the hammers, testing their heft and weight. The handles were ornately carved and looked made of some special, black wood.

Olivar and his apprentice went to work. Gunther didn't understand the mechanics or magic of it, but gradually, billowing, huge thunderheads began to climb into the skies around the mountaintops ringing the valley.

Another man showed up, out of breath as if he'd run a long way, and introduced himself as a stormcaller, also. He joined Olivar and the avarian at their work, and the storms built more quickly thereafter, growing heavy and dark with wind and rain.

"It's lightning we'll be wantin', boys, and plenty of it!" Magnus yelled to the stormcallers over the gusting storm front.

The fires roared and the wind howled, and hail pelted down upon the wooden shingles of the roof over the forge. Torrents of rain began to fall, and gushing gouts of water were channeled off the roof into channels cut into the ground.

Gunther had never seen anything like this storm the callers had summoned. Lightning flashed and thunder crashed continuously, and through it all, the smiths waited grim-faced around the dwarven statue, hammers poised.

All of a sudden, a quick series of flashes erupted from every direction, all the mountaintops taking nearly simultaneous lightning strikes at their summits.

"That's it!" Magnus shouted. "Here it comes!"

The twelve great copper tubes all coming to a point just over the statue's head erupted with a blinding flash of light and heat that all but knocked Gunther off his feet. The twelve channeled bolts of lightning joined into one massive burst that exploded into the storm copper dwarf with a deafening crack and huge shower of sparks.

"Quick, lads!" Magnus cried. All the smiths hammered furiously at the statue, which looked almost molten. It appeared that their blows softened the copper, made it more malleable.

"Consistency's right. Quench it, now!" Magnus yelled. "Hold on, boys!" Each of the smiths grabbed a support pole nearby and hugged it for dear life.

And Gunther saw why as a brace of dwarves above the forge threw open a floodgate, and a great rush of water roared into the forge. Apparently, the statue was too big to lift and carry to a quenching pool, so flooding the entire forge had been the only alternative. An explosion of steam erupted as the water hit the fires of the forge, and all was chaos for upward of a minute as the tsunami swept through.

The dwarves at the floodgate wrestled it closed, and the storm water drained away, leaving the ruined forge behind.

The bedraggled smiths let go of the posts, shaking water out of their clothing and beards. Gunther limped forward as quickly as his leg would go to see how the statue had fared.

Except the statue was gone.

In its place, on the ground, a man lay. The spitting image of the statue from before.

"A healer, quick!" Magnus called, kneeling next to the prone man.

Mina raced forward and poured what had to be all the healing she had into the man.

Everyone held their breaths, the anticipation unbearable, the silence complete.

A gasp of returning breath.

A low groan.

He was alive. They'd done it. The rokken in the statue lived once more as a flesh-and-bone dwarf.

Sha'Li waited until Rosana called in Rynn from the last watch of the night to approach the camp, creeping in like a thief after their valuables. Her heart was heavy, her cheek cold. She might have upheld her vows, but she could not live with the person it made her into. She had to face the consequences of her actions.

"There you are!" Raina exclaimed in relief. "We were worried about you!"

Confused, Sha'Li's gaze snapped to Eben, who stared down fixedly at the ground, refusing to look at her. He did tell them what she'd done, didn't he? But as Rosana passed her a bowl and Will moved over on a log to make room for her to sit as if nothing was amiss, she had to assume that Eben had not told them she'd betrayed the party's trust and let Kerryl go.

At least Raina would side with her if it came to an argument.

She'd watched them all night long, remembering moments with each of them, how welcome they'd made her and how good it had felt to have friends. To be part of a group. To have a shared higher purpose.

Tarryn sat down beside her, and Sha'Li said shyly, "For you, I whittled these." She laid a bow and a dozen arrow shafts at the kindari's feet. "An archer, Eben said you were. Fletching the arrows still need. And tips. Sinew have I not for a pull string, but when next a large creature I hunt, sinew will I harvest for thee."

The kindari stared at her as if she'd grown a second head.

"What?" she asked gruffly.

Tarryn launched herself at Sha'Li and wrapped her in a horribly embarrassing hug while the others grinned like fools around the fire. "That's the nicest thing anyone's ever done for me!" the elf exclaimed.

"Nice, I am not," she replied sharply.

Eben grunted across the fire but held his tongue. Was it his plan, then, to say nothing to the others of what she'd done? Why would he protect her like that?

Raina grinned at her over Tarryn's shoulder. "Get over it, Sha'Li. You're nicer than any of us."

The healer's faith in her might as well have been a dagger straight to her heart. Scowling to hide her pain, she scooped out a bowl of the hot cereal Rosana had cooked for them this morning as a celebration for yesterday's victory. It tasted like paste and was about the same consistency. *Bah.* Human food—horrible stuff.

Rosana spoke up. "Cerebus was able to take me to the spirit realm last night to rescue those children's spirits."

If she'd had eyebrows, she would have lifted them at that announcement.

The gypsy continued, "It made me think. What if Cerebus could help you, Sha'Li?"

Alarmed, she muttered, "To spirit realm I wish not to go."

"No, I mean with reversing Tarryn's condition."

"You mean my curse," the kindari said bitterly. "Call it what it is."

Raina stood and went over to the unicorn, who was standing quietly to one side of their camp this morning, apparently dozing. She put a hand on his shoulder for a moment. "He says he is weakened at the moment but will do what he can to help you, Sha'Li."

She frowned. "No healer am I. Know what to do, I do not." Truly, she had no desire to fool around with rituals and magic and unicorns. But how could she refuse after what she had done last night? She owed them this. She glanced up and caught Eben's accusing stare on her before he turned away.

"I'll help," Raina volunteered. "Let's do it now before anyone else attacks us. Tarryn, you might want to lie down."

Frowning, Sha'Li moved over beside Raina and squatted beside the kindari. She felt movement behind her and smelled grass and sunshine. A warm, white presence entered her mind.

"You put your hands on Tarryn thus." Raina laid her hand on Tarryn's knee, and Sha'Li did the same to Tarryn's shoulder. "Now imagine the curse flowing out of Tarryn."

"To where will it go?" Sha'Li asked practically.

"Into me," a foreign voice murmured in her mind. Sha'Li jumped and looked around wildly. The unicorn bobbed its head up and down at her. Kerryl Moonrunner could *keep* his talent for speaking to animals. That was unsettling.

"Like this," Raina said. Warm, soothing magic flowed into her. Sha'Li needed no healing, but the magic felt nice nonetheless. She concentrated on letting it pass through her and into Tarryn.

"Sense the taint within Tarryn that is not part of her, and focus on pushing it out," Raina suggested.

That made a certain sense to Sha'Li. She'd always been able to taste when water was polluted and to cleanse it of foreign substances by concentrating upon it. This was similar, but on a much larger scale.

The mark upon her cheek began to burn. At the moment, she wasn't overly fond of the thing, and the pain of it was sharp. Still, out of long habit, she murmured an invocation to Lunimar to help her purify this worthy kindari. It was what her grandfather, a Tribe of the Moon shaman, would have done, and it seemed appropriate now.

A soft nose touched her shoulder, and a third strand of magic joined Raina's spirit magic and her own purifying energy. The strand was green and growing and contained all the nurturing magics of nature. The three energies twined together as they flowed into Tarryn, wrapping around the scout's spirit and gathering up the darkness from it, carrying it away from the kindari.

Time ceased to have meaning as Sha'Li focused her whole being on collecting every last bit of that foreign magic from Tarryn and absorbing it into the braided strands of healing and cleansing. If she was going to do this thing, she was going to do it to the best of her ability.

At last, the process was complete. Only Tarryn remained, and the cord of magical energy was black and fouled, having drawn all of Kerryl's curse into it. Abruptly, the rope snapped away from Tarryn and away from Sha'Li, recoiling hard . . . into Cerebus.

A great cracking sound behind Sha'Li made her jump and open her eyes. And behind her stood the unicorn, sides heaving, body dripping with sweat, and . . . *oh no.* Its horn was cracked. A dark, broken line ran the length of the glistening horn.

Raina leaped to her feet. "Cerebus!" She ran to the beast's head and put her hands on the horn, flowing so much healing into the horn that Sha'Li could actually see the magic. For a second, Sha'Li actually thought Raina turned the slightest bit translucent. The healer must have been pouring everything she had into the beast's horn. Which was impressive. She'd seen the human heal *dozens* of wounded people at a time and still have magic left over.

At length, Rosana drew Raina away from the unicorn. "That's enough. You'll kill yourself."

It was possible for a healer to die from healing?

"Is it enough, Cerebus?" Raina gasped. "I have more."

Sha'Li heard the voice echo in her head. "Enough, human child. You have saved my horn. With time, it will heal."

Raina's legs collapsed, and Sha'Li lunged forward in time to catch her and ease her to the ground. Dryly, she commented, "To eat again, I suppose Raina will want." The magic casters always wanted to eat everything in sight after they used their magic.

Indeed, it took most of the morning for Raina to recover

from whatever she'd done to the unicorn. Sha'Li was secretly glad to rest and eat the brace of quail Rynn hunted, Will prepared, and Eben cooked, for she, too, was feeling exceptionally tired and weak. Even Rosana seemed to be drooping this morn.

Only Tarryn was bright eyed and bushy tailed. She spent the morning pulling strands from her silk vest and twisting them into a bowstring. The elf trimmed feathers from the quail and fletched her arrows, as well, and by noon was practicing shooting at a nearby tree, getting the feel of her makeshift bow and arrows.

Eben studiously avoided her, and she didn't push him to talk to her or even acknowledge her existence. The fact that he hadn't betrayed her in retaliation for her betrayal of him was humbling. And it saddened her. She was in the wrong, and they both knew it. Furthermore, there wasn't anything she could do about it. Kerryl was long gone, and they would likely not get another shot at capturing the nature guardian again.

Sha'Li scouted a reasonably dry route for the party to the north and west, out of the swamp. She turned down Tarryn's help and did the scouting alone.

For once, she was glad to be leaving her native home. She would have liked to visit her village, but the shame of what she'd done was too much for her to face her grandfather right now. He would want to show off her tribe mark to everyone in the village, and she was not worthy of it.

The unicorn took his leave of them, declaring that his herd had lost its way and needed reminding of it. When Raina questioned him on that, he said something cryptic about the unicorns having forgotten that they were, in fact, unicorns. As the king of their kind, it was his responsibility to teach them how to be unicorns once more.

Raina asked Cerebus, "When it is time to wake Gawaine, how shall I call you to him?"

The unicorn answered simply, "I will come." And with a flash of glistening white hide, the beast disappeared.

"Where went it?" Sha'Li asked, looking around in surprise.

Rynn answered, "Unicorns are said to have the ability to instantly transport themselves from one place to another. As soon as Cerebus was free of that magical mud that had the property of preventing him from teleporting, he was able to leave anytime he wanted to."

But he'd stayed to help Rosana . . . and to help her. She was humbled by the honor.

That evening, as they sat by a blazing campfire, Eben sat down beside her. "Sha'Li, do you think you could do the same thing for Kendrick that you did for Tarryn? Remove Kerryl's curse?"

She frowned and looked over at Raina, who frowned back thoughtfully. "Newly made was Tarryn. Not deeply woven into her spirit was the curse. And help from Raina and Cerebus I had. Much more difficult to fix Kendrick would it be. But impossible it is not."

She dared not risk looking at Eben as she spoke the words.

To her shock, Eben actually reacted, even if not directly to her. "One day, we *will* catch up with Kendrick again, maybe when he's done figuring out what Kerryl's up to. And we'll fix him then."

"If help I can, help I will," she replied soberly.

Eben didn't respond.

Raina felt wrung out for several days after healing Cerebus. She'd opened the gates of her healing wider open than ever before and had poured enough magic into the unicorn to heal hundreds of people. Frankly, she was surprised she'd lived through it.

In a dream, Gawaine had thanked her for helping Cerebus and then rather sternly lectured her not to pull such a stunt again without further training on how to handle large volumes of magic. She did not know if it had been an actual communication from him or just her own guilty conscience conjuring what he likely would have said. Either way, she made a mental note to request more training from the high matriarch if they ever got back to Dupree.

Over the next two weeks of travel, she practiced quieting the voices in her head the way Gawaine had shown her. Gradually, she was learning to control the echoes. Just knowing what they were had helped. It was a relief to know she was not going mad.

They had Gawaine's crown, ring, and steed now. All they had left to find were his sword, shield, and bow. And then, of course, they would have to find his body. But that was a quest for another day. Right now, they had to return to Goldeneye, give him the ampoules of change water they'd recovered from Phillipe's corpse, and get Rosana's enslavement removed.

Although Raina worried that something else was wrong with the gypsy. Ever since she'd come back from the spirit realm, Rosana had been different. She'd been pensive and preoccupied. Raina tried to talk to her about what she'd seen and done there, but the gypsy refused to talk about it. And gradually, it dawned on Raina that Rosana never cast magic anymore. Where she might have cast a spark of magic to light a fire before, now Rosana chose to struggle with flint and steel. If Will had some small cut or bruise that Rosana would have healed before, now she sent him to Raina for healing. And when Raina asked about it, Rosana mumbled an excuse about needing to recover from her spirit journey and changed the subject.

Instead of heading into the Quills to the Dominion encampment there, this time they hugged the Barbed Coast, following the stormy shore of eastern Haelos north toward the Dominion capital. Rynn called it the Great Den, and she gathered he'd been there before.

Who was Rynn, anyway? She hadn't forgotten his declaration the night they'd fought Kerryl's minions that he had the right to exercise high justice on Pierre and sentence him to death. Only a high-ranking noble could do such a thing. And then there was that odd exchange with the paxan, Olar, they'd met on the road. Olar had acted at first as if he recognized Rynn, at least until Rynn and Olar shared a mind touch and some private communication. She didn't question him about it. They all had their secrets, and he was allowed to keep his if he wished.

For her part, she did not share with the others that she visited Gawaine in his grove nearly nightly now. The others teased her about developing a great fondness for sleep and about being nigh impossible to wake up at times, and she let them.

She and Gawaine spoke on topics ranging from politics to the nature of magic. He talked about mistakes he made when he'd been king of a great elven nation—overconfidence that peace would hold forever if his subjects were happy.

His zinnzari guards briefed him on current events whenever one of them died and joined the others guarding his eternal grove. But her perspective was somewhat different from that of the Children of Zinn's, and she was able to fill in gaps for him and brief him in detail about recent events in Dupree.

He had a brilliant mind and unshakable sense of right and wrong, both of which she found immensely appealing. He seemed to enjoy her dry humor and scathingly honest observations about the people and events around her. She could not speak to anyone else thus. As she was a White Heart member, her position called for tact and diplomacy at all times. He seemed to understand that. She supposed kings were similarly constrained in not being able to speak their minds freely to even their closest advisors.

She worried that her visits were an imposition upon him, but then one of the zinnzari guards commented that until she came, he had never heard Gawaine laugh. After that, she made it her mission to bring him laughter frequently.

One afternoon, she and her companions were trudging along the coast road when they rounded a headland, and before them lay a great sprawling city. Briza, the Great Den of the Dominion. It was close to Dupree in size, but without the elaborate stone structures and towering palaces and buildings. Rather this city was made up of hundreds of low, wooden structures weathered gray by the nearby sea and many hundreds of heavy tents. Huh. They'd probably never been burned out by the Boki like Dupree had. The Night of Green Fires had been the catalyst for all major structures in Dupree being rebuilt of stone.

To the east of the city lay a long stretch of gravel shore terminating in a large dock crowded with cargo ships. To the west, a complex of large caves was visible, nestled in a line of gray cliffs. Near the cliffs a great open plain was dominated by a circle of standing stones visible even from here. Those must be *huge* up close.

Raina and her companions were eyed suspiciously as they entered the rough city, but no one challenged them outright. Briza was crowded and busy with changelings everywhere. She was fairly sure several men wearing Dominion military colors followed them, but they were hard to spot in the crush of people.

Apparently, it was some sort of market day. A great open-air bazaar had drawn a huge crowd, and merchants from far-flung corners of the world hawked weapons, suits of armor, furs, and herbal mixes that would increase a person's strength or stamina.

It was in the market that they found Goldeneye, seated in a huge tent that seemed to be a combination feasting hall and tavern, surrounded by an entourage numbering in the hundreds. Musicians played on exotic instruments, changelings of every imaginable variety crowded into the space shouting for more food and wine, serving wenches hurried to comply, and chaos ruled.

Of course, Raina and her friends were not allowed to stroll right up to Goldeneye to say hello. The cobra changeling was surrounded by a cadre of big, dangerous-looking warriors, eating and drinking with their leader.

In fact, their party was stopped at some distance from the ruler of the Dominion by a phalanx of guards and ordered to state their business. Rynn had been elected spokesman for their group. Not only did Dominion warriors seem to respect his open eye, but he'd dealt with them before and still lived.

"We come bearing something of great personal importance to your leader, Lord Goldeneye. Kindly tell him our party has arrived; he will want to see us immediately."

The guard scoffed and told them to move along.

Rynn replied patiently, "If I am speaking the truth, he will kill you for delaying us. Are you willing to take that chance?" The guard frowned, his dismissal wavering. Rynn pressed his advantage. "Perhaps you should tell your superior to speak to us."

And so it went. It took three more Dominion military officers coming over to hear out Rynn before a badger changeling finally strode over, looking annoyed. But as soon as he caught sight of them, the changeling's demeanor changed to alert scrutiny. "So. You're back. Never thought to see you again, I did."

Rynn made a formal short bow, polite, yet curt enough not to be subservient. "We have returned to report on our mission. Lord Goldeneye is going to be irritated at the length of the delay in our being presented to him. May I have your name to add to the list of soldiers who refused to let him know we have arrived?"

"Stand down, Three Eyes. I'll tell him. Stay here."

Raina wondered if Rynn used his mind powers in some way to influence the changelings he'd spoken with. Or mayhap he was just an accomplished diplomat. If so, his methods were worth studying. She could use that kind of persuasive skill.

Raina watched the big badger changeling elbow his way across the crowded tent and lean down to murmur in Goldeneye's ear, assuming he actually had ears somewhere in that cobra hood of his. Goldeneye looked up in their direction and then gestured once sharply with his hand for them to come.

He must have known it would take them a while to cross

the tent, for he returned to drinking and laughing with his cohorts. It was no easy task to push through the crowd, particularly since they were assumed to be servants or slaves not worth moving aside for.

But Rynn was patient as he led the way, and with Eben and Will elbowing along just behind him, a narrow path slowly opened for Rosana, Raina, and Tarryn. Sha'Li brought up the rear, protecting them from untoward demands to refill mugs. At length, the last few soldiers moved aside, and Goldeneye loomed before them, intimidating even while lounging at a table.

"Report," he snapped between bites on some succulent fowl carcass.

Rynn replied, "We found Kerryl Moonrunner, engaged him and his minions in combat, and recovered that which you wished us to, minus one ampoule Kerryl had already used."

"Used for what?" Goldeneye asked sharply, laying down the roasted bird.

"To transform a prisoner he held into a were-alligator. We captured her, however, and have already reversed the transformation."

"You reversed a changeling transformation?" They had the cobra changeling's undivided attention now.

"She's with us if you wish to meet her," Rynn said mildly. The paxan gestured Tarryn forward to stand beside him.

"Give me your hand," Goldeneye demanded. He took Tarryn's hand for several seconds, as if to detect whether she was truly fully kindari and not a were-creature in humanoid form. He asked abruptly, "How did he do it? How did he change you, kindari?"

Tarryn answered, "A ritual of some kind. He first kidnapped an alligator speaker and had him summon a great alligator to us. Then Kerryl used the change water, a few items he possessed, and nature magics to join my spirit and the alligator's."

"And you reversed it how?"

Tarryn looked over at Sha'Li, who stepped forward. "I used my tribe marking, nature energies, and her spirit magics." Raina winced involuntarily as Sha'Li pointed her way and that golden stare landed on her. They had all agreed that it would not be wise to mention the existence of a unicorn to anyone. Their horns were prized as great magic items, and they were relentlessly hunted by certain factions.

"Let's have my change water, then."

Rosana stepped forward, holding the pouch with the ampoules of magical water in it. "I believe, Lord Goldeneye, that we had a bargain."

Raina thought she spotted a hint of amusement in the changeling's expression. But it was hard to tell with those vertical pupils of his and reptilian features. He held out his hand, and Rosana laid the pouch in it. He looked inside and nodded in satisfaction.

"I have to say, I did not expect you to succeed."

A disturbance caused Goldeneye to look away from them as one of his lieutenants said, "There's a problem up near the Ringstones. A brawl of some kind has erupted."

"Kondo, go deal with it," Goldeneye ordered.

"Yes, my lord." A huge rhinoceros changeling stood up, wiped his mouth on the sleeve of his shirt, and shoved his way out of the tent.

"Tell me how you captured a were-alligator."

"I assure you, it was with utmost difficulty, my lord," Rynn replied dryly. "A were-boar, two were-rats, and a host of boglins also fought against us."

Raina listened as Rynn told of the fight, recalling mainly her terror and frantic racing around in the woods trying to find her friends and heal them before they all died. Their injuries had been terrible in that fight. It had taken all her skill to keep them from dying. She'd healed the boglins she'd come across enough for them to stagger away from the fighting, as well.

Although Rynn described the fight in the style of an epic bard, she was surprised to realize that he wasn't actually embellishing the truth of what had happened at all. It had been an intensely dangerous fight. She winced a little as he launched into a description of the various wounds, poisons, and deaths she had fixed during the battle. Worse, Goldeneye's gaze narrowed as he clearly did the math in his head of how much healing she'd performed.

"And you did all this healing he describes by yourself?" the cobra changeling asked her.

"Well, yes. Sister Rosana is a capable healer in her own right, but her magic was more useful for combat-related spells."

"How many dagger wounds can you heal in one sun cycle?" Goldeneye asked.

"I don't know. A lot."

"Define a lot." It was easy to forget that keen intelligence was at work behind Goldeneye's grotesque and animalistic features until he said something like that.

"Several hundred, I suppose."

Jaws dropped around Goldeneye, and guffaws of disbelief erupted. But his stare never wavered from hers. She probably ought to look away lest he try to enslave her as he had Rosana, but for some reason, she did not think he would. This man knew more of the Empire, more of what her colors represented than he was letting on. He might not honor the neutrality of her colors, but he understood the implications of them.

Without looking away from her, he said, "Does she speak truth, paxan?"

"Yes."

Another runner interrupted them again. "My lord, the brawling grows worse. Some elementals have shown up and joined in the fighting. Kondo Ironhide sends word that it gets out of hand."

Goldeneye made a sound of exasperation and stood up. "Fine. I'll go take care of it."

Rosana spoke quickly, "You have not removed my . . . curse. You promised."

"Come along, then," he threw over his shoulder as he strode out of the tent. He was easy to follow, for everyone jumped out of his way and gave wide berth to him.

Now that Raina looked, the tent had emptied a fair bit while they had spoken to Goldeneye. Had his soldiers been quietly called away to deal with the disturbance, or had they left to join in the fun? Bracing for a long bout of healing cuts and bruises, she followed along in the snake changeling's wake.

They headed uphill, winding through the rough city. This place was built on the principle of functionality and not beauty or permanence. They emerged into a vast open area that, while not paved, was built upon wind-scrubbed stone.

The fight was hard to miss. Knots of changelings fought with elementals and with one another all over the space, and a huge melee with Kondo Ironhide at its core took place not far away from them. The rhinoceros changeling was throwing aside anyone who dared to approach him, while some sort of simian changeling clung to his back, ineffectively knocking him on the head with one fist.

Raina'd expected fisticuffs with the occasional chair leg or length of firewood as a weapon. But these warriors were going at one another with claws and swords, axes, maces, spears, and any other manner of weapons. She was stunned by the violence of it.

Goldeneye himself grunted in surprise at the sight.

"Do your people often beat one another's brains out?" Rynn asked him.

"Often enough. But not like this."

As they looked on, a group of six humanoids raced out from behind one of the humongous standing stones ringing the plain and dived into the fight. But they were not just any people, nor even changelings. Some appeared to be made of burning fire, others shaped like wispy, windblown representations of humans. *Elementals.*

Raina stared in horror as they cut and slashed their way across the open space, mowing down everything in their path.

"Is it a slave uprising?" Will asked, looking confused.

"I do not keep elemental slaves."

She was intrigued at Goldeneye's restraint. She frankly would have expected him to take one look at this fight and wade in, sword swinging, and start chopping people down with that inhuman speed of his. But instead, he was assessing the situation coolly, learning the lay of the battlefield, as it were.

Another group of elementals burst around one of the inner standing stones. They looked around aggressively, spied Lord Goldeneye, and charged straight at him and his immediate lieutenants. Raina and her friends were forced to retreat to get away from the fight that ensued between the elementals and Goldeneye's men.

While the outer circle of stones was made of some light gray stone, the inner circle of stones was tall and black, absorbing light and reflecting none of it back, lending the stones an inky hue.

"Nullstone," Sha'Li breathed. She walked toward the stones, and Raina followed suit, fascinated by the unusual stones.

Eben kept pace with her. "Have you ever seen anything like it?" he asked in wonder. "I must touch that stone."

She could feel it calling to her, singing in her blood. Was the nullstone magic?

"Raina!" Rosana shook her arm. "Stop!"

"Stop what?" she asked, continuing to walk forward.

"Come with me, right now."

Raina frowned. "No. I have to go look at the stones. Sha'Li says they're made of nullstone."

"Sha'Li is under the same compulsion you are to go to the middle of the rings. You must come away now. Please. Trust me." Rosana bodily blocked her path, forcing her to stop.

"I have to go. Move, Rosana."

Instead, the gypsy hooked her arm in Raina's and stubbornly tugged her back toward the outer stones. Raina yanked her arm, trying to free it, but the gypsy hung on doggedly. They passed the outer stones, and Rosana stopped. She asked cautiously, "How are you feeling now?"

"Fine. What was that all about?"

"You tell me. You, Eben, Sha'Li, and Tarryn all took off for the inner circle at the same time and didn't want to come back."

Raina glanced at the tall nullstones and didn't feel any particular need to examine them more closely. Especially since any number of Dominion warriors were brawling like Diamond fighters around the stones at the moment.

Rynn said grimly, "There's some sort of mental effect at work here. A compulsion to go to the middle of the Ringstones."

"Those changelings in the middle of the stones look as if they want to kill someone," Will commented.

Rynn nodded. "Where there's one mental effect at work, it's possible that there is another. Perhaps their aggression is being triggered somehow in the same way you four were drawn toward the center stones."

"We should let Goldeneye know," Raina suggested reluctantly.

The others nodded and moved around the outer ring of stones to where Goldeneye was trying unsuccessfully to get a group of his men to stop fighting with one another. At the moment, everyone was separated and being held by other warriors, but the combatants looked determined to take up where they'd left off as soon as they were freed.

"My lord Goldeneye," Rynn said, "we believe mental effects are at work within the circles." He explained briefly the others' compulsion to go to the inner ring.

"Why didn't it affect you?" Goldeneye asked tersely.

"I have a certain resistance to mental attacks inherent to my race. As for the boy and the gypsy, who knows? But they were safe."

Raina knew why Will was safe. Undoubtedly Bloodroot protected him. But Rosana? Why did she suddenly have the mental resistance of a paxan?

Another group of elementals emerged from the inner ring, moving fast. They clearly planned to break through the line of Dominion changelings starting to form around the outer ring of stones as more Dominion warriors came up to the Ringstones to see what all the fuss was about.

The aggression she'd expected from Goldeneye before surfaced now. The cobra changeling whipped out swords from the crossed scabbards on his back and shoved through the warriors who would have protected him. He stepped inside the outer stones, and she watched closely to see if he, too, was drawn to the middle of the circle.

Goldeneye caught the fastest elemental on the edge of his sword and sliced it almost in half as the second one impaled itself on his blade. A third one leaped in between his dying comrades, heedless of them, almost as if their purpose had been to tie up Goldeneye's swords. The cobra changeling caught the third attacker with his fanged teeth, his snake half asserting itself with shocking violence. Raina recoiled from the sight, horrified.

The first elemental went gray as it died, its body losing shape and form upon Goldeneye's blade. The cobra changeling yanked his blade free and slashed at a fourth elemental as he spit out the corpse of the now gray creature he'd bitten. The entire attack had taken barely the blink of an eye, and four elementals lay dead on the ground.

A group of fighting changelings spilled out of the inner circle, rolling and tumbling across the wide space in a tangle of limbs and fur. Somewhere within that melee, the rhinoceros changeling, Kondo Ironhide, must have spotted his leader, for he charged across the open space straight at Goldeneye, head lowered, plowing through anyone and everyone in his path. A number of the changelings he knocked aside took umbrage with his passage and followed in his wake, swinging weapons at his tough hide. The result was that the brawl came to them whether they wished it or no.

"What are you doing?" Goldeneye roared at his lieutenant as the rhinoceros closed on him. "Halt!"

But Kondo was so lost in the battle rage that had claimed him that he apparently did not hear his liege lord. He swung a pair of massive clubs from side to side, smashing everything and everyone around him.

Goldeneye danced back, narrowly avoiding getting clocked by his own man. "You dare to attack me?" His cobra hood flared in warning.

One of the clubs arced down toward Goldeneye, and Rynn somehow managed to get in front of the blow and deflect the force of it away from Goldeneye's head. The blow spun Rynn into Kondo, though, and the two men fought hand to hand, Kondo's brute strength pitted against Rynn's agility and speed.

Goldeneye joined in the fray from the right, striking at his man with the flat of his sword. Meanwhile, Will dived in from the left, using his staff to pummel the rhino changeling.

The other changelings, fighting anyone and everyone, surged and heaved around Raina, buffeting her from side to side. She ducked frantically as errant blows came dangerously close to gutting her. None of these Dominion warriors would pull their punches or halt a sword swing mid-strike because of her colors. They would kill her as quickly as they cut down one of their own in this furious, senseless battle.

"Where are the elementals coming from?" Rynn shouted to Goldeneye as Kondo finally dropped, unconscious.

Raina reached for the changeling, but Goldeneye snarled, "Leave him. He is not mortally wounded." The cobra changeling was not amused at being attacked by his own lieutenant, apparently.

Another larger wave of elementals and elementally aligned humanoids emerged from the inner circle, this group followed by a screaming horde of Dominion soldiers who plowed wildly into their backs. Some of the creatures slipped through, however, and Goldeneye, Rynn, and Will stepped up to meet them.

The cobra changeling called out between sword swings,

each one resulting in the death of an elemental, "These creatures must be coming from the gate. Shouldn't be active, though. The claviger guards it."

Raina leaned down and tried to heal one of the formless gray shapes, but her magic slid off the creature as if it were not even there. *What on Urth?* "Rosana, my healing won't work on this!"

"It's not a living creature," Rosana called back.

Rynn called to her, "Elementals have no spirits. They're constructs."

Huh. Did that mean she could kill one if she wanted to? Not that she actually did want to. And then there was the problem of her having not a single damaging spell in her arsenal of memorized magic.

"Why are the Dominion warriors fighting with one another?" Raina ventured to ask. "Why are they not just attacking the elementals?"

Goldeneye must have heard her, for he sent her a piercing look. She shrugged back at him. She couldn't help noticing these things. Everyone else might be busy fighting, but she had nothing to do except heal people and watch the battle.

"Let us investigate that, shall we?" Goldeneye hissed. The threat in his voice made her skin crawl. When he got to the bottom of this brawl, heads were going to roll.

Someone came around the large stone behind them and rolled in on the party from behind, apparently targeting Rosana. Will leaped in front of her, magic crackling abruptly along his staff.

A wolverine changeling snarled, "You dare fight me, human child? I will kill you!" His voice rose with each uttered syllable until he was roaring in rage. He slashed an impressive pair of claws at Will, who parried one with each end of his staff. Sparks flew as the claws slid off the metal cladding at each end of the weapon.

A quick, short swing by Will, and he clipped the changeling hard in the side of the head. The wolverine staggered back to shake his head and clear it. A low growl started in the wolverine's throat once more as he prepared to charge. Will took a step back, pointing one end of his staff at the changeling. Magic built along its length, dancing like lightning.

"Stop!" Goldeneye yelled. He jumped in front of Will, but facing the wolverine. "Look at me, Zerrik!"

The wolverine charged, and Raina gasped. He attacked his own leader? Goldeneye ducked under the claws and came up grappling with his lieutenant. Goldeneye wrestled with the wolverine, all the while staring furiously into his man's eyes.

Of a sudden, the fight went out of the furred changeling. Goldeneye loosed him cautiously and took a step back. "You will not attack any Dominion warriors or their allies in this fight. You will not rage again, and you will target only elementals in this battle. Understood?"

"Yes, my leader."

"Go." Goldeneye waved the wolverine away. He turned to Will and said tersely, "I could not let you kill my war leader. Such a blood debt would have to be paid in kind."

Will nodded. It was probably as close to an apology as the cobra changeling ever ventured.

Goldeneye continued, "Zerrik Flay was enraged by something or someone. Let us discover who dares do this to my second-in-command." He strode angrily toward the middle of the space and the smaller ring of stones standing there. But a badger changeling stepped bravely in front of the cobra changeling, blocking his way. "Everyone who goes near the gate has become uncontrollably enraged. They attack everything in sight. The inner circle is littered with the dead and dying."

Raina flinched. "I must go heal them."

The badger shook his head at her. "As soon as you draw near the gate, you will fall into battle madness."

Goldeneye bit out, "If what you say is true about your casting capability, we don't need you going insane."

"You do not understand. It is my duty. I am sworn to

defend life. If there are dying people in there, I am obligated to help them."

"And if you go mad, understand that I will kill you," he declared.

A horde of elementals burst around one of the standing stones, and the conversation ended abruptly as Goldeneye, the badger, and Raina's friends mowed them down.

"They just keep coming," the badger changeling panted. "Every one of my men who tries to close the gate comes back out and attacks us instead—if the claviger does not throw him through the portal."

"Hence the chaos out here," Goldeneye responded in disgust. "We must close the gate."

"The claviger holds the gate open. He, too, is not in his right mind. We cannot get to him to wake him from whatever trance he's in. He is defended by a group of particularly large elementals."

"What's a claviger?" Will muttered.

Rynn muttered back, "The keeper of a gate leading to other planes. He or she wields the key to a tympan, which is an arrangement of magical stones that align the gate with the various planes at different times."

Goldeneye ordered everyone within earshot, "Those who can resist mental attacks, come to me!"

Rynn, Will, and Rosana stepped forward. Panic rushed through Raina, along with certainty that, if she did not go with them, all three of them would die.

"Enslave me," Raina blurted. Everyone turned to stare at her, and she, in turn, stared at Goldeneye. "Make me immune to the rage so I can do my job."

"You volunteer to be my slave?" Goldeneye challenged her.

"My duty is to defend life at all costs," she bit out. "We're losing time, and another wave of these creatures is about due—"

As if on command, a new group of elementals rushed around a nearby stone.

"What do they want?" Rynn grunted while kicking and spinning and flailing.

"Let one live," Raina called out to Goldeneye. "Follow it. See where it goes."

"Do it," Goldeneye ordered, blocking his badger changeling's sword with his own. The last elemental standing, a fire creature, was allowed to run away, with the badger changeling trailing it closely, ordering away all who would have killed it.

She heard some kind of shouted order from across the expansive circle to form up and charge. Dozens of snarling, growling voices yelled like soldiers rushing into battle.

Goldeneye cursed. "The jukara quartered in the caves. Someone has sent in a pack of them to attack the gate."

"Jukara?" Will asked.

Rynn answered for the cobra changeling, "Dominion's strongest warriors, mostly badger and wolverine changelings. Ferocious, skilled, and deadly to the last one."

"Great," Will muttered under his breath. "And they're all about to go crazy."

"White Heart, look at me," Goldeneye ordered tersely.

She looked into his eyes and was fascinated by the metallic golden shimmer in them. It was like a molten pool that she could lose herself in. She felt herself falling, falling . . .

"At all costs, you will not rage. Understood?" Goldeneye bit out.

The words resonated within her, sinking into her bones as incontrovertible truth. "Yes," she breathed.

"Jann, spread word throughout the city to send in only fighters with mental resistance or enslaved to me. The rest need to stay outside the outer stones. Find Vedara Sylk, my mate. She should be able to resist this and can rally the troops I need."

Eben nodded and took off with Sha'Li and Tarryn on his heels to fetch reinforcements for them. Reinforcements they would sorely need before this was all said and done if Raina did not miss her guess.

Goldeneye started toward the inner circle of stones. It was not so much that they were smaller than the outer ring of stones, but rather that this place was so massive in scale that they just looked small at first. Her friends on the left flank and Goldeneye's lieutenants on the right, they advanced.

Raina gasped when they neared the inner stones. Dead and dying changelings were strewn all over the place. When Dominion troops brawled, they apparently pulled none of their punches.

The jukara approaching from the cliff side of the Ringstones had charged straight into the inner circle, and the damage was done. They fought among themselves, and some had peeled off to attack the few sane Dominion soldiers in the area, who were trying futilely to contain the catastrophe without murdering their brethren.

Goldeneye's line approached the huge nullstones, towering easily three times Raina's height, and she felt a wave of rage press down upon her mind, pure bloodlust urging her to kill. Then, from deep inside her, Goldeneye's command rose up to push back the frenzy. At all costs, she must not rage. Resist the blood fury. The two commands fought within her for control of her mind while she watched on, a bystander in her own fate.

Another group of elementals, jann, and elementally aligned elves emerged from behind one of the inner stones. Gradually, Raina won the mental battle and remembered why she was here. She looked around, assessing where to begin healing first.

As she moved among the fallen, dodging pockets of fighting, she took note of what stood in the very center of the Ringstones. There was one last stone in the exact center of the inner ring, about the size of a table, low and flat. Upon it sat a circle of carved stones linked together into a single great disk. That must be the tympan Rynn had mentioned. In the center of the disk was some sort of opening down into the table rock. An object that looked like a large key stuck up out of the opening.

She glimpsed a figure moving on the far side of the table. The claviger. Mostly she saw his hands. They wove in an intricate pattern, leaving a momentary trail of faintly glowing lines in the air behind them. He was weaving a magical sign. And given its complex form, she would wager it was powerful magic he shaped. The claviger must have bent down for he disappeared from sight. Her next glimpse between fighters was a dark figure grabbing a large animal changeling off the ground as if he weighed no more than a child and tossing the changeling between two of the inner stones, and the body blinked out of sight.

A portal.

Open. And its master was tossing everyone he could get his hands on through it. A half dozen large elementals clustered close to the claviger, obviously tasked with protecting and defending him.

As she looked on, a streaming mass of elementals poured out from the nothingness between the two stones and into existence. *And this time they did not stop coming.*

They poured forth, more and more of them, boiling out into the circle. The maddened jukara were overtaken by the horde, and chaos exploded as the crazed Dominion changelings were overrun.

Goldeneye jumped forward, leading those with him into the battle. Raina was torn between trying to heal wounded warriors still up and fighting and trying to heal changelings already down on the ground.

The problem with healing those who'd already fallen was that first she had to determine whether or not they were dead, and if dead, were they still within the first few minutes of death when a life spell would still work? Life spells took a lot of magic, and today was not the day she wanted to test the limits of her healing capacity or run out of healing altogether.

This might have started as a brawl, but it had blown up into something worse. Much worse. The way that horde of elemental creatures was streaming through the portal, this looked like a full-scale invasion.

She spied a changeling bleeding profusely and sent a blast of life magic into his body. He sat up, took one look around, and surged upward, tackling the warrior nearest him and commencing wrestling violently for control of the second man's sword.

She swore under her breath. The enraging effect lasted even after a person lost consciousness or died, apparently. The best she would be able to do was stabilize everyone she could so they wouldn't die. If and when that cursed gate was closed, then she could go back and actually heal the wounded.

The force of elemental beings pouring through the gate had grown large enough in number to fill most of the inner circle of stones, and her friends and Goldeneye's forces were vastly outnumbered. She dived toward her companions, narrowly missing being skewered or beheaded outright several times before she reached them. Goldeneye was forming his small force into a ring, and she barely slipped inside it before claws and blades closed into a solid defensive wall.

She turned round and round, responding to shouts for healing from her friends as fast as she could. The Dominion warriors figured it out quickly and started shouting for first aid as well.

The number of elementals being slaughtered was staggering. When one died, another took his place, and when that one died, a third one stepped over the corpses of the other two.

They had to shut down the source of these endless waves of elementals, or the limited Dominion forces who could resist the rage would be overwhelmed by the sheer volume of creatures.

Some of the elementals were starting to charge the outer ring of Dominion warriors frantic to join the fight but under orders to stay beyond the outer ring of stones. Thank the stars for that small blessing.

She craned to see over, around, or between the fighters to the center stone. Between the elementals' hulking forms, she finally got her first good look at the claviger. Her blood ran cold.

Dressed in dark blue robes, his exposed skin covered in familiar runes, she recognized a Mage of Alchizzadon. The claviger was one of the mages who'd tried to force her into bearing children with one of their own against her will? What on the Lady's great green Urth was one of *those* doing *here*? The fellow was hunched over the center table protectively, as if using his body to shield the tympan and key. Whatever he was doing with them was bound to be the source of this mayhem.

She made her way through the chaos toward Goldeneye. A maddened equine changeling burst through the defensive ring and swung at her with something arm length and blunt. She threw up her arm, but too late. Her head exploded in pain, and the ground came flying up at her, knocking the breath and most of the remaining consciousness out of her.

Somewhere in a detached corner of her mind, the healer in her ticked off injuries. Concussion. Possible skull fracture. Dislocated shoulder. A couple of cracked ribs. Grave danger of accumulating trampling injuries—

Something hot and intensely painful rushed through her. *Healing.* Oww, that hurt.

A glittering crystal bracer appeared under her nose. She took Rynn's hand, and he dragged her to her feet, spinning away into the fight again as quickly as he'd appeared before she could catch the breath that had been knocked out of her to thank him.

Getting her bearings, she looked around in time to see a pair of big fire elementals charge Goldeneye from each side. Miraculously, he held them off swinging both swords so fast she could barely keep up with each blade. Still. The elementals were nicking him up here and there. Which meant they'd gotten through whatever armor or natural defenses he had.

She jumped forward and took a wild guess at how much magical energy it would take to bring him back to full health.

She shot the bolt of healing energy into him and then leaped back as one of the beings took a swing at her. A singed stripe blossomed on her tabard. Stars, she was terrible at this combat stuff! If only she'd paid more attention to the manor lads when her father had taught them the rudiments of armed combat.

She yelled over Goldeneye's shoulder, "We need to get to the mage in the middle! He's the key to closing the gate!"

The cobra didn't respond as he was still beset by the two elementals. Two more of his men rolled in on his right flank, however, and with one more round of healing from her and a hard fight, both elementals went down.

"To the tympan and key!" Goldeneye bellowed. His men ran forward with him, but Rynn, Will, and Rosana were in danger of being left behind, which would get them surrounded and cut off from the sane Dominion warriors. They would all die!

"We have to move!" she shouted frantically to her friends.

A wind elemental turned to face her, and she stumbled back, terrified. She didn't even have a weapon to protect herself! Panicked, she summoned magic to her hands and brandished it as if she could actually do anything with it.

The elemental recoiled momentarily. And in that instant's respite, something fast moving flashed past her, jumped high, and clobbered the being on the side of the head. The creature staggered, and something heavy and fast moving slammed into it from the other side. The wind elemental turned to face Rynn and Will. If her friends didn't get past this beast and fast, they were going to get left behind and overrun.

Rynn wasn't moving correctly. There was a hitch in his stride as if something was wrong with his left leg. Dodging around the elemental, she managed to throw a bolt of healing at him, hitting him in the chest.

"Duck, Raina!" Rosana shouted from behind Will.

She hadn't even seen the gypsy behind Will, so close to

his back was the girl sticking. Raina dropped into a crouch as something hot passed far too close to her head and crashed into the wind elemental's back, making it howl. Will threw an awaken spell at whatever was behind her, and a horrible odor of burning flesh arose. An *awakening* spell did all that damage?

"To me!" an inhuman voice roared in a rush of magically enhanced sound from the tabletop stone. As one, every elemental in the outer circle disengaged from whomever they fought around the edges of the space and surged inward.

Straight at her and her friends.

The entire battle was collapsing in on them.

"Run!" Rynn yelled. He leaped over the remains of the elemental he'd just dropped and raced toward her. She turned and joined him in fleeing for her life as Will and Rosana came up beside her. They approached the central stone where the fight raged and Goldeneye and his men attempted to break through the ring of guards around the claviger.

But they were out of time. The collapsing horde of elementals was almost on them. Yet again, Goldeneye's beleaguered forces were forced to fall back into a tight knot, fighting like mad not to be summarily overrun.

They were losing. At some point, healing was no longer the question, but exhaustion. Slowly but surely, Goldeneye's forces were buckling under the brunt of the sheer number of attackers they faced. That, and several of the big ones guarding the claviger had peeled away from the mage and now attacked Goldeneye and his men, as well. Horror unfolded in Raina's gut. There was nothing she could do to help the warriors, whose arms were flagging in strength and steps were slowing.

In the distance, she heard more shouting, but she was too involved, casting healing as fast as she could summon and shape it, to look up. Frantically, she reached for more healing, feeling her own reserves running low. If she died, a whole lot of people out here were going to die with her.

The entire force of elementals shifted as something large plowed into it from behind. Stars willing, that was Goldeneye's mate and whatever reinforcements she'd rounded up. The intensity of the fighting around them abated a tiny bit as some of the elementals peeled away to face whatever new threat had stepped onto the field.

She craned to see over her companions and spied a new force of Dominion warriors furiously attacking the elementals. *Thank the Lady.*

"Help has arrived!" she shouted. "We're almost there!" It wasn't exactly accurate, but the warriors around her needed some glimmer of hope to cling to as their portion of the fight became desperate. A second big elemental moved away from their beleaguered group and toward the claviger. Will hit the only remaining big elemental with some sort of damaging magic. The creature staggered, and Goldeneye and two of his lieutenants leaped on it, slashing ferociously at it. The violence of their combined attack was breathtaking.

The elemental went down. And then the fight began to turn a little. Buoyed by their small victory, the Dominion group moved in a phalanx toward the center stone. Only two of the big elementals, one wind and one fire, were left. They shoved aside the smaller elementals still emerging from the gate to attack Goldeneye's force directly.

Most of the smaller elemental beings moved away to attack Vedara and her forces, who were now circled up in the same way Goldeneye had been a minute before. At least they were relatively fresh and able to put up a stiff fight against these invading elementals.

Goldeneye's forces found their second wind and attacked fiercely, giving the pair of large elementals and a host of the smaller ones all they could handle. Still. The fighters she stood behind could not keep going like this much longer.

Someone had to do something to turn the fight.

She dodged and weaved behind them, trying to catch a glimpse of the claviger. In an opening between the elementals, she spotted him weaving another spell with his hands.

This time, he was hunched over the table and his key. If only she could pull him away from the key. Get it out of the lock, somehow . . .

"Alchizzadon!" she shouted at the top of her lungs. "Raina of Tyrel has taken the field of battle!"

The mage lurched upright and turned to stare at her. He said something she couldn't hear. And then both of the large elementals protecting him turned and headed straight for her. They cut through the warriors around her as if they were made of soft butter.

Her friends fell back to the left, and Goldeneye and his men fell back to the right. As for her, she turned and ran. It was, of course, an unwinnable race. She was human and fatigued. And they were made of pure elemental energy.

"I'm drawing them off!" she shouted. "Get the mage!"

As plans went, it wasn't great—use herself as bait to lure away the big bads so her friends could deal with the mage while he was alone and unprotected. Worse, it deprived her friends of her massive pool of healing.

She paused in her flight, grabbed Rosana's arm, and blasted her friend with all the magical energy she could hastily summon. She hoped she'd done that right. Lenora had shown her how to transfer a little piece of her magical energy to another healer just before they'd left Dupree. Raina had never tried it herself, however. Only a fraction of the magic she'd summoned would likely make its way into Rosana's spirit. But it was worth a try.

The pause had been costly, though. The elementals were almost on her now, and she shouted one last time, "Stop the mage!" Then she ran for all she was worth. Justin, who'd chased her through the woods as a child, and Cicero, who'd run her all over the colony, would be proud of her. She made it almost halfway to the outer ring of stones before she felt a hot wind on her neck.

The elementals were on her. She had nothing with which to defend herself and wouldn't have known how to, anyway. She was shocked when the creatures did not kill her on the spot. Instead, they grabbed her by both arms and commenced dragging her toward the mage waiting for her by the gate.

No. *No, no, no.* They were taking her to a Mage of Alchizzadon, and he was going to throw her through that gate to who knew where, and he and his kind would do who knew what to her! She dug in her heels and fought against the elementals with all her might. It hardly slowed them down. But every second she could buy for her friends and delay her own fate was worth it. Step by step, the elementals forced her toward that mage and the shimmering expanse of nothingness behind him.

Eben ran through the city, following a wind elemental who'd slipped past the fighting and was now racing intently toward some goal. Dominion changelings streamed past him, going the other direction, running toward the battle. Even if he could have stopped one, explained that he was following an elemental and why, the wind elemental ahead of him would have been long gone, lost in the endless, winding rows of huts and tents.

The wind elemental slowed for a moment and lifted its head, almost as if it sniffed the air, testing it for the scent of something. The creature turned and dashed off to its left. Eben followed grimly. It paused to sniff again, and this time it smiled. Eben had closed to within a dozen yards of it when the creature, without warning, ducked into a narrow alley and fetched up next to a wooden wall.

It looked like the back of a permanent building. Without any ceremony, the wind elemental blasted the wall with some sort of damage that sent splinters of demolished wood flying in every direction. Eben skidded to a stop, throwing up his arm and ducking the worst of the debris.

The elemental stepped through the hole, and Eben followed quickly. It was some sort of storehouse. Maybe a treasure trove. But if there was any system of organization in here, it eluded him. All manner of things were stacked in all manner of piles, bundles, and jumbled messes. But his quarry appeared to know what it was looking for. The elemental headed straight for the far side of the space, snatched a leather sack out of a pile, and then whirled around. It fetched up short, seeming startled to find Eben right behind it.

"Whatchya got there?" Eben asked the elemental.

The creature scowled and didn't bother to answer. It merely lifted its hand and sent a blast of wind magic at him. Just as fast, he activated his stoneskin. The wind spell buffeted him but slid past him. The elemental darted to one side, but Eben was faster, dropping his stoneskin and reaching out to snag the elemental around its nominal waist.

Using his new mace, he took a short swing at the creature, clocking it in the head several times in fast succession. It wasn't pretty, and it surely wasn't an elegant use of the weapon, but it did the trick. The elemental dropped the bag and turned into a rushing vortex of air in his arms, slipping free of his grasp and racing toward the hole in the wall. Eben scooped up the leather sack and gave chase, but the creature had a head start on him, and the bag was heavy and awkward, banging against his thigh as he ran.

He gave up the chase and stopped, huffing hard. The elemental was headed back toward the Ringstones, anyway. It would never reach the standing stones alive. A huge crowd of Dominion warriors was streaming up in that direction even as he looked on. What had that creature been sent to fetch that it was willing to sacrifice its life for?

He opened the bag to have a look.

Panic surged through Raina. She could *not* let the Mages of Alchizzadon get their hands on her again! Frantically, she summoned magic and incanted a spirit form. She felt her body shift into a formless, non-corporeal state. She drifted backward, away from her would-be captors.

The wind elemental made a grab for her, but its arms passed harmlessly through her. It growled in frustration. Then, as she stared, the creature changed. Its gray, storm-cloud form melted away, and in its place, a white, misty being stood.

But not just any white, misty being. She'd seen creatures just like it before. That was a *phantasm*. A limb-like extension formed out of the mist, its end glowing magically. The arm threw magic at her, and she ducked frantically.

"Phantasms!" she shouted. "They're not elementals. They're *phantasms*!"

The second, fiery elemental made a grab for her and also could not affect her spirit form. If she could just keep them distracted from their master for a few more seconds, it might give someone an opening to attack the mage. But it was going to have to be soon.

Will had a head start on Rynn as they both rushed the mage. But the rune-covered wretch straightened, *smiling,* and threw a whirlwind spell that anticipated Rynn's dodge and clocked him squarely in the chest. Will watched in dismay as the paxan was picked up off the ground and hurled toward the glimmering portal.

Frantic, Will put on a burst of speed, veering away from the mage toward the portal. He had to do something to stop Rynn from being thrown through, likely never to return.

Will spied a silk rope lying on the ground across the front of the portal, stretching from stone to stone, no doubt left by some hapless Dominion caster who'd tried and failed to close the portal. Somewhere, out of the depths of his being, a spell came to Will. He didn't stop and think. He just gathered the magic and cast a wall of force into the rope.

A wall of magical energy sprang into existence just as Rynn reached it. The paxan slammed into it and was thrown backward, away from the portal. He landed in a heap on the ground, gasping for breath.

A crackling sound came from Will's wall, and he stared as the massive energy of the portal broke down his magic. The wall slowly but surely dissipated.

From that unknown place deep within him from whence the wall spell had come, a veritable flood of knowledge, known but forgotten, planted in his brain and lying fallow all this time, poured into his conscious mind. So much knowledge slammed into him that he could not stop to register all of it. He gave himself over to it, trusting that his mind would know what to do with it.

He whirled and assessed the situation grimly, seeing the battle in an entirely new light. The mage was a problem. He had range, accuracy, more magical power than Will, and likely more dangerous spells. It came to him in a flash: *Control the battlefield. Manipulate the environment to your advantage.*

He leaped behind one of the nullstones and called Rynn and Rosana to join him. The gypsy got there first.

He told her tersely, "Cut all your rope into ten-foot lengths and give them to me. Here's my rope, as well. Quickly." He detached a wrapped bundle of rope from his belt.

Frantically, she measured and sawed. "Why?" she asked.

"I have a plan."

Rynn skidded behind the stone, breathing hard. The paxan downed a healing potion of some kind from his pack and looked slightly less battered. Will outlined his plan in as few words as he could while they all chopped at rope. Rynn's only response was a broad grin and, "Let's do it."

They cut up all the rope they had, and Will laid down his staff, gathering the ropes, slinging them over his shoulder. "Are you two ready? Remember, Rosie, hold off casting as long as you can."

"Got it." She nodded.

Will went first, charging into the inner circle. He threw out a rope in a line between him and the claviger and cast a wall of force. He darted forward to one side, tossing down another rope and another wall.

The claviger noticed him and threw a spell at Will as he dived to the side and laid down another rope as he rolled. Up went another wall. So it went, with Will dodging and tossing down walls. When a dozen of them formed a zigzagging progression in the general direction of the claviger, Will yelled, "Now!"

Rynn sprinted out from behind the standing stone and started running the maze Will had built for him. The claviger threw several spells at Rynn, but the walls of force repelled the magical energy in sizzling explosions of sparks that flew away harmlessly.

As they'd expected, Rynn was starting to catch up with Will, and he frantically threw down a couple of more ropes and walls, building a maze ahead of the running paxan.

A big fire elemental and a white, misty phantasm ran after Rynn. But they, too, were hampered by the walls and had to go around them or else suffer damage from touching one. Worse, walls of force threw anyone who touched them back violently from them.

Dregs. His magic was getting low. That had been the one unknown variable. Would he have enough magic to build enough walls to get Rynn to the claviger? They were only about halfway across the gap between the standing stones and the tympan.

"Need some help?" Raina panted, coming up beside him, her body just finishing assuming a corporeal form.

"Know how to cast a wall?"

"Yes."

Praise the Lady and all her minions. They might win this day yet. Will threw down several more ropes. Rynn was almost on them now. Raina cast two fast walls of time.

Will darted to one side, threw down another rope, and then darted forward and threw down another one. As fast as he could put down the ropes, Raina cast the walls, and Rynn ran the maze they built for him, dodging the elemental and the phantasm.

The fire elemental almost caught Rynn, and seeing the problem, Will cut through a gap. As Rynn streaked past, he snaked out a length of rope and threw up a new force wall. The elemental screeched to a halt only inches from the new obstacle, roaring a gout of fire in its frustration. The creature had to retrace its steps back through the maze of walls to acquire Rynn's trail once more.

Will returned to Raina, and they ran forward, building walls as they went. The claviger cursed as his magics bounced harmlessly off the network of walls closing in on him, his enemies safe behind them. It was laborious work, running, dodging, and casting walls, and the amount of magical energy they burned was staggering.

Rosana ran up behind them, her hand glowing strangely. Since when had her magics become brilliantly colored like that? Right now, her hand glowed the color of blood.

"A few more walls," he panted.

Rynn was getting close to the target. They watched the paxan weave his way among the walls, at times only a few yards from the claviger. Will looked ahead of the paxan, anticipating his path, guessing when and where he would emerge to make the attack. The timing of their plan was going to be tight.

Will ran with Raina and Rosana to a gap in the walls and crouched to one side of it. *Get ready,* he mouthed to the gypsy. One more wall to go.

Rynn made the turn Will was waiting for. Will spun out from behind cover, exposing himself to the claviger's fire. He threw down a rope while Raina incanted the magic. Using the last wall for cover, Rosana stepped out from behind him and lit up the mage with a barrage of silence spells.

The claviger was forced to defend against the curse spells, frantically throwing up new magic shields every time one of Rosana's silences brought down the previous one. Raina started sending raw magical energy into Rosana, sharing power with the gypsy.

Will threw one last wall for Rynn. The paxan ran down its length and turned the corner only feet from the furious claviger, who was still having to continuously cast shields on himself.

The thing about most mages was they had fairly scrawny bodies in comparison to warriors. Something about the magic seemed to prevent them from ever bulking up. And the need to be able to gather and cast magic meant mages had to have a lot of freedom of movement, particularly in their upper bodies, which made wearing heavy armor pretty much impossible.

Rynn closed on the mage, battering at the claviger with his hands and feet in a blindingly fast barrage that the mage simply had no defense against. In a matter of seconds, Rynn had pounded the man senseless, and the claviger dropped to the ground, unconscious.

Raina whipped out from behind the wall and threw a confining spell at the claviger. Rosana added insult to injury and cast one last silence on the mage to be safe.

They looked up hopefully at the portal, and it still shimmered between the stones.

The fire creature burst out from behind one of the other walls. It roared and charged the fallen claviger and her friends.

"Incoming!" Rosana cried. "Get away from the gate! He'll throw you through!"

Rynn reached down to grab the mage and drag him away from the gate, which was only a few feet behind two of them. Raina jumped forward to help and took the mage's arm just as the elemental attacked.

But now that they knew it *not* to be a real elemental, but rather a phantasmal representation of one, Rosana fired an awakening spell at the phantasm while Will read a scroll for dispelling enchantments. They blasted the being simultaneously, and Rynn, grinning broadly, jumped in on the attack. He obviously knew how to battle phantasms. Will joined in with his staff, and in a matter of seconds, the creature dropped.

"Is it dead?" Raina asked breathlessly.

"As dead as its sort can be," Rynn declared.

Two cadres of Dominion, one led by Goldeneye and one led by Vedara, had started into the maze of walls and were chasing the lone remaining phantasm, gradually cornering it.

"How do we close the gate?" Raina asked.

Will raced over to the tympan and yanked the narrow shaft out of the center of the elaborate carving. He thought it had had a large, ring-shaped handle on it before, but it didn't now. The teeth mounted on the arrow-like rod cleared the tympan.

Nothing happened. As he'd feared. The key had been broken.

The gate continued to shimmer between two of the nullstones. Will cursed violently inside his head. For the moment, no more phantasms bearing the aspects of elementals or elementally aligned beings were coming through. But he suspected it was only a matter of time until whatever force lay on the other side of the gate sent another stream of them through.

The Dominion forces outside the outer ring surged inward, shouting a deafening battle cry. The wave of changelings rolled over the remaining elemental phantasms, destroying every being in their path. As for the maddened changelings, piles of their comrades appeared to have landed on top of each of them, pinning them to the ground. It was not a perfect solution for the problem, but at least the brawling was contained for the moment.

Goldeneye strode up to Will. "Why is it not closed? We must kill the mage."

Raina stepped in front of the unconscious Mage of Alchizzadon. Will had to give her credit for courage if she planned to stop the Dominion leader from making his kill. "Does anyone else in town know how to close a gate?" she asked.

Goldeneye frowned. "Only the claviger holds the key and knows how to align the gate."

"Then I'd suggest you not kill this man," she replied tersely.

Goldeneye scowled fiercely at her. She visibly recoiled from the violence in his gaze. Will gave her even more credit. It was one thing to stand up for one's beliefs. It was another to do it in open defiance of such a fearsome creature.

Will asked carefully, "Is there by any chance a spare key?"

Goldeneye's scowl deepened. He would take that as a no.

Rosana tried, "Are there any elementally aligned scholars here who might be able to decipher the symbols on the stones?"

"We do not indulge in such useless learning," one of Goldeneye's lieutenants scoffed.

Will murmured, "Rynn, could you find Eben and bring him here? Mayhap he knows something about elemental magics or symbols that might tell us how to close the gate."

The paxan took off running down the hill.

Goldeneye had moved over to the unconscious mage and nudged the blue-clad body with his toe. "What got into him? Always he has been quiet like a mouse. Happy to dust off his gate and tend to it."

Will answered, "His mind must have been tampered with like everyone else's. Perhaps some creature from the other side of yon gate controlled him and compelled him to open it." The other option that he left unspoken was that someone in Goldeneye's own stronghold had done it.

"He must be killed," the cobra changeling declared.

"He must be cured," Raina contradicted gently.

Goldeneye's head whipped around, and he stared at her angrily, hood flaring. If a look from him could kill, she would already be dead. Will took a step closer to her, and brave, sweet Rosana stepped up on her left side.

Raina pitched her voice in mild, reasonable tones. "If you lose your claviger, you'll lose control of the gate. Cure him. Earn his undying gratitude for rescuing him from whatever attacked him. And the gatekeeper's masters will also owe you a great debt."

The cobra changeling considered her argument. Thankfully, his lieutenants were all occupied elsewhere, tackling battle-crazed changelings whenever one happened to break free of the pile holding it down. Goldeneye would not lose face by accepting the logic of a weak, human girl. Will just prayed the Dominion leader would go for it; otherwise, the confrontation between Goldeneye and the White Heart would turn ugly. Personally, Will had no desire to stand before Lord Justinius and explain why he'd let a White Heart member be murdered in cold blood. As it was, Will was startled that the snake changeling didn't use his enslavement of Raina to order her to step aside.

"All right," Goldeneye said suddenly. "Tie him up, and then heal him just enough to regain consciousness."

Will and Rosana did the honors, tying up the mage with lengths of rope from a few of the expired walls of force that had been the claviger's downfall. Raina stepped forward. And gasped.

Will murmured low as he checked the mage's knots, "Know him?"

She ground out, "He's the spitting image of the man the mages planned to force me to have children with. This must be that one's father."

"Remember, you can't kill him," Will warned. She looked infuriated enough to blast the claviger into tiny bits.

Jaw clenched, she glared at Will and then trickled a tiny bit of healing into the fellow. His eyes blinked open, and he began thrashing in his bindings. Goldeneye knelt on the mage's neck, however, choking the claviger into submission. The cobra changeling glared into the mage's eyes for a full minute.

"Bring the open-eyed paxan," Goldeneye ordered.

A contingent of Dominion warriors was sent to find Rynn and bring him back. Hopefully, they would bring Eben, too. The vignette froze for a full two minutes while they waited. And then Rynn and—thank the Lady—Eben raced into the Ringstones.

Goldeneye growled, "Paxan, I could use your help."

It was a huge admission from the changeling, and it shocked Will.

"Of course, my lord," Rynn murmured. He knelt beside the mage, who still turned his head feebly from side to side, half choked to death as he must have been by now. Rynn laid his hand on the side of the mage's head.

The mage's limbs twitched helplessly as Rynn and Goldeneye did whatever they did to his mind. It took several minutes, but gradually the mage's thrashing ceased. His wild gaze cleared, and finally, Goldeneye lifted his knee off the man's throat.

The mage sat up, coughing and wheezing.

Over his head, Goldeneye and Rynn exchanged a long, grim look. What had they seen inside the mage's mind? It was enough to make both of them look as if they'd seen a ghost.

"Close the gate," Goldeneye ordered the mage soberly.

"Can't," the claviger rasped. "I threw part of the key through to the dream plane while I was out of my mind."

"Can you realign the stones and shift the gate away from the home of hordes of angry phantasms at least?" Rynn asked.

"Not without a complete key."

"Where do we find another key?" Goldeneye demanded.

The mage shrugged. "I am sorry, but I am bound by death oaths never to speak of such things to an outsider. To do so would activate one of my marks and result in my immediate and permanent death."

"Does he speak truth?" Goldeneye surprised Will by asking him.

He quickly reviewed what little he knew about runes. Why hadn't he paid more attention when Aurelius had droned on and on about how powerful runes could be when used intelligently? "It's possible," he answered reluctantly.

Eben, who'd been examining the tympan and the portal while they talked, spoke up. "These are like the stone I took off an elemental earlier." He opened his sack and pulled out a large, wedge-shaped piece of stone. Indeed, the carving on it looked very similar to the smaller wedges of stone in the tympan before them.

The Mage of Alchizzadon cried, "Give that to me!" He made a grab for the stone, but Eben yanked it out of reach easily.

"Uhh, no," Eben replied sarcastically. Ignoring the ranting mage, who went on about that stone being his by birthright or some such tripe, the jann returned to his examination of the tympan, speaking low and urgently to Will. "I had a dream a while back of an army of elementals, jann, and elementally aligned races forming on the dream plane. It looked exactly like the creatures that came through here. Except the army I saw was huge. The bunch that came through today would have been but a small scouting expedition compared to the main army."

Will stared at him in dismay. "There are more where those came from?"

"Thousands more. Ever hear the story of the boy who plugged the hole in the dam with his finger?" Eben asked grimly. "That's us right now."

Will gulped. "We've got to find a way to close this gate. Now. Here's the piece of the key I pulled out before."

Eben studied the broken key and then frowned. He unhooked the mace from his back and held it beside the broken key. Huh. The number and pattern of flanges on the mace was very similar to the shape and arrangement of the teeth on the key. "What are the odds?" he muttered.

Will rolled his eyes. "Kerryl could have seen this coming. Stars know, he's been one step ahead of us the whole time. I'm really starting to want to talk to him and find out just how much he knows. Try your mace in the lock."

Eben shook his head. "There's more to it than that. These stones have to be shifted in a specific way to close the gate without opening another one."

"Can you tell how they have to be shifted?" he asked.

"I can almost see it. There's a thread . . . ." The jann trailed off, using his finger to trace a carved line in the stone from one piece to the next. "To complete the pattern, this piece would have to go here." He lifted one of the stones and replaced it with another. "But then that would mean this one had to go there." He glanced up at Will. "Quit hovering. This is going to take a while, and you're making me nervous."

Smiling a little, Will turned away.

Rosana had moved off and was assessing injuries while Raina healed the most badly injured. Goldeneye's healthy men waited, weapons in hand, guarding the gate in case any more phantasms made an appearance.

Dominion healers moved around the area, as well. It took nearly an hour for the healers to finish their work. Close to a dozen Dominion warriors resurrected on the great plaza, and Will looked away in distaste from the sight of the forming bodies.

Goldeneye came over to him. "The maze of force walls was clever. How did you know to do it?"

That was an *excellent* question. To the cobra changeling, he shrugged. "It just came to me. Seemed like a good idea, so I went with it."

"Bold. Creative. Worthy of a great battle caster," Goldeneye said quietly.

Will stared. Had he known Will's father? Recognized him as the son of Tiberius De'Vir? He dared not let his charade be pierced, and certainly not by this man, who had no vested interest in keeping Will's secrets. Belatedly, he mumbled his thanks for the compliment.

Thankfully, Eben made more awkward conversation unnecessary by announcing, "I think I have it."

Will followed Goldeneye over to the table. Eben aligned the head of his mace carefully with the center of the tympan. The claviger struggled where he was restrained and tried to break free, no doubt to stop Eben from messing with the tympan. The jann turned the mace slightly, and the entire head of the weapon slipped into the opening like . . .

. . . like a key fitting into a lock.

Carefully, the jann turned the mace, and the stones of the tympan jostled and clacked against one another.

The portal blinked out of existence. One second the shimmering skin of air was there, and the next, it was gone.

"You did it!" Will exclaimed. He and the rest of their little party closed in to pound the jann on the back and congratulate him while Eben blushed.

"Well done," Goldeneye declared. The Dominion leader turned and shouted, "I call for a feast to celebrate this day's victory!"

One thing Raina had to give the Dominion credit for: they put on a great party. Where all the organization came from to pull it off, she had no idea. But in a matter of a few hours, an even larger tent than the one they'd first found Goldeneye in earlier today—a lifetime ago—was erected. It wasn't so much a tent as it was a seemingly endless tarp of oiled skins stretched over an entire city square, and held up by poles the size of trees. Tables and benches held perhaps a third of the assembly, and the rest either stood or sat on skins unrolled on the ground. The crowd extended down side streets well into the city.

As participants in the heaviest fighting, they'd been afforded seats at the tables. Of course, they were not given a place of honor. Goldeneye could not afford to admit that he'd had help from outsiders—some of them puny, human children, no less.

Raina was just glad for a big meal. She had no idea how much magic she had cast today; but along with the magical energy she'd shared with Rosana, it had to be more than she'd ever attempted. The voices bothered her a little, but when she tried Gawaine's technique of opening herself to them and then closing them off, they retreated.

Huge platters of food were passed around in a seemingly endless stream until everyone in the massive gathering had full plates, and eventually, full bellies. Even Raina could not fathom eating another bite of the succulent roasted meat, boiled vegetables, and chewy, dark bread that comprised the meal. Simple, practical people, these Dominion. Their food, like their homes, was not fancy but functional. Filling and nourishing. And that was all she cared about at the moment.

As darkness fell, a great opening in the center of the tarp roof was pulled back, and a bonfire was built. The flames danced up at least thirty feet in the air but did not come close to reaching the tarp overhead. She stared at the bright dance of flames and let it lull her toward sleep.

"Raina!" Rynn jolted her out of her half-asleep reverie. "Goldeneye has summoned you."

"What?"

"You and Eben. Go. Don't keep him waiting."

Alarmed, she looked at the jann, who shrugged and led the way through the crowd. Drinking seemed to be the order of the evening now. The benches were rowdy, their occupants hoisting horns of ale and singing loud songs in slurred voices not even in the vicinity of a tune.

Someone grabbed her rear end, and she whipped around, hands glowing menacingly. A shout of laughter went up, and rude comments flew, but no one else made a grab for her.

She and Eben reached the head table. Goldeneye addressed the jann first. "In thanks for closing the gate today, you may keep the stone you found on that elemental you chased down."

From down the head table, the claviger rose to protest. But the rhino changeling, Kondo, put a heavy hand on the mage's shoulder and forced him back down onto the bench. Raina was amused. Gifting the piece of nullstone to Eben was a slap in the face of the Mage of Alchizzadon. She approved.

"As for you, White Heart."

Her attention jerked to the cobra changeling.

"Look into my eyes."

Reflected firelight danced off his golden irises, making them look alive with fire. It was fascinating.

"I release you from your enslavement to me, healer."

She blinked, startled, the fascination broken. The cobra

changeling had already unenslaved Rosana earlier in private. Why wait until now to do the same for her?

A commotion erupted nearby, and she was shocked to see a pair of Royal Order of the Sun guardians trying to come toward her. But they were being blocked by a brace of jukara who only let them come as far as the end of the head table.

"Raina of Tyrel," Goldeneye bellowed. "Before everyone assembled here tonight, I declare you my emissary to the Heart."

She stared, dumbfounded. He had no authority to declare her an emissary. And yet, he had just done it. She looked over at the Royal Order men, who looked equally shocked.

She spoke low and urgent, "But, my lord. I'm too young. Too inexperienced. I've barely joined the White Heart and started my training. I'm not even close to making the rank of Virtue. I'm certainly not prepared to do the work of an emissary."

"You are my emissary, or I shall have no emissary at all." He glared over at the pair of Royal Order men. "You hear me? You tell your superiors. She's mine."

Eben muttered out of the side of his mouth. "Are you sure you're unenslaved?"

"I think so," she breathed between unmoving lips. "But . . . why?" she asked Goldeneye.

He leaned across the table, gesturing her near. In a voice not pitched to carry, he said, "You showed courage to go into battle unarmed. You were willing to sacrifice yourself for the good of the group. You are skilled with magic. These are traits my people admire."

"There are other White Heart members with those same traits who are much more qualified—"

He cut her off. "The paxan and I looked into the claviger's mind today. Saw through the gate into the Realm of Dreams. A great threat comes this way. The Dominion will have need of powerful allies if it is to survive. The Heart is powerful, is it not?"

"Very."

"Then you shall be my emissary."

"Will you teach your people to honor my colors and honor all those who wear them?" she challenged.

He stared at her, the pupils of his eyes narrowed to vertical slits, weighing her words. She could actually see him examining the implications, weighing possible outcomes, and calculating his best interest. Oh yes. This creature was extremely intelligent. Much more so than one would expect of the leader of a nation of violent changeling fighters whose sole purpose was war.

At length, Goldeneye drawled, "Aye." A pause. Then he added, "And in return, you shall form an alliance between my people and yours."

With that pronouncement, he leaned back and gestured for the Royal Order of the Sun guardians to be let through.

An alliance with the Heart. Not with the governess of Dupree. And not with the Empire. Did he dare to attempt driving a wedge between the healers and their masters? It was a subtle ploy hinting at a much deeper strategy.

The Royal Order of the Sun men rushed to her side while she stared at the Dominion leader. Ignoring them, she spoke slowly. "I think everyone has underestimated you greatly, Lord Goldeneye. I shall not make that mistake." She made the deep formal curtsy that one would give to a head of state and held it as etiquette dictated, waiting to be released from the obeisance.

"Rise," Goldeneye murmured, amusement lacing his voice. "We shall get on well, you and I."

So. He knew Imperial etiquette too, did he? Now where did a cobra changeling in the wilds of an untamed continent learn that? An intriguing mystery, her new sponsor was. One she looked forward to solving.

"Come away, Initiate," one of the Royal Order of the Sun guardians said nervously. "We have a ship at the docks and will take you to safety."

"Emissary," Goldeneye corrected, his hood flaring menacingly.

"Emissary Raina," the Royal Order man corrected hastily. He urged low, "Please, come. This is no place for you."

It was her turn to be amused. "Oh, I don't know about that. I think I could grow to enjoy these warriors and their ways. They fought well today."

Enough Dominion around her heard the words that a great shout went up, and a round of toasting ensued. She nodded her farewell to Goldeneye and turned to follow the red-and-white Royal Order of the Sun tabards.

W ill sat on the deck of the gently rocking ship, leaning back against a folded sail, enjoying the sun,
warm on his upturned face. The vessel was Heart
owned and plied the coast of Dupree, trading and spreading
the good word of the Heart. The Royal Order of the Sun
guardians had been frantic to get Raina on it last night and
away from the Dominion and had offered all of her friends
passage to wherever they wanted to go if she would come
along.

He was just happy to be free for a time of pursuit from
Imperial hounds, Anton Constantine, Marikeen and her
hooded friends, Kerryl Moonrunner, and whoever else
wanted a piece of them.

"Tell me something, Will."

He smiled without opening his eyes. "Anything, Rosana,
if you'll sit down beside me and enjoy the sun."

"It feels good after that swamp, doesn't it?"

He agreed and held an arm out to her. She settled in
against his side comfortably. "Who taught you that wall of
force spell?"

"No one. I've never learned it as far as I can remember."

She sat up, and reluctantly he opened his eyes to look at
her. "How can you cast a spell you've never learned?"

"I haven't the faintest idea." Last night, he'd demanded to
know in no uncertain terms from the Bloodroot spirit inside him if it had cast the spell. And in just as uncertain
terms, the spirit had denied any knowledge of it. In fact,

overwhelming confusion had been the response from his other half.

"Bloodroot didn't do it?" Rosana asked.

"No. He's as stymied as I am."

Rynn came over and sat down cross-legged in front of them. "Have you ever checked to see if you have some sort of repressed memories?"

"No."

Raina wandered over, remarking, "It's pretty clear he's got some, or else that spell wouldn't have bubbled up out of nowhere in his mind."

They didn't know the half of it. It wasn't just the spell that had come to him. It was the other knowledge of how to take command of a battlefield, how to tactically assess the situation, to see where the points of weakness and strength were, and knowing how to turn them to his own advantage that he couldn't explain. It was *all* there inside his head.

How? Who'd put it there? And more importantly, who'd hidden it from him?

He fully expected that his father had done the teaching of it. But the hiding of it? That was a different matter entirely. "Rynn? Can your kind hide memories?"

"Of course. But understand. I can hide one specific memory. One event, perhaps a short period of time. But even the most accomplished paxan cannot shut off an entire portion of a person's mind, filled with hundreds or thousands of memories, facts, lessons, understandings."

Will frowned. *What* had done this to him? And why had his knowledge chosen yesterday to finally break open? Not that he was complaining. Yesterday could have—he corrected with his new knowledge—*would* have gone very badly had it not happened.

Who was he? *What* was he? What did this new knowledge mean for him? How would it shape him and his future?

"Well, I know one thing for sure," Rosana declared. "I

may not know where your knowledge came from or how, but I'm glad it came to you. You saved us all."

He matched her smile, but it did not reach his heart. Something had changed yesterday. Something bigger than a fight not going well. There was a reason his hidden training had broken free, and he worried that it was the harbinger of more dangerous battles to come.

He glanced up, and Rynn was studying him intently. Cursed if he didn't get the impression that the paxan was thinking the exact same thing.

Rynn called across the open deck, "Sha'Li, Eben, Tarryn! Could you join us for a minute?"

The paxan looked grim as they all assembled. He dived in without preamble. "When Goldeneye and I were tearing the enslavement away from the mind of the claviger, we saw something."

Rynn made eye contact with Will. "Something's coming. A great army assembles on the dream plane, led by someone or something with enormous elemental powers. We must be ready for it. I think perhaps this is why Will's memories surfaced yesterday. You looked into the portal, did you not, just before you cast that wall spell?"

Now that Rynn mentioned it, he had. Just a glimpse. But he'd seen a vast army stretching as far away as the eye could see across a great, misty plane.

Sha'Li snorted. "Attacked by bad dreams shall we be?"

The others chuckled. But Will's newfound way of thinking leaped ahead to the obvious question. "Who hides on the dream plane to assemble this army, and for what purpose?"

"I do not know," Rynn answered soberly. "But I do know that only a few beings on the mortal realm are powerful enough to pull it off. This being manipulates the planes themselves to hide his or her actions."

The others waxed sober as the gravity of what he'd said finally began to sink in.

"Is our effort to wake the Sleeping King the cause of this?" Raina asked.

The answer came to Will in a flash of insight. "Not directly. The fact that it is time to wake the Sleeping King is the trigger. Nonetheless, we will need him awake, and soon, if we are to prevail against whatever comes."

"Why?" Raina asked sharply.

"He is powerful. And he will know how to manipulate the planes in the same way the architect of the dreaming army does. We must find the rest of his regalia and go after his body *soon*."

"Time is against us, then?" Rynn asked.

What was this? The great paxan warrior was asking for his considered military opinion? Huh. He really must have impressed them all yesterday with his stunt. He answered Rynn's question gravely. "Time is our greatest enemy now."

Raina leaned forward. "Goldeneye saw this army on the dream plane, too?"

"Aye," Rynn replied.

Raina looked relieved. "That explains why Goldeneye made me his emissary. He, too, prepares for war."

Will responded dryly, "The Dominion always prepares for war. He merely prepares for a new enemy that he has never faced before."

They fell silent for a time, and then into it, Eben said, "I have made a decision. I am going to join my sister on the dream plane to discover who creates a dreaming army there and for what purpose."

Raina spoke gently. "Eben, you are a man of many skills, but subtlety and subterfuge are not among yours. You are not suited to be a spy."

She was right. The jann approached life directly. Head-on. He opened his mouth to say so, but Sha'Li spoke first. "Do I know why you're doing this?"

The two stared at each other for a long moment, something uncomfortable and private hanging between them, like an unresolved argument.

Sha'Li looked away first. "Sorry I am."

"It makes no difference now," Eben replied grimly. "The damage is done."

"Put it right, I will. I swear."

What on Urth were they talking about? Will glanced at the other members of the party, who seemed equally lost in the pair's cryptic exchange. Aloud, he said, "Eben, what must we say or do to talk you out of this?"

"My mind is made up. You are right, Raina. I am the unlikeliest person to be a spy. And that is why I shall succeed. My sister and her associates will not see an infiltrator when they look at me."

"When do you go?" Rynn asked unexpectedly. The paxan was endorsing this mad scheme?

"Tonight. Will you help me make the journey?" Eben responded.

Rynn bowed his head. "Aye."

Will, Raina, and Rosana argued with Eben for a solid hour after that, but neither he nor Rynn could be talked out of the plan. And Sha'Li just moved to the other end of the ship and stared broodingly out to sea.

Eventually, frustrated, Will and the healers gave up. Eben went belowdecks, and Rynn followed, presumably to discuss how they were going to transport the jann to the dream plane.

Silence fell around them. Into it, Will asked, "Raina, can you use that ring of yours to find the other pieces of Gawaine's regalia?"

"He said I could."

"You've spoken with him?" Will blurted, surprised. "When did that happen? How?"

She actually blushed. "I dream of him sometimes."

Well, well, well. It seemed as if all of them were unlocking hidden potentials these days. Eben had a talent for finding elemental energies and Sha'Li could remove taints. And then there was that change to Rosana's magic. Speaking of which . . .

"Rosana, what's up with your magic? When you cast yesterday, it was a strange color."

She jammed her hands into folds of her skirt as everyone stared at her. But she confessed reluctantly, "When I went to the spirit realm to rescue those children, something happened to me."

It was his turn to lurch upright. "Are you all right?"

"I don't know. While I was there, I cast a kind of magic I've never learned. I don't recognize it, but it scared me."

"Can you call it now?" Raina asked.

Rosana's cheeks stained with something akin to shame. "Aye."

"Does it harm you in any way?" Will asked quickly.

"Nay." A pause. "But it harms others."

"Will you show it to us?" He coaxed, "We're all family here. There's nothing to be ashamed of."

She held out her hand, took a deep breath, and summoned thick, oily, black magical energy to her palm. He'd never seen anything like it.

To his amazement, it was Sha'Li, who'd come rushing from the other end of the deck to stare at Rosana's hand, who breathed, "That's death magic. A most rare and powerful form of magical energy."

Rosana closed her fist convulsively. She jammed her hand back under her skirt. "But I'm a healer," she whispered.

Rynn spoke kindly. "We must all accept who we are and embrace our true forms. Once you are at peace with your nature, you will be both a bringer of death and life."

Will winced mentally. He, too, would have to make peace with himself. But first, he had to understand who he really was. Thankfully, they had a long journey ahead of them and time on their hands for him to explore this heretofore unknown side of himself. The sailors said it would take nearly two months to make the trip down the coast of Haelos to Dupree.

As the others drifted away, he lay back down on his folded sail and let the sun warm his face once more. He had a feeling there would not be too many more moments of sunlit rest before the coming storm.

Aurelius stepped off the Black Ship *Valiant* onto the pier in Dupree. He was ready for the sensation of the ground rolling beneath his feet, but that did not make it any easier to walk in a reasonably straight line down the dock.

It was good to be home, squalid buildings, muddy streets, rough-dressed peasants and all. He looked forward to sleeping in his own bed and catching up on the local news. Will and the others should be back from their visit to Shepard's Rest to check out the lead on Kendrick Hyland. He was eager to hear what they'd found. But first, he had a letter to deliver.

A rather strange old crone had approached him as he left the Imperial Seat to head for the Imperial docks. She'd pressed the letter into his hand and told him rather imperiously never to let it out of his possession and to deliver it personally to High Matriarch Lenora of Dupree. And then she'd disappeared into the crowd at the docks without another word.

Curious to find out its contents, he made his way to the Heart house and was duly shown to Lenora's office. He went through the ritual of her asking how his trip had been and if the weather had been good for the crossing of the Abyssmal Sea. And then he took out the letter.

"This was given to me just before I left Koth with a request to deliver it to you." He passed it to Lenora.

"Who's it from?"

"An old lady gave it to me. I got the impression she was not its author, but merely a messenger."

"A mystery, then," Lenora murmured as she broke the seal. She unfolded the parchment and read quickly, a look of dismay crossing her features.

"Bad news?" he inquired.

"Ygrielle, a powerful mage and old acquaintance of mine, has written to inform me that the magics she and I were hoping to prevent Rosana from learning have somehow been discovered by her, anyway."

"Rosana, the young gypsy girl who cannot hit the broad side of a barn with a spell?" he asked, surprised.

"Her aim has improved greatly, and her nerves have steadied. She will make a fine combat healing caster in time."

"And what dangerous magic has she unlocked?" he asked.

Lenora pursed her mouth, a sure sign that what words came next would be edited. "Ancestral magic from her familial line."

"You know her family, then? I was under the impression she was one of your many orphans."

"That is because I wished for the world to have that impression. Nay, I know full well who she is. And so do you."

"Me?" He stared, surprised. "I know nothing of her!"

"You know a great deal about the daughter of Gregor and Ygrala Beltane. Gregor's wife was Ygrielle's daughter."

"Rosana's grandmother wrote that letter to you?"

"Yes. And it is she who gave Rosana into my care, she who asked for my help in protecting Rosana from that which would awaken her ancient family magics."

"Which are?"

"Death magics."

He slammed back in his chair, stunned. "The child can cast death magic?"

"She couldn't when she left Dupree a few months back. But according to this missive, something has happened to unlock it in her."

"And how would this Ygrielle know that Rosana has learned death magic?"

"You likely are familiar with Ygrielle by her nickname: the Blood Witch."

Aurelius swore long and hard. The granddaughter of the Blood Witch herself was among the party of young adventurers he'd assembled? Great stars above, the fates really had been conspiring to influence events. The Blood Witch was said to be one of the most powerful magical researchers alive anywhere, although what exactly she researched was a matter of mystery and speculation. She was known to study gypsies, though.

"Well, well, well. They've a death caster among them, now, do they?" he ruminated. "I'd say the odds of success just went up for our young friends."

Lenora shook her head. "They've just put a great light upon themselves that the Empire will not be able to ignore."

"The Empire will have to catch them first," he retorted.

"But can they stay one step ahead of Maximillian?"

"They must, Lenora. They must."

"Promise me you will do everything in your power to help them," she said urgently.

"I swear upon the noble blood of my forefathers."

"We are all in this together now," she muttered. "For better or worse. We shall all succeed or fail as one."

C icero breathed in the clean air and familiar scents of home. His kindari village was only a few leagues away now. It might be called the Sorrow Wold, but he knew every tree and trail of it and ran through it with joy in his heart. It had been a very long journey home from guarding the young mage, Raina, as she fled Tyrel a year ago.

Before long, he came to the clearing he sought. A house caught a stray shaft of sunlight, and a burly spider changeling looked up from splitting wood.

"Is she home?" Cicero asked, breathing a little hard. "I come from Dupree with news."

The spider changeling pointed with his hatchet toward the front door and went back to hammering a wedge into a log.

Cicero knocked on the front door, and a female voice bid him enter. He stepped inside and bowed cautiously to a female spider changeling known to his kind as the Black Widow. He found her repugnant physically, and he was not fond of how she styled herself superior to the kindari in the area. They were all Children of Zinn, the Great Spider, after all. How was it that she was more special than his people?

Just because her husband had been the spider speaker didn't make her the next speaker.

"What brings you to my parlor this fine day, young Cicero?"

Her sibilant syllables sent a shiver down his spine. He realized with surprise that several more spider changelings perched in chairs around the darkened room, silently listening. "I deliver a message."

"From whom?"

"An ancient being on the dream plane called the Laird of Dalmigen."

The Black Widow hissed in surprise. "Now there is a name I have not heard in a very long time. What is this message?"

"He sends you his greetings and bids me to tell you that a great conflict is coming. You and yours must be ready for it."

"From whence comes this threat?" the widow asked tersely.

"He did not say. Only that you would know what must be done."

"Ahh," she said in comprehension. "It's time, is it?" She looked over at her fellow spider changelings. "The long wait is over. It is time for the Great Circle to rise."

He had no idea what she spoke of, and frankly, he wasn't sure he wanted to know.

"Tell me of your journey, Cicero. From the beginning, and leave out nothing."

"It started in the manor house in Tyrel. The second daughter of the house was celebrating her sixteenth birthday . . . "

Endellian looked out across the assemblage in the Great Throne Room. Tonight's feast was grander than most, the food and drink flowing even more freely than usual. She suspected her father had done it intentionally to put the court into an especially festive mood. But why? He had yet to make an appearance and the hour was growing late. Bored, the revelers were consuming more and more, becoming less and less restrained.

She had some of her father's ability to see into minds, but not, of course, his awesome power at manipulating them. When he'd been gathering power to create her, he had not seen fit to share that particular gift. A fact which made her more than a little bitter at times.

At long last, the chamberlain stepped forward and, using the fantastic acoustics of the hall, proclaimed the arrival of his Most Resplendent Majesty, Maximillian the Third, Emperor of the Eternal Empire of Koth.

As always, the tiniest ripple of jealousy flowed through her. It was a hard lot being heir to a throne occupied by an immortal being. It was always there in front of her, visible but unattainable. All the glory, all the power. Just out of reach, never hers.

Along with everyone else, she made a deep obeisance and held it while her father took his place on the great Throne of the Black Flame. His sonorous voice rolled out across the enormous room, magnified by magic and the acoustics of the throne itself. "Rise."

An expectant rustle filled the hall. Along with the assembled kings and queens, ambassadors, and advisors ordered to this night's feasting, she waited to hear why they had all been called together.

"Grand Marshal Korovo, step forward," her father intoned.

A moment passed while Korovo separated himself from the others, made his way up the steps of the tall dais, and knelt before Maximillian.

"Rise, Grand Marshal, and serve me. I bid you to form a new legion. The Legion of the Vast. Train it as you will. And when it is battle hardened, I bid you to set sail for Haelos and conquer the entire continent for the greater glory of Koth and my name. Bring that untamed land to heel once and for all. Bring it into the fold of Kothite possessions: loyal, dutiful, and obedient."

Korovo's voice rang out clear and strong across the great hall. "So shall it be."

Read on for a preview of

THE WANDERING WAR

CINDY DEES
AND
BILL FLIPPIN

Available in Winter 2018
from Tom Doherty Associates

TOR ®
fantasy

A TOR BOOK

Read on for a preview of

THE
WANDERING
WAR

CINDY DEES
and
BILL FLIPPIN

I t started with a prickle down Hemlocke's spine. Nothing much, but enough to cause the faintest spark of awareness in her sleeping mind. *Something was not right.*

Out of all her kind, she was the one who'd been created and empowered to act as a sentinel, exquisitely sensitive to the continent the humans called Haelos and to all its living creatures, aware even in the deepest of restorative slumbers when a threat stirred.

Slowly, slowly, blood began to seep through her veins, bringing a hint of warmth to her curled body and the beginning of thought to her dreamless mind. She'd been asleep a long time in her dark, watery lair. Her injuries at the hands of the Kothite invaders had been serious, and full healing could be measured in centuries. Her body might be nearly whole, but her spirit was still weak.

Not so weak, though, that she could not protect Haelos from its enemies. She waited patiently for her mind to come to sharp alertness, her claws to regain their deadly strength, her massive, scaled body to come to a fully active state, her great wings to unfurl. And when they did . . .

Then she would fly.

M adness! Unthinkable! Absolutely not!"
    Raina gazed sympathetically at the sputtering Heart patriarch and his equally agitated fellow matriarchs and patriarchs. Outrageous though it surely was, nonetheless, she had been raised to the rank of emissary in the White Heart

by Lord Goldeneye, leader of the great Dominion colony of changelings in the north of Haelos. He had no authority to do so, of course, but that had not stopped him.

High Matriarch Lenora had called this conclave of Heart leaders from across the settled lands of Haelos to discuss the matter, but the truth of it was that, no matter how much they blustered, their hands were tied. They needed the entrée to the heretofore impenetrable Dominion; hence they had no choice but to recognize her rank in the offshoot branch of the healer's guild, no matter how unorthodox it might be.

"She's a child!" a matriarch down the table spat in disgust. "The girl's hardly fit to be a White Heart initiate, let alone an emissary equal in rank to one of us."

The *girl* was sitting right here, hearing every word of their tirade. And she'd done a decent job of being a White Heart initiate, thank you very much. It hadn't always been easy, by the Lady. Even if she wouldn't be eighteen until springtime, age was not only measured in years but also in experience.

The Heart had three branches. The regular Heart to which most healers belonged. Then there was the White Heart, the pacifist branch of healers sworn to defend all life, to which Raina belonged, for better or worse. Lastly, there was the Royal Order of the Sun, the militaristic arm of the Heart, responsible for defending Heart chapters, their members, and the all-important resurrection Heartstones.

To Raina's vast relief, the Royal Order also took responsibility for protecting White Heart members from harm since she and her brethren were unable to protect themselves. Most of the Dominion's warriors had expressed a strong desire to kill her for being weak and spineless during her recent stint as a prisoner of that aggressive changeling army. They'd taught her to be abjectly grateful for the swords and shields that had hovered over her protectively since her return to Dupree.

At tonight's meeting, the Royal Order of the Sun was represented by Lord Justinius, knight commander of the entire order in Haelos. So far, he'd sat tense and taciturn at

Lenora's right hand and not participated in the discussion. Raina suspected he saw the strategic necessity of letting her new rank stand and furthermore saw the advantage of finally having an emissary to the Dominion, her tender age notwithstanding.

Lenora patiently let the matriarchs and patriarchs bellyache their fill, which took a while. Raina had taken just about as many insults to her age, intelligence, training, and skills as she could tolerate before their complaints finally wound down to a trickle and then ceased.

The high matriarch said with admirable calm from beside Raina, "Thank you for your comments. I appreciate your candor, but here's the thing. Never in the history of the Heart has *any* Dominion settlement, *anywhere*, allowed a member of the Heart to act as an envoy to it. We simply cannot turn down this opportunity."

"Agreed!" the sputtering patriarch from before exclaimed. "Let us send a more seasoned Heart member to Goldeneye with all due haste."

It was all Raina could do not to call him a fool for even suggesting such a thing. Lord Goldeneye would not stand for a substitute. They would be lucky to get their replacement emissary back alive, let alone with his or her mind intact.

She opened her mouth to tell the man so, but Lord Justinius sent her a brief, quelling look and a small shake of his head.

The big knight leaned forward ponderously, leather gambeson creaking under his chain mail, to weigh in at last. "Ladies and gentlemen. We are in full agreement that we have been presented with a rare opportunity, and we cannot turn away from it. However, I have met Lord Goldeneye, and he is not the sort to be trifled with. If this young lady is the one he chose, I guarantee you, he will accept no other. I shall send one of my most experienced knights to guard her, and he will be fully capable of advising her should she need guidance."

She studied Justinius while the others buzzed and Lenora

tried unsuccessfully to quiet them. What was his game? Did Lord Justinius wish merely to plant an observer in his enemy's stronghold, perhaps co-opting control of her mission for his order?

Or did he aim higher? Did he dare hope for a rapprochement between the Royal Order of the Sun and the Dominion itself? The idea skirted perilously near treason. The Dominion's leaders openly declared themselves sworn enemies of Koth, nearly as openly as they declared their intent to conquer all the lands of Urth for themselves.

"*The enemy of my enemy?*" she murmured under the hubbub for Justinius's ears only.

"Silence!" he hissed in alarm.

Lord Justinius didn't deny her implication. But he did push abruptly to his feet, towering over them all in his armor and weapons while she stared at him in shock.

The others fell mostly silent, and his voice cut across the last few protests. "It is settled. I will send Sir Lakanos to Dupree to accompany her. He is a skilled warrior who will earn the respect of the Dominion and is subtle enough to help Raina manage the nuances of this assignment. When do you leave for the Great Den, Emissary?"

"Lord Goldeneye told me to return in the summer."

"Very well. When the days lengthen and the wheat ripens, look for my knight."

She bowed her head respectfully. "Yes, my lord."

Downstairs in the big common room with its heavy-beamed ceilings and plenty of cots for the ill and injured, the Heart door opened to let in twilight's chill, and a crowd of drunken soldiers spilled inside loudly. The gypsy healer Rosana, scowled as Will Cobb peeled away from his boisterous cronies, members of the elite Imperial Special Forces unit who called themselves the Talons of Koth. He wasn't a member of the unit, but they were recruiting him hard to join them. And to her chagrin, he was letting them.

"The lot of you are sloshed again?" she complained, hands planted in dragon wings of irritation on her hips.

"'Ey there, Rosie," Will called, overloud, his words slurring slightly. "We're here to get our blood purified so we can start drinking anew."

"What brilliant tactician thought up that idea?" she snapped.

"Me, of course." Will made an exaggerated bow in her general direction. "Will Cobb, tactical genius extraordinaire, at your service."

"I see your ego hasn't suffered any bruises after your training with Captain Krugar," she replied tartly.

Will had come to the Heart daily for the past two weeks for treatment of various contusions, cuts, and even a few cracked ribs after his sparring sessions with the Imperial Army officer. Unfortunately, Will's ego was growing right along with his prodigious combat skills.

Something had happened to him a few months back during the pitched fight to close a portal to the dream plane up in Dominion territory. He'd unlocked some sort of repressed memories of martial training from his childhood. He'd gone from being able to handle himself reasonably well in a fight to a highly skilled battle caster in the blink of an eye. Rumor had it he was actually beating Krugar on a semiregular basis in their weapons training now.

She ought to cut him some slack, forgive him for his abrupt surge of arrogant confidence, but it still rubbed her the wrong way. She preferred her humble cobbler's son from a tiny village in the Wylde Wold to this swaggering young man.

Maybe Will's attitude was influenced by the tree spirit trapped in the wooden disk that had grown onto his chest a year back. Bloodroot was the tree lord of death, destruction, and rage, after all. Ever since their unnatural union, Will had struggled against bouts of anger, jealousy, and quick temper.

Sometimes Rosana despaired of hanging on to the sweet lad who'd rescued her from an orc attack on a deserted road in the western woods over a year ago and won her heart in the process.

"C'mon, Rosie. Give us some potions," Will cajoled.

He opened his arms, and she scooted out of reach, swatting at his hands. "You know that is not how Heart resources are used."

Commander Thanon, leader of the Talons, threw an arm across Will's shoulder. "We'll pay for the potions. Twice—no, triple—their worth. I've got gold."

Rosana's scowl deepened. With triple the cost of the potions in gold, she could replace the ones she used on these fools with many more potions to heal the needy who poured through the Heart's front door in a never-ending stream. "Fine," she huffed. "But show me the gold first."

Raina heard a commotion downstairs and recognized the voices. Grabbing her white cloak boldly emblazoned with the royal blue symbol of the White Heart, she headed down to the big common room.

One of the men lolling about with Will spied her and peeled away from the others. She recognized the Imperial Army officer, a handsome young man entirely too cocky for his own good. He was a paxan, with a closed third eye in the middle of his forehead, and he made an exaggerated bow to her. "Greetings, my lady fair. Mine eyes rejoice at the sight of thy beauty."

She rolled her eyes. "Good evening, Commander Thanon. I see you and your friends have been celebrating again. Is there some occasion I am not aware of to warrant this revelry?"

"Merely the fact of being alive, my lovely Raina."

"I am not yours, sir," she replied a shade sharply. She turned to Will, her good friend and traveling companion of the past year. "I have some news to celebrate and was hoping you and Rosana could join me and our friends for a drink."

He frowned foggily, and she impatiently placed her glowing hand on his elbow, murmured an incant, and released magic that would purify his blood of the alcohol flowing through it.

Rosana stepped out into the main room holding a fistful of glass vials. "I've got the purification potions. Hand over the gold you promised."

"Take the gold, but keep the potions," Raina told her. "I'll take care of these louts."

"Hey!" A general cry went up from the soldiers, but they crowded around readily enough to accept her healing.

Irritated at their obnoxious behavior, Raina declined to trickle the healing slowly into the men to minimize discomfort. Rather, she slammed the healing into each man at combat speed, ensuring maximum pain as it did its work, coursing through their blood, cleansing the alcohol from it.

Thanon was last. Raina was tall, but Thanon was taller by nearly a head and smiled down at her entirely too intimately for her comfort. His attention zinged across her skin like a vibrating wire and made her more nervous than she liked to admit. He murmured low, "I shall relish the pain because it is you who causes it, my lady."

She really wished he would quit calling her that. Just to be contrary, she trickled his healing into him slowly enough not to cause the slightest discomfort. "I would not dream of hurting an important Imperial officer such as yourself, Commander. After all, I am but a lowly commoner."

He grinned broadly. "My dear, you are anything but common."

The twinkle in his eyes was hard to resist, but he was not the first handsome young man to flirt with her since her return from the Dominion lands. She stepped back and said formally, "I must go."

"Form up, men," Thanon ordered crisply, entirely sober now.

The Talons fell into a marching formation and departed the Heart with sharp efficiency.

"Shall we go find Eben, Rynn, and Sha'Li?" she asked Rosana and Will.

The three of them set out across Dupree, the capital city of the Imperial Kothite colony in Haelos, in search of their friends. Raina barely noticed the pair of Royal Order of the Sun guardians who fell in behind them, but she was still glad for their presence.

They arrived at what had been Landsgrave Hyland's residence until his permanent death. Leland's foster son and their friend, Eben, still lived there. The young jann, an elementally aligned humanoid, grabbed his cloak eagerly when he heard the plan to go out on the town and celebrate Raina's promotion in rank.

Rynn, a magnificently handsome paxan with golden hair and brilliant blue eyes—three *open* blue eyes, to be exact—was also pleased to join them, although his enthusiasm was more measured. He paused to don a filigree headband that covered the third eye in the middle of his forehead before sweeping on his cloak and pulling its deep hood far forward to hide his damningly illegal open eye.

All members of the paxan race had third eyes; it was just that most were permanently closed. Imperial law dictated that all open-eyed paxan were to be arrested on sight and turned over to the Empire. No one knew what happened to them once in Imperial custody, but it could not possibly be good.

The party, now numbering five, rang a great brass bell down by the dock and passed along an invitation for Sha'Li to join them to the lizardman who rose out of the water at their call. He knew who the black-scaled lizardman girl was and agreed to pass the message along to her.

Eben seemed relieved when Sha'Li didn't join them, which made Raina frown. Something had happened between him and Sha'Li in the Angor Swamp a few months back. Once the best of friends, Eben refused to even speak of the lizardman girl now. It pained Raina to see two of her dearest friends so estranged.

They headed for the Hungry Horde Inn, a favorite watering hole of young artisans in Dupree. The ale was hearty, the food plentiful, and none of it too expensive. Tonight, Raina treated her friends to dinner and drinks, unaccustomed to having a bit of gold jingling around in her belt pouch. High Matriarch Lenora had given the coins to her before she left the Heart earlier, calling it her allowance as an emissary. Apparently, emissaries required spending money to conduct business in a manner commensurate with their rank.

"Look at you!" Will exclaimed. "All grown up and financially independent!"

She laughed. "I wouldn't go so far as to say I'm independent. The Heart provides me with my cash and resources. And I do have to earn it by doing a job."

Rynn looked concerned. "When must you return to the Dominion?"

"This summer. And Lord Justinius has offered to provide a knight escort for me."

"More like a babysitter," Rosana teased.

Raina rolled her eyes at the characterization but could not deny its truth.

They talked and laughed about nothing in particular through the evening. It was a welcome change after the stress and danger of the past few months. They'd sought, and ultimately found, another piece of the Sleeping King's regalia that they would need to wake the ancient elven king one day. Furthermore, they'd finally found their good friend Kendrick Hyland, who'd been kidnapped last year. Unfortunately, he'd chosen to stay with his captor, nature guardian Kerryl Moonrunner, and to retain the were-curse Kerryl had put upon him.

Raina worried about Kendrick and shared his grief at the permanent death of his father, Landsgrave Leland

Hyland, who had been like a father to her since she arrived in Dupree.

Sha'Li, their lizardman friend, never showed up at the pub. Whether she didn't receive the invitation or simply chose to ignore it, Raina couldn't guess. Sha'Li spent most of her time underwater in the lizardman settlement near Dupree, rather than roaming the streets of the human city where most people eyed Sha'Li's kind with suspicion, if not outright hostility.

Not that the lizardmen had done anything to earn the enmity of the locals—or the Kothite regime, for that matter. They were just . . . alien. Technically, Raina supposed they were nothing more than simple animal changelings—part animal and part human, but their reptilian features and scaled bodies unsettled even Raina at a visceral level. Strange appearance aside, though, Sha'Li had been as loyal and supportive a friend as Raina had ever had. No matter how hard Sha'Li would have protested if she said it aloud, Raina thought the girl had a deeply noble soul.

"Hey, look who's here!" a familiar voice boomed behind Raina, shaking her from her ruminations.

What was Thanon doing here? She swiveled on the bench, scowling to see the military officer and a half dozen of his men piling into the pub. Had they followed Will? Or worse, her?

"The hour grows late," Raina announced in disgust. "I'm going back to the Heart. Rosana, do you wish to come with me or have Will bring you back later?"

The other healer answered, "I'll come with you and your escort."

The two girls piled out of the corner of the pub, and Raina pressed a few coins into the hand of the bartender. "Keep the ales flowing for my friends, if you will."

"Consider it done," the fellow replied, grinning.

Raina stepped out into the evening, and two Royal Order of the Sun guardians emerged from the shadows beside the pub, falling in behind her. It had started to snow while they'd been in the pub, a fine, crystalline dusting coating every horizontal surface and hiding the usual mud and muck of the cobbled streets in early spring.

"Wait up!" Thanon called from the doorway of the pub. "I'll walk you home."

She sighed and summoned a smile. It was not as if she could tell him not to bother. He was a high-ranking Imperial officer, and the way she heard it, he was also the governess's favorite. He fell in beside her, sparing a nod and grin for the Royal Order guards.

"You're incorrigible," she muttered as he held out his forearm expectantly, forcing her to rest her hand on it or else be openly rude to the man.

"Irresistible, aren't I?"

"And modest, too," she replied dryly.

"My finest quality."

They walked in silence for a few minutes. Then Thanon commented, "In Koth, everybody talks about how squalid and filthy Haelos is, but seeing it like this, quiet and covered in a coat of new fallen snow, it's actually rather quaint. Pretty."

Raina considered the half-timbered buildings jostling for space on the cobblestone street. Dupree was by far the grandest place she'd ever been in her life, born and raised as she'd been at the very westernmost edge of civilization in Haelos. Sprawling up the side of two great hills and sloping down to the expansive Bay of Dupree, close to five thousand people lived in the city's tall, narrow buildings and winding streets.

"Where's the most beautiful place you've ever been?" she asked Thanon, whose many badges and blazons on his uniform spoke of a long military career and travels all over Urth. No matter that the man looked to be no older than his mid- to late twenties. It must be nice to age at the rate of a long-lived race like the paxan.

He glanced down at her. "The most beautiful place I've seen is wherever you are," he answered. One corner of his mouth lifted in a grin.

She couldn't help but laugh. "Truly. Incorrigibility is your gift."

The slate roofs and black-painted timbers around them wore their fluffy coats of sparkling snow with quiet dignity. Their footsteps melted behind them, leaving a trail of footprints to mark their passing through the still streets. The evening was serene, as if a blanket of peace and calm lay over the entire world this night. The past several months of life-threatening danger and never-ending stress fell away, leaving her feeling as weightless as the flakes settling gently around her toward earthly rest.

The avenue they trod spilled into the large square in front of the towering House of the Healing Heart, a sprawling, four-story-tall structure taking up most of one side of the square. The tall dome of the central Heartstone tower in its private courtyard within the Heart headquarters peeked above the main building's roof. It was an elaborately carved and gilded rotunda as befitted a place where people could magically be restored from fully dead to alive.

Thanon escorted her across the broad expanse of pristine snow covering Heart Square and stopped at the foot of the wide, shallow steps leading up to the glowing front doors of the blond stone edifice.

"I shall leave you here and wish you sweet dreams, my lady."

"Safe travels and a good night to you, Commander Thanon," she replied formally.

"I have spent part of it with you. It is already a good night."

Stars, that man missed no opportunity to lay on the charm. Were all courtiers like that? She would not know. Funny, but the past year had taught her a great deal about just how much she did not know of the world. An urge to travel, to see more and learn more surged through her.

"C'mon. I'm cold," Rosana muttered, starting up the broad steps.

Raina followed the ever-practical Rosana inside, out of the snow and out of the night's quiet magic.

When the girls left the pub, Eben ordered a round of ales for himself, Will, and Rynn. He was surprised and pleased when the barkeep informed him that their White Heart friend had covered their tab for the rest of the evening. That was good of Raina. Beneath all that deep thinking and political maneuvering she lived for, she was a decent sort. Good heart.

"All right, boys. I need your advice," Will declared. "It's about Rosana."

"Give her whatever she wants and don't cross that gypsy temper of hers, man." Eben laughed.

Will punched him playfully in the upper arm. "No, you fool. I want to propose to her, but I have to figure out just the perfect way to do it."

Eben grinned. "About time you got around to it."

Everyone had known the pair was sweet on one another and would end up together for much longer than the two of them had known it. Rosana smoothed out the rough edges of Will's temper, and he helped her be braver and more confident.

Will turned to Rynn. "I figure a pretty fellow like you has lots of experience with women. How do girls like to be proposed to?"

Rynn squawked. "How should I know? I've never proposed to anyone!"

Will groaned, and Eben declared to him, "You're on your own on this one, my friend."

Rynn piped up jovially, "Good luck with it."

Will scowled and downed the entire contents of his mug, then stared morosely into the remnants of foam clinging to the sides of the tankard, which frankly amused Eben to no end. Not that he would tell Will that and risk rousing Will's formidable temper.

Rynn emptied his mug and slammed it down on the rough, board table. "A gift," he declared.

Will looked up, frowning.

"Give her a gift. Something significant to both of you. Something that will make her cry and feel all emotional. Then spring your proposal on her, and she'll be swept away and say yes."

Eben frowned. "Isn't that trickery?"

Rynn shrugged. "Either he wants the girl or he doesn't. All's fair in love and war."

The barkeep brought them three more brimming mugs, and Eben sipped this one a bit more temperately.

"What gift would make her cry?" Will wondered aloud.

Eben and Rynn both shrugged, their limited store of wedding proposal advice exhausted.

"What of you, Eben? Any young women in your near future?" Rynn asked.

This last mug of ale was hitting Eben hard all of a sudden, and he had to concentrate to form an answer to his friend's question. "No time for love. I have to help my sister, Marikeen. Get to the dream plane. Protect her from whatever goes on there." He asked Rynn abruptly, "Can you help me? You're good with all that dream plane stuff, right?"

Rynn nodded modestly.

"I know you can take me there. You did it when I first saw my sister on the dream plane. Can we do that again? Watch me sleep or whatever it is you do, and take me to Marikeen." Whew. The pub's dirty plaster walls and low, blackened ceiling were starting to spin.

Rynn mumbled, "Sure, fine. Are you all right, Eben? You look like you want to pass out. Maybe we should go back to Hyland House . . ." The paxan started to push to his feet but collapsed back to the bench, blinking hard. "Whoa. I'm a little dizzy."

"Can't hold your booze?" Will teased, jabbing Rynn with an elbow, but half missing and tipping himself partway over.

Rynn gave Will a shove back upright and then grabbed Eben's hand across the table. "I'll help you find your sister. I promise, my friend."

"You're a good man. No matter how many eyes . . ." Why were words so hard to enunciate clearly all of a sudden?

"Thanks. Not so bad yourself for a jann," Rynn mumbled, frowning and appearing to work hard to focus on Eben's face.

Rynn's brilliant blue eyes whirled like a kaleidoscope, and Eben grinned stupidly. "Look . . . funny . . ."

"Feel . . . funny . . ." Rynn sighed back.

Eben felt himself starting to tip over and pulled against Rynn's hand to right himself. Rynn was leaning at an odd angle, too, and he did his best to prop up the paxan, not that it helped one whit.

A new voice intruded from somewhere above Eben's head. Eben squinted and made out the barkeep, flanked by two burly young men who looked like his sons. The fellow's words only sluggishly formed meaning in Eben's sotted brain. "Too bad the girls left, but ye three'll still bring me a pretty penny from Anton and his boys. He's got quite the bounty out on ye. Sweet dreams, then."

Eben glanced across the table at Rynn in dawning horror. The paxan stared back blearily, looking appalled. Will toppled sideways into Rynn just as Eben and Rynn fell forward in unison and passed out.

R aina hurried up the Heart's front steps behind Rosana. She loved how the broad stones were worn a little in the middle, testament to the thousands of feet that had trod these stones in search of healing over the years.

The glow around the front doors blinked out as someone inside removed the key from the wizard's lock for them. Raina followed Rosana inside, and the wizard's lock went back up behind them, the magically protected doors glowing once more.

Raina shook like a dog, giggling as Rosana did the same and they pelted each other with melted droplets of snow.

"A moment of your time, Emissary," High Matriarch Lenora said from near the big hearth across the room.

Raina crossed to where the woman sat in a deep armchair, a quilt spread across her lap. Raina sank into the matching chair, relieved that the common room was empty of sick or wounded supplicants for a change. She supposed most people stayed at home on a night like this, tucked into their warm beds, rather than venturing out and getting hurt.

"How may I serve you, High Matriarch?"

"I hear Commander Thanon and his men escorted you and your friends out this evening."

"They did."

"And that young Thanon brought you home?"

"He walked with me, yes." She did not correct Lenora for calling Thanon young. The high matriarch knew as well as anyone that a paxan could be hundreds of years old and look one-tenth his or her age.

"Tell me something, Raina. Why do you choose to move about Dupree in the company of Imperial soldiers rather than entrusting your safety to the Royal Order of the Sun?"

Caution surged through Raina. The high matriarch was as subtle as anyone she'd ever known. Even the simplest question had the potential to be fraught with layers of meaning.

"Has the Royal Order complained?" Raina asked.

"They would never dream of complaining about such a thing, but it does bother them that you do not seem to trust them."

Raina forced herself to take a moment to honestly consider the question. Clearly, there was import to the matter or else Lenora would not have brought it up. Perhaps Raina was unknowingly committing some grave breach of Heart etiquette and the high matriarch was too polite to say so outright. Or maybe the Royal Order of the Sun was embarrassed that the new emissary shunned them in favor of an elite military unit.

Or perhaps this was a deeper gambit by the Royal Order

of the Sun to position itself as Raina's primary source of support and advice going forward. They had already managed to become her sole guardians and advisors once she went north to the Dominion.

She knew herself to be an extraordinary mage and was moving quickly into a position of unusual power compliments of her relationship with the Dominion. Of course, others would see her as a political tool to be possessed and wielded.

But as she considered the question, the truth was rawer and uglier than she'd realized. She was *afraid*.

Raina admitted reluctantly, "When the Dominion kidnapped me and my friends, I was utterly helpless. They gagged and bound me so I could not cast magic, and they did not acknowledge the neutrality of my colors. They showed me just how weak I truly am in hostile situations. I understand now that healers who wear White Heart colors are exquisitely vulnerable to the violence and cruelty of a wild place like Haelos."

"Make no mistake, child. Everywhere on Urth is rife with violence and cruelty. Haelos has no special claim to either."

"And because of my White Heart vows, I am as a babe in the woods, completely unable to defend myself should anyone wish me harm."

Lenora remained silent, studying Raina intently.

At length, Raina continued, "Thanon and his men make me feel safe. They're heavily armed, highly skilled warriors, and travel in packs. They display their lethality without apology. They're formidable soldiers whom others would do well not to cross."

"I would remind you that the reputation of the Royal Order of the Sun is no less formidable. You can trust the Order, Raina. Lord Justinius chooses and trains his men and women with great care. They will lay down their lives for you to the last one of them."

"But that's the problem! I don't want anyone to die for me!"

"Are you saying that you value Thanon and his men's

lives less than Justinius's and his men's? Is that why you choose to travel with the Talons? You would rather see them die for you?"

Raina stared into the sluggish fire, shocked. Was that what she had been doing without even being aware of it? Stars, this business of being in the White Heart was hard. Apparently, she must give everyone around her an equal opportunity to die on her behalf in addition to healing those around her evenhandedly.

"It is the nature of your work that others will leap to protect you from harm, Raina. You may not like it, but you must not stop them."

"And yet my colors force me to try. It goes against everything I stand for to let others die protecting me."

"Then I must counsel you to do nothing nor go anywhere that will put your life at risk."

Hah. As if that was going to happen anytime soon. She and her friends still had to find a way to wake the Sleeping King. And that path was fraught with immense danger.

Her thoughts must have shown upon her face, for Lenora murmured, "You cannot have it both ways. There are consequences to all our decisions, all our actions. The course you have chosen is perilous in the extreme. You must be prepared to lead fine warriors to their deaths on behalf of your colors. And, I might add, on behalf of the quest you have chosen to undertake."

She got the feeling Lenora was warning her of more than a Royal Order guardian dying someday. Did the high matriarch know of some new threat to Raina and her friends as they searched for the means to wake the Sleeping King?

"Furthermore," Lenora continued, "you must accept that those warriors freely chose their path. You must let them walk it."

Raina stared at the older healer, who stared back. She was missing some hidden message Lenora was trying to convey.

The high matriarch said soberly, "Sometimes the things we do are larger than our small lives."